STAR WARS
THE EMPIRE STRIKES BACK

STAR
THE EMPIRE
STRIKES BACK
WARS

A Random House SCREEN COMIX™ Book

Random House
New York

THE EMPIRE STRIKES BACK

Directed by
Irvin Kershner

Produced by
Gary Kurtz

Screenplay by
Leigh Brackett and Lawrence Kasdan

Story by George Lucas

Executive Producer
George Lucas

For Lucasfilm
Senior Editor: Robert Simpson
Creative Director: Michael Siglain
Art Director: Troy Alders
Project Manager, Digital & Video Assets: LeAndre Thomas
Lucasfilm Art Department: Phil Szostak
Lucasfilm Story Group: Pablo Hidalgo, Matt Martin, and Emily Shkoukani

© & ™ 2020 Lucasfilm Ltd. All rights reserved. Published in the United States
by Random House Children's Books, an imprint of Penguin Random House LLC,
1745 Broadway, New York, NY 10019, and in Canada by Penguin Random House
Canada Limited, Toronto, in conjunction with Disney Enterprises, Inc. Screen Comix
is a trademark of Penguin Random House LLC. Random House and the Random House
colophon are registered trademarks of Penguin Random House LLC.

ISBN 978-0-7364-4145-2
rhcbooks.com

Printed in the United States of America
10 9 8 7 6 5 4 3 2 1

A long time ago in a galaxy far, far away....

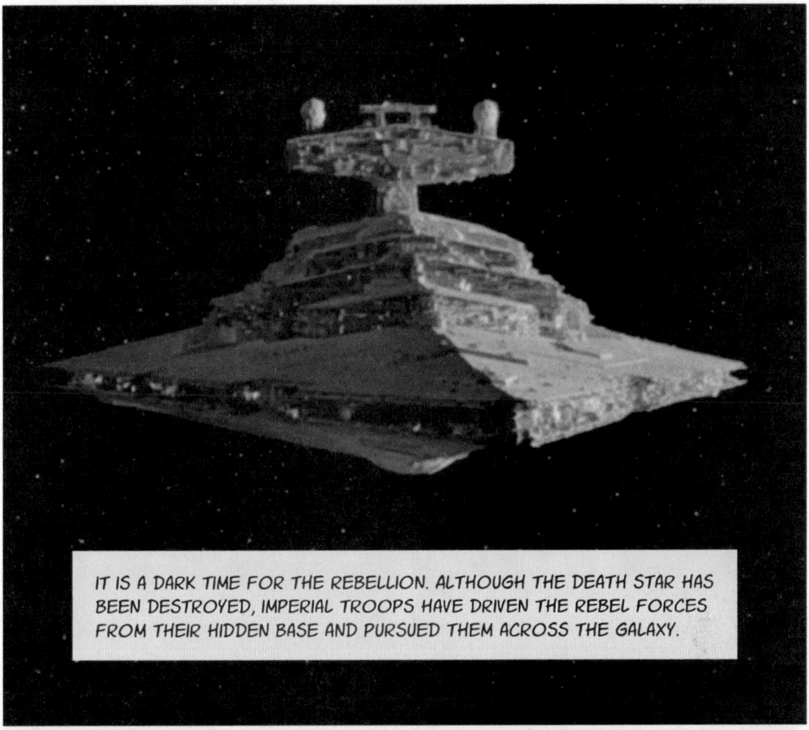
IT IS A DARK TIME FOR THE REBELLION. ALTHOUGH THE DEATH STAR HAS BEEN DESTROYED, IMPERIAL TROOPS HAVE DRIVEN THE REBEL FORCES FROM THEIR HIDDEN BASE AND PURSUED THEM ACROSS THE GALAXY.

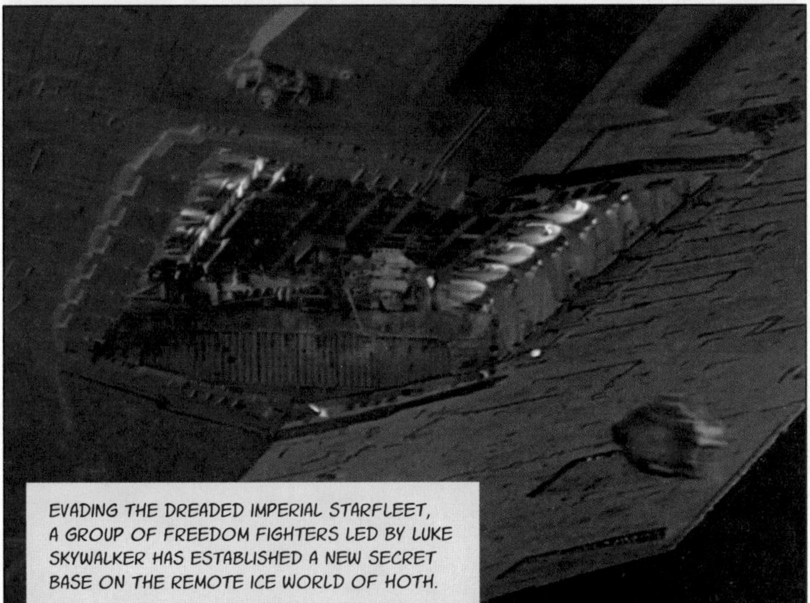
EVADING THE DREADED IMPERIAL STARFLEET, A GROUP OF FREEDOM FIGHTERS LED BY LUKE SKYWALKER HAS ESTABLISHED A NEW SECRET BASE ON THE REMOTE ICE WORLD OF HOTH.

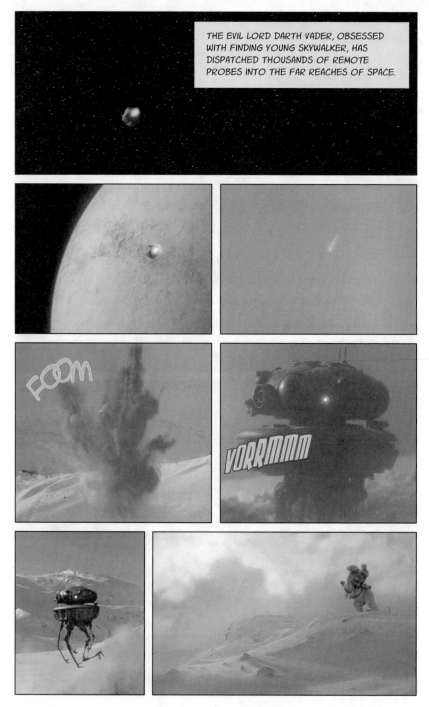

THE EVIL LORD DARTH VADER, OBSESSED WITH FINDING YOUNG SKYWALKER, HAS DISPATCHED THOUSANDS OF REMOTE PROBES INTO THE FAR REACHES OF SPACE.

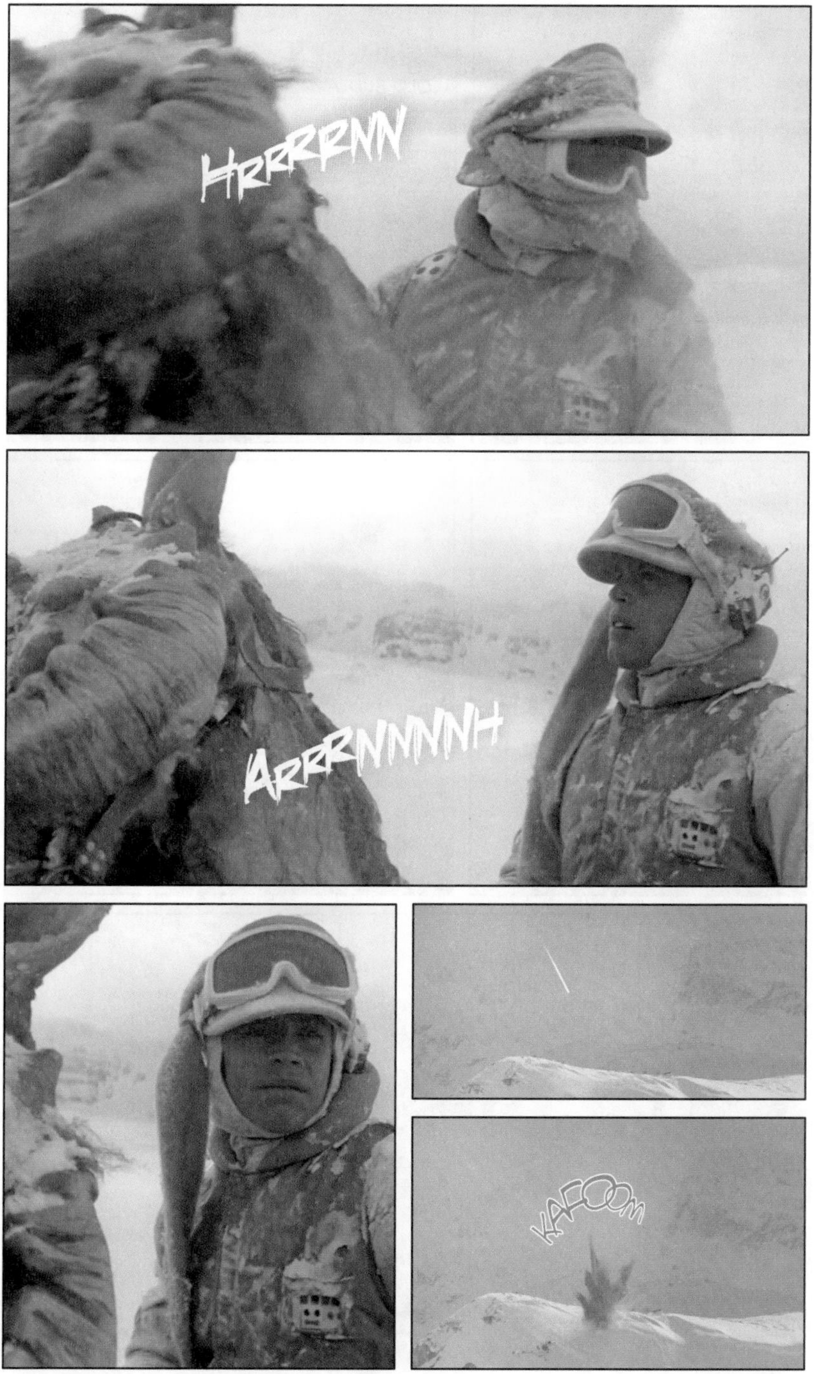
HRRRRNN
ARRRNNNNH
KAFOOM

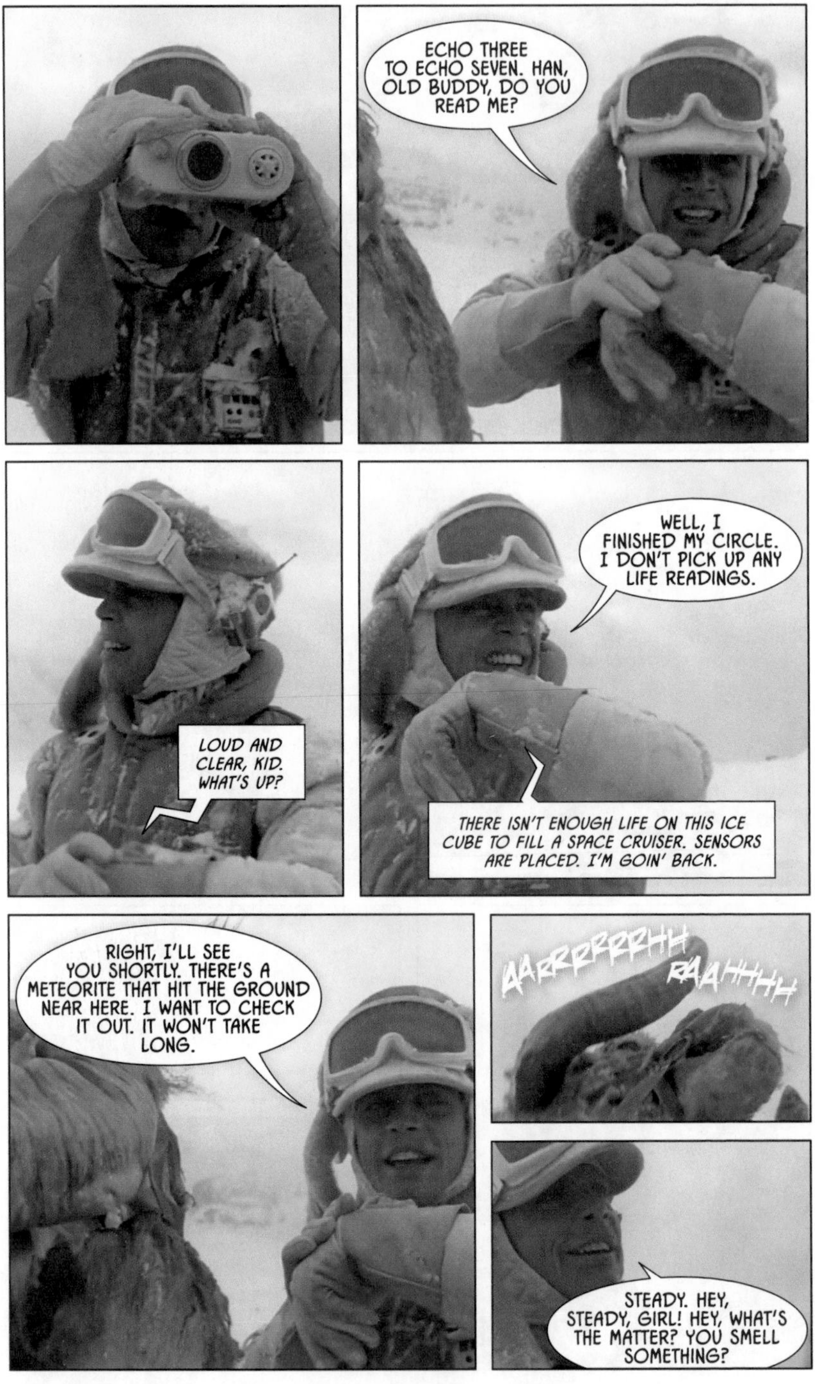
ECHO THREE TO ECHO SEVEN. HAN, OLD BUDDY, DO YOU READ ME?
LOUD AND CLEAR, KID. WHAT'S UP?
WELL, I FINISHED MY CIRCLE. I DON'T PICK UP ANY LIFE READINGS.
THERE ISN'T ENOUGH LIFE ON THIS ICE CUBE TO FILL A SPACE CRUISER. SENSORS ARE PLACED. I'M GOIN' BACK.
RIGHT, I'LL SEE YOU SHORTLY. THERE'S A METEORITE THAT HIT THE GROUND NEAR HERE. I WANT TO CHECK IT OUT. IT WON'T TAKE LONG.
AARRRRRRHH
RAAHHHH
STEADY. HEY, STEADY, GIRL! HEY, WHAT'S THE MATTER? YOU SMELL SOMETHING?

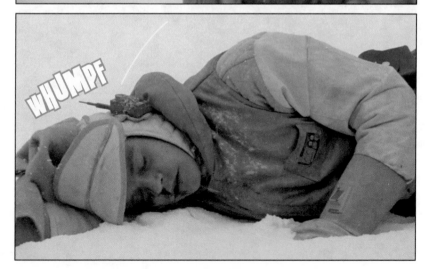

RRRAARRRRGGHHHHHHHHHH

AGH!

WHUMPF

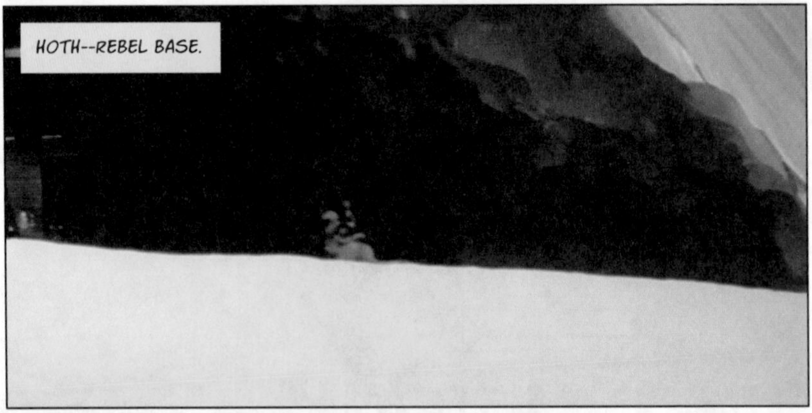
HOTH--REBEL BASE.

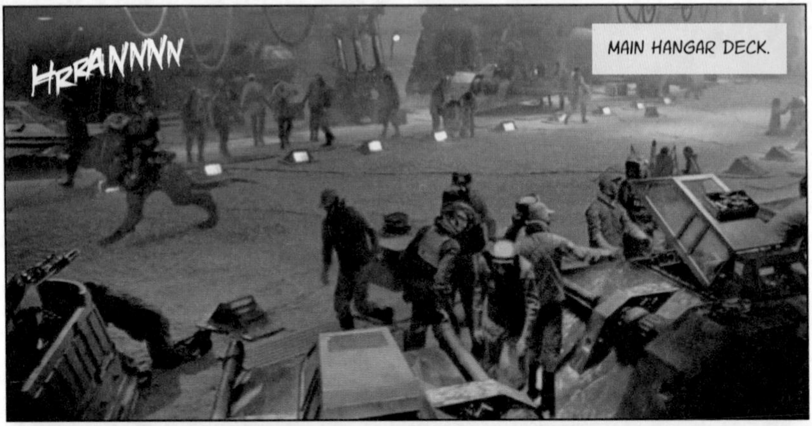
HRRANNNN
MAIN HANGAR DECK.

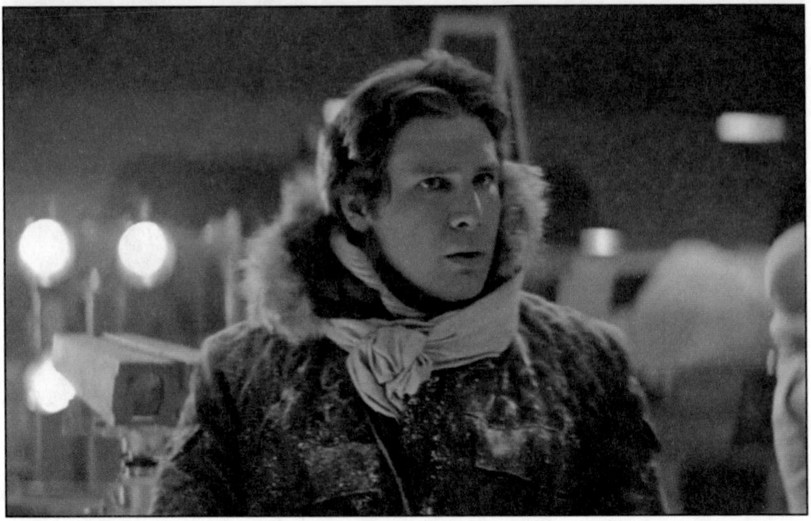

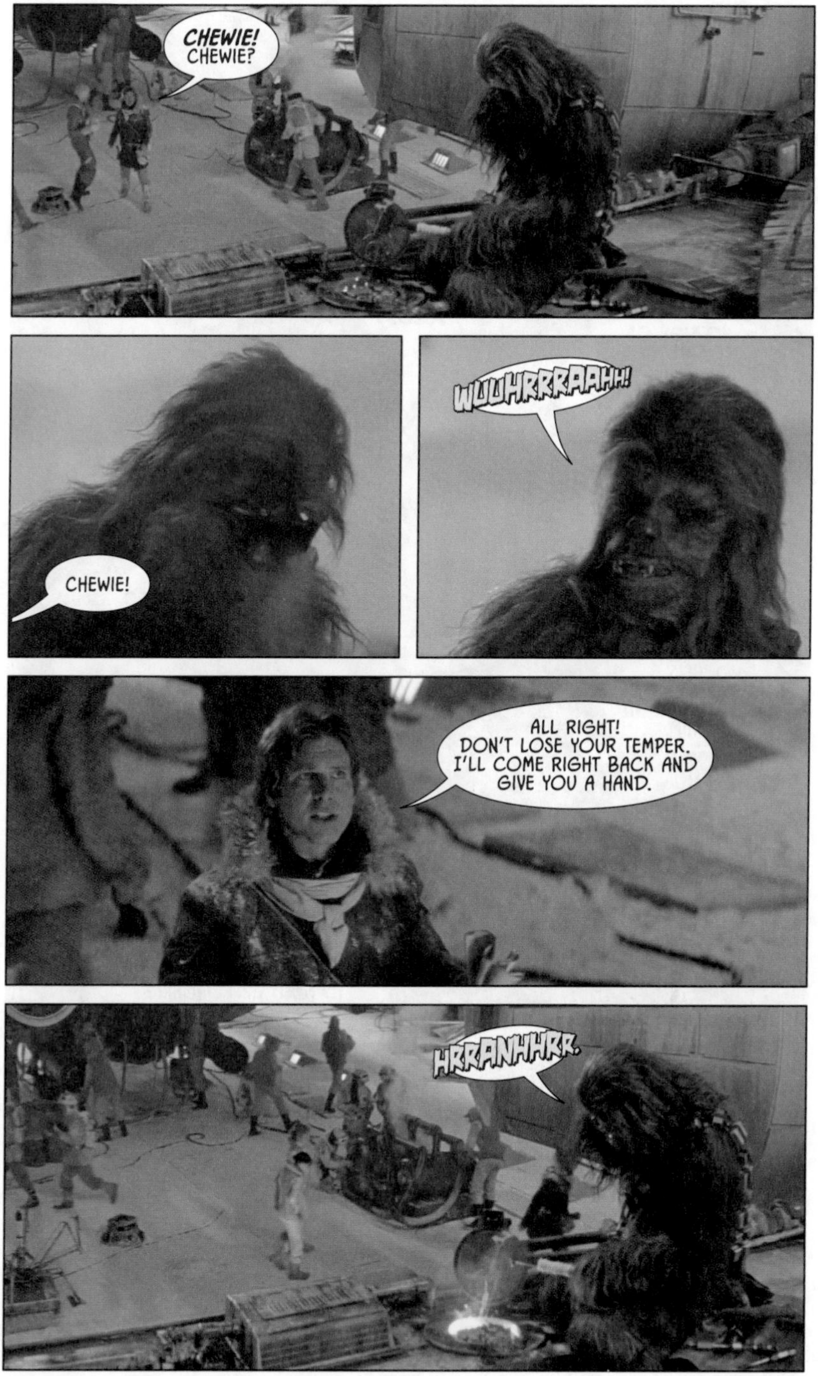
CHEWIE! CHEWIE?
CHEWIE!
WUUHRRRAAHH!
ALL RIGHT! DON'T LOSE YOUR TEMPER. I'LL COME RIGHT BACK AND GIVE YOU A HAND.
HRRANHHRR.

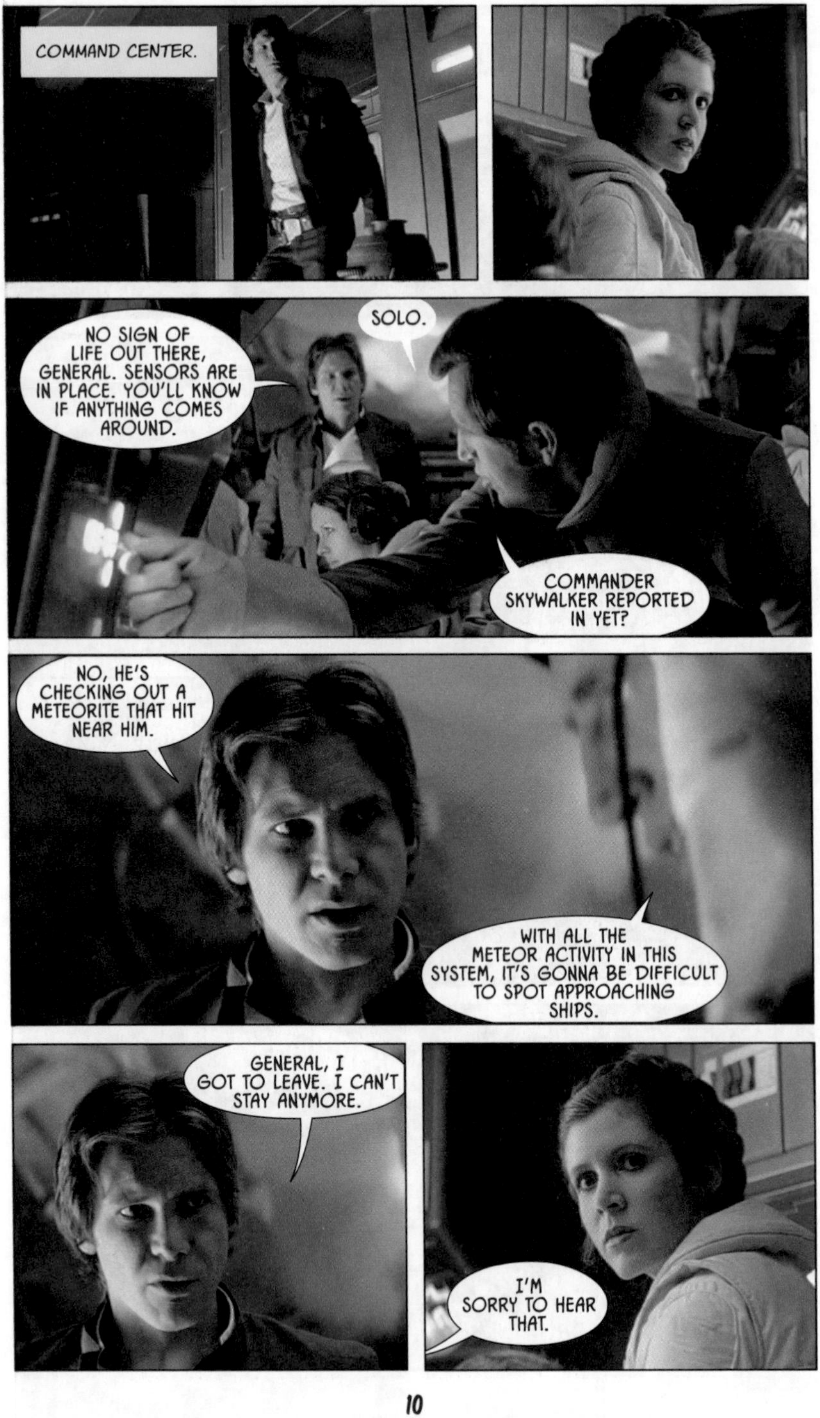
COMMAND CENTER.
NO SIGN OF LIFE OUT THERE, GENERAL. SENSORS ARE IN PLACE. YOU'LL KNOW IF ANYTHING COMES AROUND.
SOLO.
COMMANDER SKYWALKER REPORTED IN YET?
NO, HE'S CHECKING OUT A METEORITE THAT HIT NEAR HIM.
WITH ALL THE METEOR ACTIVITY IN THIS SYSTEM, IT'S GONNA BE DIFFICULT TO SPOT APPROACHING SHIPS.
GENERAL, I GOT TO LEAVE. I CAN'T STAY ANYMORE.
I'M SORRY TO HEAR THAT.

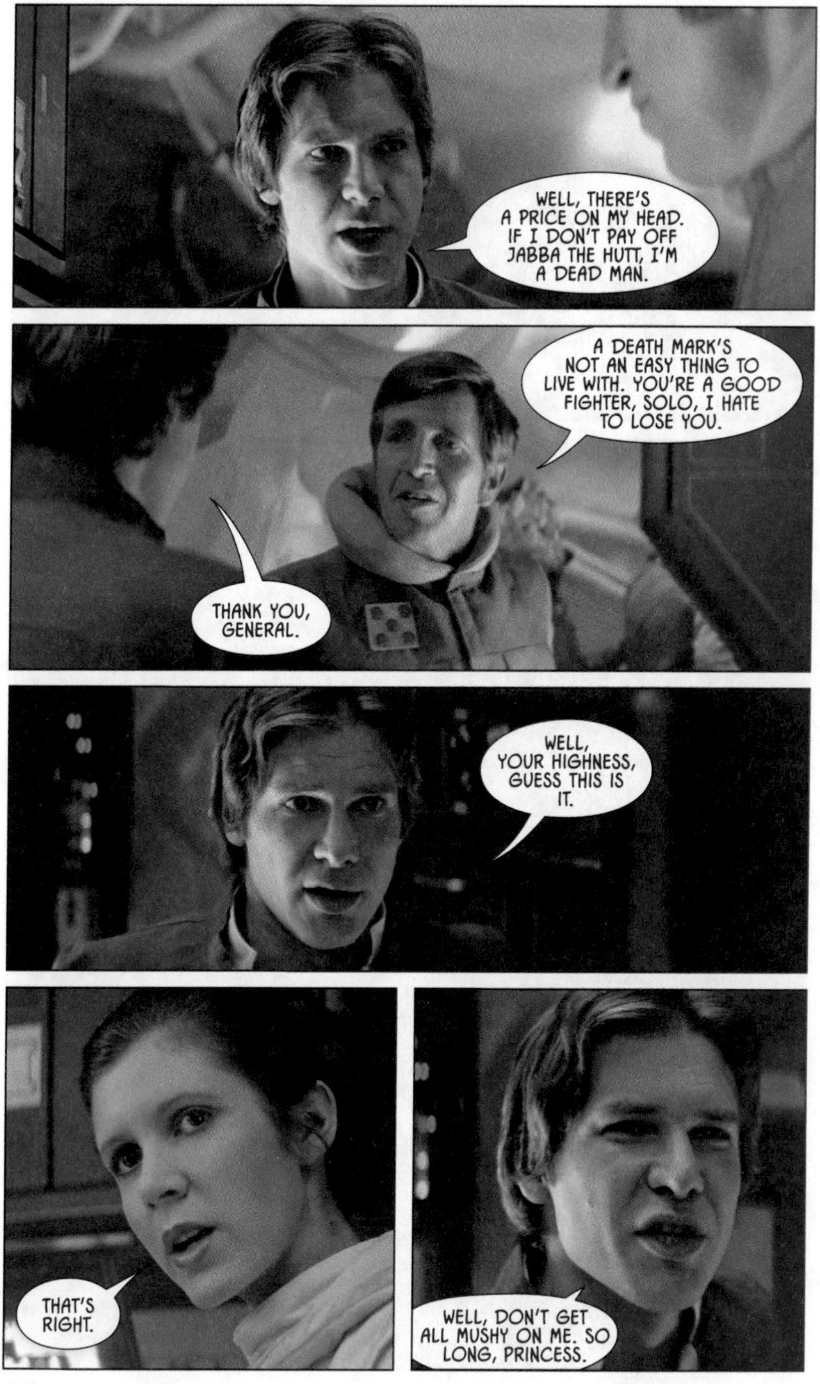
WELL, THERE'S A PRICE ON MY HEAD. IF I DON'T PAY OFF JABBA THE HUTT, I'M A DEAD MAN.
A DEATH MARK'S NOT AN EASY THING TO LIVE WITH. YOU'RE A GOOD FIGHTER, SOLO, I HATE TO LOSE YOU.
THANK YOU, GENERAL.
WELL, YOUR HIGHNESS, GUESS THIS IS IT.
THAT'S RIGHT.
WELL, DON'T GET ALL MUSHY ON ME. SO LONG, PRINCESS.

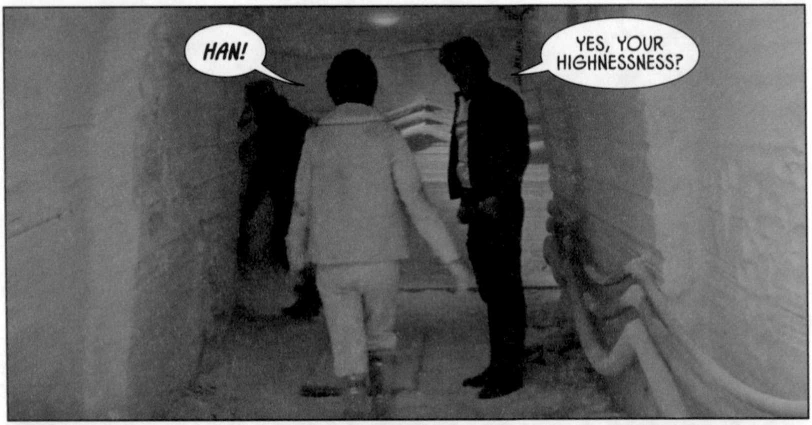
HAN!
YES, YOUR HIGHNESSNESS?

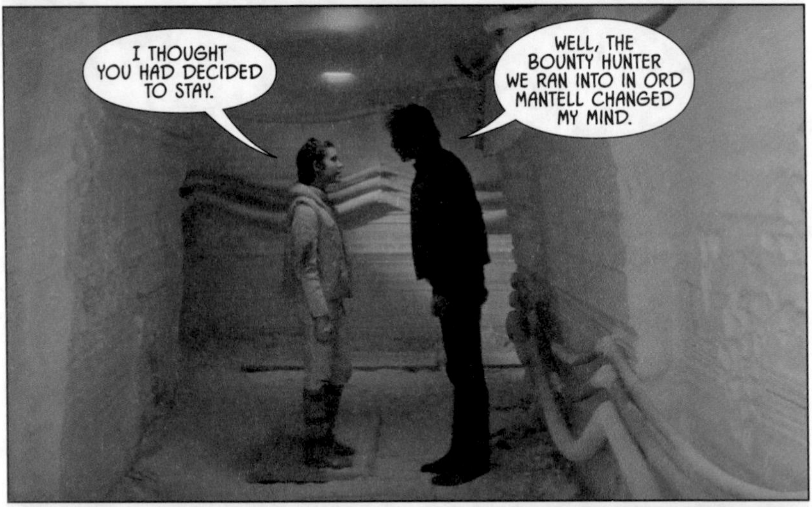
I THOUGHT YOU HAD DECIDED TO STAY.
WELL, THE BOUNTY HUNTER WE RAN INTO IN ORD MANTELL CHANGED MY MIND.

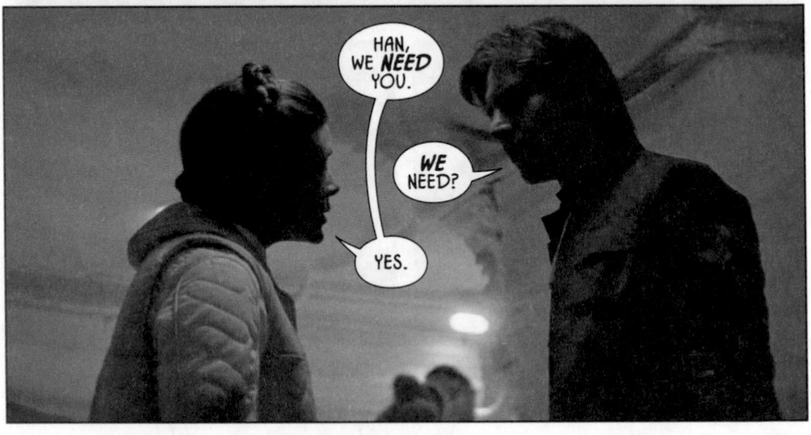
HAN, WE NEED YOU.
WE NEED?
YES.

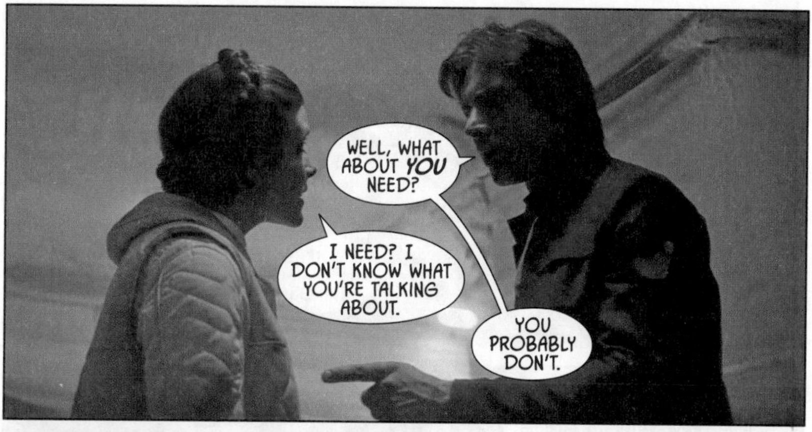
WELL, WHAT ABOUT YOU NEED?
I NEED? I DON'T KNOW WHAT YOU'RE TALKING ABOUT.
YOU PROBABLY DON'T.

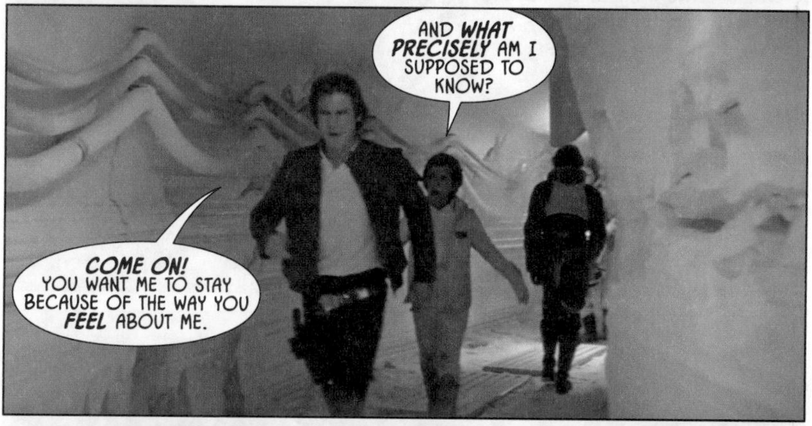
AND WHAT PRECISELY AM I SUPPOSED TO KNOW?
COME ON! YOU WANT ME TO STAY BECAUSE OF THE WAY YOU FEEL ABOUT ME.

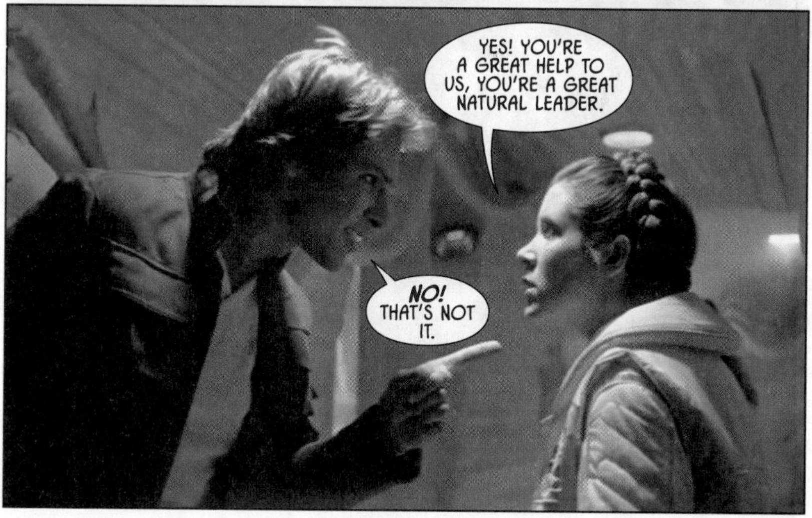
YES! YOU'RE A GREAT HELP TO US, YOU'RE A GREAT NATURAL LEADER.
NO! THAT'S NOT IT.

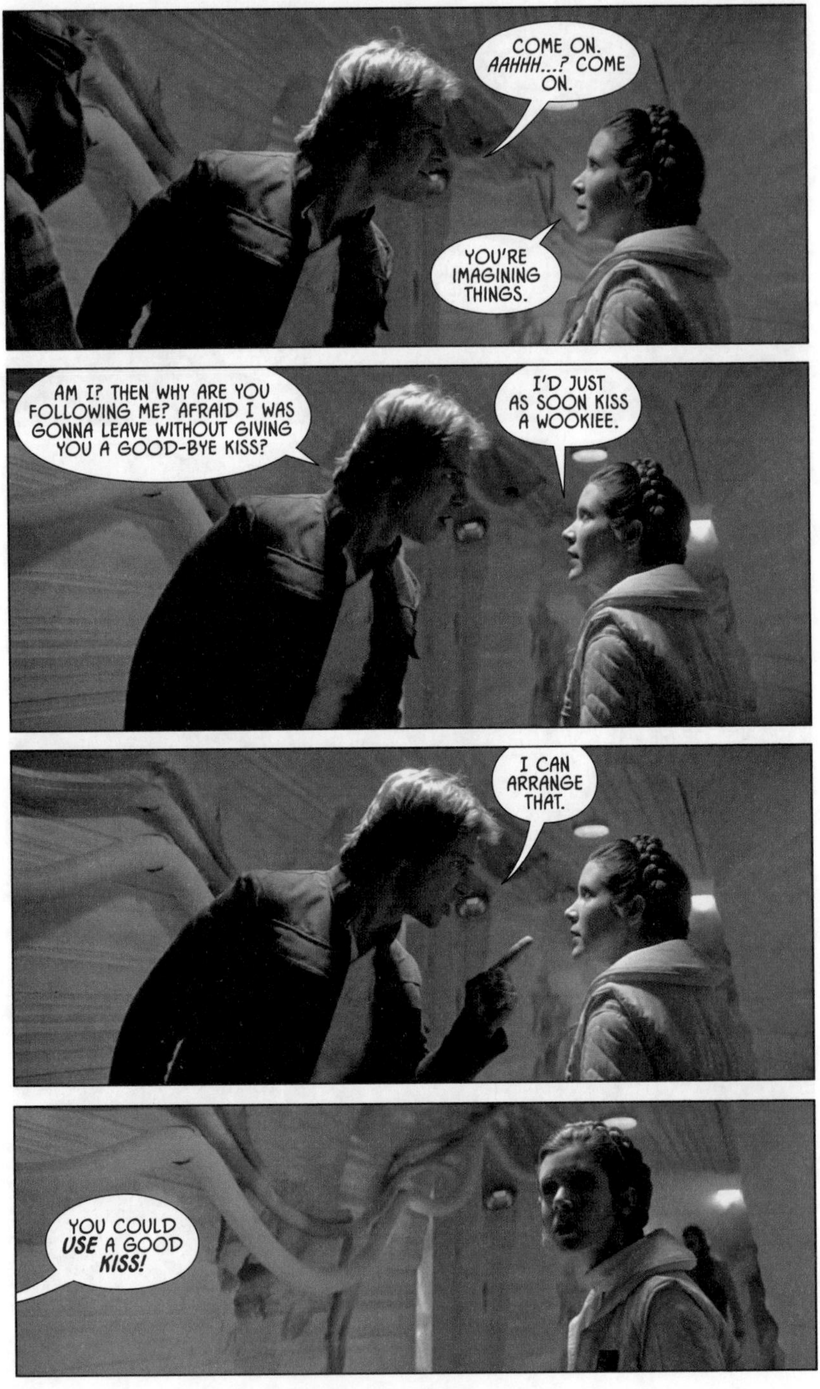
COME ON. AAHHH...? COME ON.
YOU'RE IMAGINING THINGS.
AM I? THEN WHY ARE YOU FOLLOWING ME? AFRAID I WAS GONNA LEAVE WITHOUT GIVING YOU A GOOD-BYE KISS?
I'D JUST AS SOON KISS A WOOKIEE.
I CAN ARRANGE THAT.
YOU COULD *USE* A GOOD *KISS!*

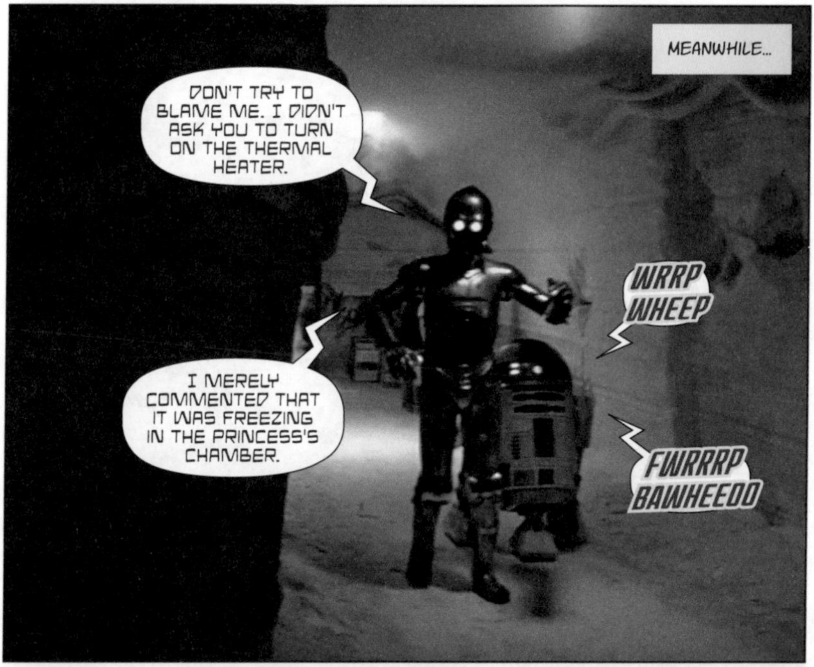
MEANWHILE...
DON'T TRY TO BLAME ME. I DIDN'T ASK YOU TO TURN ON THE THERMAL HEATER.
WRRP WHEEP
I MERELY COMMENTED THAT IT WAS FREEZING IN THE PRINCESS'S CHAMBER.
FWRRRP BAWHEEDO

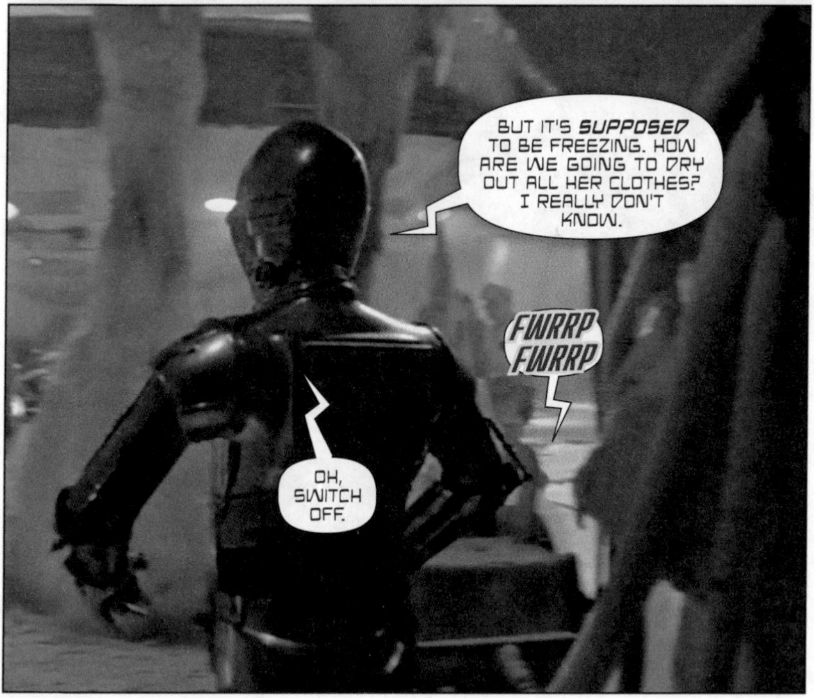
BUT IT'S *SUPPOSED* TO BE FREEZING. HOW ARE WE GOING TO DRY OUT ALL HER CLOTHES? I REALLY DON'T KNOW.
FWRRP FWRRP
OH, SWITCH OFF.

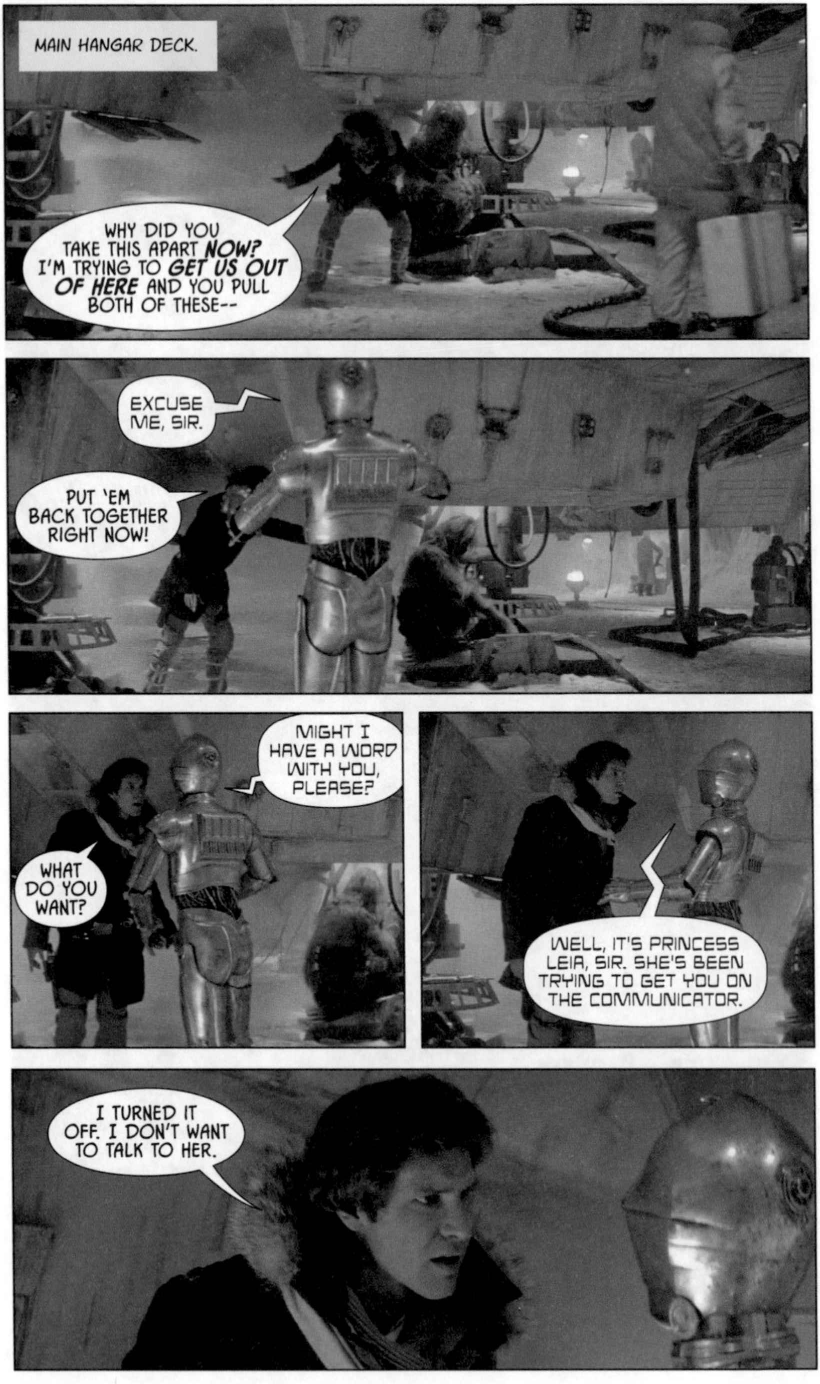
MAIN HANGAR DECK.
WHY DID YOU TAKE THIS APART NOW? I'M TRYING TO GET US OUT OF HERE AND YOU PULL BOTH OF THESE--
EXCUSE ME, SIR.
PUT 'EM BACK TOGETHER RIGHT NOW!
MIGHT I HAVE A WORD WITH YOU, PLEASE?
WHAT DO YOU WANT?
WELL, IT'S PRINCESS LEIA, SIR. SHE'S BEEN TRYING TO GET YOU ON THE COMMUNICATOR.
I TURNED IT OFF. I DON'T WANT TO TALK TO HER.

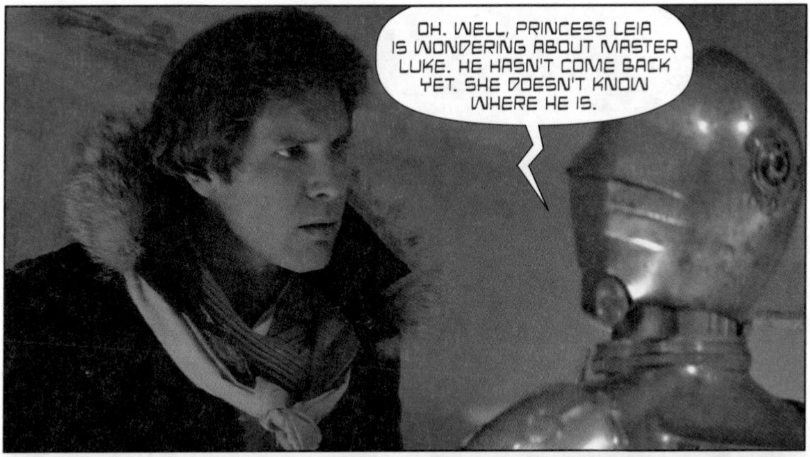
OH. WELL, PRINCESS LEIA IS WONDERING ABOUT MASTER LUKE. HE HASN'T COME BACK YET. SHE DOESN'T KNOW WHERE HE IS.

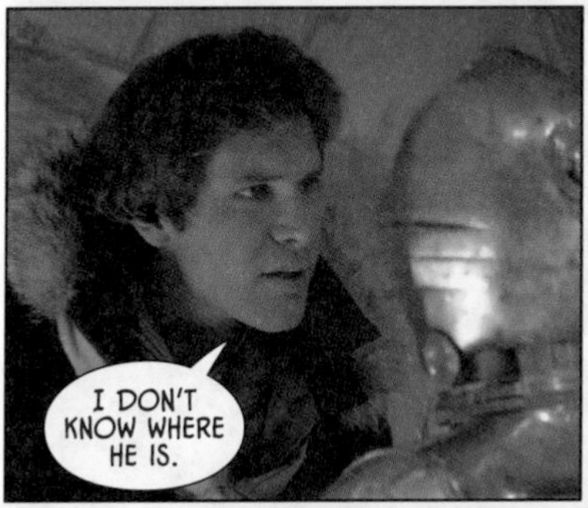
I DON'T KNOW WHERE HE IS.

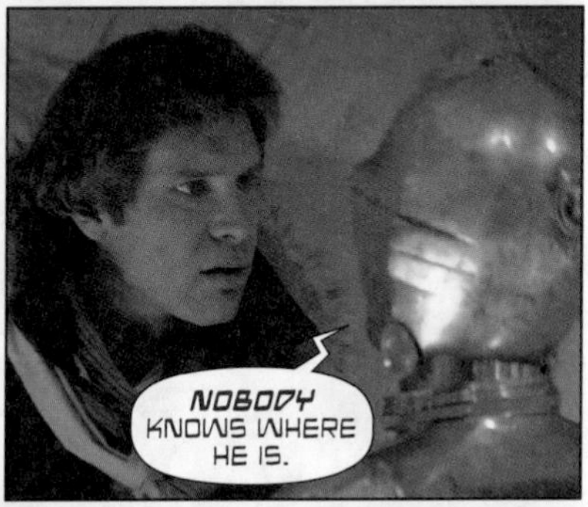
NOBODY KNOWS WHERE HE IS.

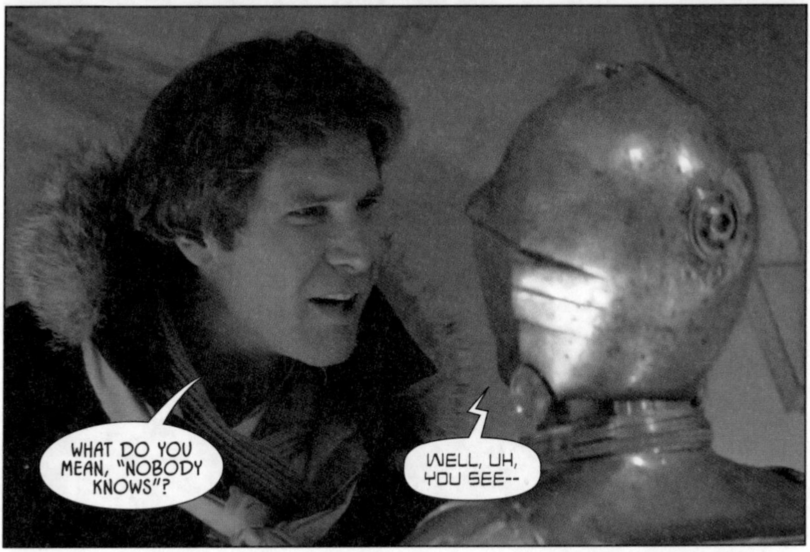
WHAT DO YOU MEAN, "NOBODY KNOWS"?
WELL, UH, YOU SEE--

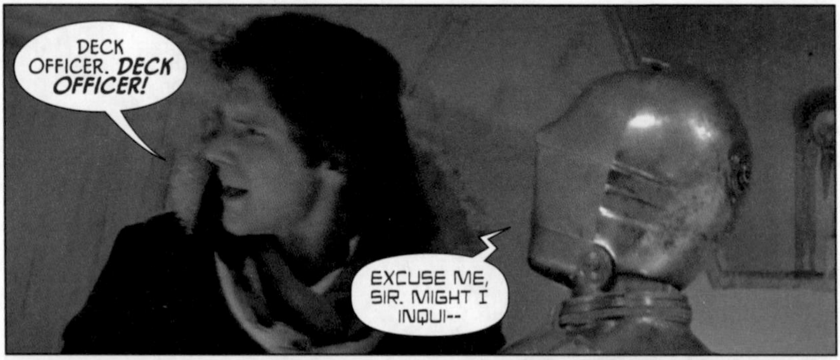
DECK OFFICER. DECK OFFICER!
EXCUSE ME, SIR. MIGHT I INQUI--

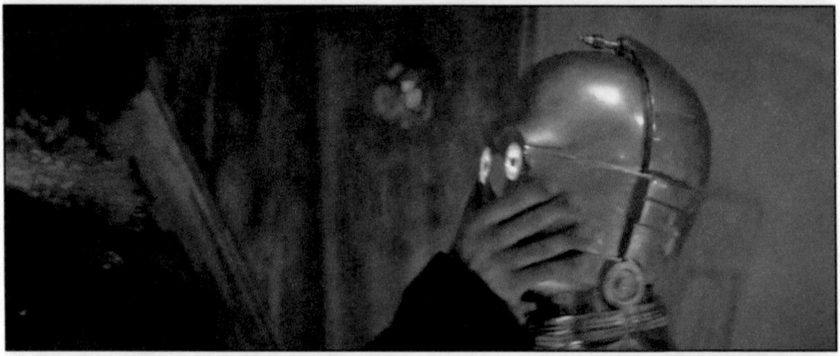

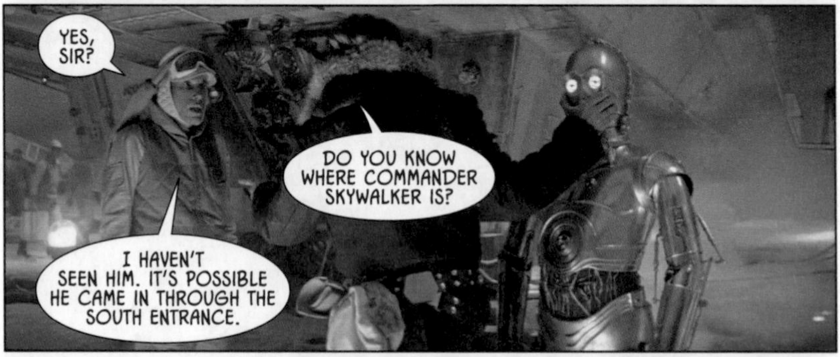
YES, SIR?
DO YOU KNOW WHERE COMMANDER SKYWALKER IS?
I HAVEN'T SEEN HIM. IT'S POSSIBLE HE CAME IN THROUGH THE SOUTH ENTRANCE.

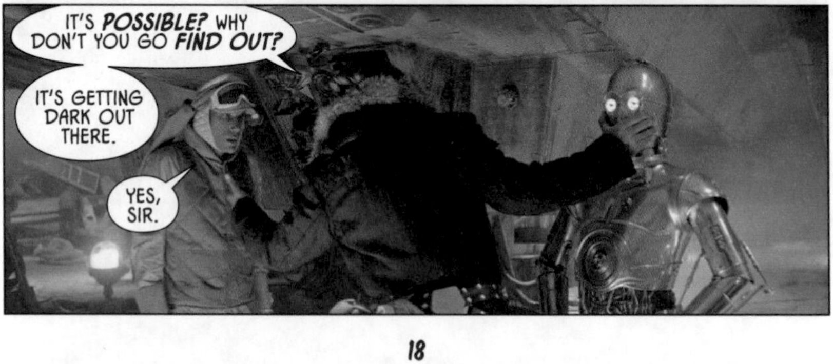
IT'S POSSIBLE? WHY DON'T YOU GO FIND OUT?
IT'S GETTING DARK OUT THERE.
YES, SIR.

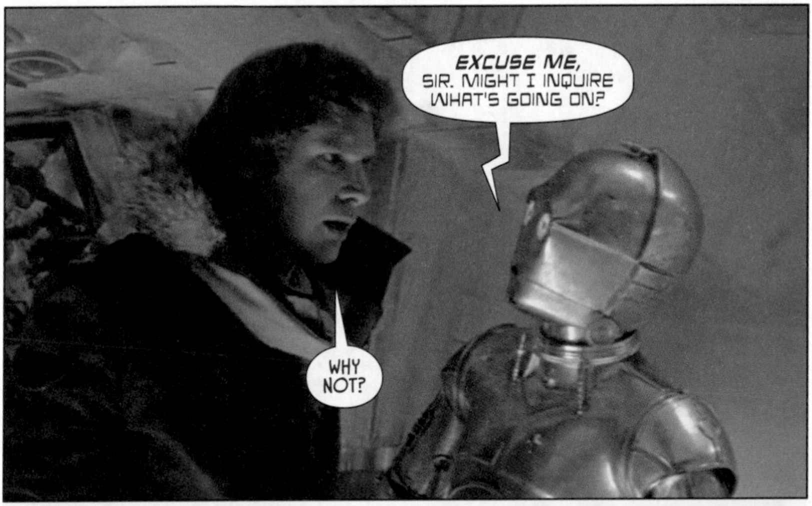
EXCUSE ME,
SIR. MIGHT I INQUIRE
WHAT'S GOING ON?
WHY
NOT?

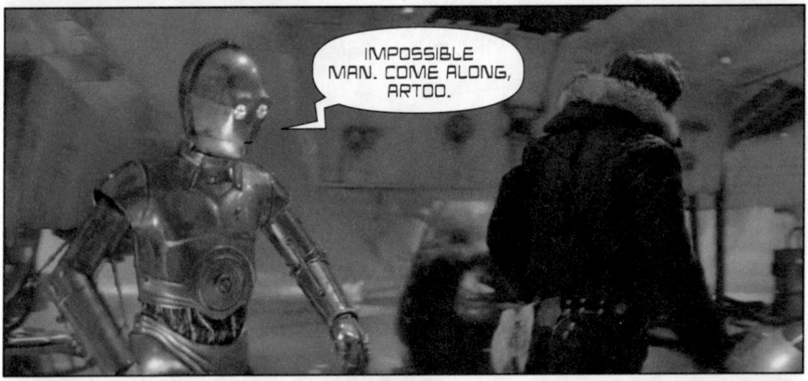
IMPOSSIBLE
MAN. COME ALONG,
ARTOO.

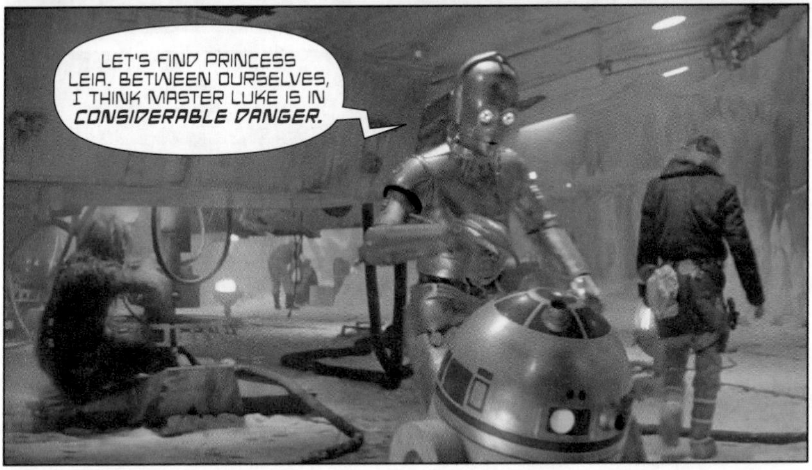
LET'S FIND PRINCESS
LEIA. BETWEEN OURSELVES,
I THINK MASTER LUKE IS IN
CONSIDERABLE DANGER.

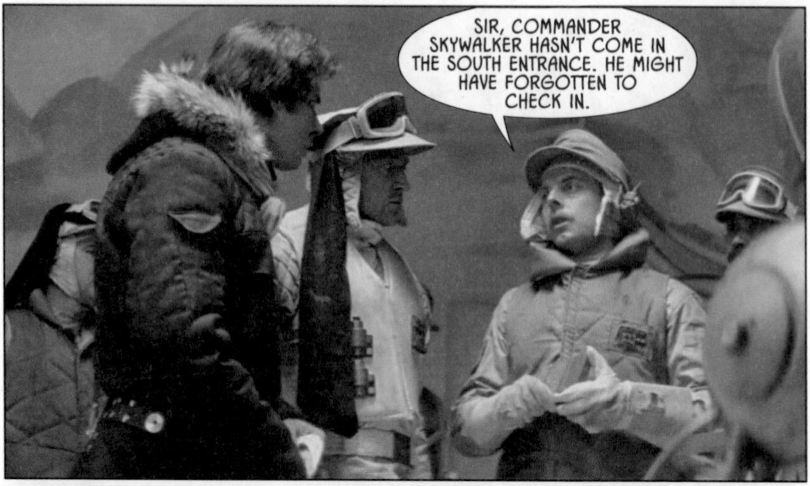
SIR, COMMANDER SKYWALKER HASN'T COME IN THE SOUTH ENTRANCE. HE MIGHT HAVE FORGOTTEN TO CHECK IN.

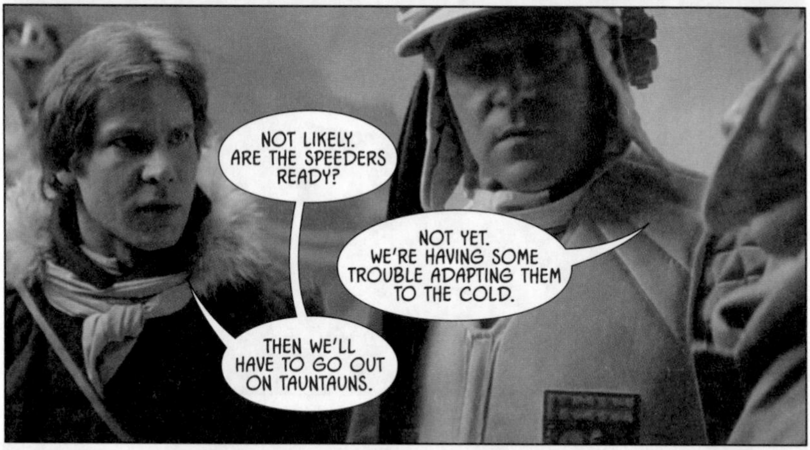
NOT LIKELY. ARE THE SPEEDERS READY?
NOT YET. WE'RE HAVING SOME TROUBLE ADAPTING THEM TO THE COLD.
THEN WE'LL HAVE TO GO OUT ON TAUNTAUNS.

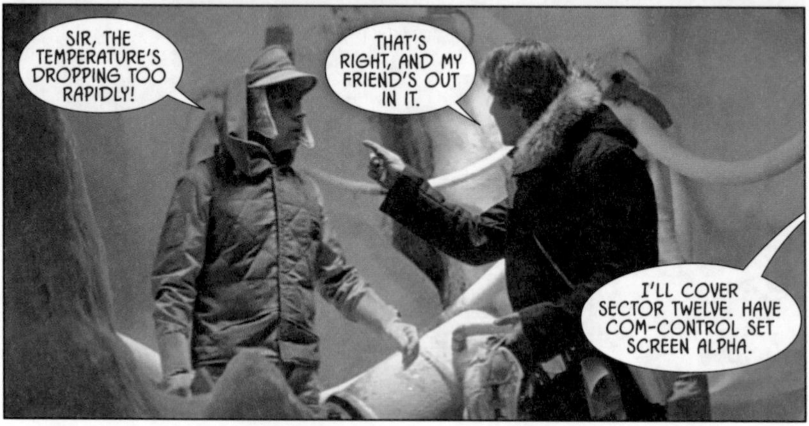
SIR, THE TEMPERATURE'S DROPPING TOO RAPIDLY!
THAT'S RIGHT, AND MY FRIEND'S OUT IN IT.
I'LL COVER SECTOR TWELVE. HAVE COM-CONTROL SET SCREEN ALPHA.

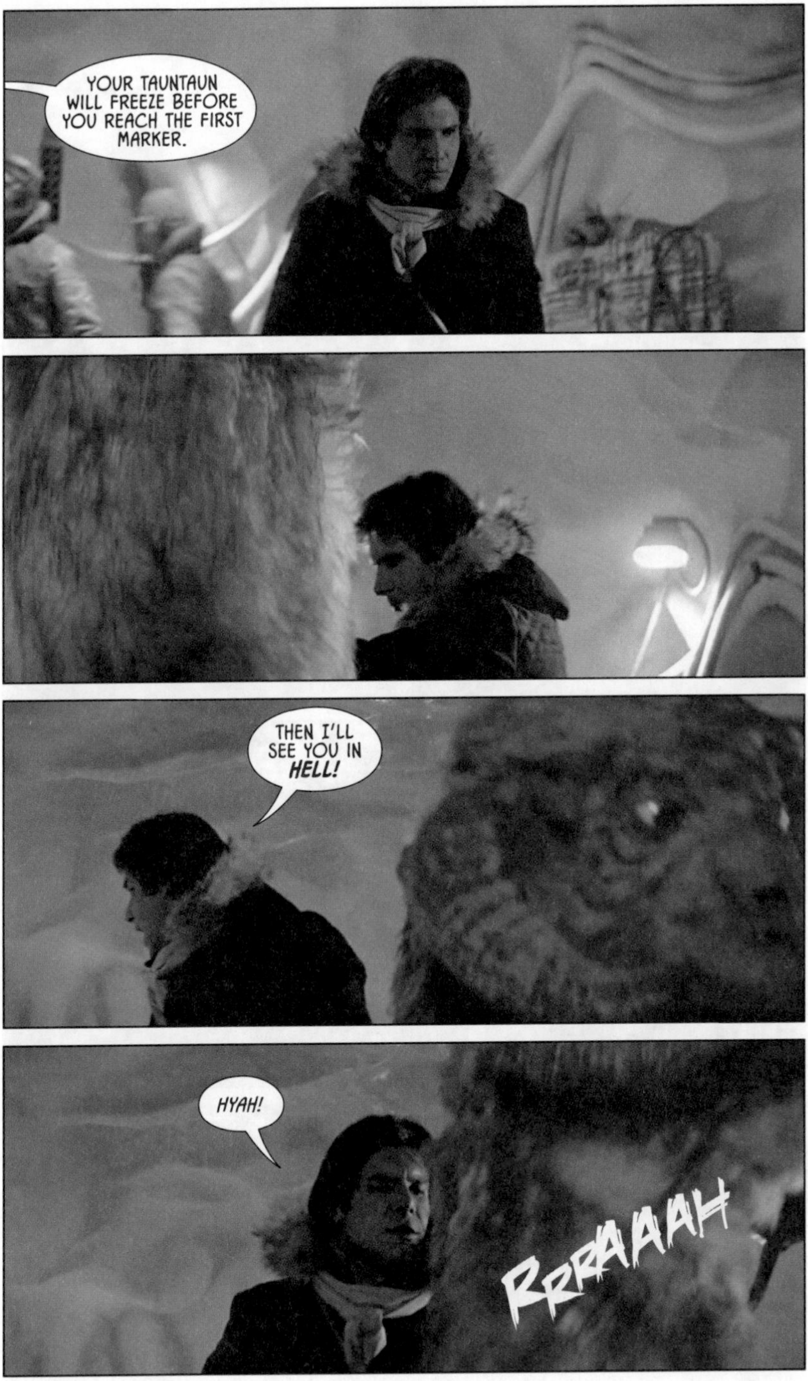
YOUR TAUNTAUN WILL FREEZE BEFORE YOU REACH THE FIRST MARKER.
THEN I'LL SEE YOU IN *HELL!*
HYAH!
RRRAAAH

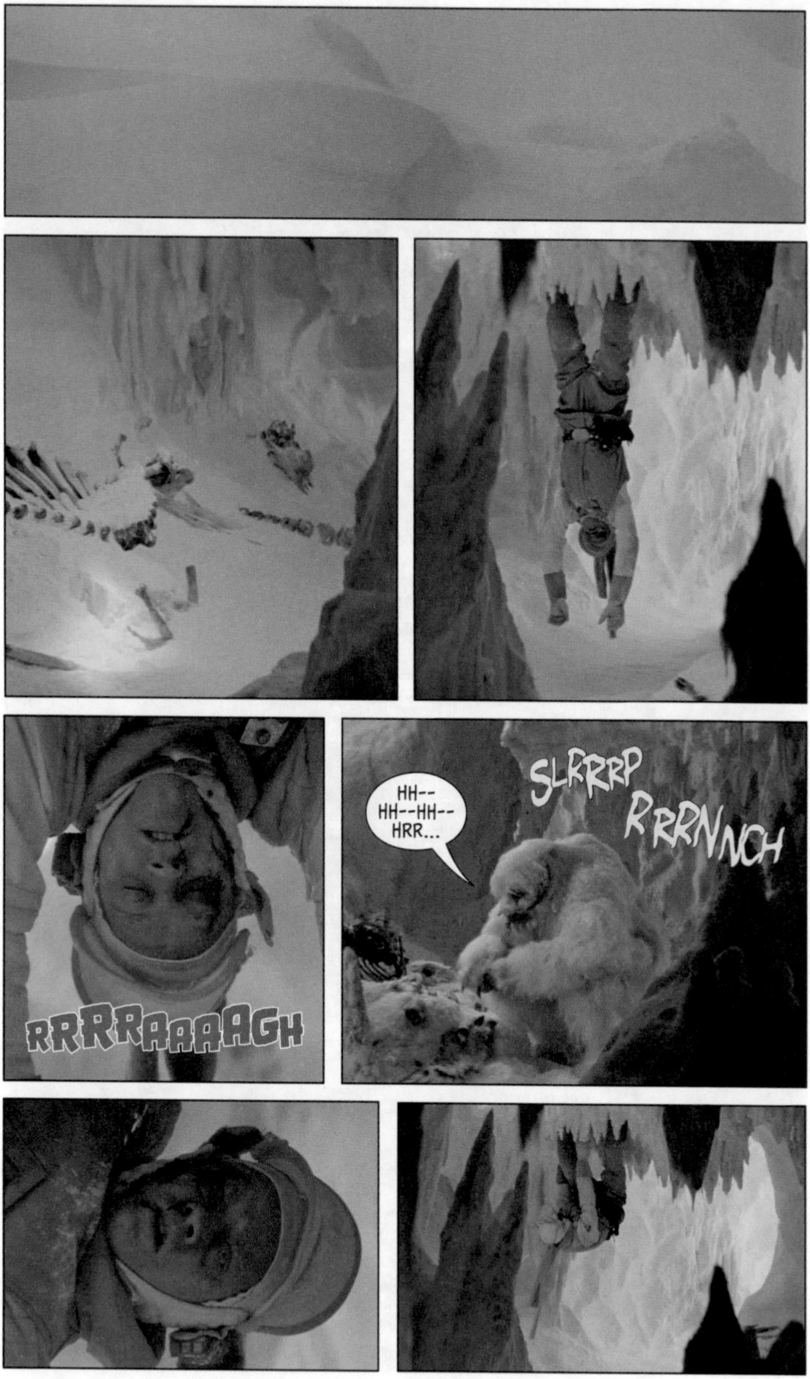
RRRRAAAAAGH
HH--
HH--HH--
HRR...
SLRRRP
RRRNNCH

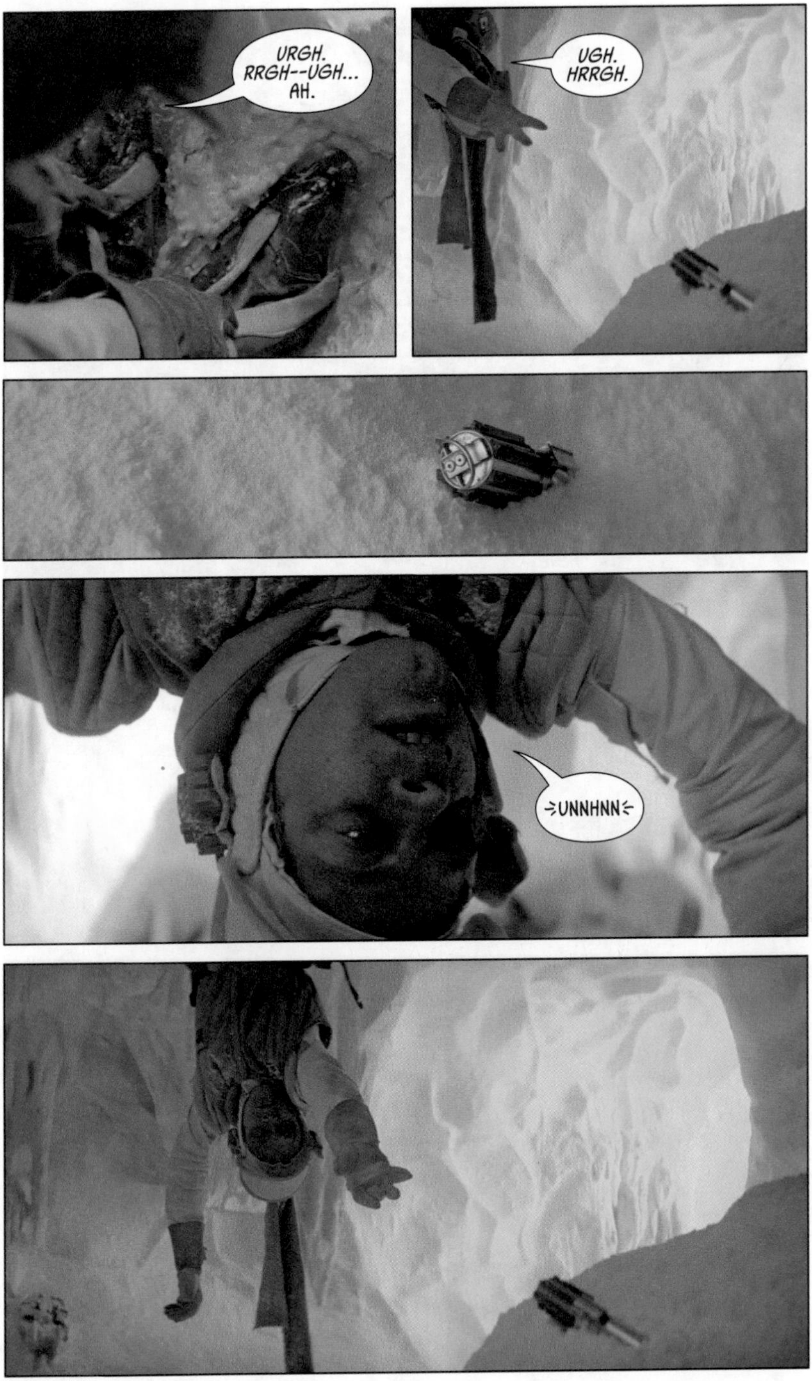
URGH. RRGH--UGH... AH.
UGH. HRRGH.
UNNHNN

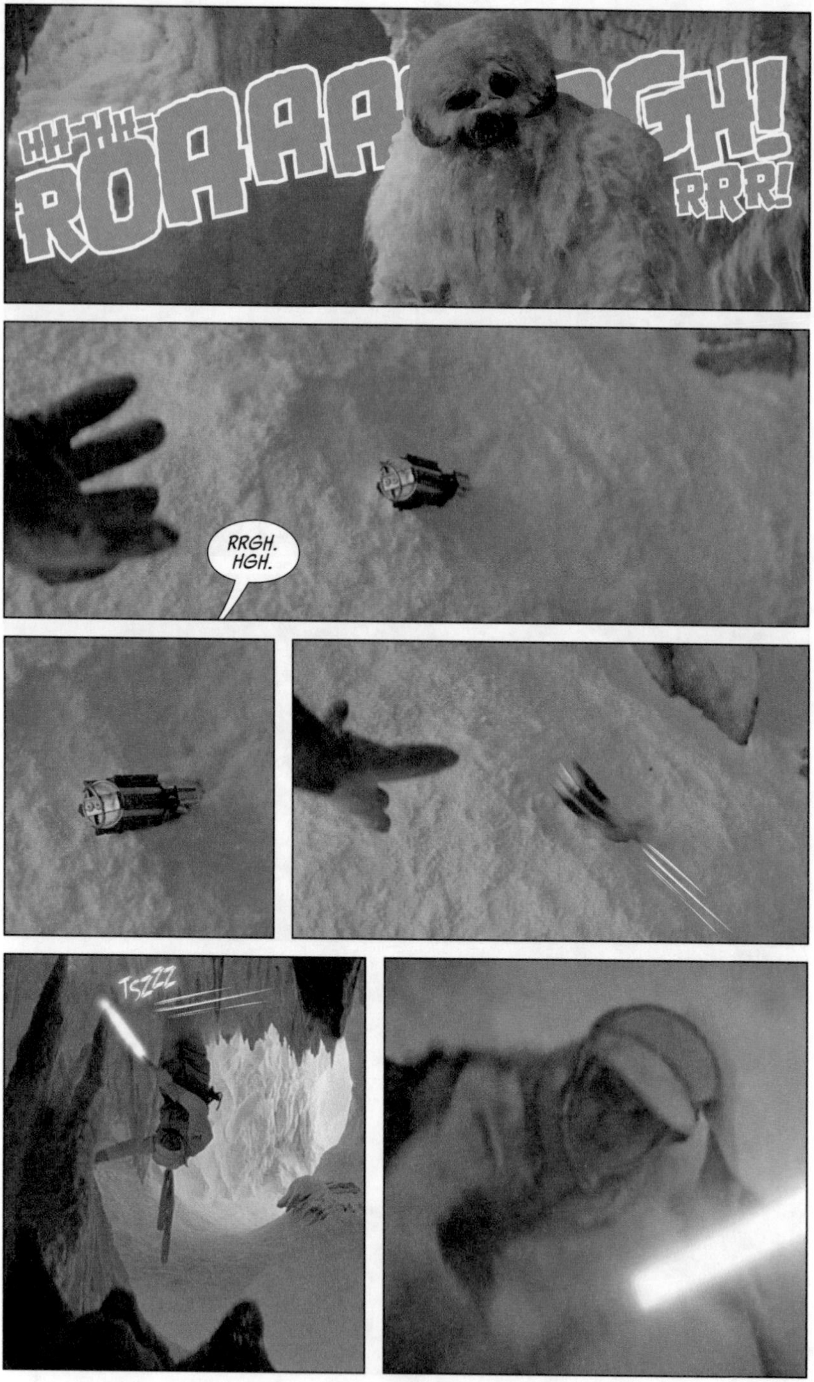
HH-HH-
ROAAAAGH!
RRR!
RRGH. HGH.
TSZZZ

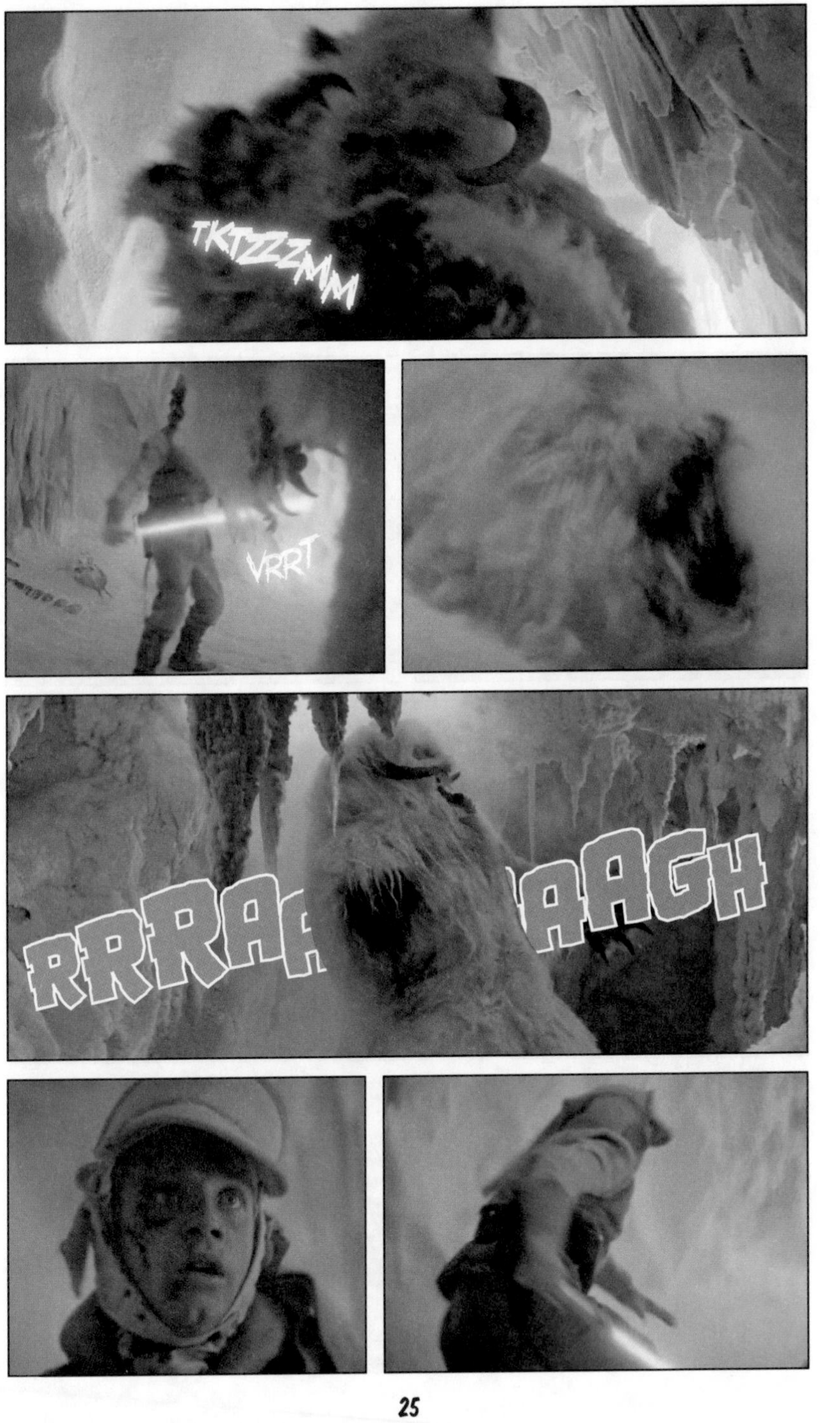
TKTZZZMMM
VRRT
RRRAA
AAGH

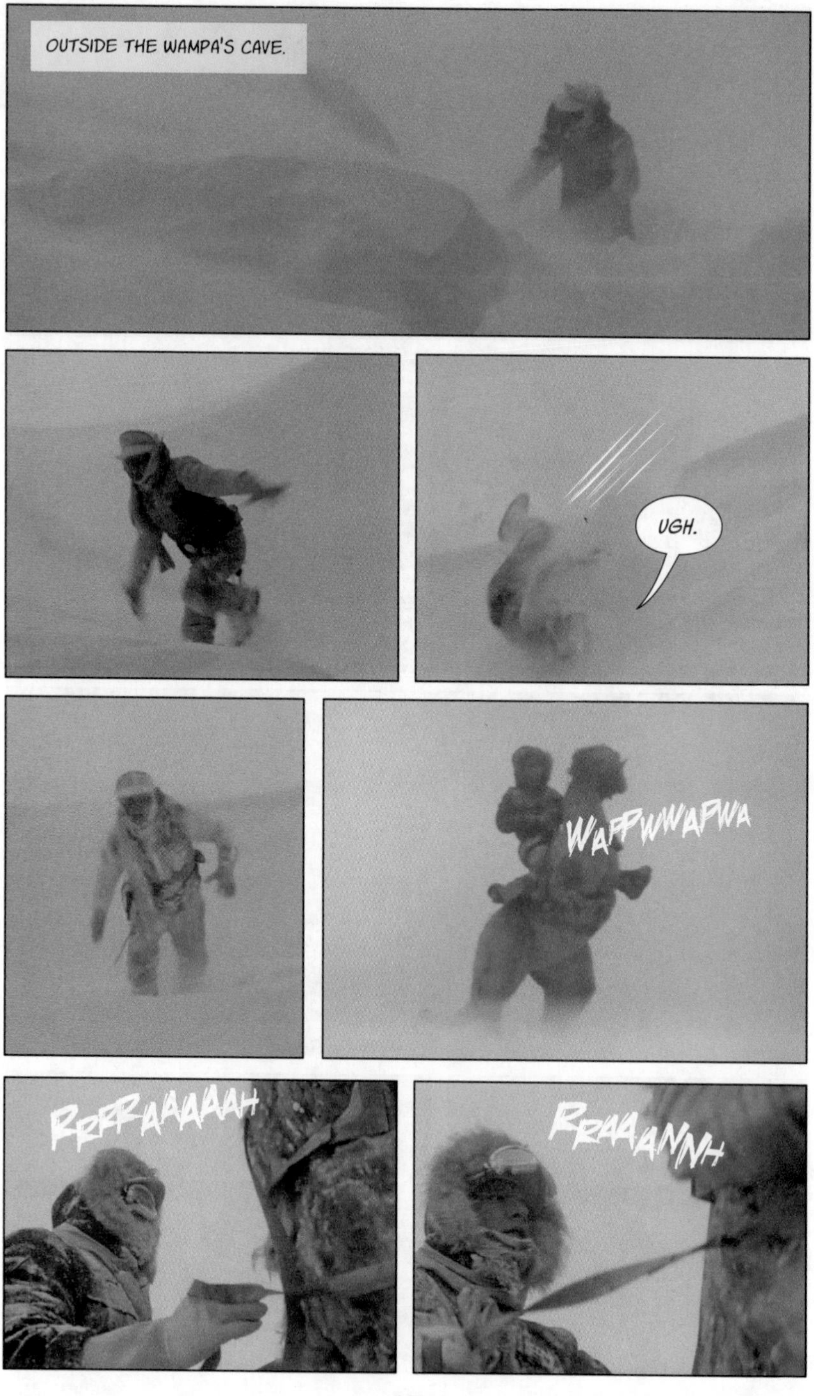
OUTSIDE THE WAMPA'S CAVE.
UGH.
WAPPWWAPWA
RRRRAAAAAH
RRAAANNH

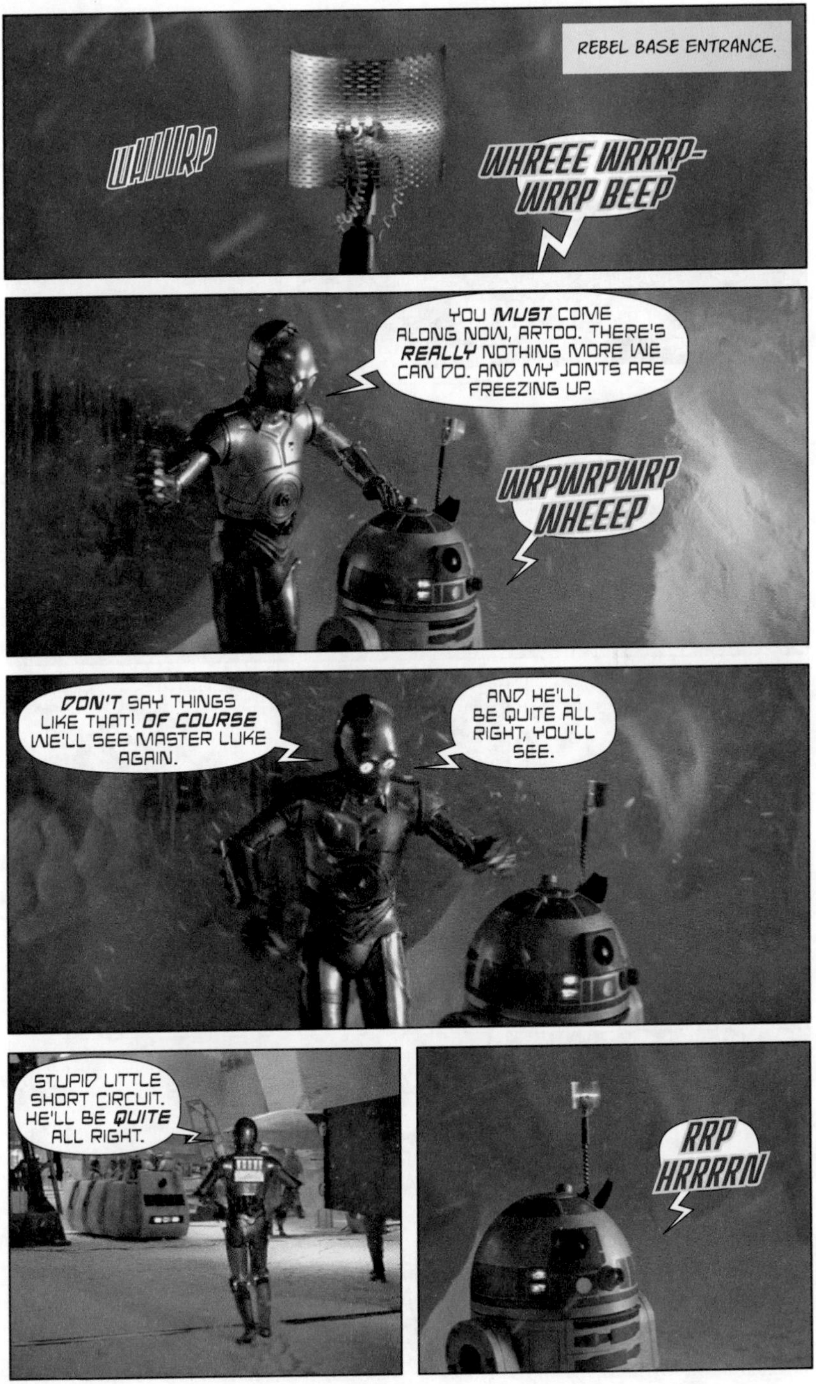
REBEL BASE ENTRANCE.
WHIIIRP
WHREEE WRRRP-WRRP BEEP
YOU MUST COME ALONG NOW, ARTOO. THERE'S REALLY NOTHING MORE WE CAN DO. AND MY JOINTS ARE FREEZING UP.
WRPWRPWRP WHEEEP
DON'T SAY THINGS LIKE THAT! OF COURSE WE'LL SEE MASTER LUKE AGAIN.
AND HE'LL BE QUITE ALL RIGHT, YOU'LL SEE.
STUPID LITTLE SHORT CIRCUIT. HE'LL BE QUITE ALL RIGHT.
RRP HRRRRN

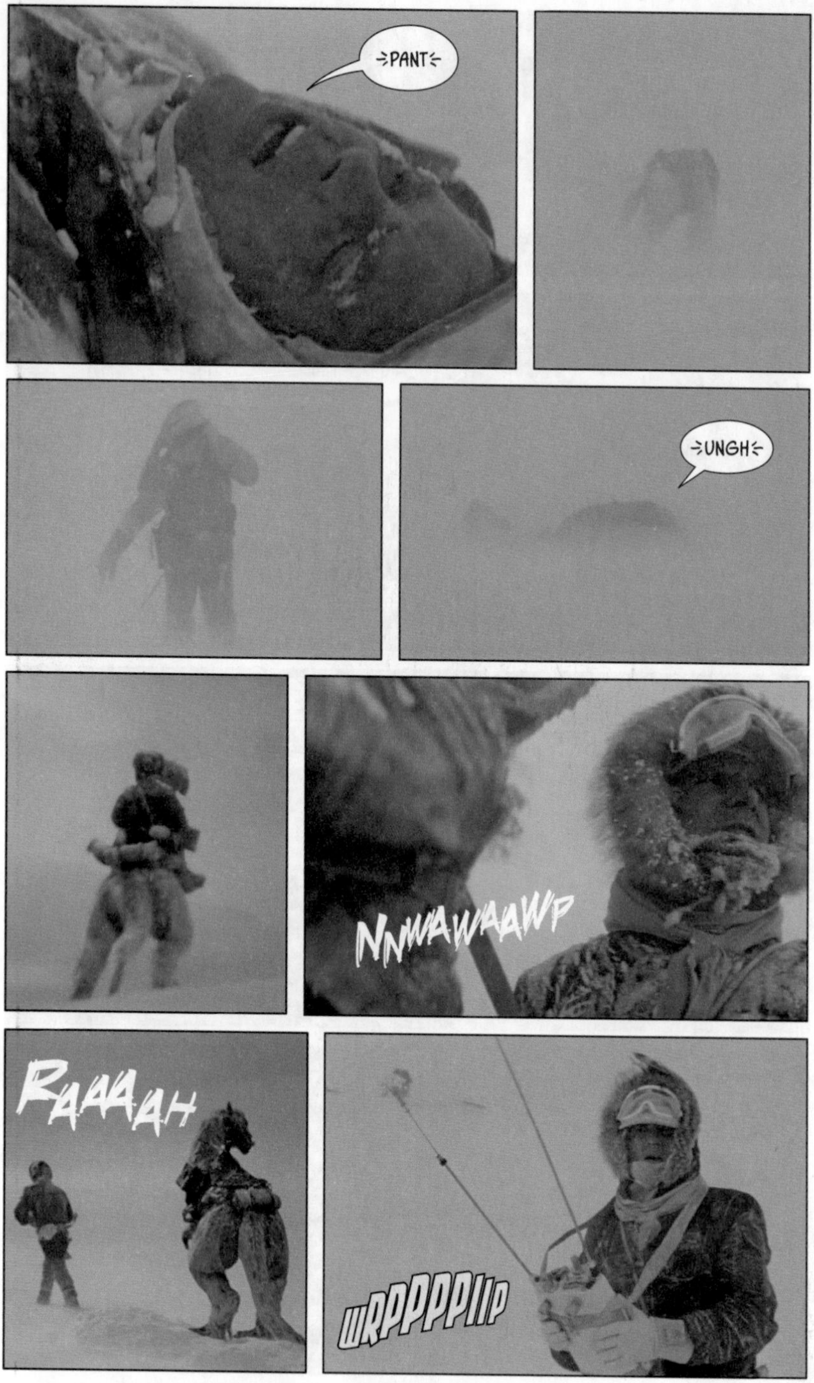
PANT
UNGH
NNWAWAAWP
RAAAAH
WRPPPPIIP

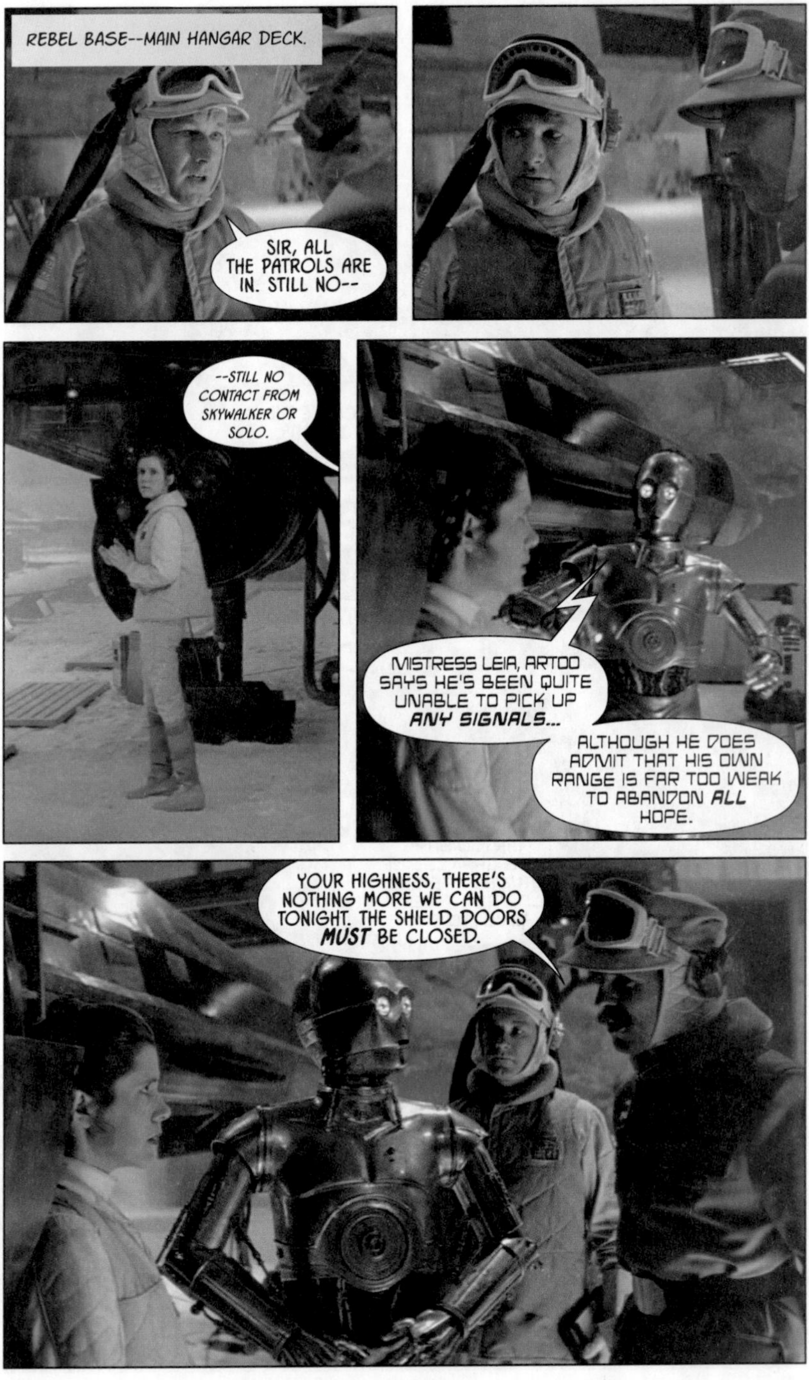
REBEL BASE--MAIN HANGAR DECK.
SIR, ALL THE PATROLS ARE IN. STILL NO--
--STILL NO CONTACT FROM SKYWALKER OR SOLO.
MISTRESS LEIA, ARTOO SAYS HE'S BEEN QUITE UNABLE TO PICK UP ANY SIGNALS...
ALTHOUGH HE DOES ADMIT THAT HIS OWN RANGE IS FAR TOO WEAK TO ABANDON ALL HOPE.
YOUR HIGHNESS, THERE'S NOTHING MORE WE CAN DO TONIGHT. THE SHIELD DOORS MUST BE CLOSED.

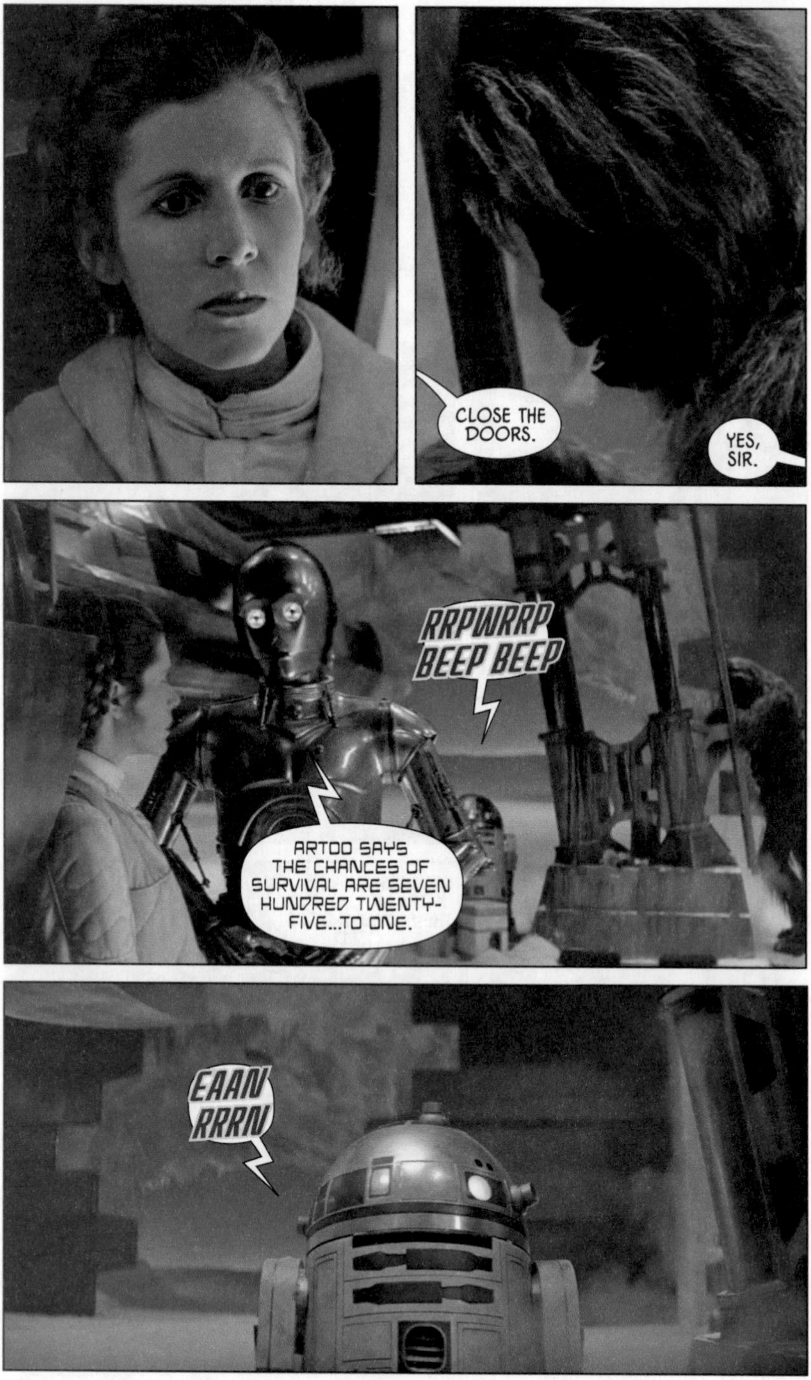
CLOSE THE DOORS.
YES, SIR.
RRPWRRP BEEP BEEP
ARTOO SAYS THE CHANCES OF SURVIVAL ARE SEVEN HUNDRED TWENTY-FIVE...TO ONE.
EAAN RRRN

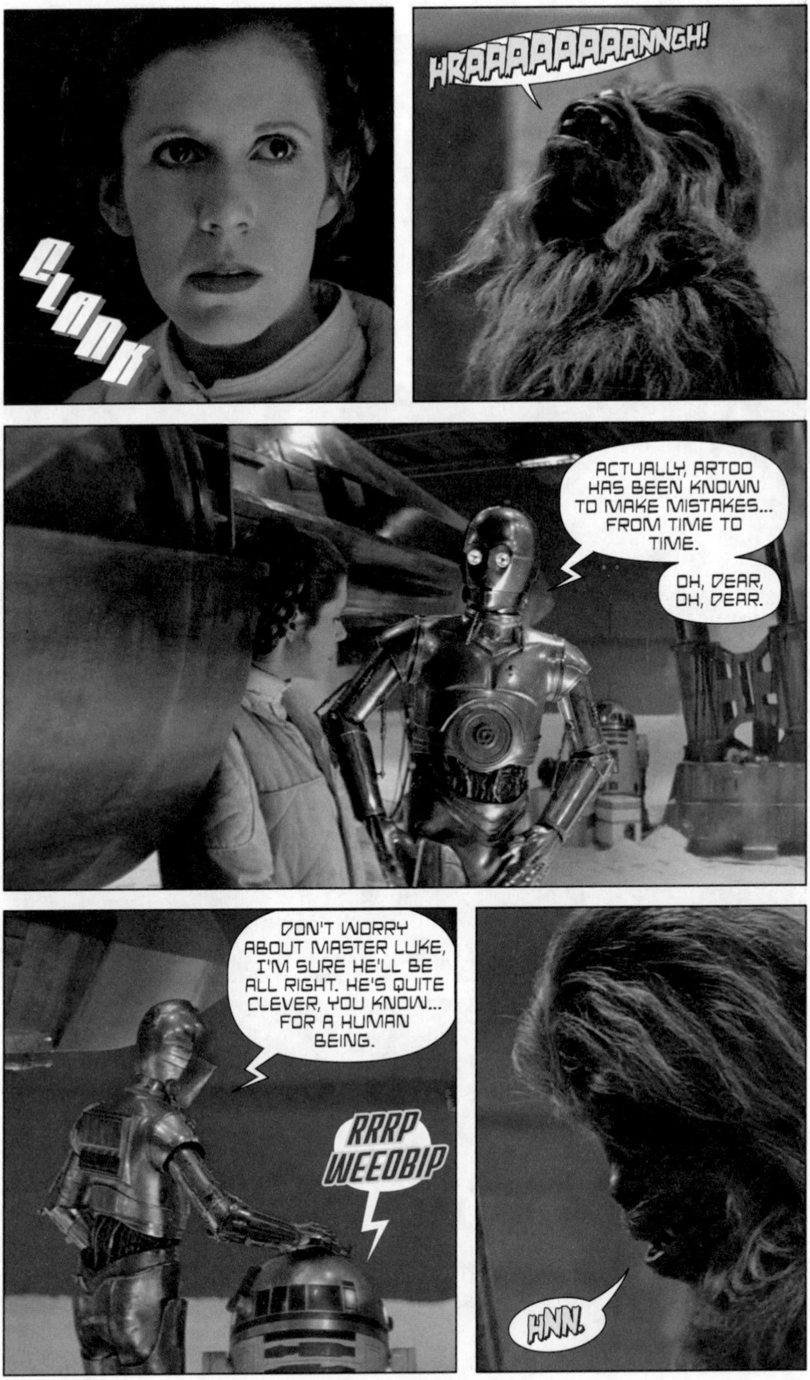
CLANK
HRAAAAAAAANNGH!
ACTUALLY, ARTOO HAS BEEN KNOWN TO MAKE MISTAKES... FROM TIME TO TIME.
OH, DEAR, OH, DEAR.
DON'T WORRY ABOUT MASTER LUKE, I'M SURE HE'LL BE ALL RIGHT. HE'S QUITE CLEVER, YOU KNOW... FOR A HUMAN BEING.
RRRP WEEDBIP
HNN.

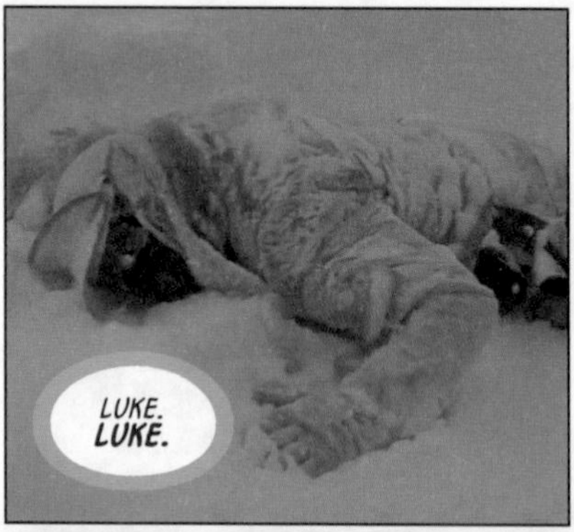
LUKE.
LUKE.

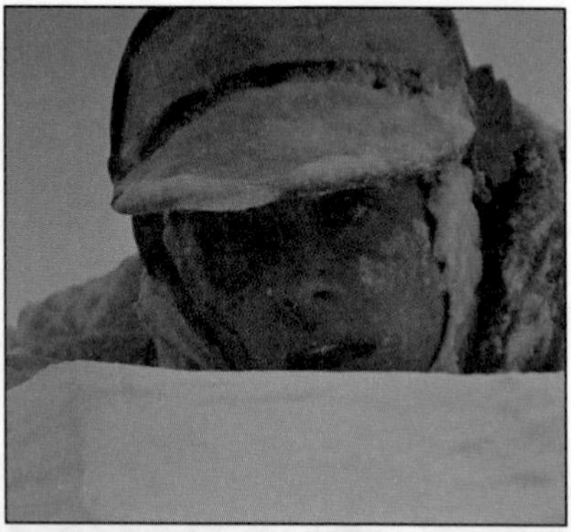

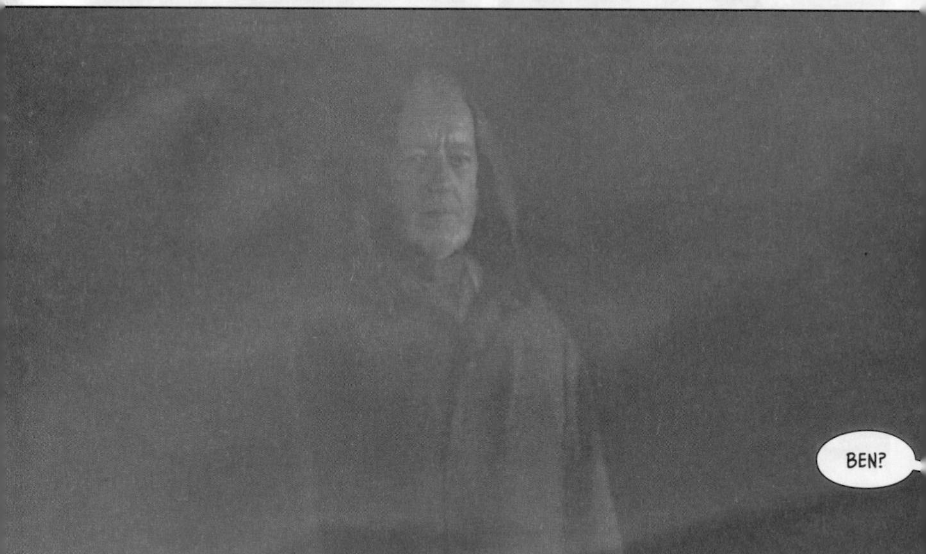
BEN?

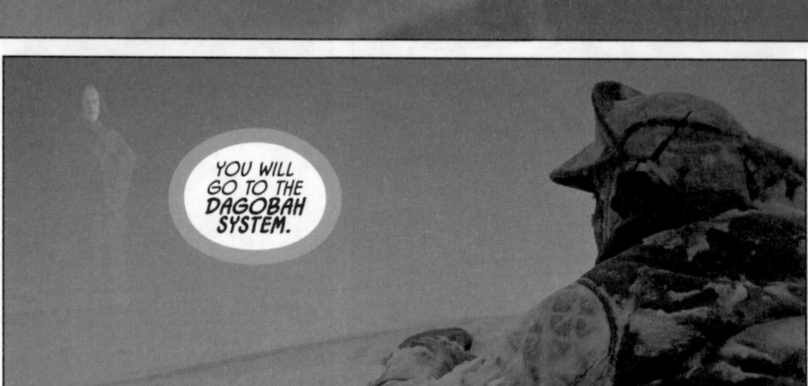
YOU WILL GO TO THE DAGOBAH SYSTEM.

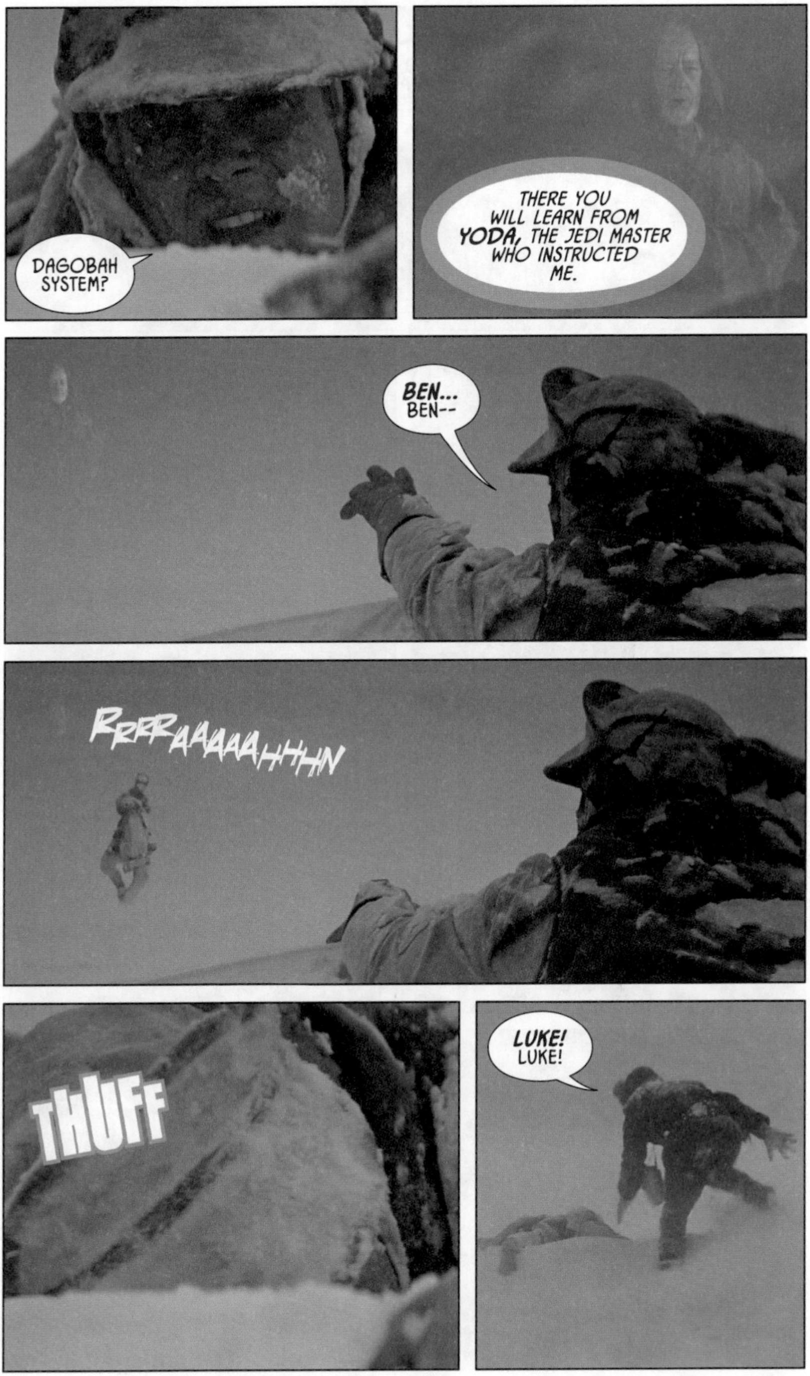
DAGOBAH SYSTEM?
THERE YOU WILL LEARN FROM YODA, THE JEDI MASTER WHO INSTRUCTED ME.
BEN... BEN--
RRRRAAAAAAHHHHN
THUFF
LUKE! LUKE!

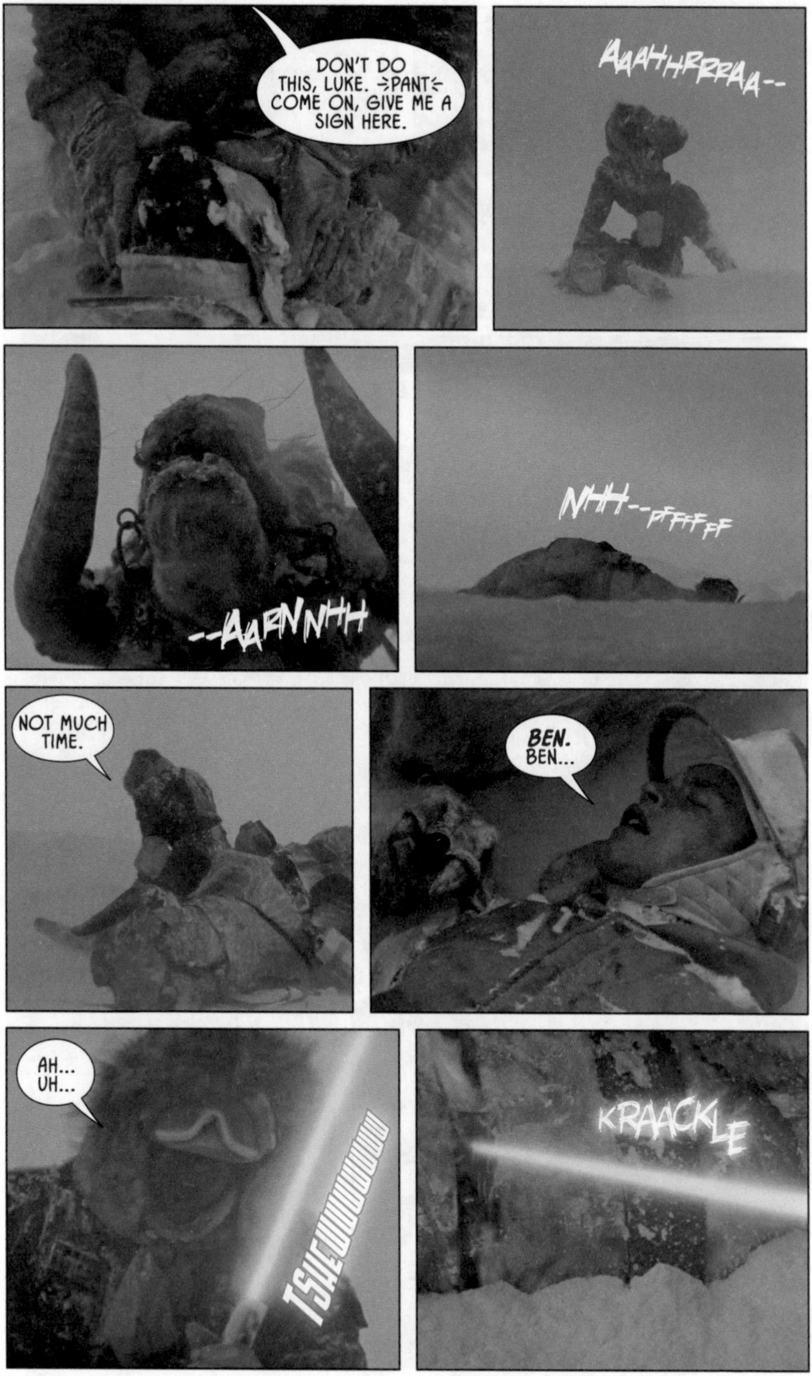

DON'T DO THIS, LUKE. ⋺PANT⋲ COME ON, GIVE ME A SIGN HERE.
AAAHHRRRAA--
--AARNNHH
NHH--PFFFFF
NOT MUCH TIME.
BEN. BEN...
AH... UH...
TSHEWWWWWW
KRAACKLE

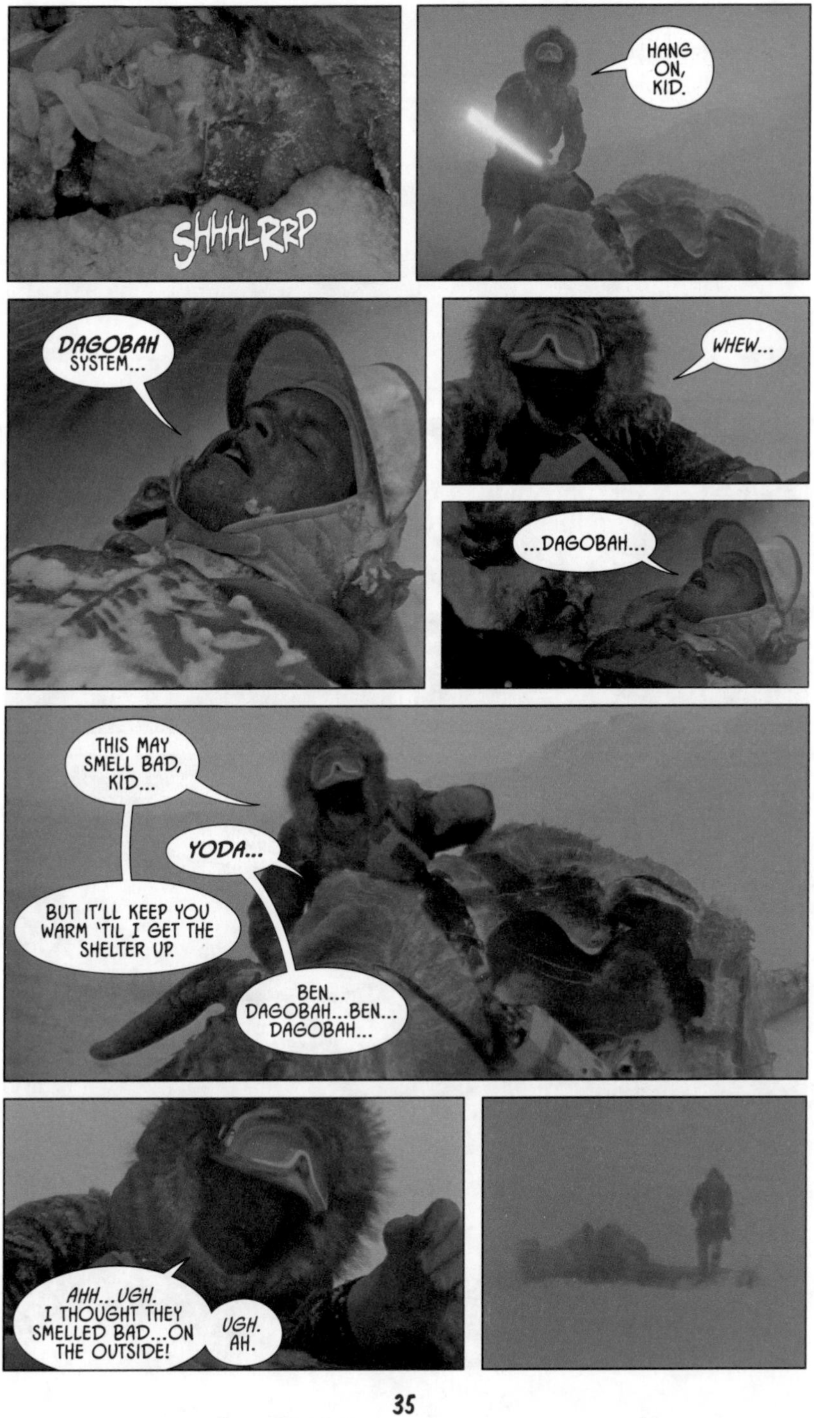
SHHHLRRP
HANG ON, KID.
DAGOBAH SYSTEM...
WHEW...
...DAGOBAH...
THIS MAY SMELL BAD, KID...
YODA...
BUT IT'LL KEEP YOU WARM 'TIL I GET THE SHELTER UP.
BEN... DAGOBAH...BEN... DAGOBAH...
AHH...UGH. I THOUGHT THEY SMELLED BAD...ON THE OUTSIDE!
UGH. AH.

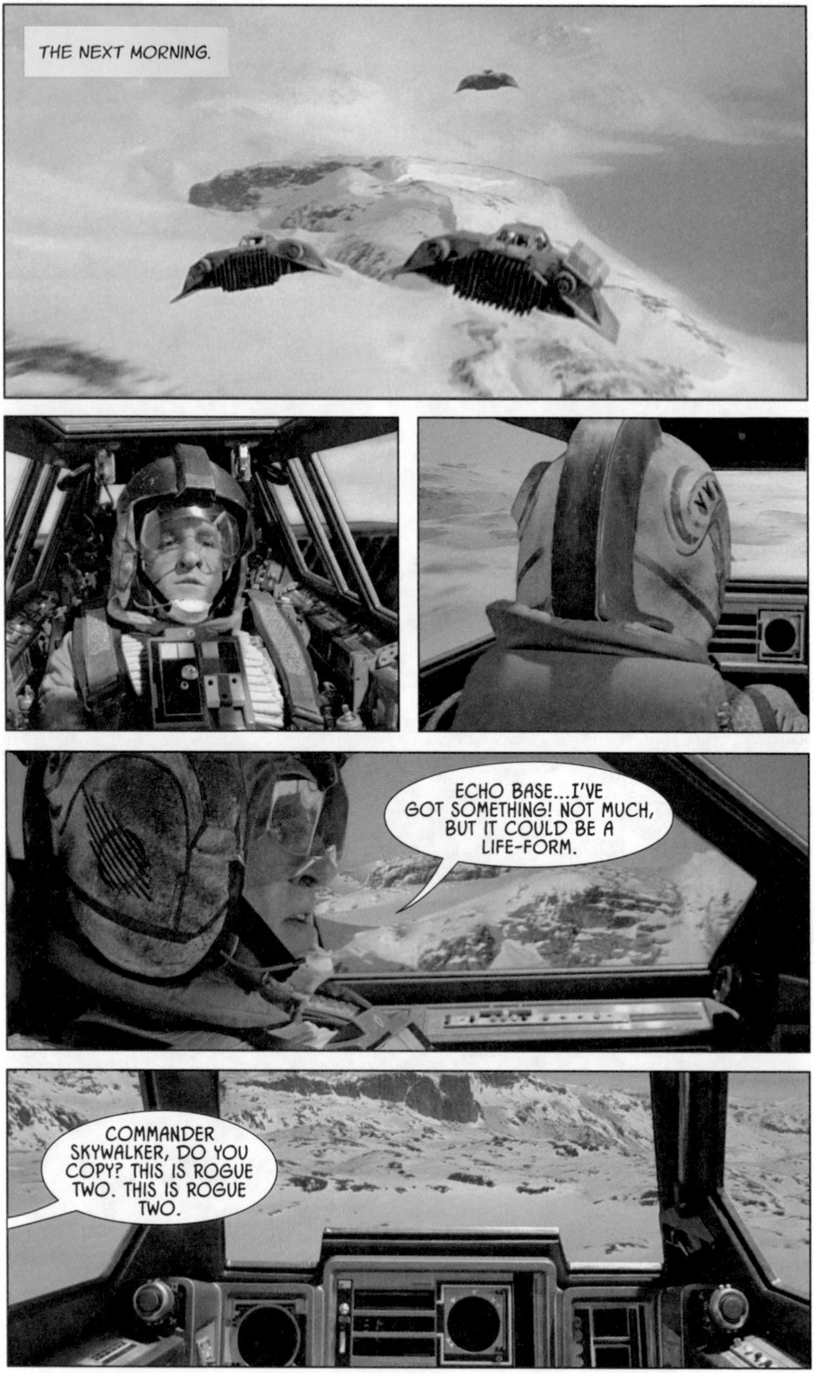
THE NEXT MORNING.
ECHO BASE...I'VE GOT SOMETHING! NOT MUCH, BUT IT COULD BE A LIFE-FORM.
COMMANDER SKYWALKER, DO YOU COPY? THIS IS ROGUE TWO. THIS IS ROGUE TWO.

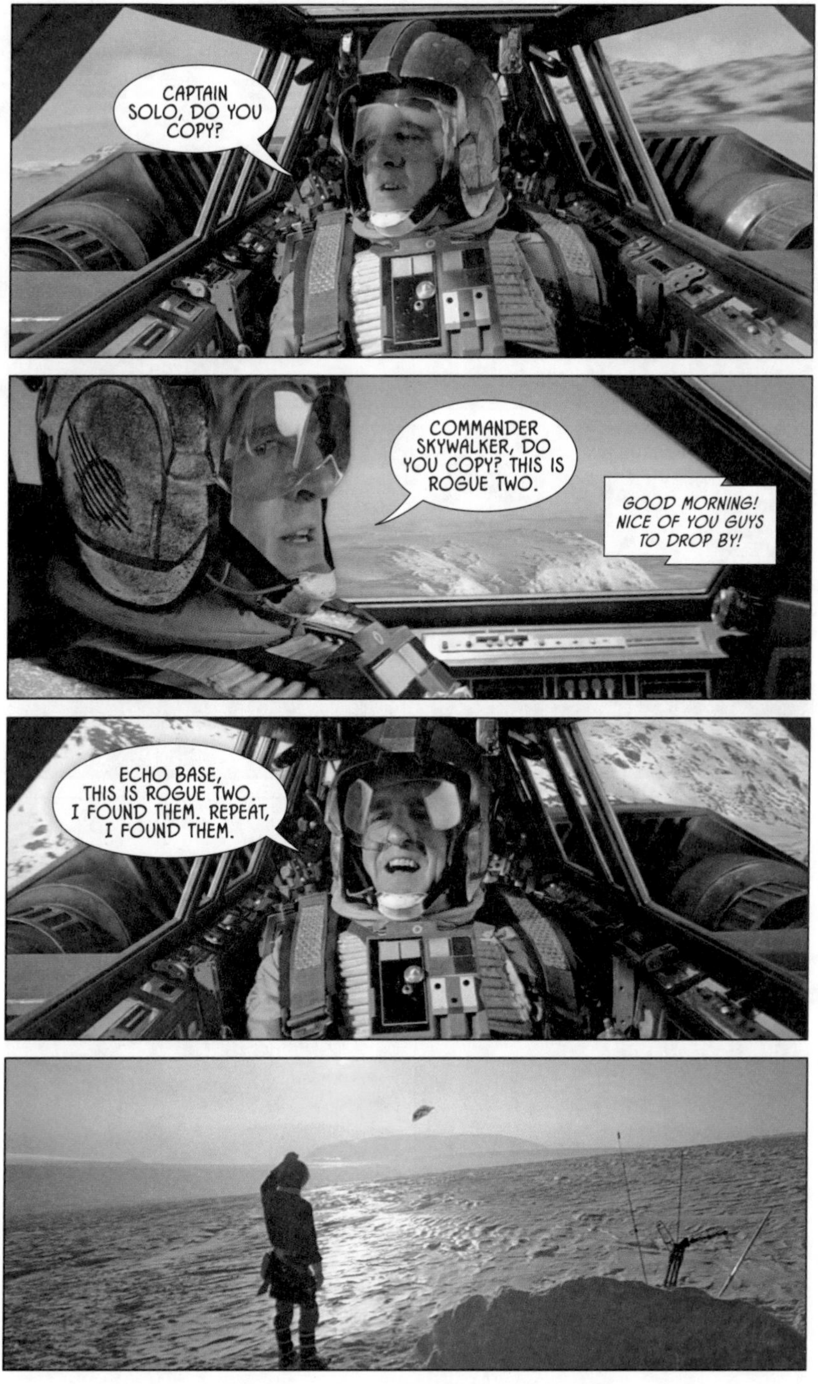
CAPTAIN SOLO, DO YOU COPY?
COMMANDER SKYWALKER, DO YOU COPY? THIS IS ROGUE TWO.
GOOD MORNING! NICE OF YOU GUYS TO DROP BY!
ECHO BASE, THIS IS ROGUE TWO. I FOUND THEM. REPEAT, I FOUND THEM.

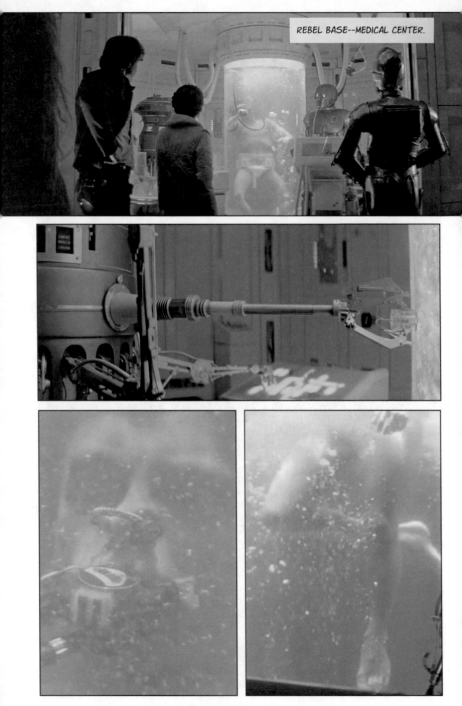

REBEL BASE--MEDICAL CENTER.

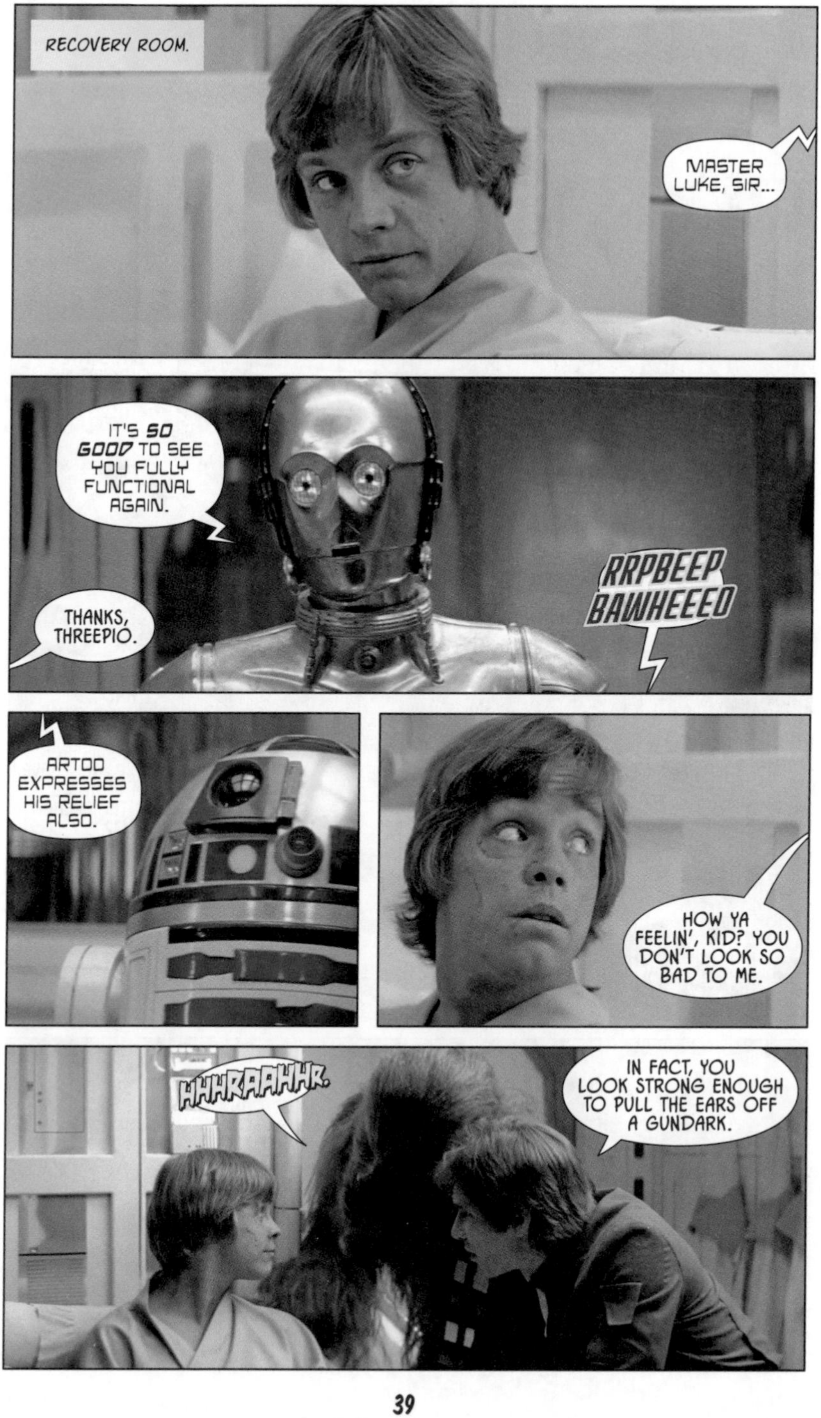
RECOVERY ROOM.
MASTER LUKE, SIR...
IT'S SO GOOD TO SEE YOU FULLY FUNCTIONAL AGAIN.
THANKS, THREEPIO.
RRPBEEP BAWHEEED
ARTOO EXPRESSES HIS RELIEF ALSO.
HOW YA FEELIN', KID? YOU DON'T LOOK SO BAD TO ME.
HHHRAAHHR.
IN FACT, YOU LOOK STRONG ENOUGH TO PULL THE EARS OFF A GUNDARK.

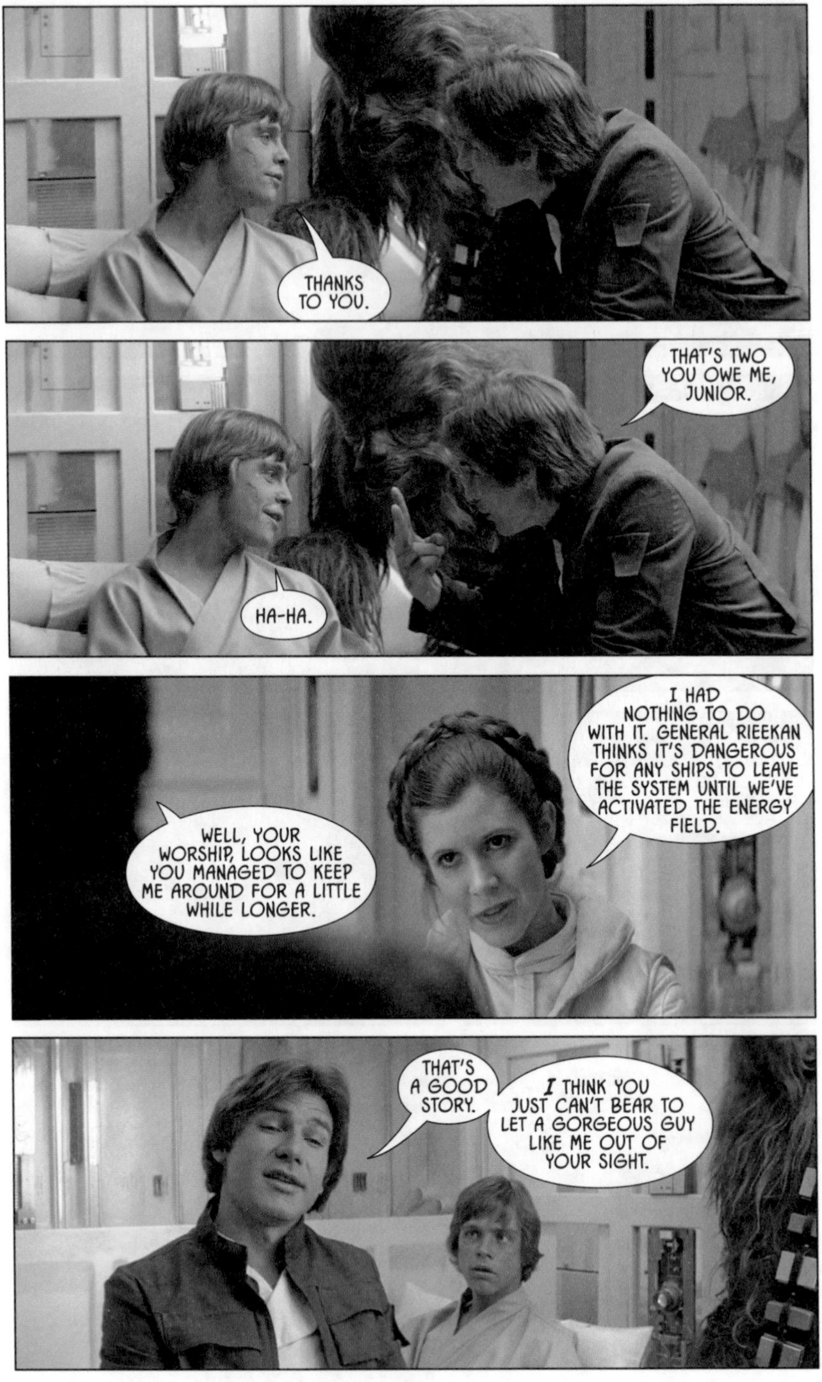
THANKS TO YOU.
THAT'S TWO YOU OWE ME, JUNIOR.
HA-HA.
WELL, YOUR WORSHIP, LOOKS LIKE YOU MANAGED TO KEEP ME AROUND FOR A LITTLE WHILE LONGER.
I HAD NOTHING TO DO WITH IT. GENERAL RIEEKAN THINKS IT'S DANGEROUS FOR ANY SHIPS TO LEAVE THE SYSTEM UNTIL WE'VE ACTIVATED THE ENERGY FIELD.
THAT'S A GOOD STORY.
I THINK YOU JUST CAN'T BEAR TO LET A GORGEOUS GUY LIKE ME OUT OF YOUR SIGHT.

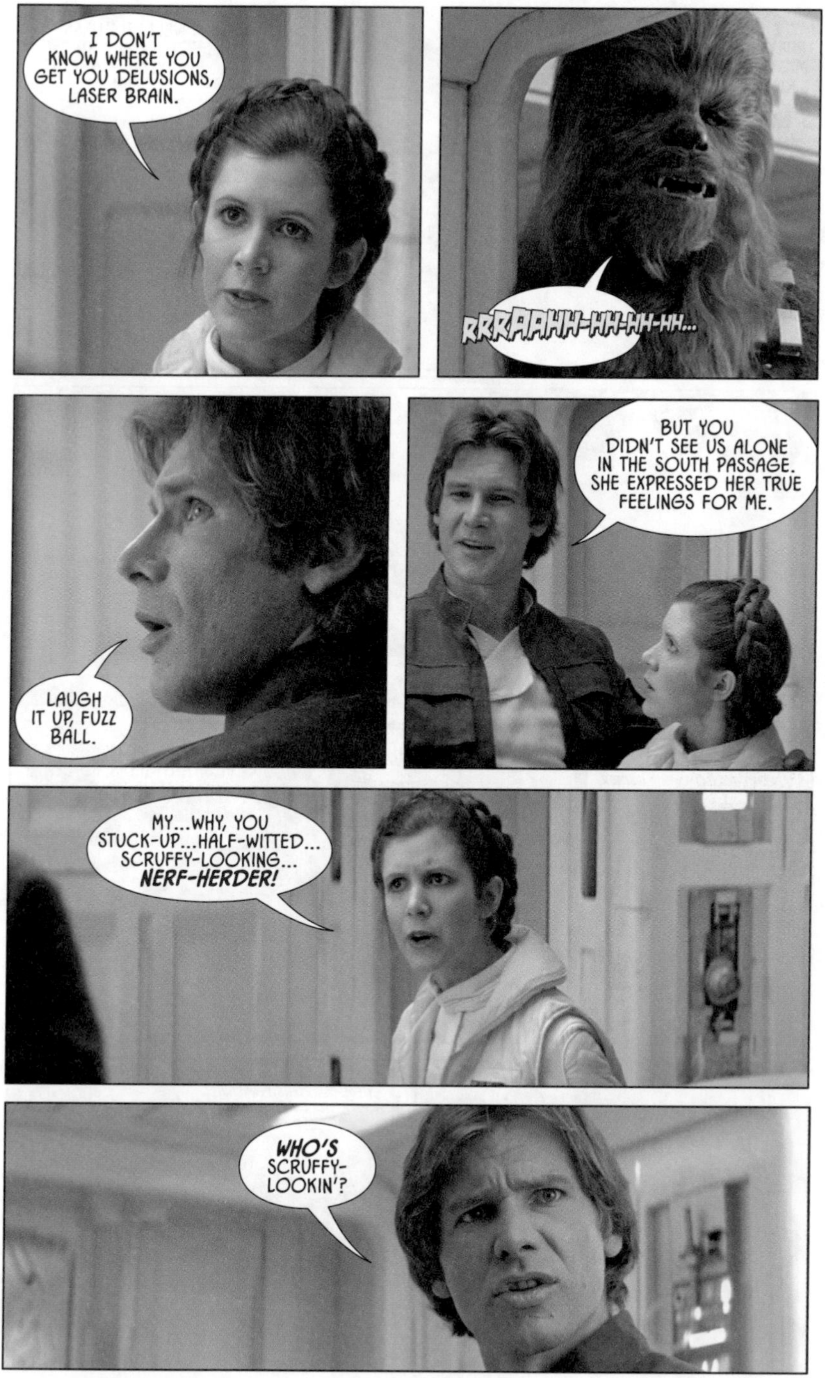
I DON'T KNOW WHERE YOU GET YOU DELUSIONS, LASER BRAIN.
RRRAAHH-HH-HH-HH...
LAUGH IT UP, FUZZ BALL.
BUT YOU DIDN'T SEE US ALONE IN THE SOUTH PASSAGE. SHE EXPRESSED HER TRUE FEELINGS FOR ME.
MY...WHY, YOU STUCK-UP...HALF-WITTED... SCRUFFY-LOOKING... NERF-HERDER!
WHO'S SCRUFFY-LOOKIN'?

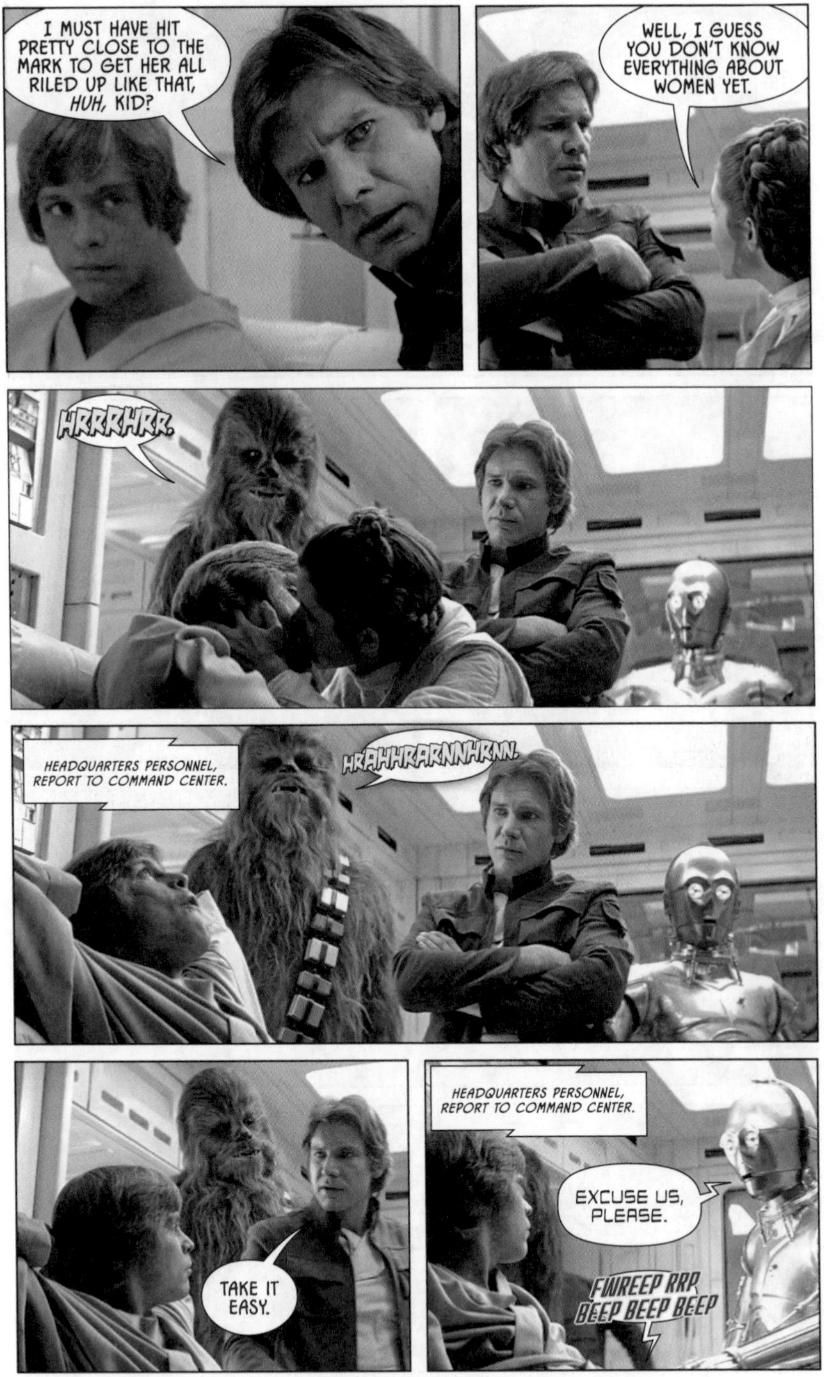
I MUST HAVE HIT PRETTY CLOSE TO THE MARK TO GET HER ALL RILED UP LIKE THAT, HUH, KID?
WELL, I GUESS YOU DON'T KNOW EVERYTHING ABOUT WOMEN YET.
HRRRHRR.
HEADQUARTERS PERSONNEL, REPORT TO COMMAND CENTER.
HRAHHRARNNHRNN.
TAKE IT EASY.
HEADQUARTERS PERSONNEL, REPORT TO COMMAND CENTER.
EXCUSE US, PLEASE.
FWREEP RRP BEEP BEEP BEEP

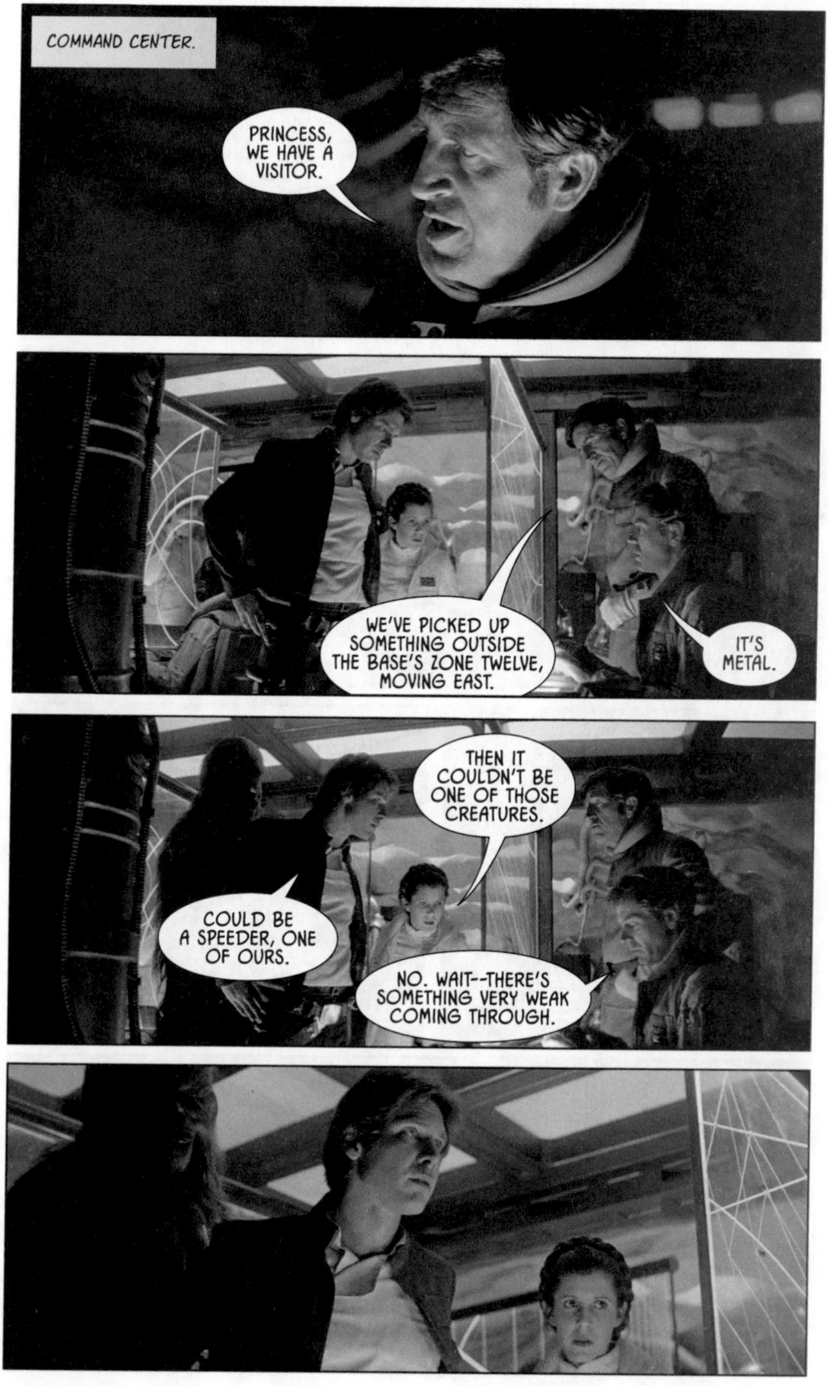
COMMAND CENTER.
PRINCESS, WE HAVE A VISITOR.
WE'VE PICKED UP SOMETHING OUTSIDE THE BASE'S ZONE TWELVE, MOVING EAST.
IT'S METAL.
THEN IT COULDN'T BE ONE OF THOSE CREATURES.
COULD BE A SPEEDER, ONE OF OURS.
NO. WAIT--THERE'S SOMETHING VERY WEAK COMING THROUGH.

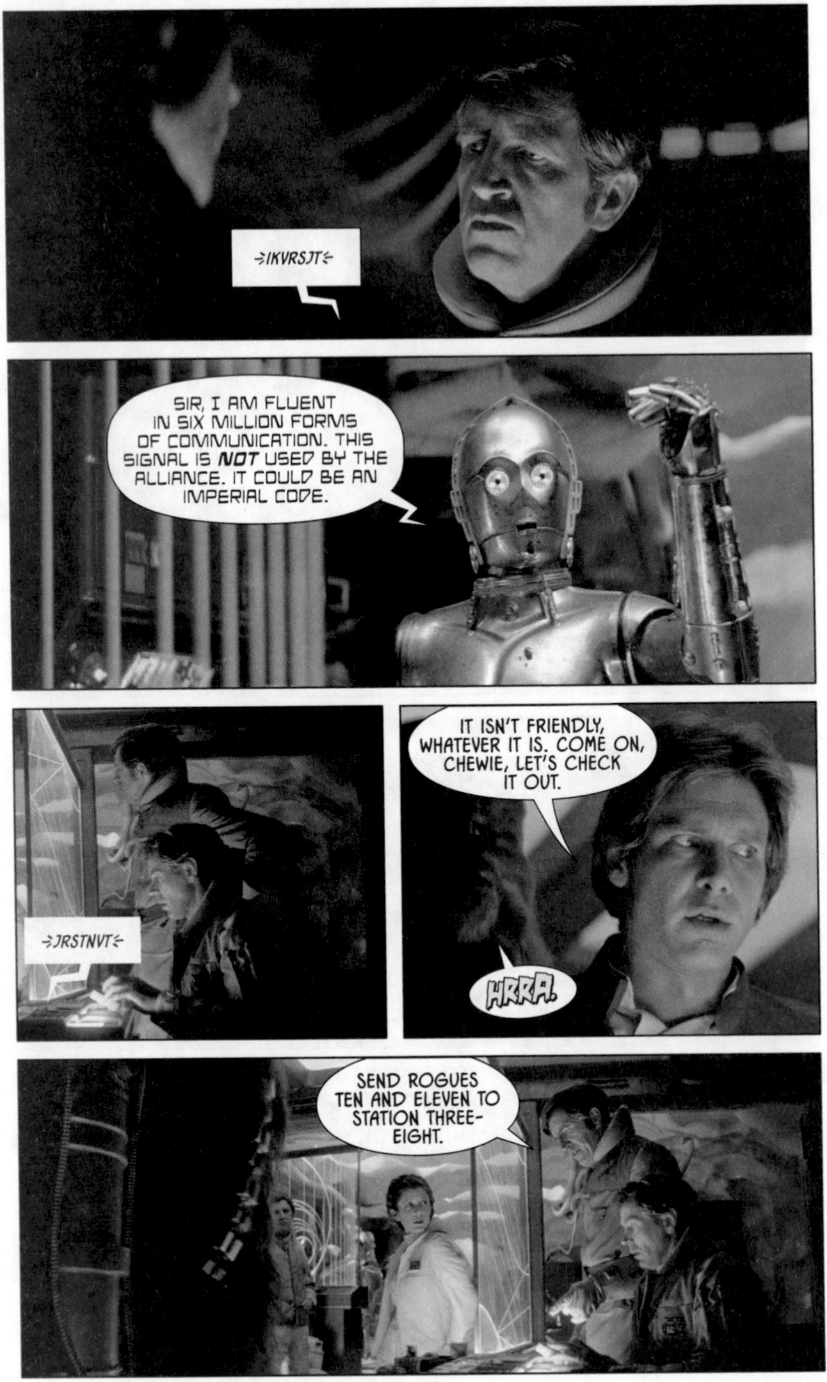

⇒IKVRSJT⇐
SIR, I AM FLUENT IN SIX MILLION FORMS OF COMMUNICATION. THIS SIGNAL IS **NOT** USED BY THE ALLIANCE. IT COULD BE AN IMPERIAL CODE.
⇒JRSTNVT⇐
IT ISN'T FRIENDLY, WHATEVER IT IS. COME ON, CHEWIE, LET'S CHECK IT OUT.
HRRA.
SEND ROGUES TEN AND ELEVEN TO STATION THREE-EIGHT.

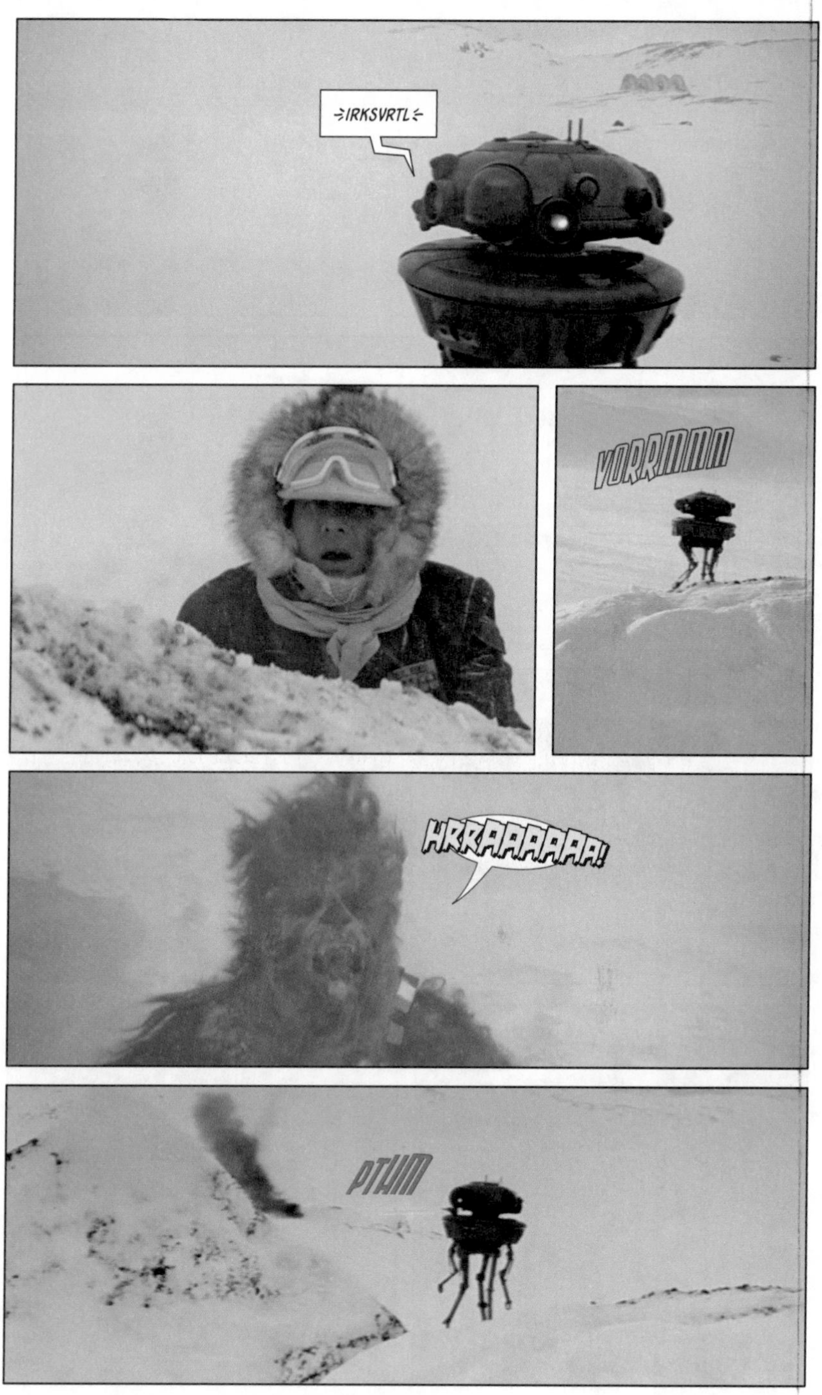
⚟IRKSVRTL⚞
VORRMMM
HRRAAAAAAA!
PTUM

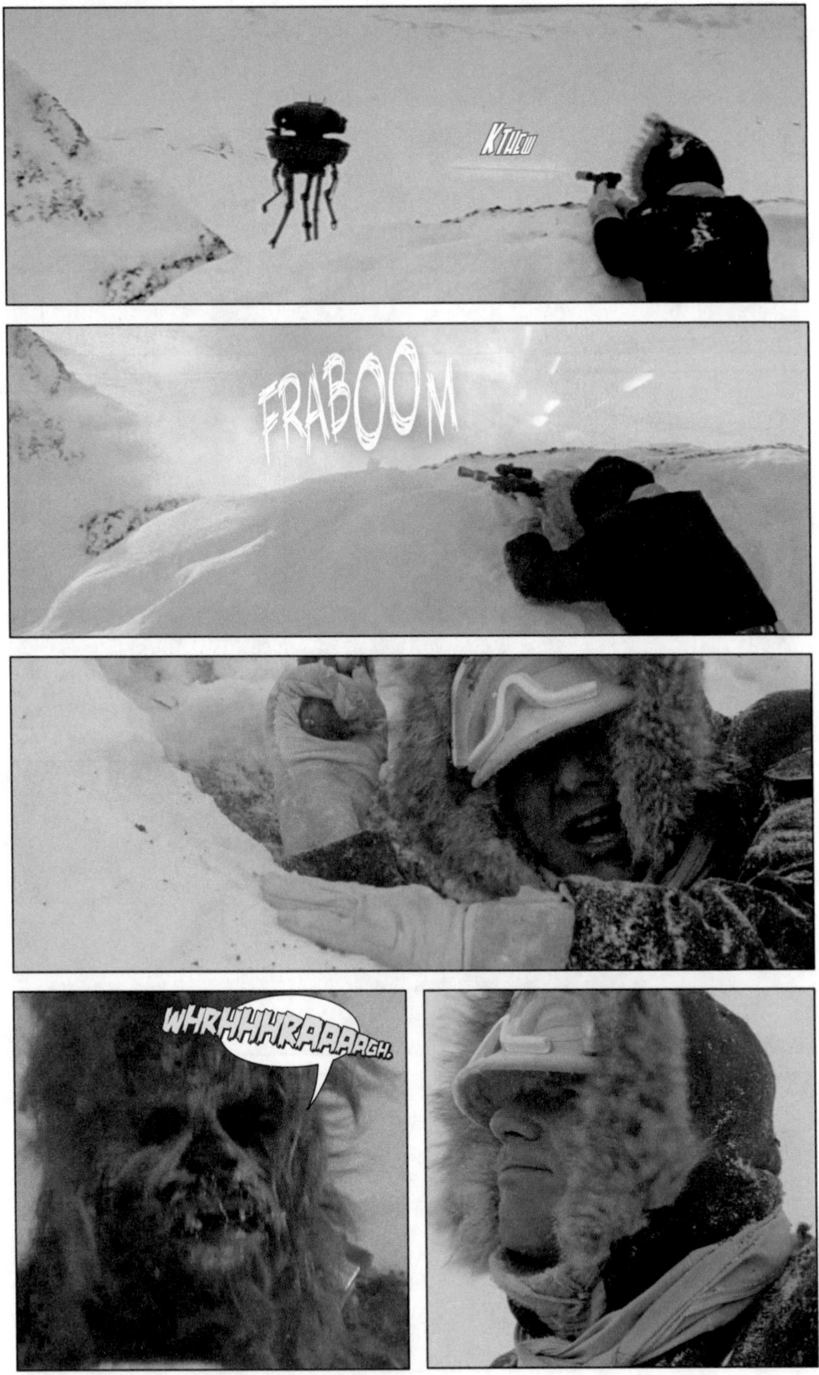
KTHEW
FRABOOM
WHRHHHHRAAAAAGH.

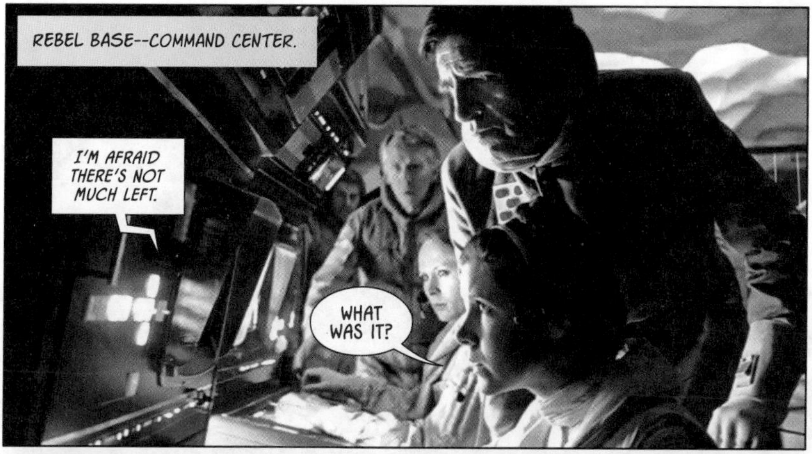
REBEL BASE--COMMAND CENTER.
I'M AFRAID THERE'S NOT MUCH LEFT.
WHAT WAS IT?

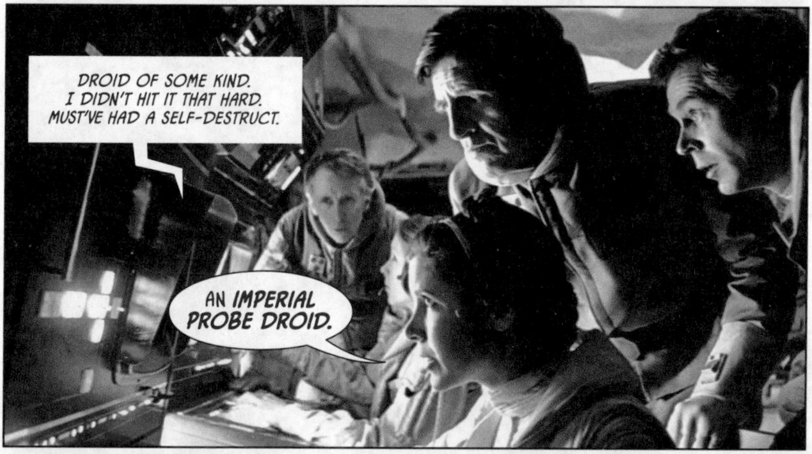
DROID OF SOME KIND. I DIDN'T HIT IT THAT HARD. MUST'VE HAD A SELF-DESTRUCT.
AN IMPERIAL PROBE DROID.

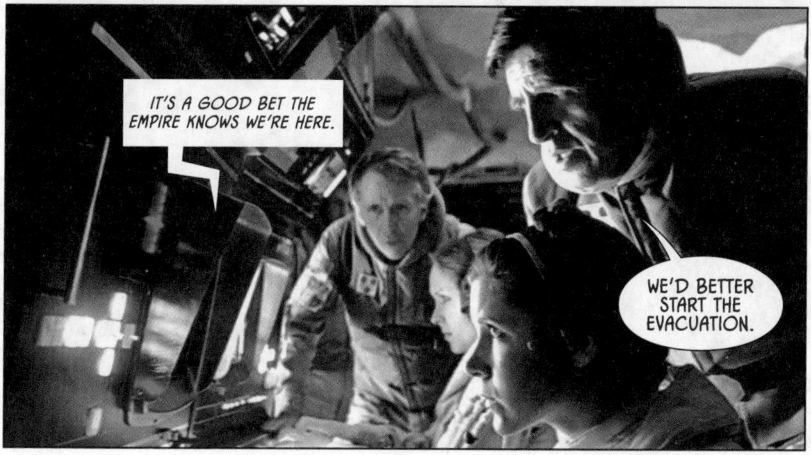
IT'S A GOOD BET THE EMPIRE KNOWS WE'RE HERE.
WE'D BETTER START THE EVACUATION.

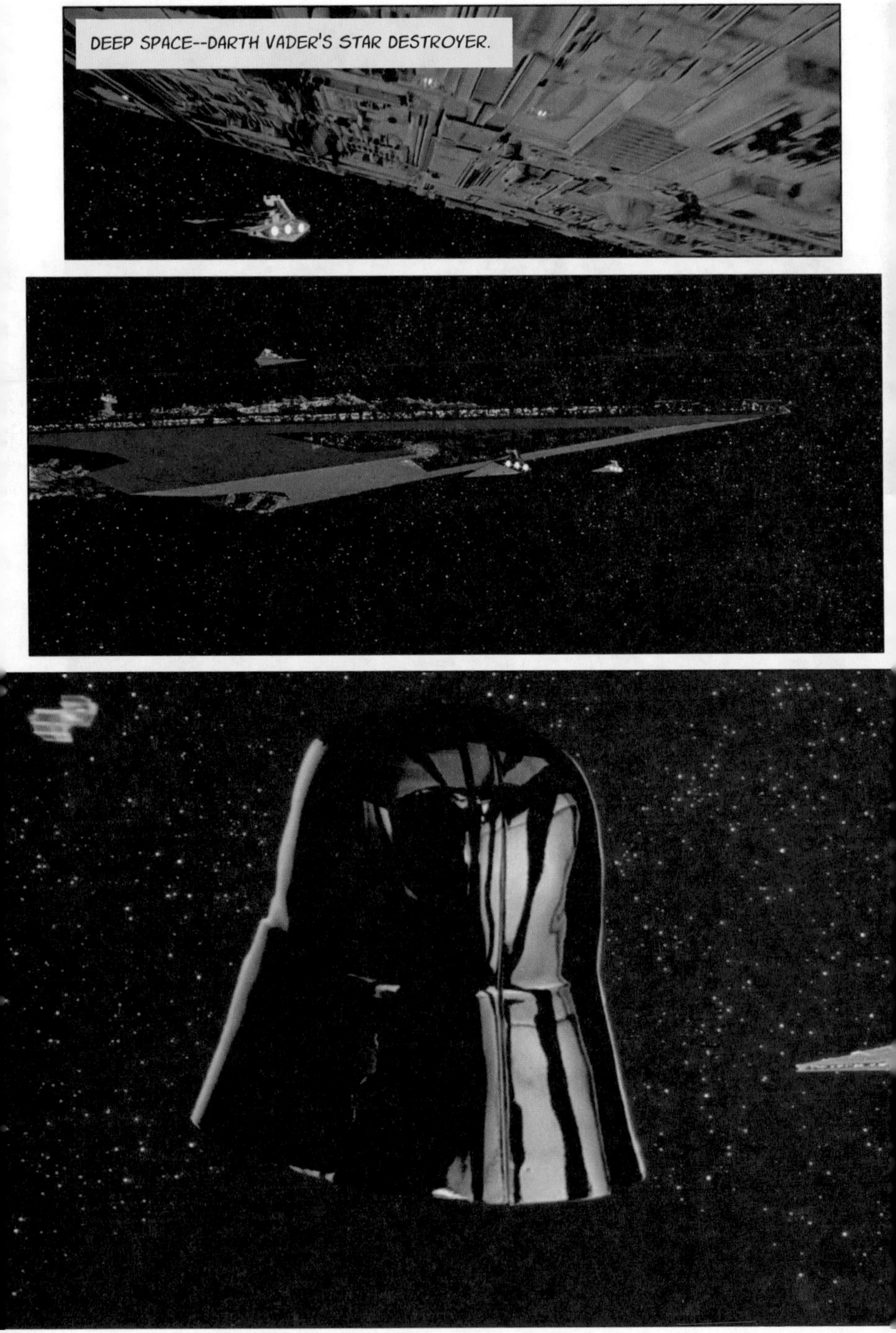
DEEP SPACE--DARTH VADER'S STAR DESTROYER.

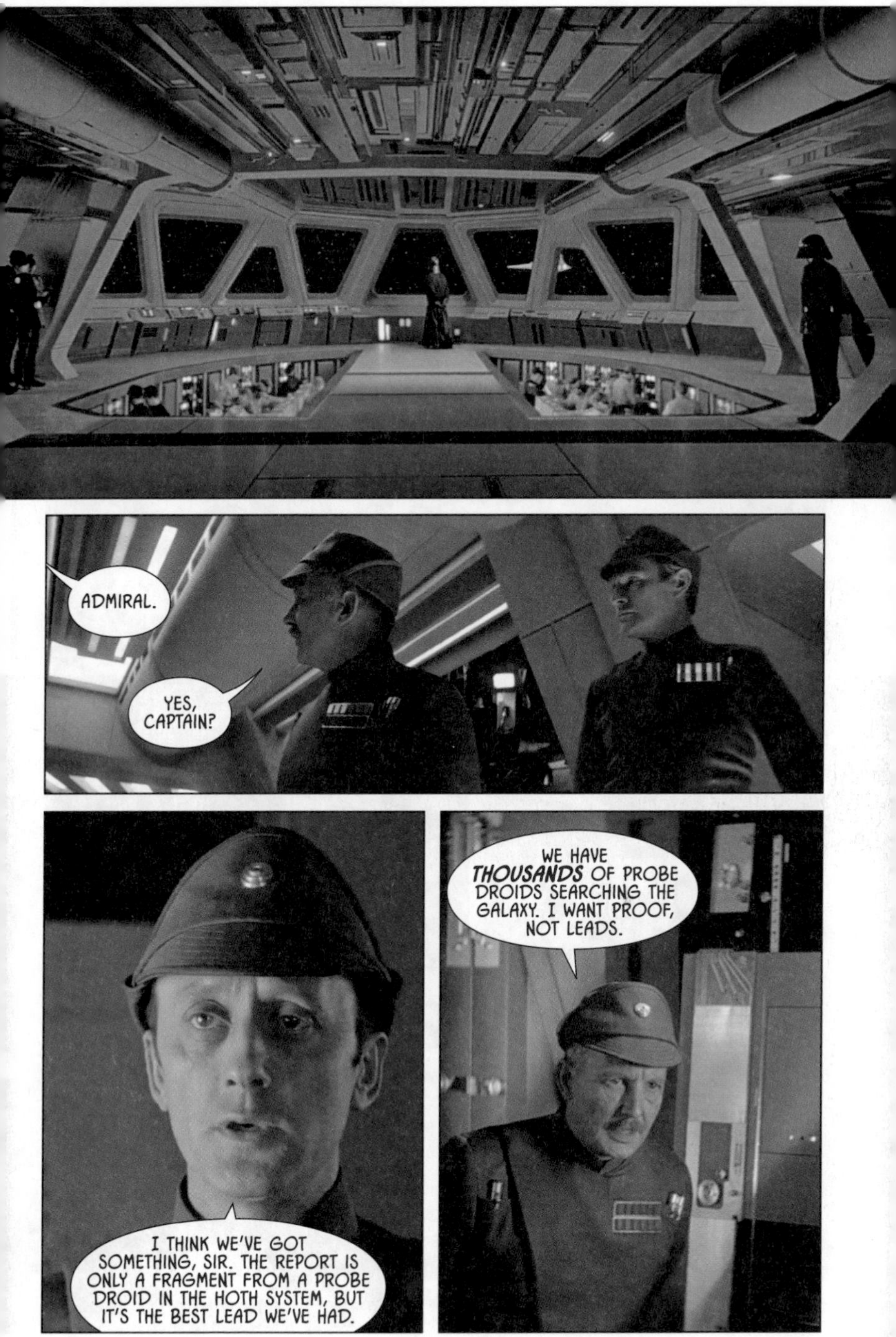
ADMIRAL.
YES, CAPTAIN?
I THINK WE'VE GOT SOMETHING, SIR. THE REPORT IS ONLY A FRAGMENT FROM A PROBE DROID IN THE HOTH SYSTEM, BUT IT'S THE BEST LEAD WE'VE HAD.
WE HAVE *THOUSANDS* OF PROBE DROIDS SEARCHING THE GALAXY. I WANT PROOF, NOT LEADS.

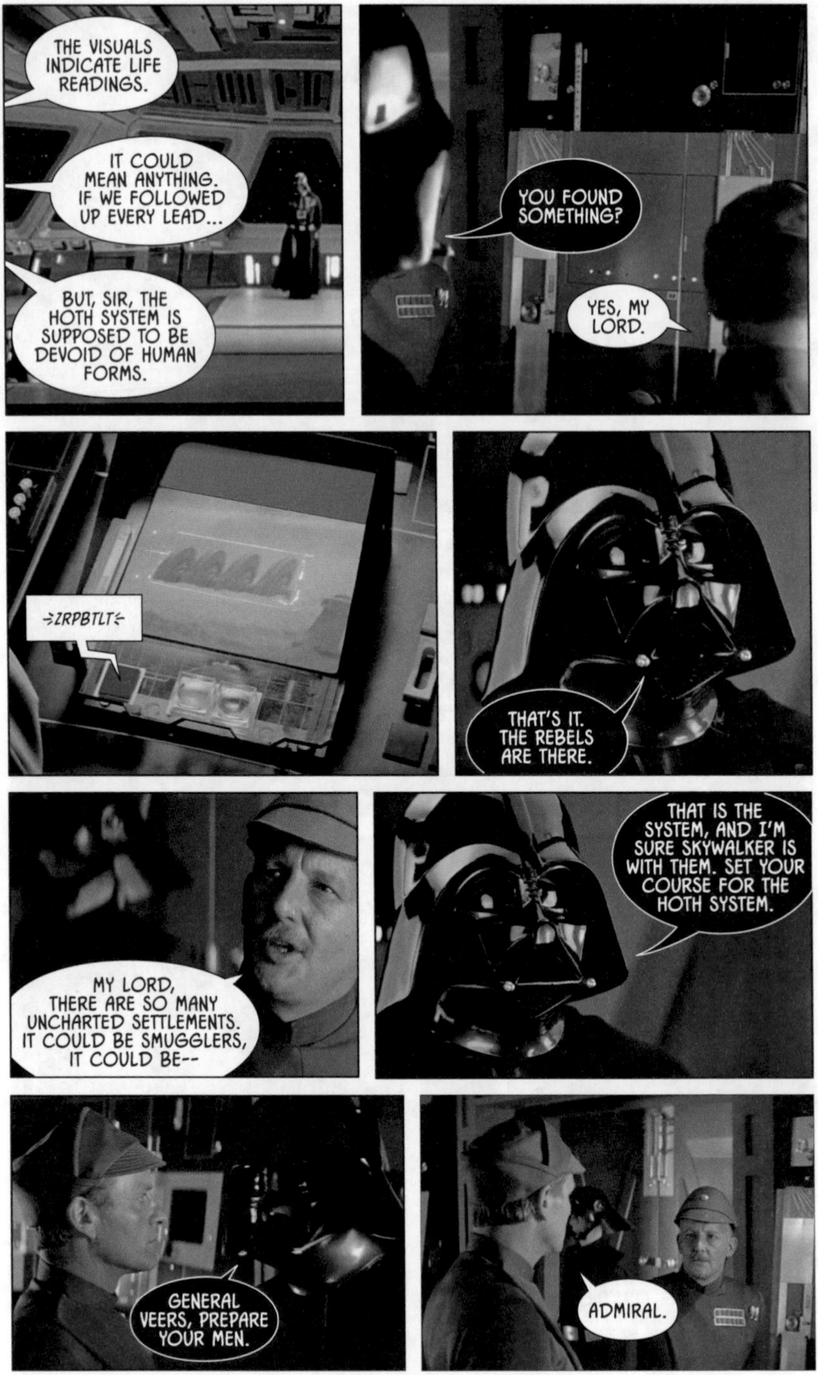
THE VISUALS INDICATE LIFE READINGS.
IT COULD MEAN ANYTHING. IF WE FOLLOWED UP EVERY LEAD...
BUT, SIR, THE HOTH SYSTEM IS SUPPOSED TO BE DEVOID OF HUMAN FORMS.
YOU FOUND SOMETHING?
YES, MY LORD.
ZRPBTLT
THAT'S IT. THE REBELS ARE THERE.
MY LORD, THERE ARE SO MANY UNCHARTED SETTLEMENTS. IT COULD BE SMUGGLERS, IT COULD BE--
THAT IS THE SYSTEM, AND I'M SURE SKYWALKER IS WITH THEM. SET YOUR COURSE FOR THE HOTH SYSTEM.
GENERAL VEERS, PREPARE YOUR MEN.
ADMIRAL.

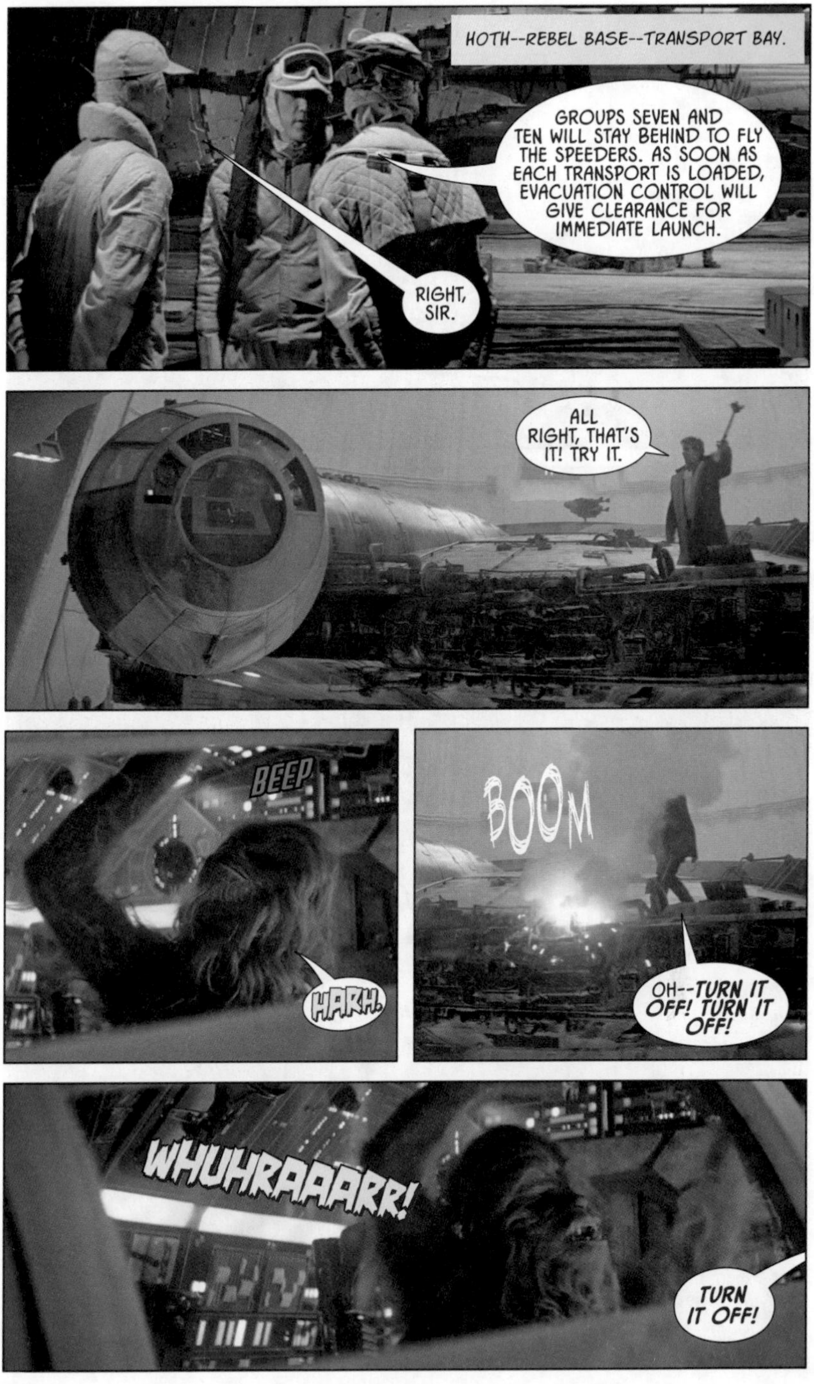
HOTH--REBEL BASE--TRANSPORT BAY.
GROUPS SEVEN AND TEN WILL STAY BEHIND TO FLY THE SPEEDERS. AS SOON AS EACH TRANSPORT IS LOADED, EVACUATION CONTROL WILL GIVE CLEARANCE FOR IMMEDIATE LAUNCH.
RIGHT, SIR.
ALL RIGHT, THAT'S IT! TRY IT.
BEEP
HARH.
BOOM
OH--TURN IT OFF! TURN IT OFF!
WHUHRAAARR!
TURN IT OFF!

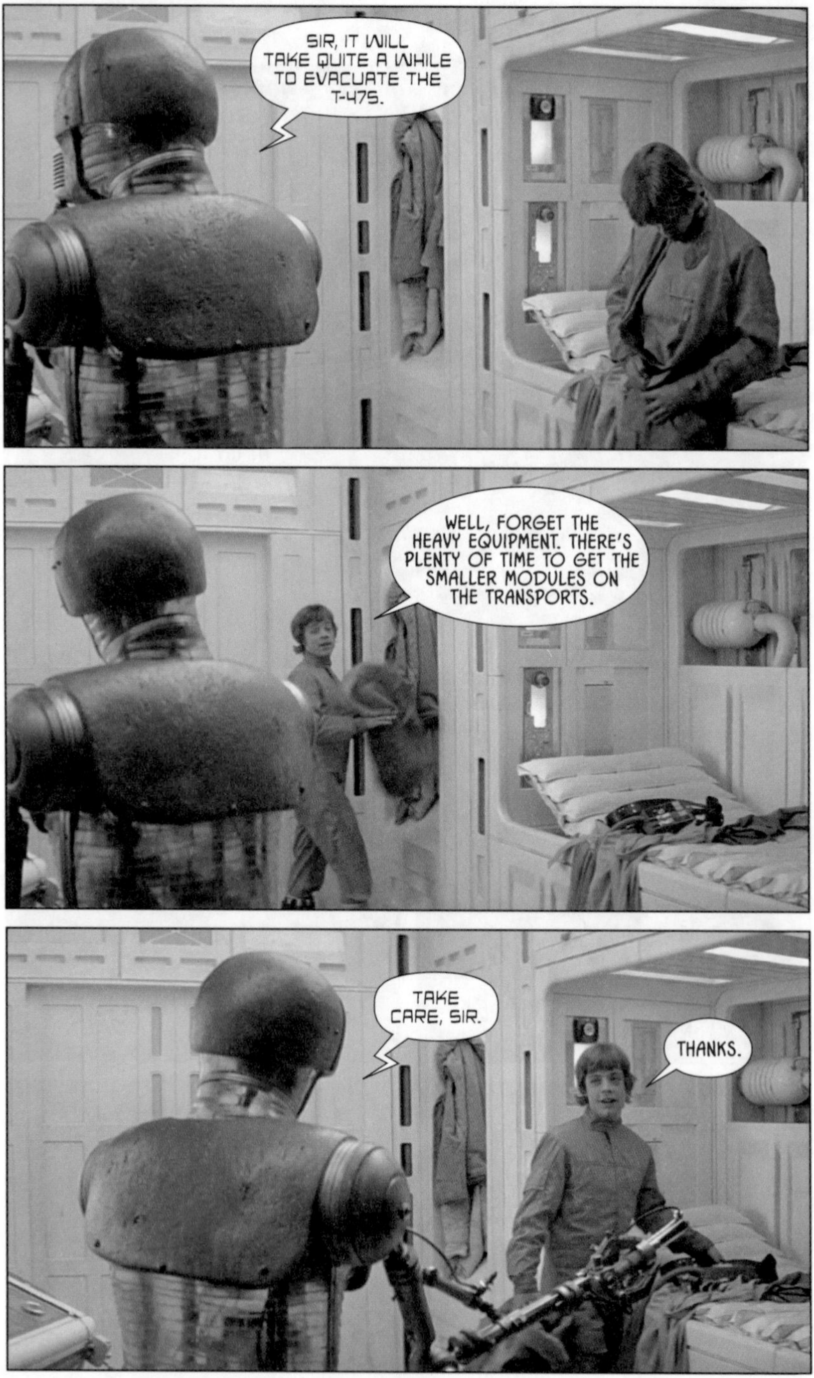
SIR, IT WILL TAKE QUITE A WHILE TO EVACUATE THE T-47S.
WELL, FORGET THE HEAVY EQUIPMENT. THERE'S PLENTY OF TIME TO GET THE SMALLER MODULES ON THE TRANSPORTS.
TAKE CARE, SIR.
THANKS.

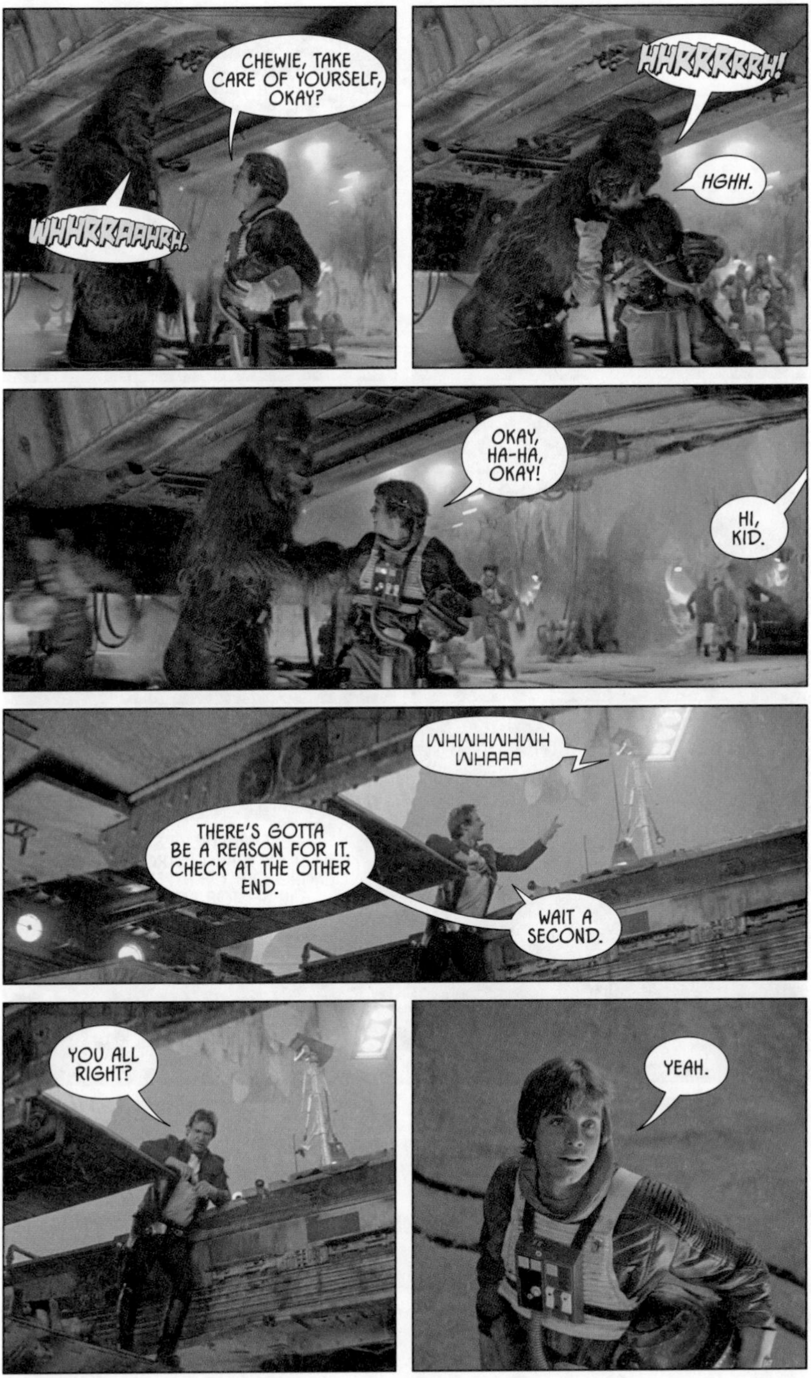
CHEWIE, TAKE CARE OF YOURSELF, OKAY?
WHHRRAAHRH.
HHRRRRRH!
HGHH.
OKAY, HA-HA, OKAY!
HI, KID.
WHWHWHWH WHAAA
THERE'S GOTTA BE A REASON FOR IT. CHECK AT THE OTHER END.
WAIT A SECOND.
YOU ALL RIGHT?
YEAH.

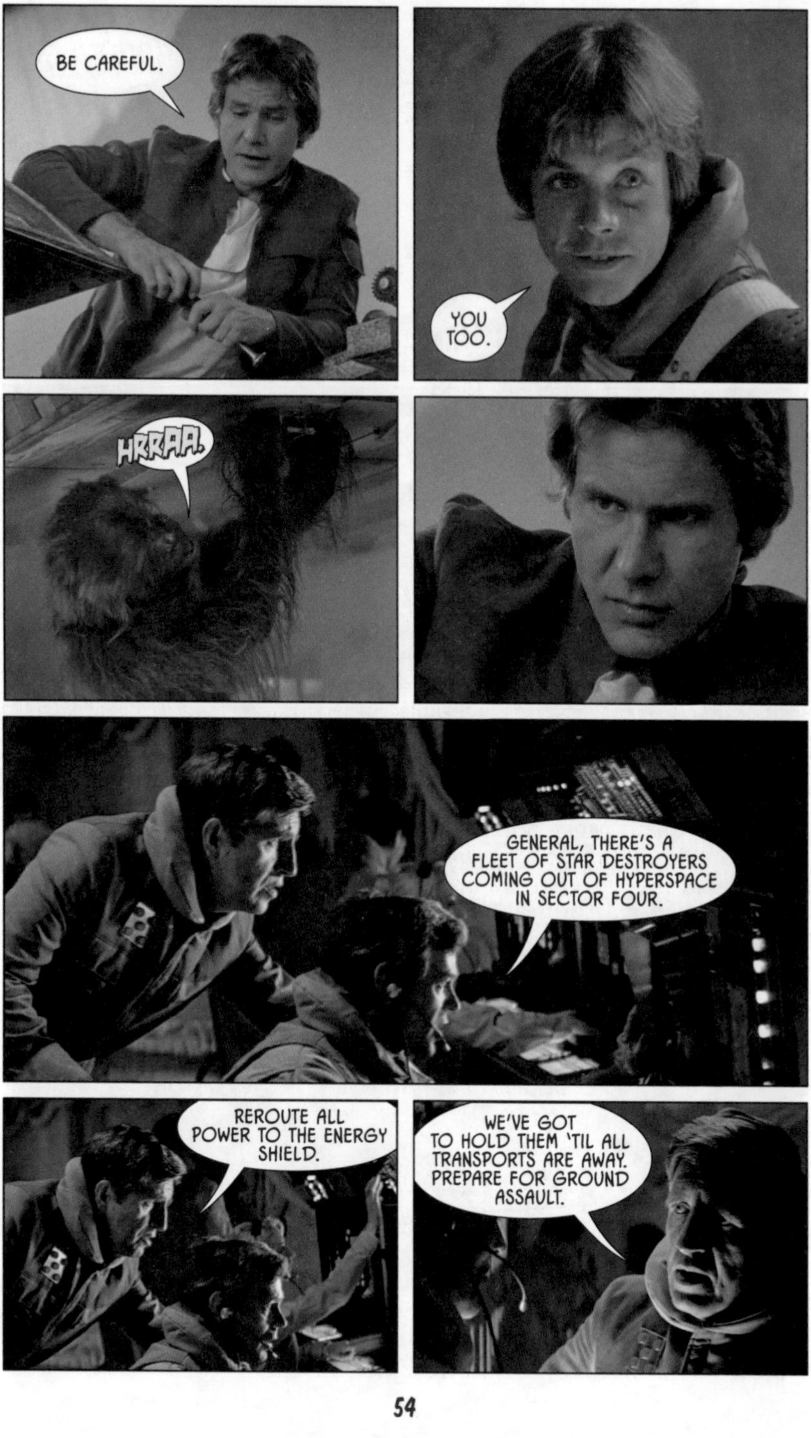
BE CAREFUL.
YOU TOO.
HRRAA.
GENERAL, THERE'S A FLEET OF STAR DESTROYERS COMING OUT OF HYPERSPACE IN SECTOR FOUR.
REROUTE ALL POWER TO THE ENERGY SHIELD.
WE'VE GOT TO HOLD THEM 'TIL ALL TRANSPORTS ARE AWAY. PREPARE FOR GROUND ASSAULT.

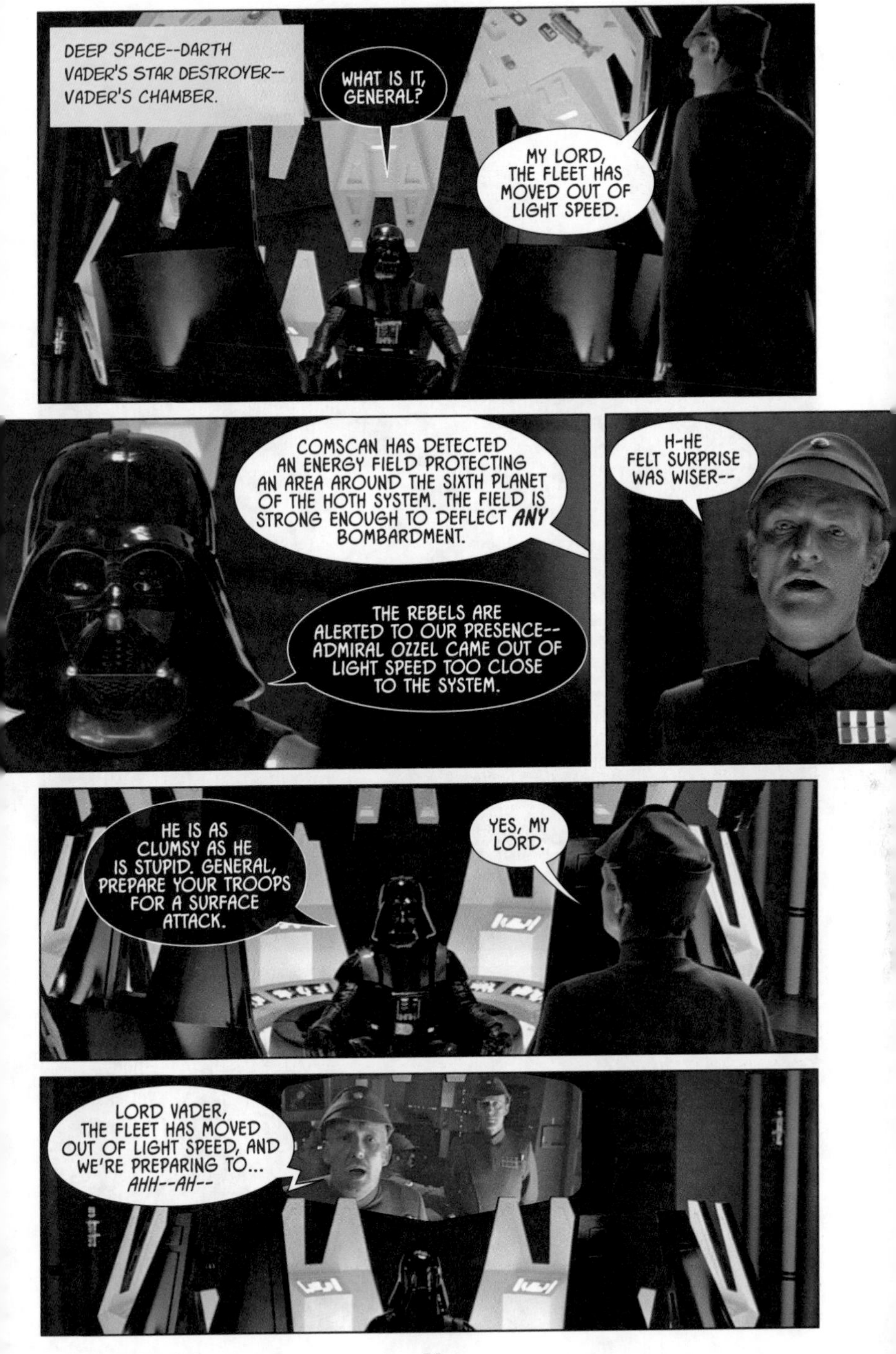
DEEP SPACE--DARTH VADER'S STAR DESTROYER--VADER'S CHAMBER.
WHAT IS IT, GENERAL?
MY LORD, THE FLEET HAS MOVED OUT OF LIGHT SPEED.
COMSCAN HAS DETECTED AN ENERGY FIELD PROTECTING AN AREA AROUND THE SIXTH PLANET OF THE HOTH SYSTEM. THE FIELD IS STRONG ENOUGH TO DEFLECT ANY BOMBARDMENT.
THE REBELS ARE ALERTED TO OUR PRESENCE--ADMIRAL OZZEL CAME OUT OF LIGHT SPEED TOO CLOSE TO THE SYSTEM.
H-HE FELT SURPRISE WAS WISER--
HE IS AS CLUMSY AS HE IS STUPID. GENERAL, PREPARE YOUR TROOPS FOR A SURFACE ATTACK.
YES, MY LORD.
LORD VADER, THE FLEET HAS MOVED OUT OF LIGHT SPEED, AND WE'RE PREPARING TO... AHH--AH--

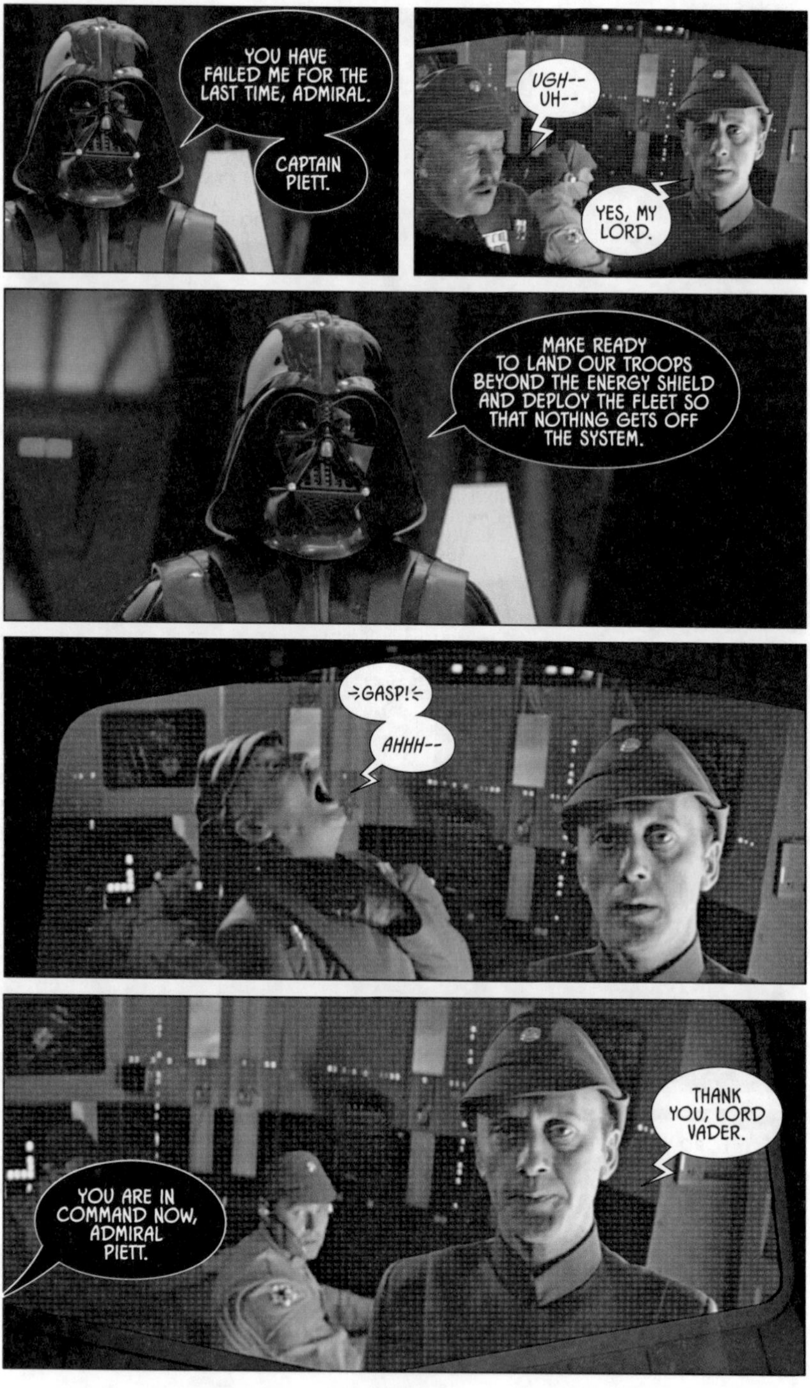
YOU HAVE FAILED ME FOR THE LAST TIME, ADMIRAL.
CAPTAIN PIETT.
UGH-- UH--
YES, MY LORD.
MAKE READY TO LAND OUR TROOPS BEYOND THE ENERGY SHIELD AND DEPLOY THE FLEET SO THAT NOTHING GETS OFF THE SYSTEM.
GASP!
AHHH--
THANK YOU, LORD VADER.
YOU ARE IN COMMAND NOW, ADMIRAL PIETT.

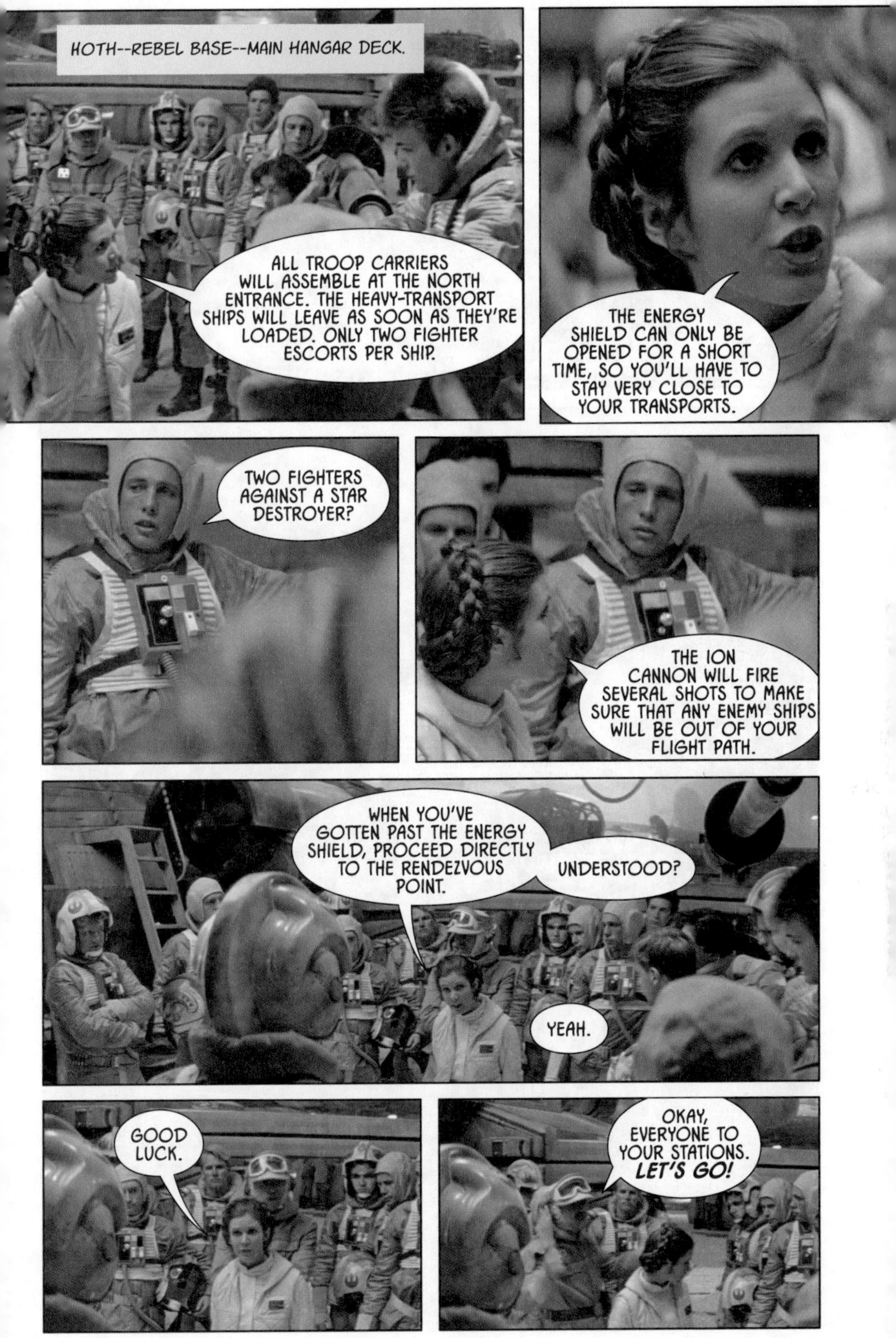
HOTH--REBEL BASE--MAIN HANGAR DECK.
ALL TROOP CARRIERS WILL ASSEMBLE AT THE NORTH ENTRANCE. THE HEAVY-TRANSPORT SHIPS WILL LEAVE AS SOON AS THEY'RE LOADED. ONLY TWO FIGHTER ESCORTS PER SHIP.
THE ENERGY SHIELD CAN ONLY BE OPENED FOR A SHORT TIME, SO YOU'LL HAVE TO STAY VERY CLOSE TO YOUR TRANSPORTS.
TWO FIGHTERS AGAINST A STAR DESTROYER?
THE ION CANNON WILL FIRE SEVERAL SHOTS TO MAKE SURE THAT ANY ENEMY SHIPS WILL BE OUT OF YOUR FLIGHT PATH.
WHEN YOU'VE GOTTEN PAST THE ENERGY SHIELD, PROCEED DIRECTLY TO THE RENDEZVOUS POINT.
UNDERSTOOD?
YEAH.
GOOD LUCK.
OKAY, EVERYONE TO YOUR STATIONS. *LET'S GO!*

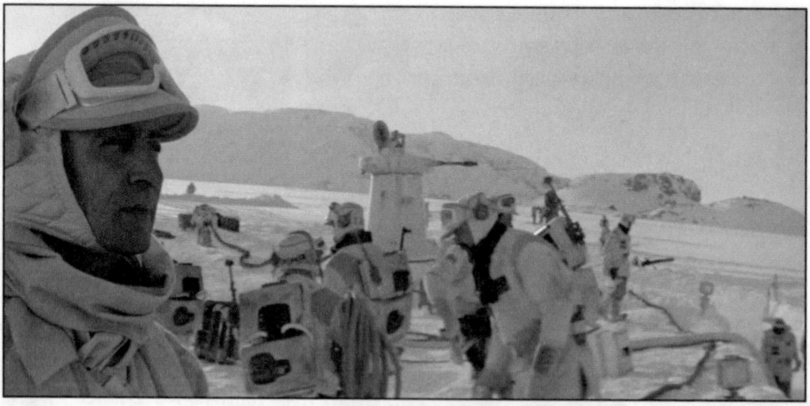

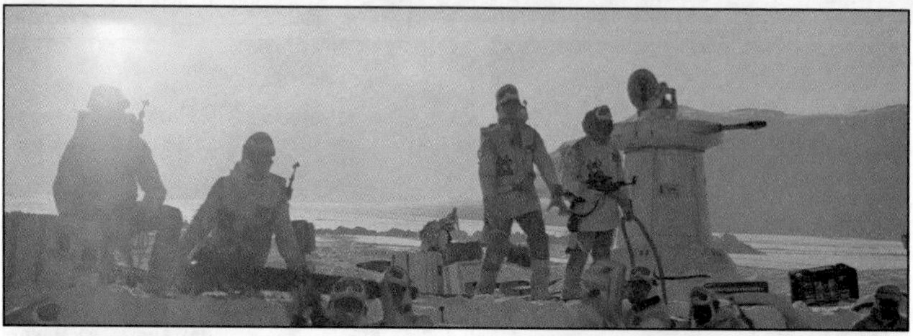

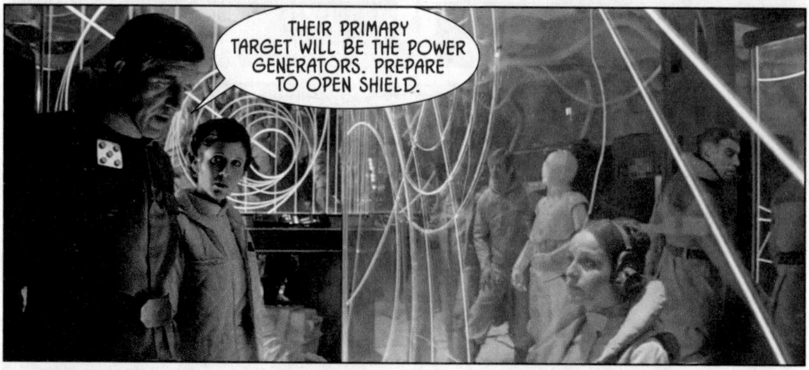
THEIR PRIMARY TARGET WILL BE THE POWER GENERATORS. PREPARE TO OPEN SHIELD.

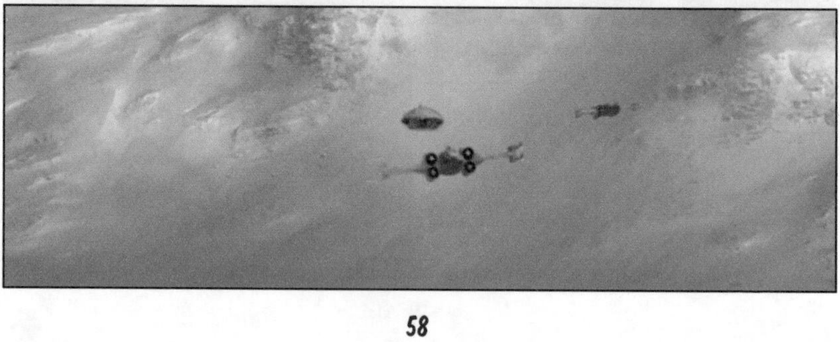

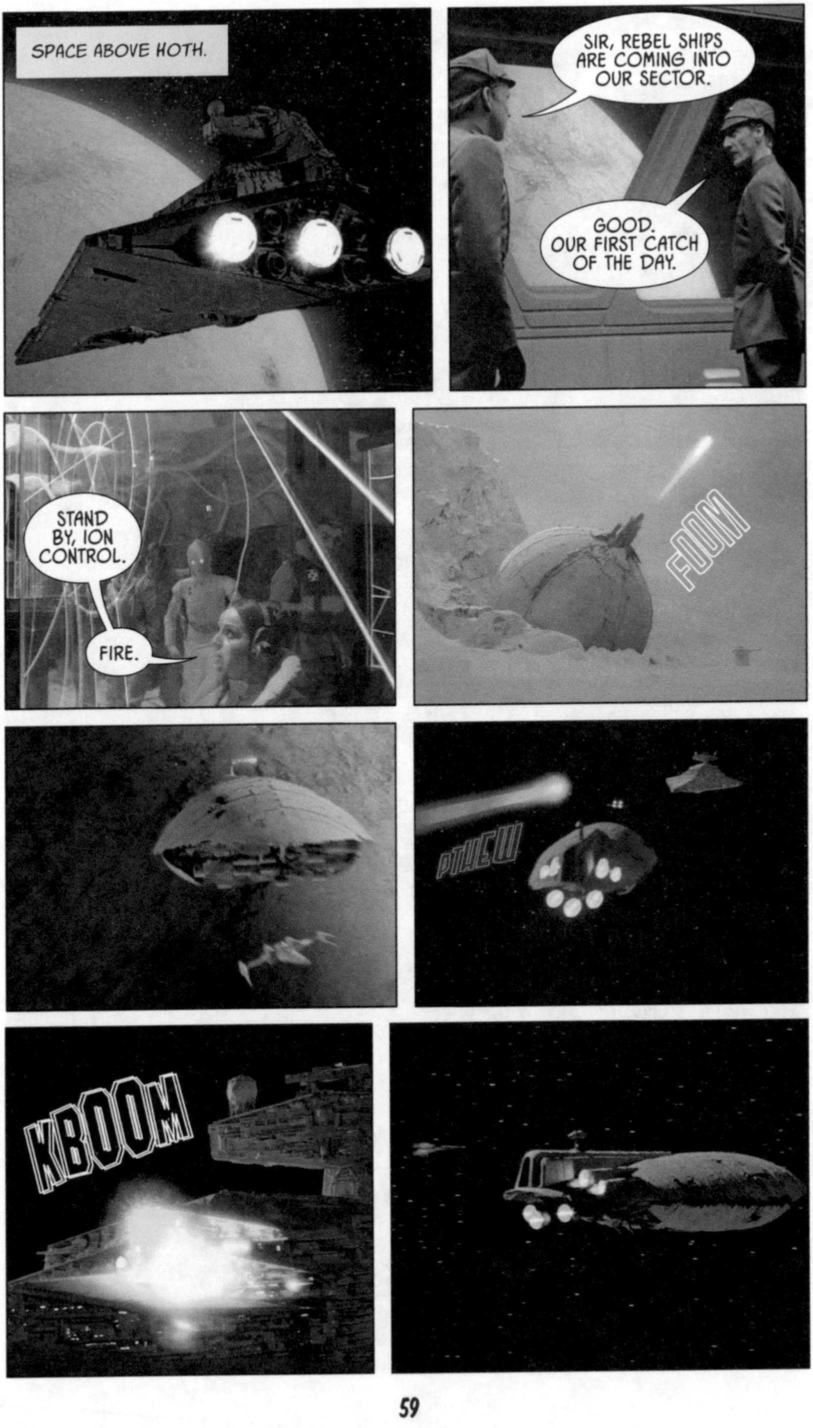
SPACE ABOVE HOTH.
SIR, REBEL SHIPS ARE COMING INTO OUR SECTOR.
GOOD. OUR FIRST CATCH OF THE DAY.
STAND BY, ION CONTROL.
FIRE.
FOOM
PTHEW
KBOOM

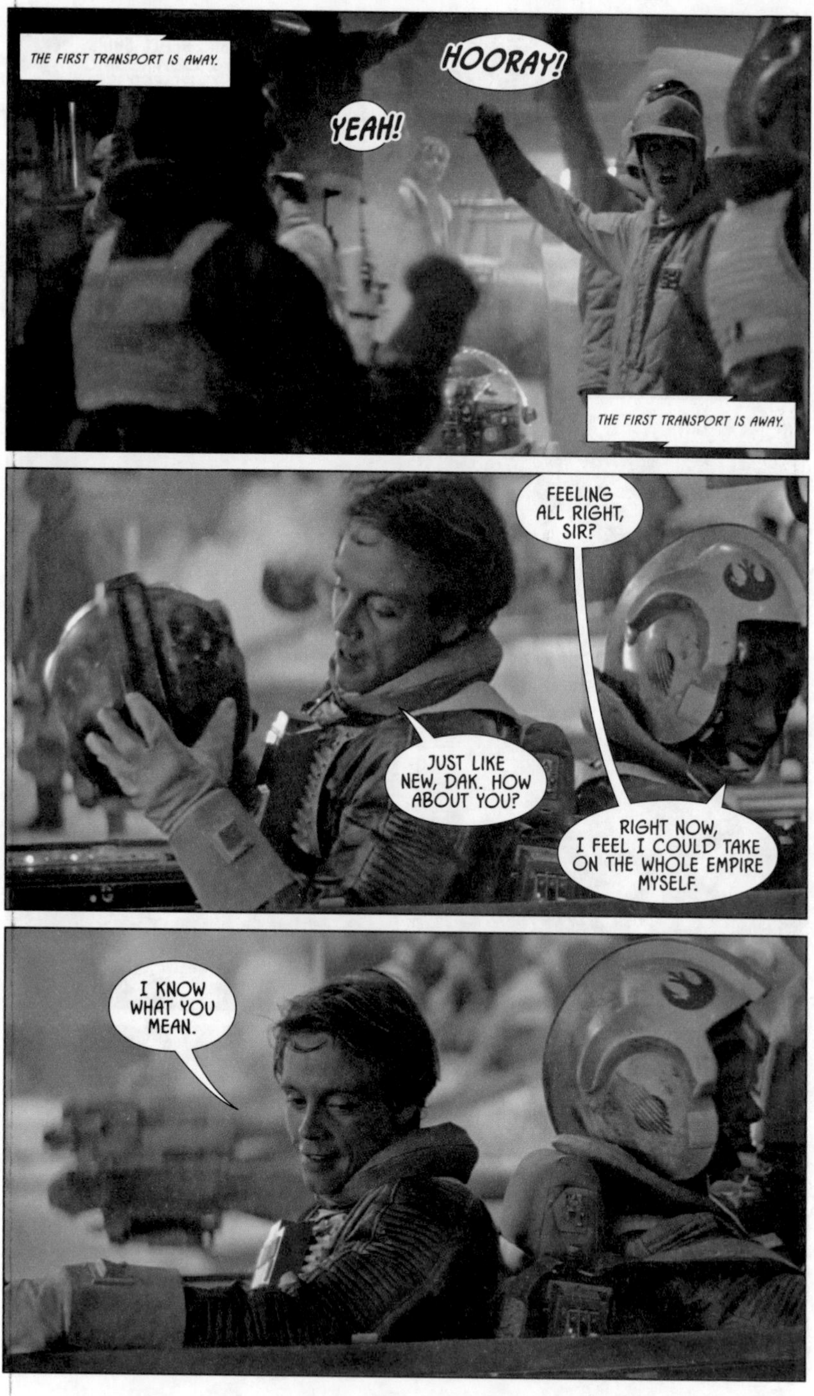
THE FIRST TRANSPORT IS AWAY.
HOORAY!
YEAH!
THE FIRST TRANSPORT IS AWAY.
FEELING ALL RIGHT, SIR?
JUST LIKE NEW, DAK. HOW ABOUT YOU?
RIGHT NOW, I FEEL I COULD TAKE ON THE WHOLE EMPIRE MYSELF.
I KNOW WHAT YOU MEAN.

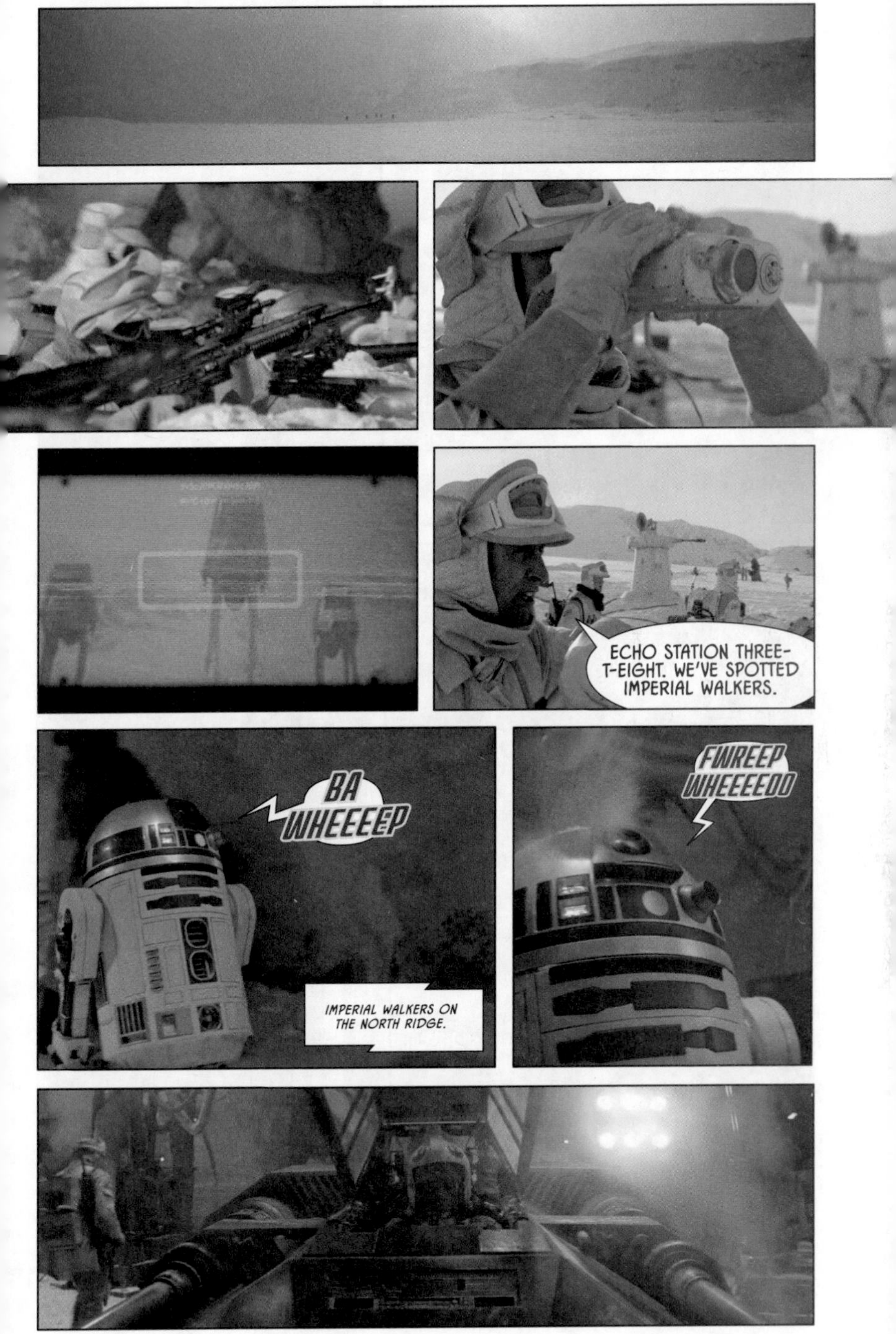
ECHO STATION THREE-T-EIGHT. WE'VE SPOTTED IMPERIAL WALKERS.
BA WHEEEEEP
IMPERIAL WALKERS ON THE NORTH RIDGE.
FWREEP WHEEEEEOO

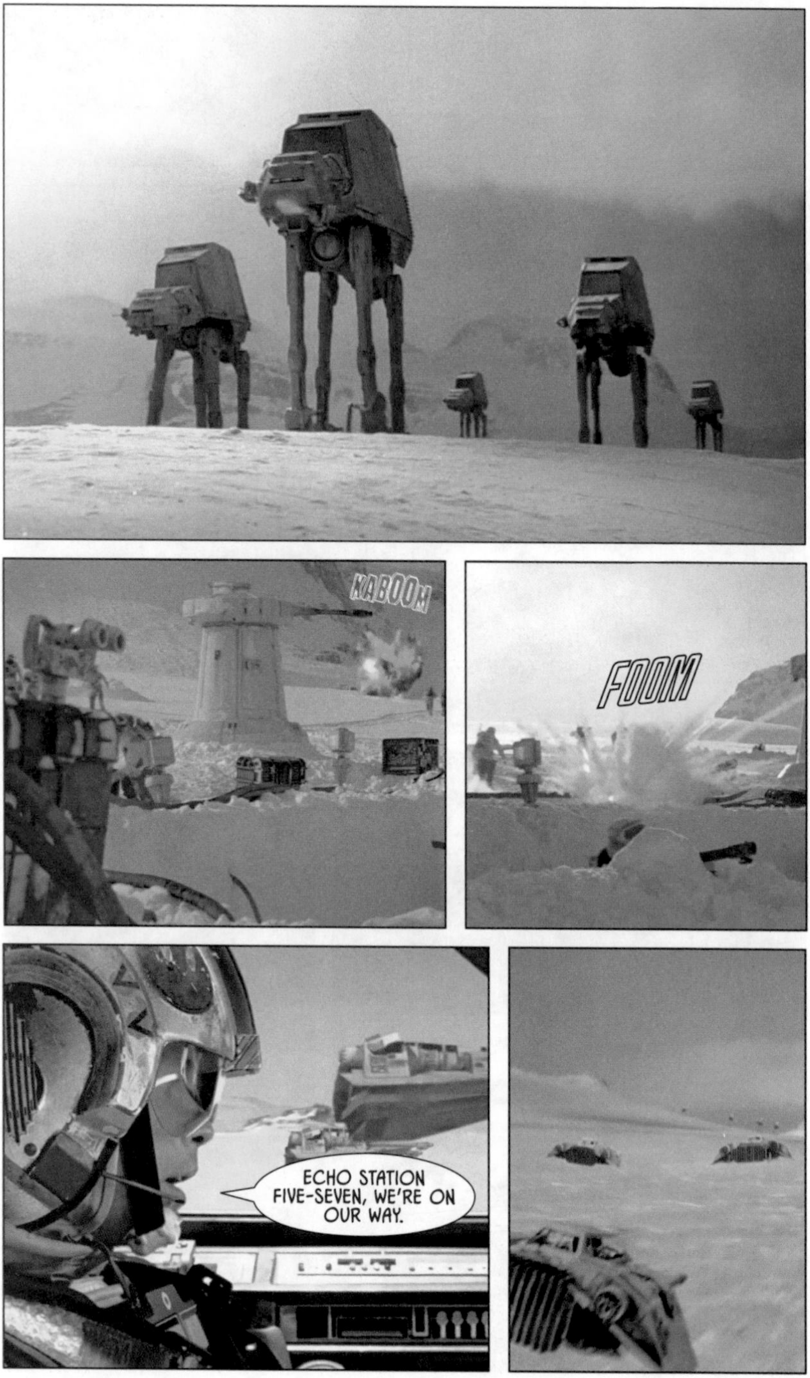
KABOOM
FOOM
ECHO STATION FIVE-SEVEN, WE'RE ON OUR WAY.

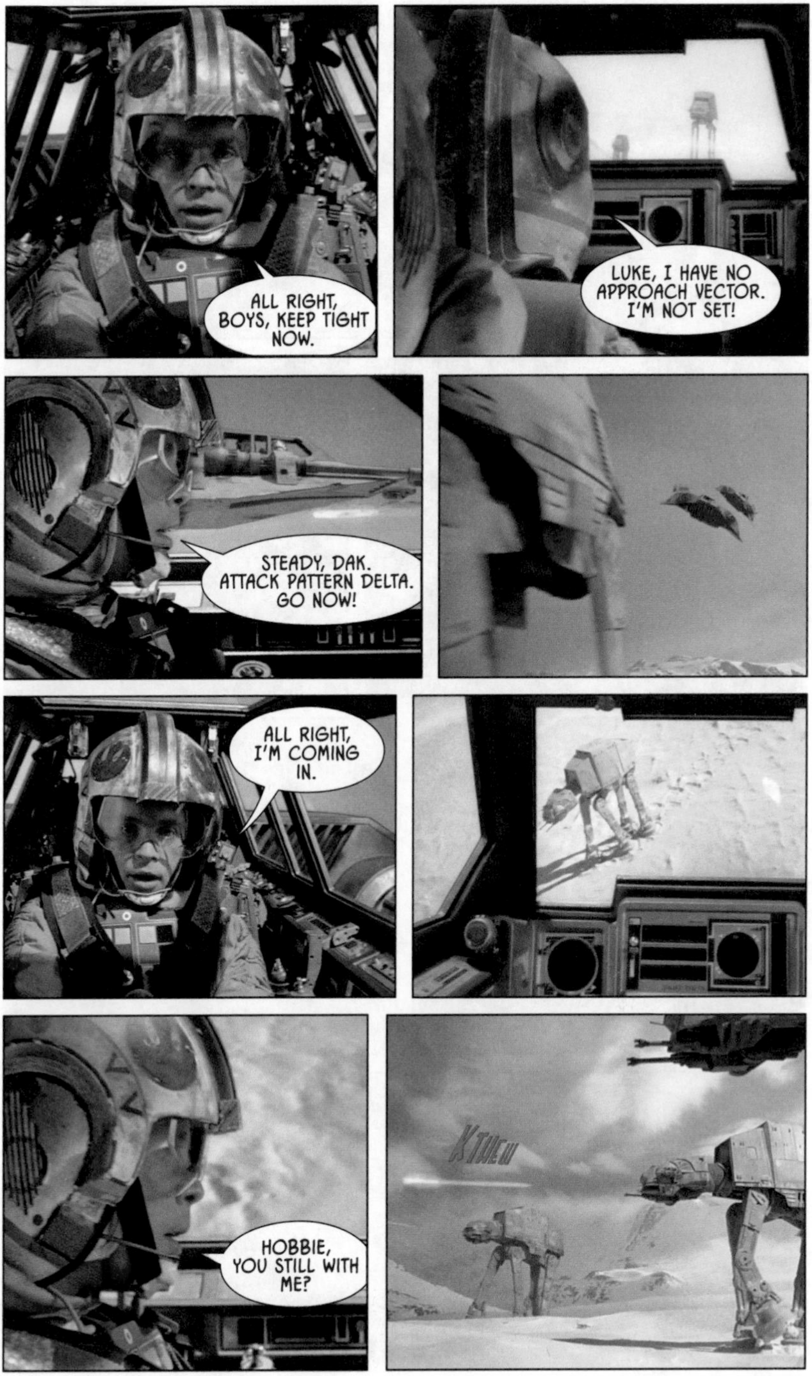
ALL RIGHT, BOYS, KEEP TIGHT NOW.
LUKE, I HAVE NO APPROACH VECTOR. I'M NOT SET!
STEADY, DAK. ATTACK PATTERN DELTA. GO NOW!
ALL RIGHT, I'M COMING IN.
HOBBIE, YOU STILL WITH ME?
KTHEW

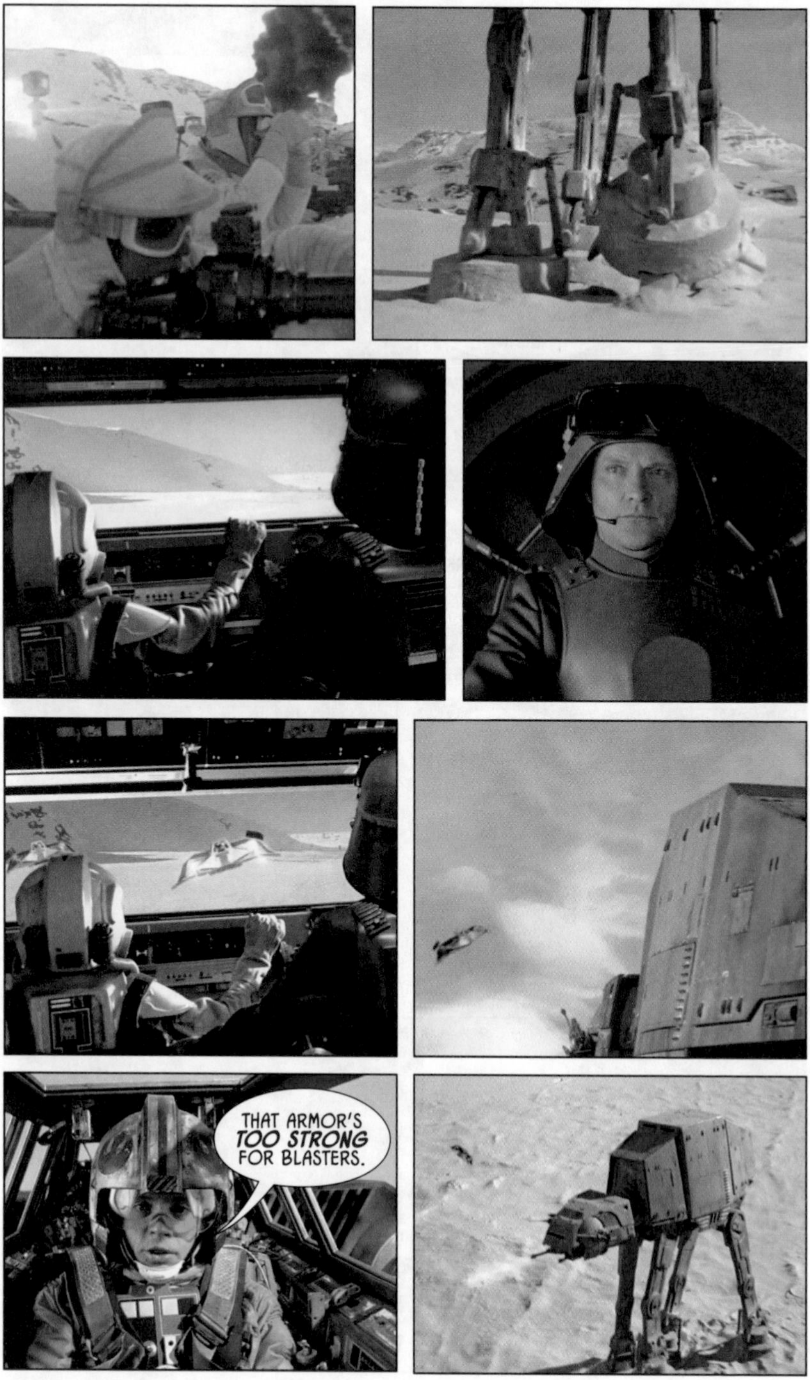
THAT ARMOR'S *TOO STRONG* FOR BLASTERS.

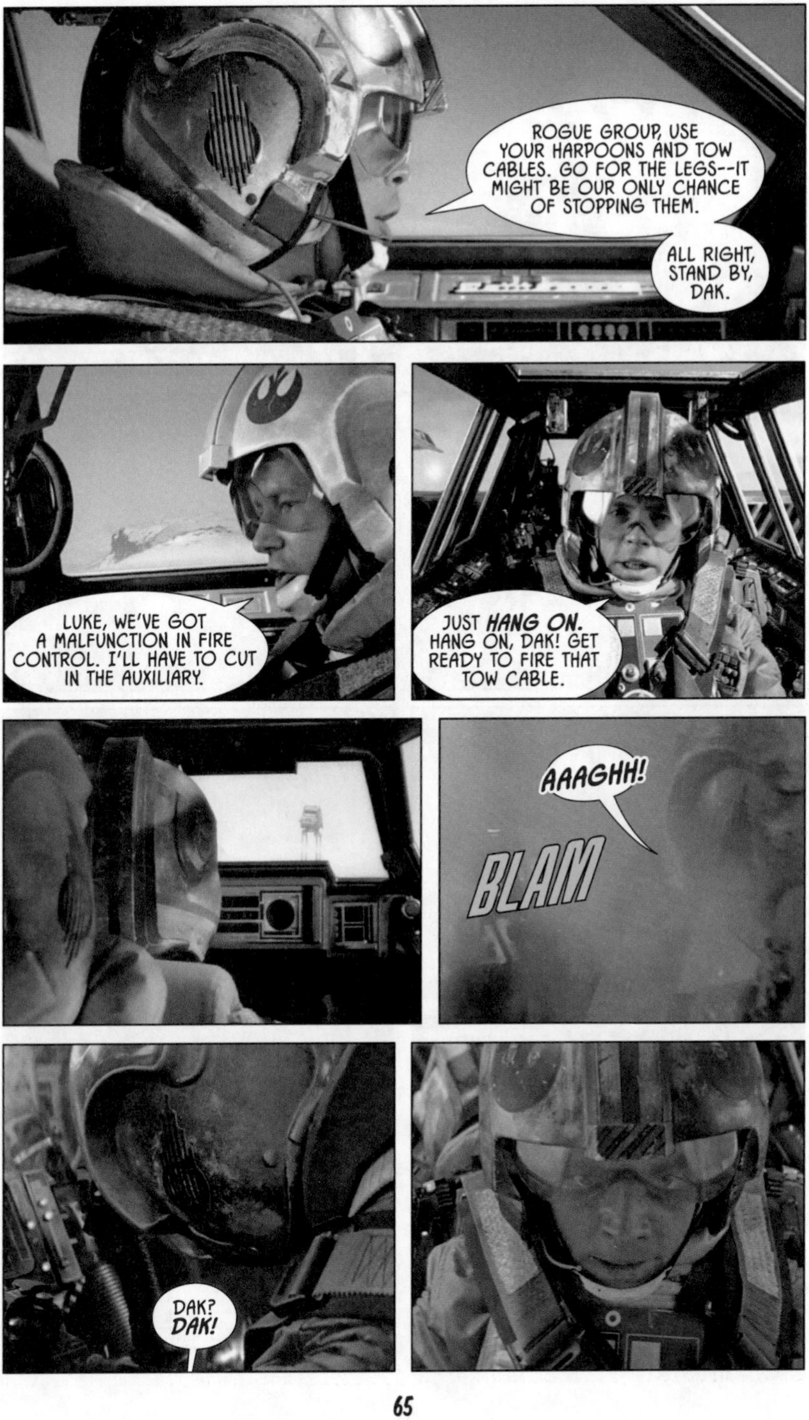
ROGUE GROUP, USE YOUR HARPOONS AND TOW CABLES. GO FOR THE LEGS--IT MIGHT BE OUR ONLY CHANCE OF STOPPING THEM.
ALL RIGHT, STAND BY, DAK.
LUKE, WE'VE GOT A MALFUNCTION IN FIRE CONTROL. I'LL HAVE TO CUT IN THE AUXILIARY.
JUST **HANG ON.** HANG ON, DAK! GET READY TO FIRE THAT TOW CABLE.
AAAGHH!
BLAM
DAK? ***DAK!***

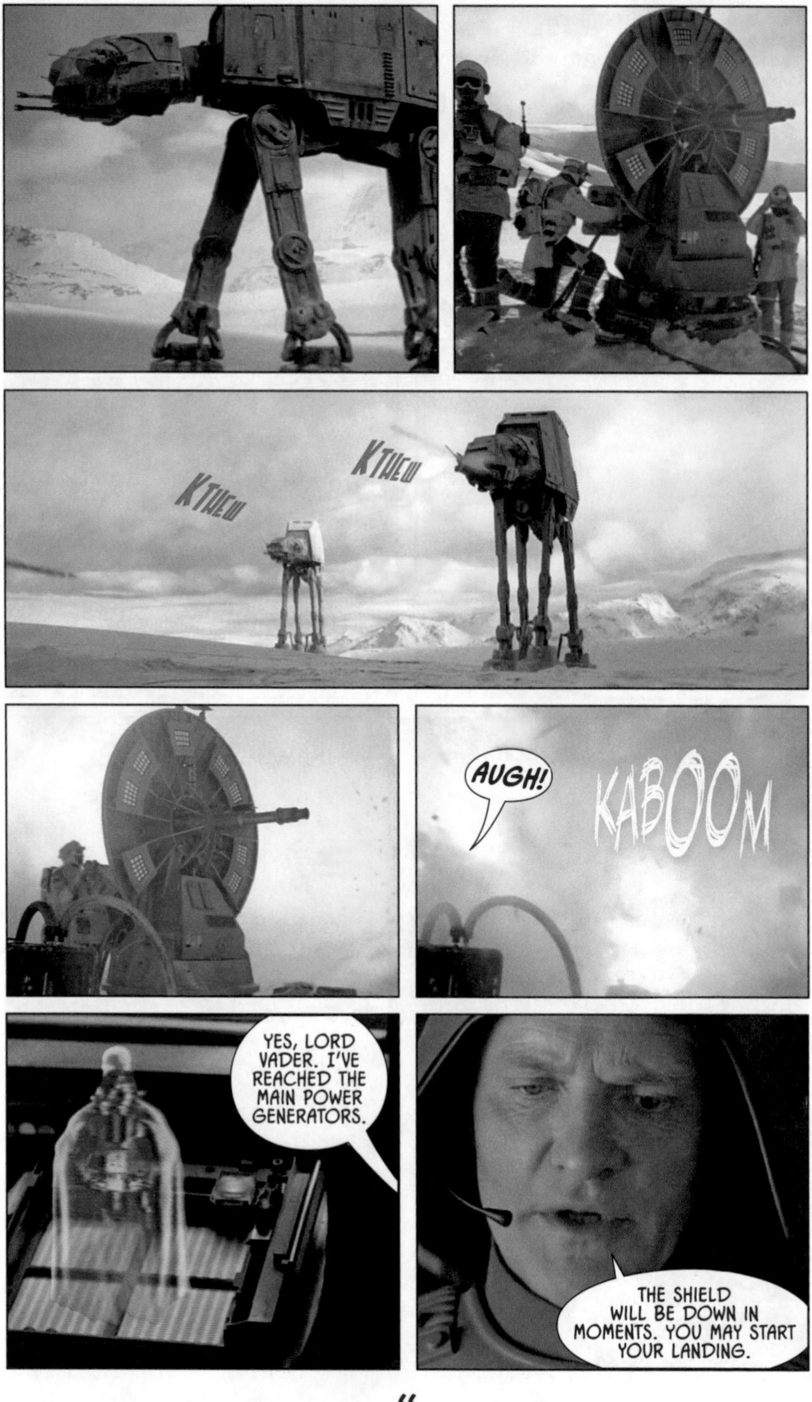

KTWEW
KTWEW
AUGH!
KABOOM
YES, LORD VADER. I'VE REACHED THE MAIN POWER GENERATORS.
THE SHIELD WILL BE DOWN IN MOMENTS. YOU MAY START YOUR LANDING.

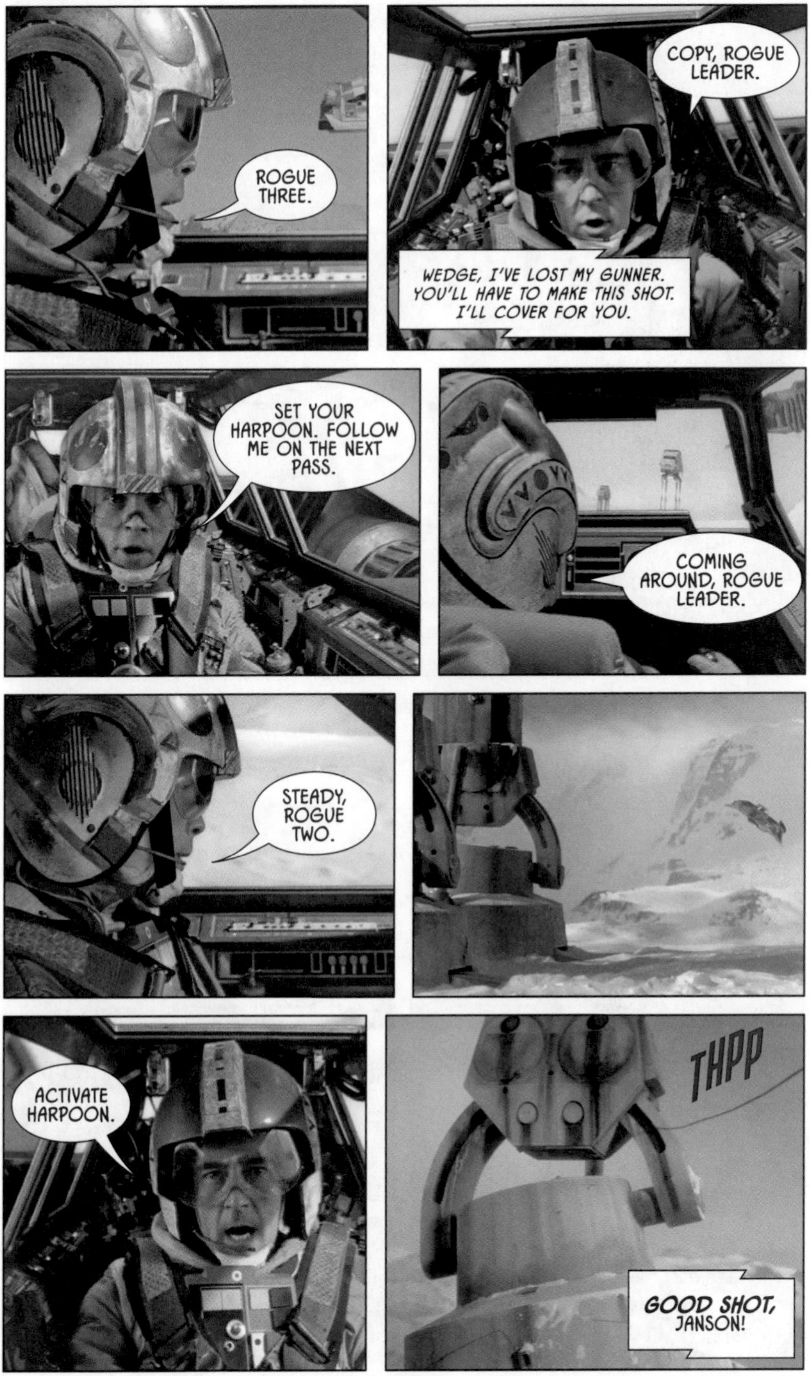
ROGUE THREE.
COPY, ROGUE LEADER.
WEDGE, I'VE LOST MY GUNNER. YOU'LL HAVE TO MAKE THIS SHOT. I'LL COVER FOR YOU.
SET YOUR HARPOON. FOLLOW ME ON THE NEXT PASS.
COMING AROUND, ROGUE LEADER.
STEADY, ROGUE TWO.
ACTIVATE HARPOON.
THPP
GOOD SHOT, JANSON!

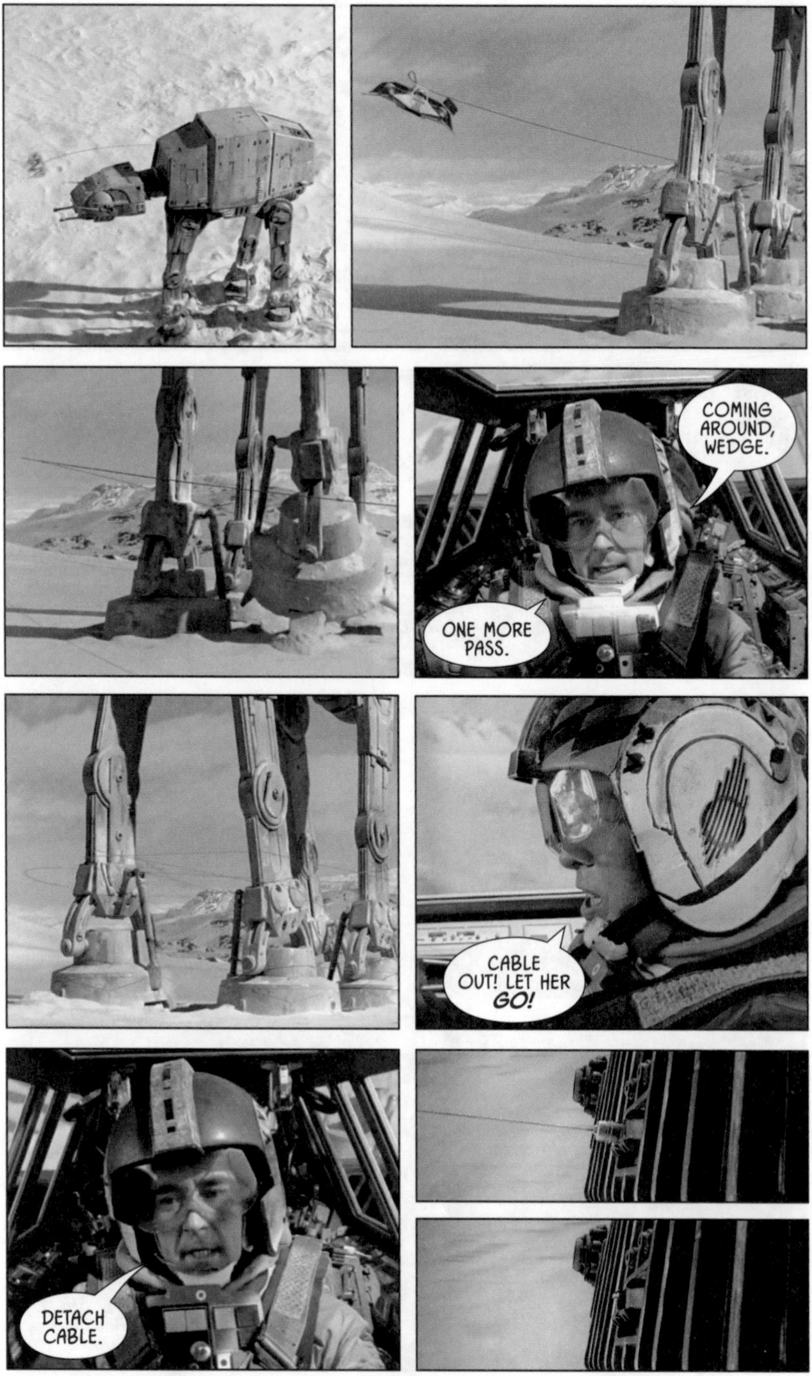
COMING AROUND, WEDGE.
ONE MORE PASS.
CABLE OUT! LET HER GO!
DETACH CABLE.

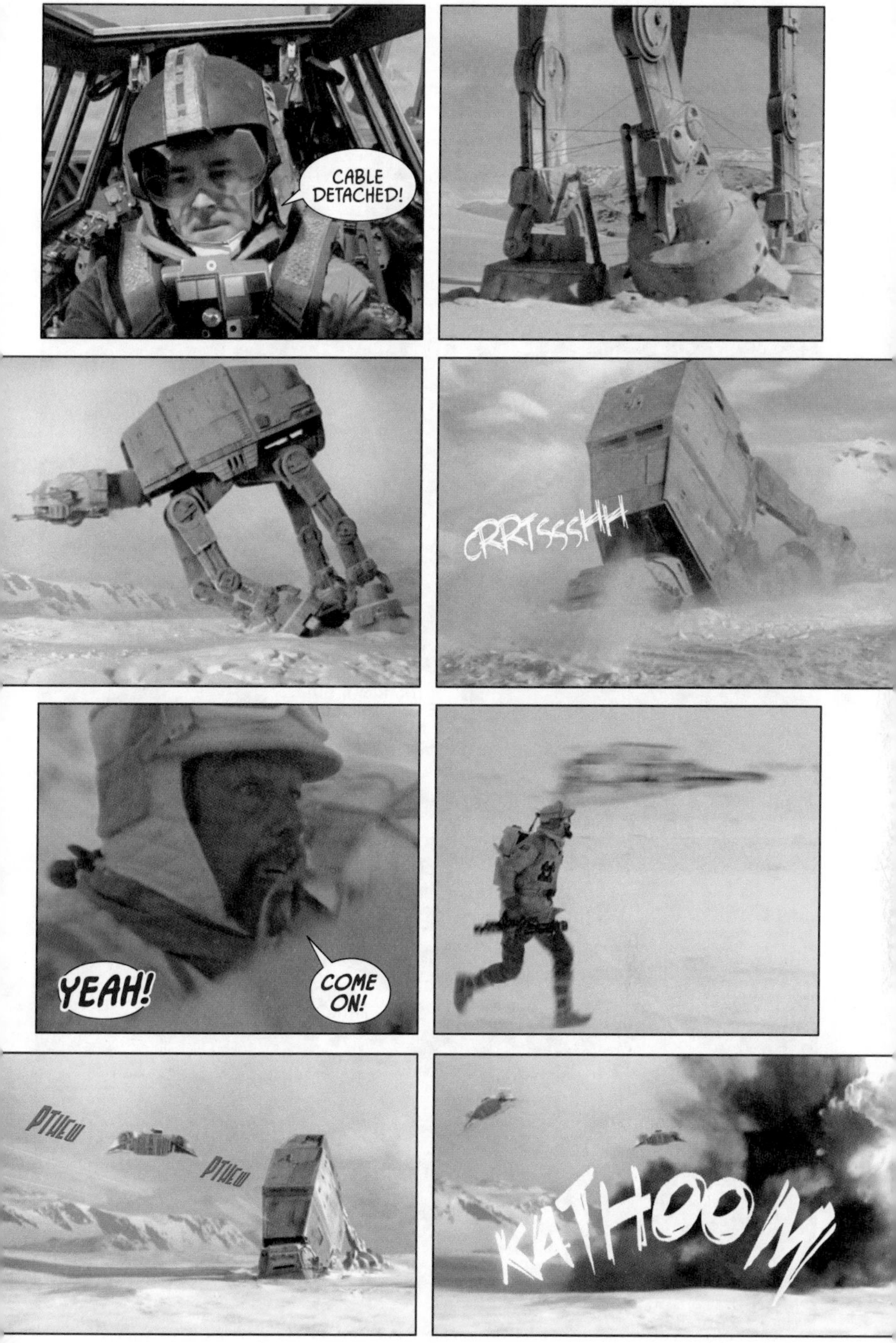
CABLE DETACHED!
CRRTSSSHHH
YEAH!
COME ON!
PTHEW
PTHEW
KATHOOM

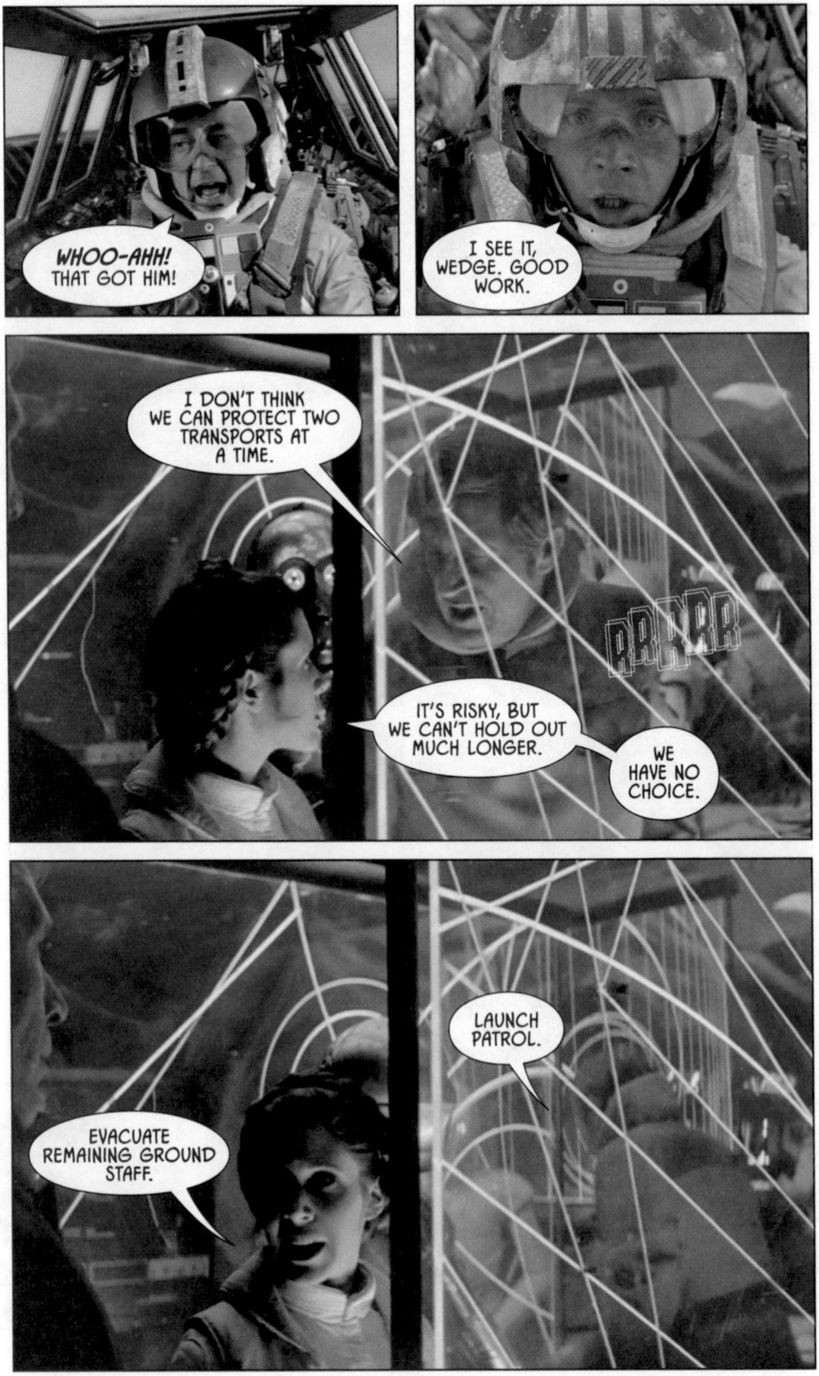
WHOO-AHH! THAT GOT HIM!
I SEE IT, WEDGE. GOOD WORK.
I DON'T THINK WE CAN PROTECT TWO TRANSPORTS AT A TIME.
RRRRR
IT'S RISKY, BUT WE CAN'T HOLD OUT MUCH LONGER.
WE HAVE NO CHOICE.
LAUNCH PATROL.
EVACUATE REMAINING GROUND STAFF.

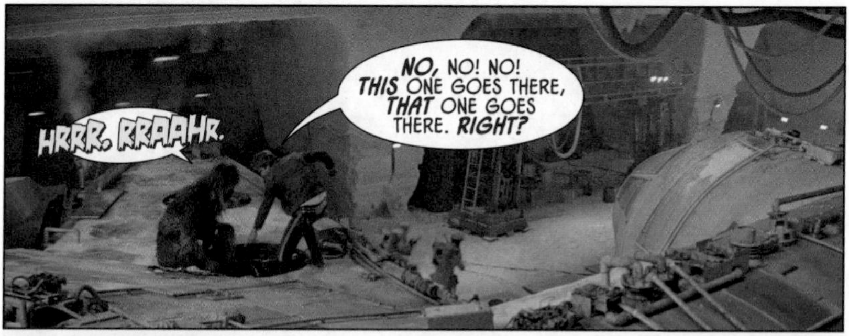
HRRR. RRAAHR.
NO, NO! NO! THIS ONE GOES THERE, THAT ONE GOES THERE. RIGHT?

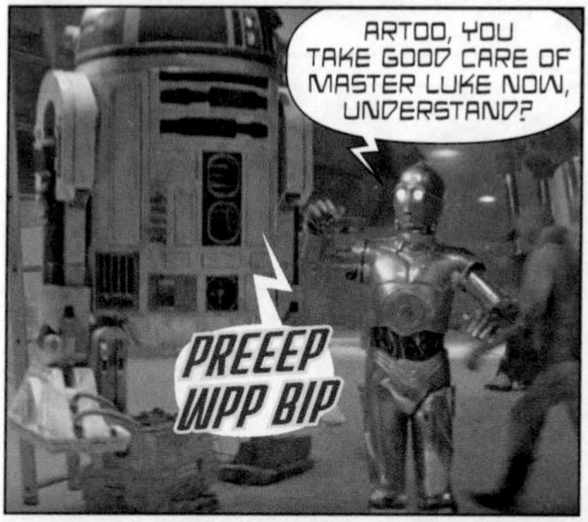
ARTOO, YOU TAKE GOOD CARE OF MASTER LUKE NOW, UNDERSTAND?
PREEEP WPP BIP

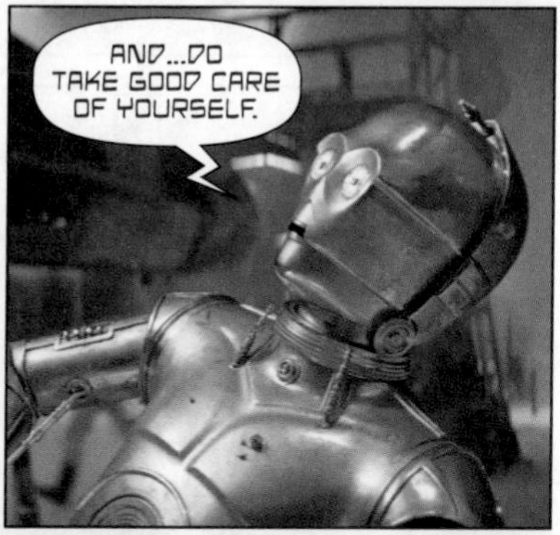
AND...DO TAKE GOOD CARE OF YOURSELF.

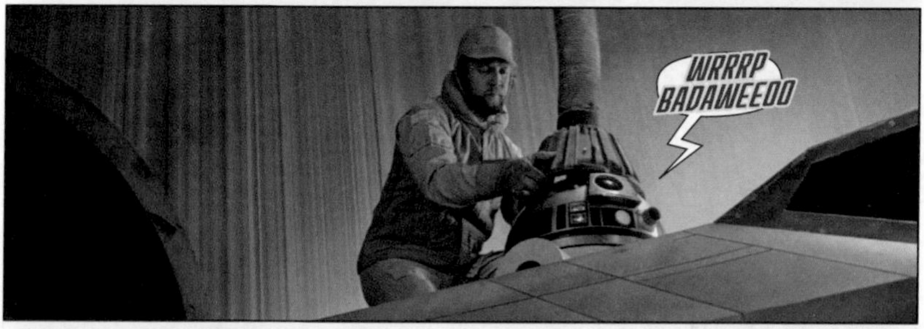
WRRRP BADAWEEDO

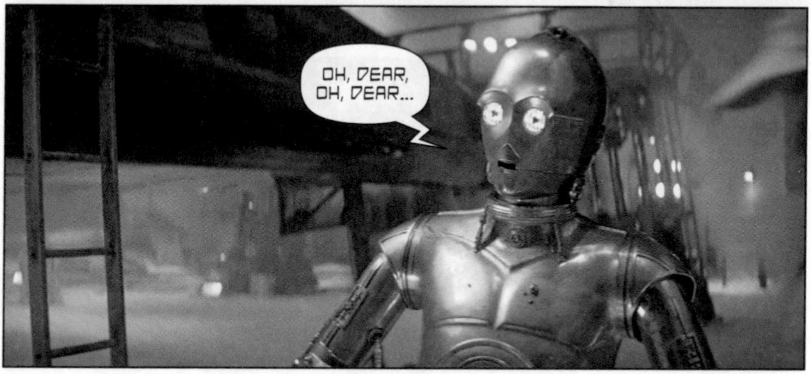
OH, DEAR, OH, DEAR...

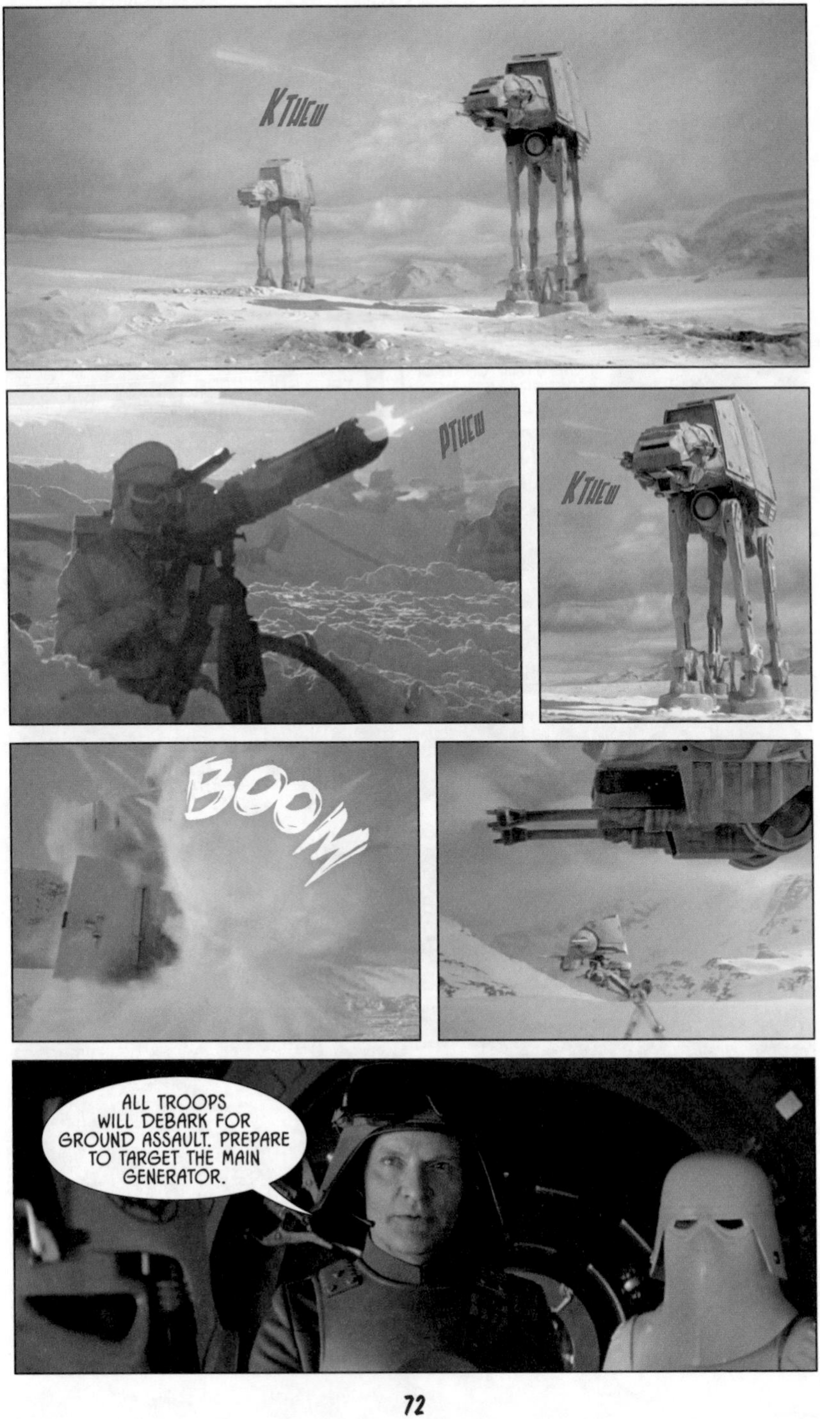
KTHEW
PTHEW
KTHEW
BOOM
ALL TROOPS WILL DEBARK FOR GROUND ASSAULT. PREPARE TO TARGET THE MAIN GENERATOR.

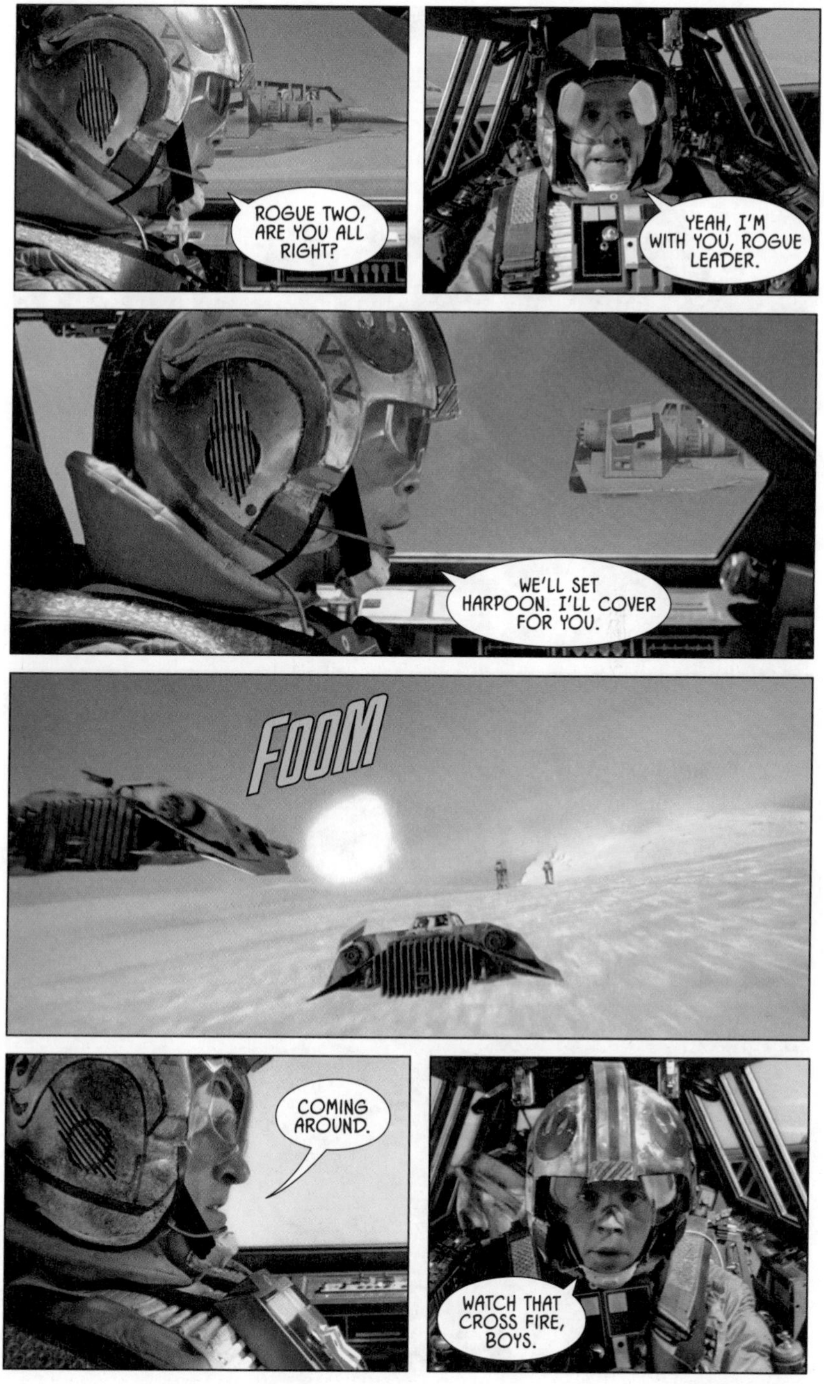
ROGUE TWO, ARE YOU ALL RIGHT?
YEAH, I'M WITH YOU, ROGUE LEADER.
WE'LL SET HARPOON. I'LL COVER FOR YOU.
FOOM
COMING AROUND.
WATCH THAT CROSS FIRE, BOYS.

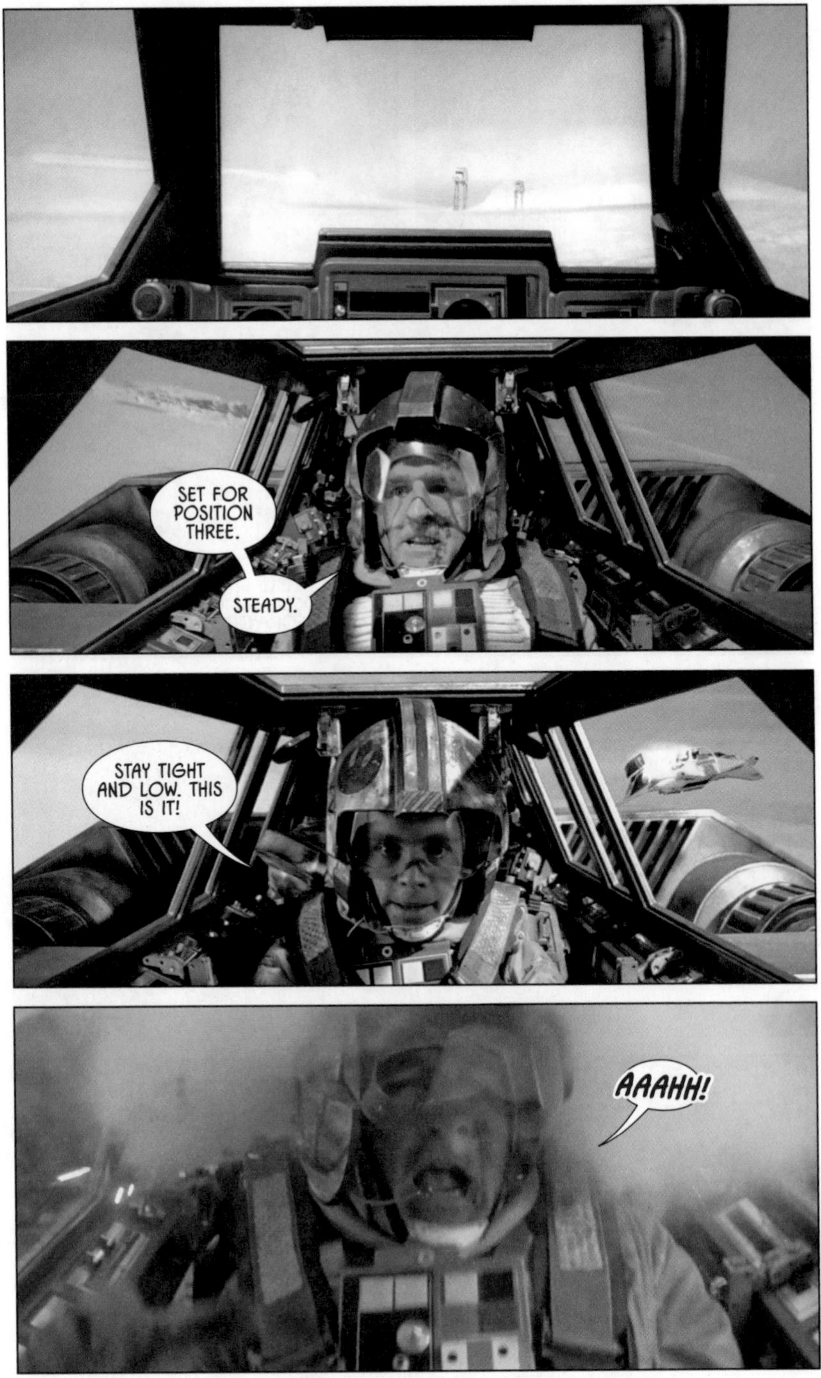
SET FOR POSITION THREE.
STEADY.
STAY TIGHT AND LOW. THIS IS IT!
AAAHH!

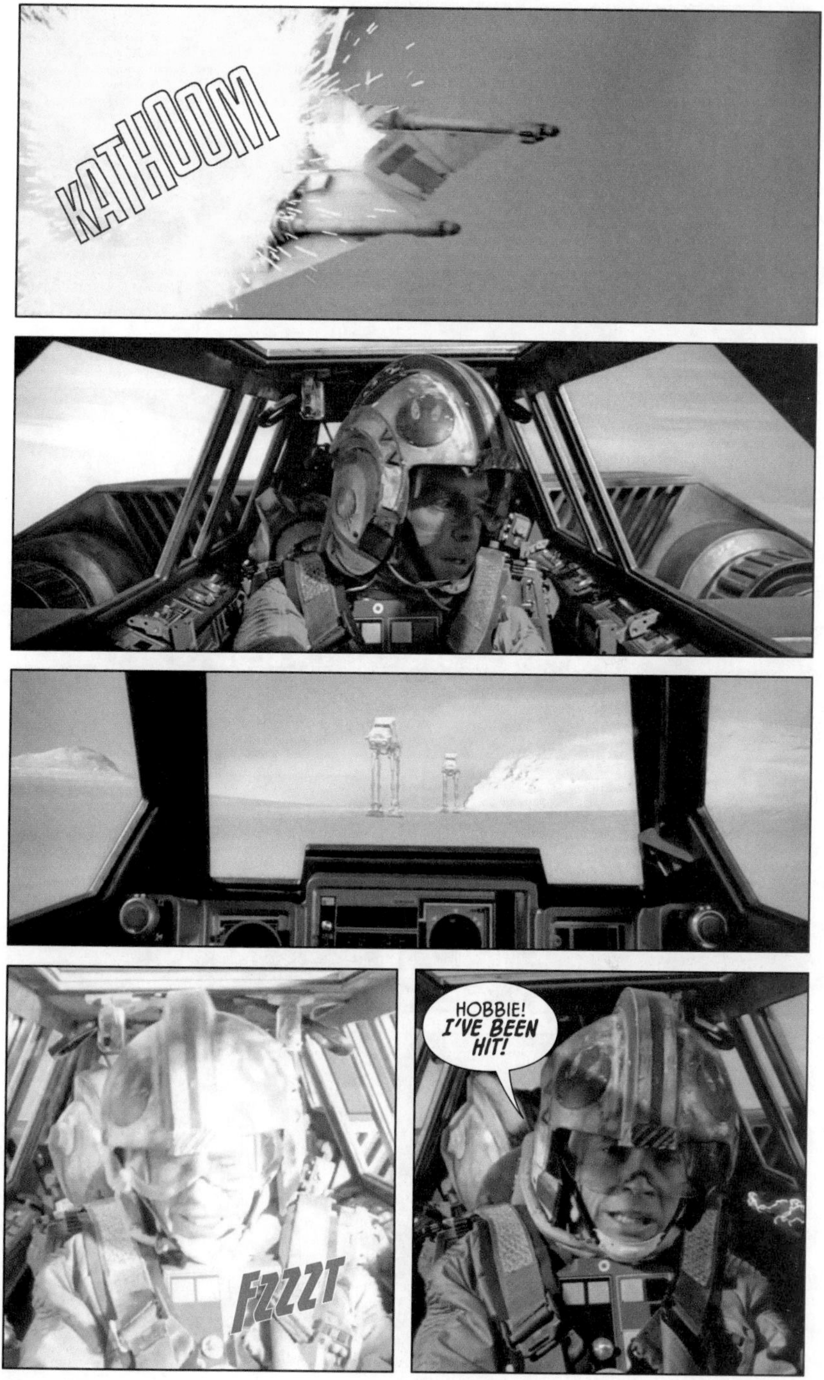
KATHOOM
HOBBIE!
I'VE BEEN HIT!
FZZZT

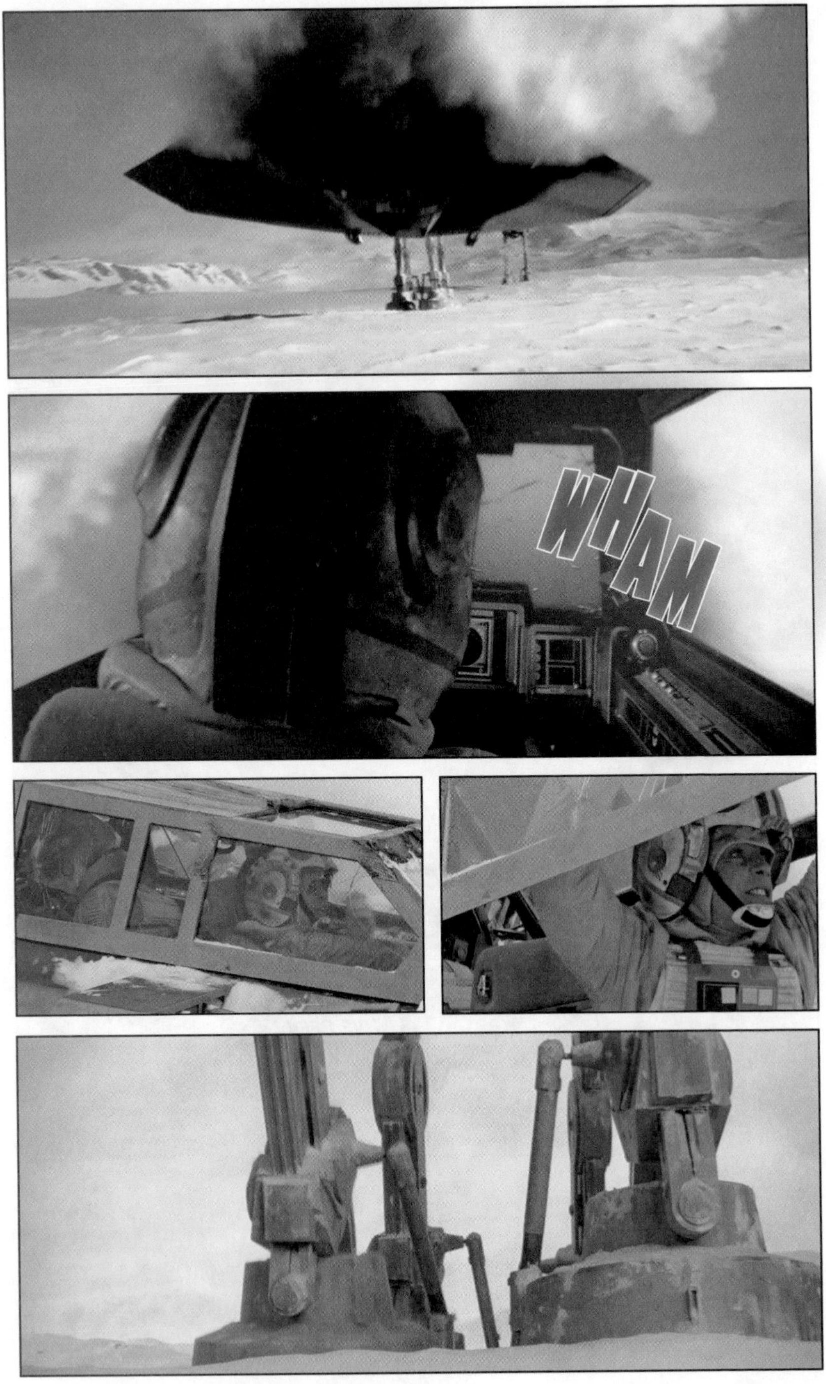
WHAM

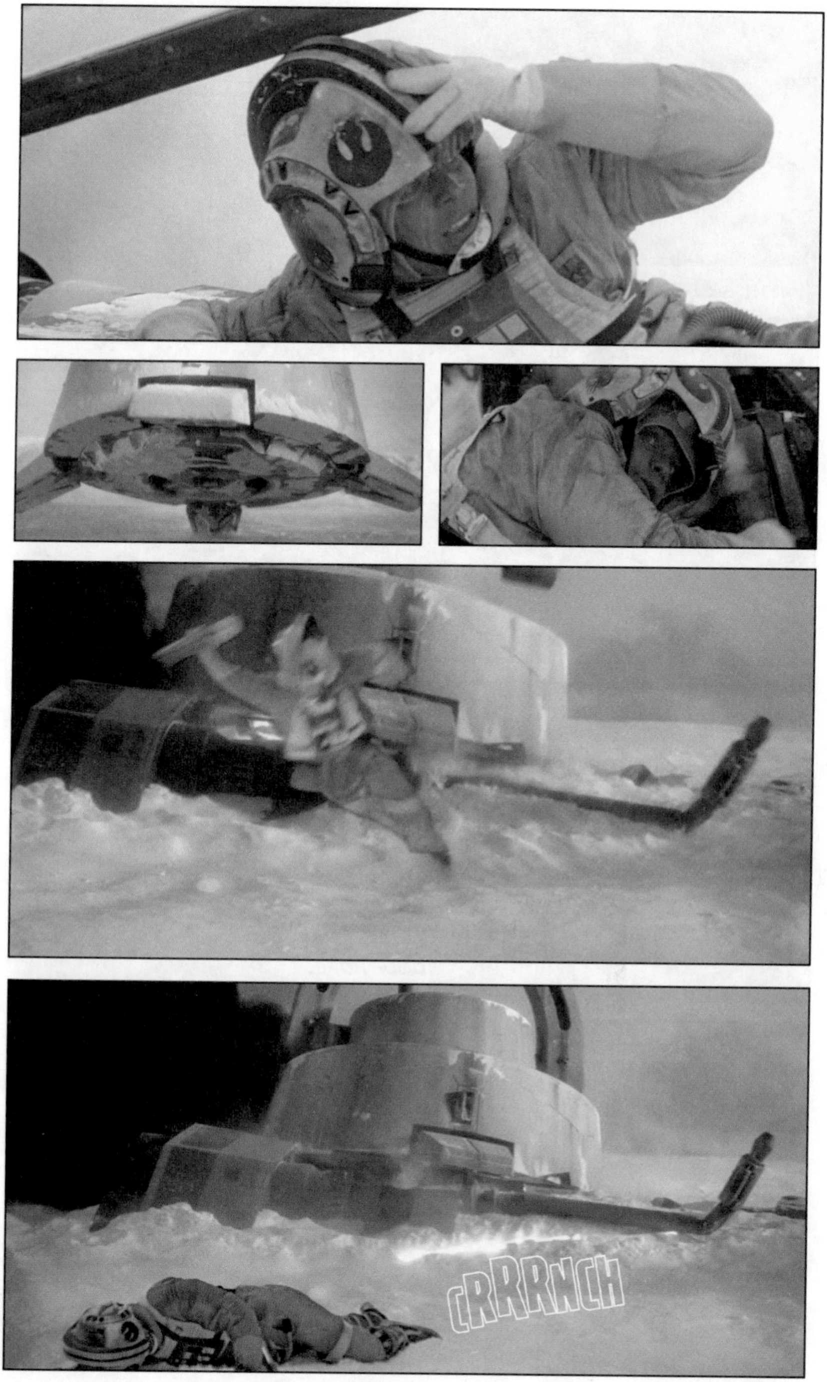
cRRRNCH

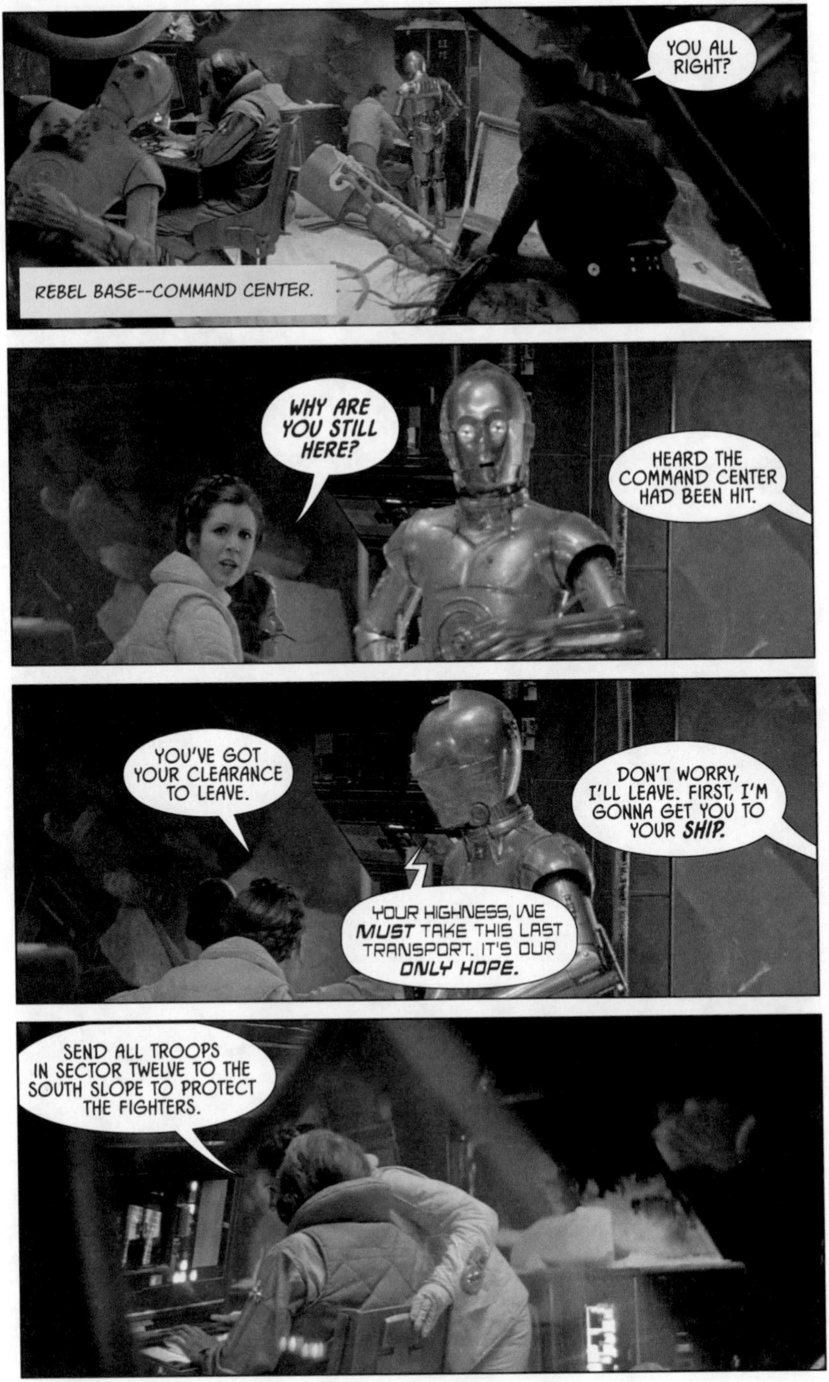
REBEL BASE--COMMAND CENTER.
YOU ALL RIGHT?
WHY ARE YOU STILL HERE?
HEARD THE COMMAND CENTER HAD BEEN HIT.
YOU'VE GOT YOUR CLEARANCE TO LEAVE.
DON'T WORRY, I'LL LEAVE. FIRST, I'M GONNA GET YOU TO YOUR SHIP.
YOUR HIGHNESS, WE MUST TAKE THIS LAST TRANSPORT. IT'S OUR ONLY HOPE.
SEND ALL TROOPS IN SECTOR TWELVE TO THE SOUTH SLOPE TO PROTECT THE FIGHTERS.

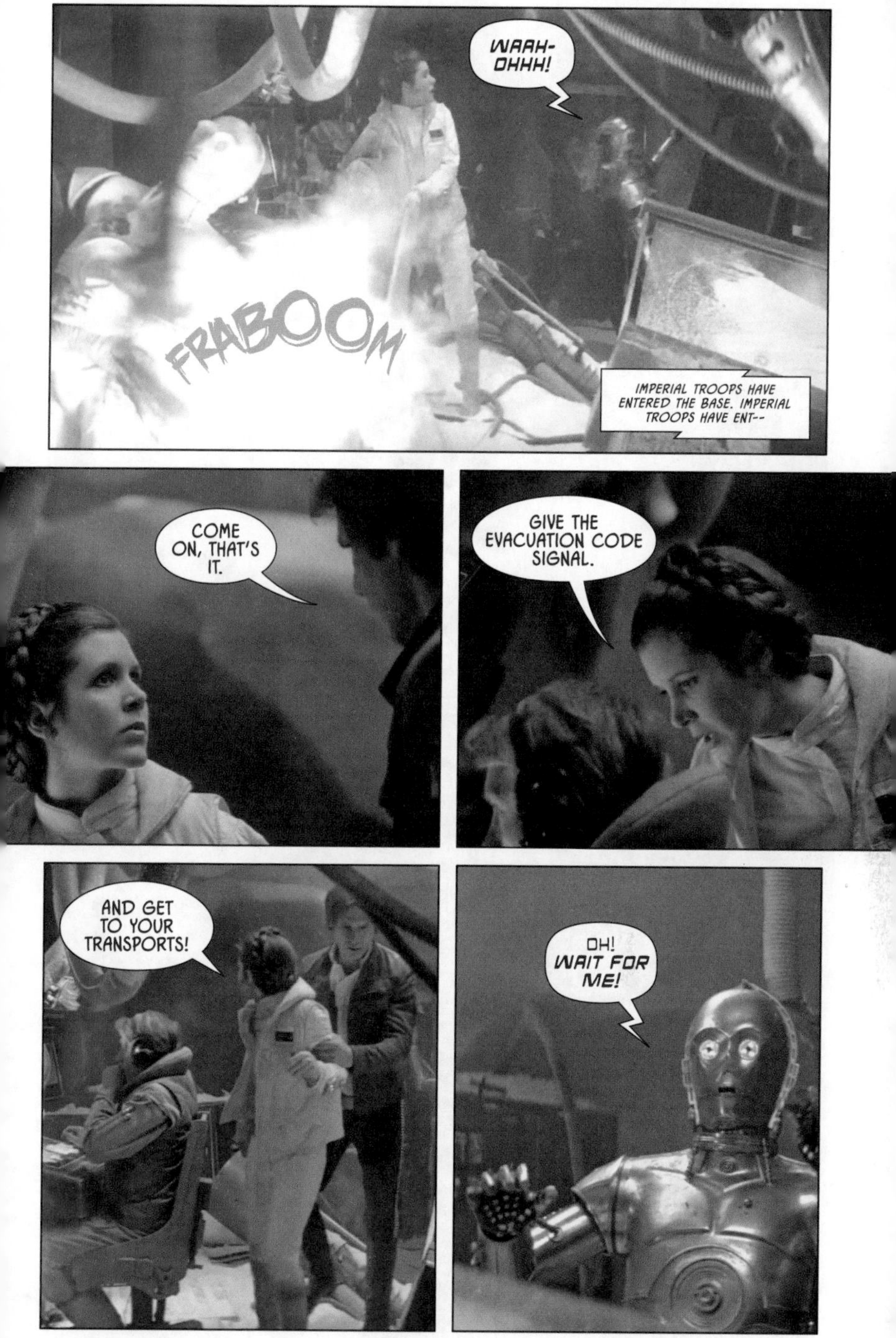
WAAH-
OHHH!
FRABOOM
IMPERIAL TROOPS HAVE ENTERED THE BASE. IMPERIAL TROOPS HAVE ENT--
COME ON, THAT'S IT.
GIVE THE EVACUATION CODE SIGNAL.
AND GET TO YOUR TRANSPORTS!
OH! WAIT FOR ME!

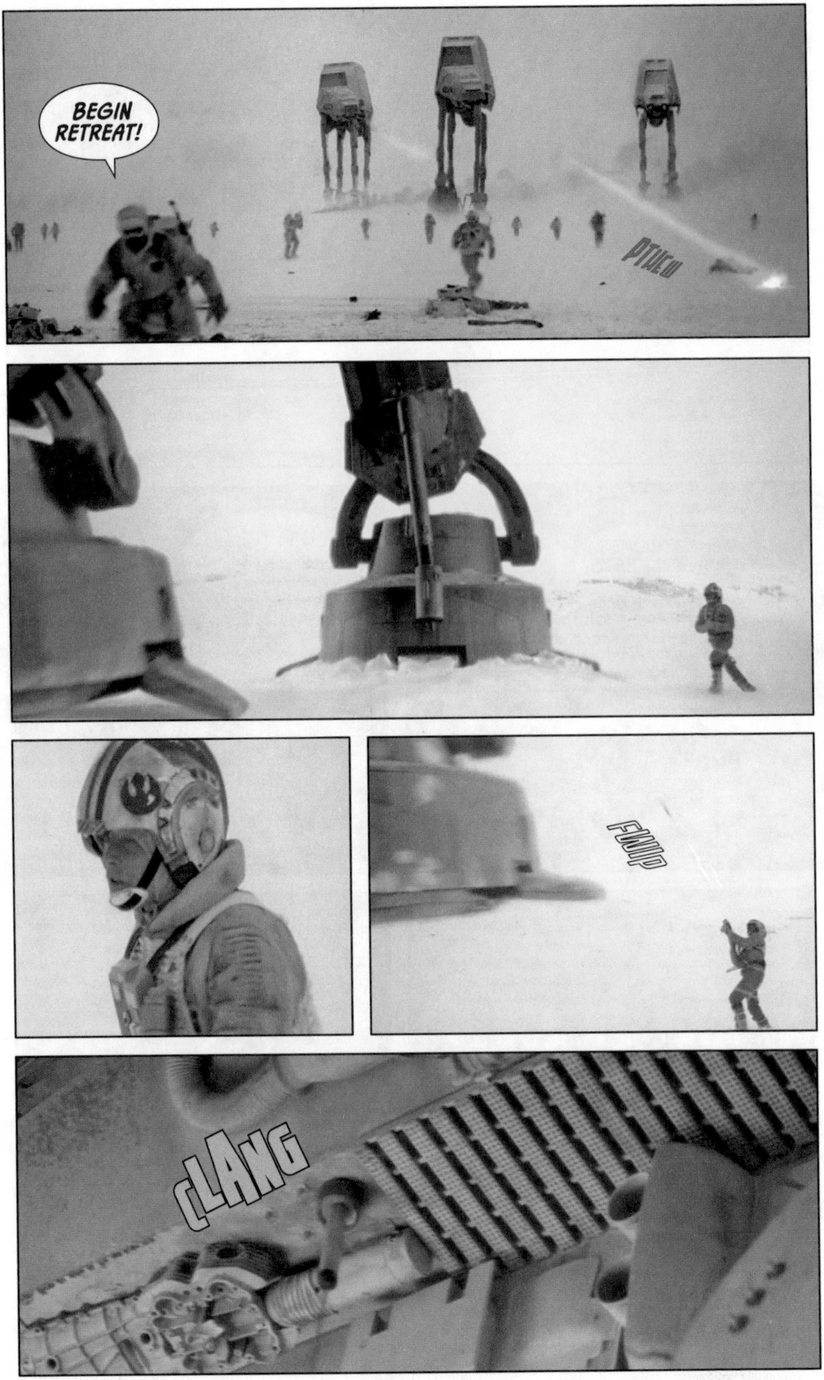
BEGIN RETREAT!
PTIEU
FWIP
CLANG

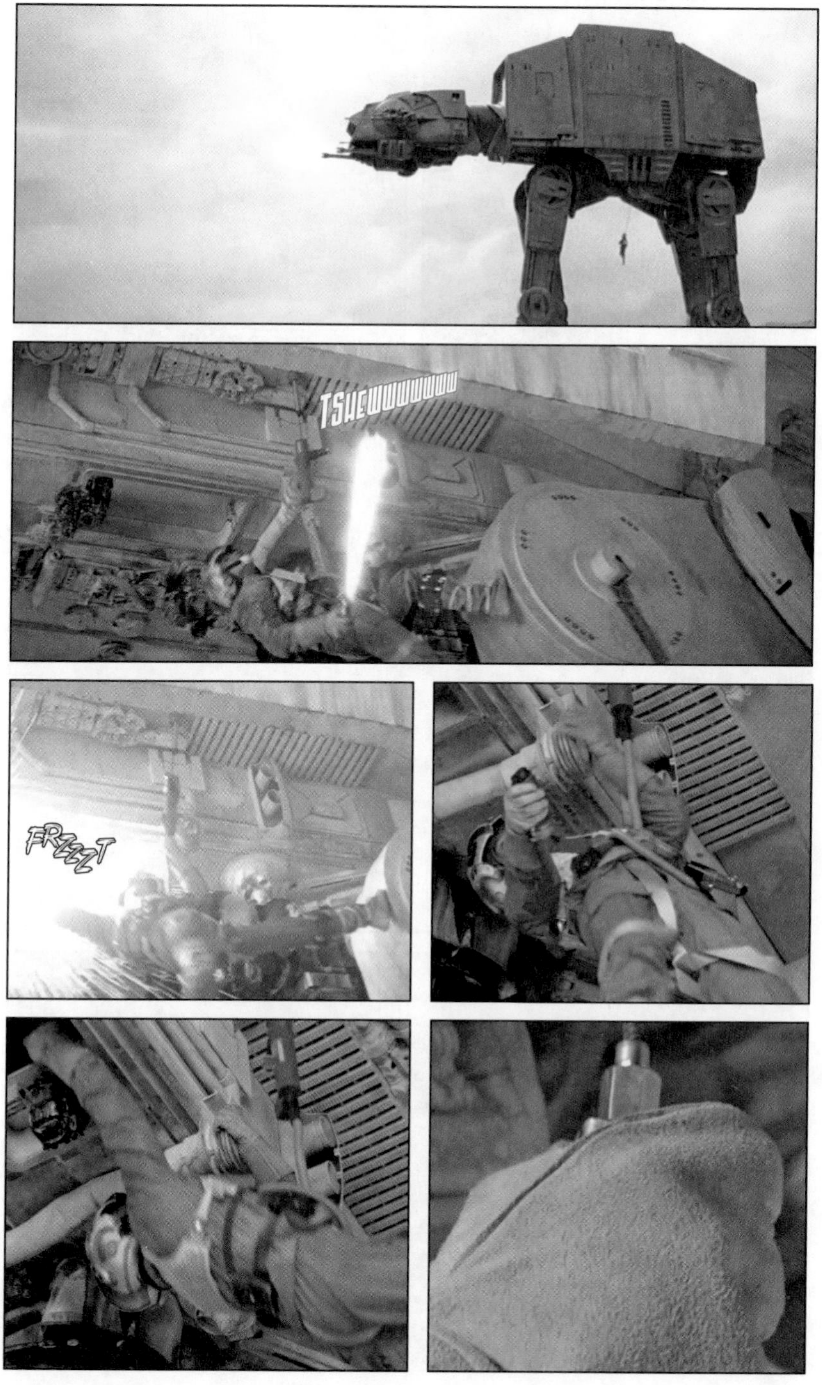
TSHEWWWWWWW
FRZZZT

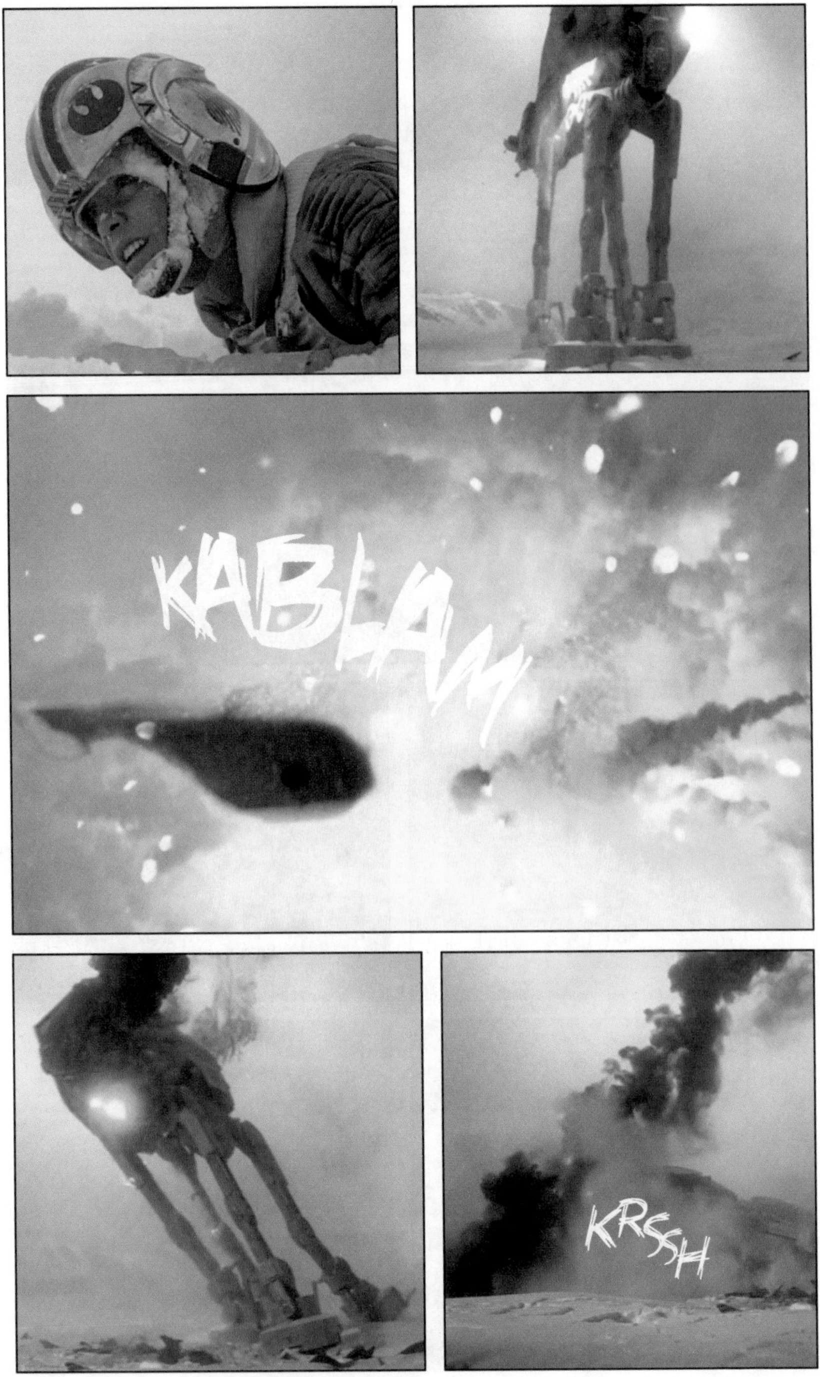
KABLAM
KRSSH

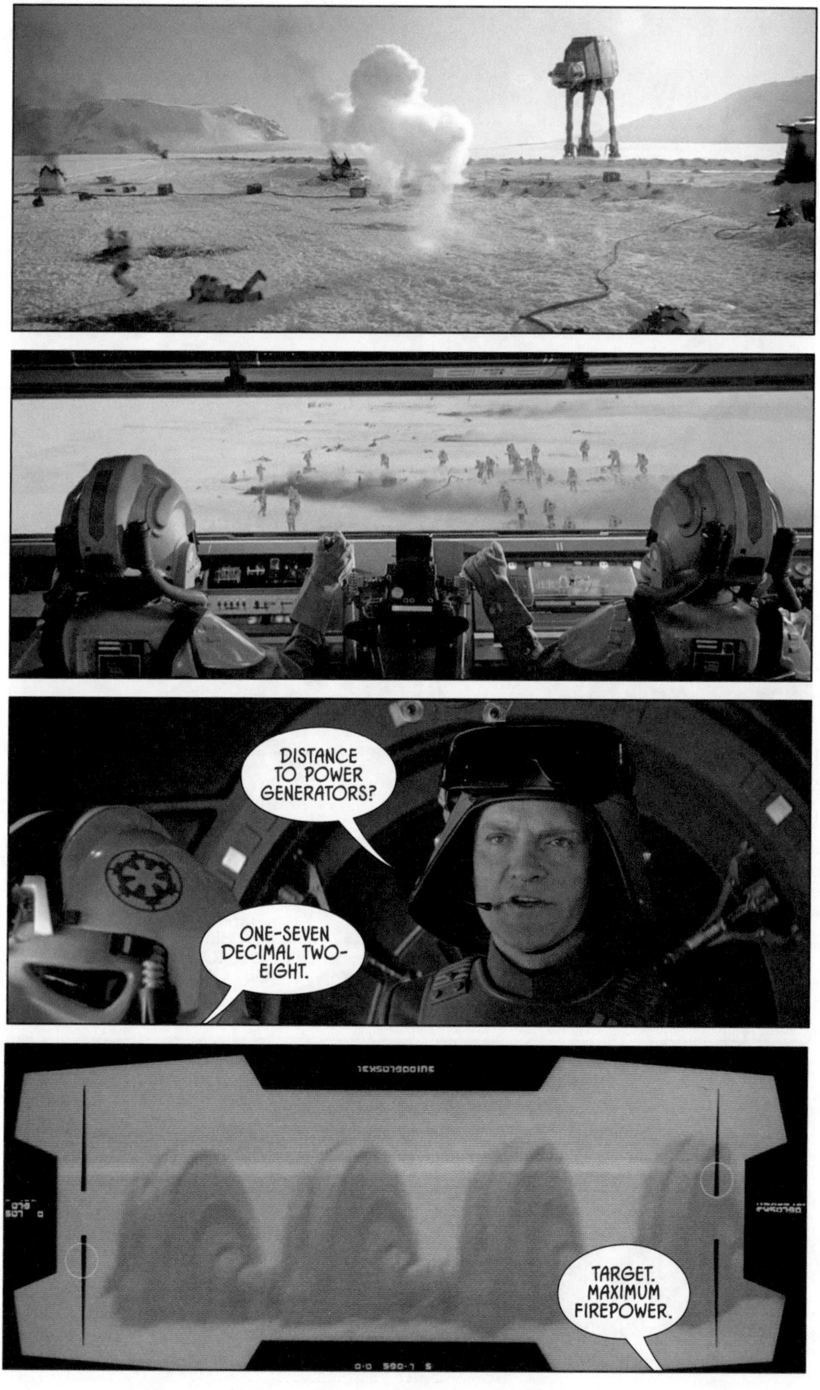
DISTANCE TO POWER GENERATORS?
ONE-SEVEN DECIMAL TWO-EIGHT.
TARGET. MAXIMUM FIREPOWER.

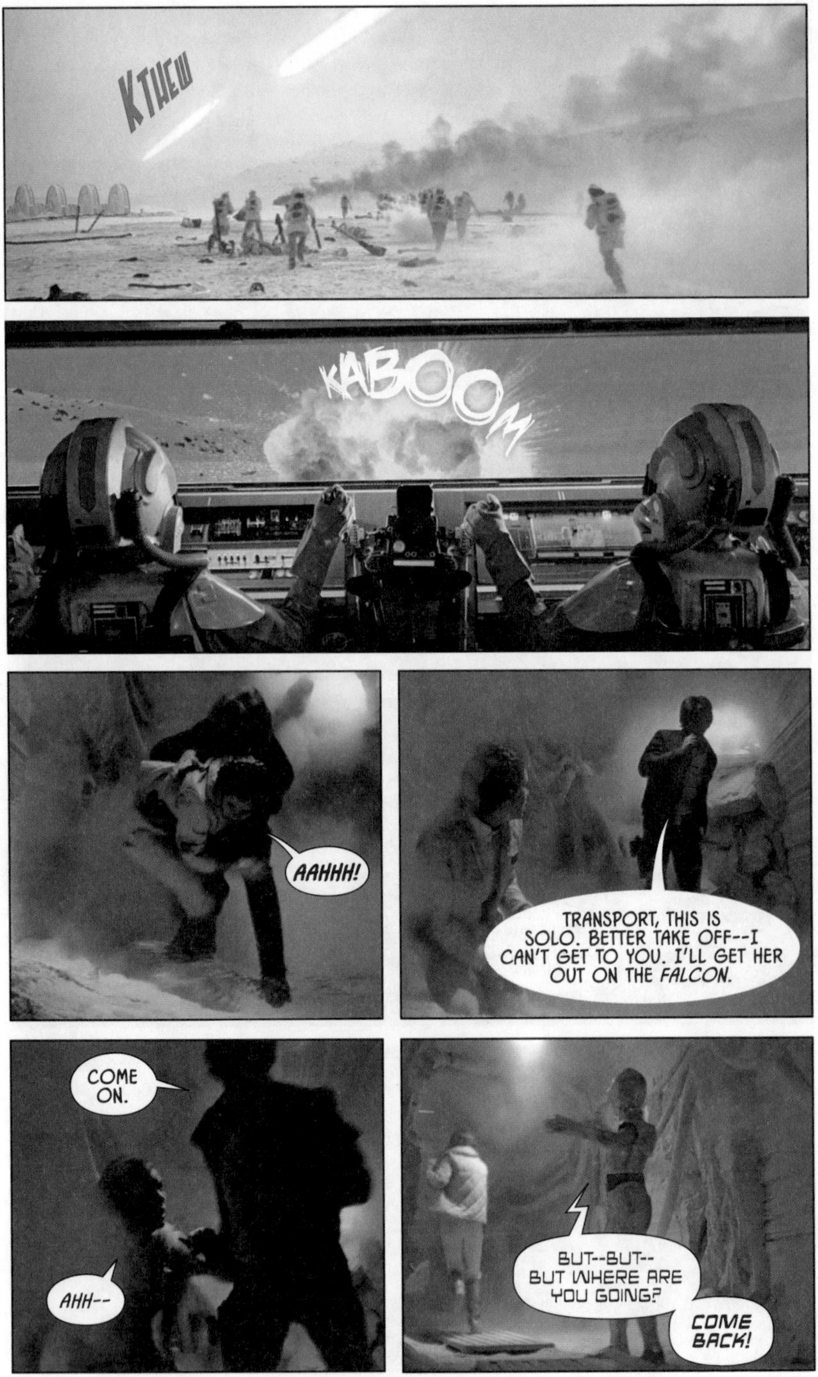
KTHEW
KABOOM
AAHHH!
TRANSPORT, THIS IS SOLO. BETTER TAKE OFF--I CAN'T GET TO YOU. I'LL GET HER OUT ON THE *FALCON*.
COME ON.
AHH--
BUT--BUT-- BUT WHERE ARE YOU GOING?
COME BACK!

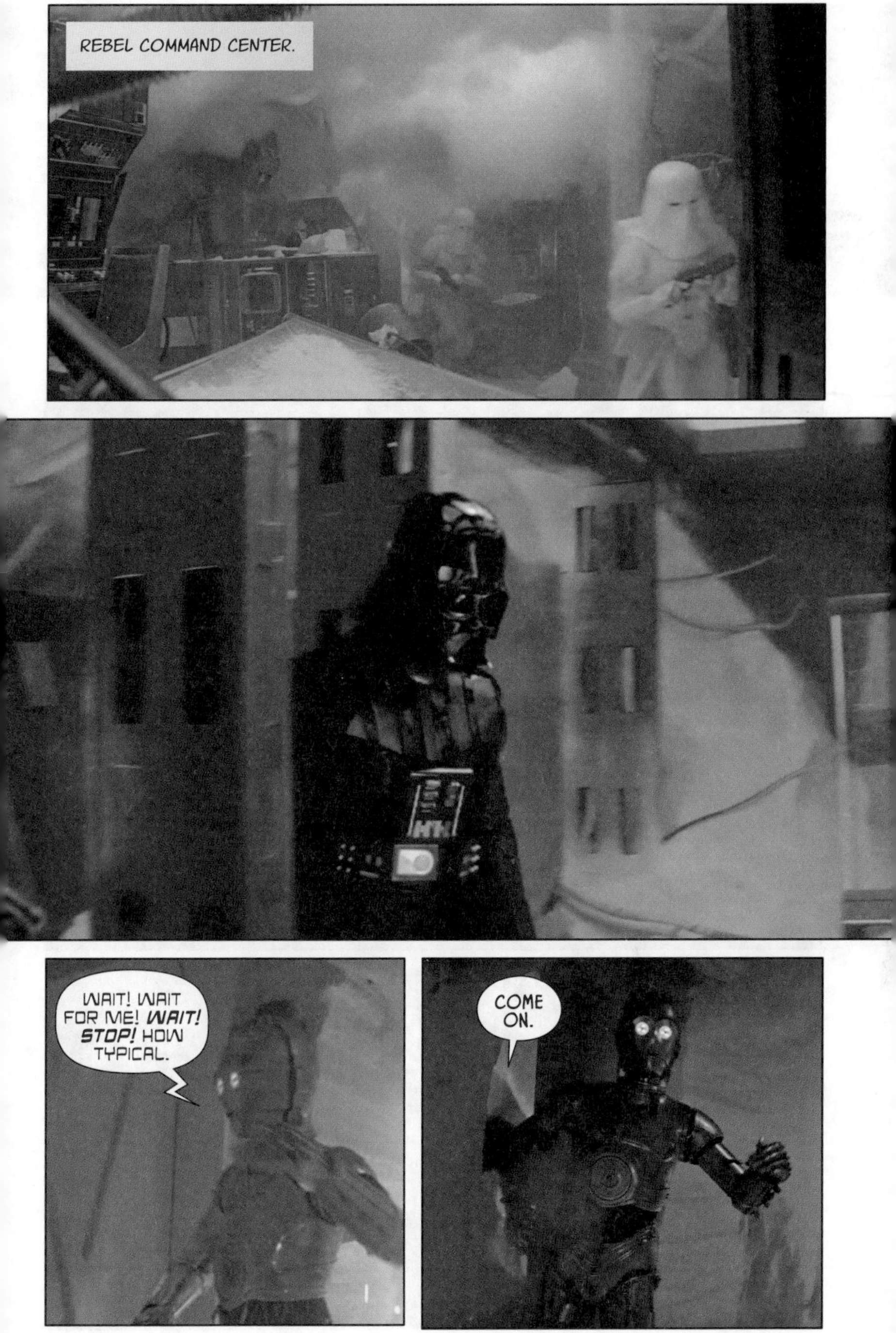
REBEL COMMAND CENTER.
WAIT! WAIT FOR ME! WAIT! STOP! HOW TYPICAL.
COME ON.

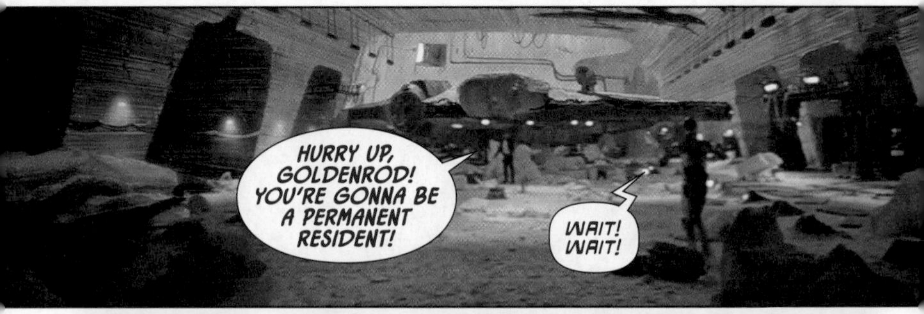
HURRY UP, GOLDENROD! YOU'RE GONNA BE A PERMANENT RESIDENT!
WAIT! WAIT!

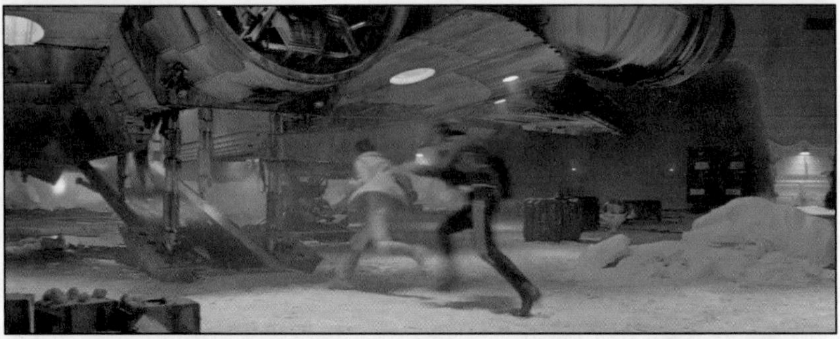

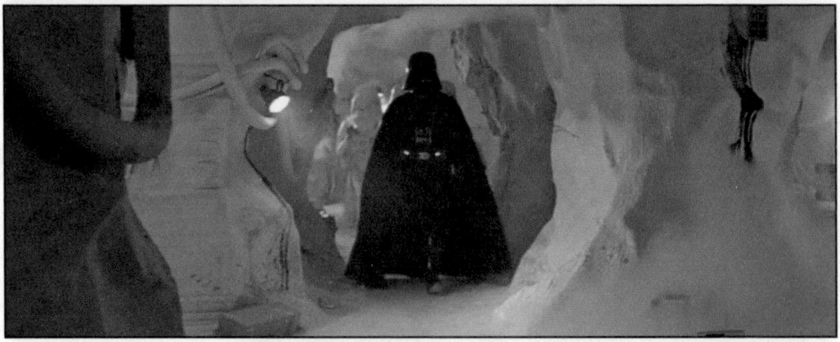

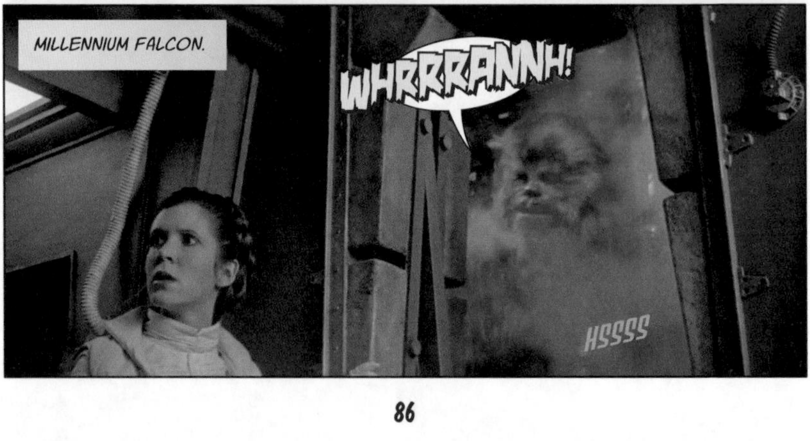
MILLENNIUM FALCON.
WHRRRANNH!
HSSSS

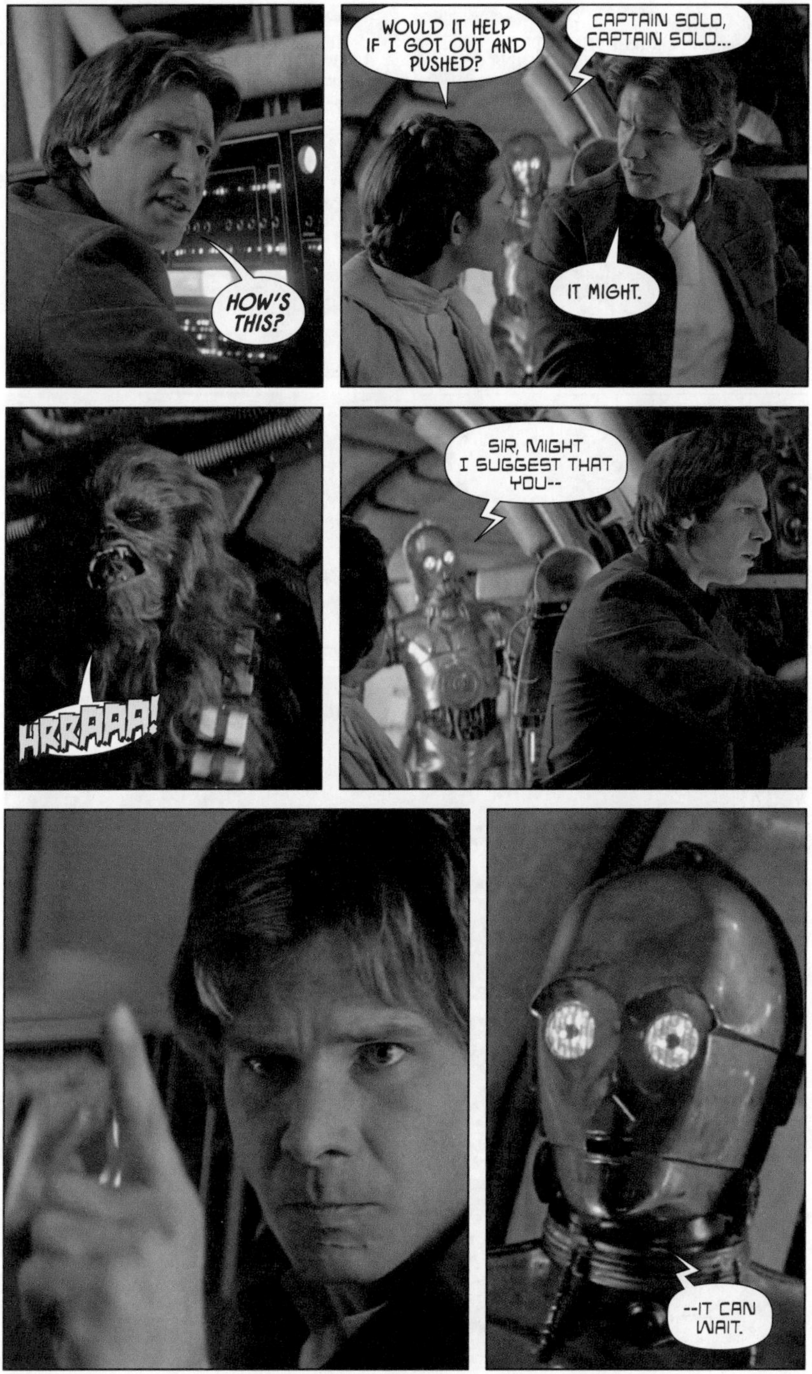
HOW'S THIS?
WOULD IT HELP IF I GOT OUT AND PUSHED?
CAPTAIN SOLO, CAPTAIN SOLO...
IT MIGHT.
HRRAAA!
SIR, MIGHT I SUGGEST THAT YOU--
--IT CAN WAIT.

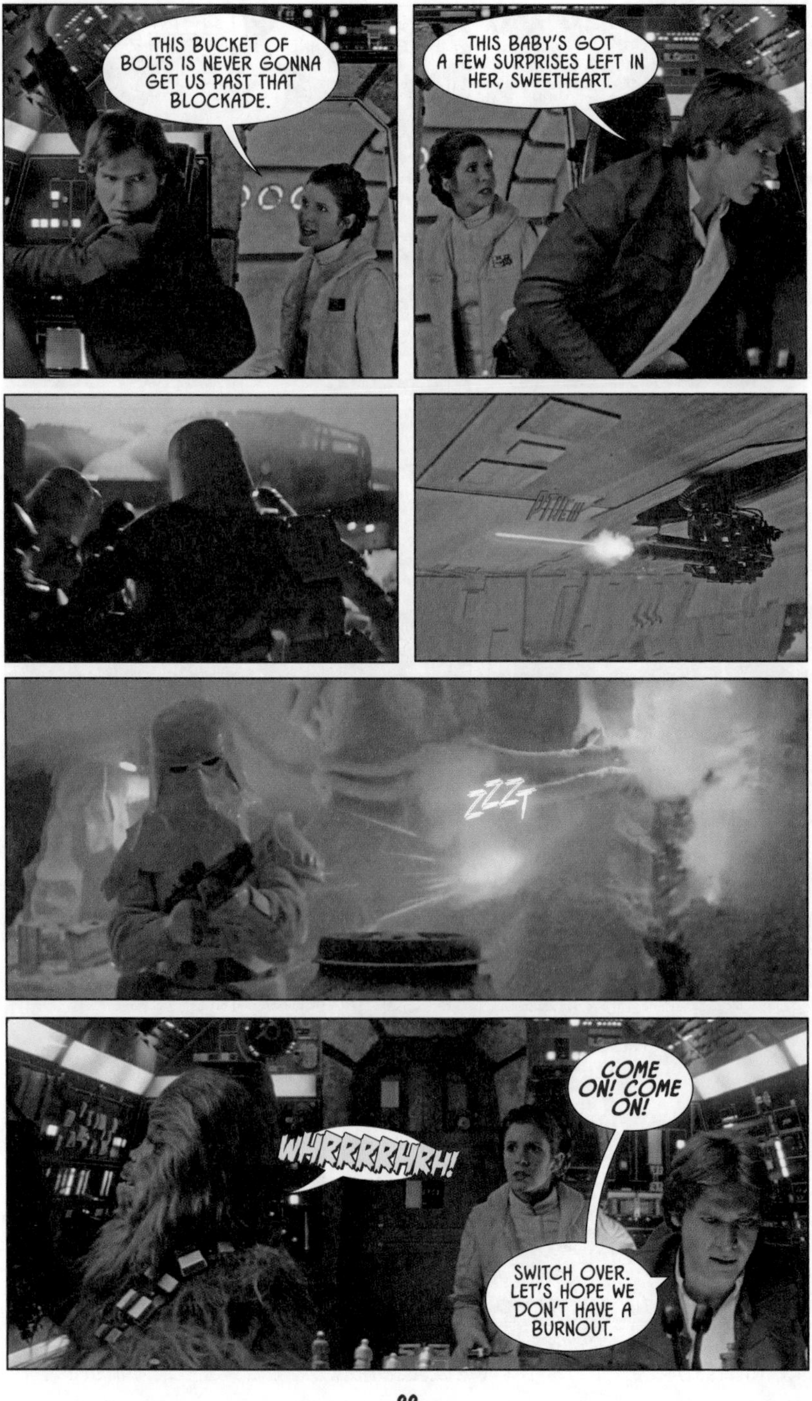
THIS BUCKET OF BOLTS IS NEVER GONNA GET US PAST THAT BLOCKADE.
THIS BABY'S GOT A FEW SURPRISES LEFT IN HER, SWEETHEART.
PTTEW
ZZZT
WHRRRRHRH!
COME ON! COME ON!
SWITCH OVER. LET'S HOPE WE DON'T HAVE A BURNOUT.

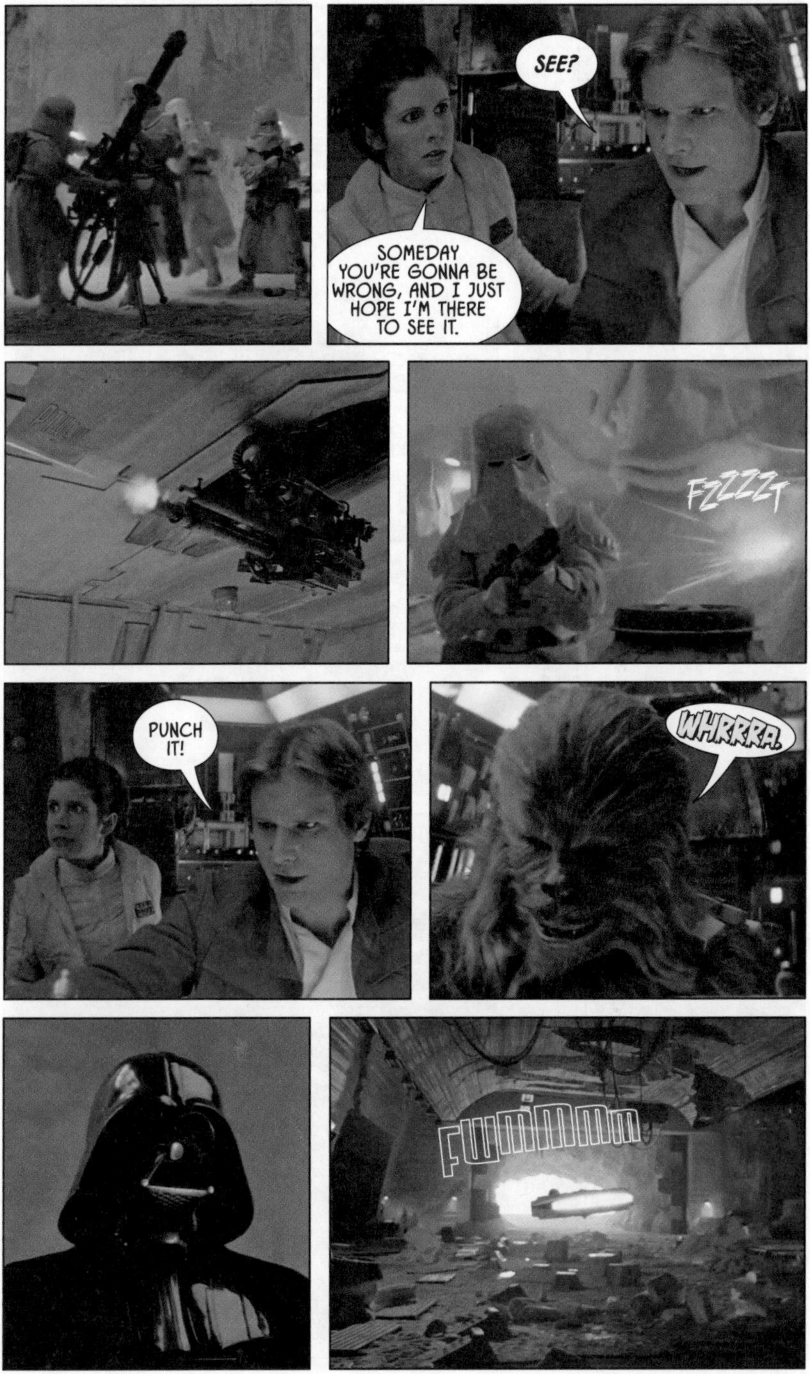
SEE?
SOMEDAY YOU'RE GONNA BE WRONG, AND I JUST HOPE I'M THERE TO SEE IT.
FZZZZT
PUNCH IT!
WHRRRA.
FUMMMM

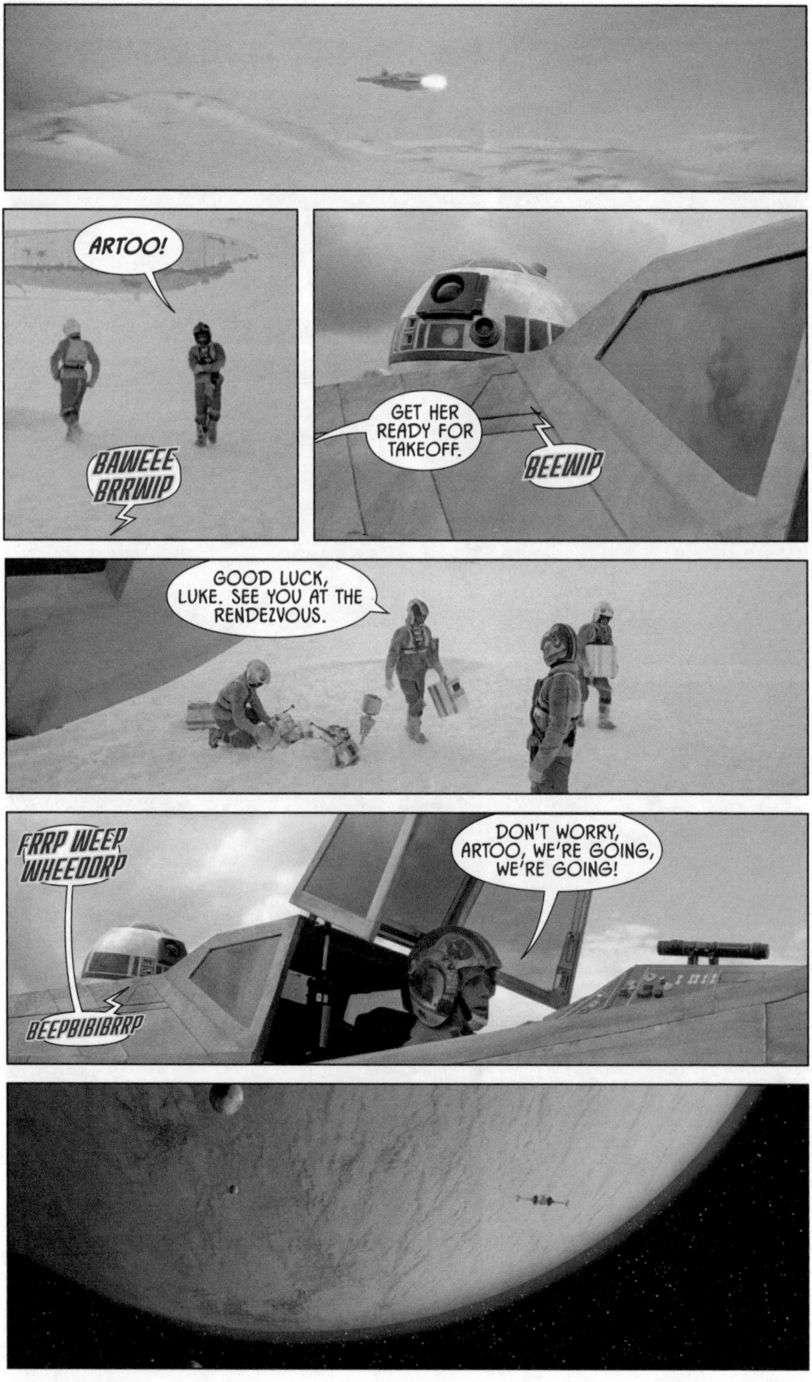
ARTOO!
BAWEEE BRRWIP
GET HER READY FOR TAKEOFF.
BEEWIP
GOOD LUCK, LUKE. SEE YOU AT THE RENDEZVOUS.
FRRP WEEP WHEEDORP
BEEPBIBIBRRP
DON'T WORRY, ARTOO, WE'RE GOING, WE'RE GOING!

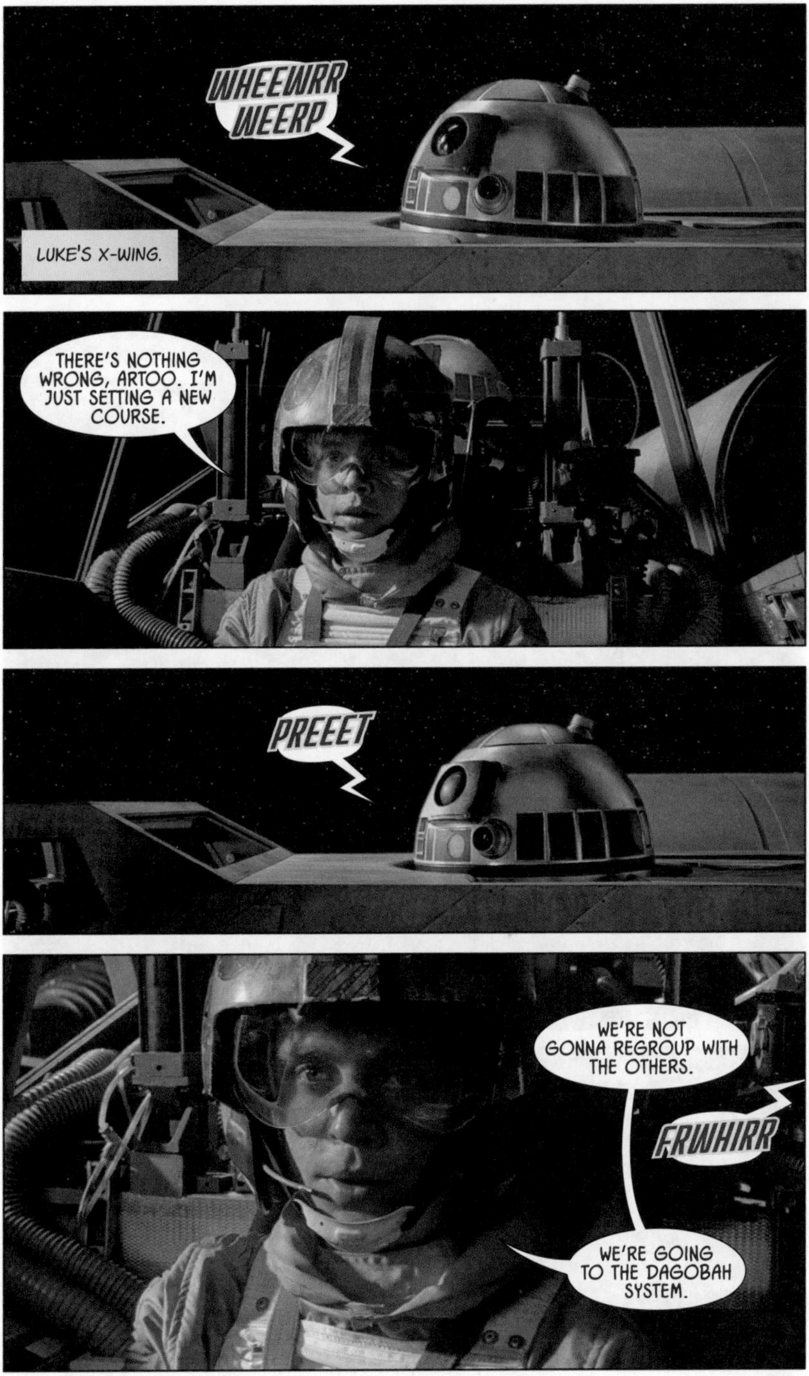
WHEEWRR WEERP
LUKE'S X-WING.
THERE'S NOTHING WRONG, ARTOO. I'M JUST SETTING A NEW COURSE.
PREEET
WE'RE NOT GONNA REGROUP WITH THE OTHERS.
FRWHIRR
WE'RE GOING TO THE DAGOBAH SYSTEM.

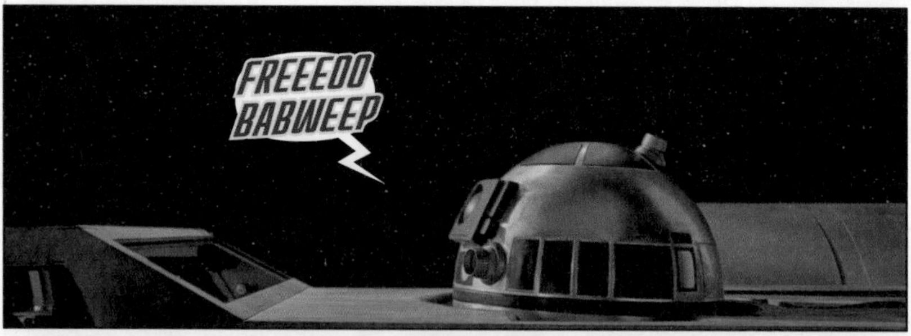
FREEEDO
BABWEEP

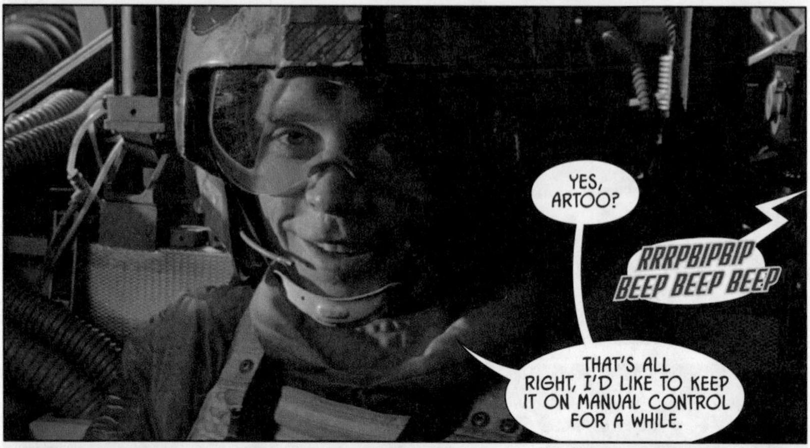
YES, ARTOO?
RRRPBIPBIP
BEEP BEEP BEEP
THAT'S ALL RIGHT, I'D LIKE TO KEEP IT ON MANUAL CONTROL FOR A WHILE.

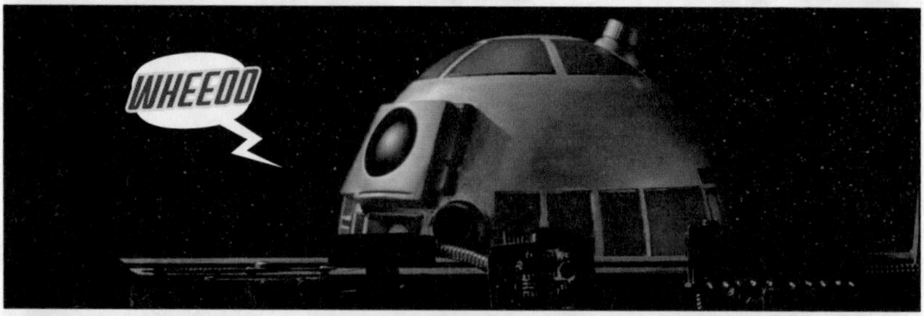
WHEEOO

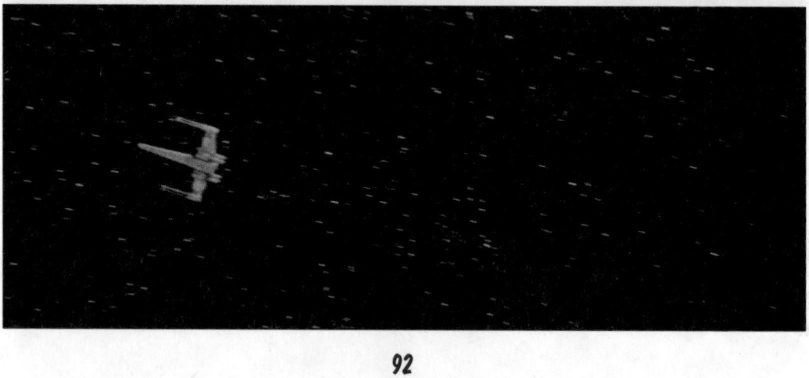

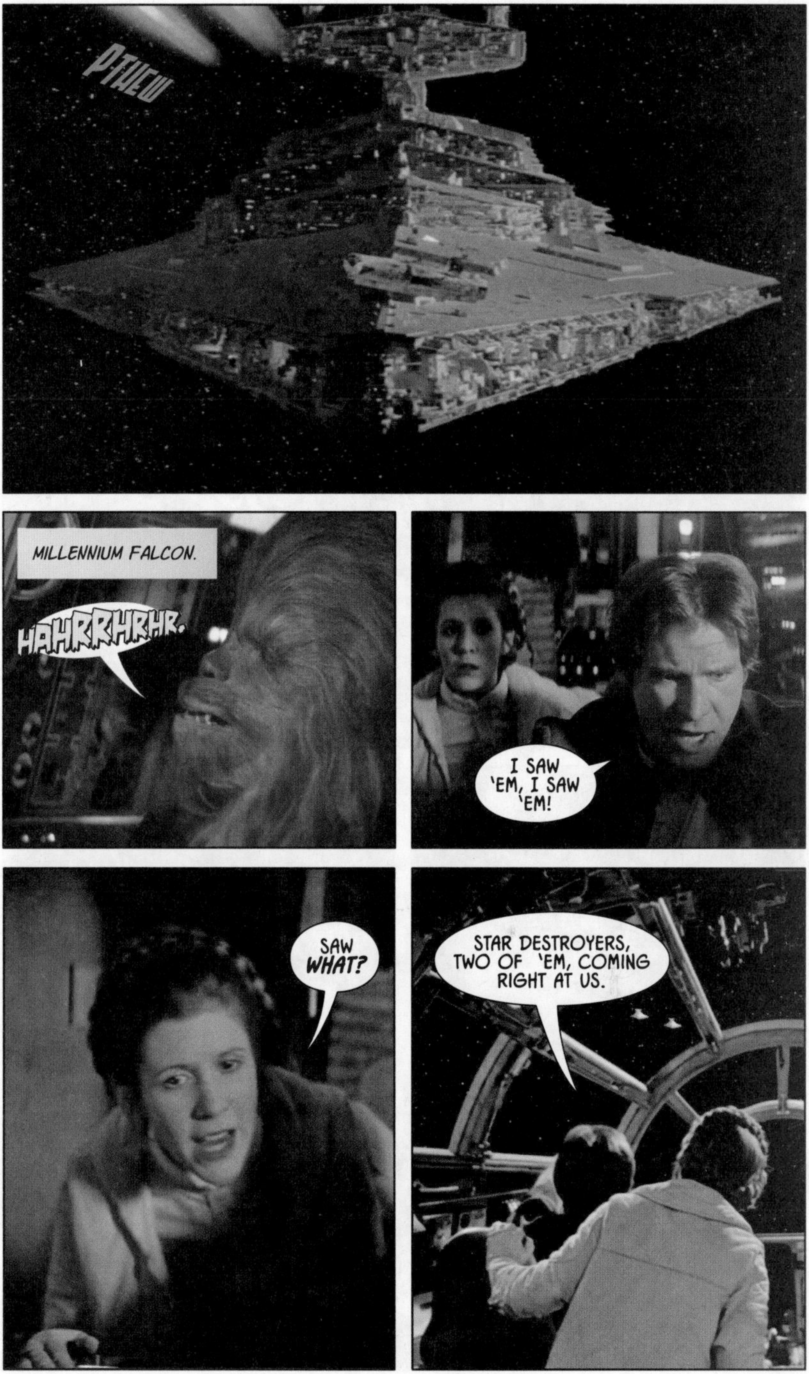
PTHEW
MILLENNIUM FALCON.
HAHRRHRHR.
I SAW 'EM, I SAW 'EM!
SAW WHAT?
STAR DESTROYERS, TWO OF 'EM, COMING RIGHT AT US.

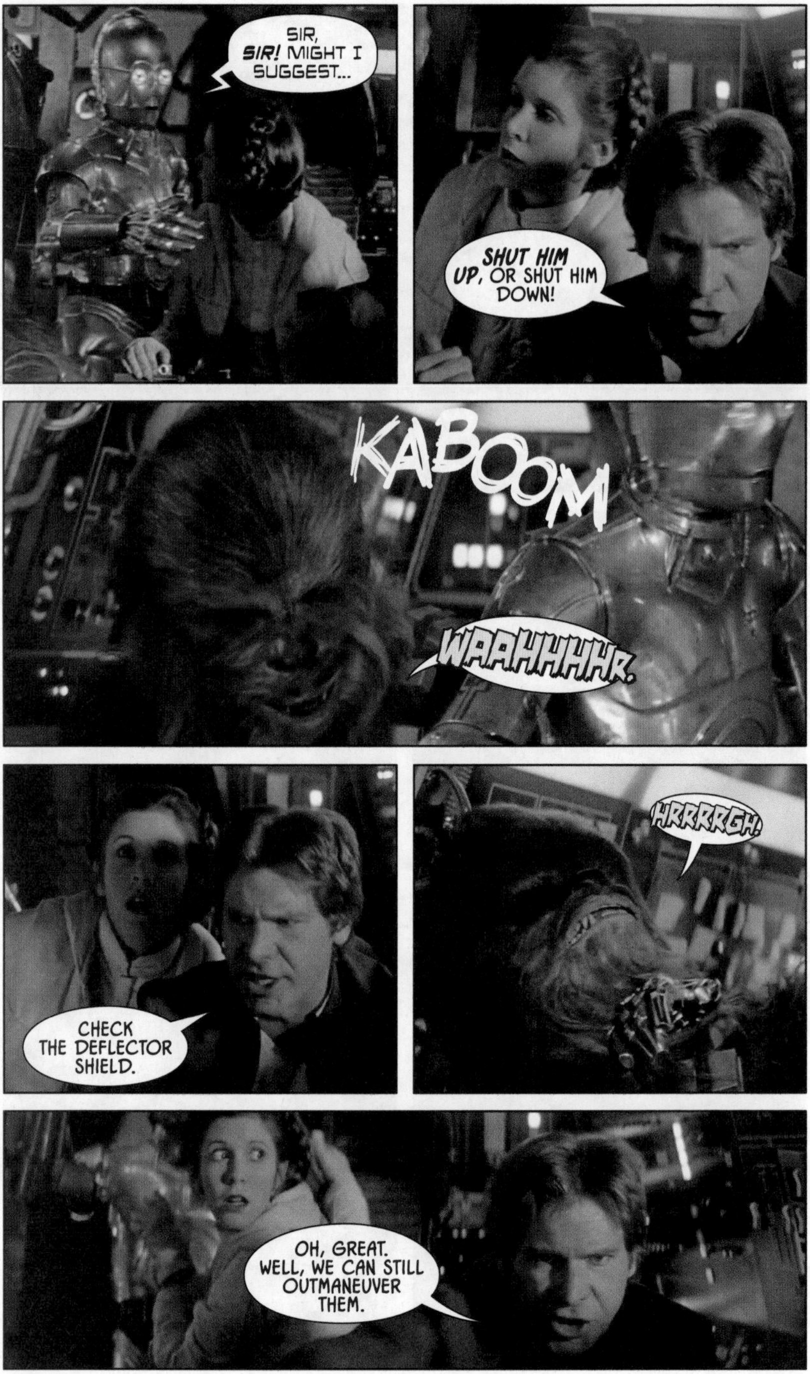
SIR, SIR! MIGHT I SUGGEST...
SHUT HIM UP, OR SHUT HIM DOWN!
KABOOM
WAAHHHHR.
CHECK THE DEFLECTOR SHIELD.
HRRRRGH.
OH, GREAT. WELL, WE CAN STILL OUTMANEUVER THEM.

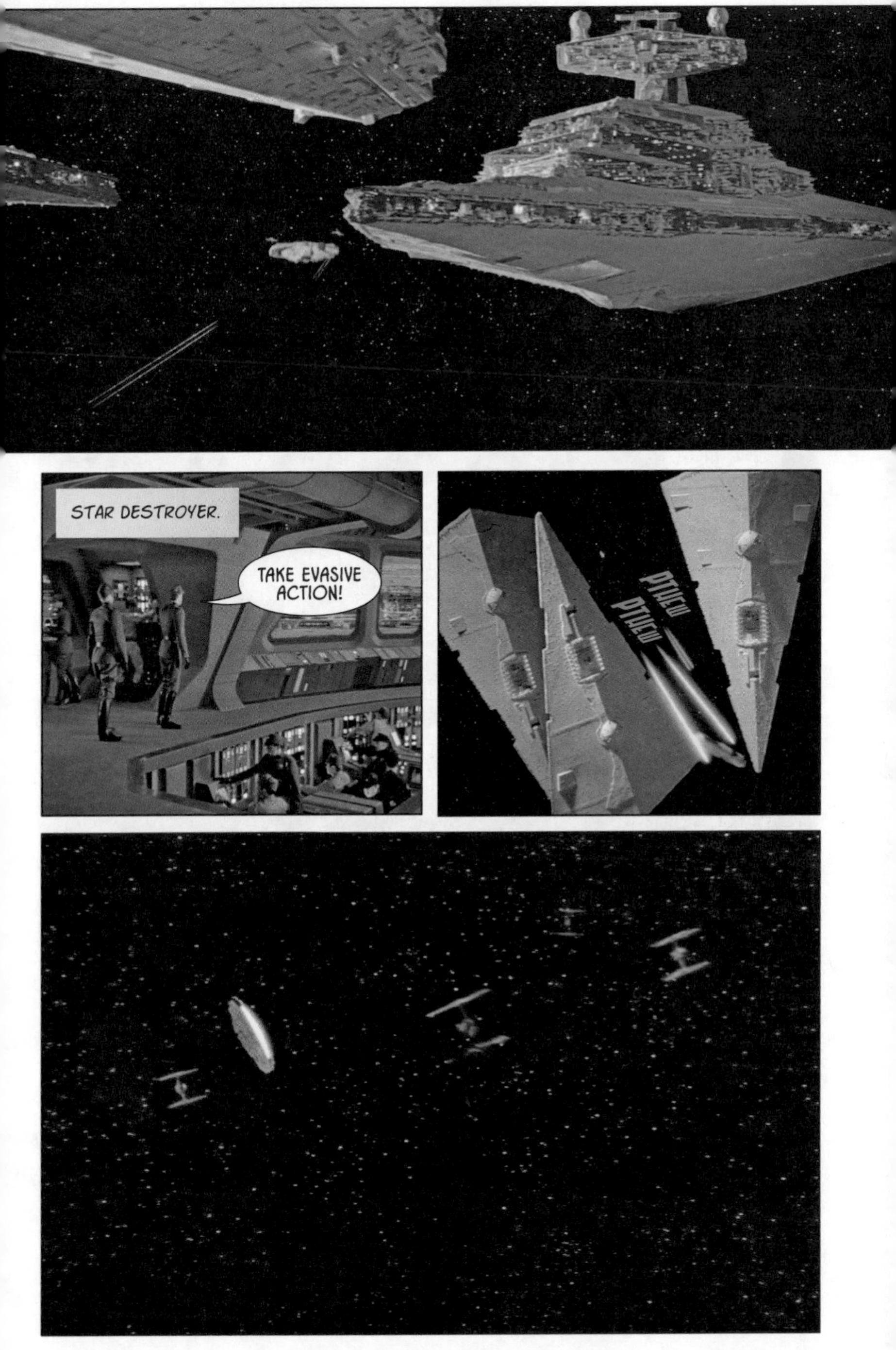
STAR DESTROYER.
TAKE EVASIVE ACTION!
PTWEW
PTWEW

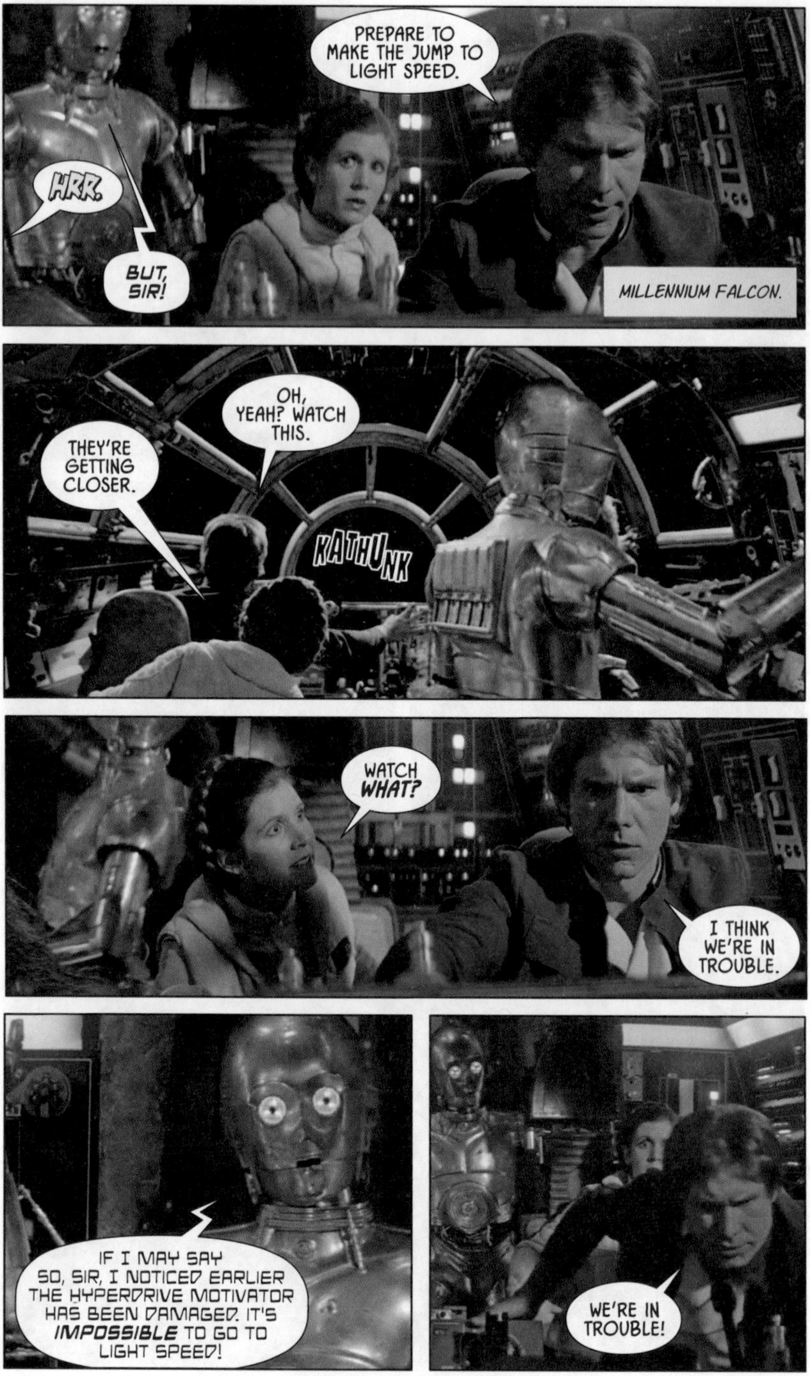
PREPARE TO MAKE THE JUMP TO LIGHT SPEED.
HRR.
BUT, SIR!
MILLENNIUM FALCON.
THEY'RE GETTING CLOSER.
OH, YEAH? WATCH THIS.
KATHUNK
WATCH WHAT?
I THINK WE'RE IN TROUBLE.
IF I MAY SAY SO, SIR, I NOTICED EARLIER THE HYPERDRIVE MOTIVATOR HAS BEEN DAMAGED. IT'S IMPOSSIBLE TO GO TO LIGHT SPEED!
WE'RE IN TROUBLE!

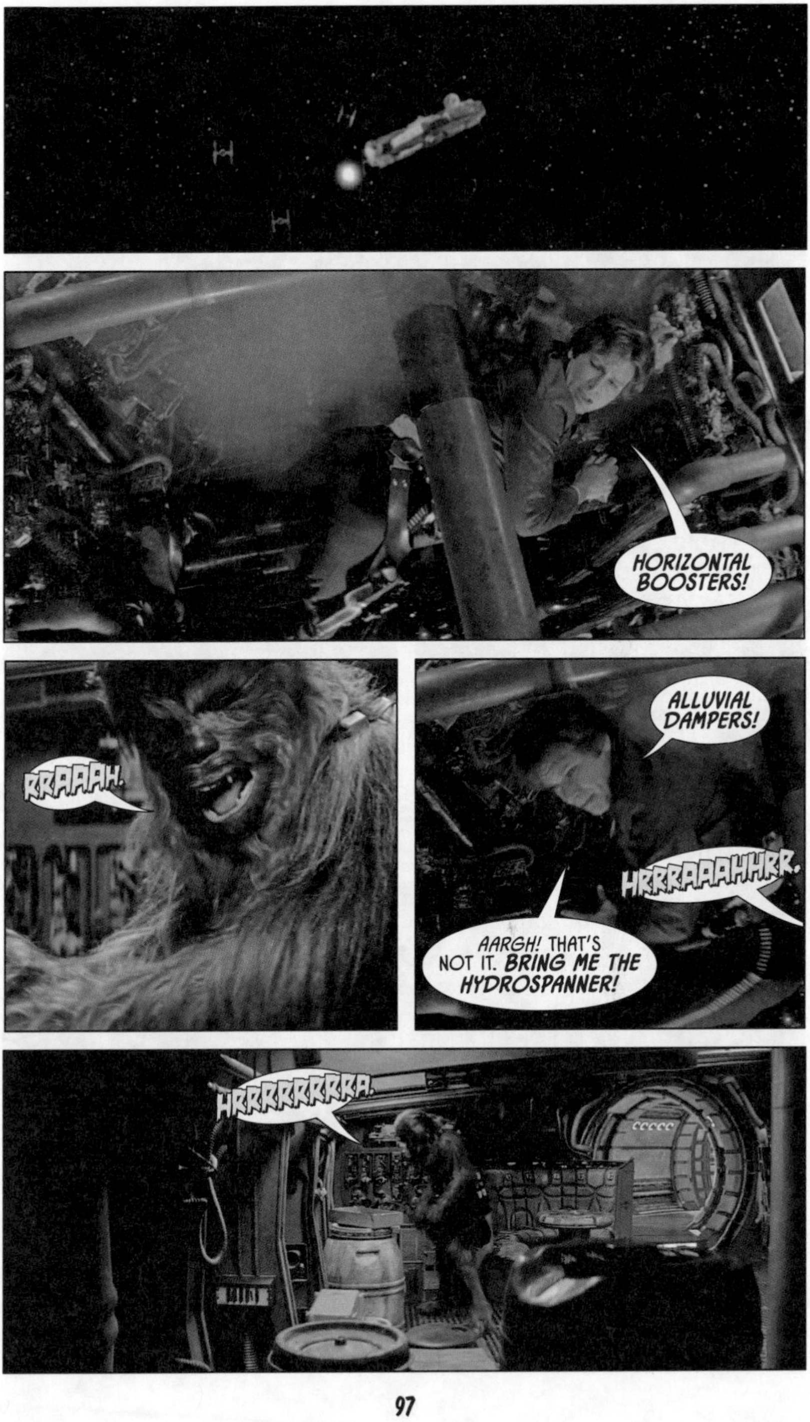
HORIZONTAL BOOSTERS!
RRAAAH.
ALLUVIAL DAMPERS!
HRRRAAAHHRR.
AARGH! THAT'S NOT IT. BRING ME THE HYDROSPANNER!
HRRRRRRRRA.

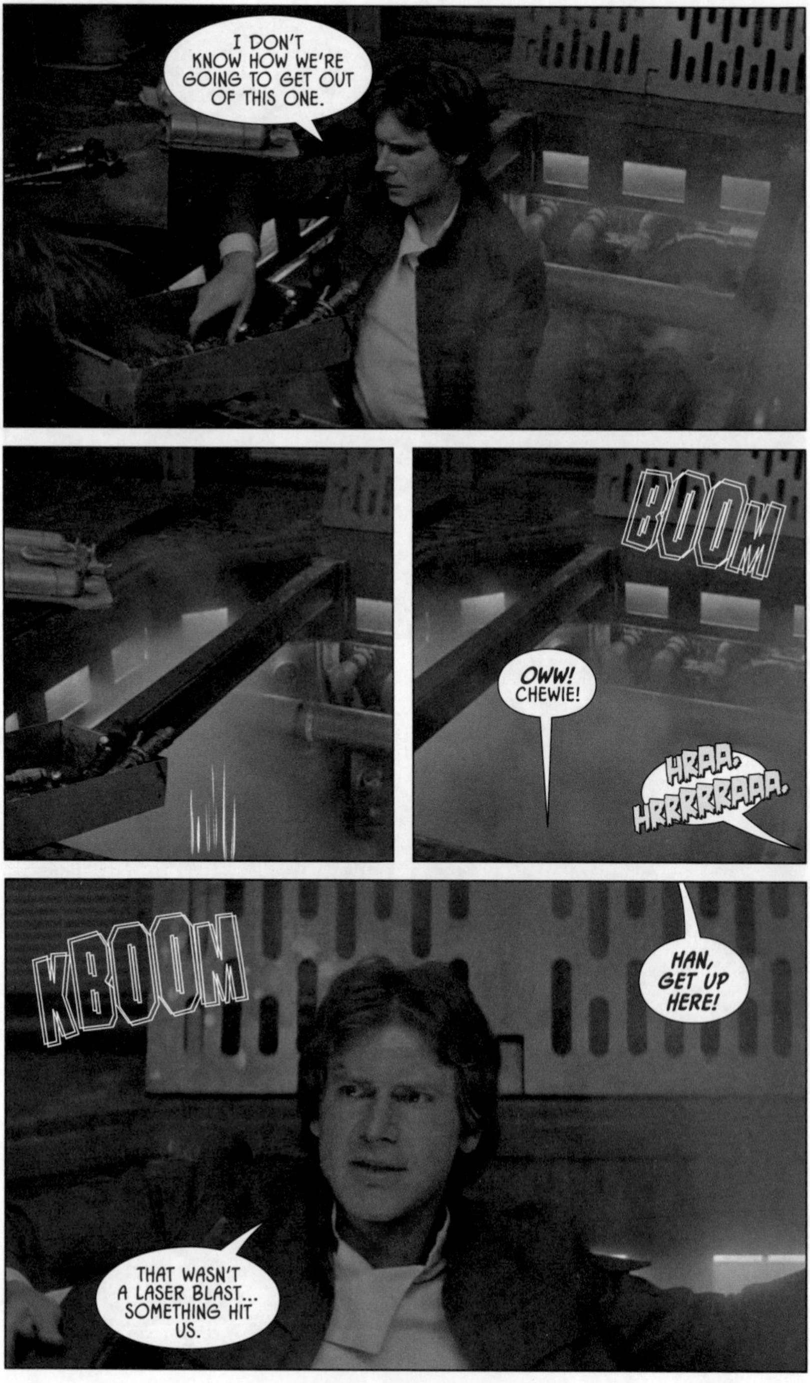
I DON'T KNOW HOW WE'RE GOING TO GET OUT OF THIS ONE.
BOOM
OWW! CHEWIE!
HRAA. HRRRRAAA.
KBOOM
HAN, GET UP HERE!
THAT WASN'T A LASER BLAST... SOMETHING HIT US.

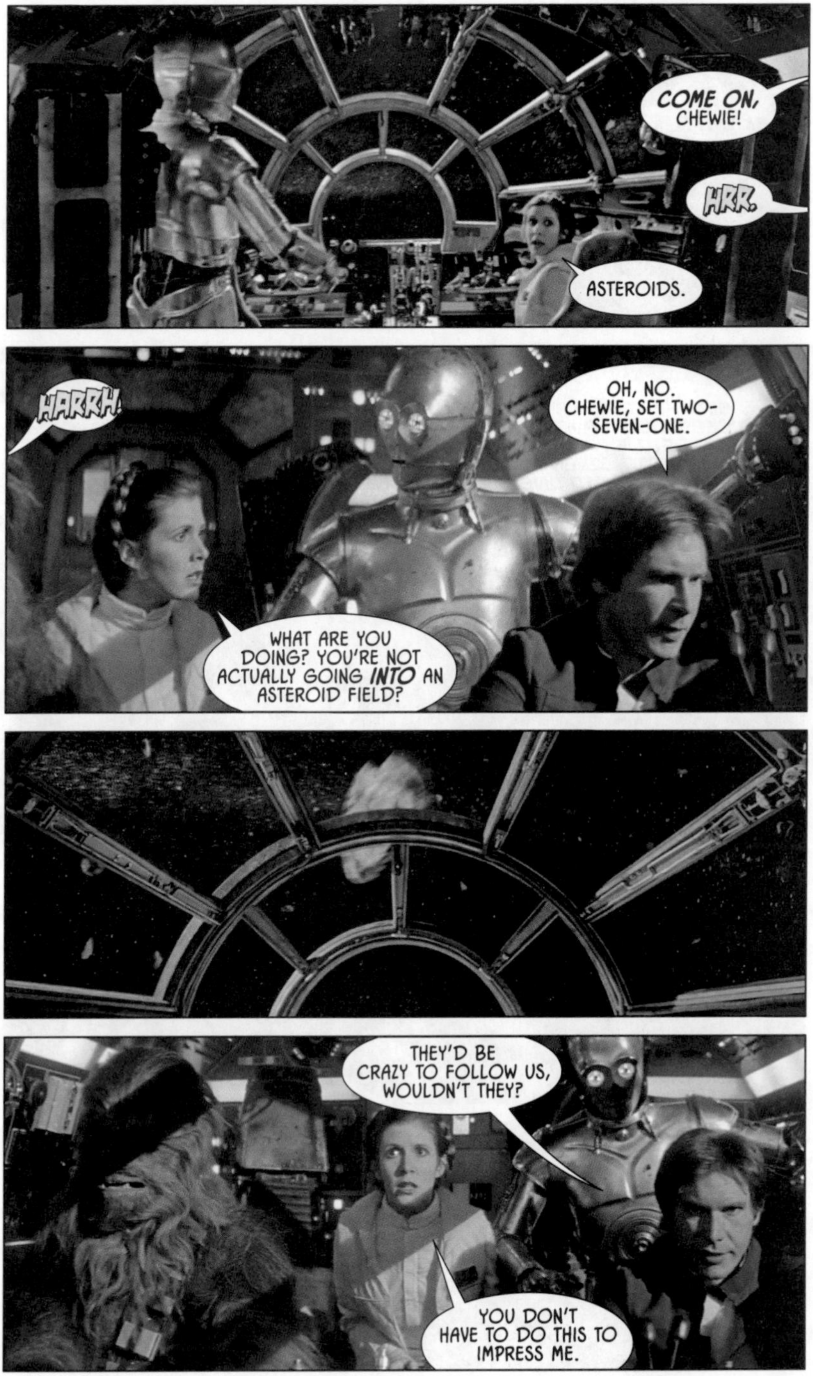
COME ON, CHEWIE!
HRR.
ASTEROIDS.
HARRH!
OH, NO. CHEWIE, SET TWO-SEVEN-ONE.
WHAT ARE YOU DOING? YOU'RE NOT ACTUALLY GOING *INTO* AN ASTEROID FIELD?
THEY'D BE CRAZY TO FOLLOW US, WOULDN'T THEY?
YOU DON'T HAVE TO DO THIS TO IMPRESS ME.

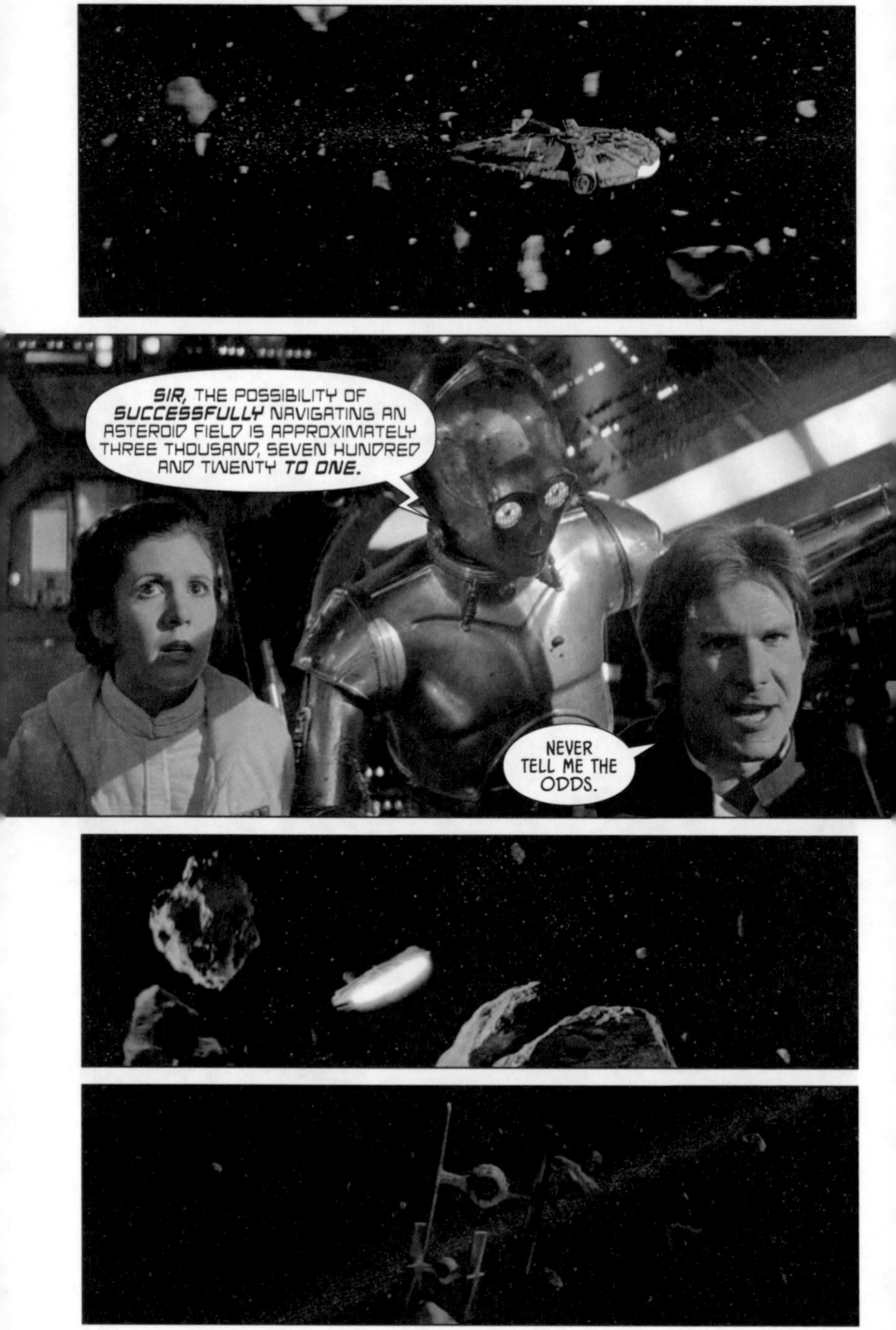
SIR, THE POSSIBILITY OF SUCCESSFULLY NAVIGATING AN ASTEROID FIELD IS APPROXIMATELY THREE THOUSAND, SEVEN HUNDRED AND TWENTY TO ONE.
NEVER TELL ME THE ODDS.

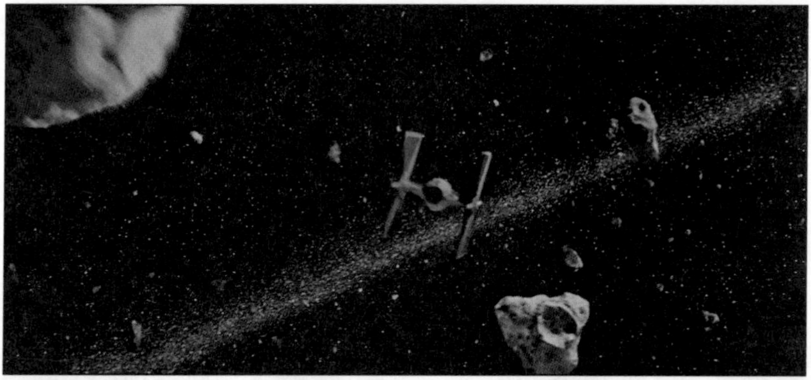

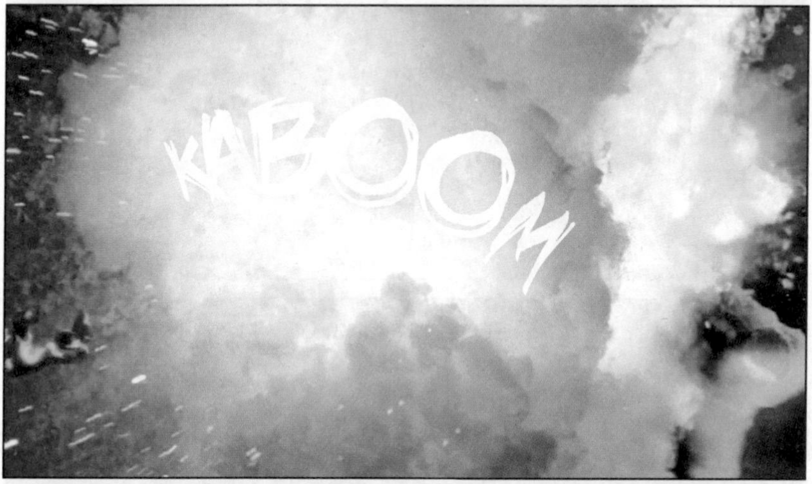
KABOOM

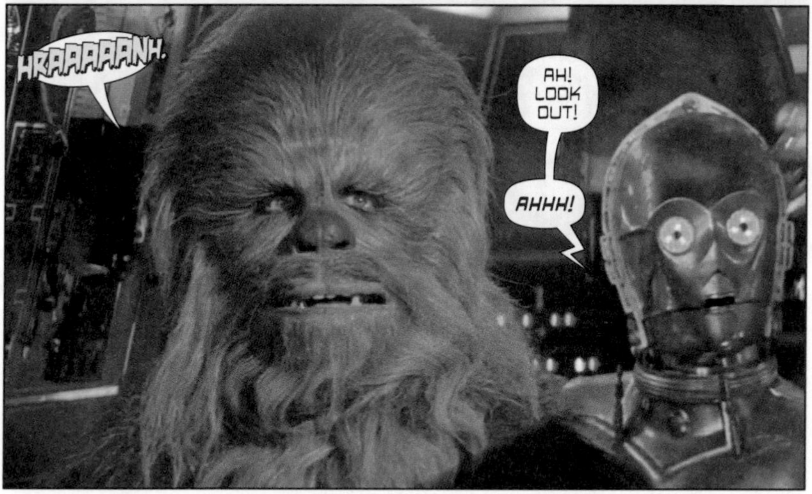
HRAAAAAANH.
AH! LOOK OUT!
AHHH!

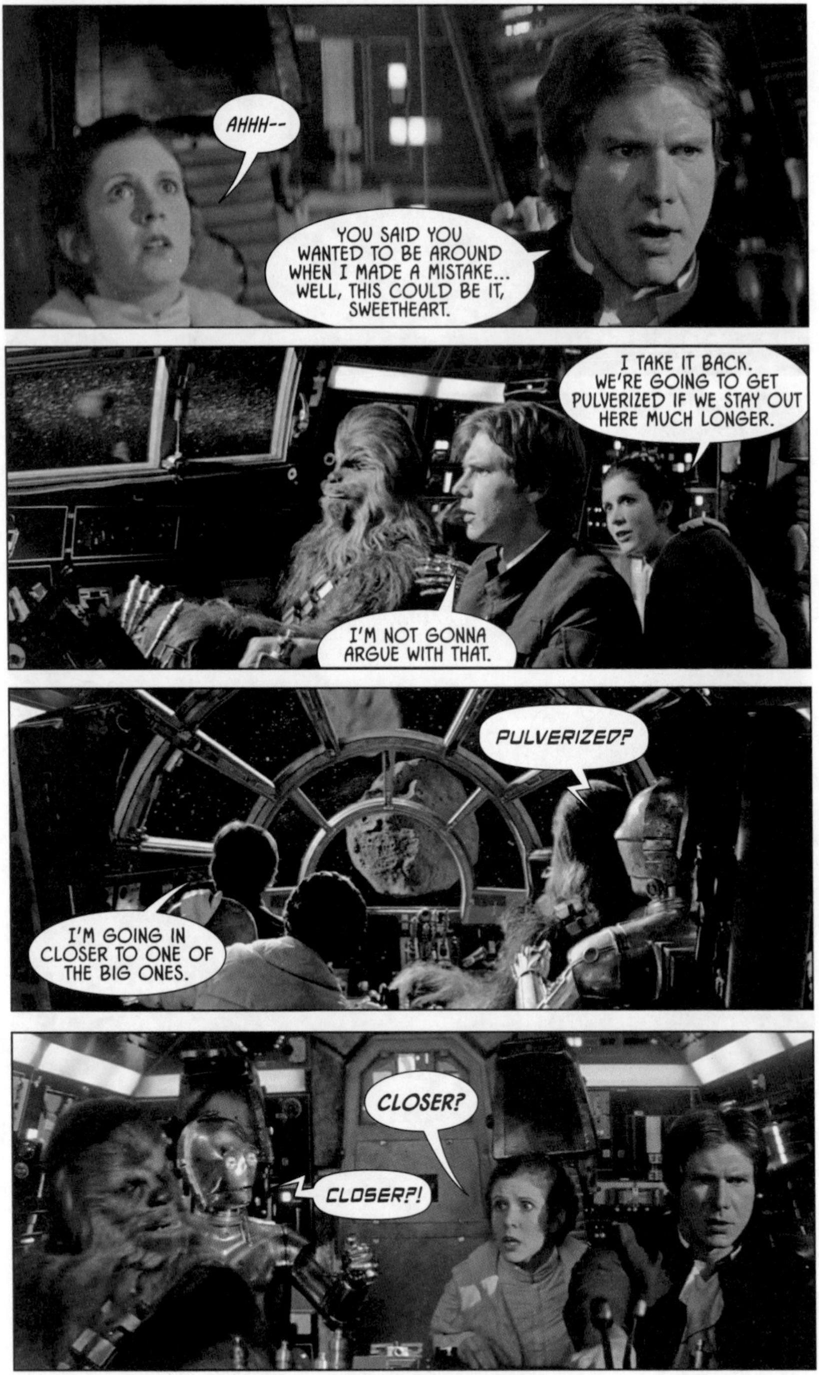
AHHH--
YOU SAID YOU WANTED TO BE AROUND WHEN I MADE A MISTAKE... WELL, THIS COULD BE IT, SWEETHEART.
I TAKE IT BACK. WE'RE GOING TO GET PULVERIZED IF WE STAY OUT HERE MUCH LONGER.
I'M NOT GONNA ARGUE WITH THAT.
PULVERIZED?
I'M GOING IN CLOSER TO ONE OF THE BIG ONES.
CLOSER?
CLOSER?!

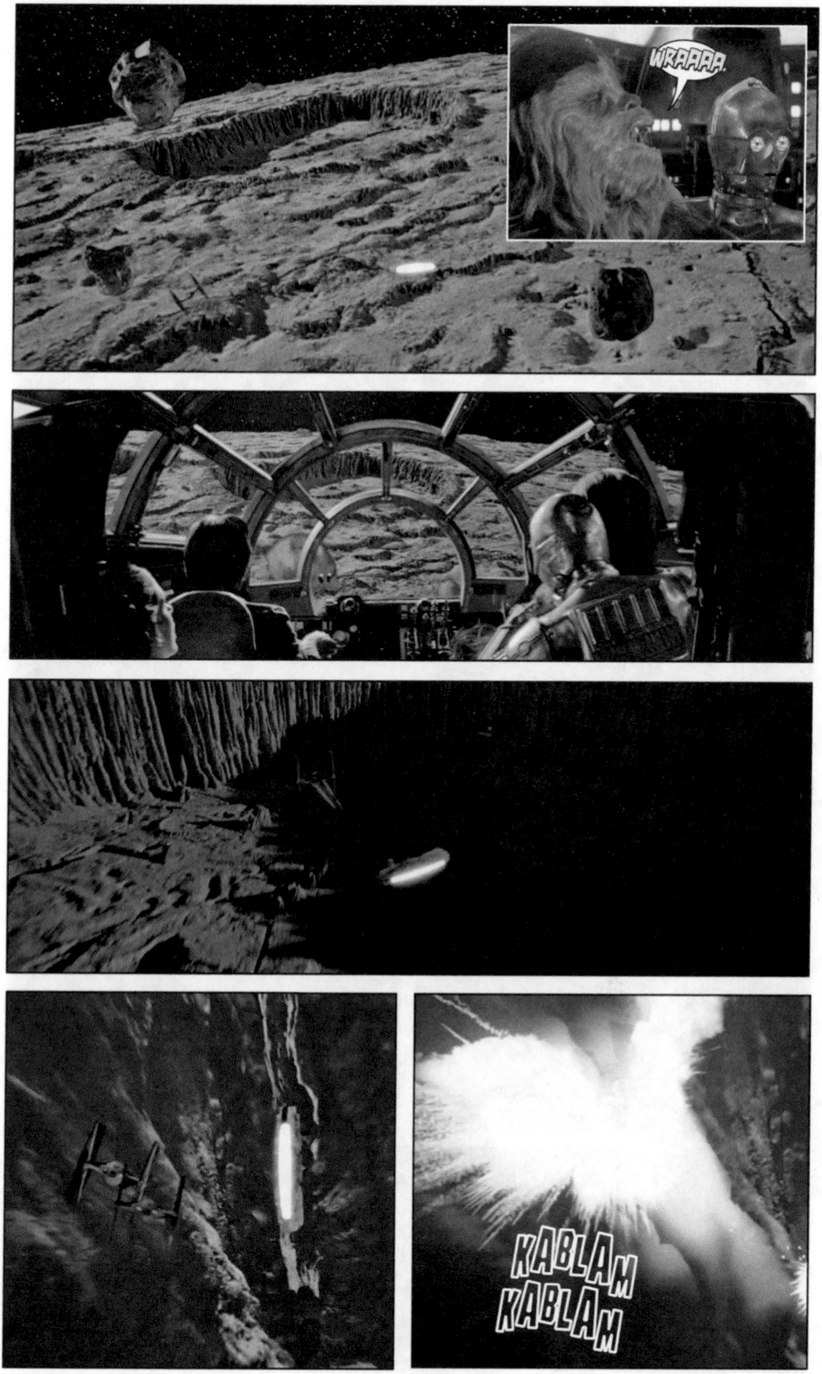
WRAAAA.
KABLAM
KABLAM

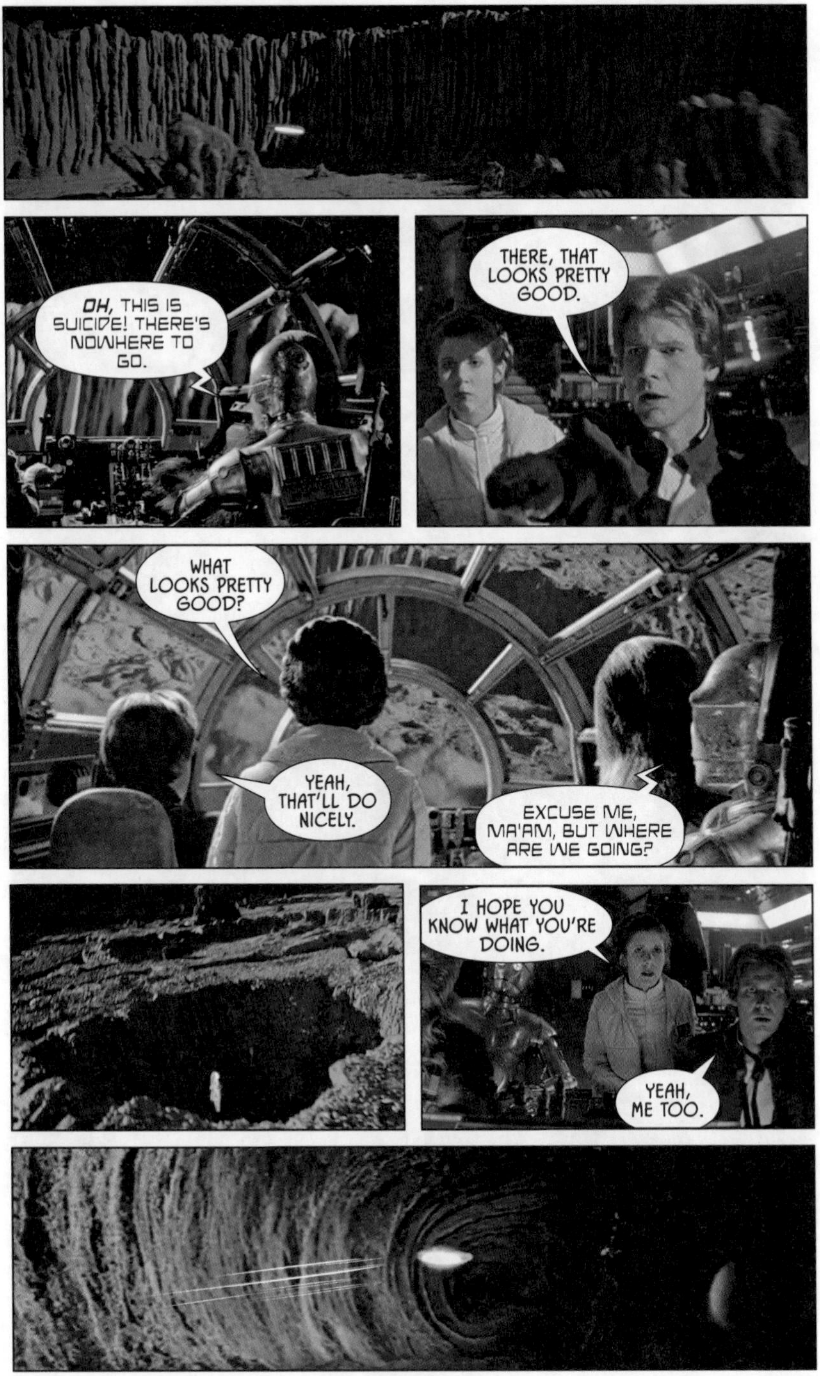
OH, THIS IS SUICIDE! THERE'S NOWHERE TO GO.
THERE, THAT LOOKS PRETTY GOOD.
WHAT LOOKS PRETTY GOOD?
YEAH, THAT'LL DO NICELY.
EXCUSE ME, MA'AM, BUT WHERE ARE WE GOING?
I HOPE YOU KNOW WHAT YOU'RE DOING.
YEAH, ME TOO.

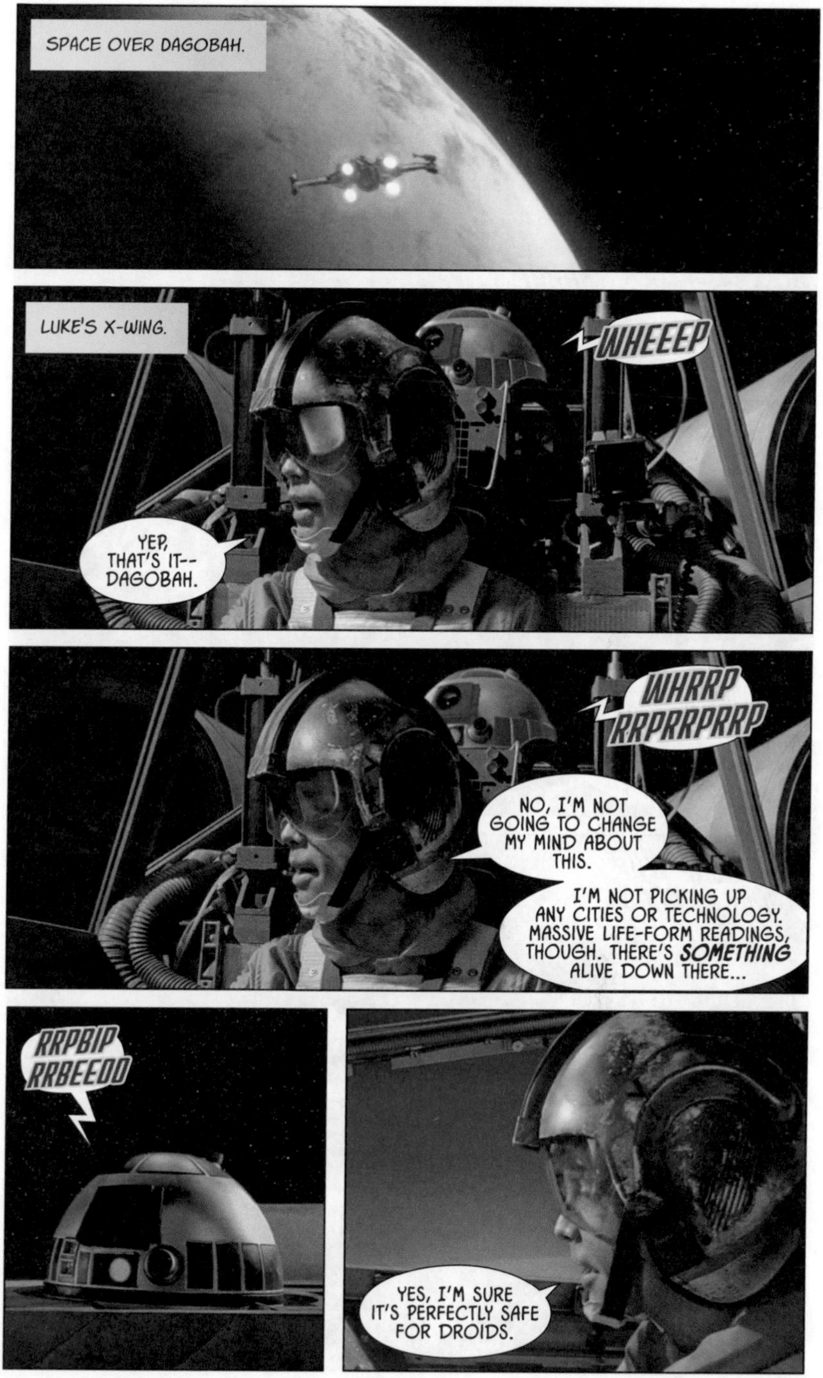
SPACE OVER DAGOBAH.
LUKE'S X-WING.
WHEEEP
YEP, THAT'S IT-- DAGOBAH.
WHRRP RRPRRPRRP
NO, I'M NOT GOING TO CHANGE MY MIND ABOUT THIS.
I'M NOT PICKING UP ANY CITIES OR TECHNOLOGY. MASSIVE LIFE-FORM READINGS, THOUGH. THERE'S *SOMETHING* ALIVE DOWN THERE...
RRPBIP RRBEEDO
YES, I'M SURE IT'S PERFECTLY SAFE FOR DROIDS.

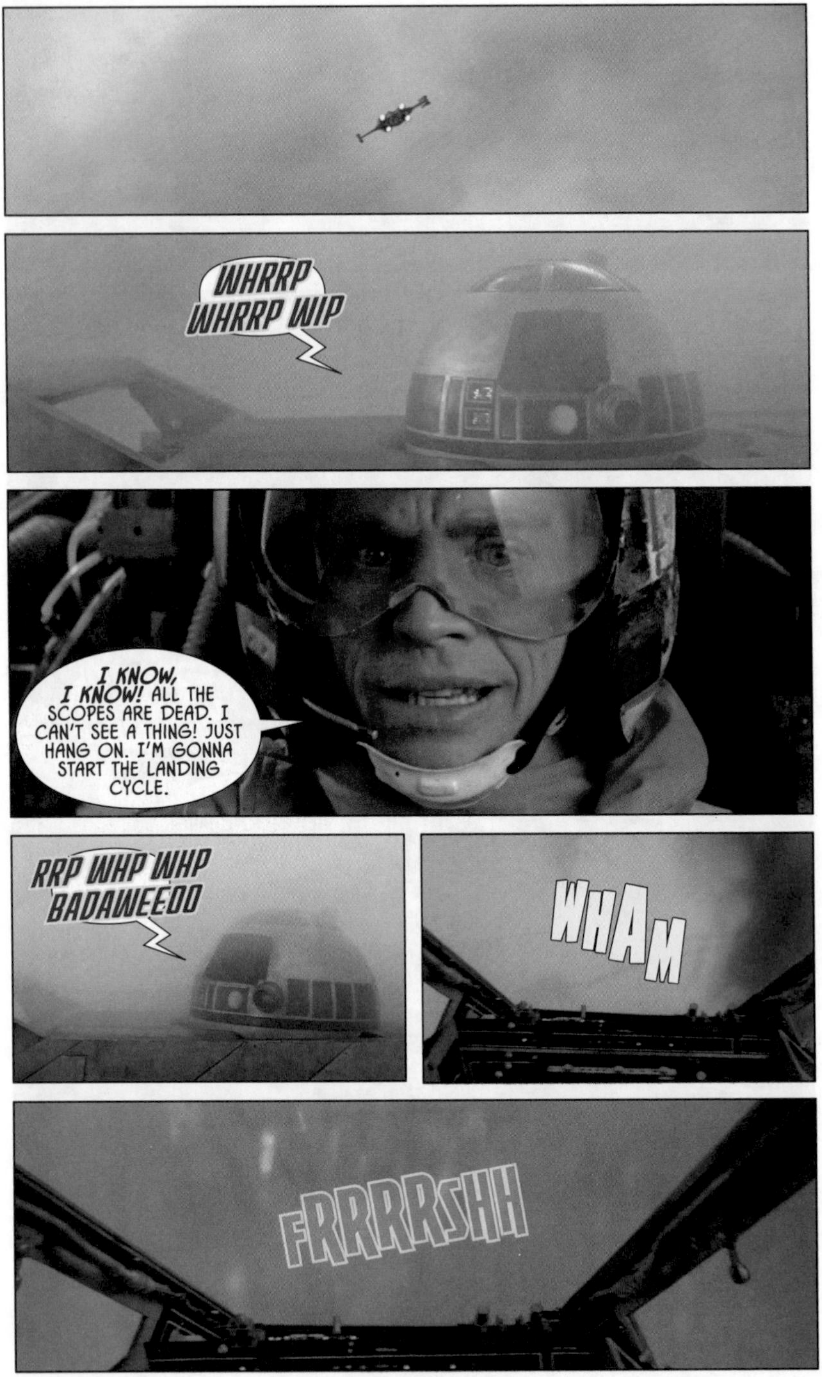
WHRRP WHRRP WIP
I KNOW, I KNOW! ALL THE SCOPES ARE DEAD. I CAN'T SEE A THING! JUST HANG ON. I'M GONNA START THE LANDING CYCLE.
RRP WHP WHP BADAWEEDOO
WHAM
FRRRRSHH

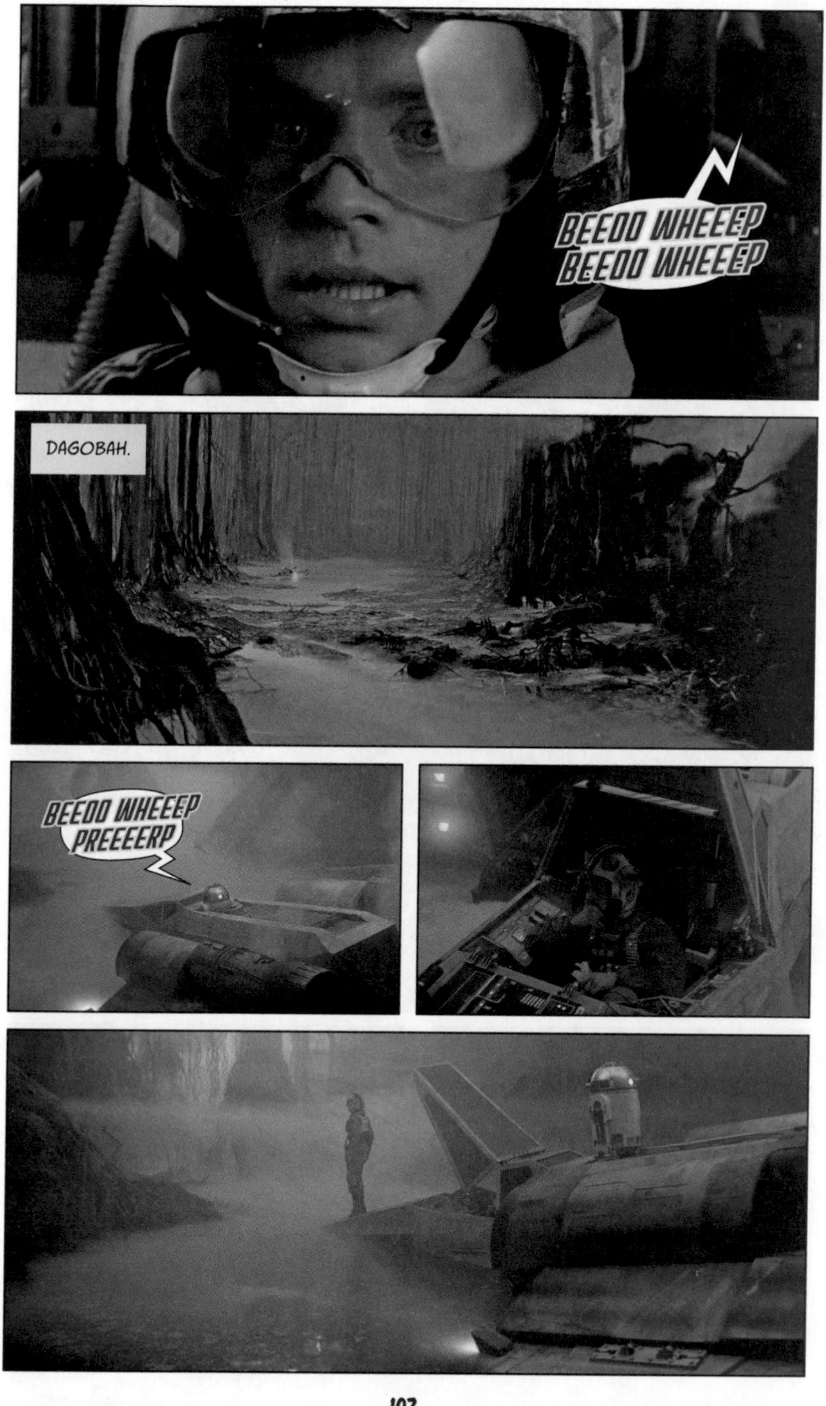
BEEDO WHEEEP
BEEDO WHEEEP
DAGOBAH.
BEEDO WHEEEP
PREEEERP

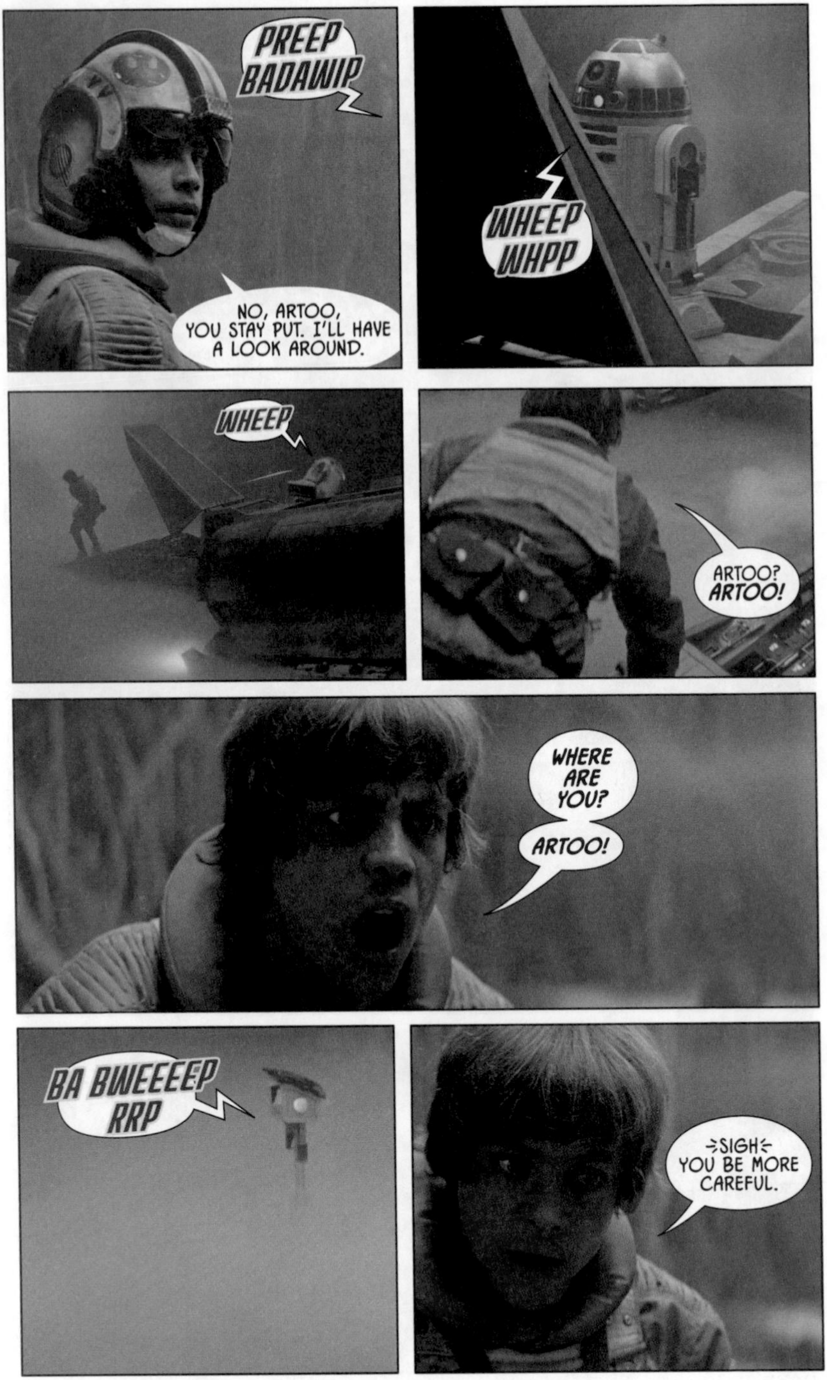
PREEP BADAWIP
NO, ARTOO, YOU STAY PUT. I'LL HAVE A LOOK AROUND.
WHEEP WHPP
WHEEP
ARTOO? ARTOO!
WHERE ARE YOU?
ARTOO!
BA BWEEEEP RRP
⇒SIGH⇐ YOU BE MORE CAREFUL.

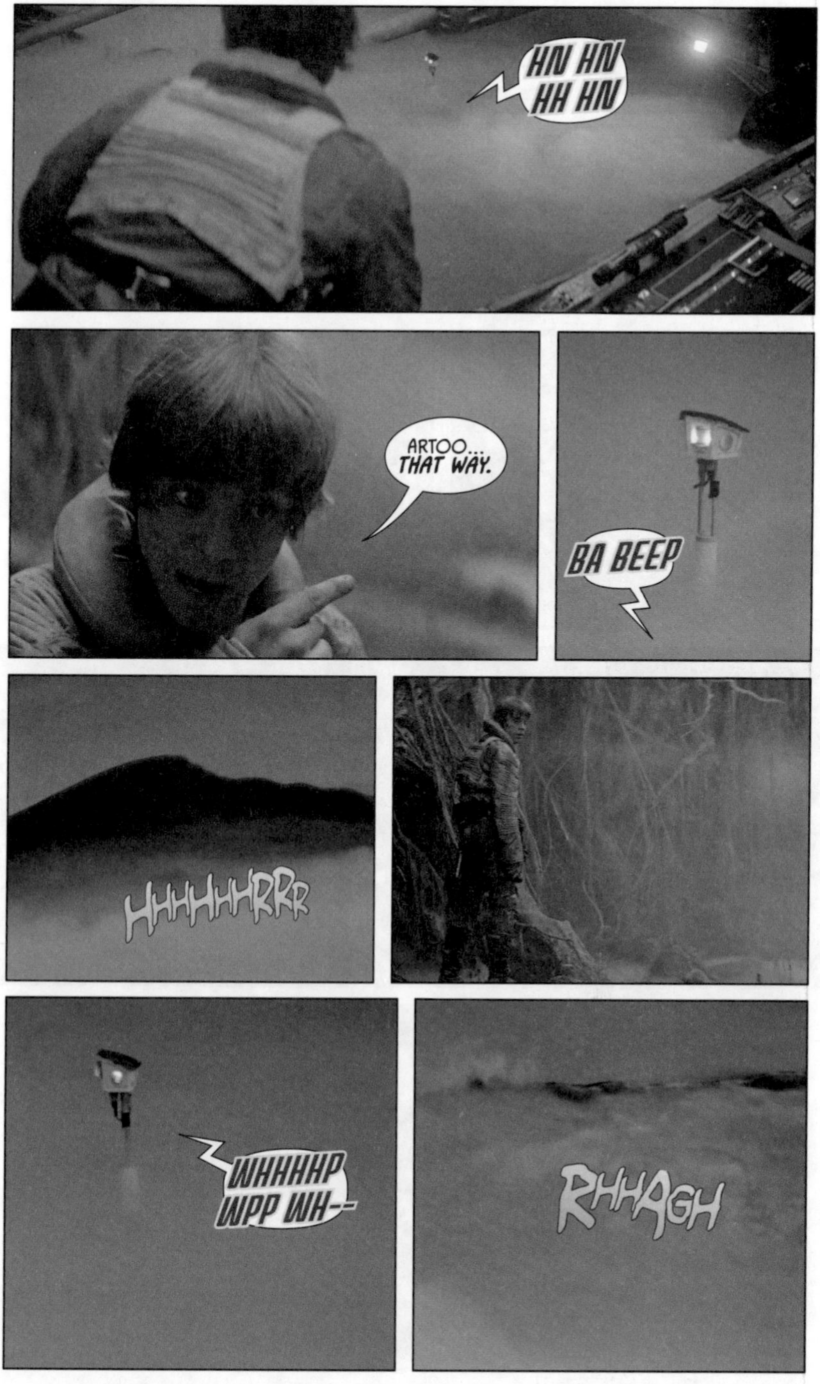
HN HN
HH HN
ARTOO... THAT WAY.
BA BEEP
HHHHHRRR
WHHHHP WPP WH--
RHHAGH

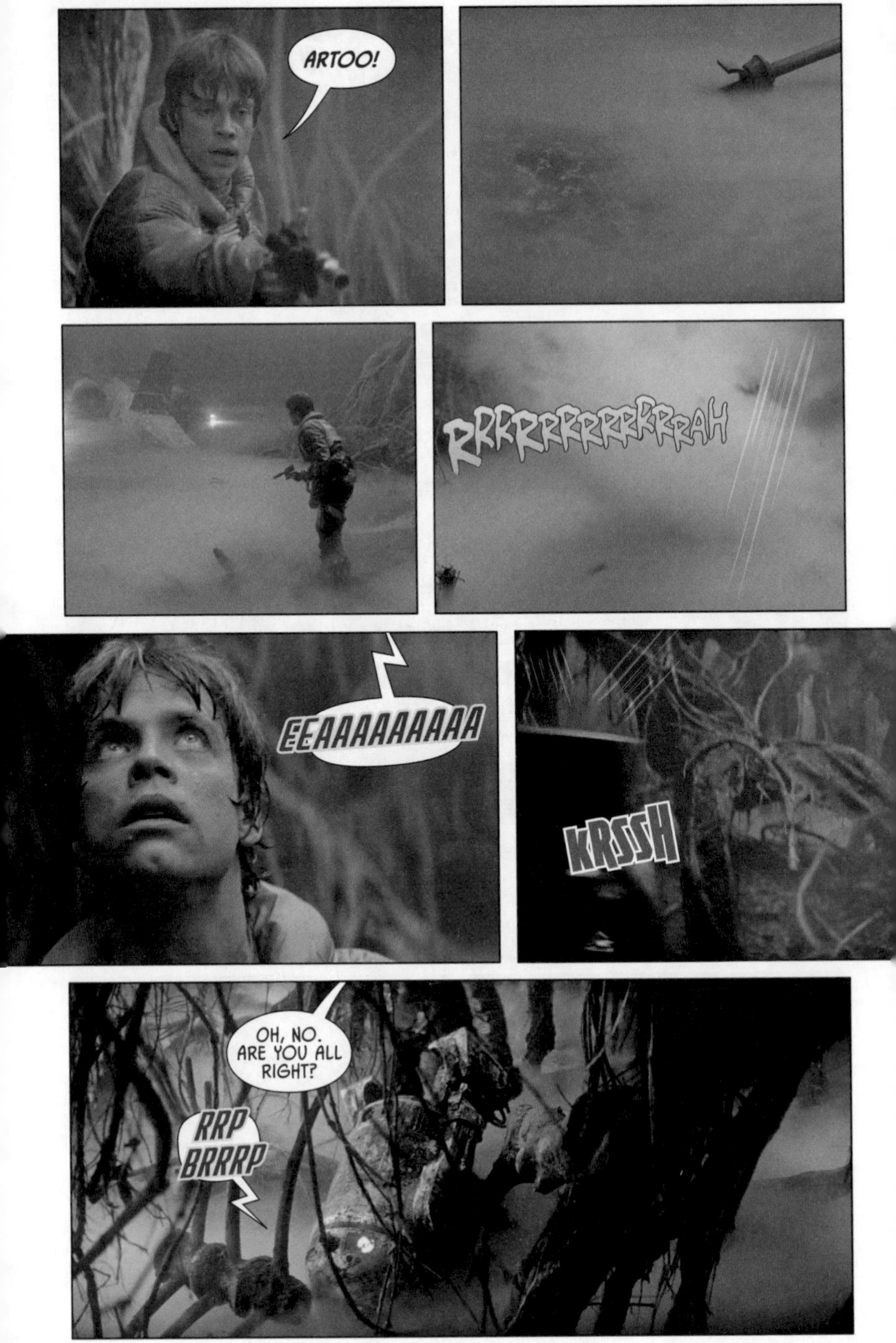
ARTOO!
RRRRRRRRRRRRAH
EEAAAAAAAAAA
KRSSH
OH, NO. ARE YOU ALL RIGHT?
RRP BRRRP

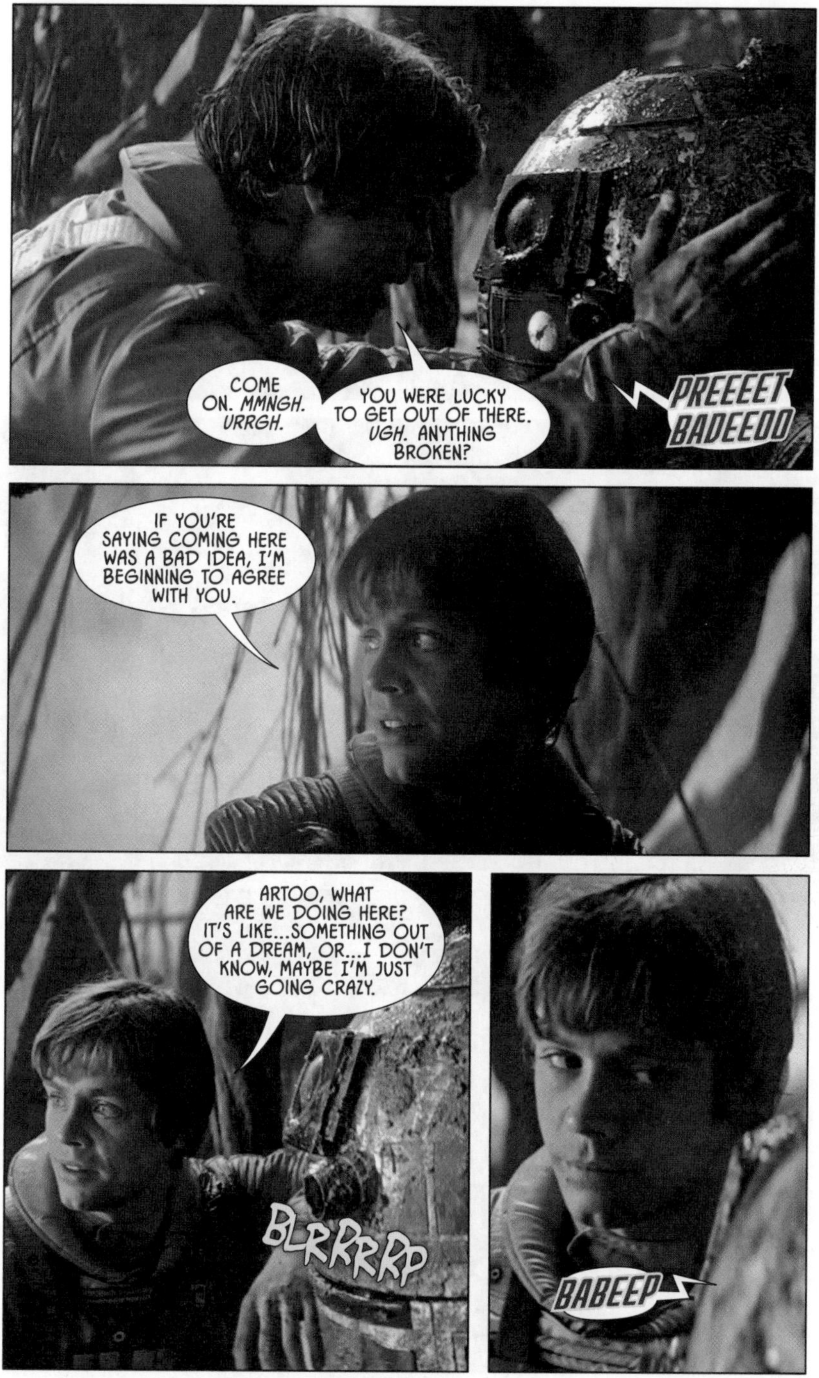
COME ON. MMNGH. URRGH.
YOU WERE LUCKY TO GET OUT OF THERE. UGH. ANYTHING BROKEN?
PREEEET BADEEOO
IF YOU'RE SAYING COMING HERE WAS A BAD IDEA, I'M BEGINNING TO AGREE WITH YOU.
ARTOO, WHAT ARE WE DOING HERE? IT'S LIKE...SOMETHING OUT OF A DREAM, OR...I DON'T KNOW, MAYBE I'M JUST GOING CRAZY.
BLRRRRP
BABEEP

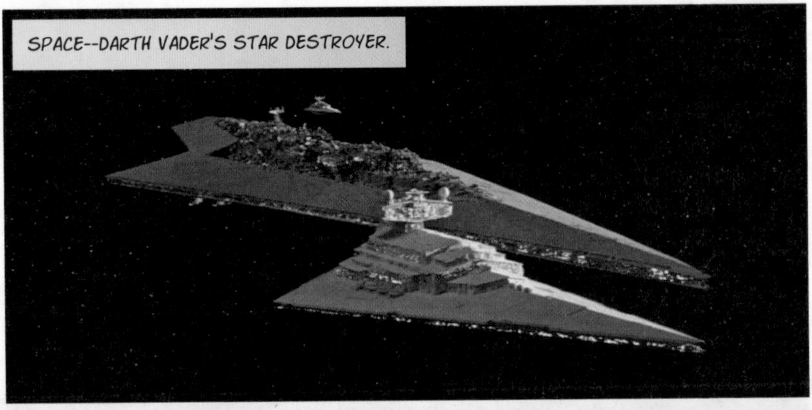
SPACE--DARTH VADER'S STAR DESTROYER.

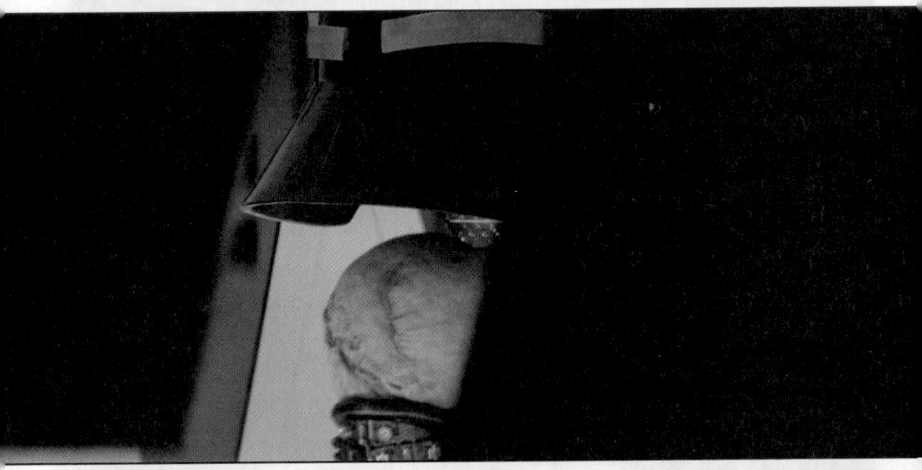

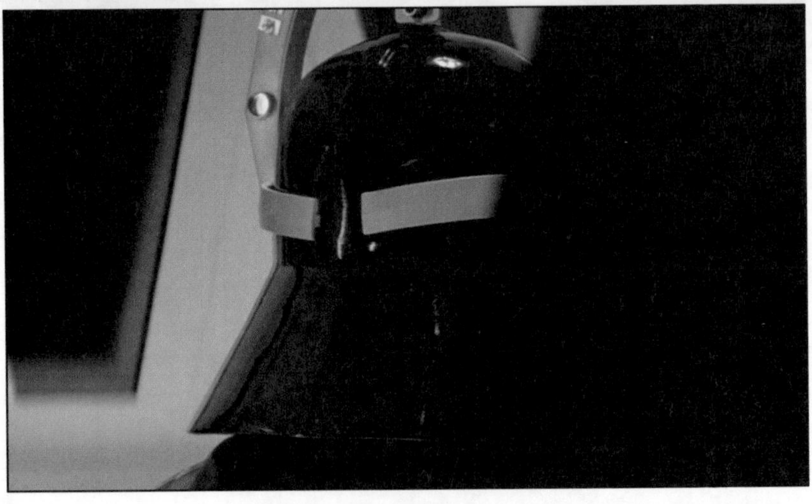

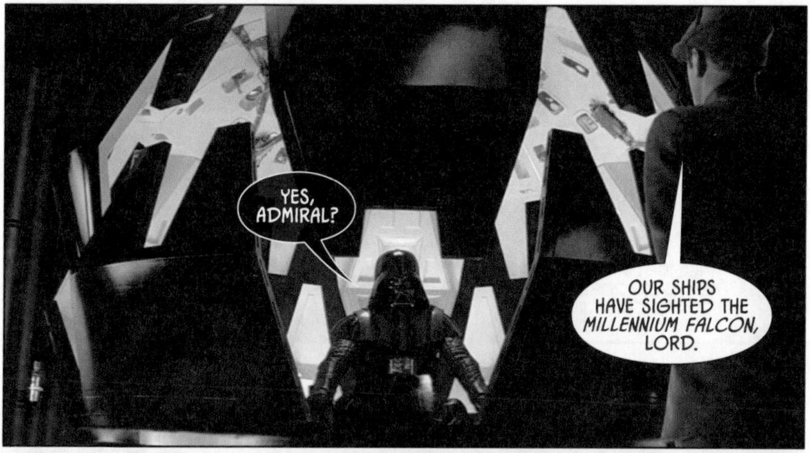
YES, ADMIRAL?
OUR SHIPS HAVE SIGHTED THE *MILLENNIUM FALCON*, LORD.

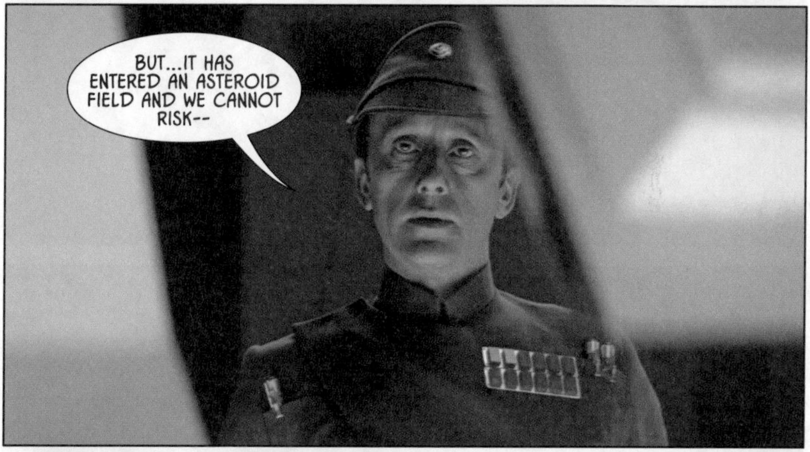
BUT...IT HAS ENTERED AN ASTEROID FIELD AND WE CANNOT RISK--

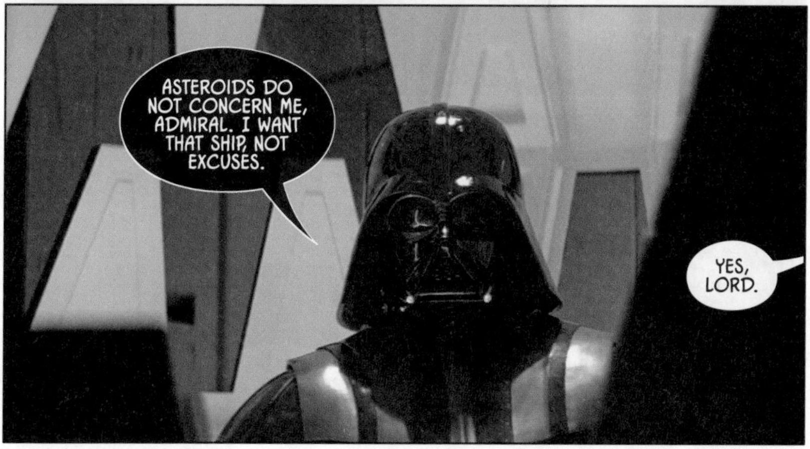
ASTEROIDS DO NOT CONCERN ME, ADMIRAL. I WANT THAT SHIP, NOT EXCUSES.
YES, LORD.

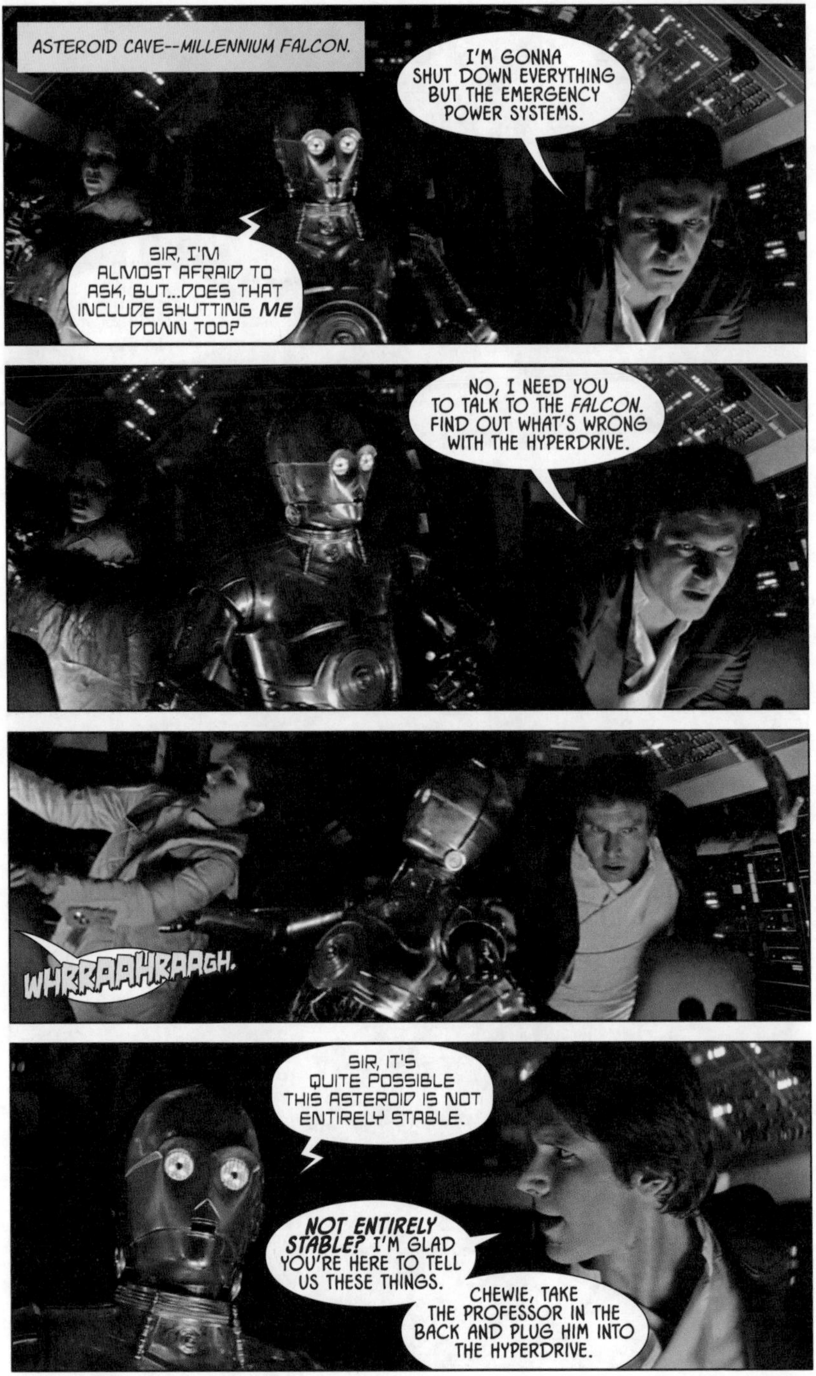

ASTEROID CAVE--MILLENNIUM FALCON.
I'M GONNA SHUT DOWN EVERYTHING BUT THE EMERGENCY POWER SYSTEMS.
SIR, I'M ALMOST AFRAID TO ASK, BUT...DOES THAT INCLUDE SHUTTING *ME* DOWN TOO?
NO, I NEED YOU TO TALK TO THE *FALCON*. FIND OUT WHAT'S WRONG WITH THE HYPERDRIVE.
WHRRAAHRAAGH.
SIR, IT'S QUITE POSSIBLE THIS ASTEROID IS NOT ENTIRELY STABLE.
NOT ENTIRELY STABLE? I'M GLAD YOU'RE HERE TO TELL US THESE THINGS.
CHEWIE, TAKE THE PROFESSOR IN THE BACK AND PLUG HIM INTO THE HYPERDRIVE.

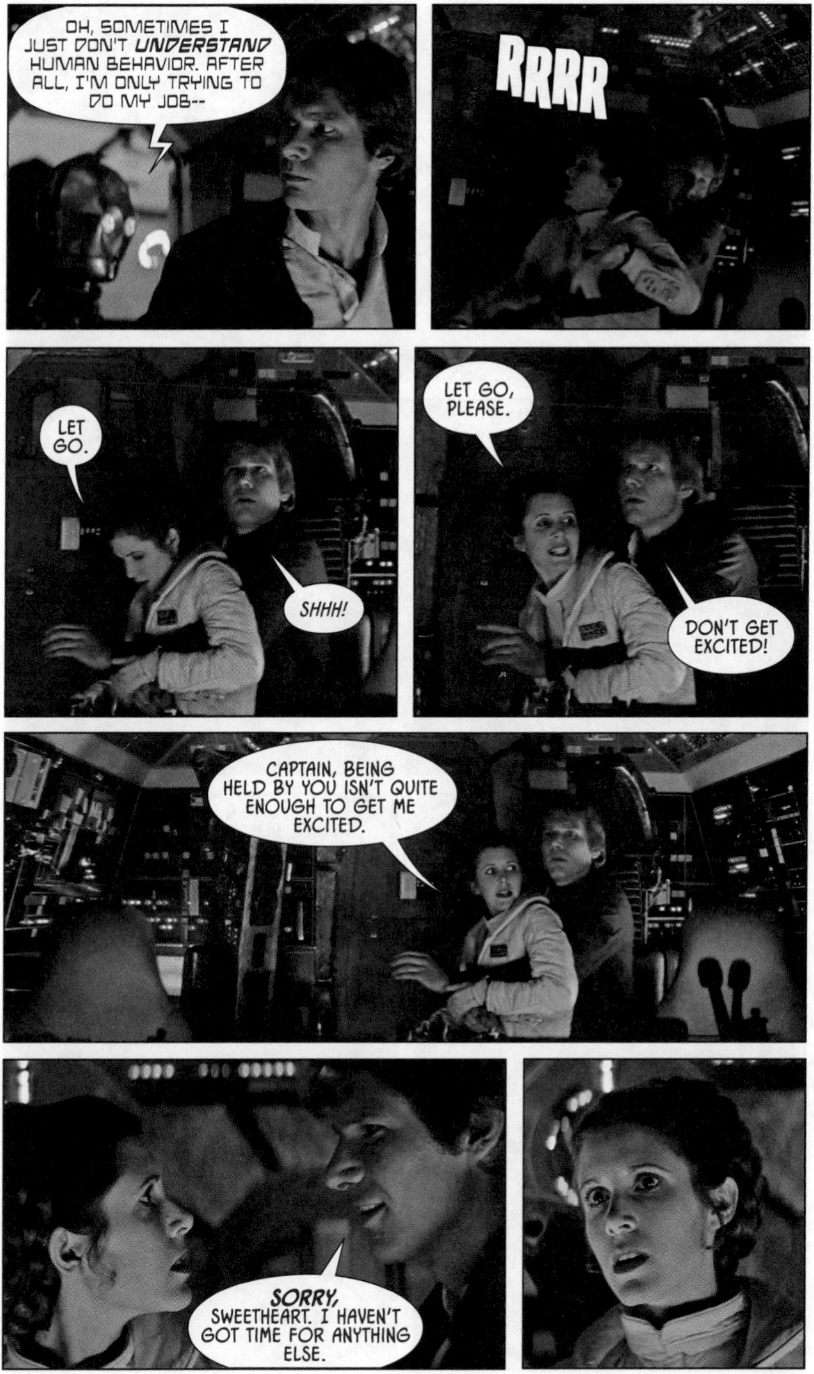
OH, SOMETIMES I JUST DON'T UNDERSTAND HUMAN BEHAVIOR. AFTER ALL, I'M ONLY TRYING TO DO MY JOB--
RRRR
LET GO.
SHHH!
LET GO, PLEASE.
DON'T GET EXCITED!
CAPTAIN, BEING HELD BY YOU ISN'T QUITE ENOUGH TO GET ME EXCITED.
SORRY, SWEETHEART. I HAVEN'T GOT TIME FOR ANYTHING ELSE.

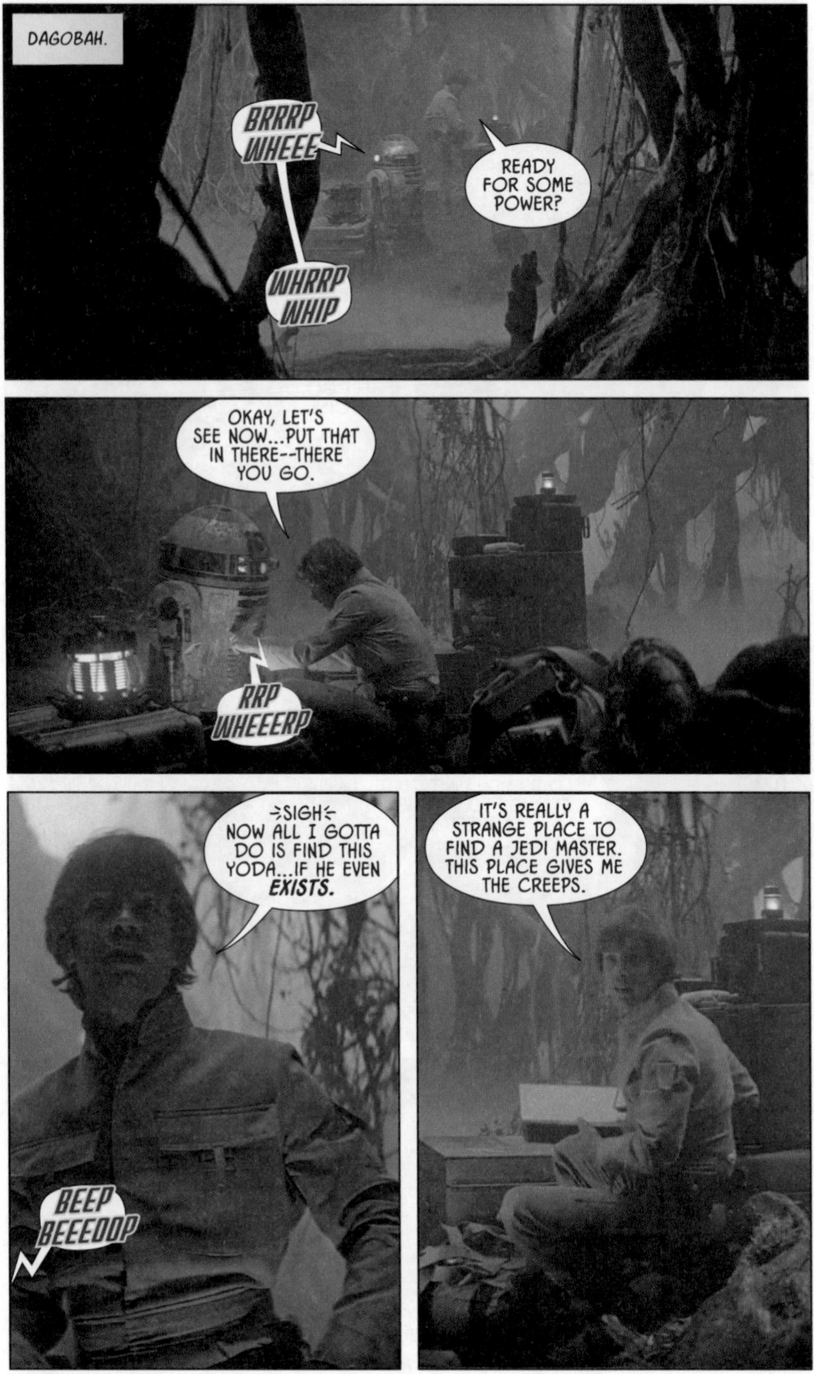
DAGOBAH.
BRRRP WHEEE
READY FOR SOME POWER?
WHRRP WHIP
OKAY, LET'S SEE NOW...PUT THAT IN THERE--THERE YOU GO.
RRP WHEEERP
SIGH
NOW ALL I GOTTA DO IS FIND THIS YODA...IF HE EVEN **EXISTS.**
BEEP BEEEDOP
IT'S REALLY A STRANGE PLACE TO FIND A JEDI MASTER. THIS PLACE GIVES ME THE CREEPS.

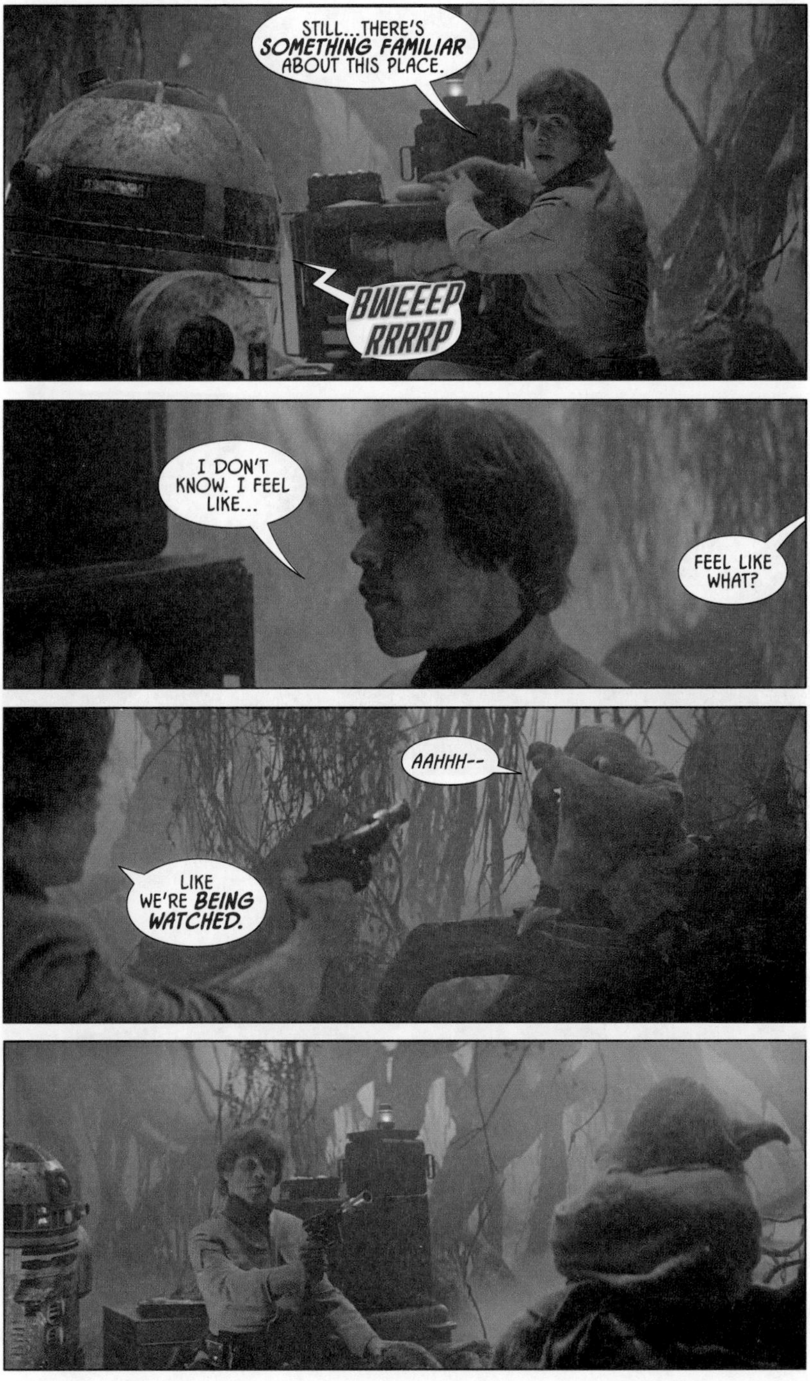
STILL...THERE'S SOMETHING FAMILIAR ABOUT THIS PLACE.
BWEEEP RRRRP
I DON'T KNOW. I FEEL LIKE...
FEEL LIKE WHAT?
AAHHH--
LIKE WE'RE BEING WATCHED.

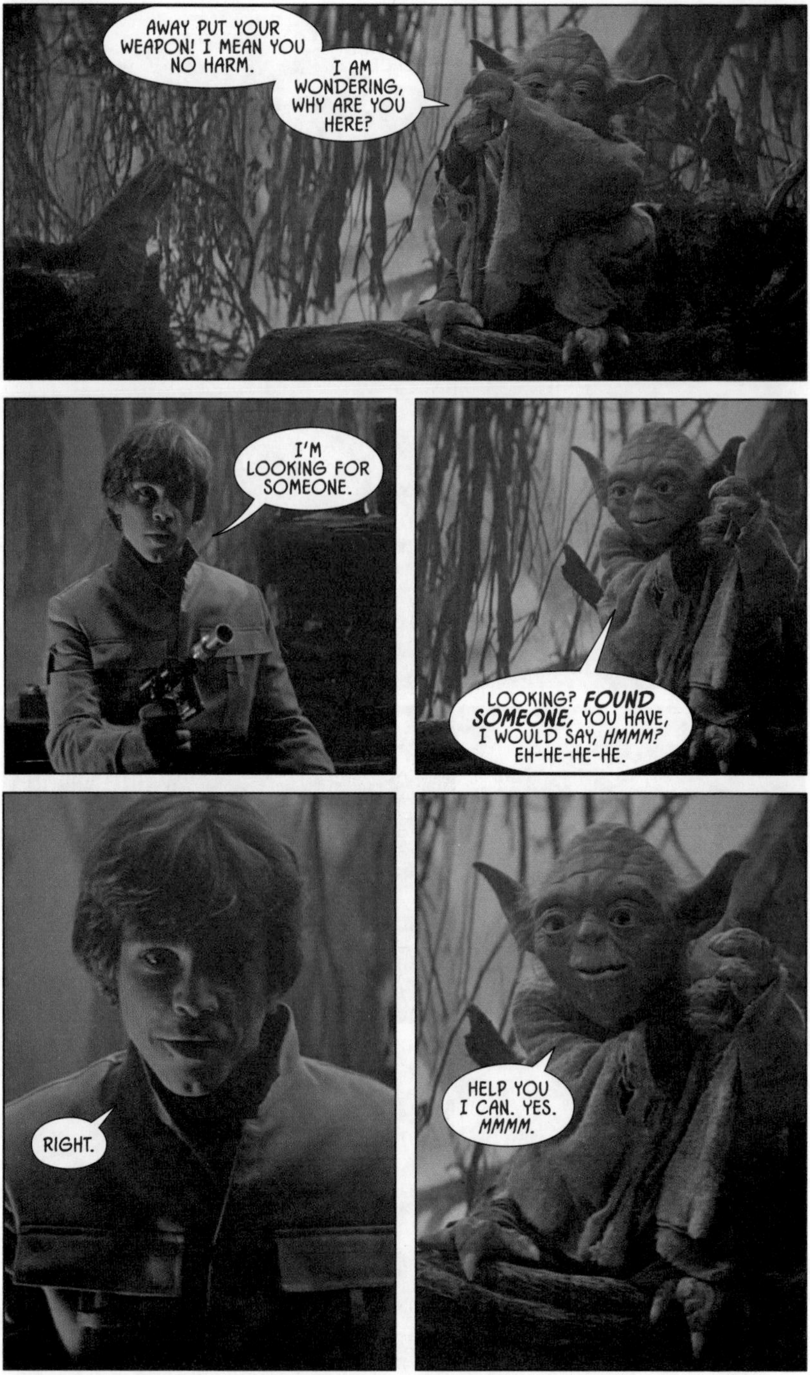
AWAY PUT YOUR WEAPON! I MEAN YOU NO HARM.
I AM WONDERING, WHY ARE YOU HERE?
I'M LOOKING FOR SOMEONE.
LOOKING? *FOUND SOMEONE,* YOU HAVE, I WOULD SAY, *HMMM?* EH-HE-HE-HE.
RIGHT.
HELP YOU I CAN. YES. *MMMM.*

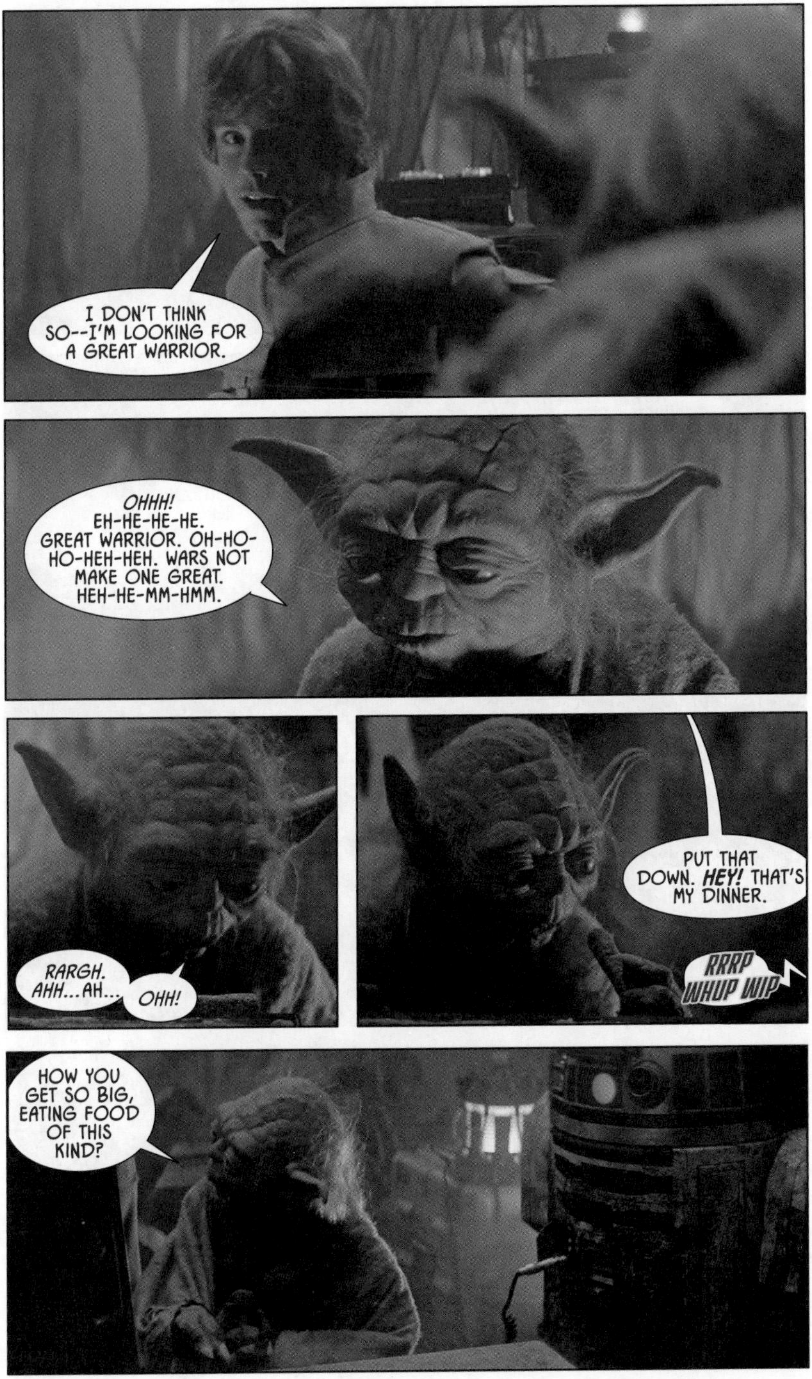
I DON'T THINK SO--I'M LOOKING FOR A GREAT WARRIOR.
OHHH! EH-HE-HE-HE. GREAT WARRIOR. OH-HO-HO-HEH-HEH. WARS NOT MAKE ONE GREAT. HEH-HE-MM-HMM.
RARGH. AHH...AH...
OHH!
PUT THAT DOWN. HEY! THAT'S MY DINNER.
RRRP WHUP WIP
HOW YOU GET SO BIG, EATING FOOD OF THIS KIND?

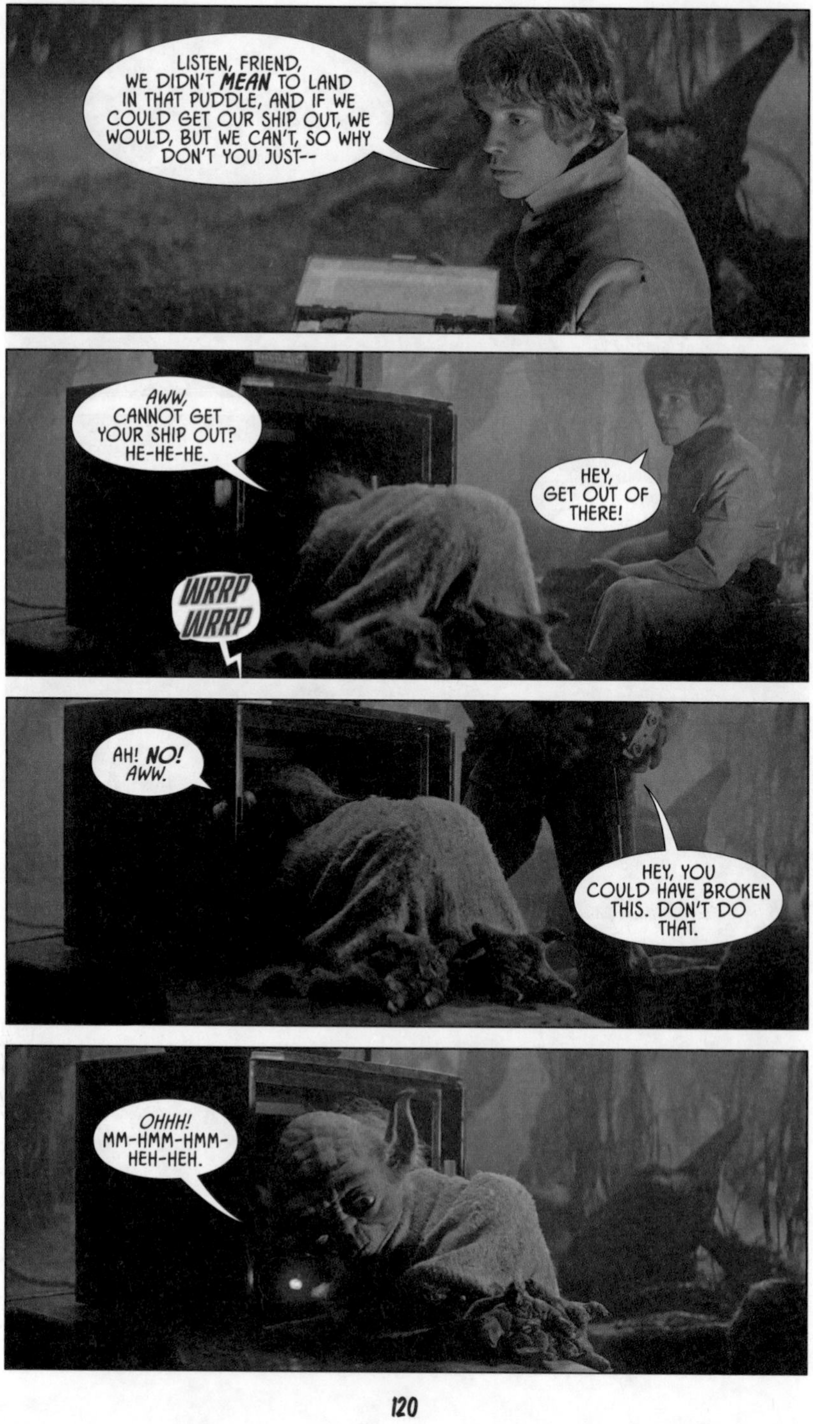
LISTEN, FRIEND, WE DIDN'T *MEAN* TO LAND IN THAT PUDDLE, AND IF WE COULD GET OUR SHIP OUT, WE WOULD, BUT WE CAN'T, SO WHY DON'T YOU JUST--
AWW, CANNOT GET YOUR SHIP OUT? HE-HE-HE.
HEY, GET OUT OF THERE!
WRRP WRRP
AH! *NO!* AWW.
HEY, YOU COULD HAVE BROKEN THIS. DON'T DO THAT.
OHHH! MM-HMM-HMM-HEH-HEH.

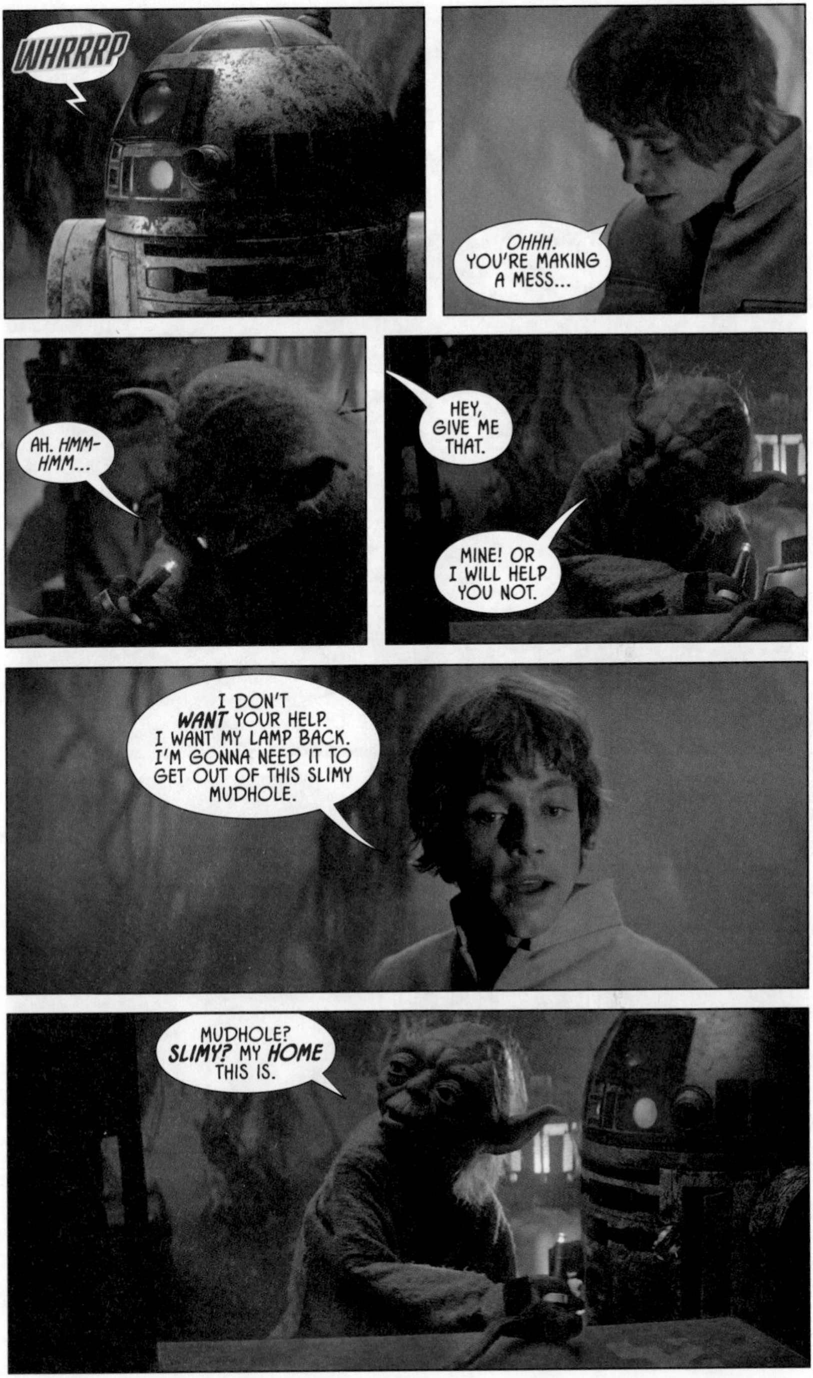
WHRRRP
OHHH. YOU'RE MAKING A MESS...
AH. HMM-HMM...
HEY, GIVE ME THAT.
MINE! OR I WILL HELP YOU NOT.
I DON'T WANT YOUR HELP. I WANT MY LAMP BACK. I'M GONNA NEED IT TO GET OUT OF THIS SLIMY MUDHOLE.
MUDHOLE? SLIMY? MY HOME THIS IS.

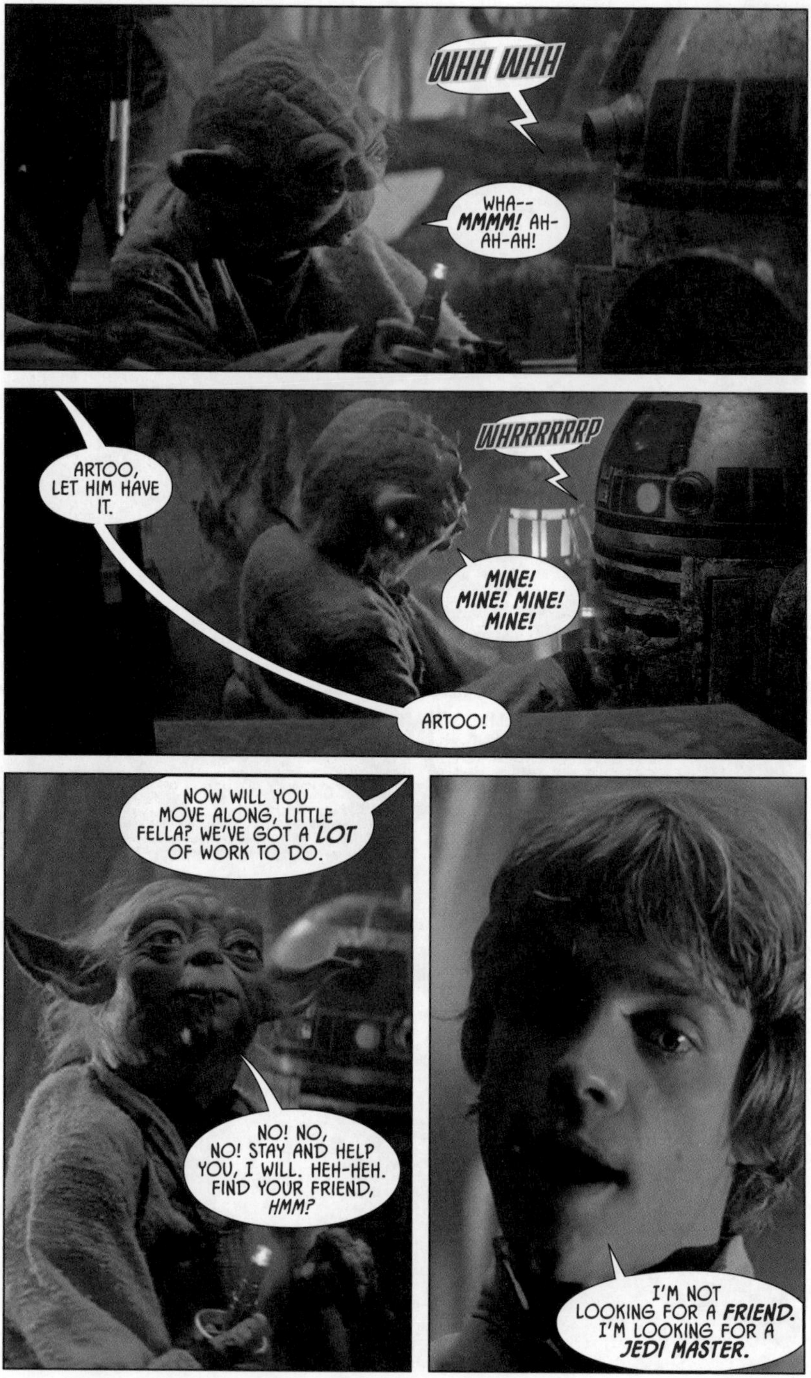
WHH WHH
WHA-- MMMM! AH-AH-AH!
ARTOO, LET HIM HAVE IT.
WHRRRRRRP
MINE! MINE! MINE! MINE!
ARTOO!
NOW WILL YOU MOVE ALONG, LITTLE FELLA? WE'VE GOT A LOT OF WORK TO DO.
NO! NO, NO! STAY AND HELP YOU, I WILL. HEH-HEH. FIND YOUR FRIEND, HMM?
I'M NOT LOOKING FOR A FRIEND. I'M LOOKING FOR A JEDI MASTER.

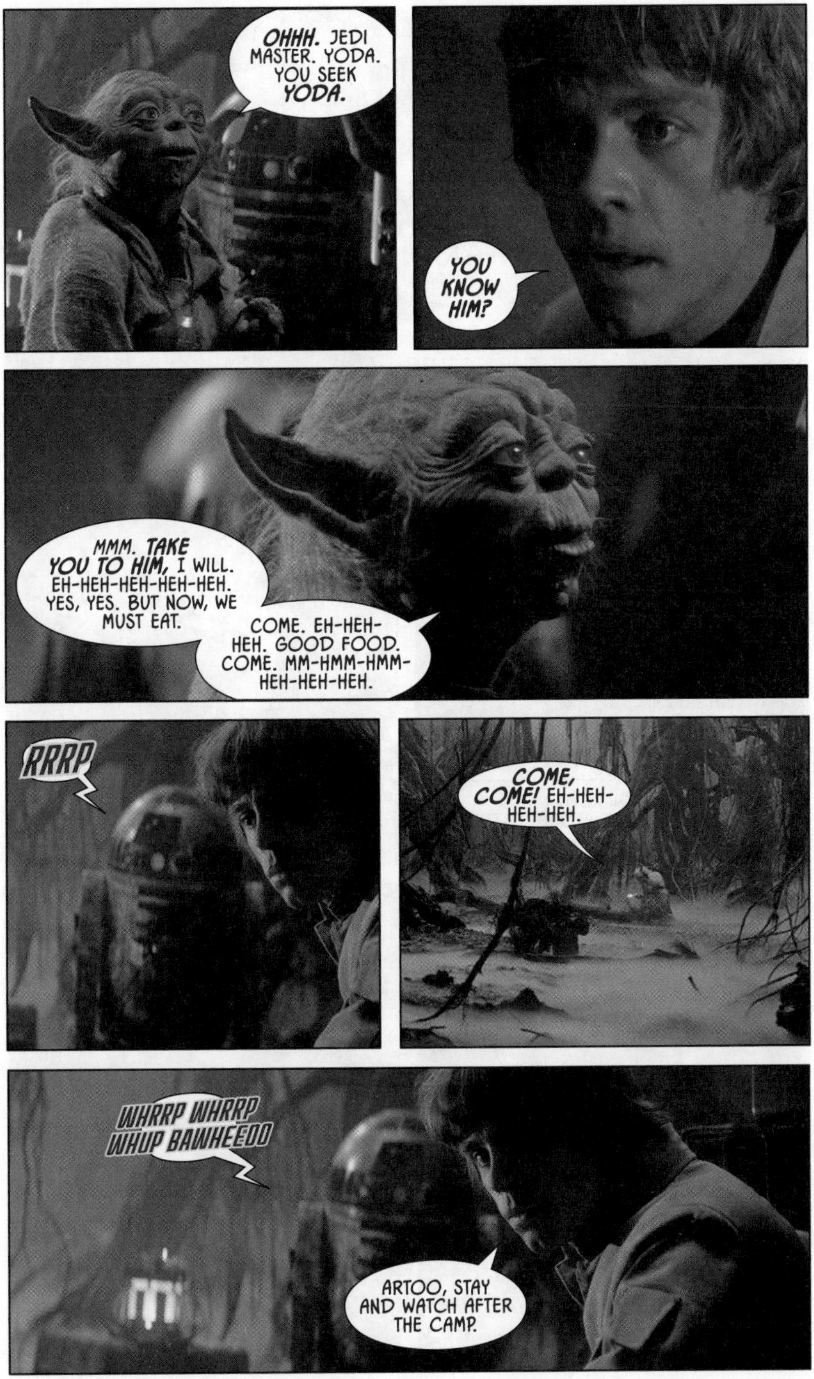
OHHH. JEDI MASTER. YODA. YOU SEEK YODA.
YOU KNOW HIM?
MMM. TAKE YOU TO HIM, I WILL. EH-HEH-HEH-HEH-HEH. YES, YES. BUT NOW, WE MUST EAT.
COME. EH-HEH-HEH. GOOD FOOD. COME. MM-HMM-HMM-HEH-HEH-HEH.
RRRP
COME, COME! EH-HEH-HEH-HEH.
WHRRP WHRRP WHUP BAWHEEDO
ARTOO, STAY AND WATCH AFTER THE CAMP.

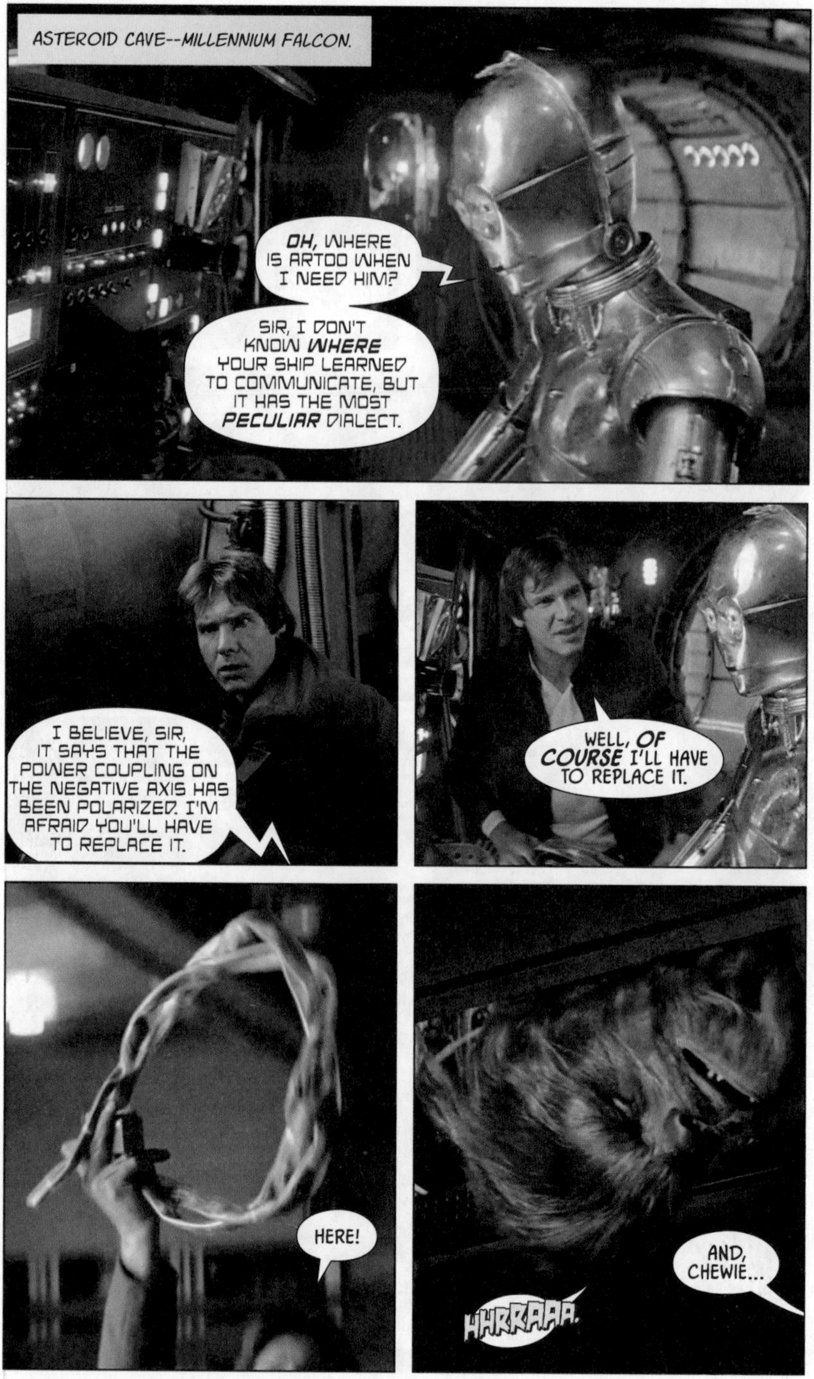

ASTEROID CAVE--MILLENNIUM FALCON.
OH, WHERE IS ARTOO WHEN I NEED HIM?
SIR, I DON'T KNOW WHERE YOUR SHIP LEARNED TO COMMUNICATE, BUT IT HAS THE MOST PECULIAR DIALECT.
I BELIEVE, SIR, IT SAYS THAT THE POWER COUPLING ON THE NEGATIVE AXIS HAS BEEN POLARIZED. I'M AFRAID YOU'LL HAVE TO REPLACE IT.
WELL, OF COURSE I'LL HAVE TO REPLACE IT.
HERE!
AND, CHEWIE...
HHRRAAA.

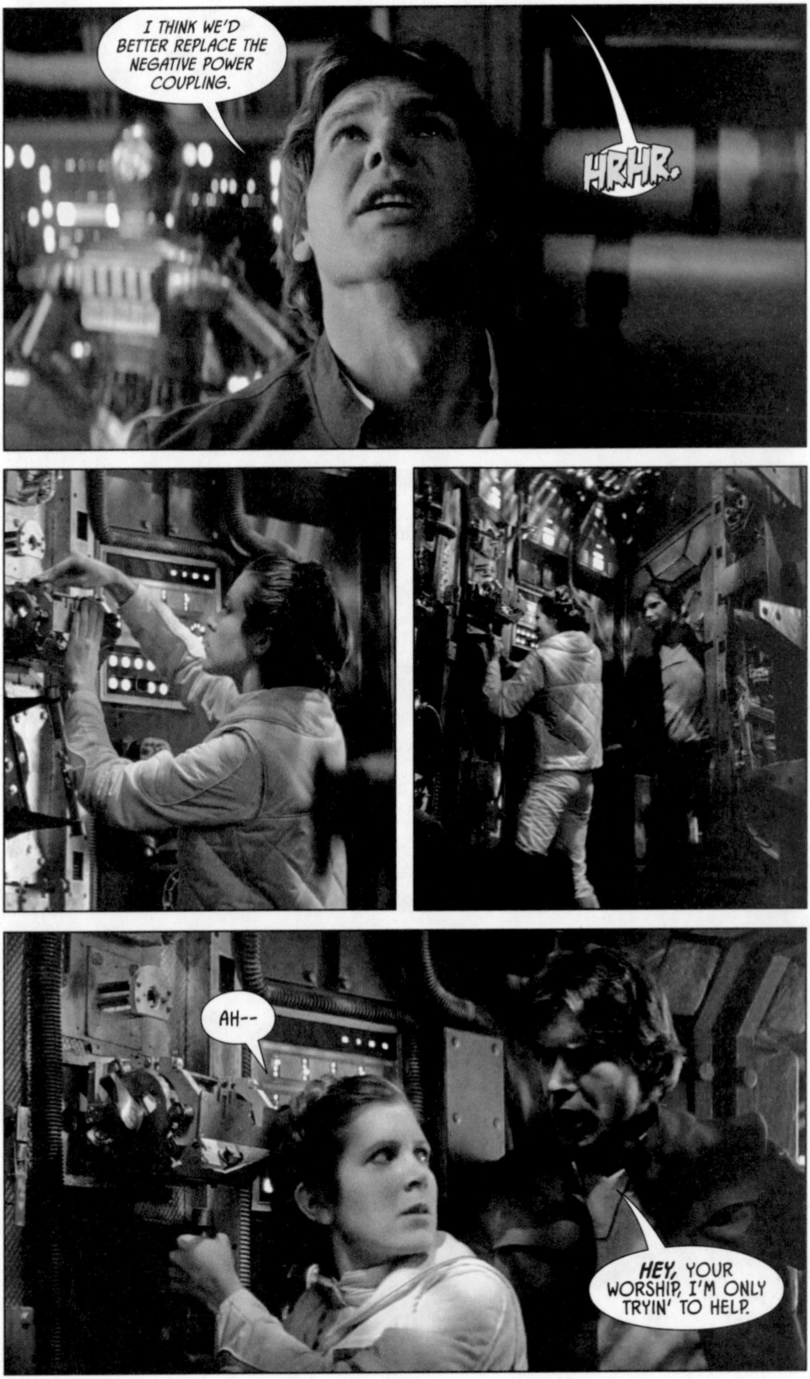
I THINK WE'D BETTER REPLACE THE NEGATIVE POWER COUPLING.
HRHR.
AH--
HEY, YOUR WORSHIP, I'M ONLY TRYIN' TO HELP.

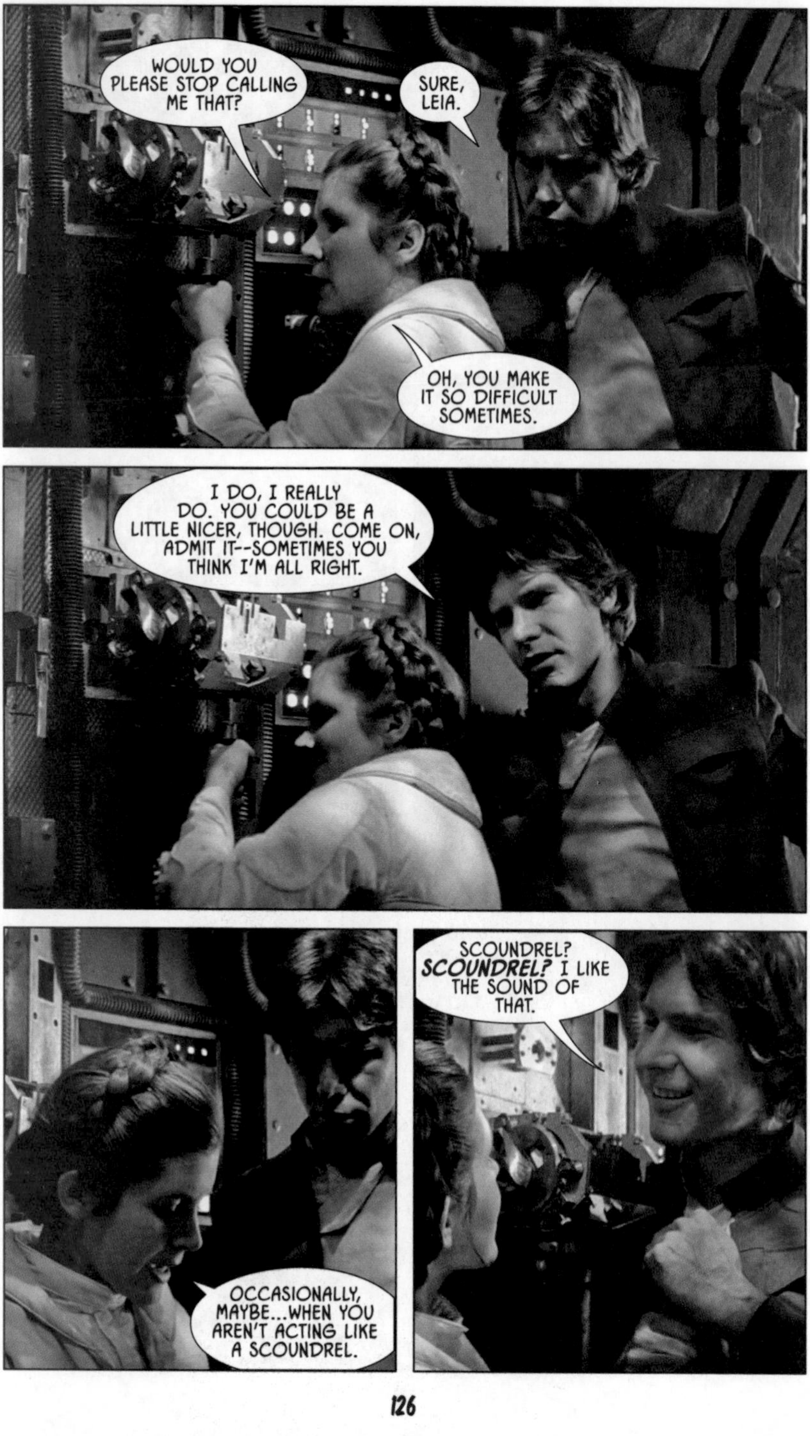
WOULD YOU PLEASE STOP CALLING ME THAT?
SURE, LEIA.
OH, YOU MAKE IT SO DIFFICULT SOMETIMES.
I DO, I REALLY DO. YOU COULD BE A LITTLE NICER, THOUGH. COME ON, ADMIT IT--SOMETIMES YOU THINK I'M ALL RIGHT.
OCCASIONALLY, MAYBE...WHEN YOU AREN'T ACTING LIKE A SCOUNDREL.
SCOUNDREL? SCOUNDREL? I LIKE THE SOUND OF THAT.

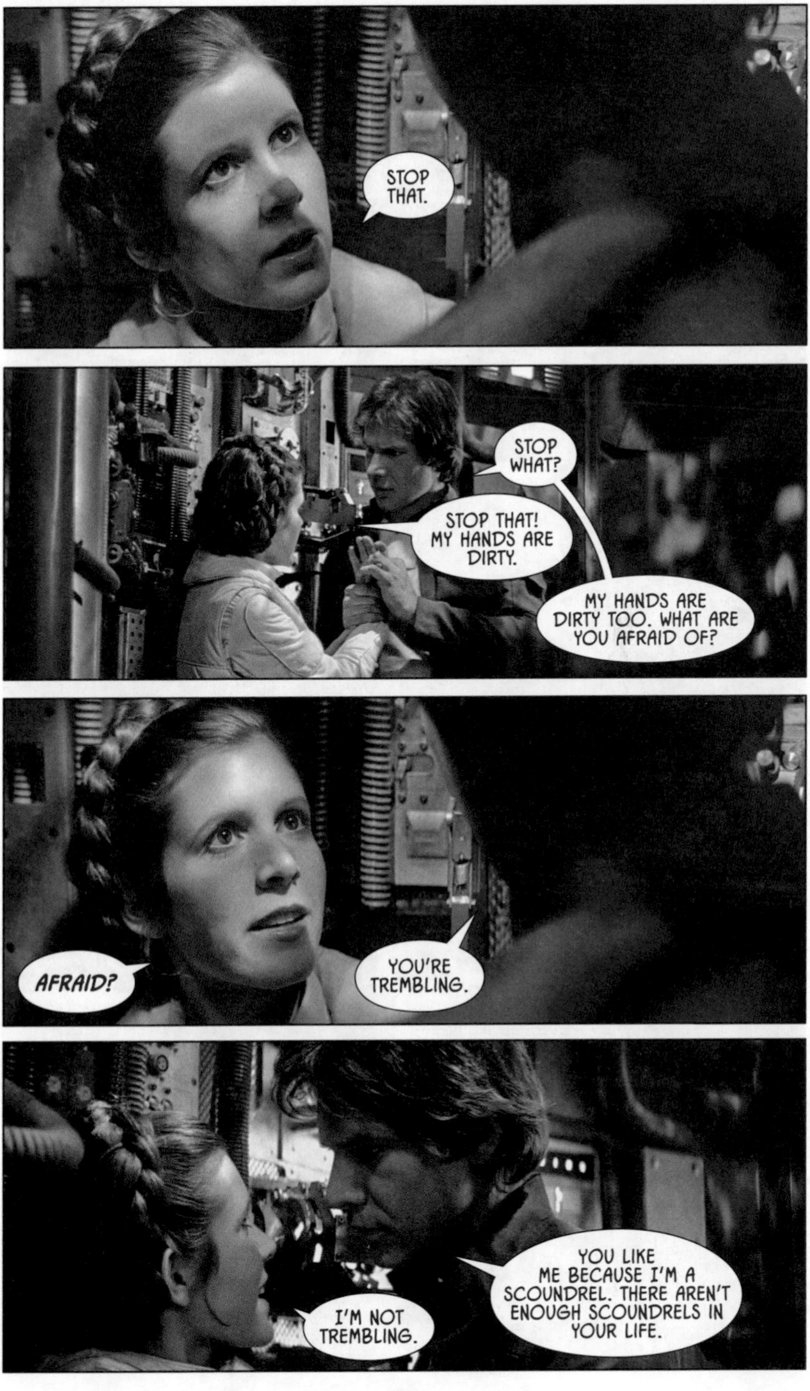
STOP THAT.
STOP WHAT?
STOP THAT! MY HANDS ARE DIRTY.
MY HANDS ARE DIRTY TOO. WHAT ARE YOU AFRAID OF?
AFRAID?
YOU'RE TREMBLING.
I'M NOT TREMBLING.
YOU LIKE ME BECAUSE I'M A SCOUNDREL. THERE AREN'T ENOUGH SCOUNDRELS IN YOUR LIFE.

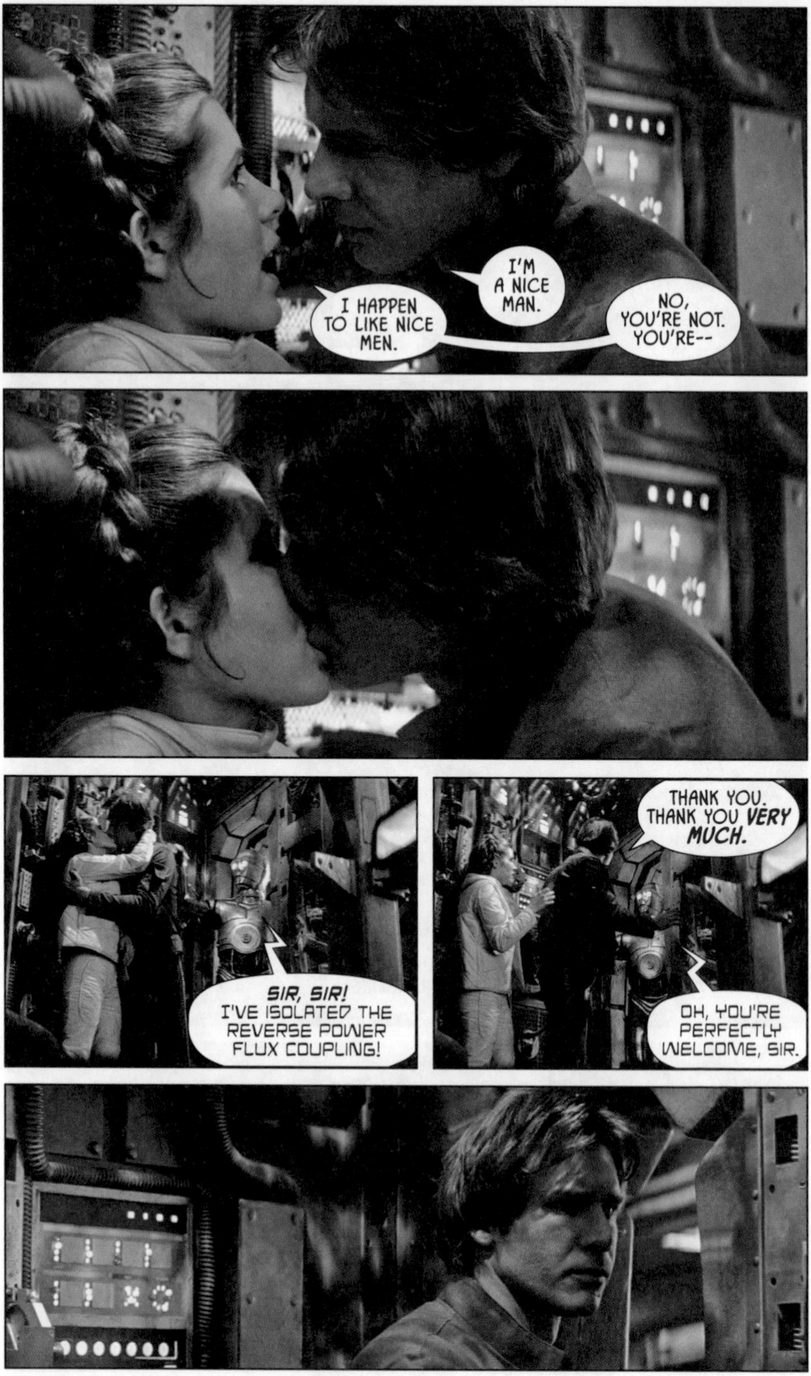

I HAPPEN TO LIKE NICE MEN.
I'M A NICE MAN.
NO, YOU'RE NOT. YOU'RE--
SIR, SIR! I'VE ISOLATED THE REVERSE POWER FLUX COUPLING!
THANK YOU. THANK YOU VERY MUCH.
OH, YOU'RE PERFECTLY WELCOME, SIR.

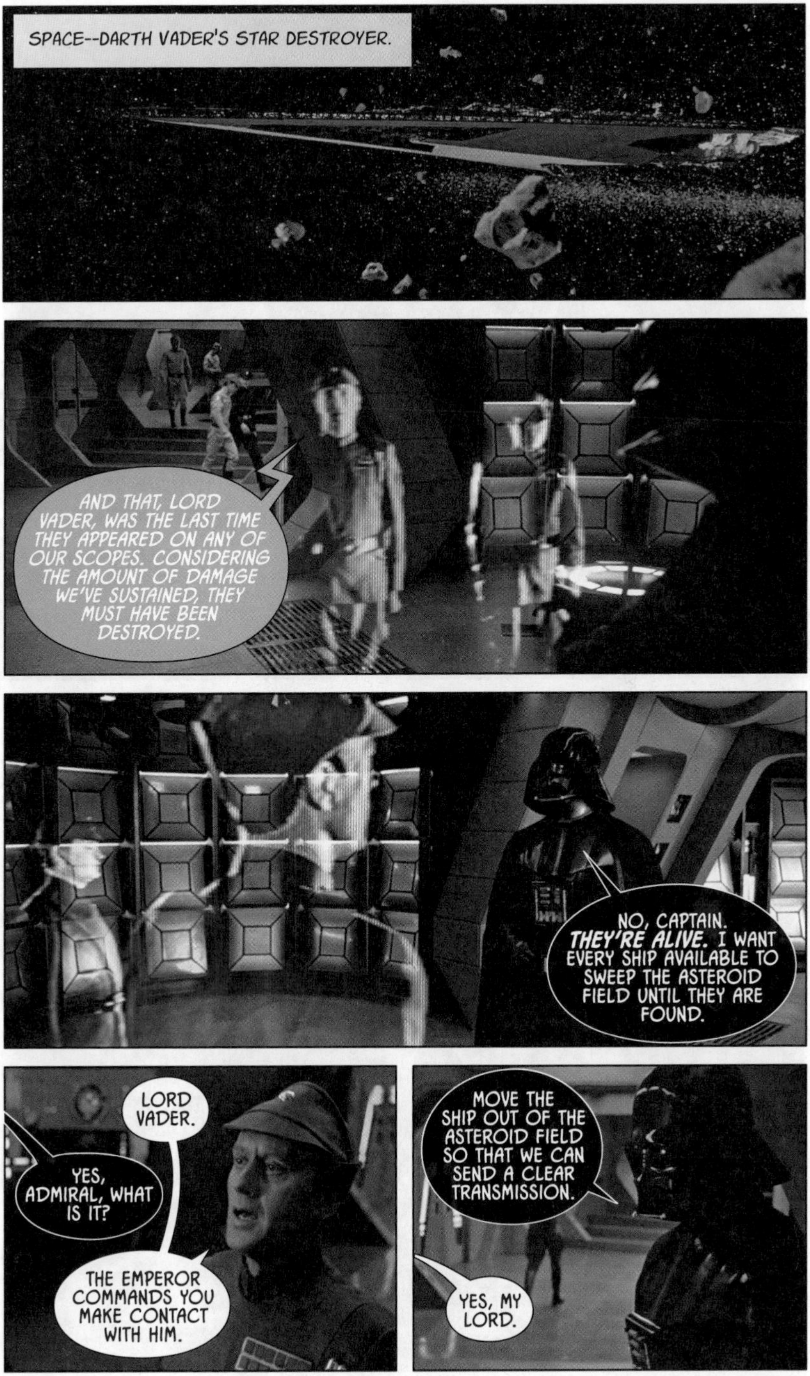
SPACE--DARTH VADER'S STAR DESTROYER.
AND THAT, LORD VADER, WAS THE LAST TIME THEY APPEARED ON ANY OF OUR SCOPES. CONSIDERING THE AMOUNT OF DAMAGE WE'VE SUSTAINED, THEY MUST HAVE BEEN DESTROYED.
NO, CAPTAIN. ***THEY'RE ALIVE.*** I WANT EVERY SHIP AVAILABLE TO SWEEP THE ASTEROID FIELD UNTIL THEY ARE FOUND.
LORD VADER.
YES, ADMIRAL, WHAT IS IT?
THE EMPEROR COMMANDS YOU MAKE CONTACT WITH HIM.
MOVE THE SHIP OUT OF THE ASTEROID FIELD SO THAT WE CAN SEND A CLEAR TRANSMISSION.
YES, MY LORD.

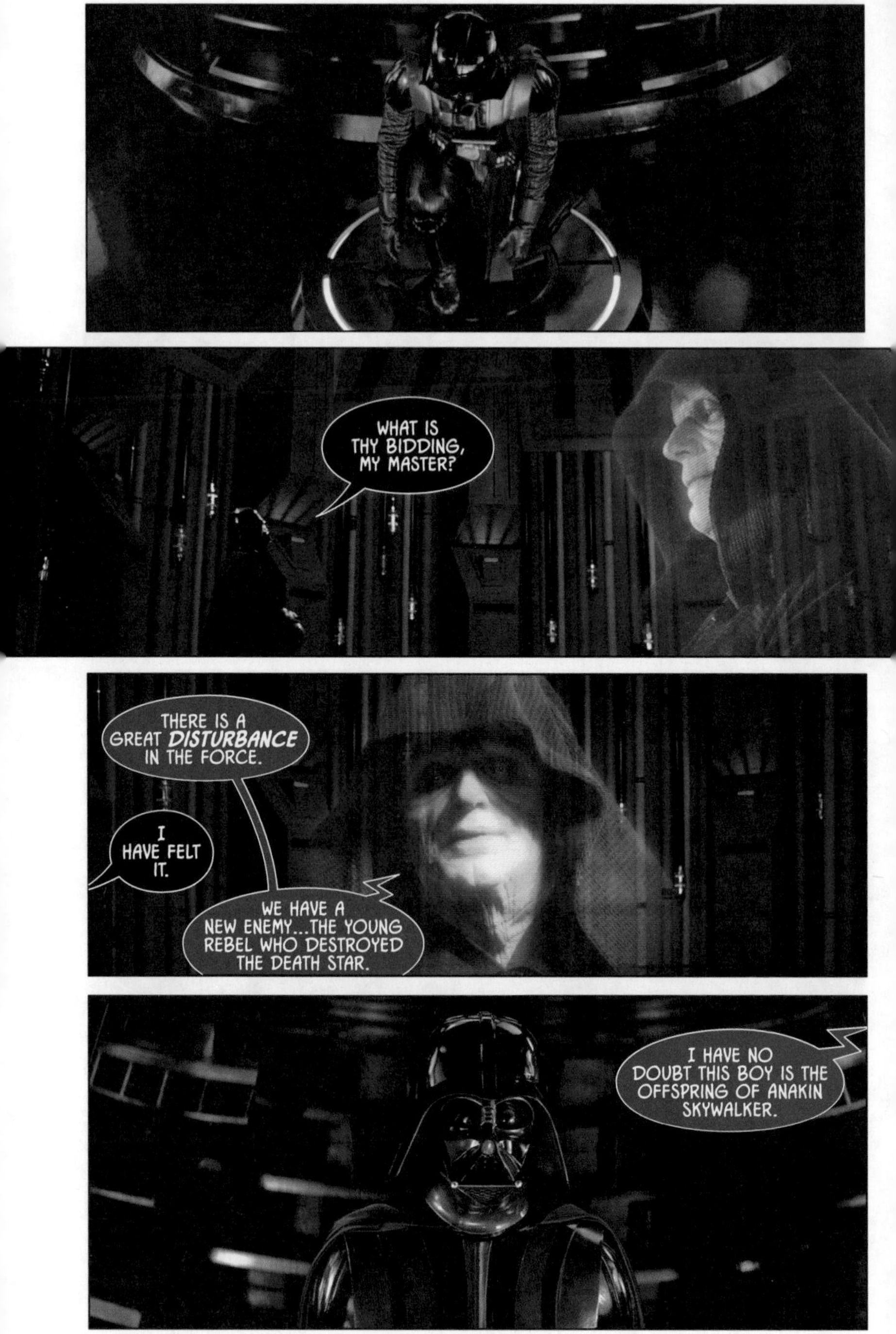
WHAT IS THY BIDDING, MY MASTER?
THERE IS A GREAT DISTURBANCE IN THE FORCE.
I HAVE FELT IT.
WE HAVE A NEW ENEMY...THE YOUNG REBEL WHO DESTROYED THE DEATH STAR.
I HAVE NO DOUBT THIS BOY IS THE OFFSPRING OF ANAKIN SKYWALKER.

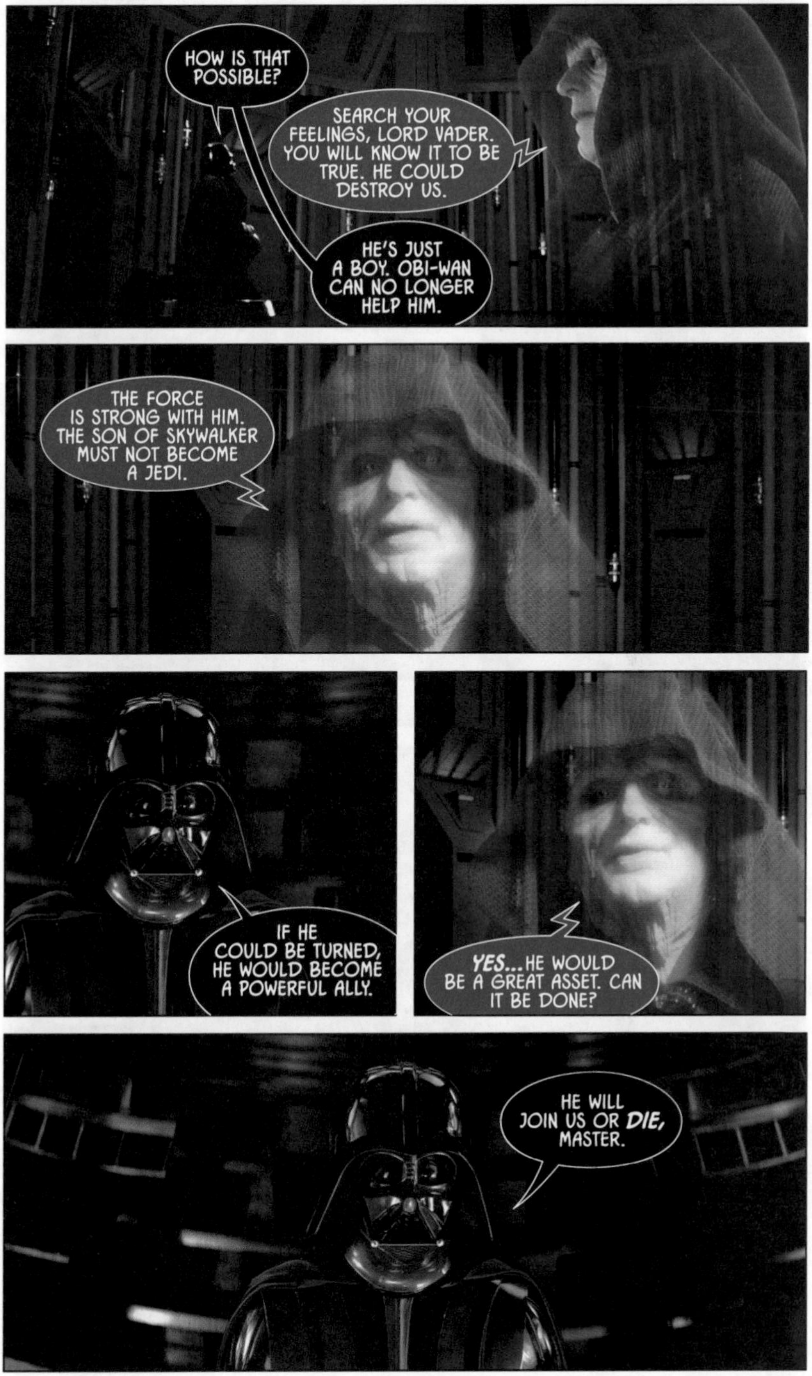
HOW IS THAT POSSIBLE?
SEARCH YOUR FEELINGS, LORD VADER. YOU WILL KNOW IT TO BE TRUE. HE COULD DESTROY US.
HE'S JUST A BOY. OBI-WAN CAN NO LONGER HELP HIM.
THE FORCE IS STRONG WITH HIM. THE SON OF SKYWALKER MUST NOT BECOME A JEDI.
IF HE COULD BE TURNED, HE WOULD BECOME A POWERFUL ALLY.
YES...HE WOULD BE A GREAT ASSET. CAN IT BE DONE?
HE WILL JOIN US OR DIE, MASTER.

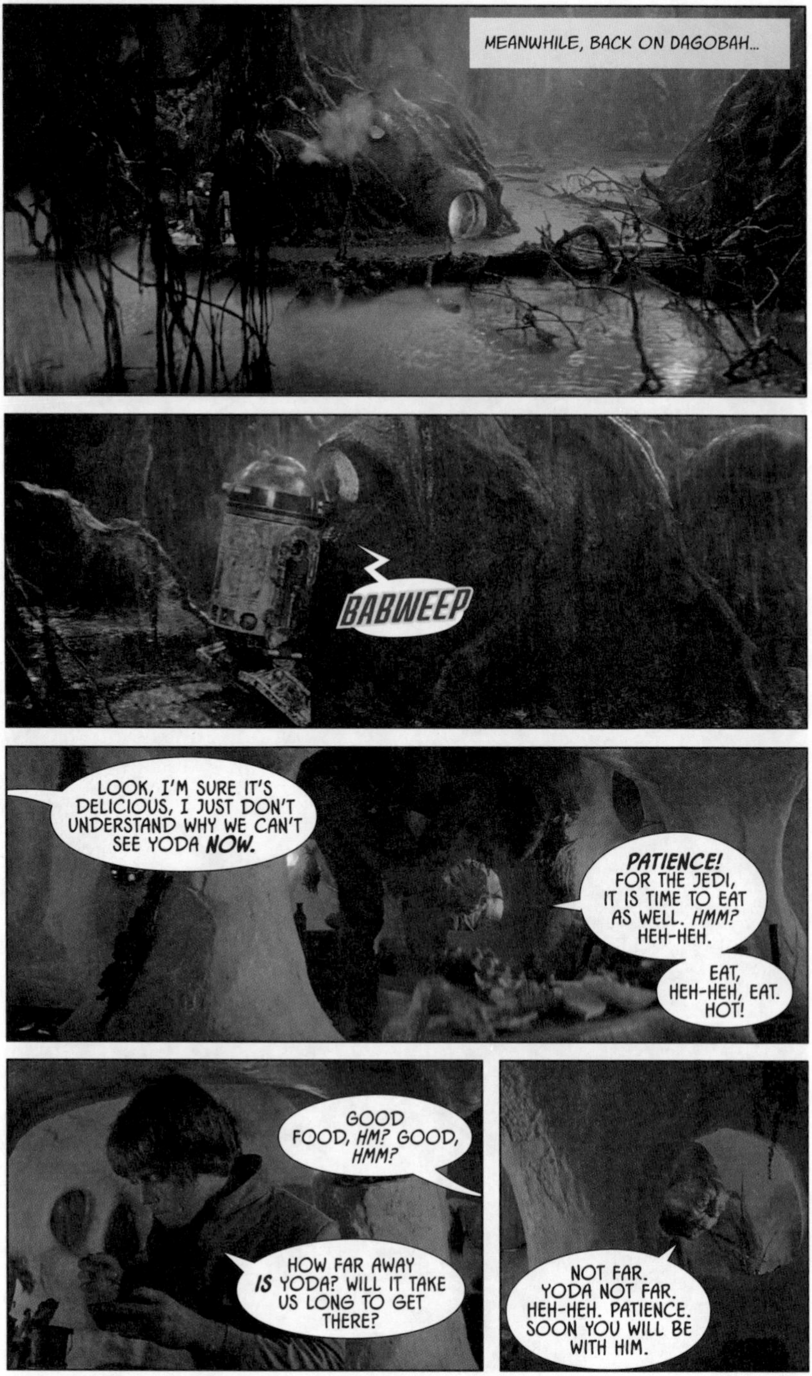
MEANWHILE, BACK ON DAGOBAH...
BABWEEP
LOOK, I'M SURE IT'S DELICIOUS, I JUST DON'T UNDERSTAND WHY WE CAN'T SEE YODA NOW.
PATIENCE! FOR THE JEDI, IT IS TIME TO EAT AS WELL. HMM? HEH-HEH.
EAT, HEH-HEH, EAT. HOT!
GOOD FOOD, HM? GOOD, HMM?
HOW FAR AWAY IS YODA? WILL IT TAKE US LONG TO GET THERE?
NOT FAR. YODA NOT FAR. HEH-HEH. PATIENCE. SOON YOU WILL BE WITH HIM.

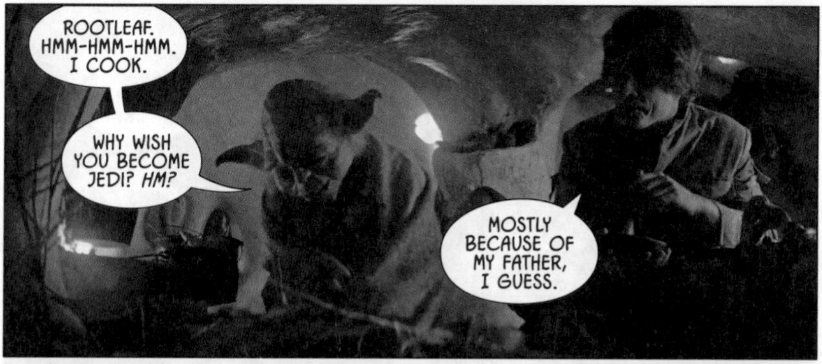
ROOTLEAF. HMM-HMM-HMM. I COOK.
WHY WISH YOU BECOME JEDI? *HM?*
MOSTLY BECAUSE OF MY FATHER, I GUESS.

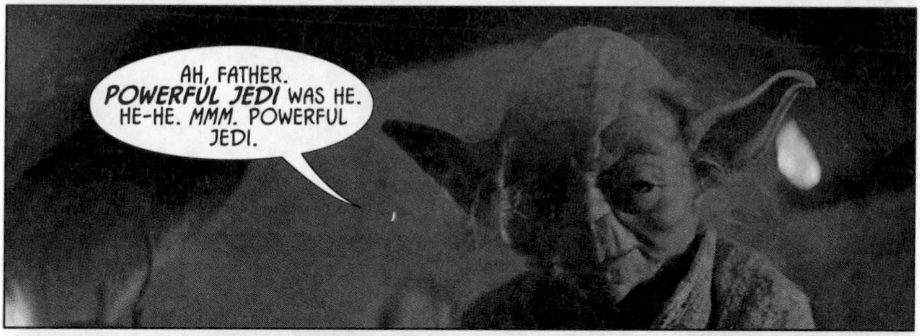
AH, FATHER. ***POWERFUL JEDI*** WAS HE. HE-HE. *MMM.* POWERFUL JEDI.

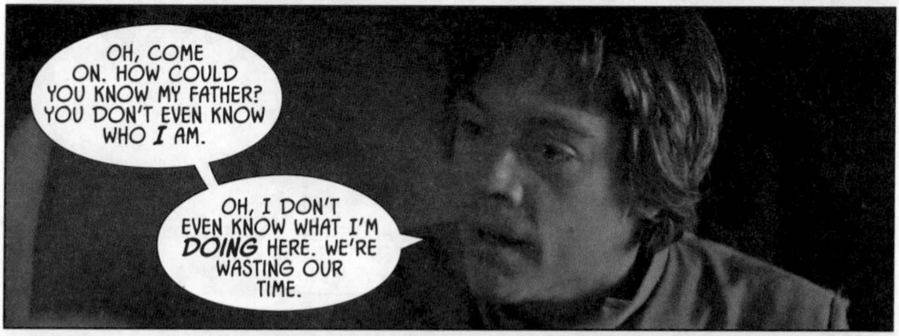
OH, COME ON. HOW COULD YOU KNOW MY FATHER? YOU DON'T EVEN KNOW WHO ***I*** AM.
OH, I DON'T EVEN KNOW WHAT I'M ***DOING*** HERE. WE'RE WASTING OUR TIME.

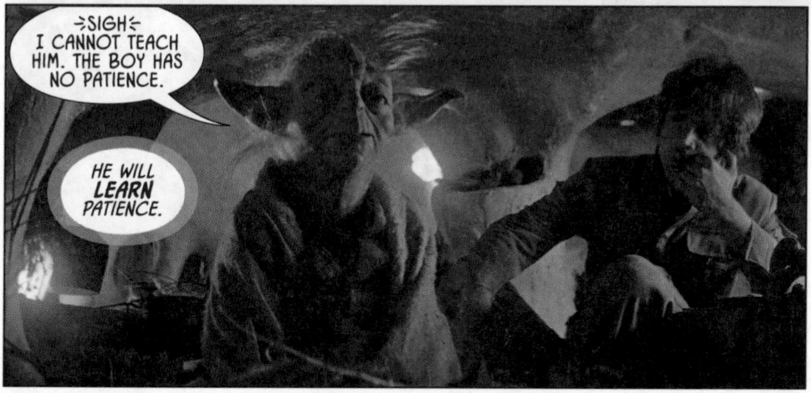
⇒SIGH⇐ I CANNOT TEACH HIM. THE BOY HAS NO PATIENCE.
HE WILL ***LEARN*** *PATIENCE.*

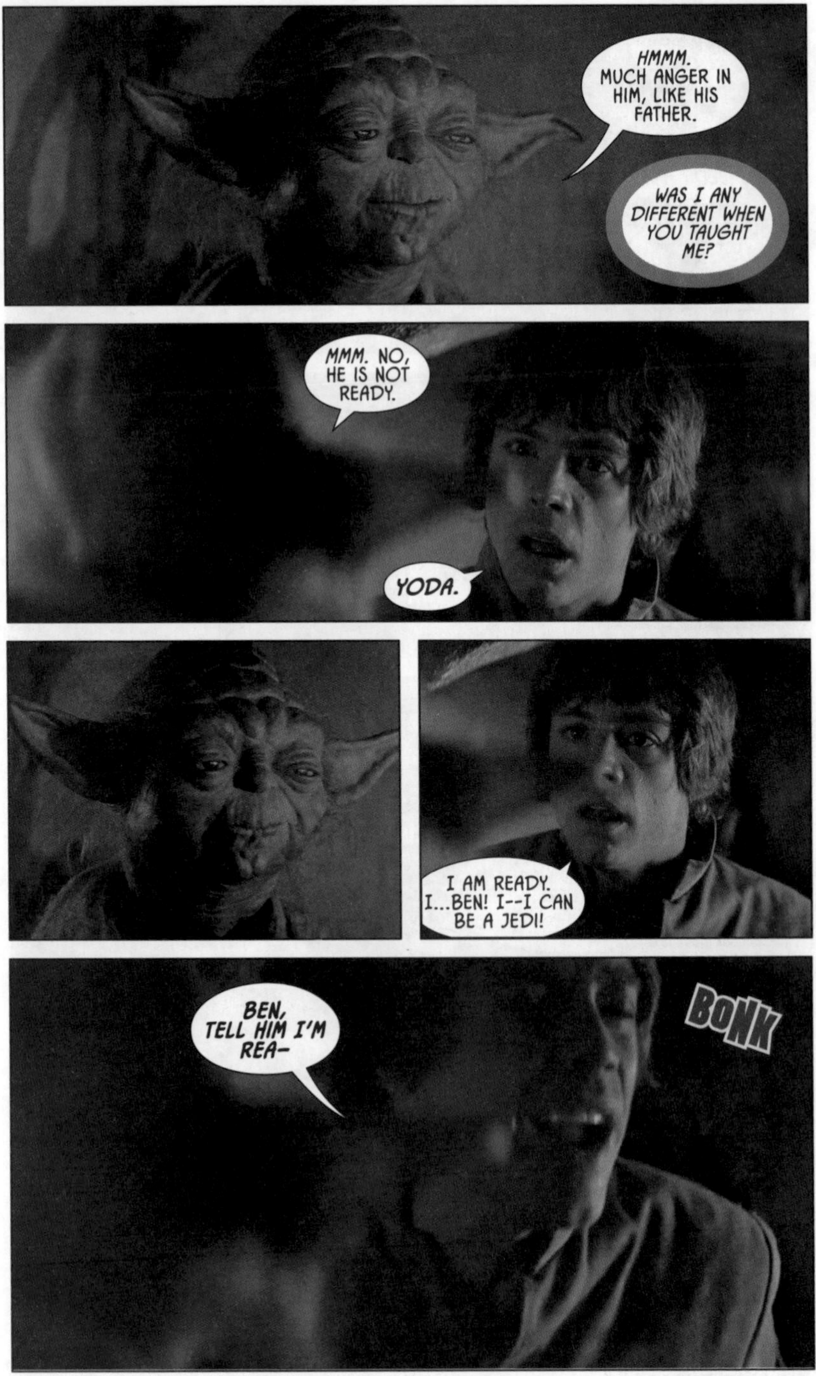
HMMM. MUCH ANGER IN HIM, LIKE HIS FATHER.
WAS I ANY DIFFERENT WHEN YOU TAUGHT ME?
MMM. NO, HE IS NOT READY.
YODA.
I AM READY. I...BEN! I--I CAN BE A JEDI!
BEN, TELL HIM I'M REA-
BONK

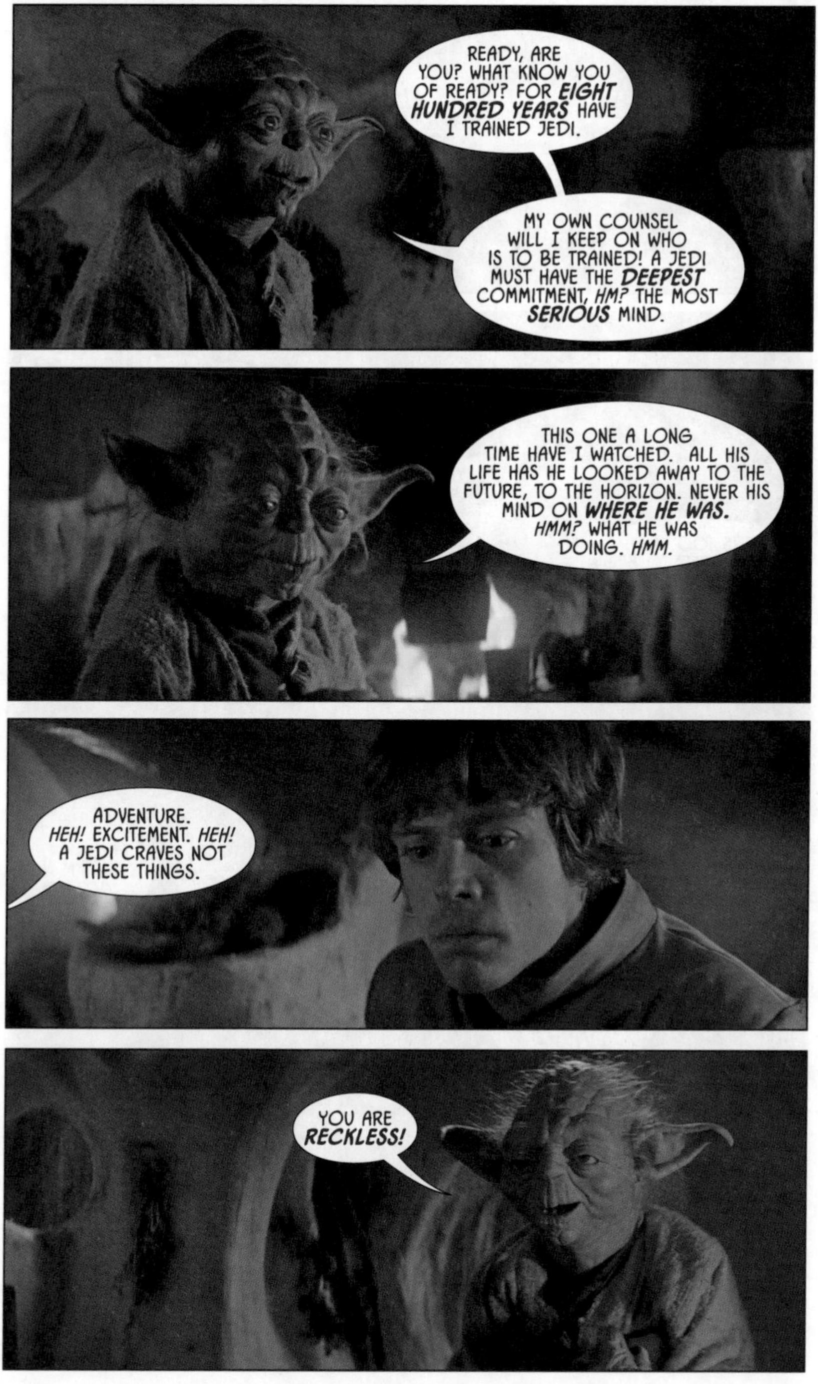
READY, ARE YOU? WHAT KNOW YOU OF READY? FOR EIGHT HUNDRED YEARS HAVE I TRAINED JEDI.
MY OWN COUNSEL WILL I KEEP ON WHO IS TO BE TRAINED! A JEDI MUST HAVE THE DEEPEST COMMITMENT, HM? THE MOST SERIOUS MIND.
THIS ONE A LONG TIME HAVE I WATCHED. ALL HIS LIFE HAS HE LOOKED AWAY TO THE FUTURE, TO THE HORIZON. NEVER HIS MIND ON WHERE HE WAS. HMM? WHAT HE WAS DOING. HMM.
ADVENTURE. HEH! EXCITEMENT. HEH! A JEDI CRAVES NOT THESE THINGS.
YOU ARE RECKLESS!

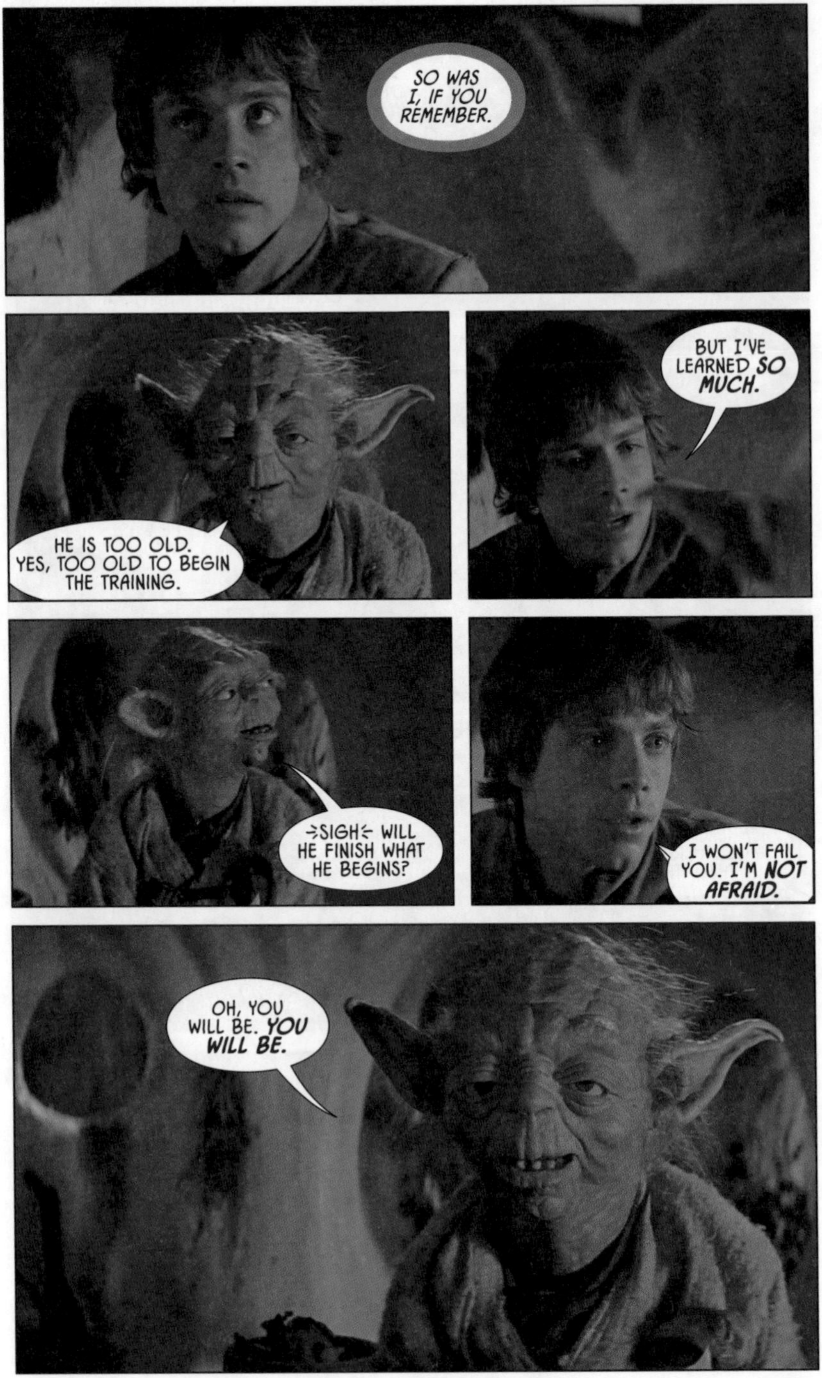
SO WAS I, IF YOU REMEMBER.
HE IS TOO OLD. YES, TOO OLD TO BEGIN THE TRAINING.
BUT I'VE LEARNED **SO MUCH.**
⋟SIGH⋞ WILL HE FINISH WHAT HE BEGINS?
I WON'T FAIL YOU. I'M **NOT AFRAID.**
OH, YOU WILL BE. **YOU WILL BE.**

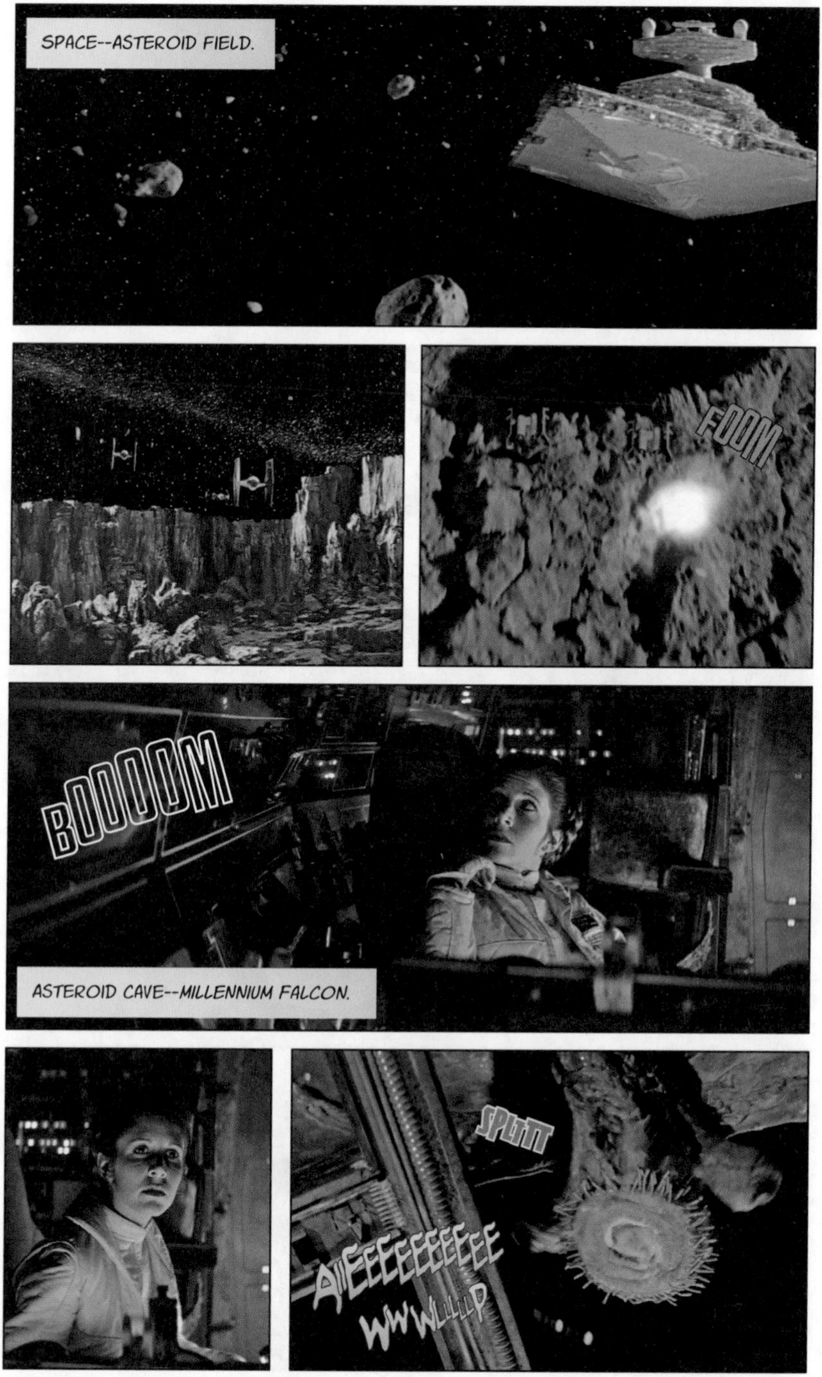
SPACE--ASTEROID FIELD.
FOOM
BOOOOM
ASTEROID CAVE--MILLENNIUM FALCON.
SPLTTT
AIIEEEEEEEEEE
WWWLLLLLP

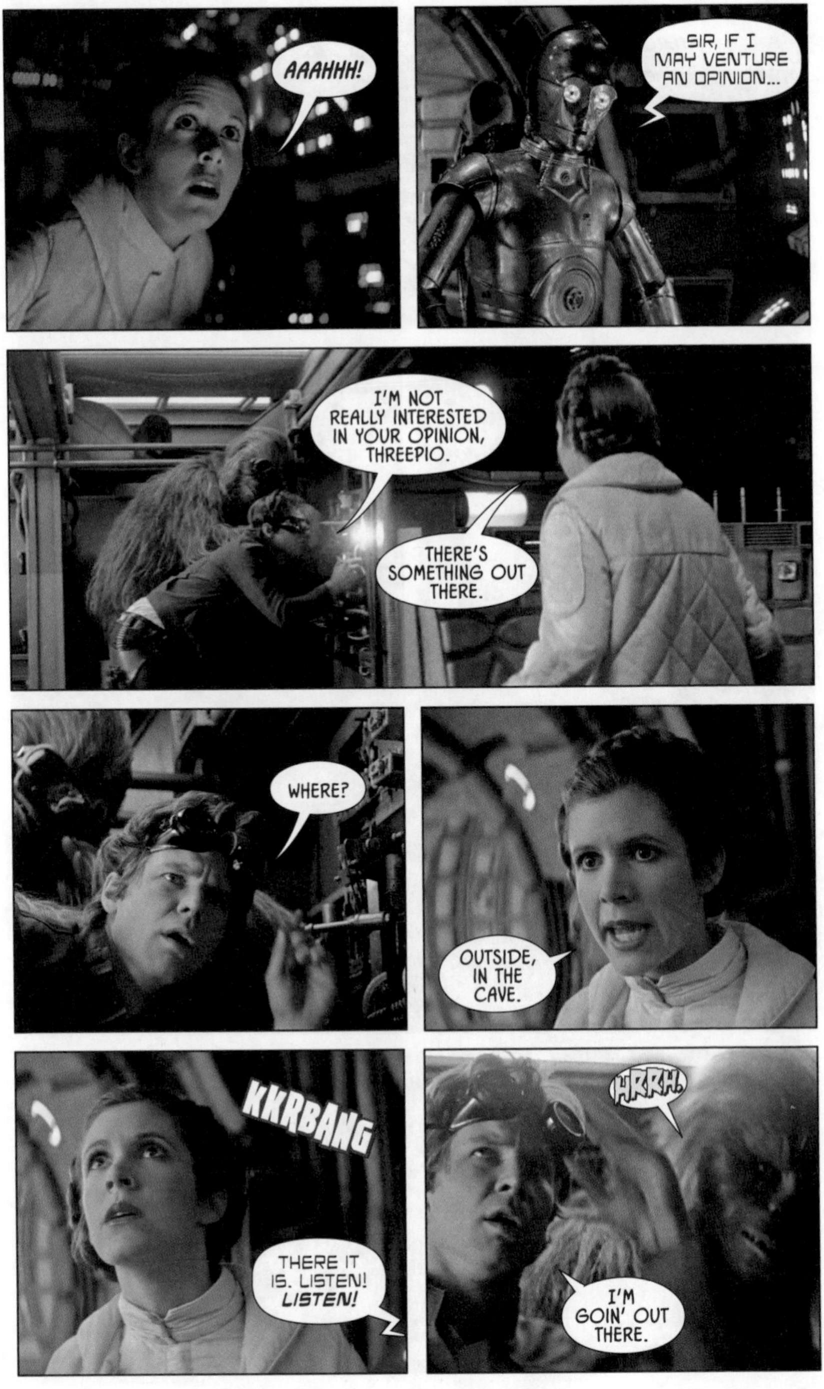
AAAHHH!
SIR, IF I MAY VENTURE AN OPINION...
I'M NOT REALLY INTERESTED IN YOUR OPINION, THREEPIO.
THERE'S SOMETHING OUT THERE.
WHERE?
OUTSIDE, IN THE CAVE.
KKRBANG
THERE IT IS. LISTEN! LISTEN!
HRRH.
I'M GOIN' OUT THERE.

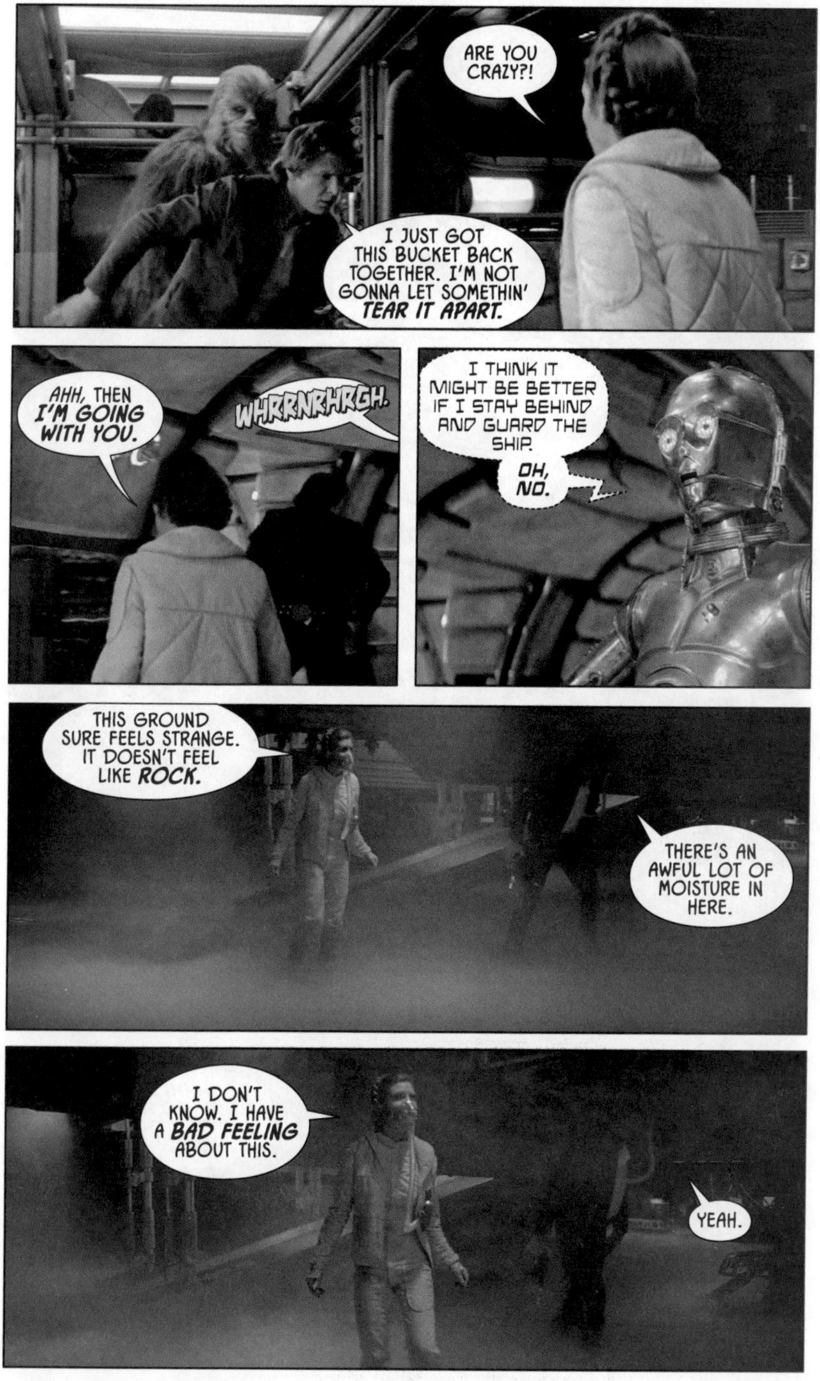
ARE YOU CRAZY?!
I JUST GOT THIS BUCKET BACK TOGETHER. I'M NOT GONNA LET SOMETHIN' TEAR IT APART.
AHH, THEN I'M GOING WITH YOU.
WHRRNRHRGH.
I THINK IT MIGHT BE BETTER IF I STAY BEHIND AND GUARD THE SHIP.
OH, NO.
THIS GROUND SURE FEELS STRANGE. IT DOESN'T FEEL LIKE ROCK.
THERE'S AN AWFUL LOT OF MOISTURE IN HERE.
I DON'T KNOW. I HAVE A BAD FEELING ABOUT THIS.
YEAH.

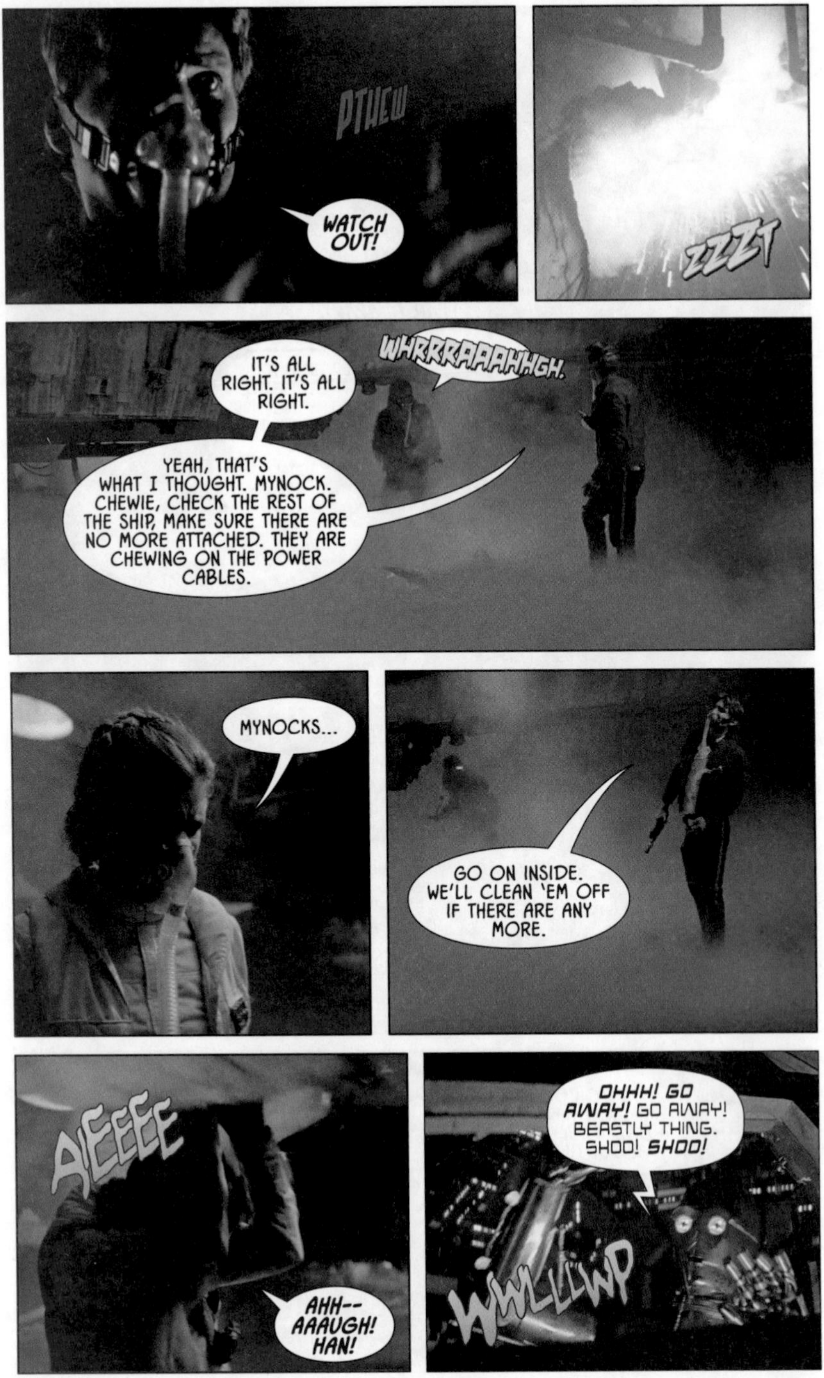
PTHEW
WATCH OUT!
ZZZT
WHRRRAAAHHGH.
IT'S ALL RIGHT. IT'S ALL RIGHT.
YEAH, THAT'S WHAT I THOUGHT. MYNOCK. CHEWIE, CHECK THE REST OF THE SHIP, MAKE SURE THERE ARE NO MORE ATTACHED. THEY ARE CHEWING ON THE POWER CABLES.
MYNOCKS...
GO ON INSIDE. WE'LL CLEAN 'EM OFF IF THERE ARE ANY MORE.
AIEEEE
AHH-- AAAUGH! HAN!
OHHH! GO AWAY! GO AWAY! BEASTLY THING. SHOO! SHOO!
WWLLLWP

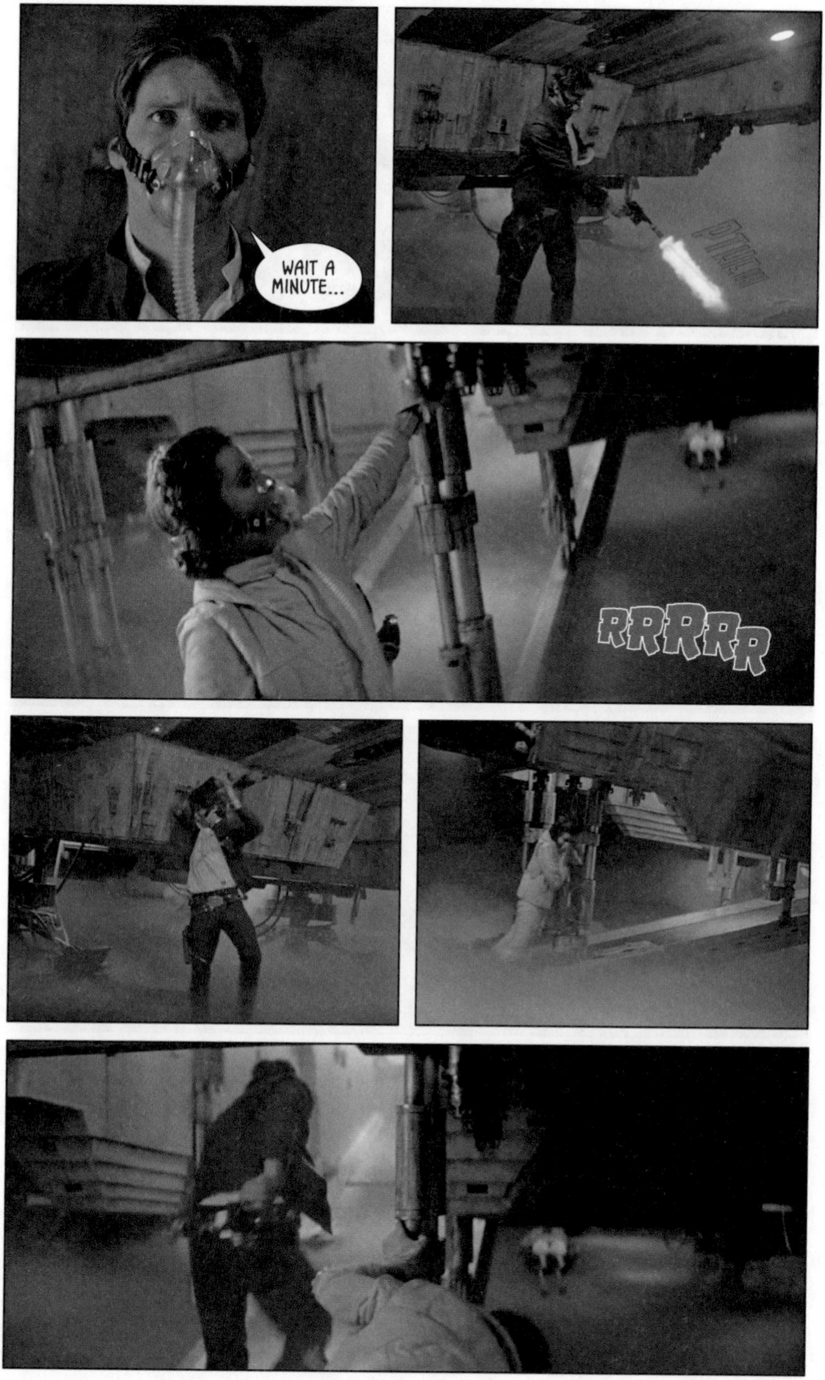
WAIT A MINUTE...
RRRRRR

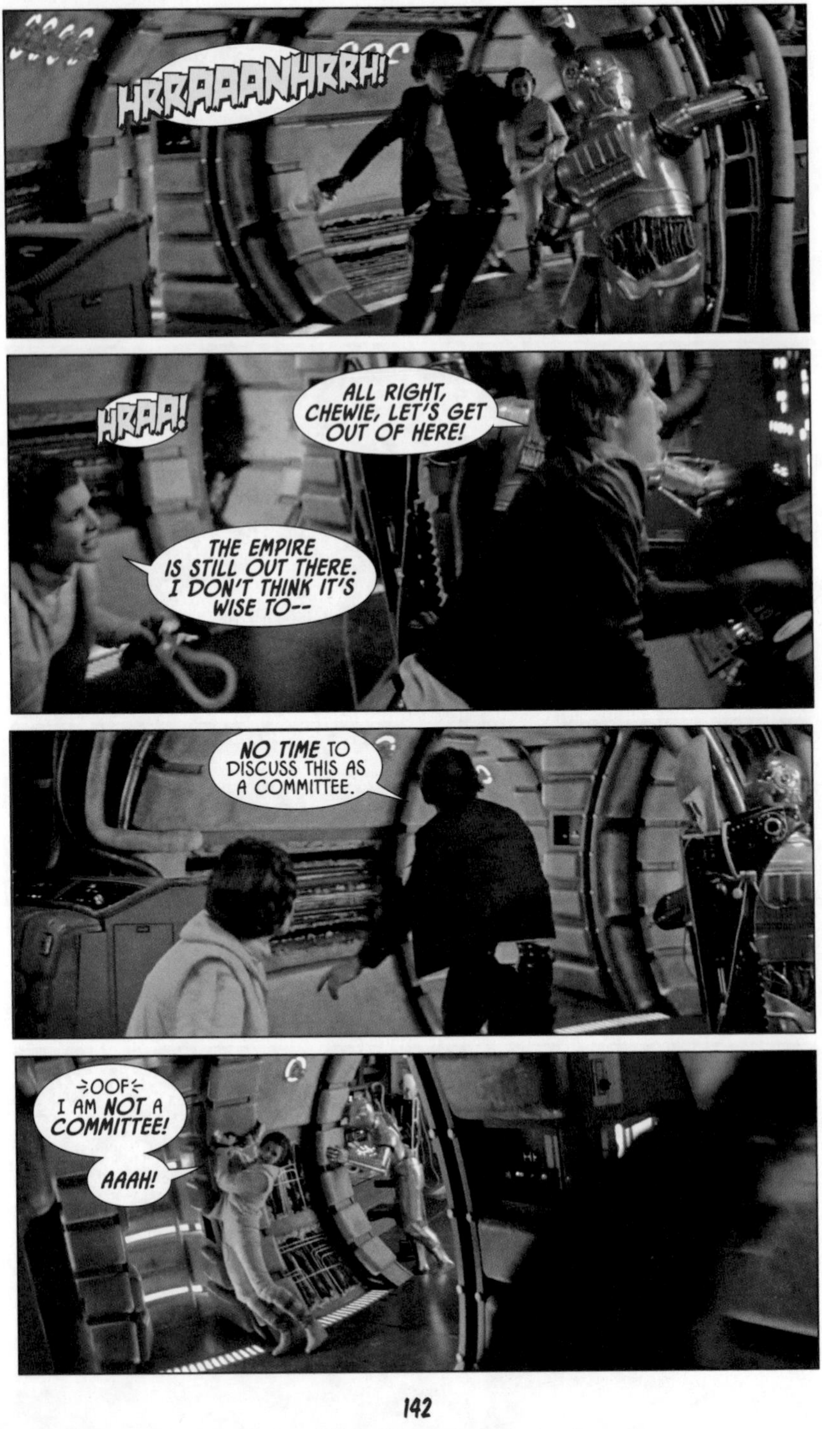
HRRAAANHRRH!
HRAA!
ALL RIGHT, CHEWIE, LET'S GET OUT OF HERE!
THE EMPIRE IS STILL OUT THERE. I DON'T THINK IT'S WISE TO--
NO TIME TO DISCUSS THIS AS A COMMITTEE.
OOF
I AM **NOT** A COMMITTEE!
AAAH!

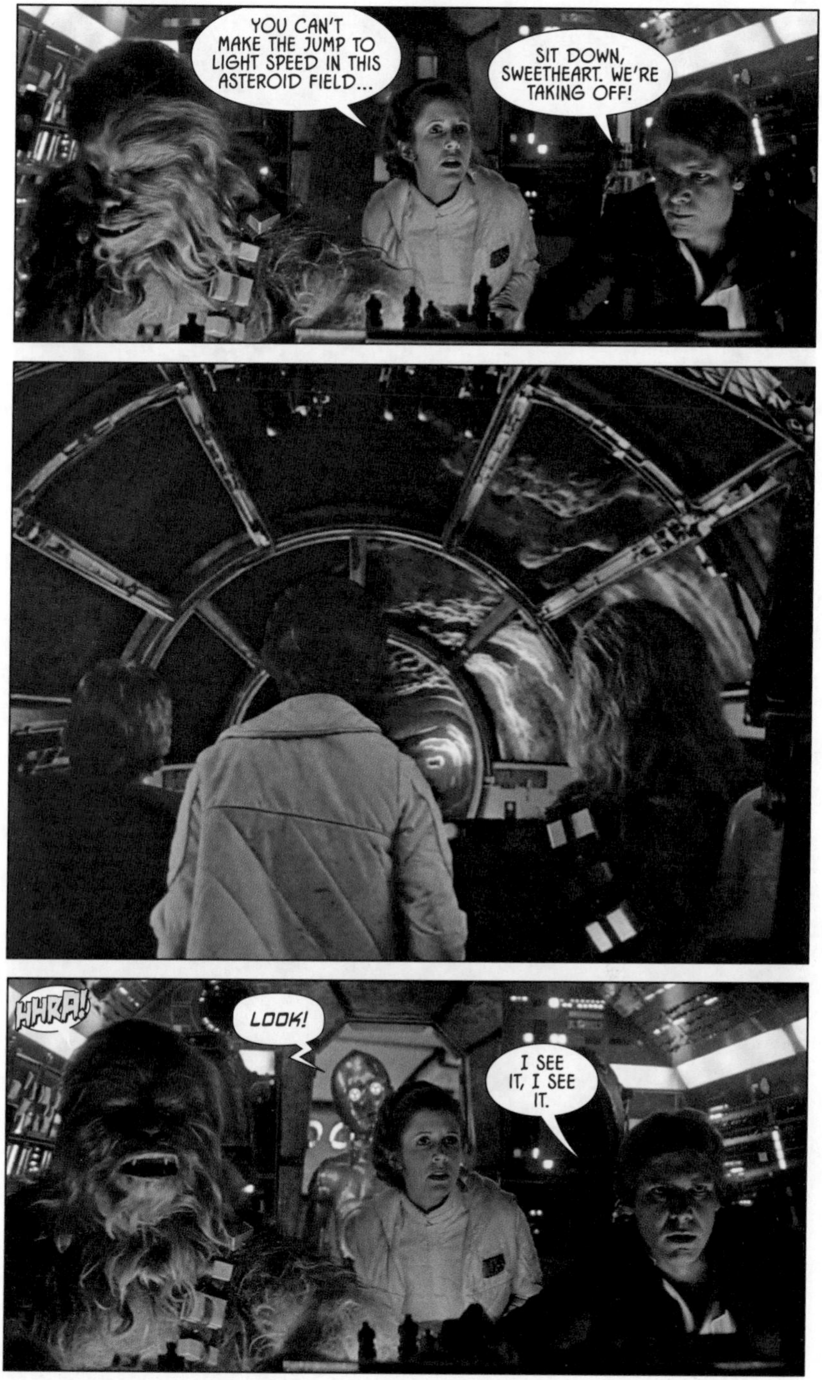
YOU CAN'T MAKE THE JUMP TO LIGHT SPEED IN THIS ASTEROID FIELD...
SIT DOWN, SWEETHEART. WE'RE TAKING OFF!
HHRA!
LOOK!
I SEE IT, I SEE IT.

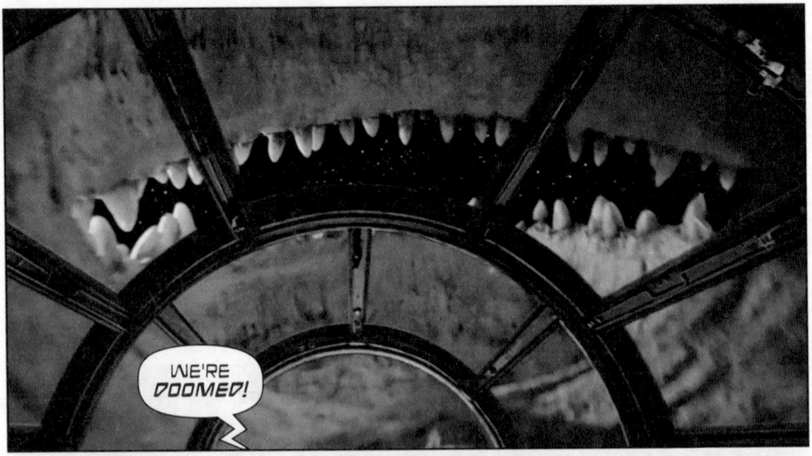
WE'RE DOOMED!

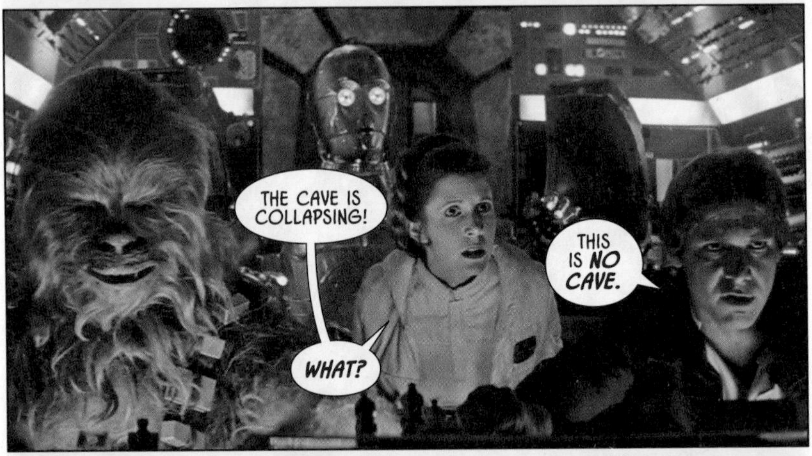
THE CAVE IS COLLAPSING!
THIS IS NO CAVE.
WHAT?

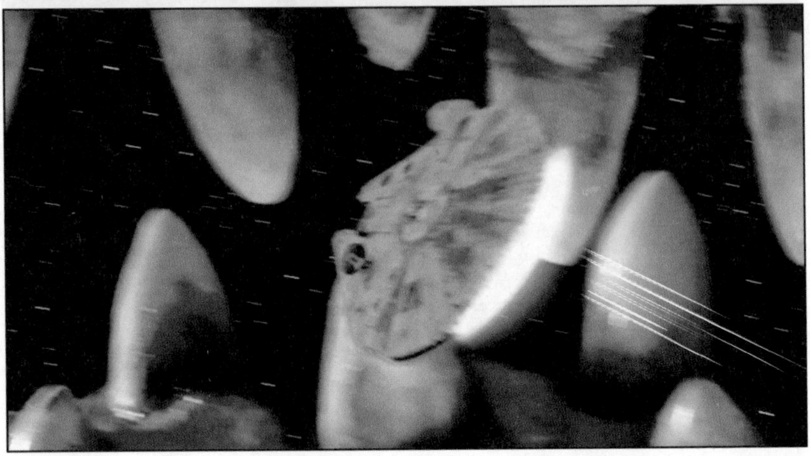

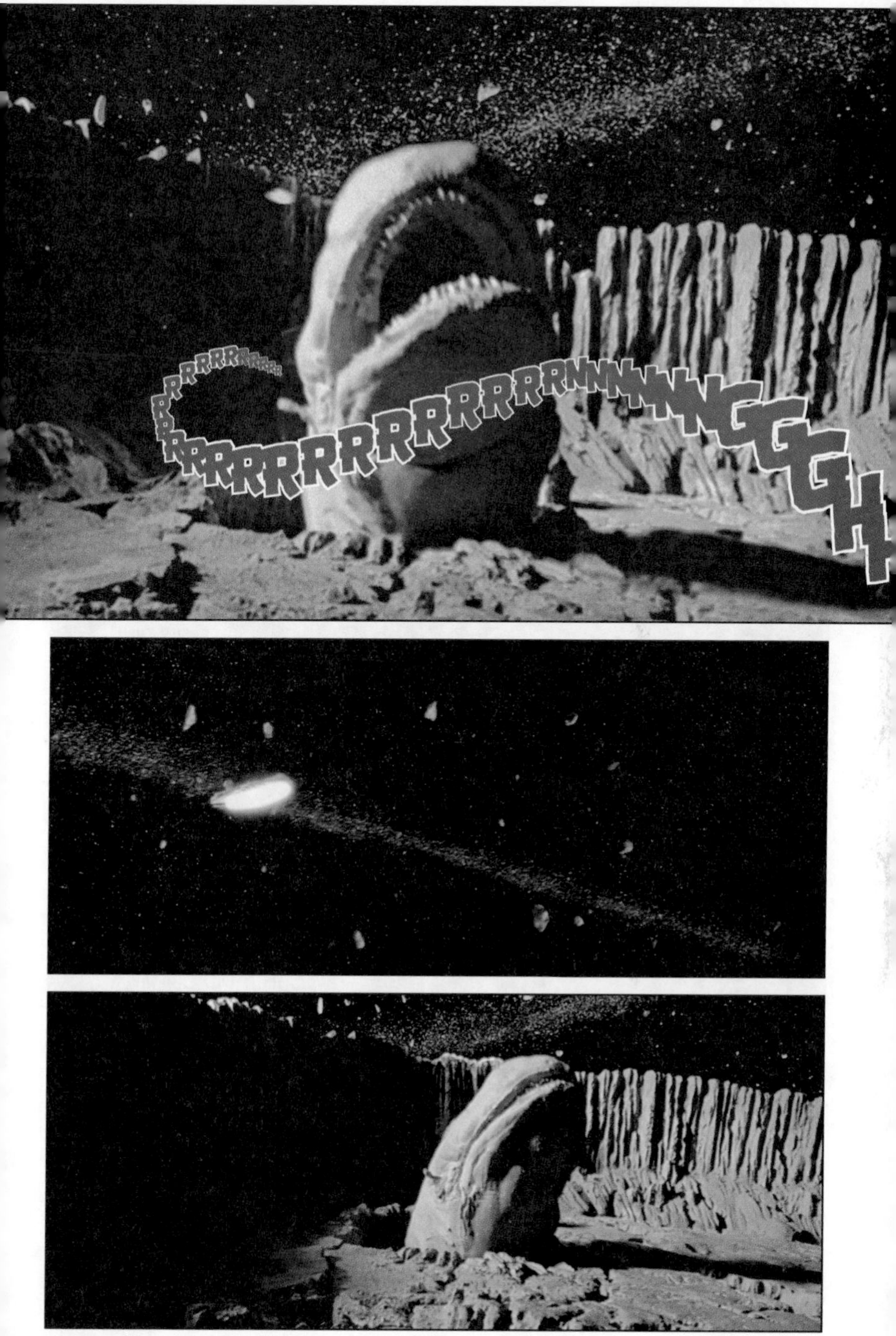
RRRRRRRRRRRRRRRRRRRRRRRRRRRNNNNNNNGGGH

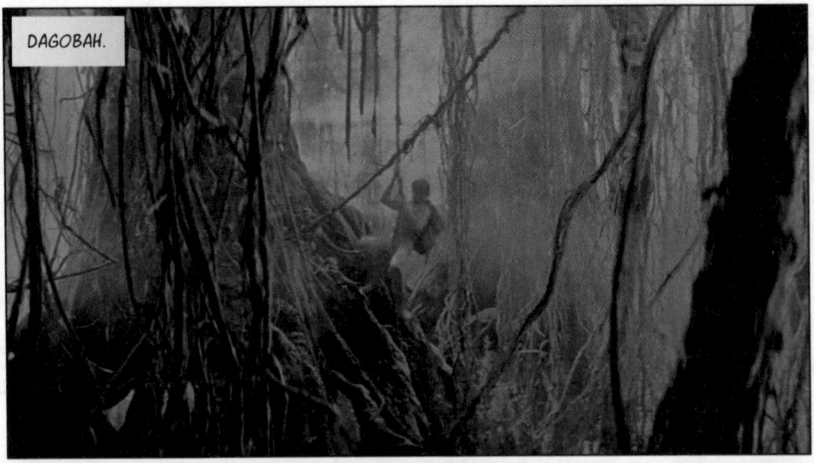
DAGOBAH.

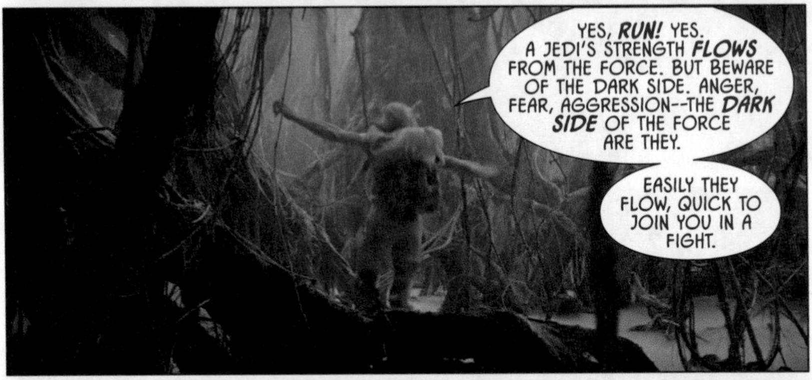
YES, **RUN!** YES. A JEDI'S STRENGTH **FLOWS** FROM THE FORCE. BUT BEWARE OF THE DARK SIDE. ANGER, FEAR, AGGRESSION--THE **DARK SIDE** OF THE FORCE ARE THEY.
EASILY THEY FLOW, QUICK TO JOIN YOU IN A FIGHT.

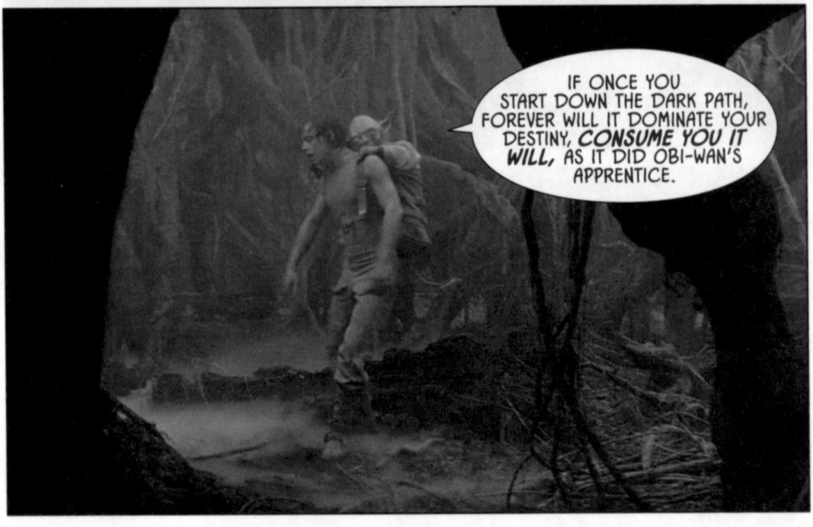
IF ONCE YOU START DOWN THE DARK PATH, FOREVER WILL IT DOMINATE YOUR DESTINY, **CONSUME YOU IT WILL,** AS IT DID OBI-WAN'S APPRENTICE.

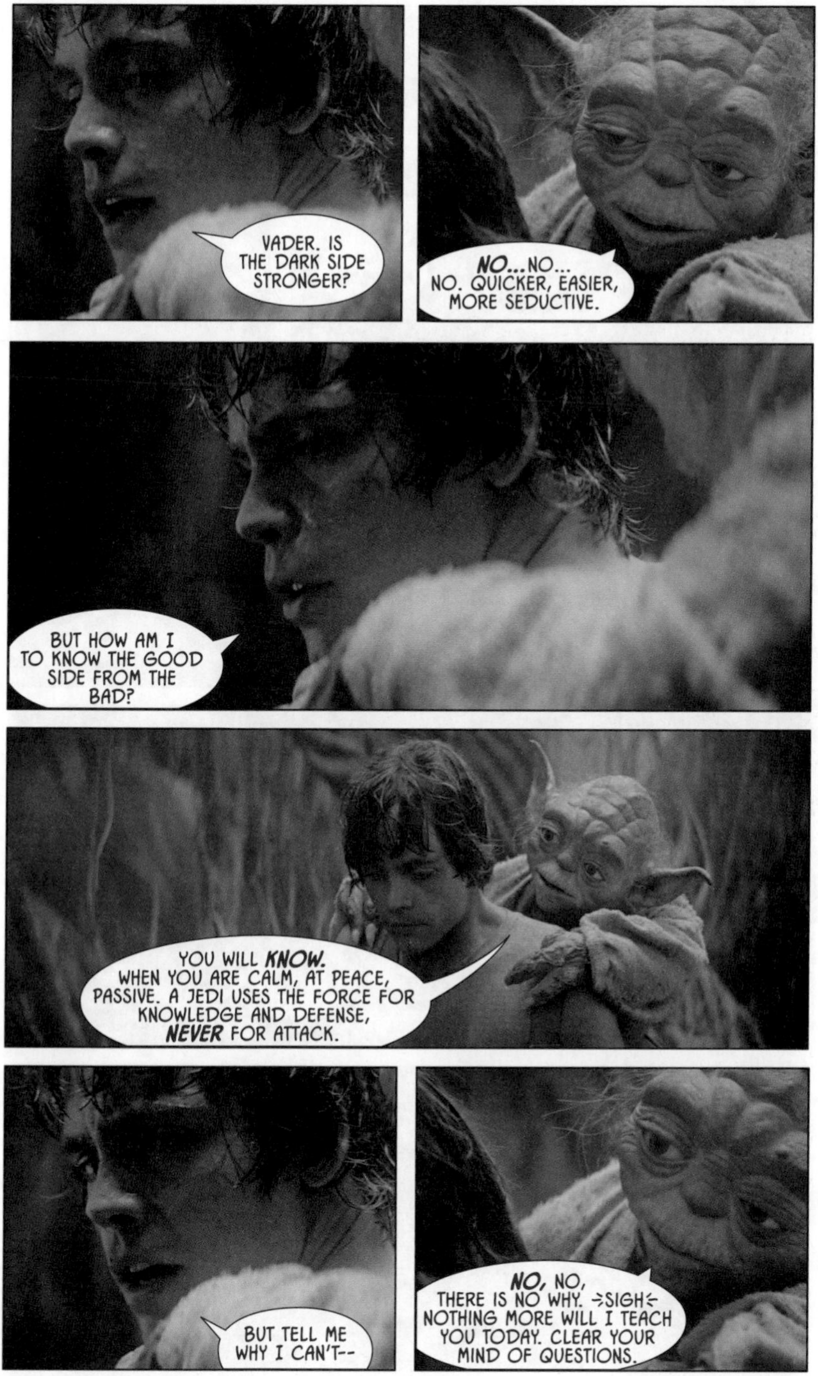
VADER. IS THE DARK SIDE STRONGER?
NO...NO... NO. QUICKER, EASIER, MORE SEDUCTIVE.
BUT HOW AM I TO KNOW THE GOOD SIDE FROM THE BAD?
YOU WILL KNOW. WHEN YOU ARE CALM, AT PEACE, PASSIVE. A JEDI USES THE FORCE FOR KNOWLEDGE AND DEFENSE, NEVER FOR ATTACK.
BUT TELL ME WHY I CAN'T--
NO, NO, THERE IS NO WHY. ⇒SIGH⇐ NOTHING MORE WILL I TEACH YOU TODAY. CLEAR YOUR MIND OF QUESTIONS.

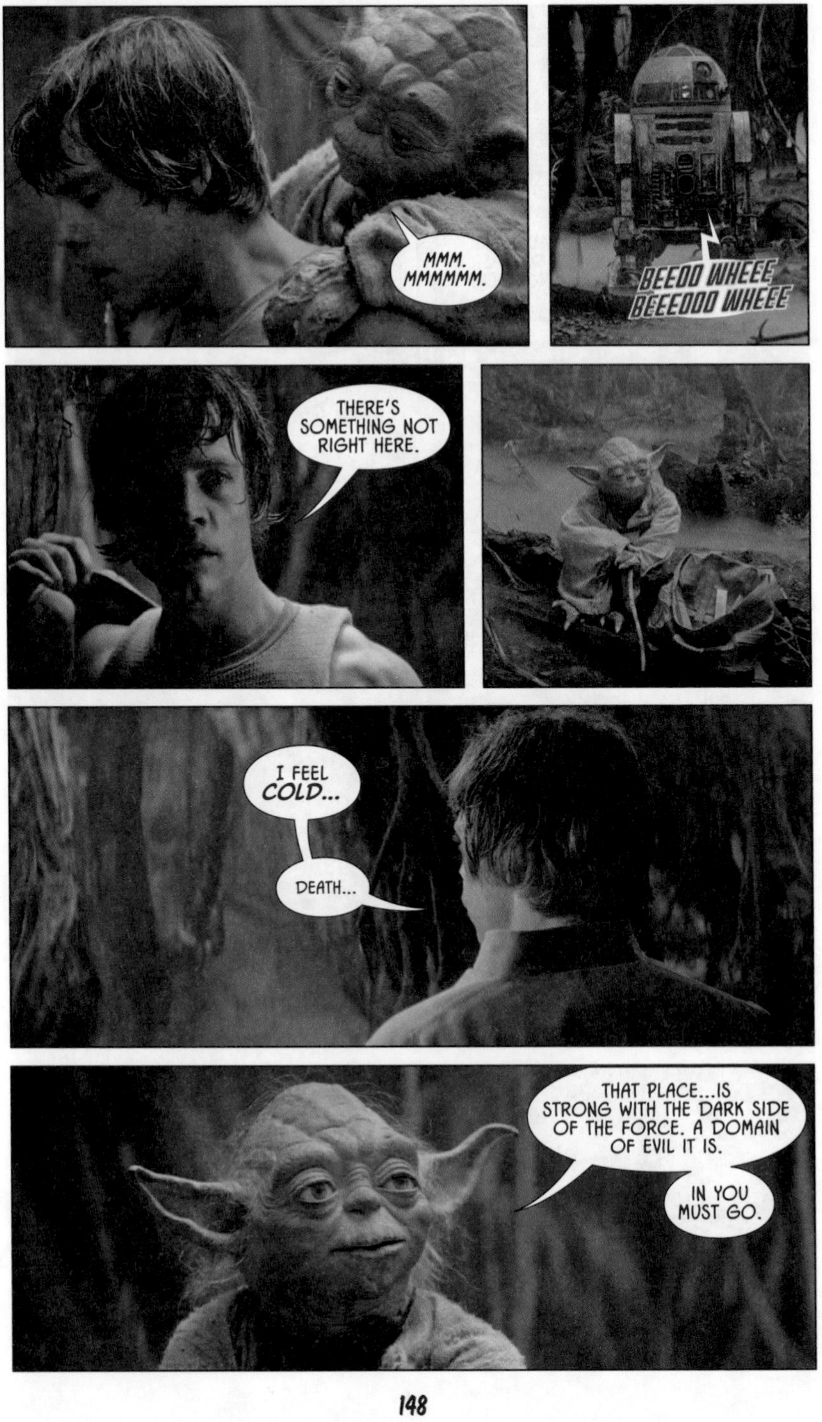
MMM.
MMMMMM.
BEEOO WHEEE
BEEEOOO WHEEE
THERE'S SOMETHING NOT RIGHT HERE.
I FEEL COLD...
DEATH...
THAT PLACE...IS STRONG WITH THE DARK SIDE OF THE FORCE. A DOMAIN OF EVIL IT IS.
IN YOU MUST GO.

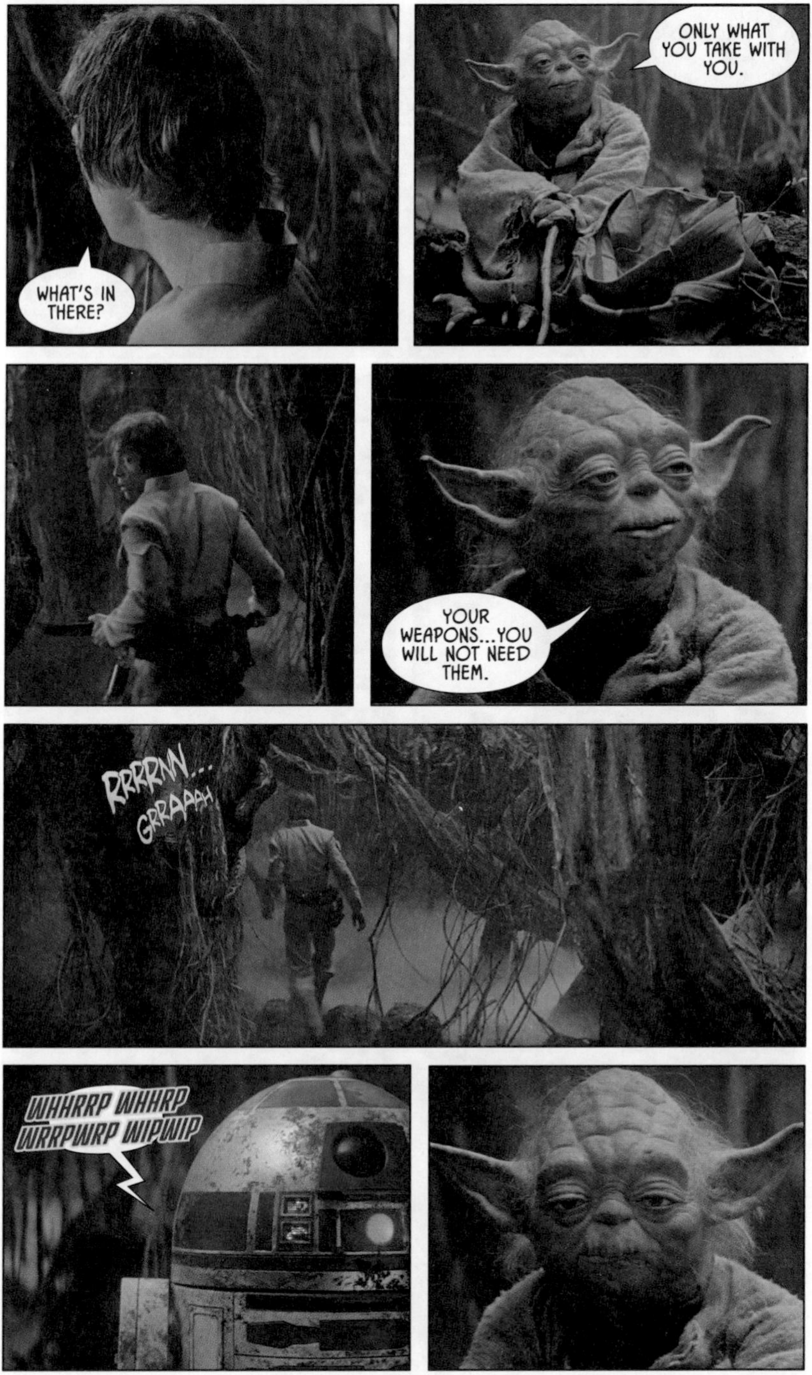
WHAT'S IN THERE?
ONLY WHAT YOU TAKE WITH YOU.
YOUR WEAPONS...YOU WILL NOT NEED THEM.
RRRRNN...
GRRAAAH
WHHRRP WHHRP WRRPWRP WIPWIP

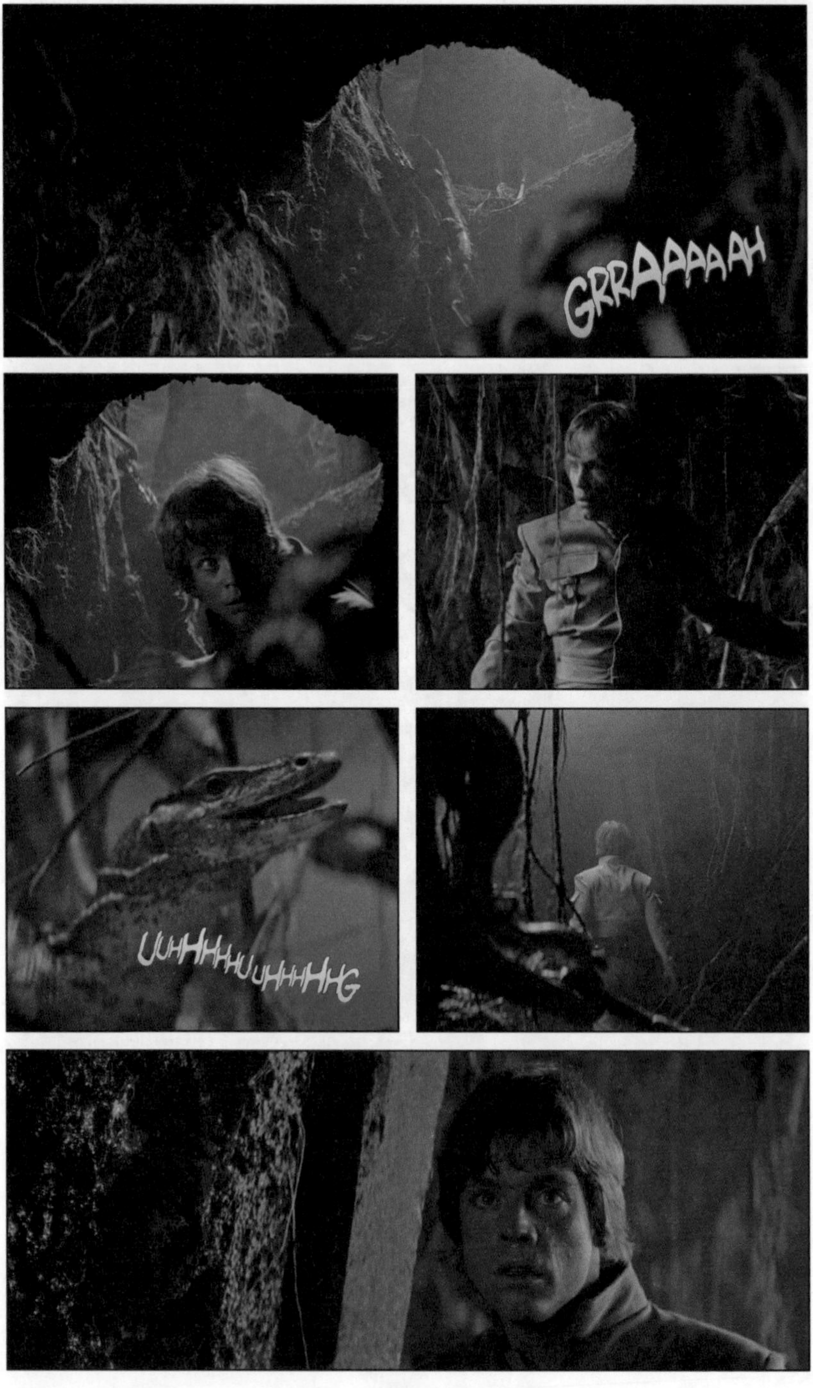
GRRAAAAAH
UUHHHHUUHHHHHG

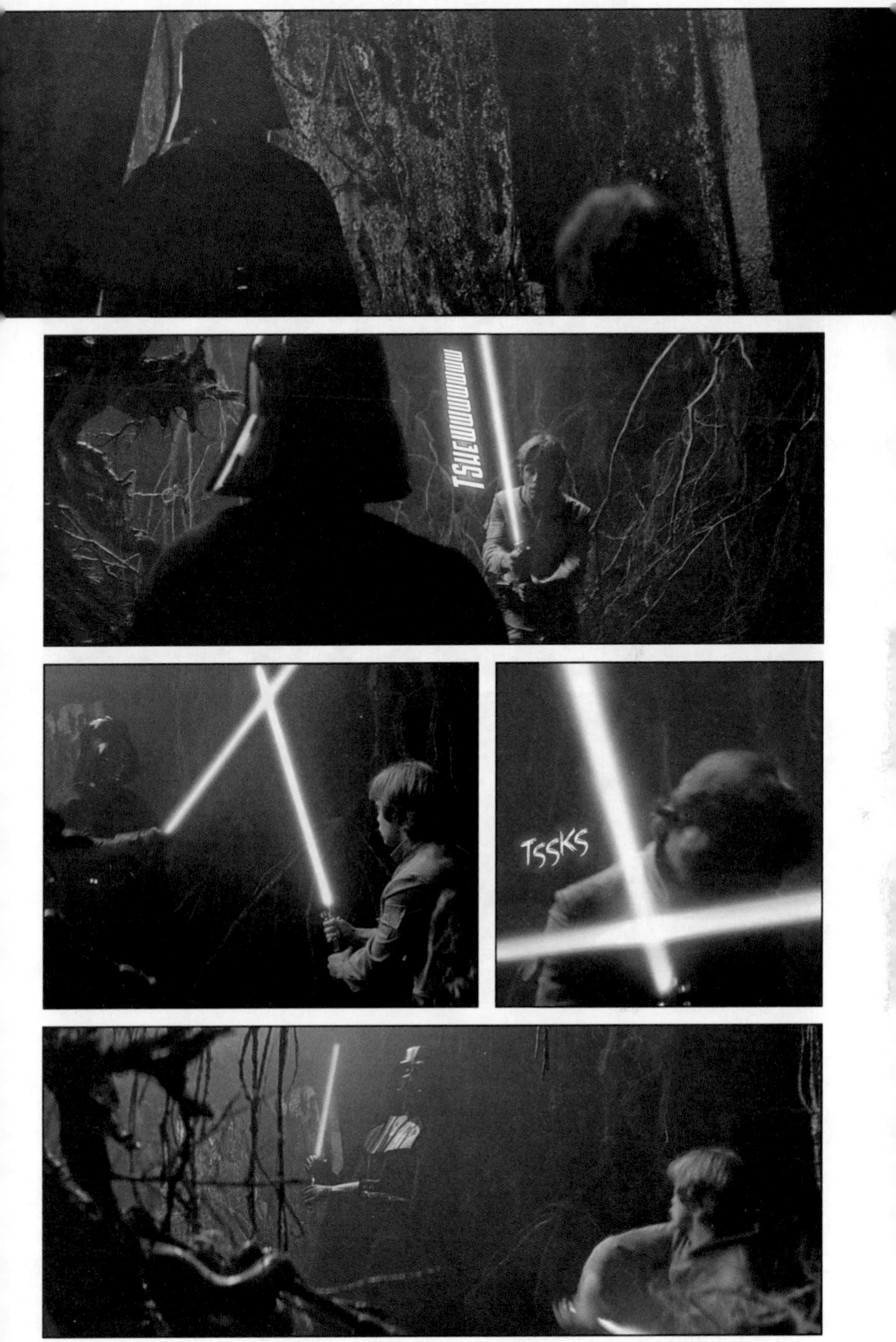
TSHEWWWWWWWW
TSSKS

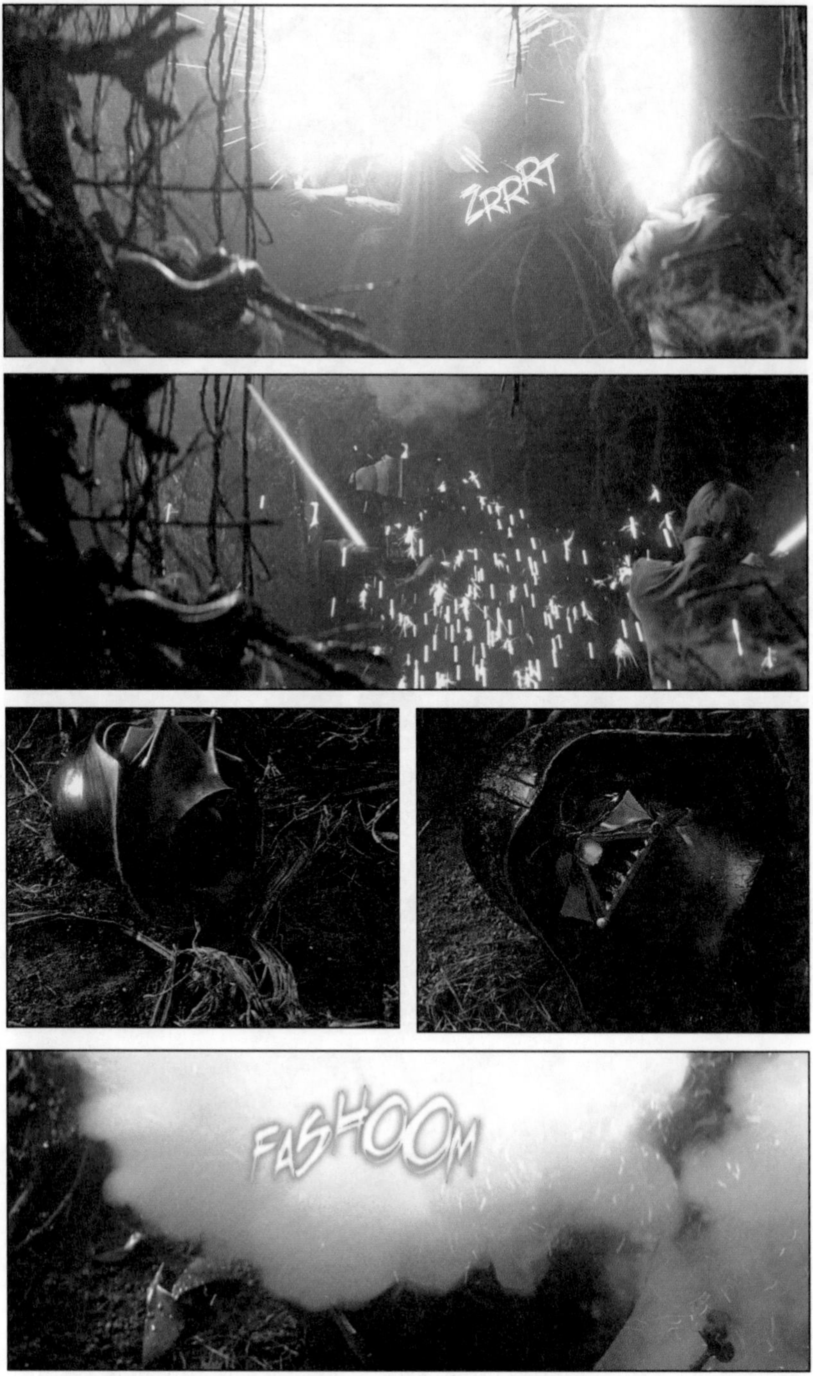
ZRRRT
FASHOOM

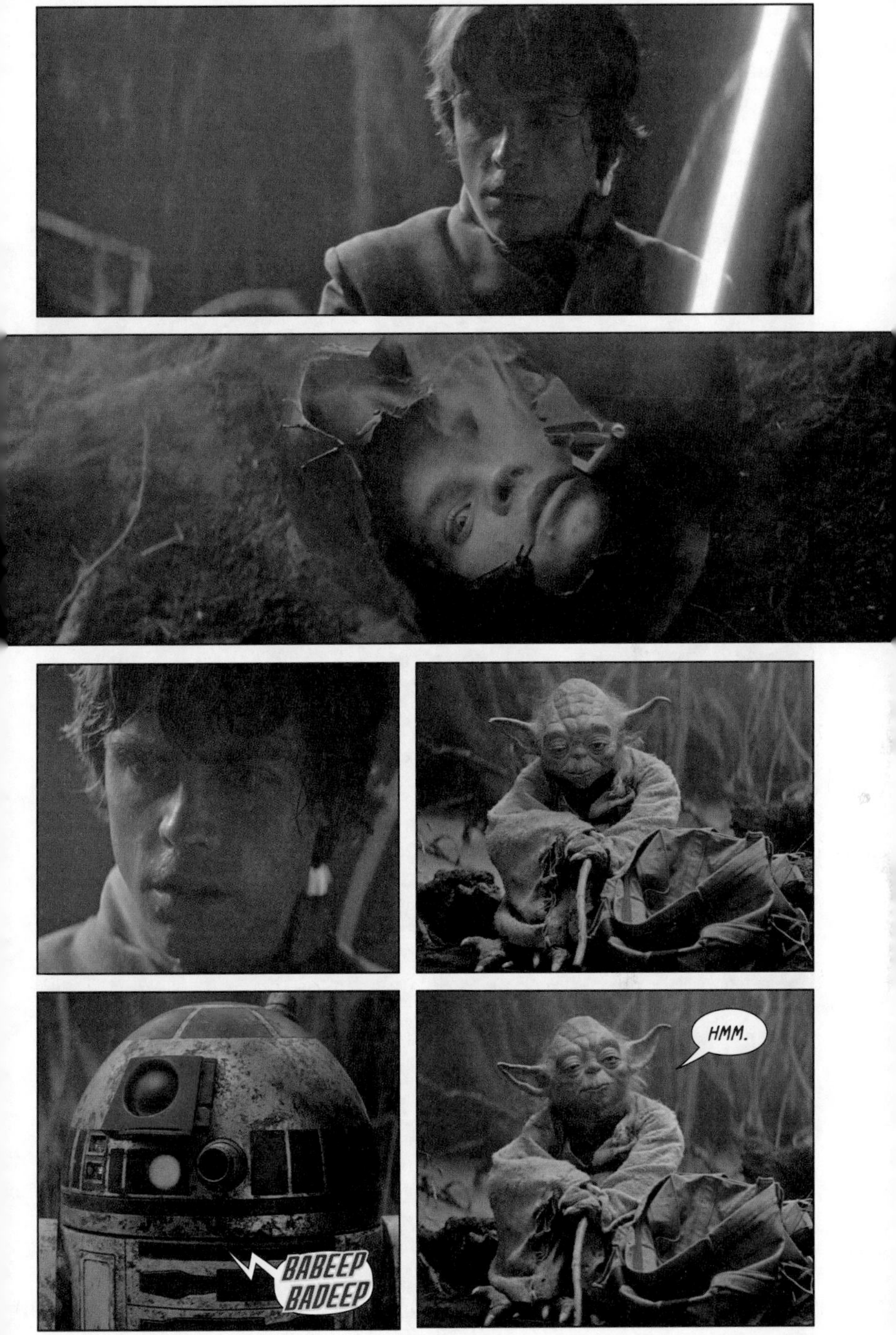
BABEEP BADEEP
HMM.

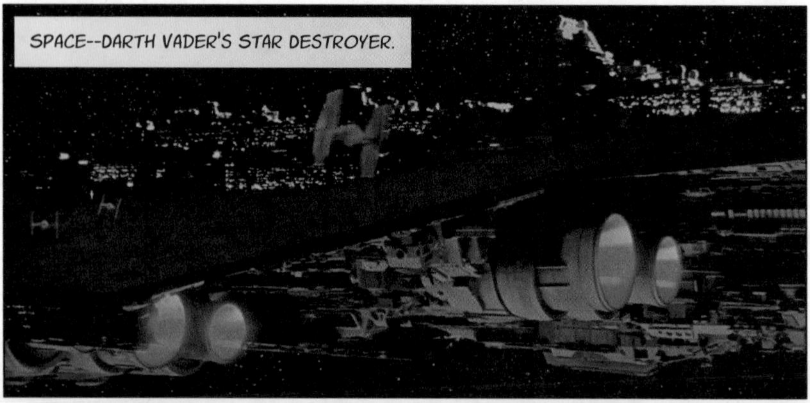
SPACE--DARTH VADER'S STAR DESTROYER.

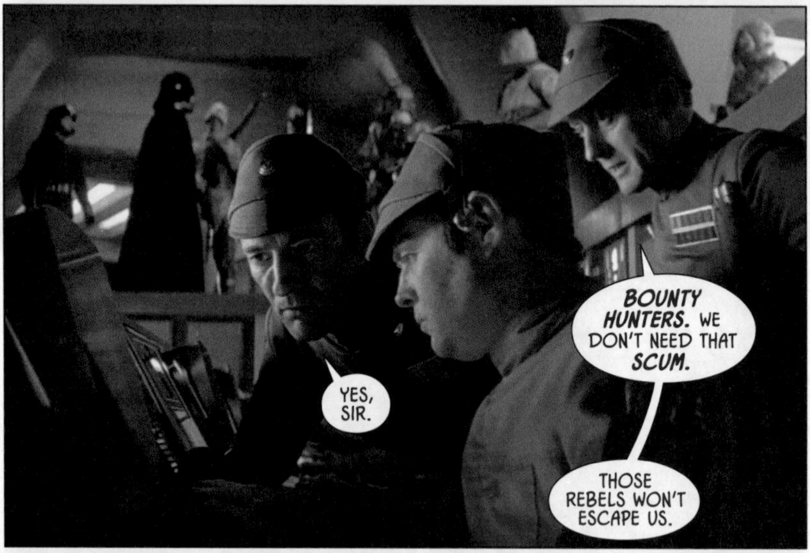
BOUNTY HUNTERS. WE DON'T NEED THAT SCUM.
YES, SIR.
THOSE REBELS WON'T ESCAPE US.

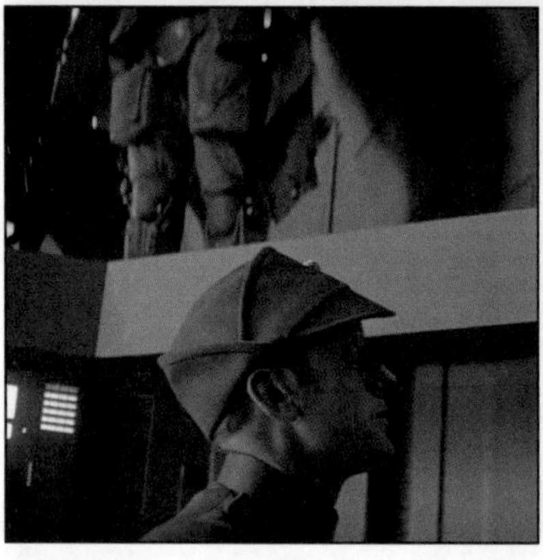

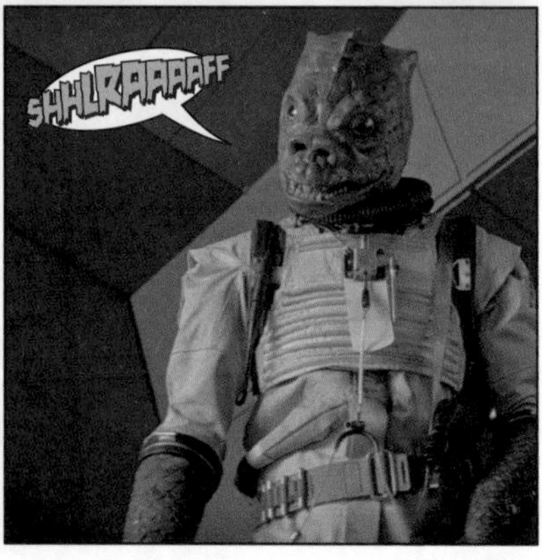
SHHLRAAAAFF

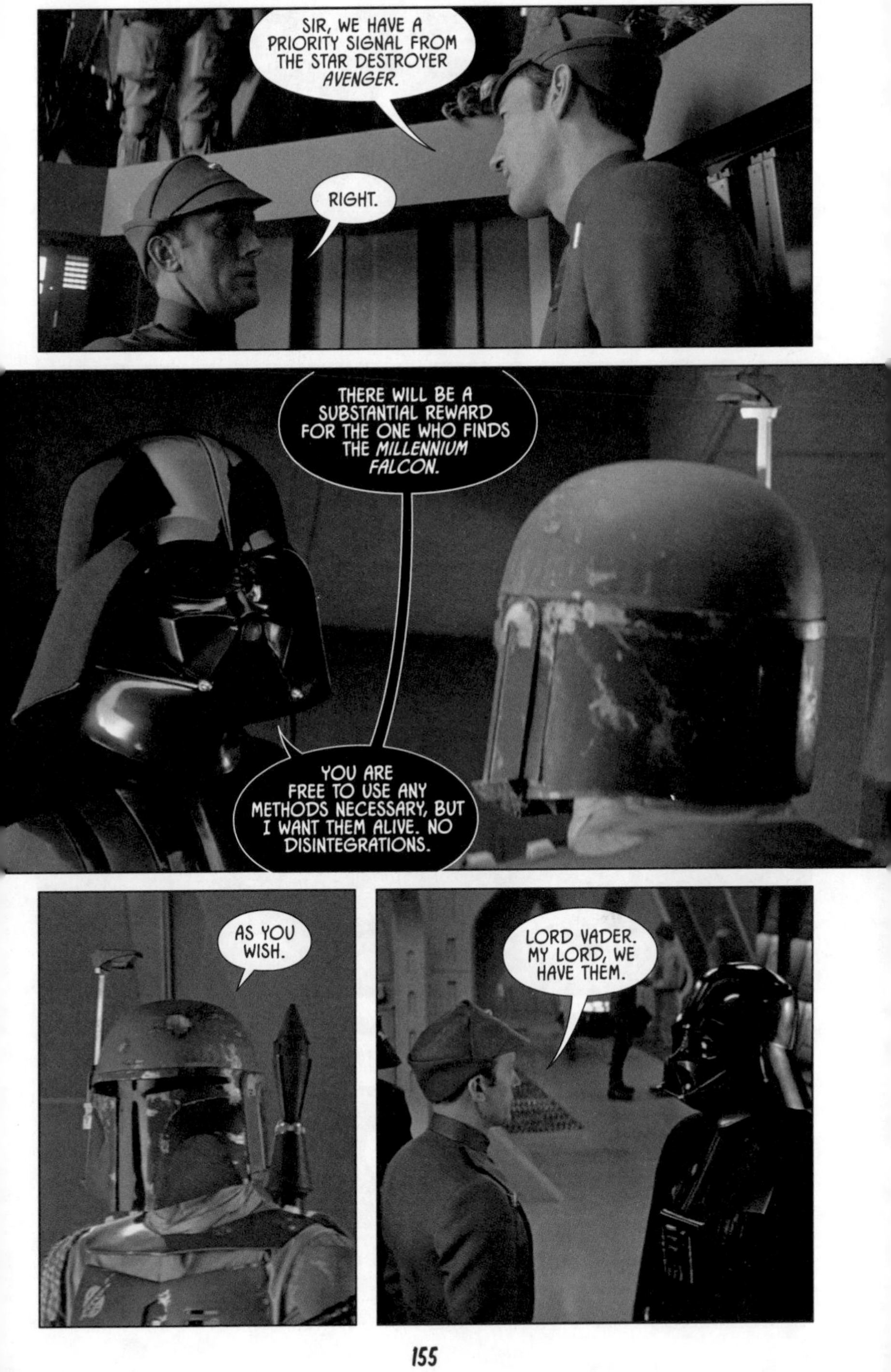
SIR, WE HAVE A PRIORITY SIGNAL FROM THE STAR DESTROYER *AVENGER*.
RIGHT.
THERE WILL BE A SUBSTANTIAL REWARD FOR THE ONE WHO FINDS THE *MILLENNIUM FALCON*.
YOU ARE FREE TO USE ANY METHODS NECESSARY, BUT I WANT THEM ALIVE. NO DISINTEGRATIONS.
AS YOU WISH.
LORD VADER. MY LORD, WE HAVE THEM.

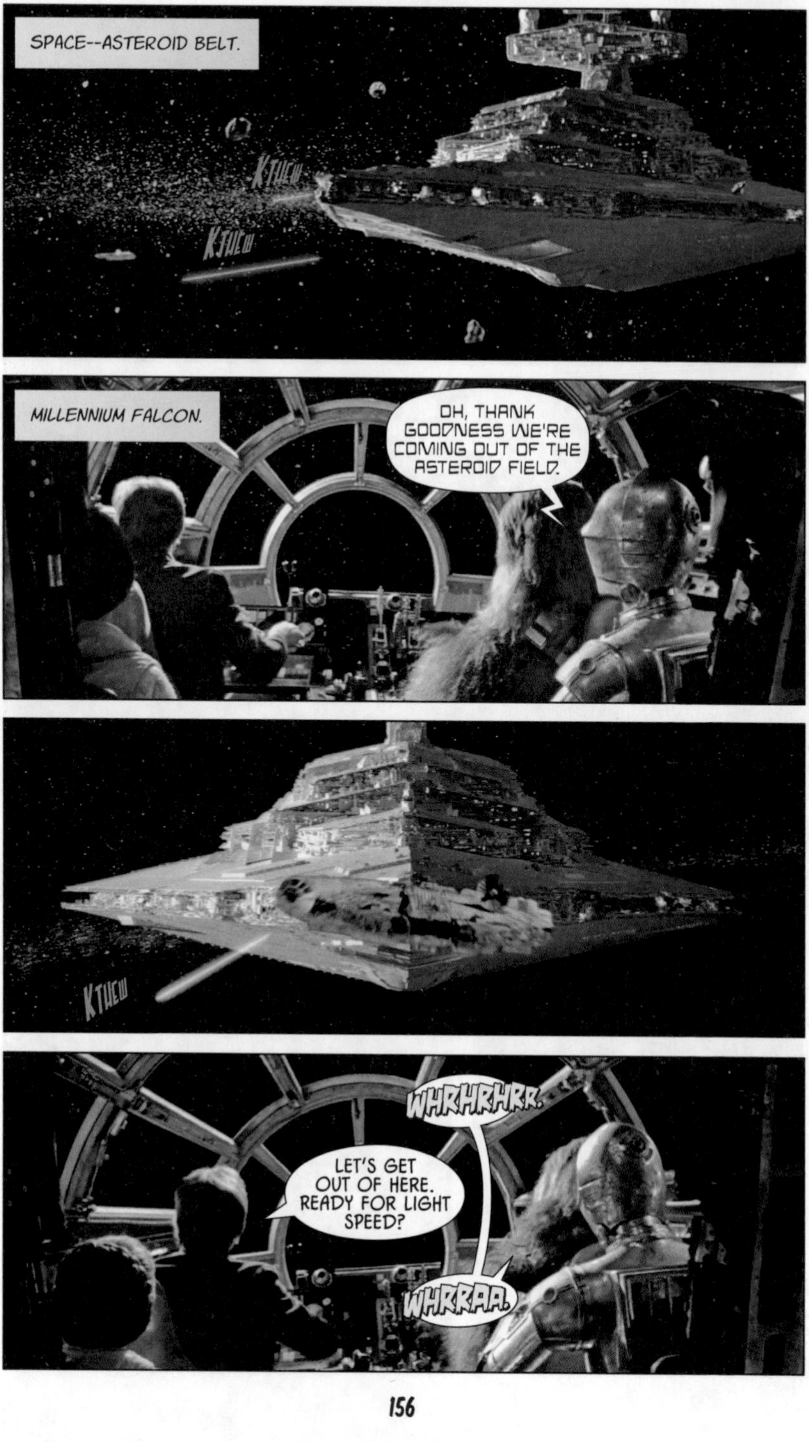
SPACE--ASTEROID BELT.
KTHEW
KTHEW
MILLENNIUM FALCON.
OH, THANK GOODNESS WE'RE COMING OUT OF THE ASTEROID FIELD.
KTHEW
WHRHRHRR.
LET'S GET OUT OF HERE. READY FOR LIGHT SPEED?
WHRRAA.

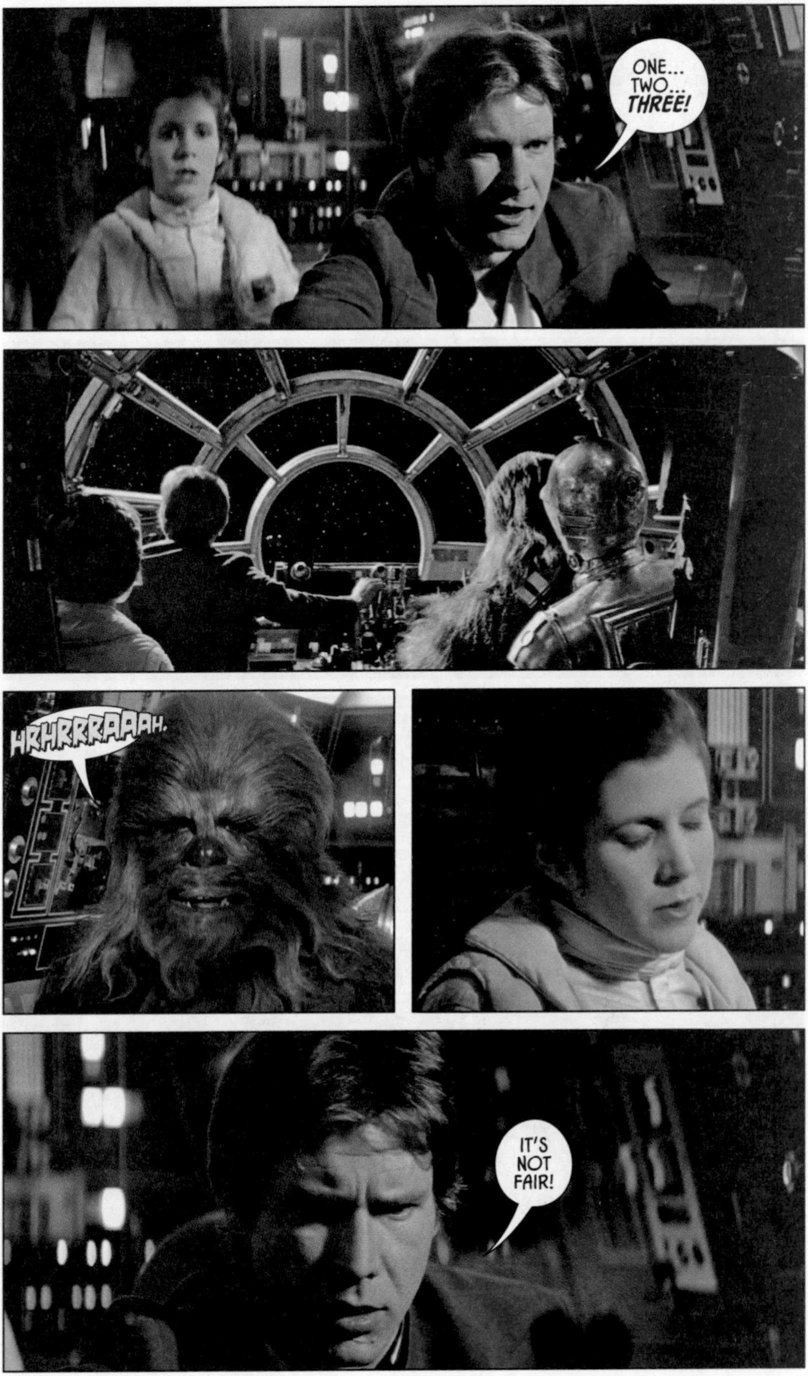
ONE... TWO... THREE!
HRHRRRAAAH.
IT'S NOT FAIR!

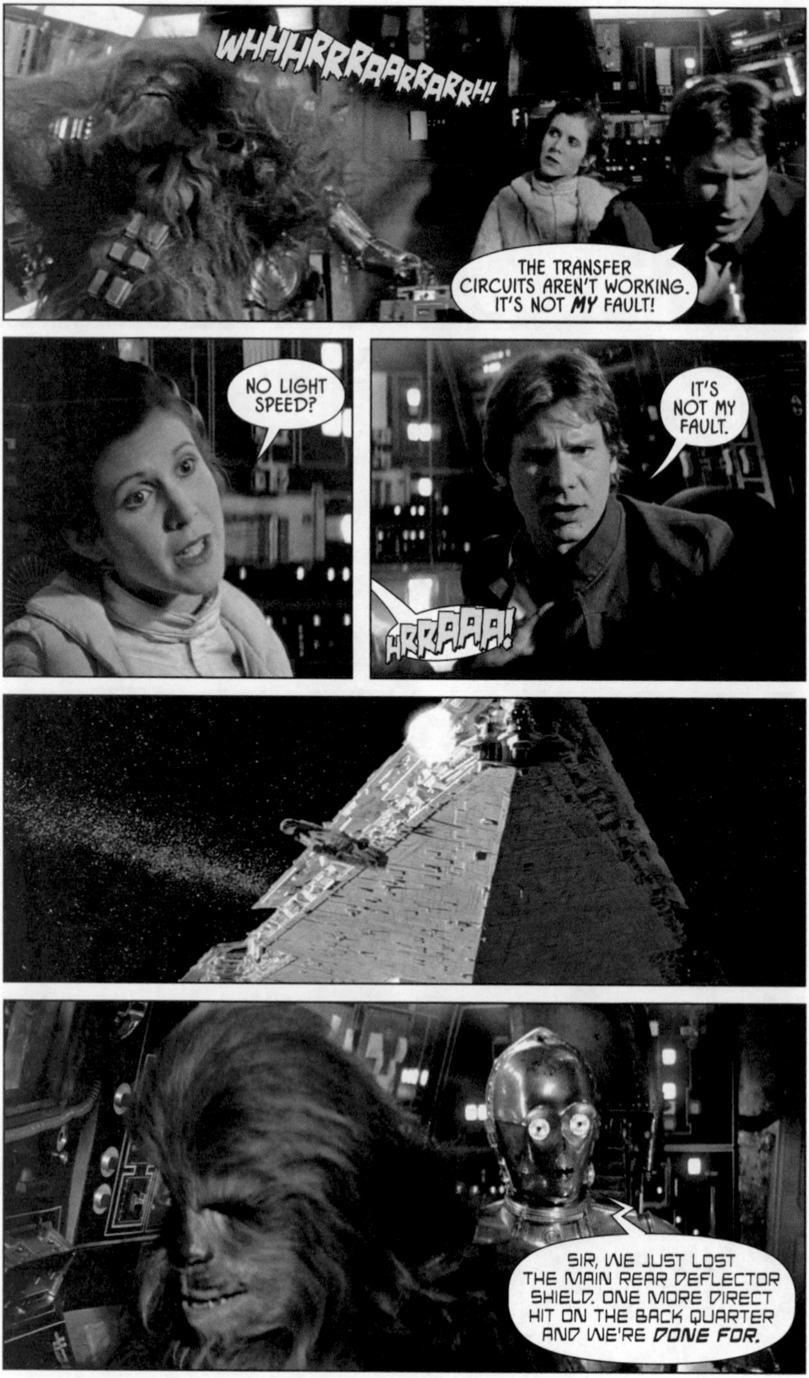
WHHHRRRAARRARRH!
THE TRANSFER CIRCUITS AREN'T WORKING. IT'S NOT *MY* FAULT!
NO LIGHT SPEED?
IT'S NOT MY FAULT.
HRRAAA!
SIR, WE JUST LOST THE MAIN REAR DEFLECTOR SHIELD. ONE MORE DIRECT HIT ON THE BACK QUARTER AND WE'RE *DONE FOR.*

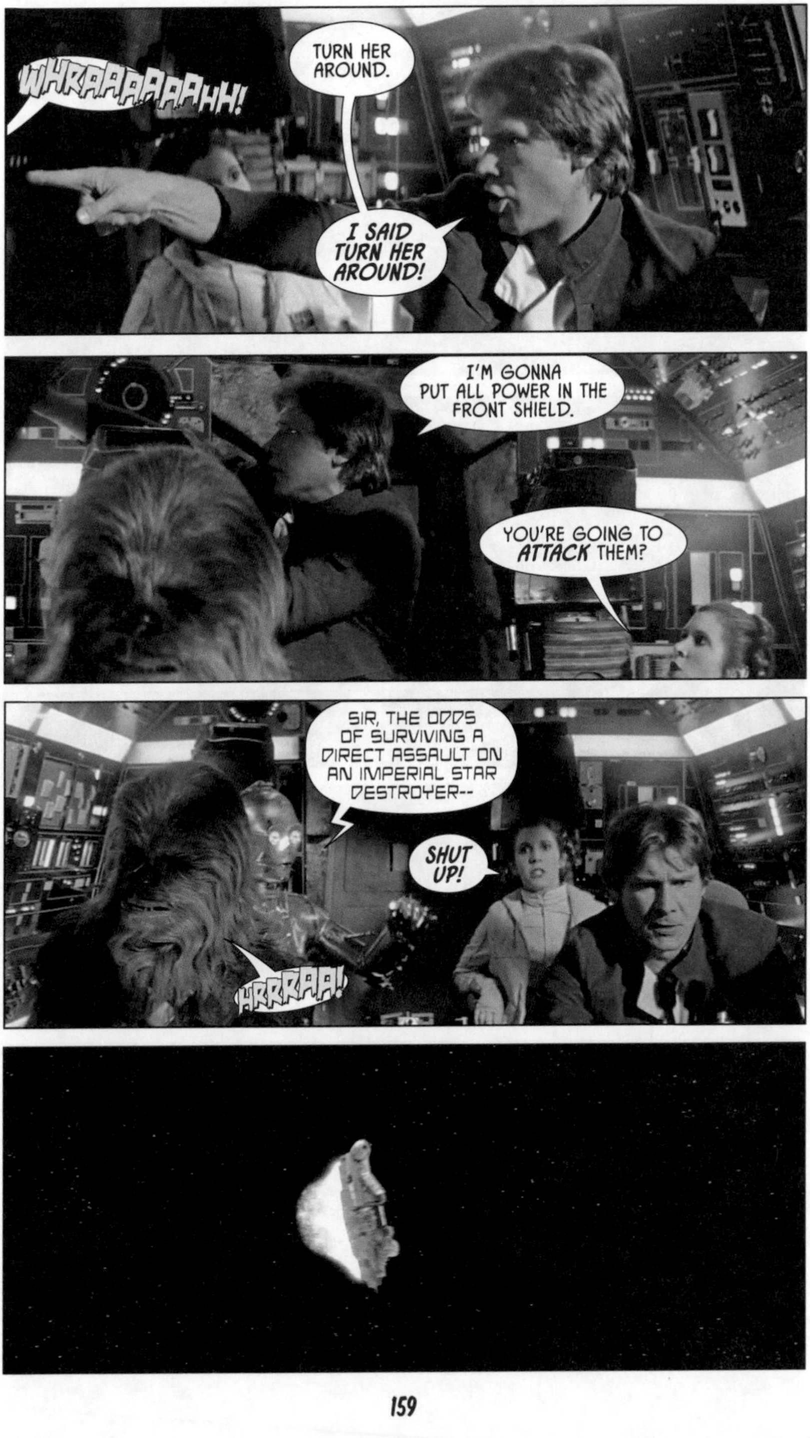
WHRAAAAAAAHH!
TURN HER AROUND.
I SAID TURN HER AROUND!
I'M GONNA PUT ALL POWER IN THE FRONT SHIELD.
YOU'RE GOING TO ATTACK THEM?
SIR, THE ODDS OF SURVIVING A DIRECT ASSAULT ON AN IMPERIAL STAR DESTROYER--
SHUT UP!
HRRRAA!

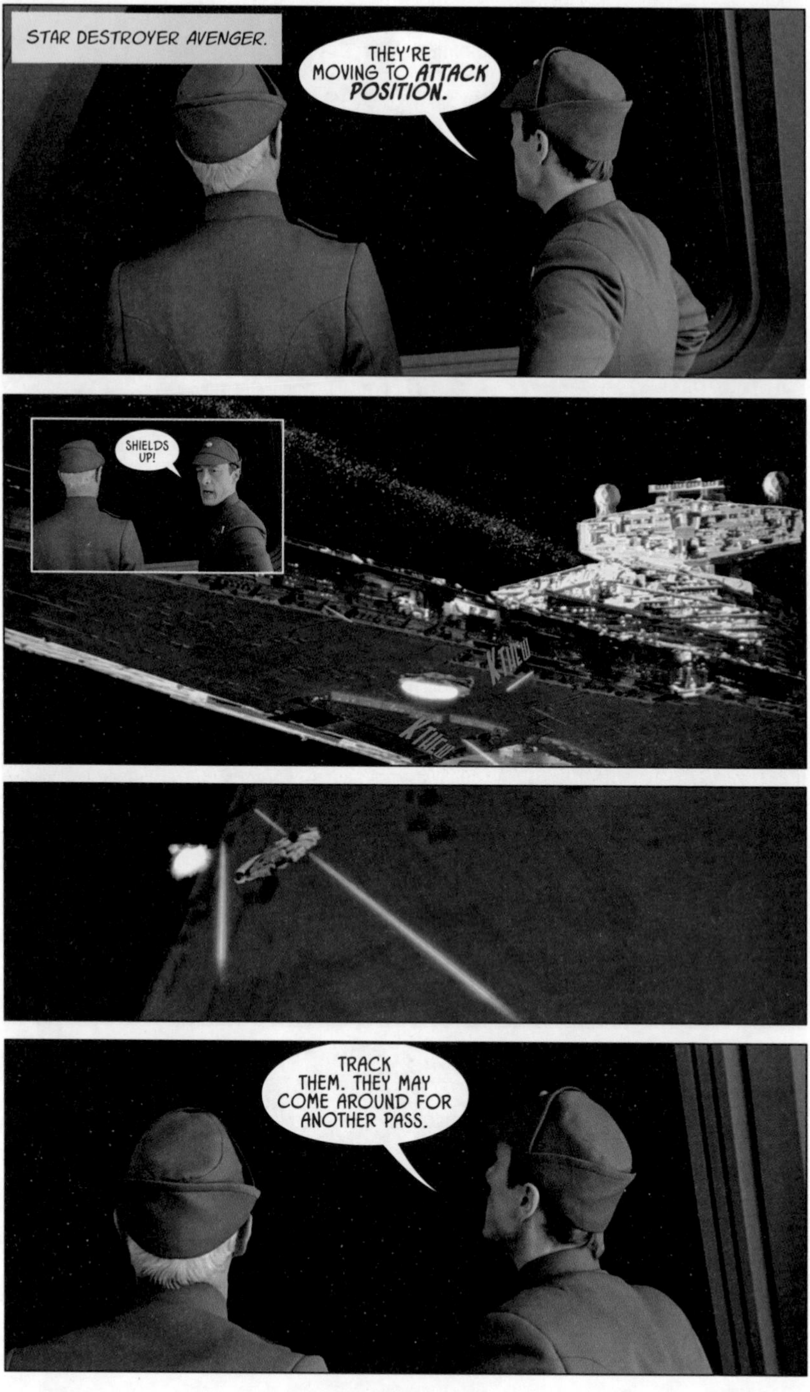
STAR DESTROYER AVENGER.
THEY'RE MOVING TO ATTACK POSITION.
SHIELDS UP!
KTHEW
KTHEW
TRACK THEM. THEY MAY COME AROUND FOR ANOTHER PASS.

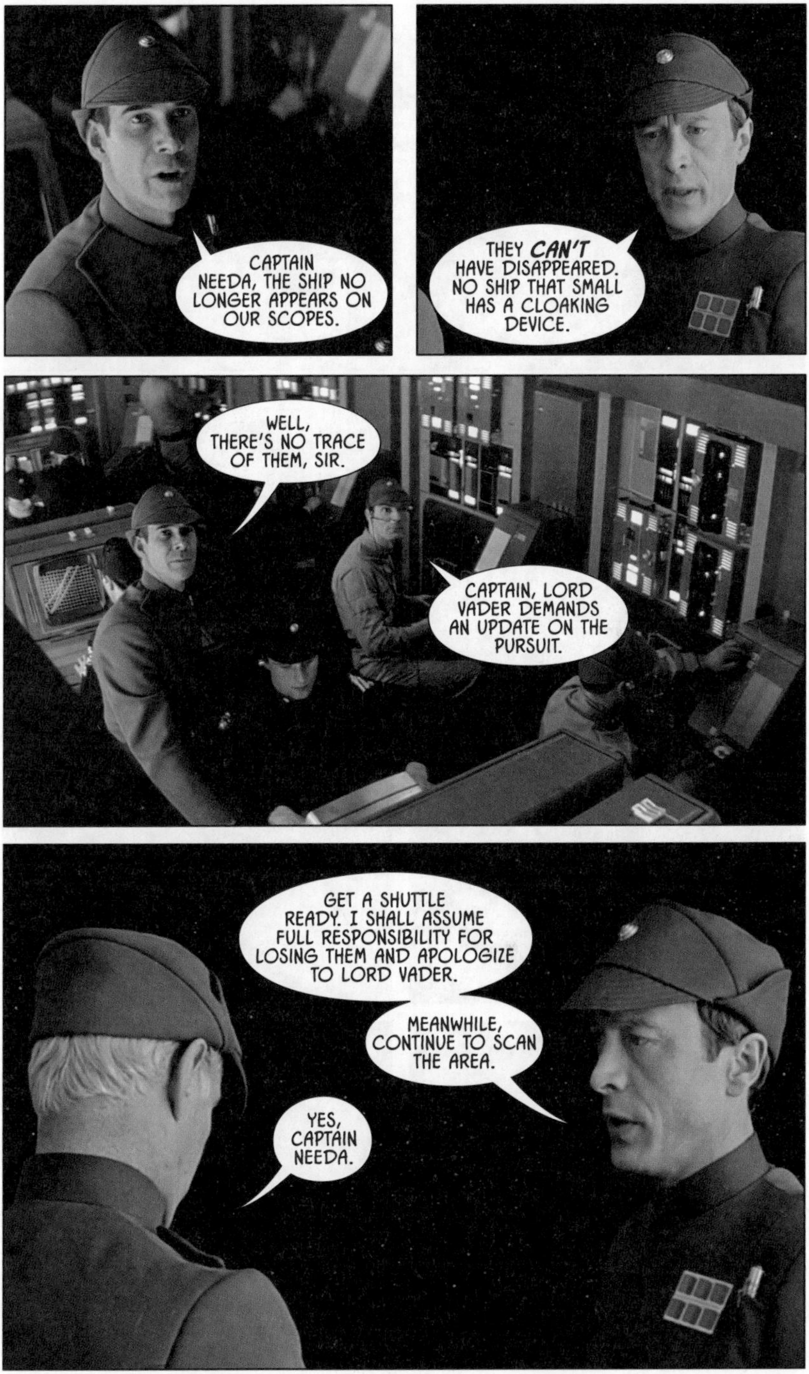
CAPTAIN NEEDA, THE SHIP NO LONGER APPEARS ON OUR SCOPES.
THEY CAN'T HAVE DISAPPEARED. NO SHIP THAT SMALL HAS A CLOAKING DEVICE.
WELL, THERE'S NO TRACE OF THEM, SIR.
CAPTAIN, LORD VADER DEMANDS AN UPDATE ON THE PURSUIT.
GET A SHUTTLE READY. I SHALL ASSUME FULL RESPONSIBILITY FOR LOSING THEM AND APOLOGIZE TO LORD VADER.
MEANWHILE, CONTINUE TO SCAN THE AREA.
YES, CAPTAIN NEEDA.

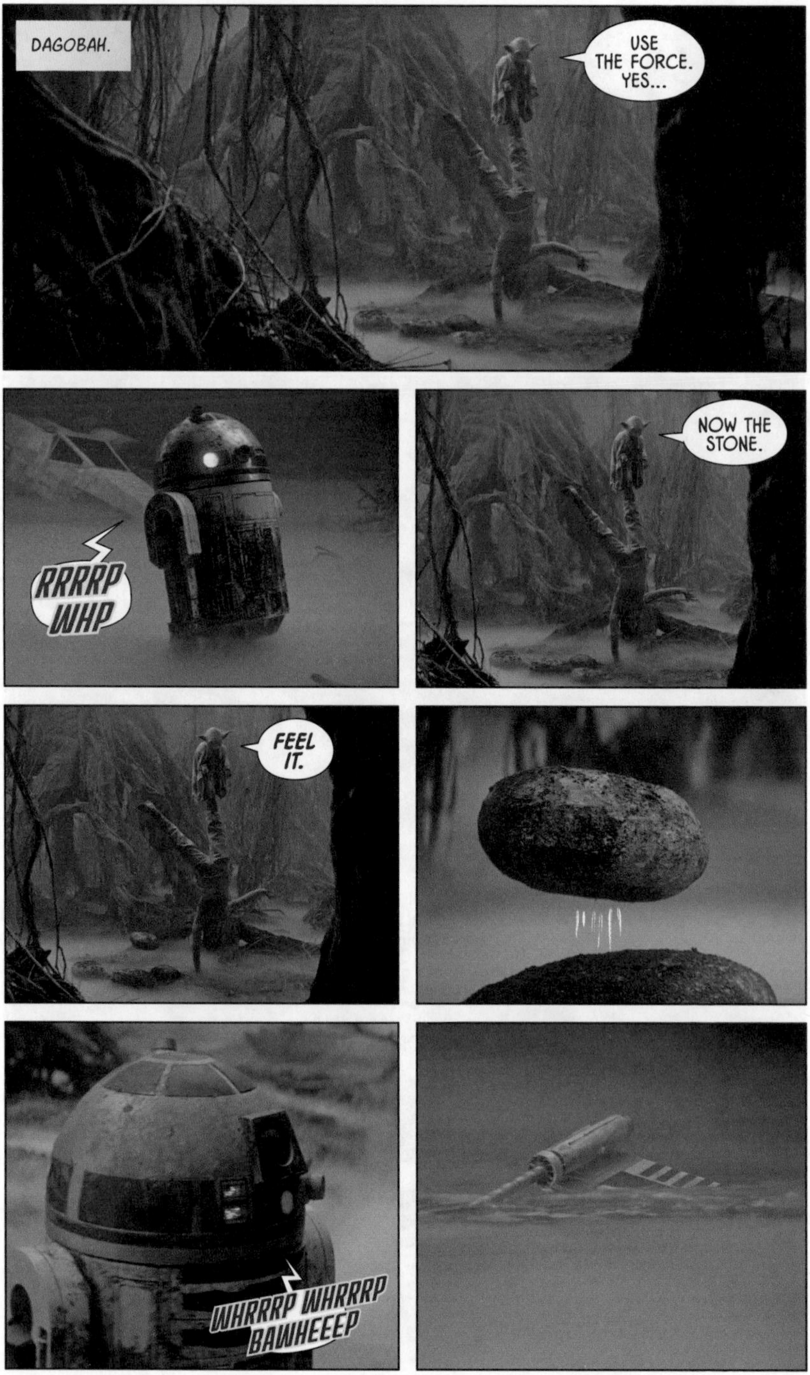
DAGOBAH.
USE THE FORCE. YES...
RRRRP WHP
NOW THE STONE.
FEEL IT.
WHRRRP WHRRRP BAWHEEEP

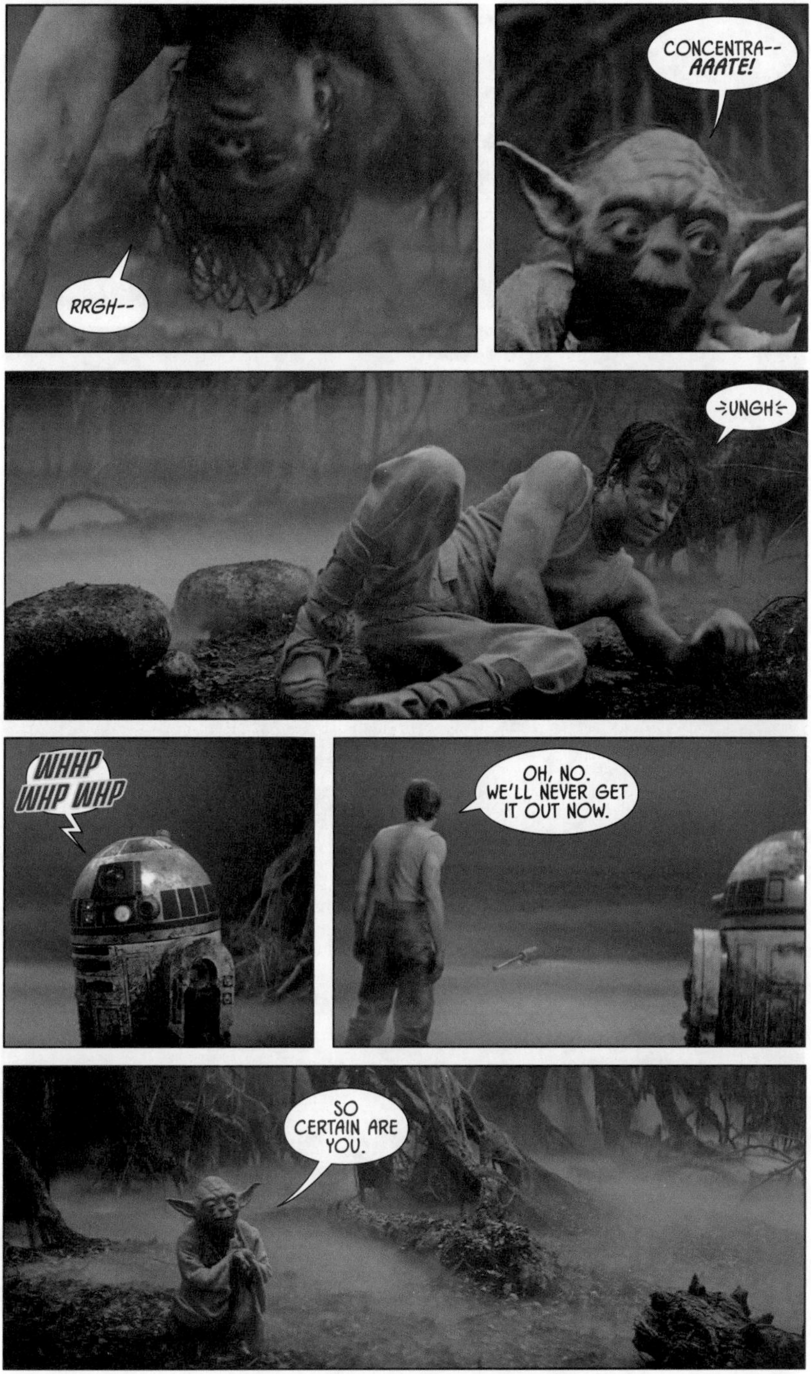
RRGH--
CONCENTRA-- AAATE!
UNGH
WHHP WHP WHP
OH, NO. WE'LL NEVER GET IT OUT NOW.
SO CERTAIN ARE YOU.

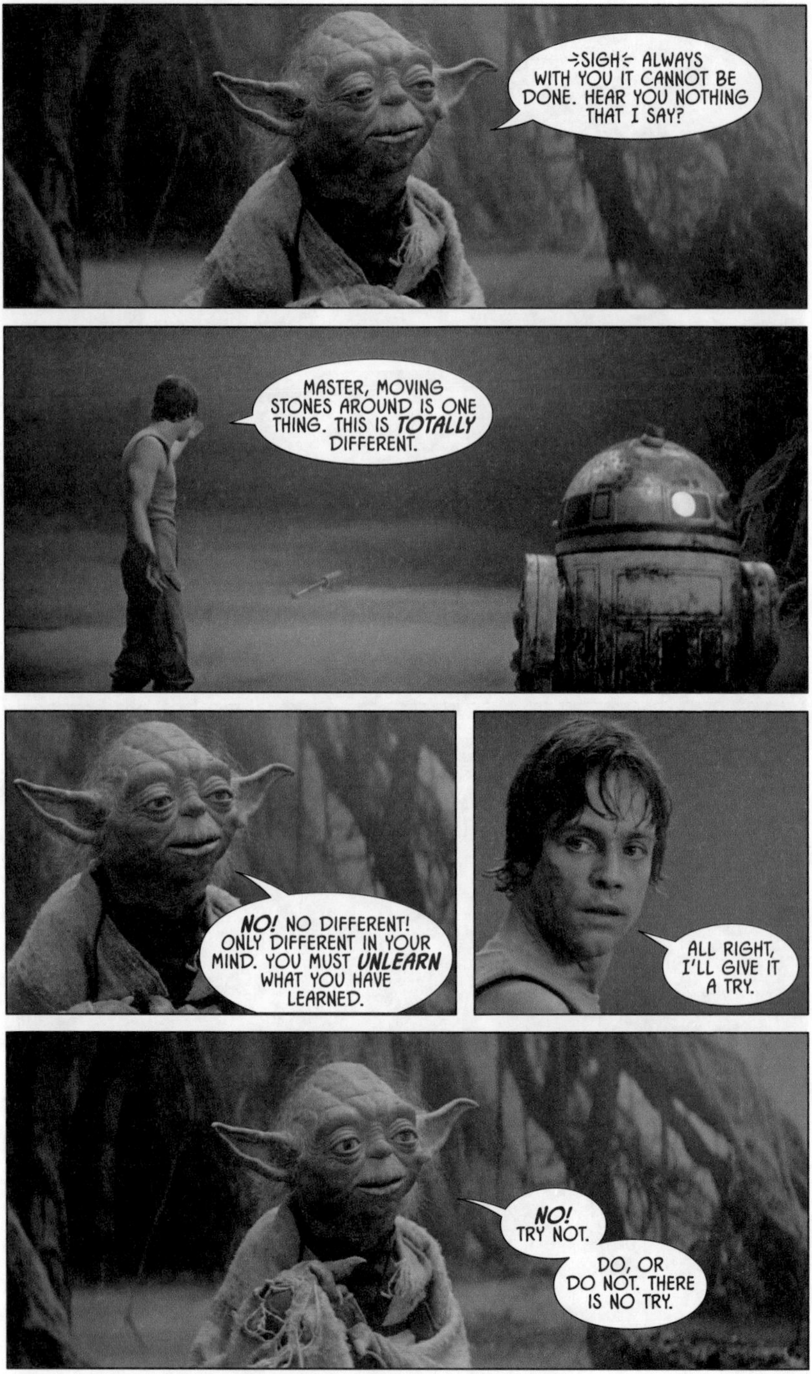
⇒SIGH⇐ ALWAYS WITH YOU IT CANNOT BE DONE. HEAR YOU NOTHING THAT I SAY?
MASTER, MOVING STONES AROUND IS ONE THING. THIS IS TOTALLY DIFFERENT.
NO! NO DIFFERENT! ONLY DIFFERENT IN YOUR MIND. YOU MUST UNLEARN WHAT YOU HAVE LEARNED.
ALL RIGHT, I'LL GIVE IT A TRY.
NO! TRY NOT.
DO, OR DO NOT. THERE IS NO TRY.

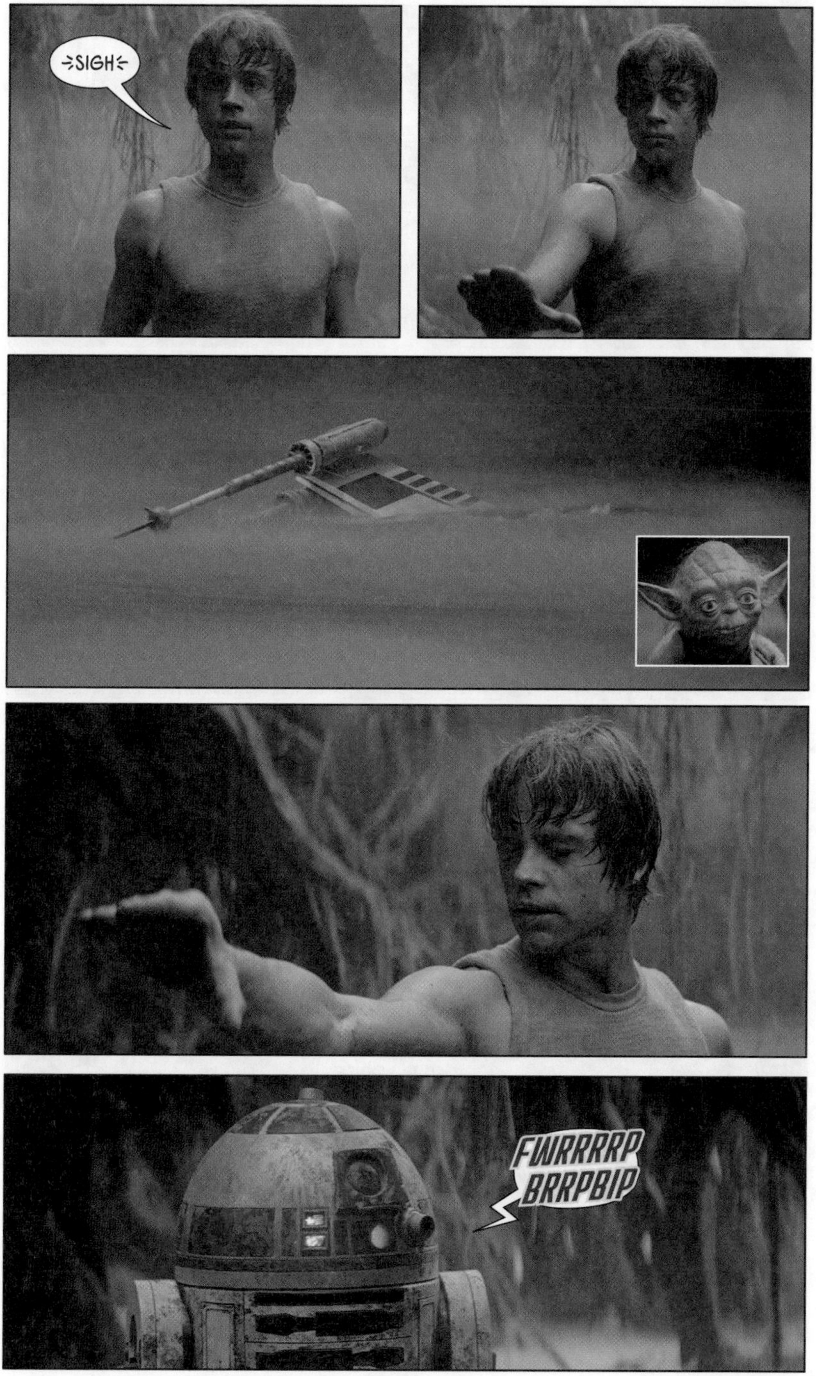

⋟SIGH⋞
FWRRRRP BRRPBIP

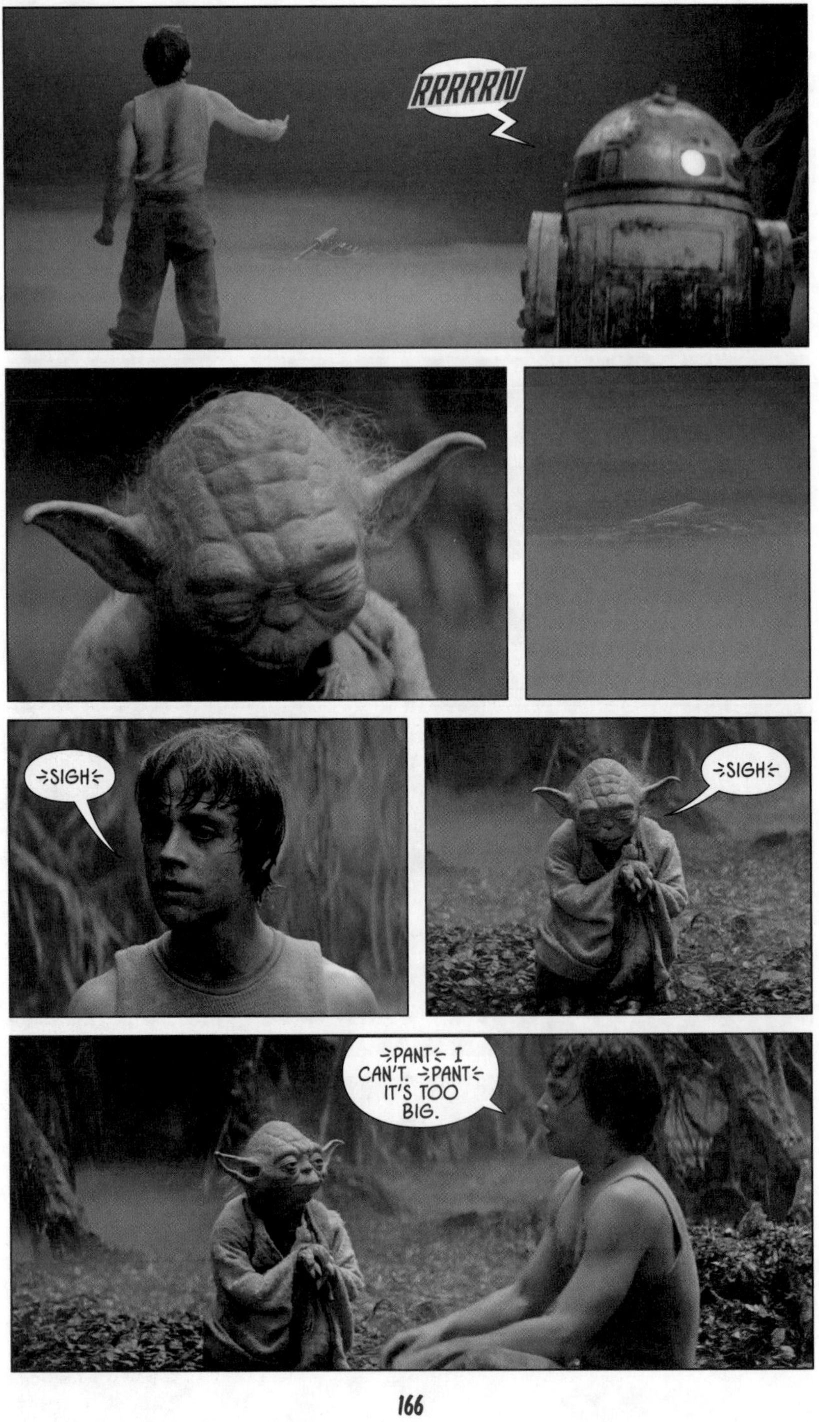
RRRRRN
≑SIGH≑
≑SIGH≑
≑PANT≑ I CAN'T. ≑PANT≑ IT'S TOO BIG.

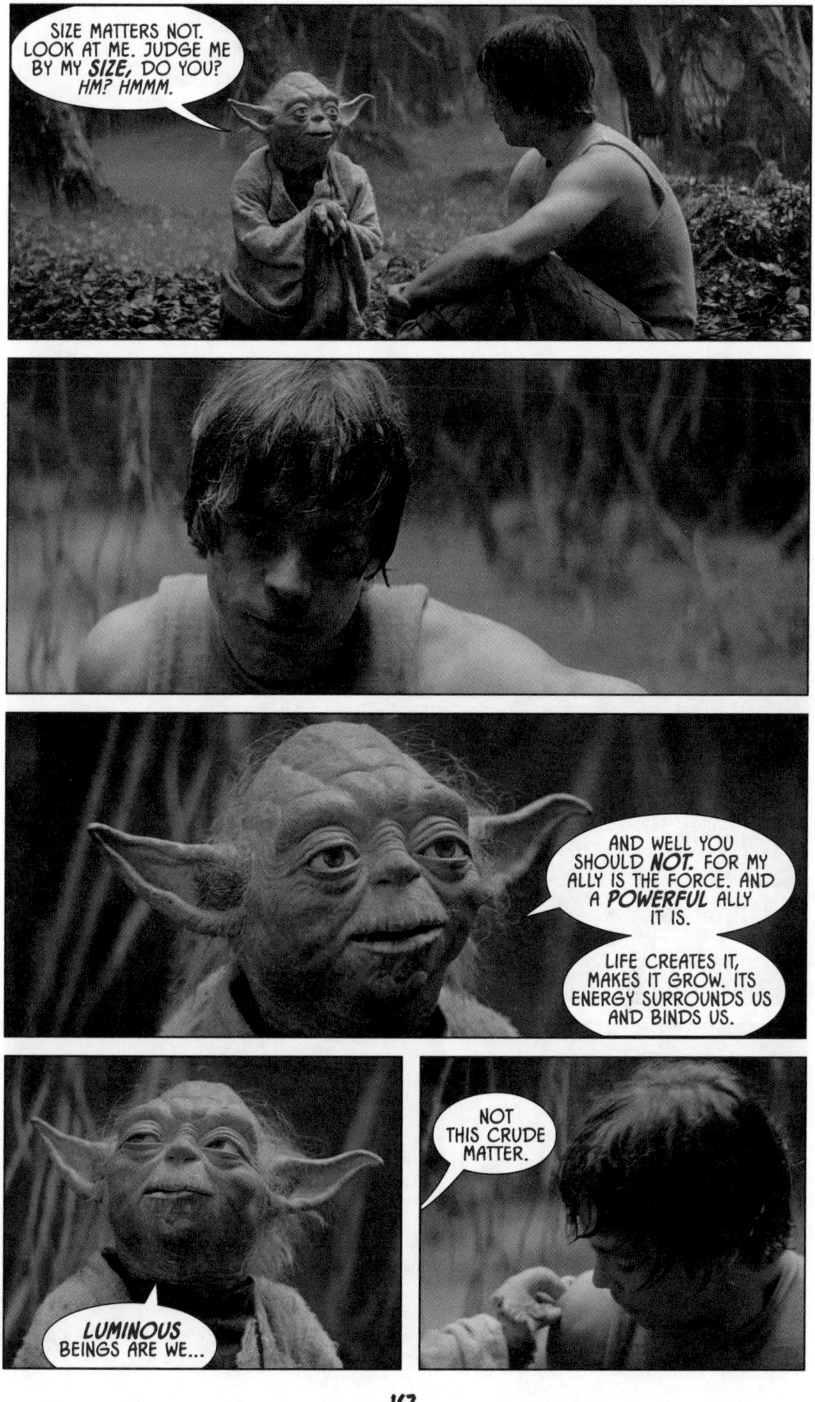
SIZE MATTERS NOT. LOOK AT ME. JUDGE ME BY MY SIZE, DO YOU? HM? HMMM.
AND WELL YOU SHOULD NOT. FOR MY ALLY IS THE FORCE. AND A POWERFUL ALLY IT IS.
LIFE CREATES IT, MAKES IT GROW. ITS ENERGY SURROUNDS US AND BINDS US.
LUMINOUS BEINGS ARE WE...
NOT THIS CRUDE MATTER.

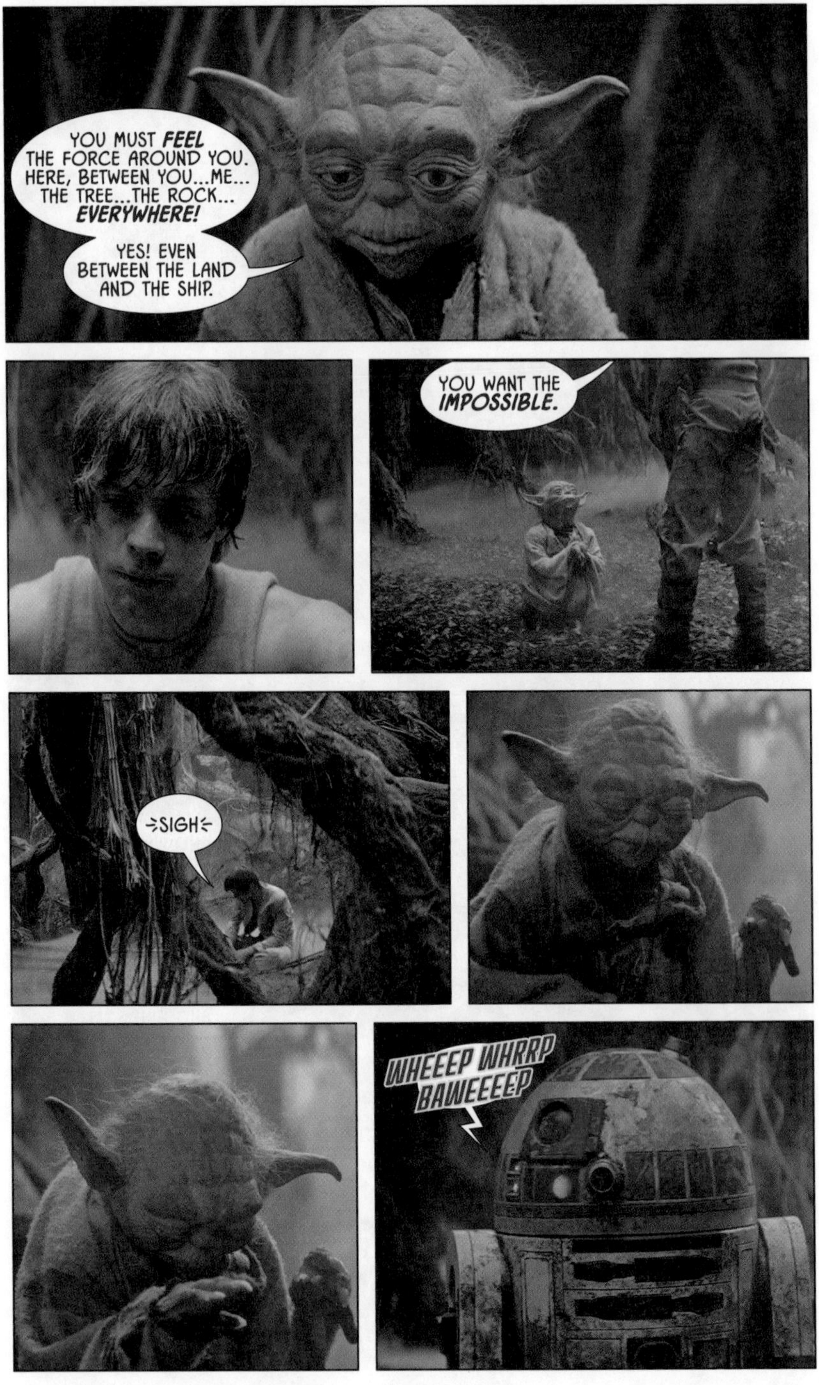
YOU MUST FEEL THE FORCE AROUND YOU. HERE, BETWEEN YOU...ME... THE TREE...THE ROCK... EVERYWHERE!
YES! EVEN BETWEEN THE LAND AND THE SHIP.
YOU WANT THE IMPOSSIBLE.
SIGH
WHEEEP WHRRP BAWEEEEP

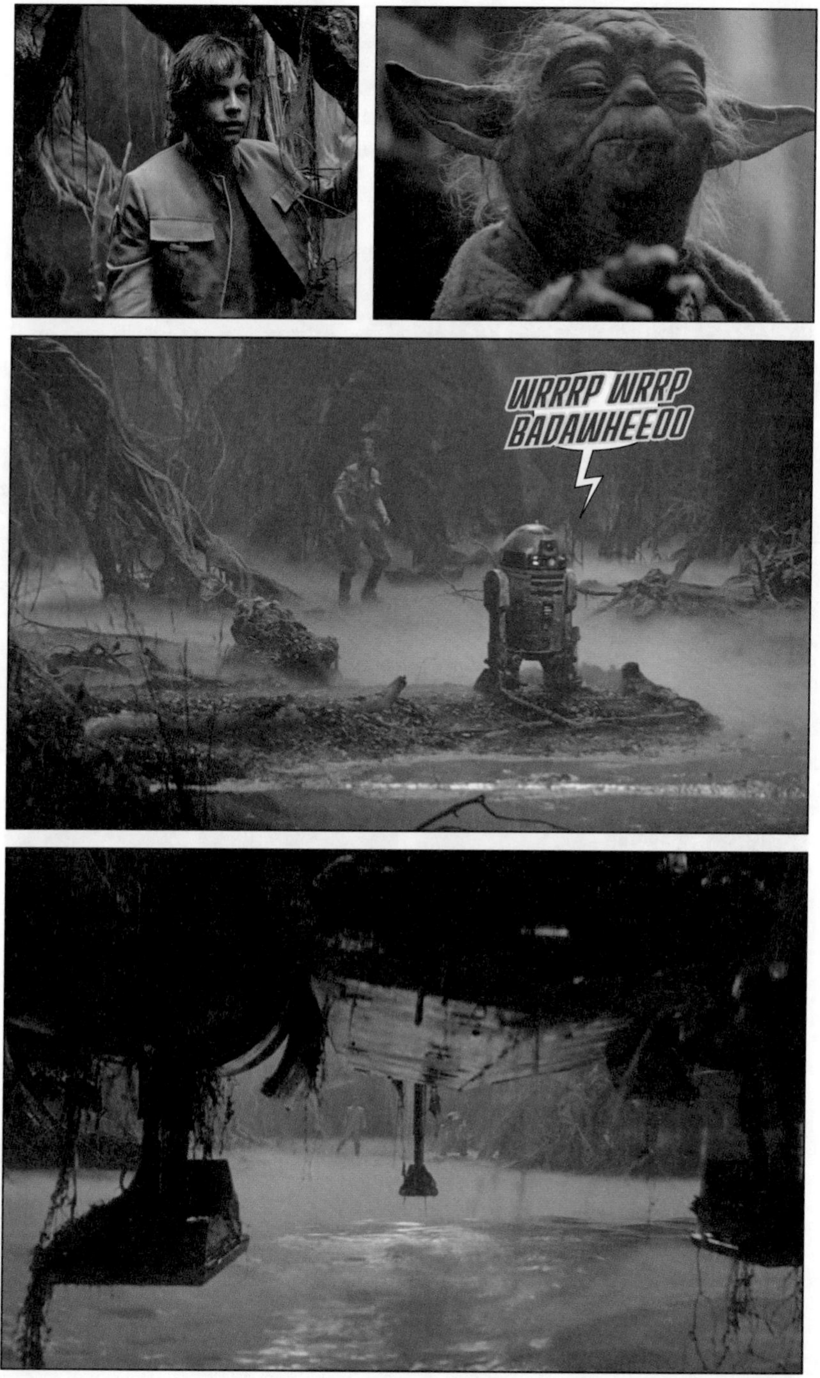
WRRRP WRRP BADAWHEEDO

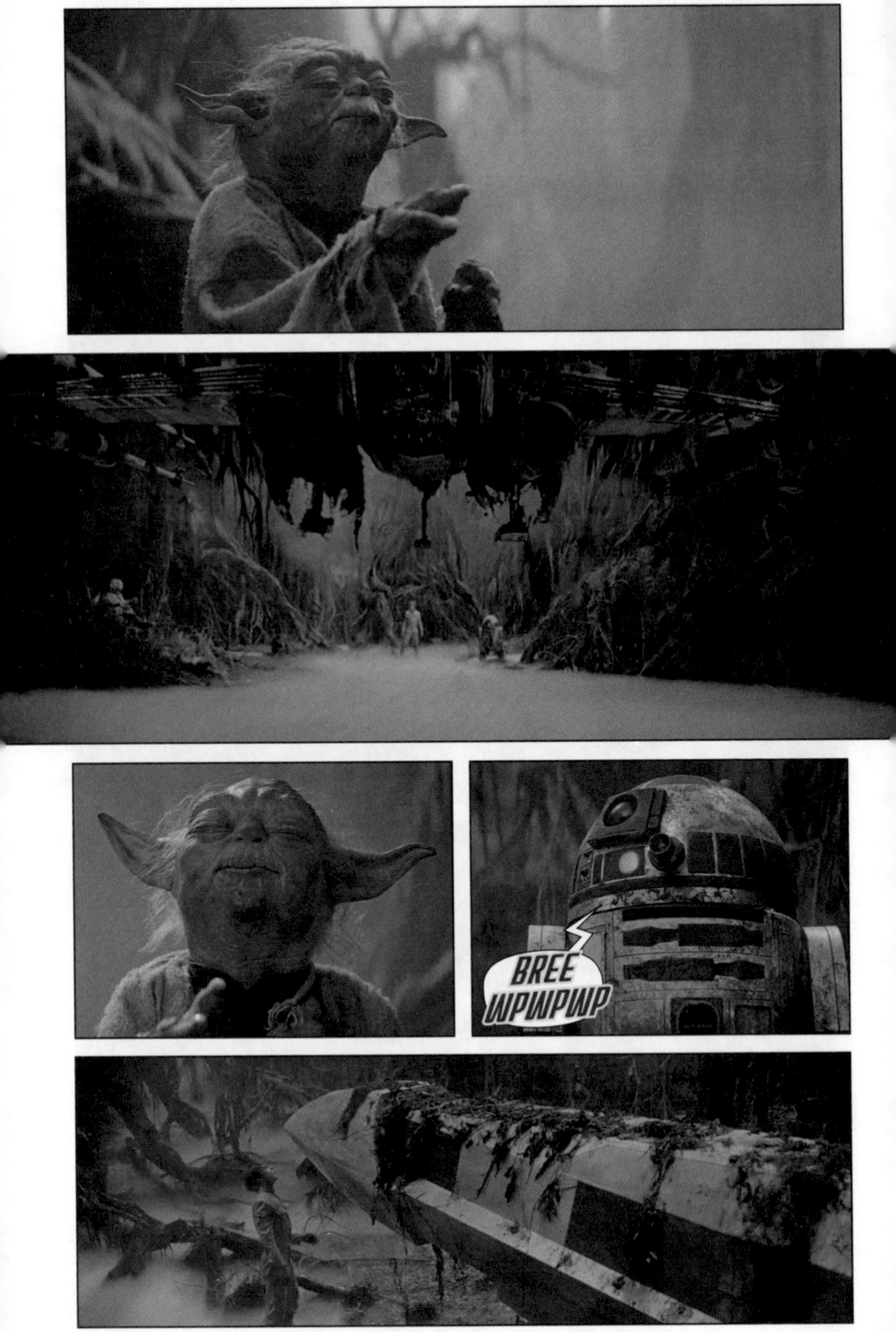
BREE WPWPWP

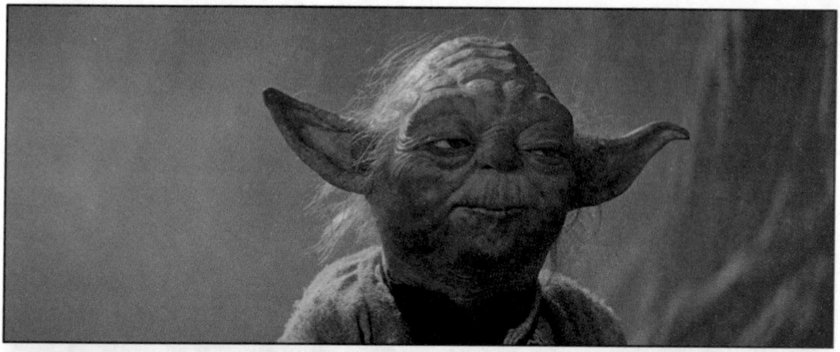

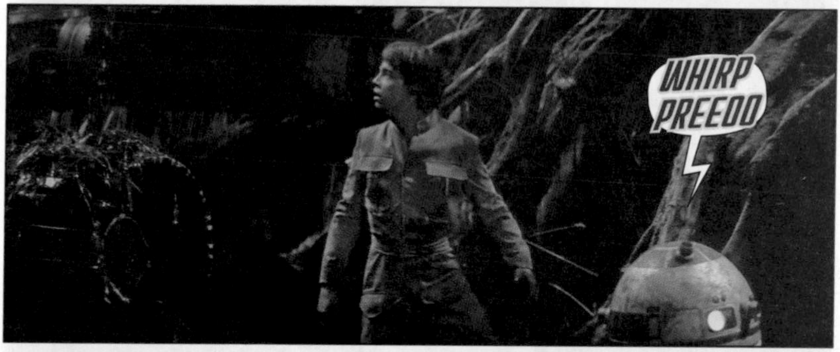
WHIRP PREEDO

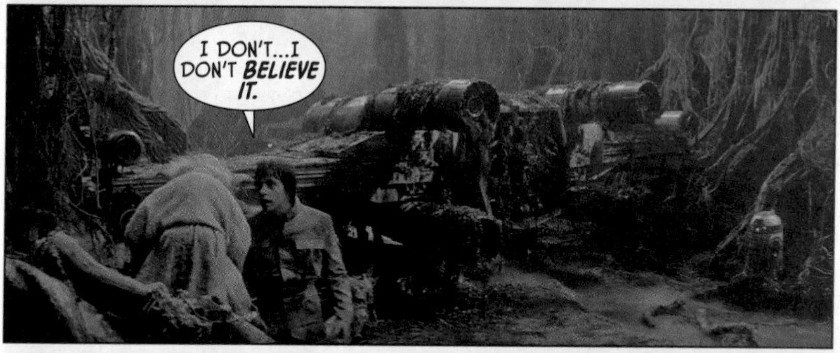
I DON'T...I DON'T BELIEVE IT.

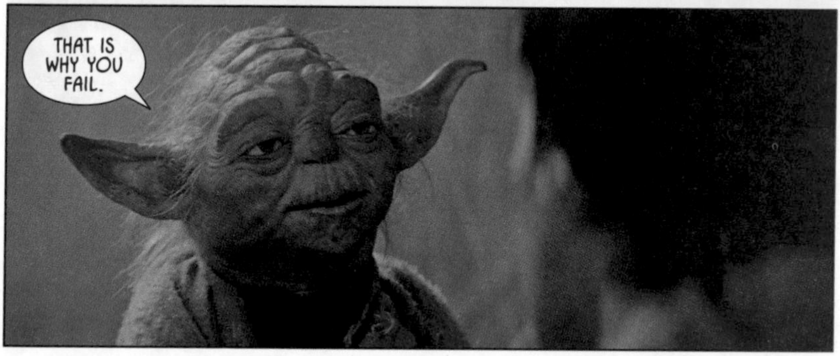
THAT IS WHY YOU FAIL.

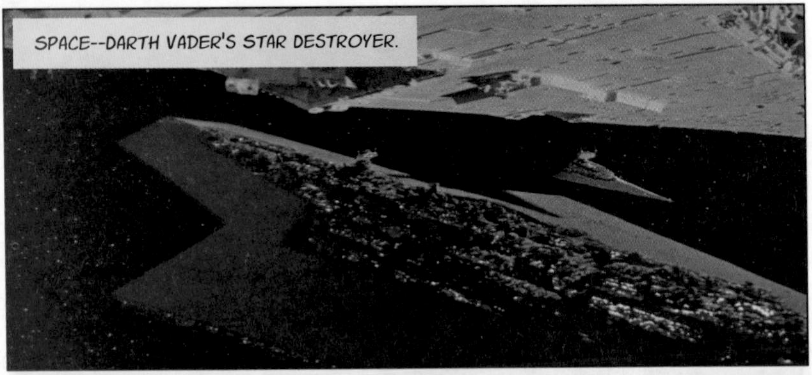
SPACE--DARTH VADER'S STAR DESTROYER.

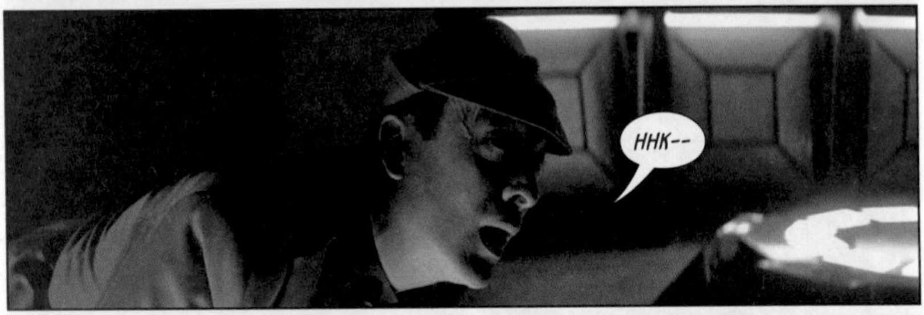
HHK--

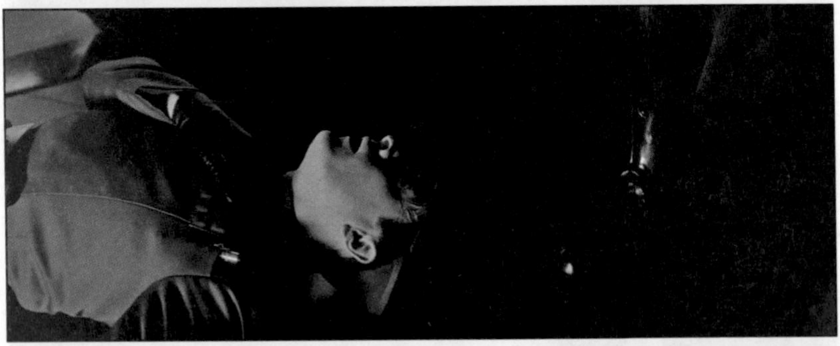

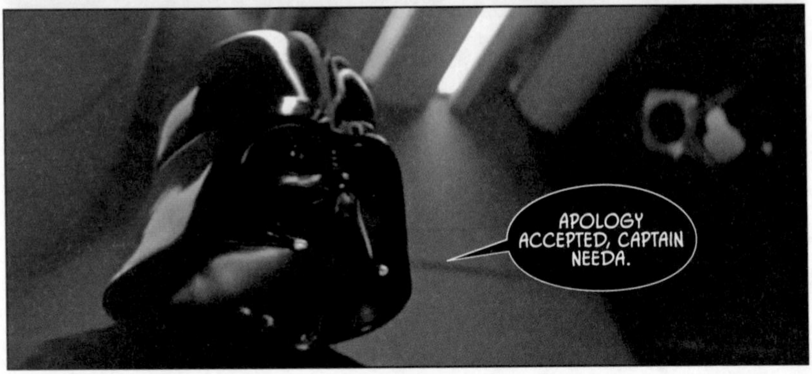
APOLOGY ACCEPTED, CAPTAIN NEEDA.

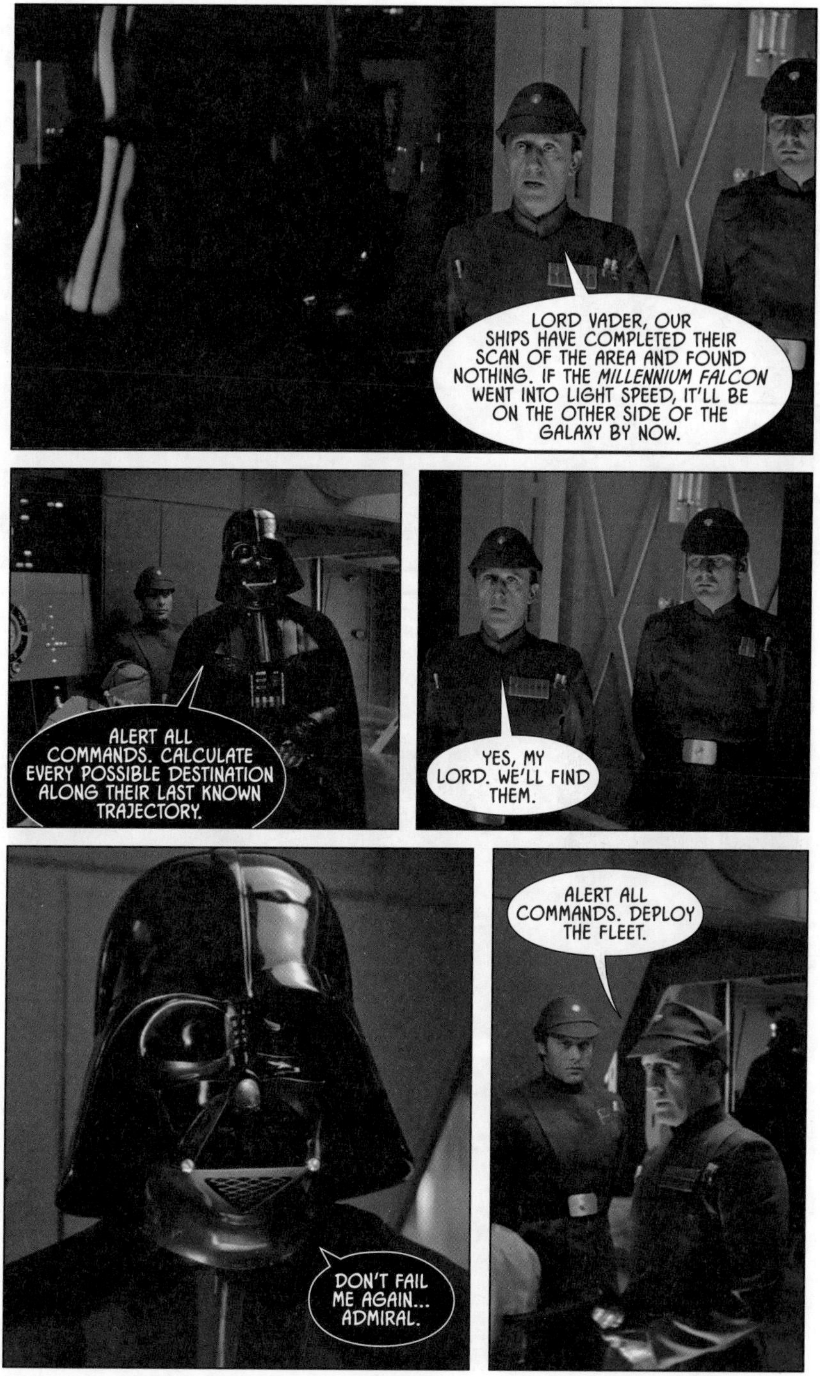
LORD VADER, OUR SHIPS HAVE COMPLETED THEIR SCAN OF THE AREA AND FOUND NOTHING. IF THE *MILLENNIUM FALCON* WENT INTO LIGHT SPEED, IT'LL BE ON THE OTHER SIDE OF THE GALAXY BY NOW.
ALERT ALL COMMANDS. CALCULATE EVERY POSSIBLE DESTINATION ALONG THEIR LAST KNOWN TRAJECTORY.
YES, MY LORD. WE'LL FIND THEM.
DON'T FAIL ME AGAIN... ADMIRAL.
ALERT ALL COMMANDS. DEPLOY THE FLEET.

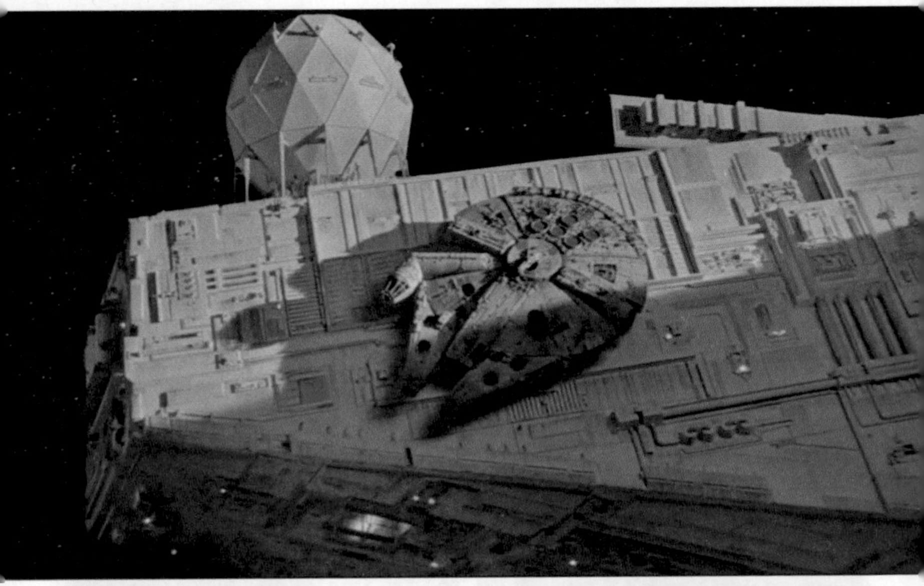

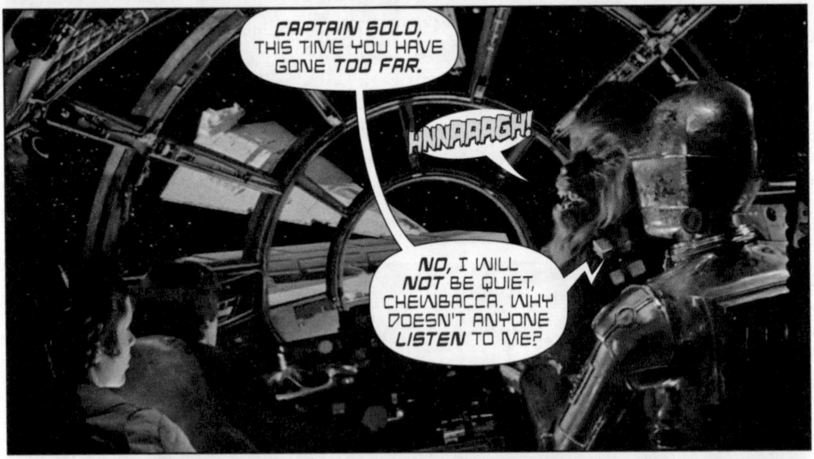
CAPTAIN SOLO, THIS TIME YOU HAVE GONE TOO FAR.
HNNAAAGH!
NO, I WILL NOT BE QUIET, CHEWBACCA. WHY DOESN'T ANYONE LISTEN TO ME?

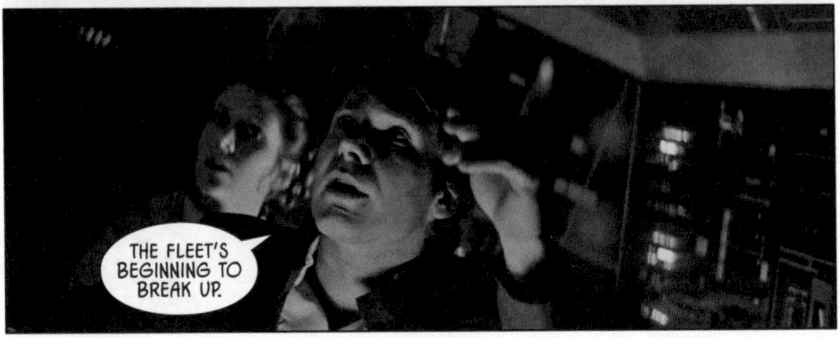
THE FLEET'S BEGINNING TO BREAK UP.

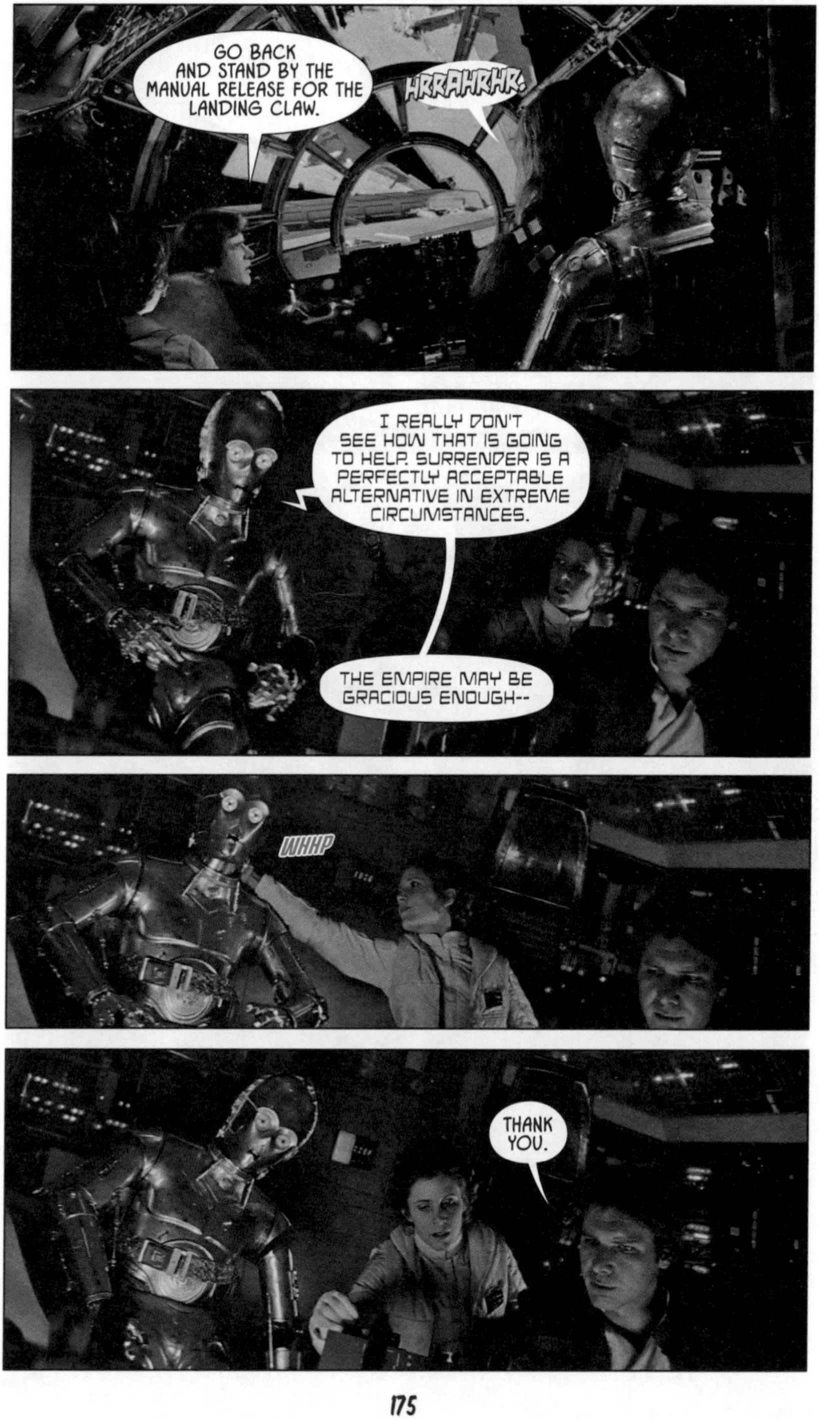
GO BACK AND STAND BY THE MANUAL RELEASE FOR THE LANDING CLAW.
HRRAHRHR!
I REALLY DON'T SEE HOW THAT IS GOING TO HELP. SURRENDER IS A PERFECTLY ACCEPTABLE ALTERNATIVE IN EXTREME CIRCUMSTANCES.
THE EMPIRE MAY BE GRACIOUS ENOUGH--
WHHP
THANK YOU.

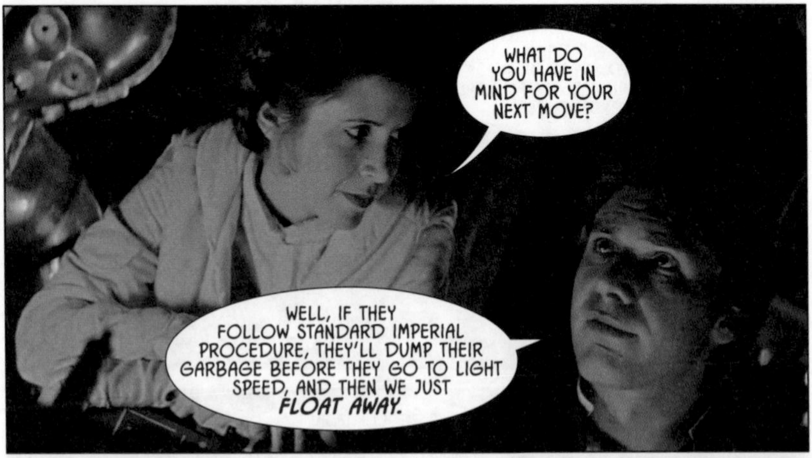
WHAT DO YOU HAVE IN MIND FOR YOUR NEXT MOVE?
WELL, IF THEY FOLLOW STANDARD IMPERIAL PROCEDURE, THEY'LL DUMP THEIR GARBAGE BEFORE THEY GO TO LIGHT SPEED, AND THEN WE JUST *FLOAT AWAY.*

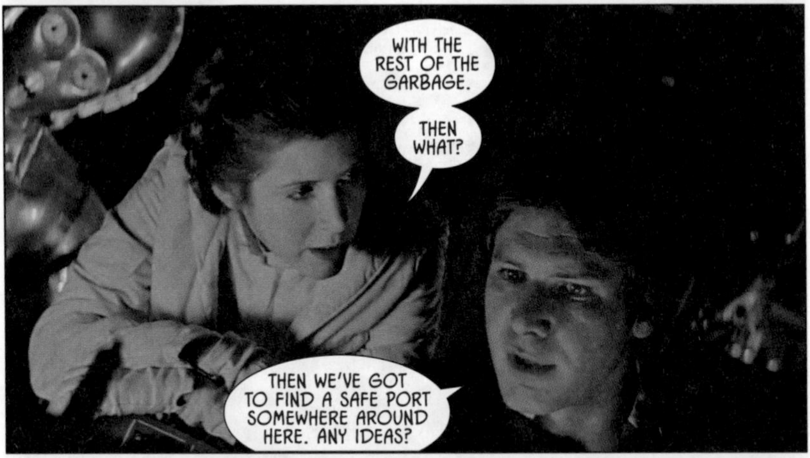
WITH THE REST OF THE GARBAGE.
THEN WHAT?
THEN WE'VE GOT TO FIND A SAFE PORT SOMEWHERE AROUND HERE. ANY IDEAS?

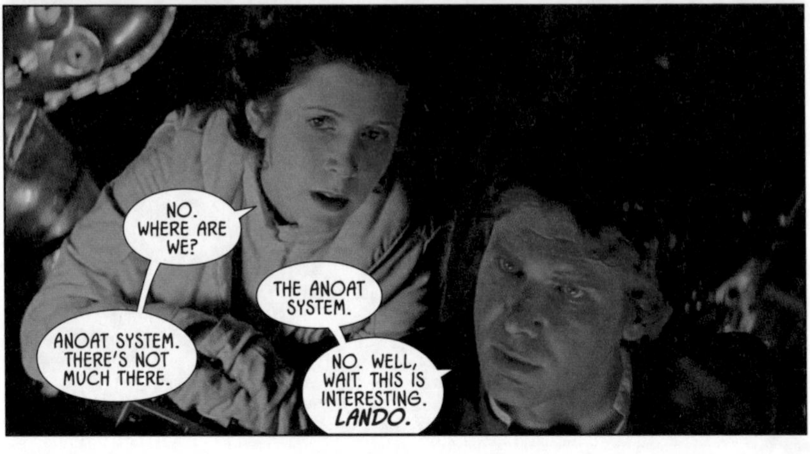
NO. WHERE ARE WE?
THE ANOAT SYSTEM.
ANOAT SYSTEM. THERE'S NOT MUCH THERE.
NO. WELL, WAIT. THIS IS INTERESTING. *LANDO.*

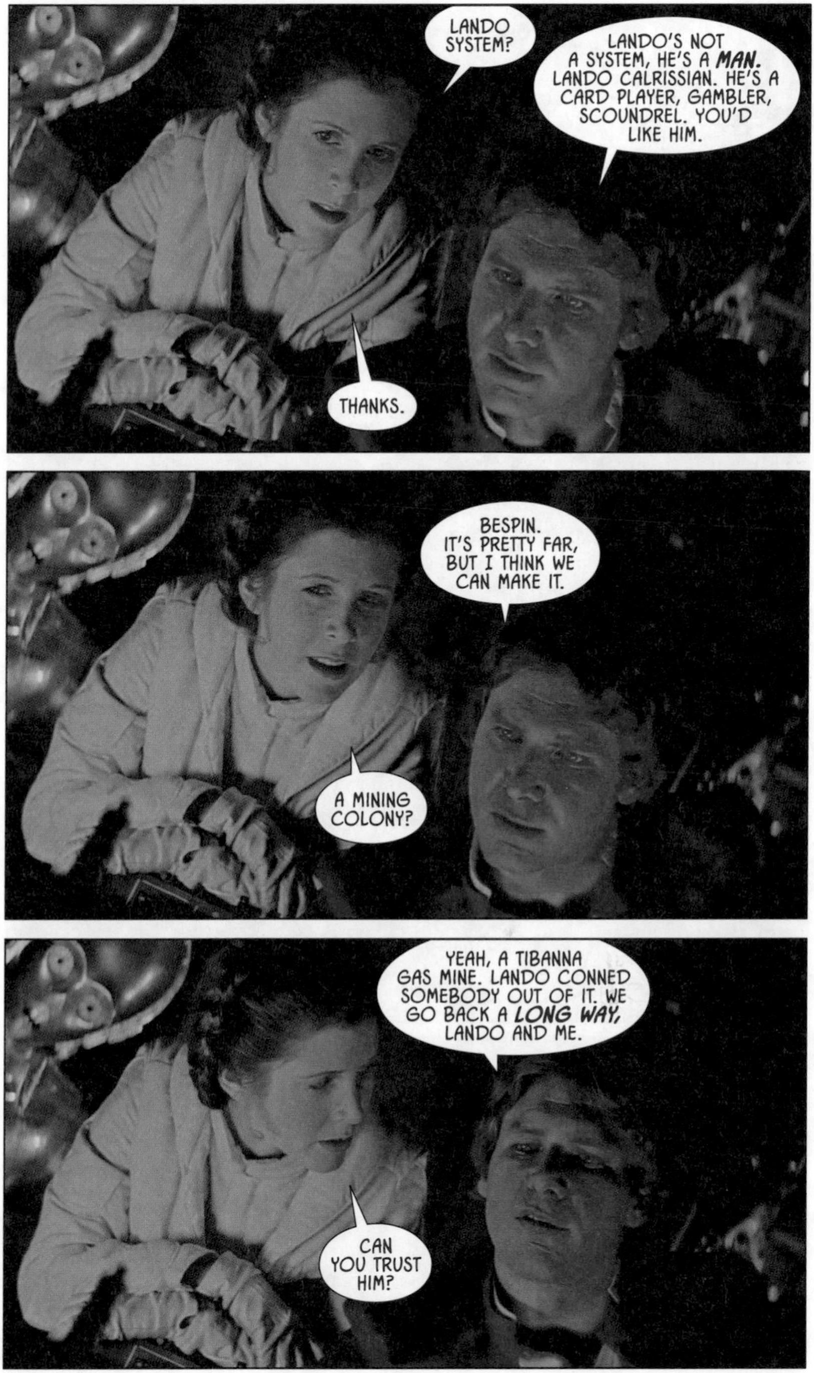
LANDO SYSTEM?
LANDO'S NOT A SYSTEM, HE'S A **MAN.** LANDO CALRISSIAN. HE'S A CARD PLAYER, GAMBLER, SCOUNDREL. YOU'D LIKE HIM.
THANKS.
BESPIN. IT'S PRETTY FAR, BUT I THINK WE CAN MAKE IT.
A MINING COLONY?
YEAH, A TIBANNA GAS MINE. LANDO CONNED SOMEBODY OUT OF IT. WE GO BACK A ***LONG WAY,*** LANDO AND ME.
CAN YOU TRUST HIM?

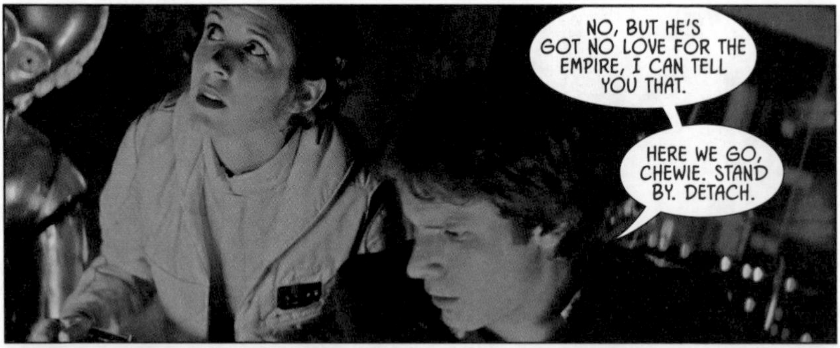
NO, BUT HE'S GOT NO LOVE FOR THE EMPIRE, I CAN TELL YOU THAT.
HERE WE GO, CHEWIE. STAND BY. DETACH.

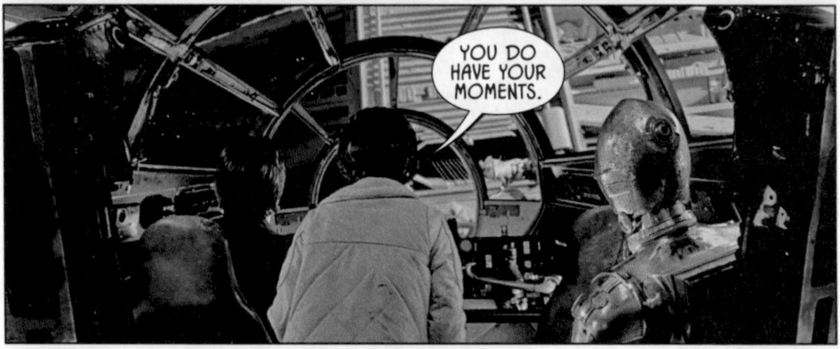
YOU DO HAVE YOUR MOMENTS.

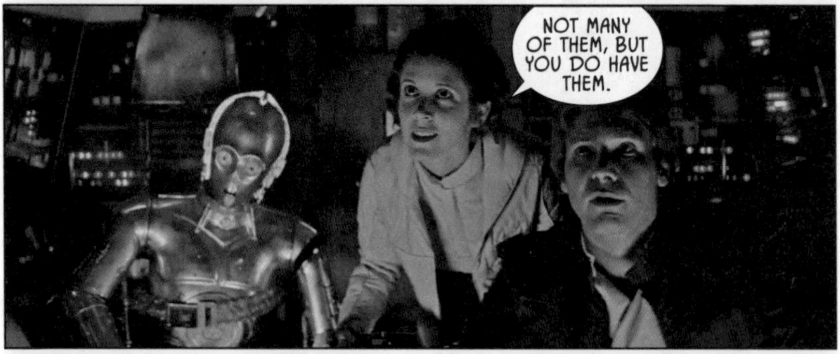
NOT MANY OF THEM, BUT YOU DO HAVE THEM.

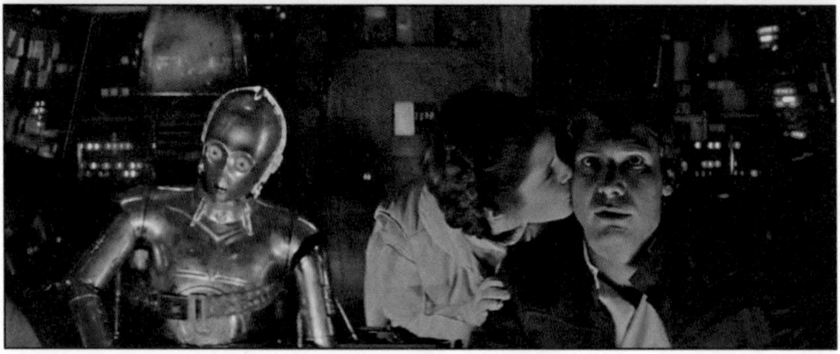

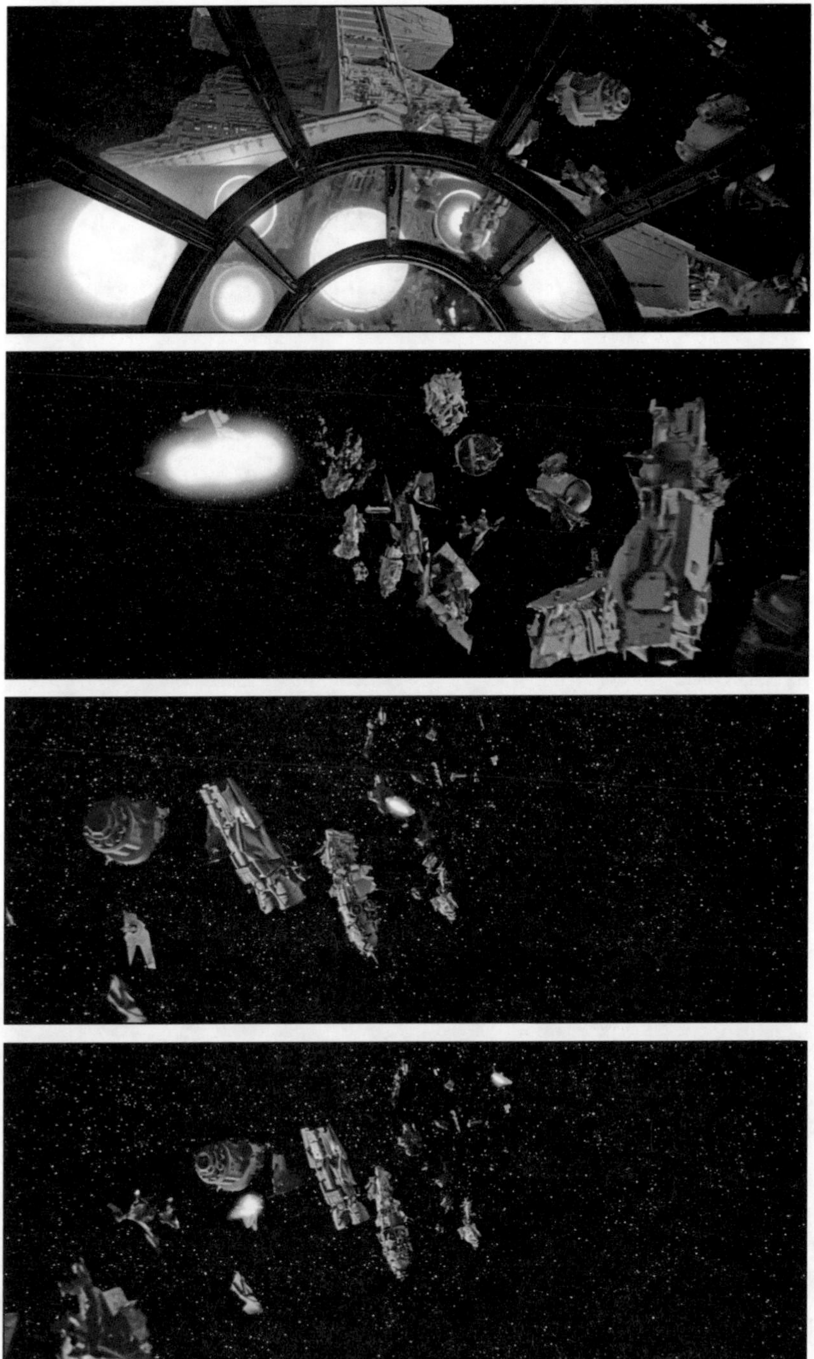

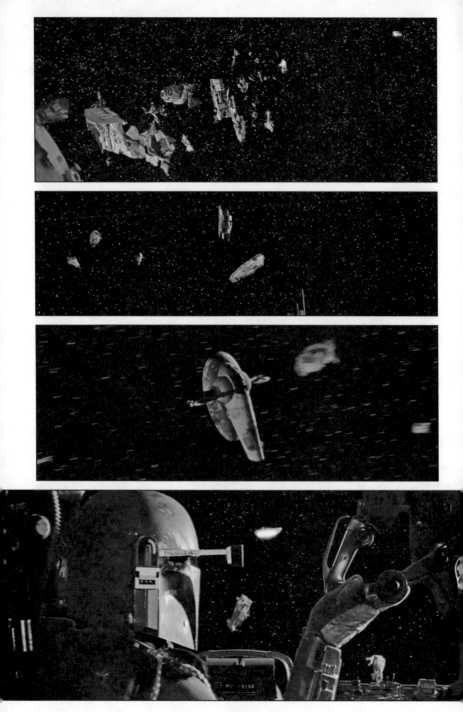

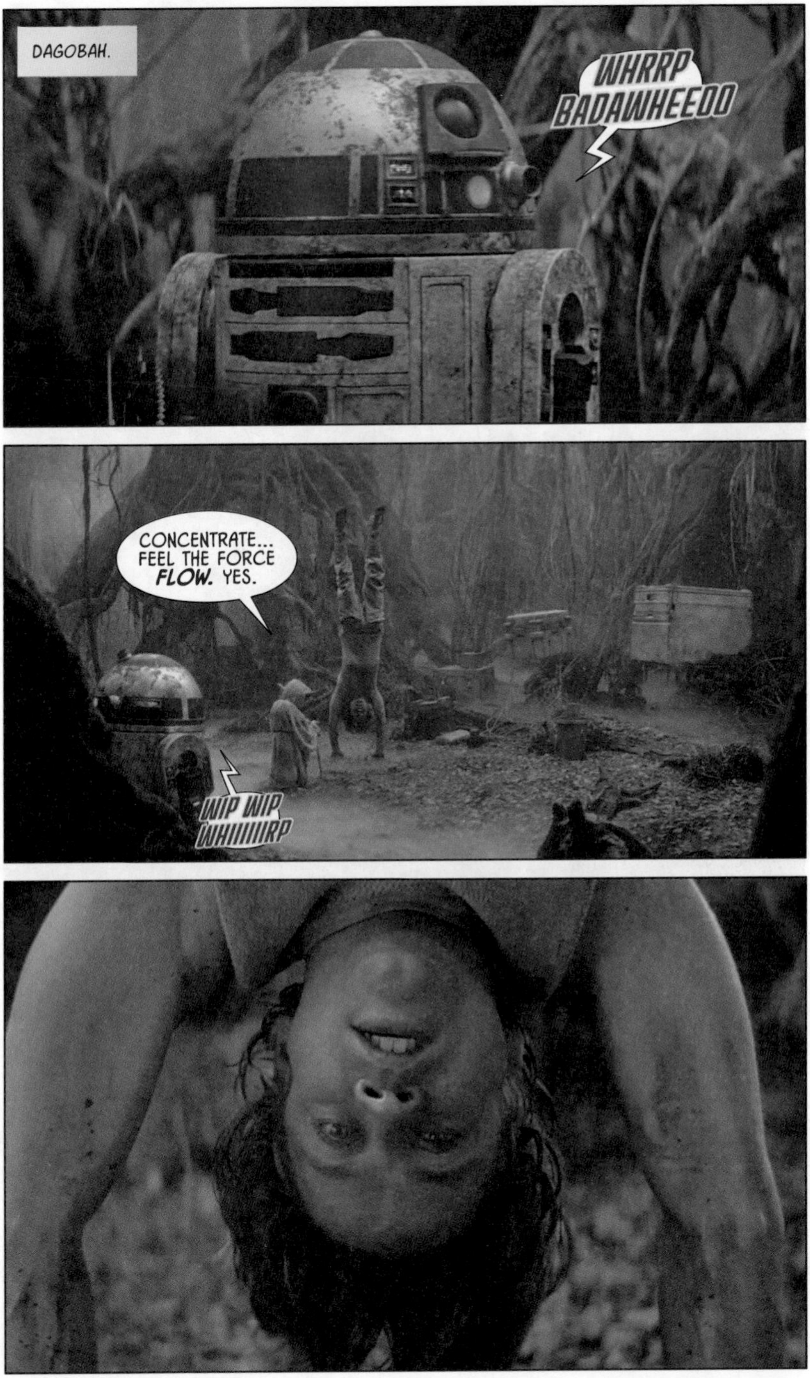
DAGOBAH.
WHRRP BADAWHEEDO
CONCENTRATE... FEEL THE FORCE FLOW. YES.
WIP WIP WHIIIIIRP

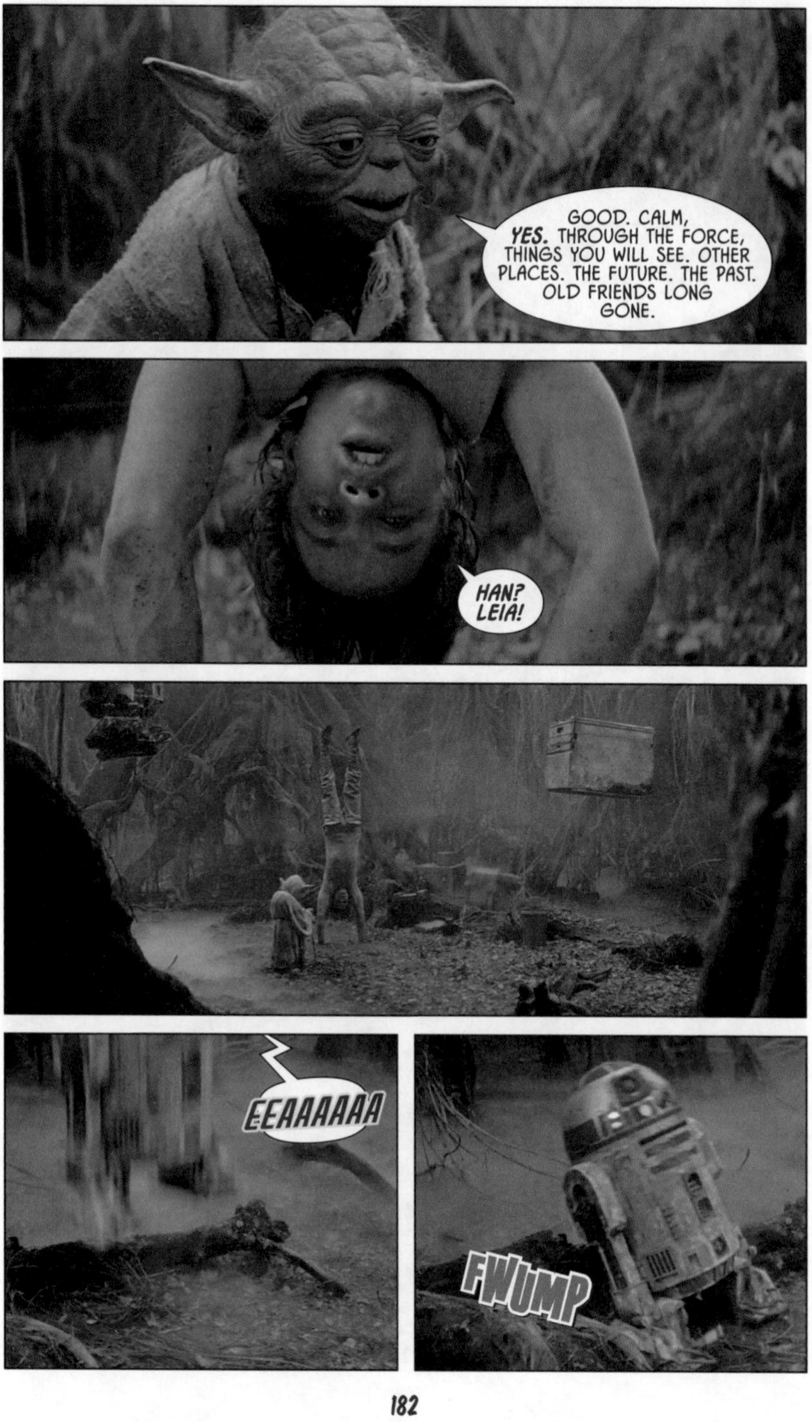
GOOD. CALM, **YES.** THROUGH THE FORCE, THINGS YOU WILL SEE. OTHER PLACES. THE FUTURE. THE PAST. OLD FRIENDS LONG GONE.
HAN? LEIA!
EEAAAAAA
FWUMP

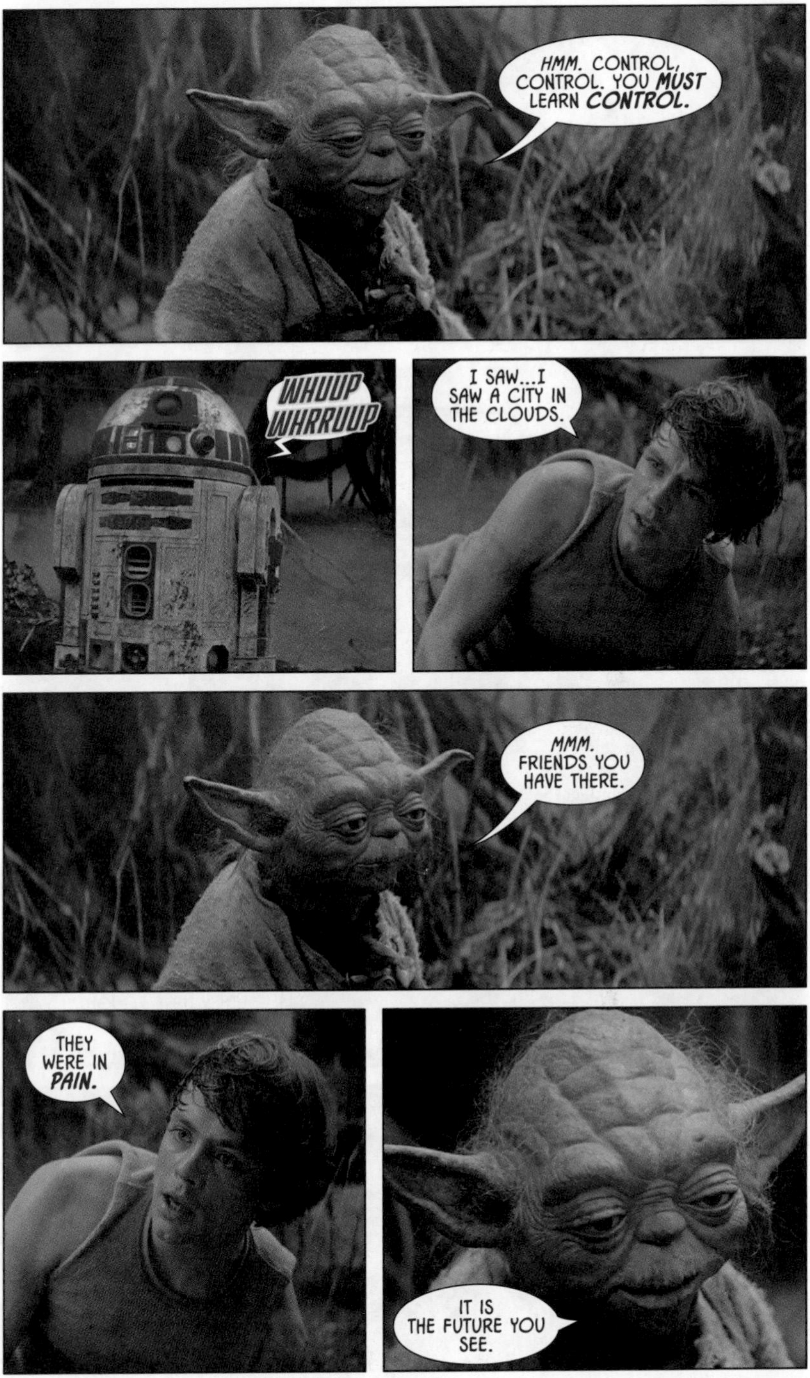
HMM. CONTROL, CONTROL. YOU MUST LEARN CONTROL.
WHUUP WHRRUUP
I SAW...I SAW A CITY IN THE CLOUDS.
MMM. FRIENDS YOU HAVE THERE.
THEY WERE IN PAIN.
IT IS THE FUTURE YOU SEE.

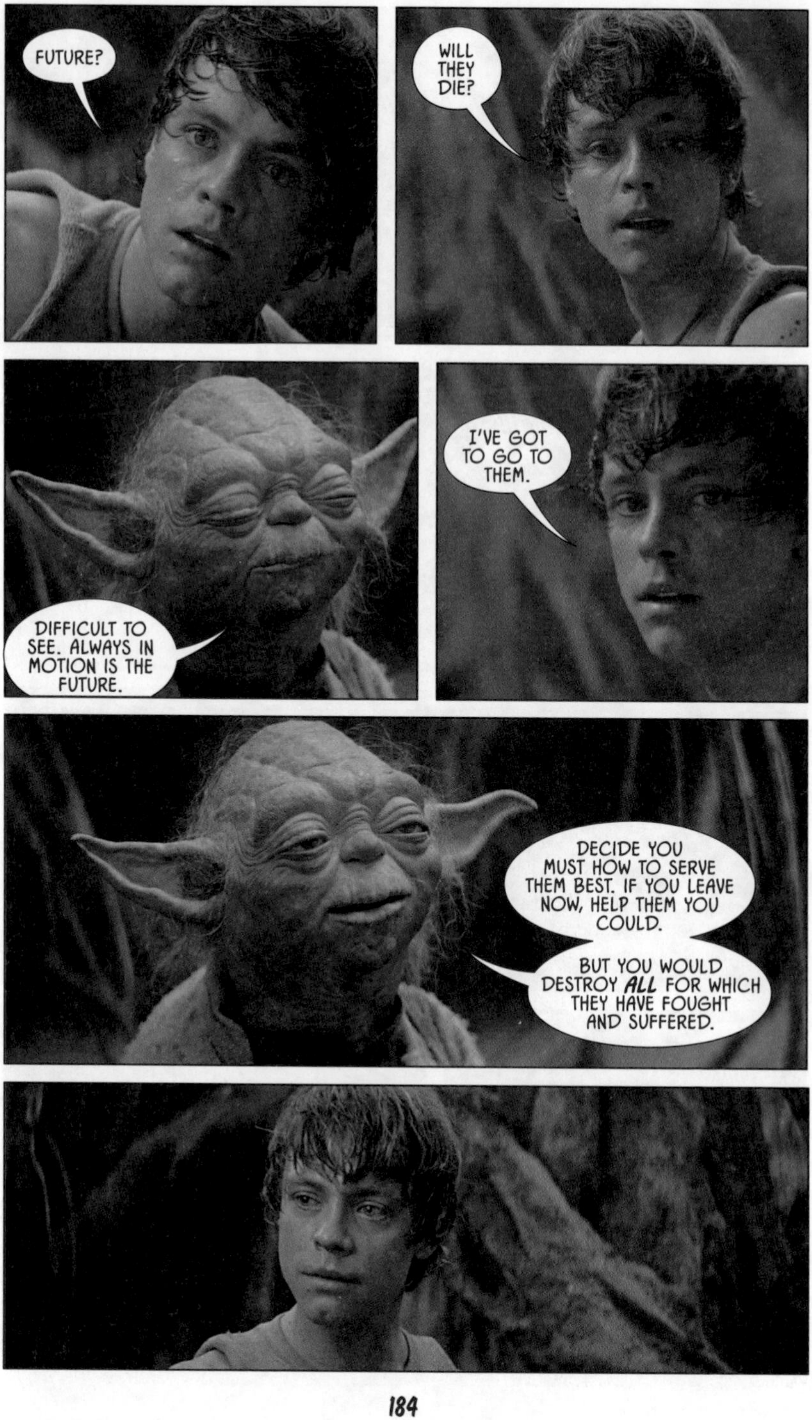
FUTURE?
WILL THEY DIE?
DIFFICULT TO SEE. ALWAYS IN MOTION IS THE FUTURE.
I'VE GOT TO GO TO THEM.
DECIDE YOU MUST HOW TO SERVE THEM BEST. IF YOU LEAVE NOW, HELP THEM YOU COULD.
BUT YOU WOULD DESTROY *ALL* FOR WHICH THEY HAVE FOUGHT AND SUFFERED.

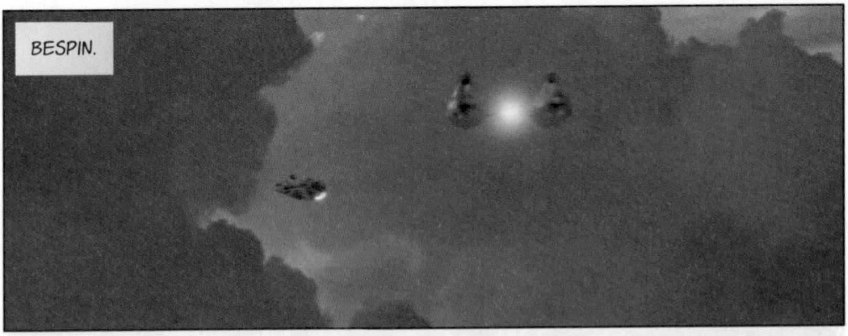
BESPIN.

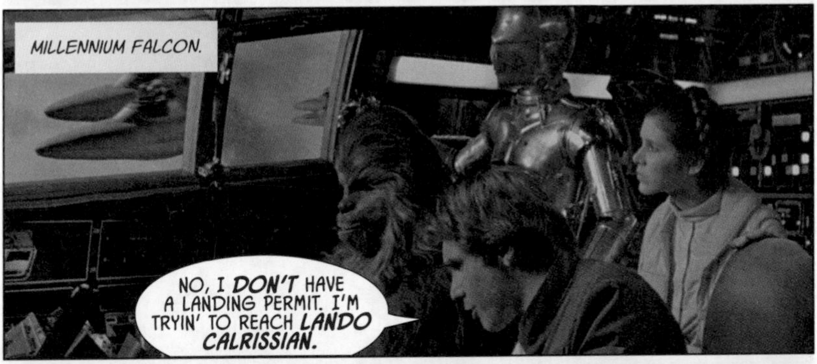
MILLENNIUM FALCON.
NO, I DON'T HAVE A LANDING PERMIT. I'M TRYIN' TO REACH LANDO CALRISSIAN.

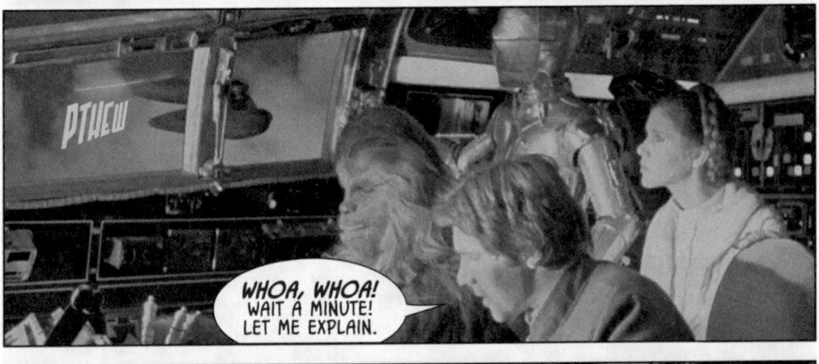
PTHEW
WHOA, WHOA! WAIT A MINUTE! LET ME EXPLAIN.

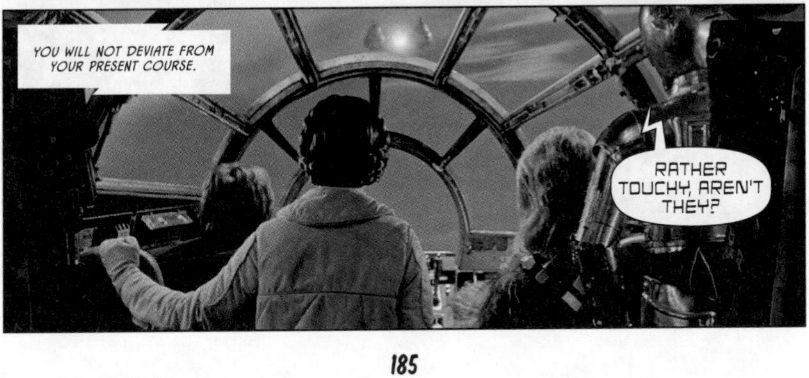
YOU WILL NOT DEVIATE FROM YOUR PRESENT COURSE.
RATHER TOUCHY, AREN'T THEY?

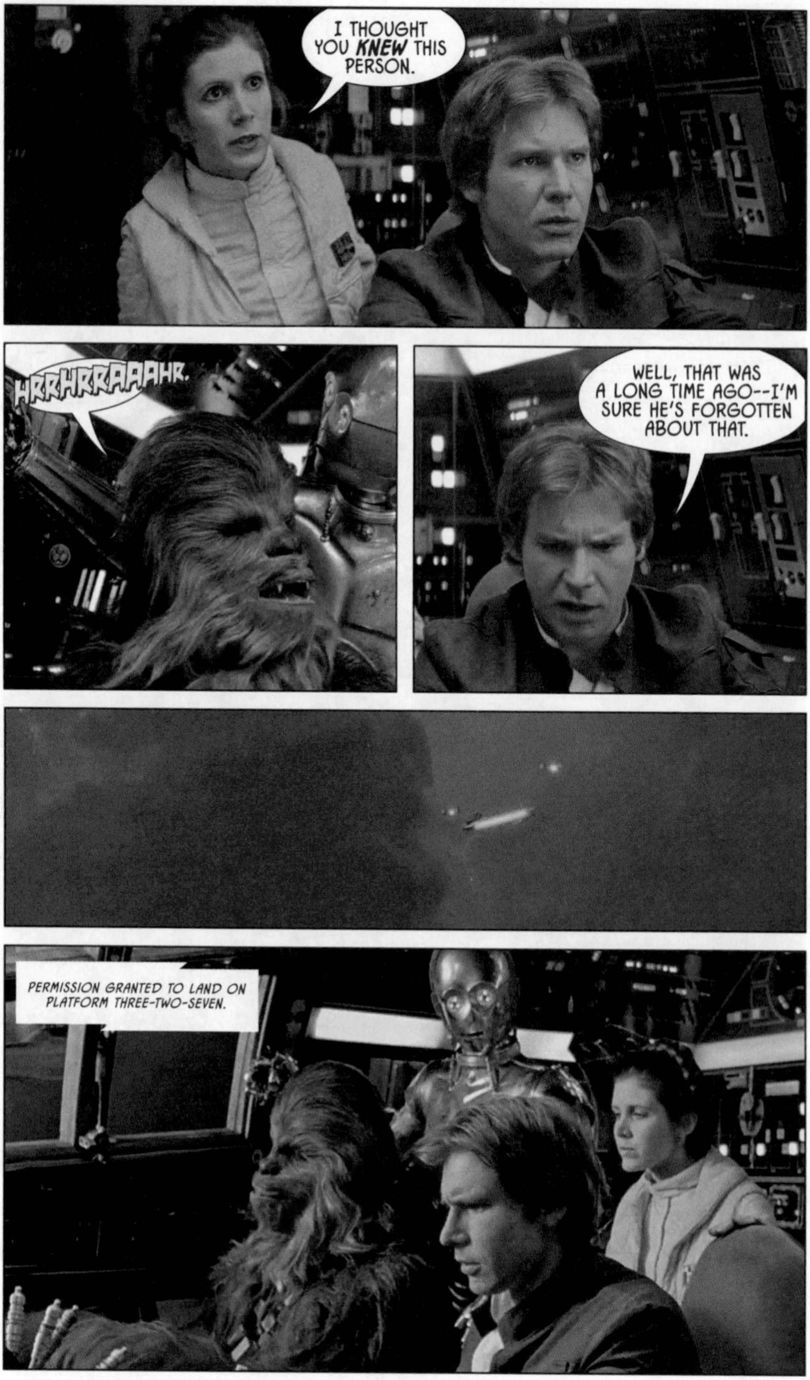
I THOUGHT YOU KNEW THIS PERSON.
HRRHRRAAAHR.
WELL, THAT WAS A LONG TIME AGO--I'M SURE HE'S FORGOTTEN ABOUT THAT.
PERMISSION GRANTED TO LAND ON PLATFORM THREE-TWO-SEVEN.

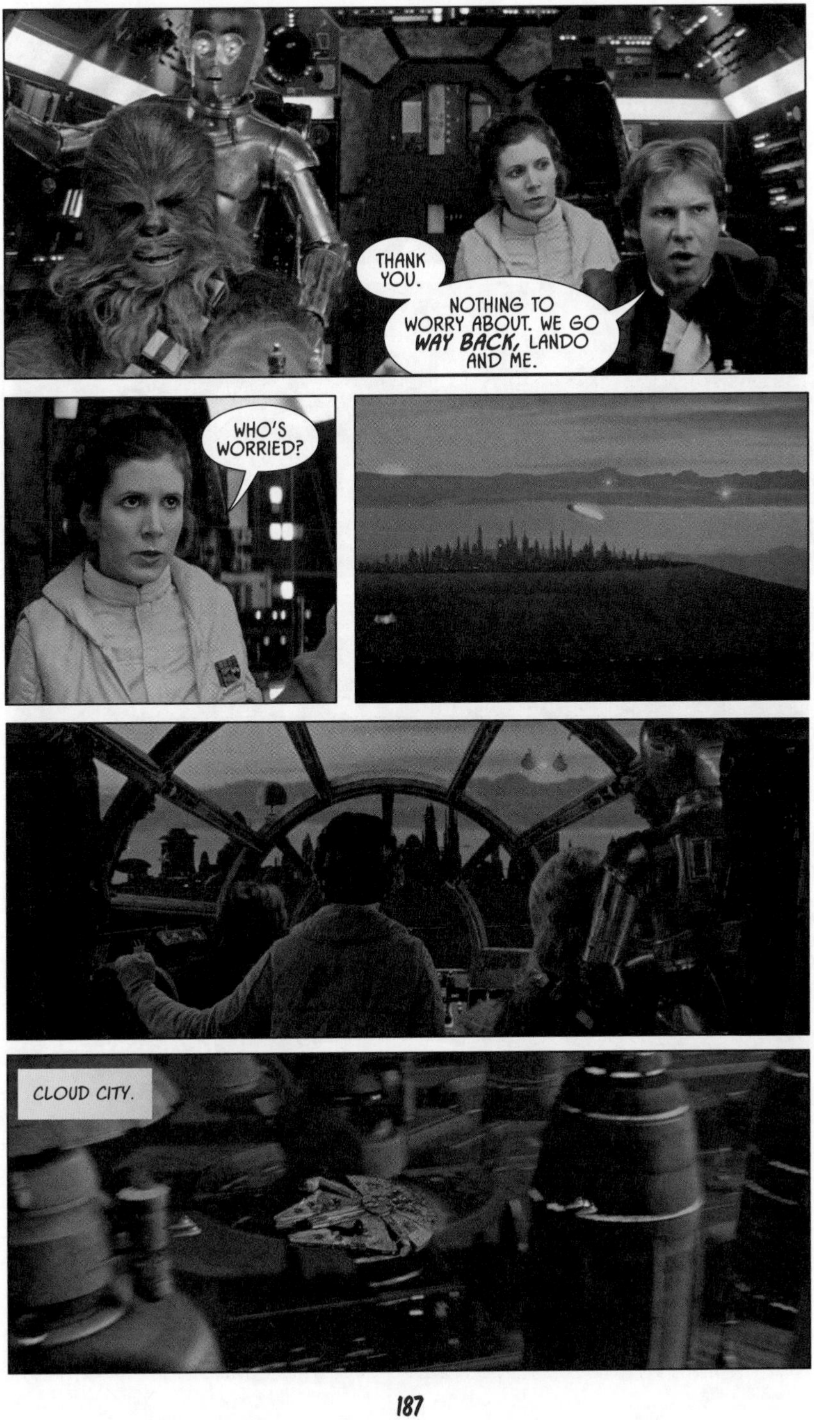
THANK YOU.
NOTHING TO WORRY ABOUT. WE GO WAY BACK, LANDO AND ME.
WHO'S WORRIED?
CLOUD CITY.

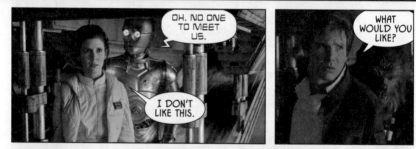

OH. NO ONE TO MEET US.

I DON'T LIKE THIS.

WHAT WOULD YOU LIKE?

WELL, THEY DID LET US LAND.

LOOK, DON'T WORRY. EVERYTHING'S GONNA BE FINE. *TRUST ME.*

HRHRRGHRRAAA.

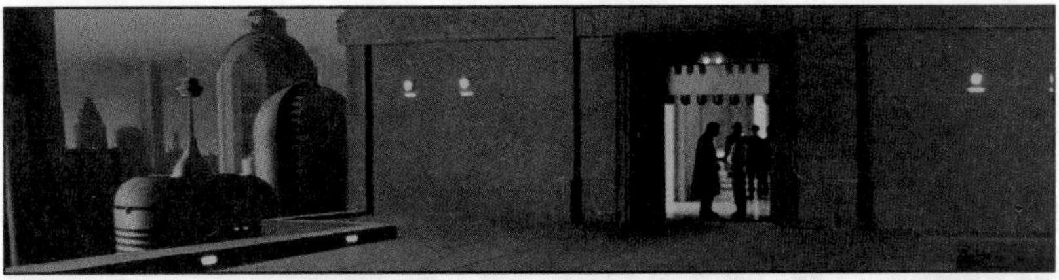

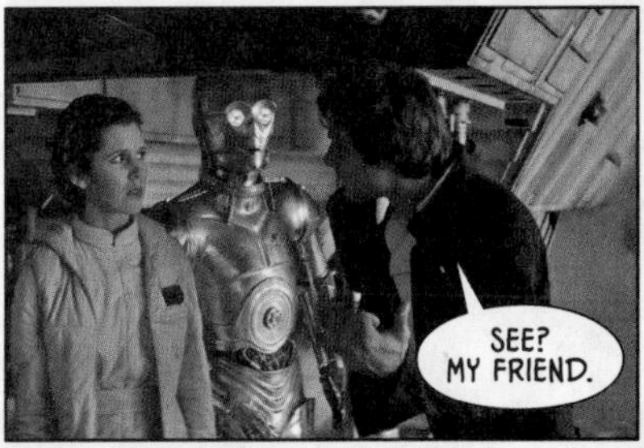
SEE?
MY FRIEND.

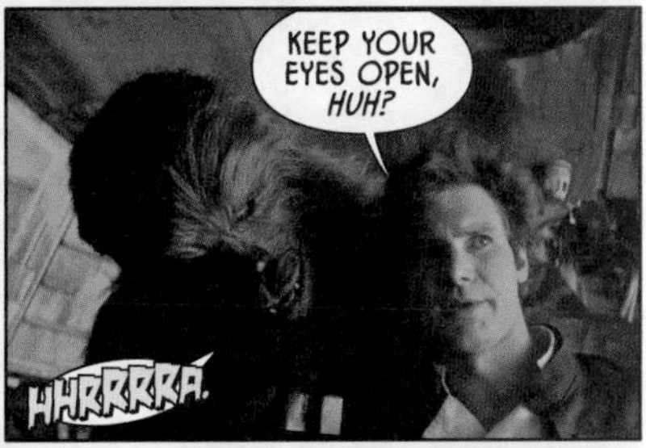
KEEP YOUR
EYES OPEN,
HUH?
HWRRRRA.

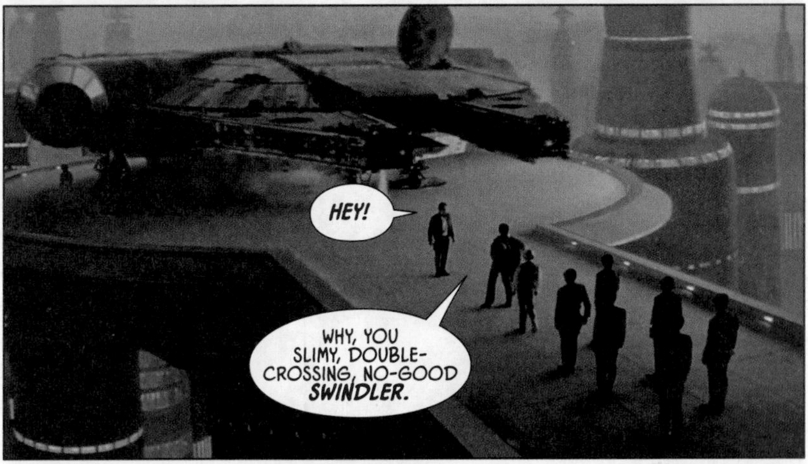
HEY!
WHY, YOU
SLIMY, DOUBLE-
CROSSING, NO-GOOD
SWINDLER.

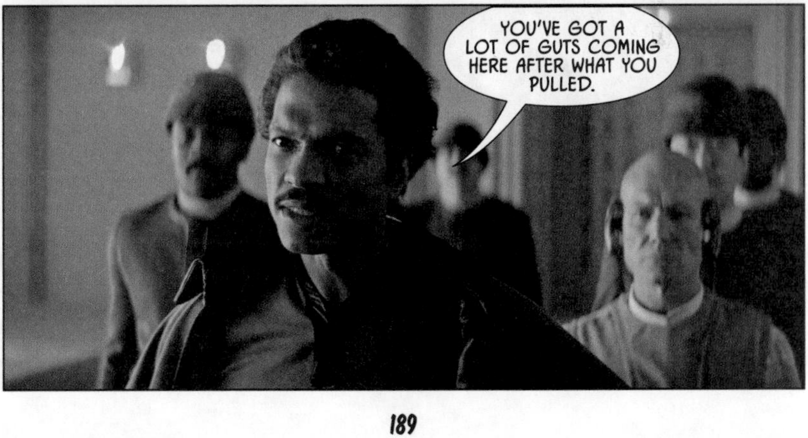
YOU'VE GOT A
LOT OF GUTS COMING
HERE AFTER WHAT YOU
PULLED.

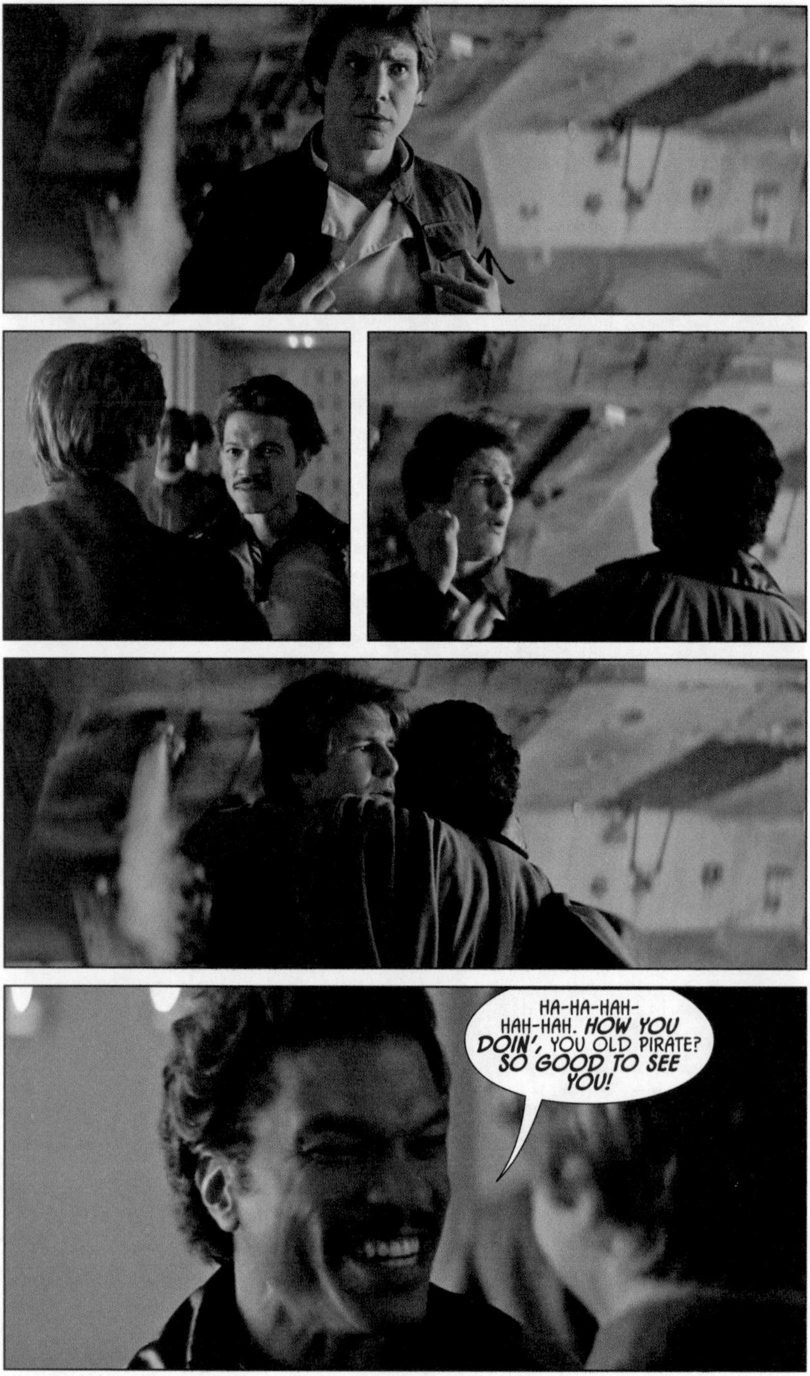
HA-HA-HAH-HAH-HAH. HOW YOU DOIN', YOU OLD PIRATE? SO GOOD TO SEE YOU!

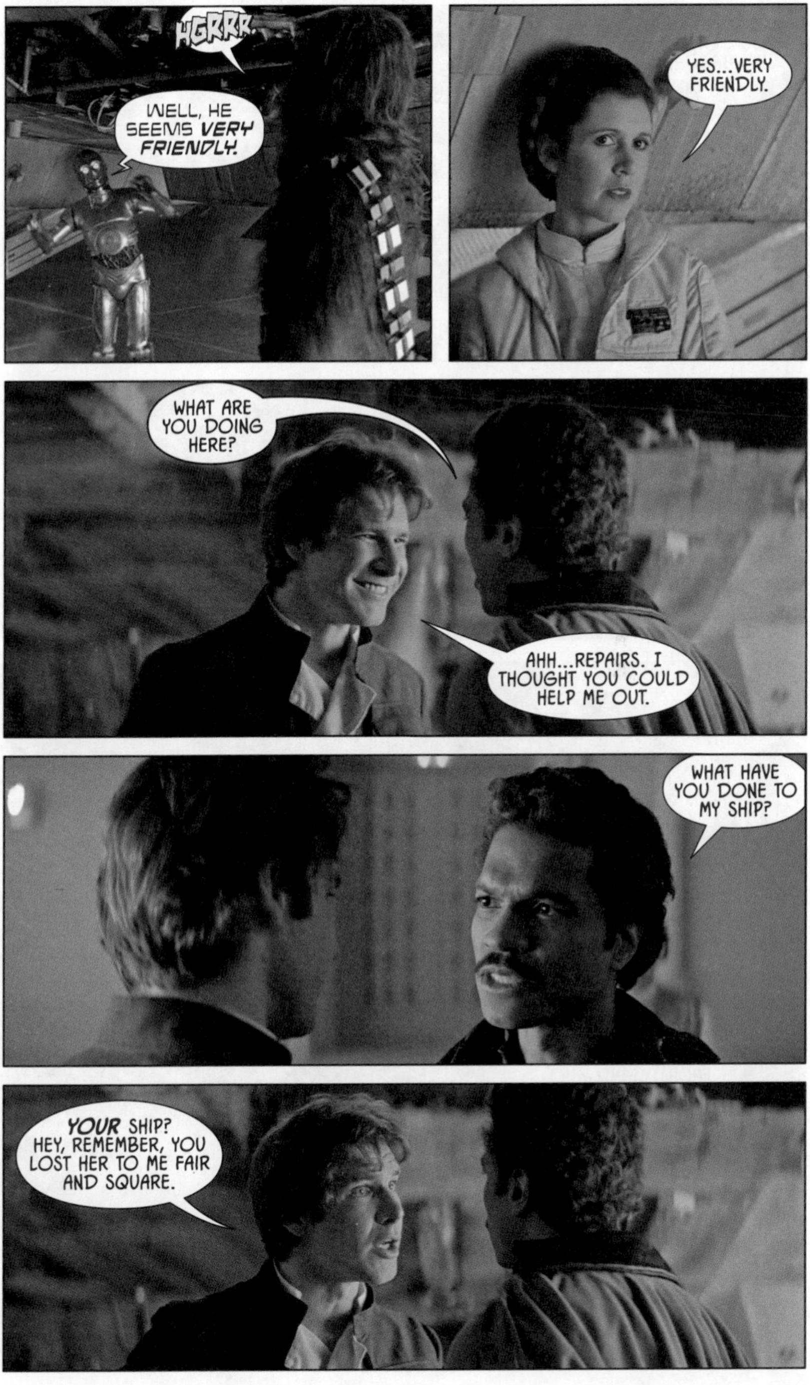
HGRRR.
WELL, HE SEEMS VERY FRIENDLY.
YES...VERY FRIENDLY.
WHAT ARE YOU DOING HERE?
AHH...REPAIRS. I THOUGHT YOU COULD HELP ME OUT.
WHAT HAVE YOU DONE TO MY SHIP?
YOUR SHIP? HEY, REMEMBER, YOU LOST HER TO ME FAIR AND SQUARE.

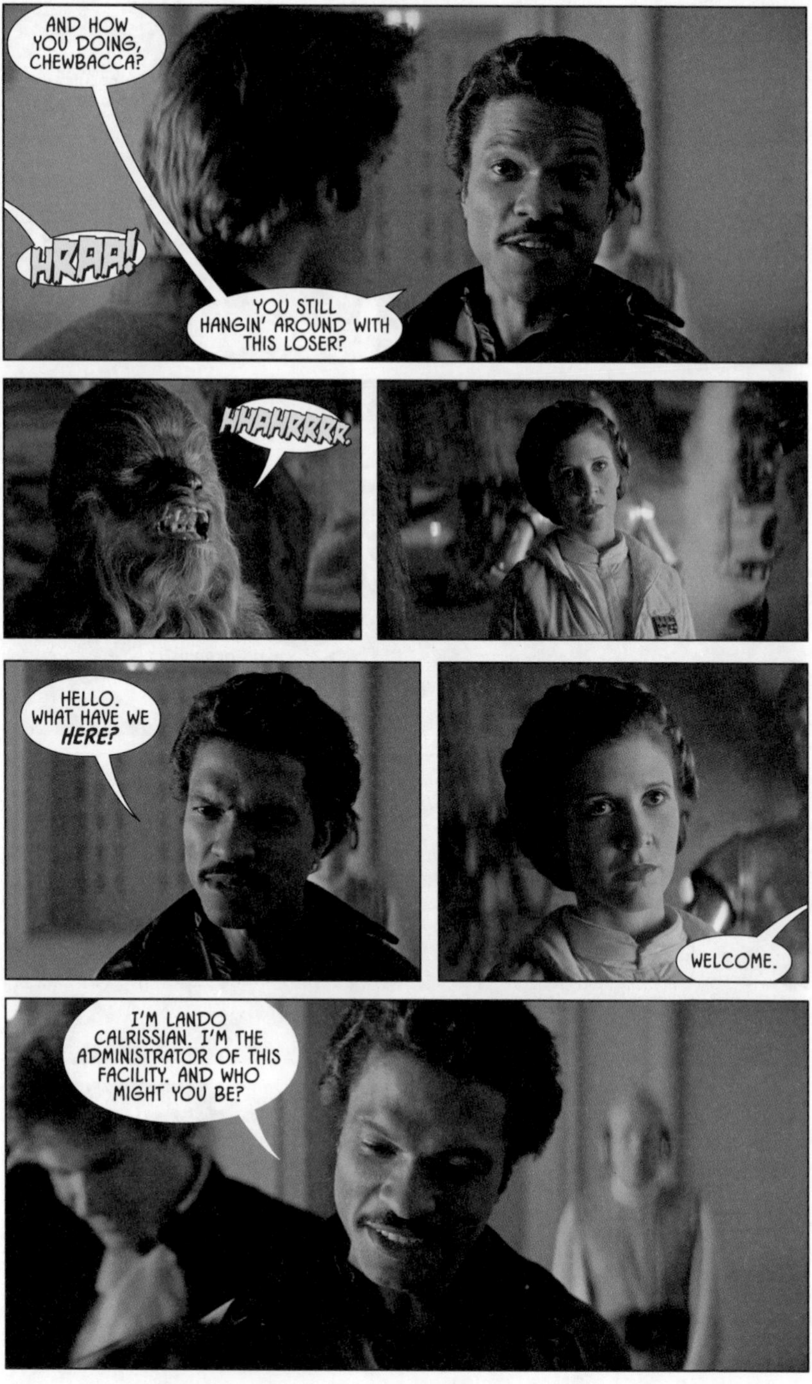
AND HOW YOU DOING, CHEWBACCA?
HRAA!
YOU STILL HANGIN' AROUND WITH THIS LOSER?
WHAHRRRR.
HELLO. WHAT HAVE WE *HERE?*
WELCOME.
I'M LANDO CALRISSIAN. I'M THE ADMINISTRATOR OF THIS FACILITY. AND WHO MIGHT YOU BE?

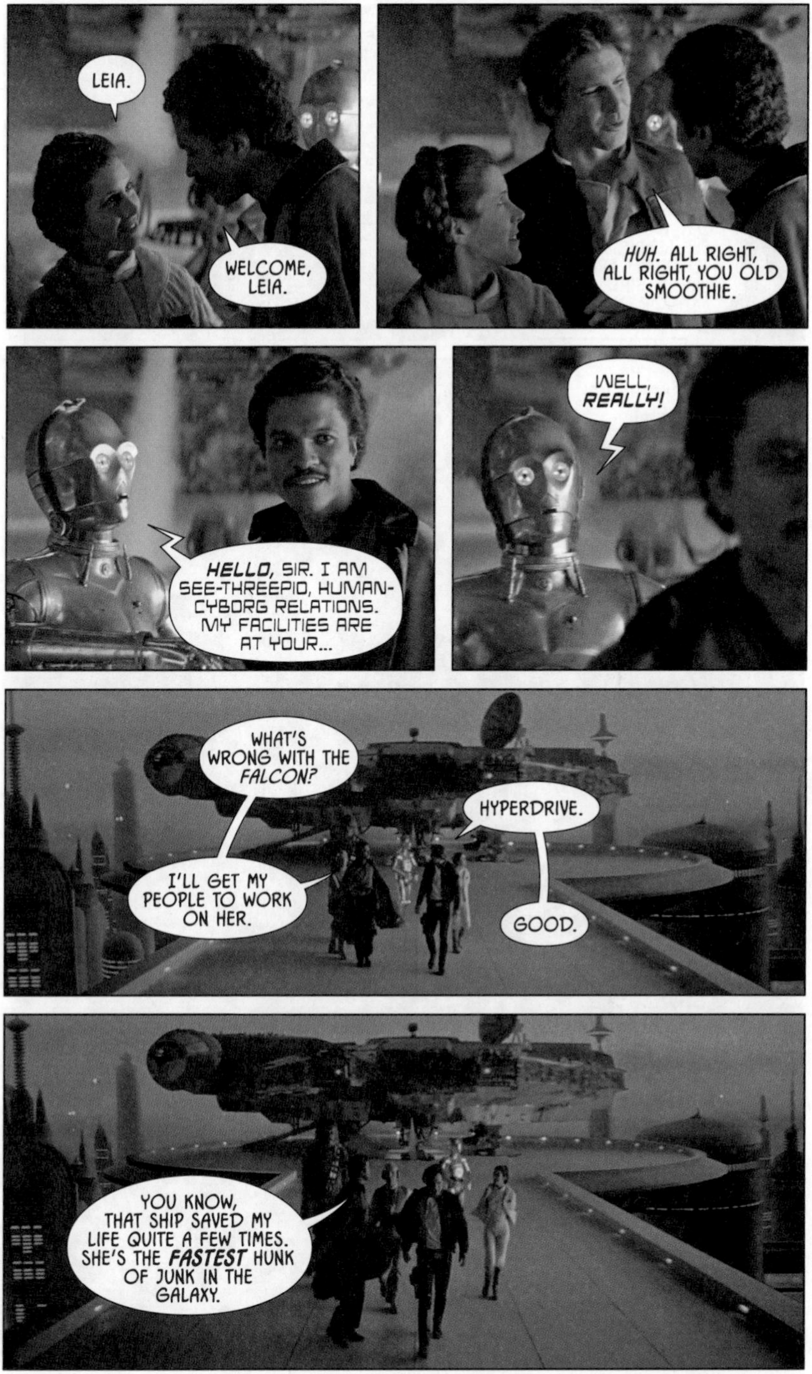
LEIA.
WELCOME, LEIA.
HUH. ALL RIGHT, ALL RIGHT, YOU OLD SMOOTHIE.
HELLO, SIR. I AM SEE-THREEPIO, HUMAN-CYBORG RELATIONS. MY FACILITIES ARE AT YOUR...
WELL, REALLY!
WHAT'S WRONG WITH THE FALCON?
HYPERDRIVE.
I'LL GET MY PEOPLE TO WORK ON HER.
GOOD.
YOU KNOW, THAT SHIP SAVED MY LIFE QUITE A FEW TIMES. SHE'S THE FASTEST HUNK OF JUNK IN THE GALAXY.

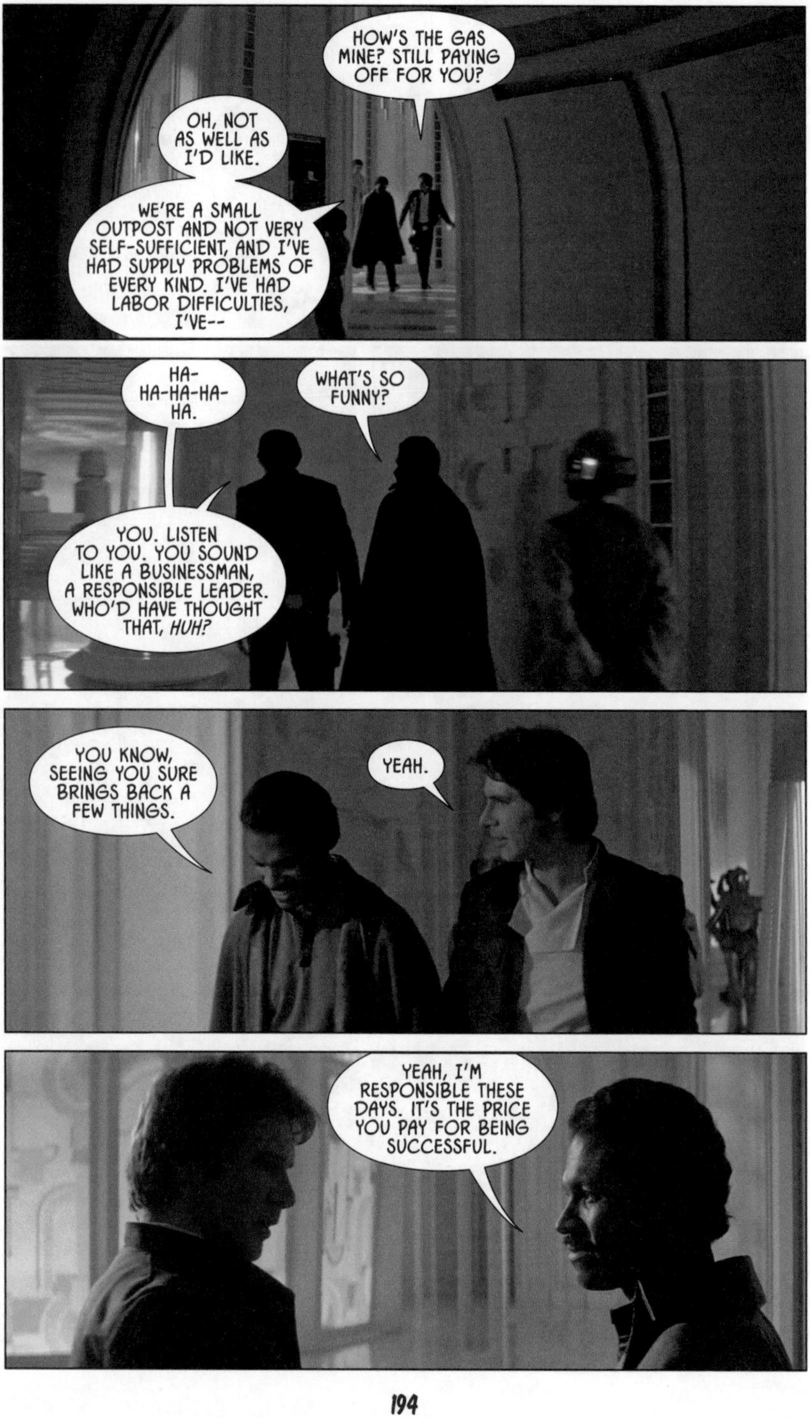
HOW'S THE GAS MINE? STILL PAYING OFF FOR YOU?
OH, NOT AS WELL AS I'D LIKE.
WE'RE A SMALL OUTPOST AND NOT VERY SELF-SUFFICIENT, AND I'VE HAD SUPPLY PROBLEMS OF EVERY KIND. I'VE HAD LABOR DIFFICULTIES, I'VE--
HA-HA-HA-HA-HA.
WHAT'S SO FUNNY?
YOU. LISTEN TO YOU. YOU SOUND LIKE A BUSINESSMAN, A RESPONSIBLE LEADER. WHO'D HAVE THOUGHT THAT, *HUH?*
YOU KNOW, SEEING YOU SURE BRINGS BACK A FEW THINGS.
YEAH.
YEAH, I'M RESPONSIBLE THESE DAYS. IT'S THE PRICE YOU PAY FOR BEING SUCCESSFUL.

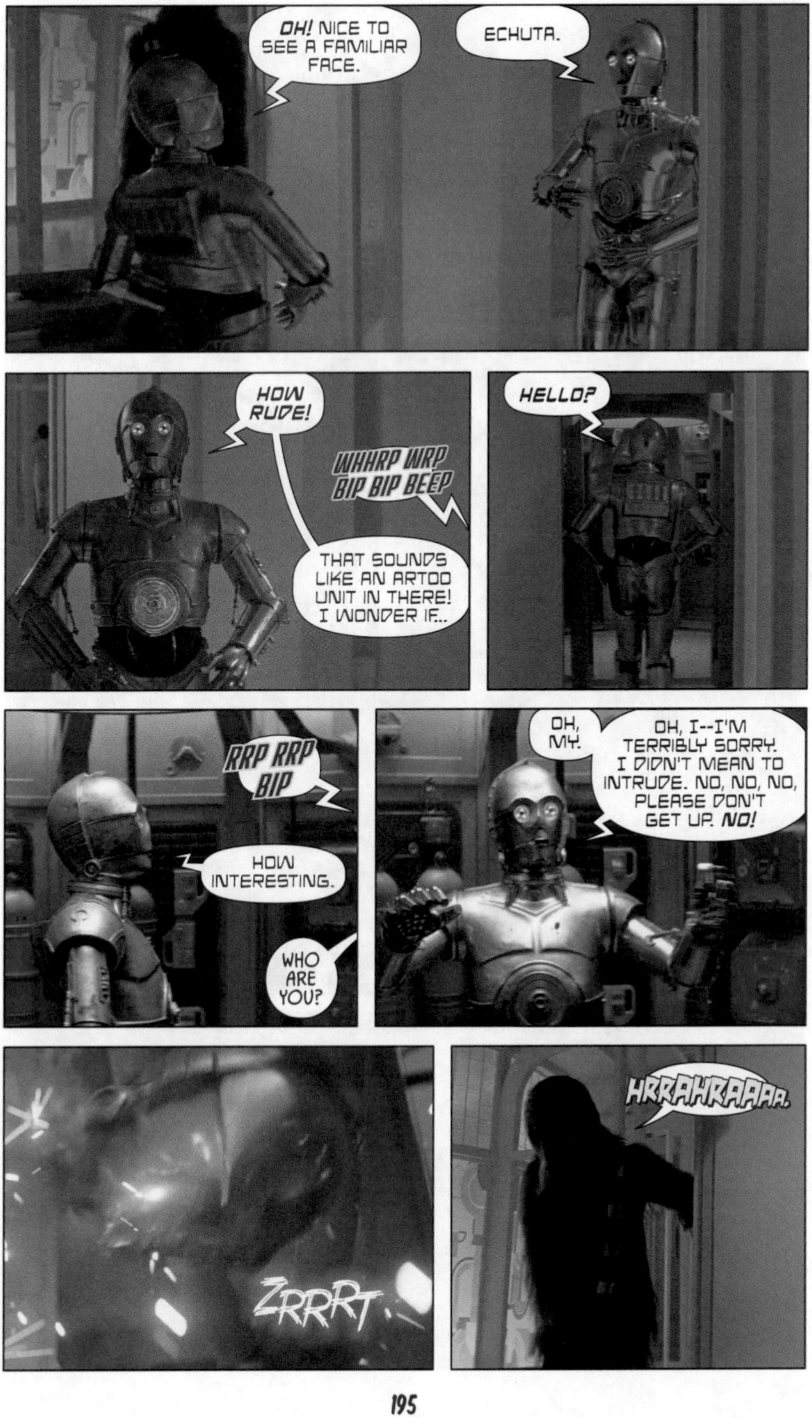
OH! NICE TO SEE A FAMILIAR FACE.
ECHUTA.
HOW RUDE!
WHHRP WRP BIP BIP BEEP
THAT SOUNDS LIKE AN ARTOO UNIT IN THERE! I WONDER IF...
HELLO?
RRP RRP BIP
HOW INTERESTING.
WHO ARE YOU?
OH, MY.
OH, I--I'M TERRIBLY SORRY. I DIDN'T MEAN TO INTRUDE. NO, NO, NO, PLEASE DON'T GET UP. NO!
ZRRRT
HRRAHRAAAA.

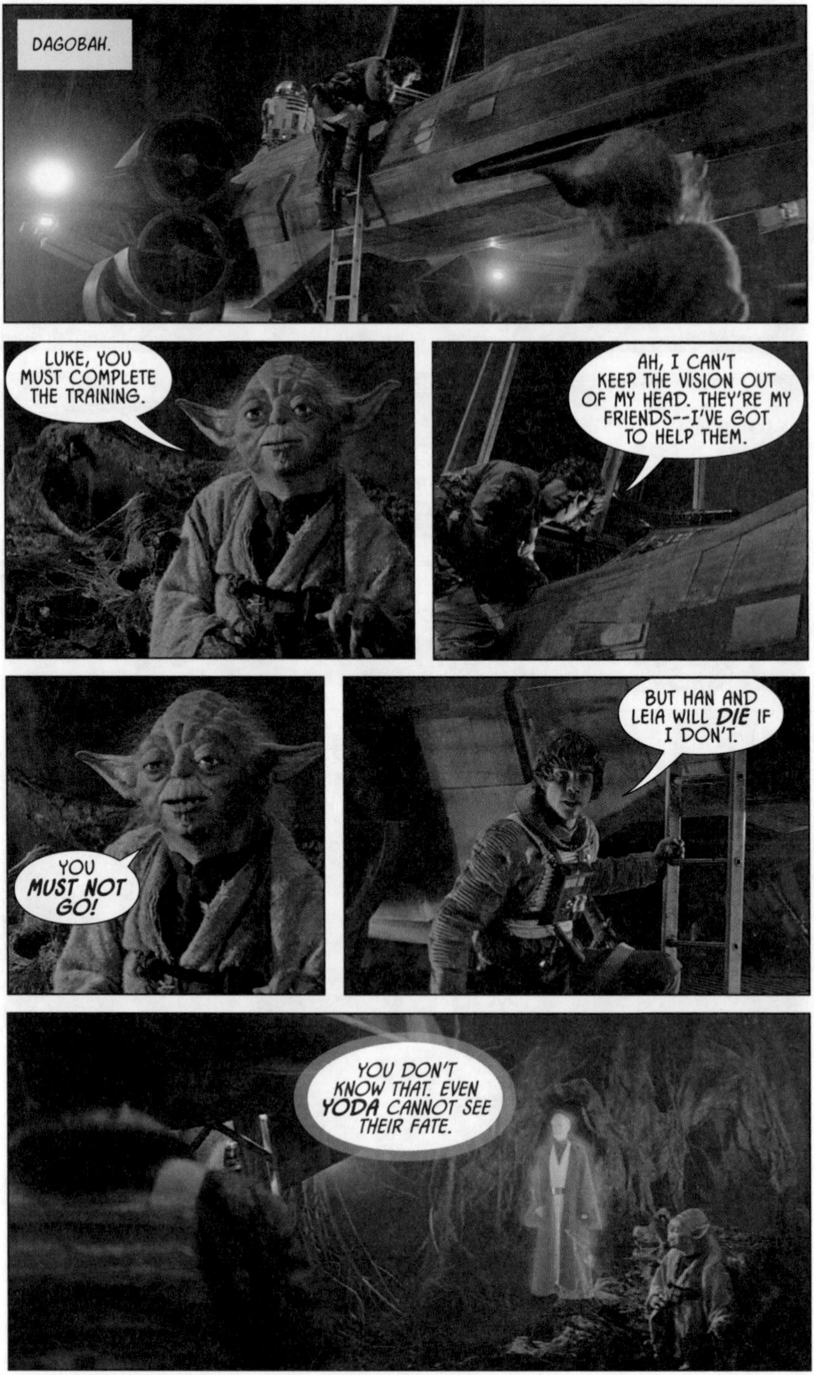
DAGOBAH.
LUKE, YOU MUST COMPLETE THE TRAINING.
AH, I CAN'T KEEP THE VISION OUT OF MY HEAD. THEY'RE MY FRIENDS--I'VE GOT TO HELP THEM.
YOU MUST NOT GO!
BUT HAN AND LEIA WILL DIE IF I DON'T.
YOU DON'T KNOW THAT. EVEN YODA CANNOT SEE THEIR FATE.

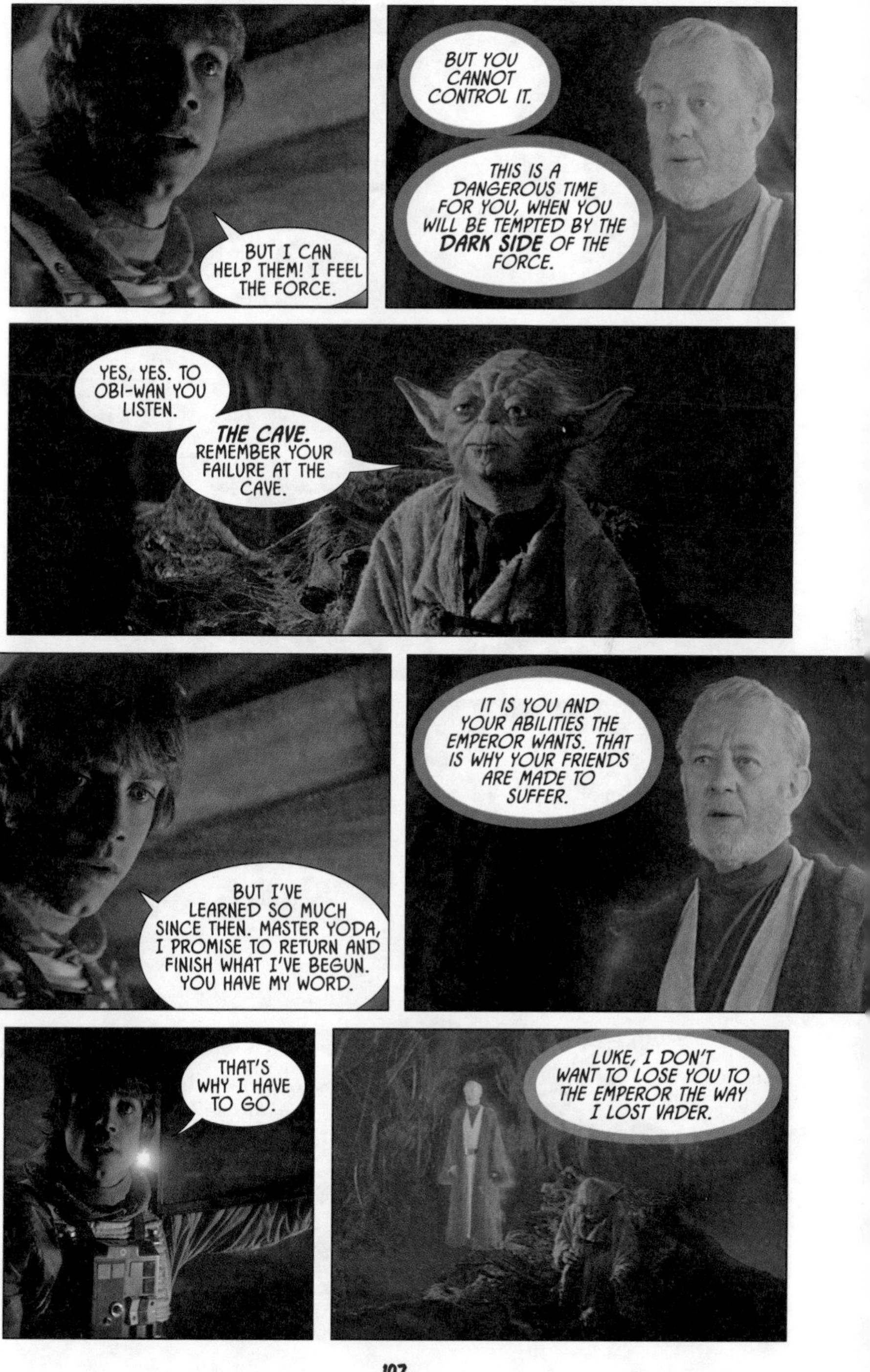
BUT I CAN HELP THEM! I FEEL THE FORCE.
BUT YOU CANNOT CONTROL IT.
THIS IS A DANGEROUS TIME FOR YOU, WHEN YOU WILL BE TEMPTED BY THE DARK SIDE OF THE FORCE.
YES, YES. TO OBI-WAN YOU LISTEN.
THE CAVE. REMEMBER YOUR FAILURE AT THE CAVE.
BUT I'VE LEARNED SO MUCH SINCE THEN. MASTER YODA, I PROMISE TO RETURN AND FINISH WHAT I'VE BEGUN. YOU HAVE MY WORD.
IT IS YOU AND YOUR ABILITIES THE EMPEROR WANTS. THAT IS WHY YOUR FRIENDS ARE MADE TO SUFFER.
THAT'S WHY I HAVE TO GO.
LUKE, I DON'T WANT TO LOSE YOU TO THE EMPEROR THE WAY I LOST VADER.

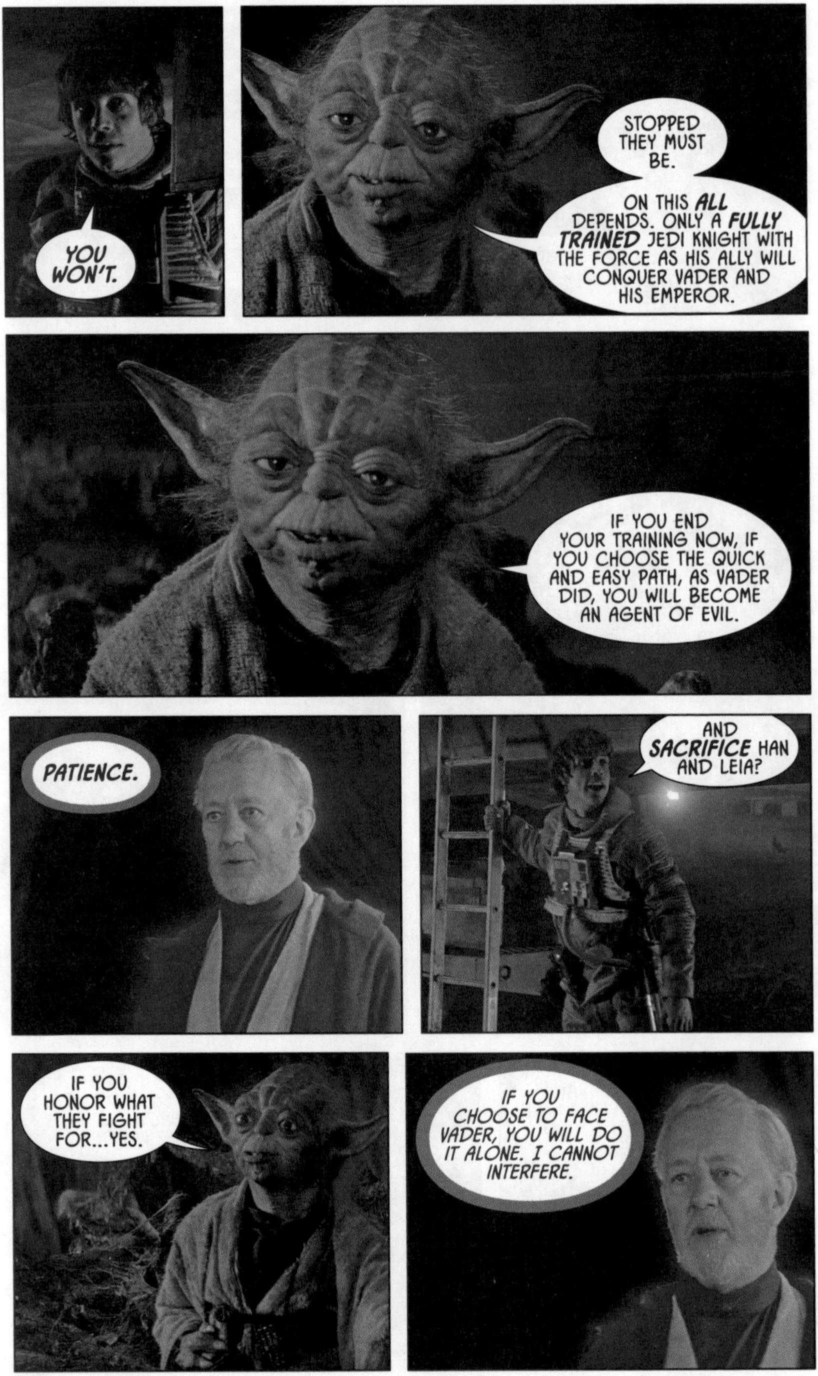
YOU WON'T.
STOPPED THEY MUST BE.
ON THIS ALL DEPENDS. ONLY A FULLY TRAINED JEDI KNIGHT WITH THE FORCE AS HIS ALLY WILL CONQUER VADER AND HIS EMPEROR.
IF YOU END YOUR TRAINING NOW, IF YOU CHOOSE THE QUICK AND EASY PATH, AS VADER DID, YOU WILL BECOME AN AGENT OF EVIL.
PATIENCE.
AND SACRIFICE HAN AND LEIA?
IF YOU HONOR WHAT THEY FIGHT FOR...YES.
IF YOU CHOOSE TO FACE VADER, YOU WILL DO IT ALONE. I CANNOT INTERFERE.

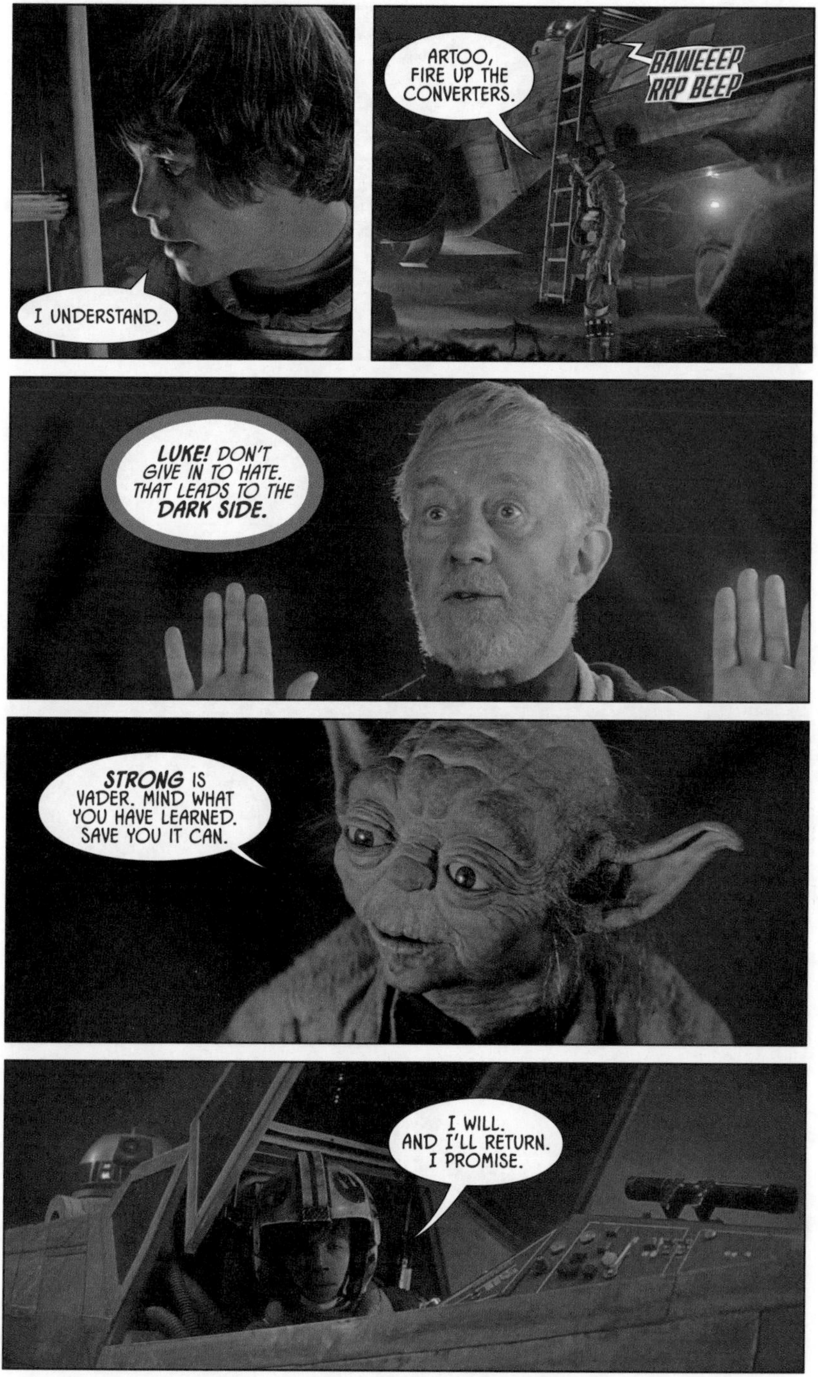
I UNDERSTAND.
ARTOO, FIRE UP THE CONVERTERS.
BAWEEEP RRP BEEP
LUKE! DON'T GIVE IN TO HATE. THAT LEADS TO THE DARK SIDE.
STRONG IS VADER. MIND WHAT YOU HAVE LEARNED. SAVE YOU IT CAN.
I WILL. AND I'LL RETURN. I PROMISE.

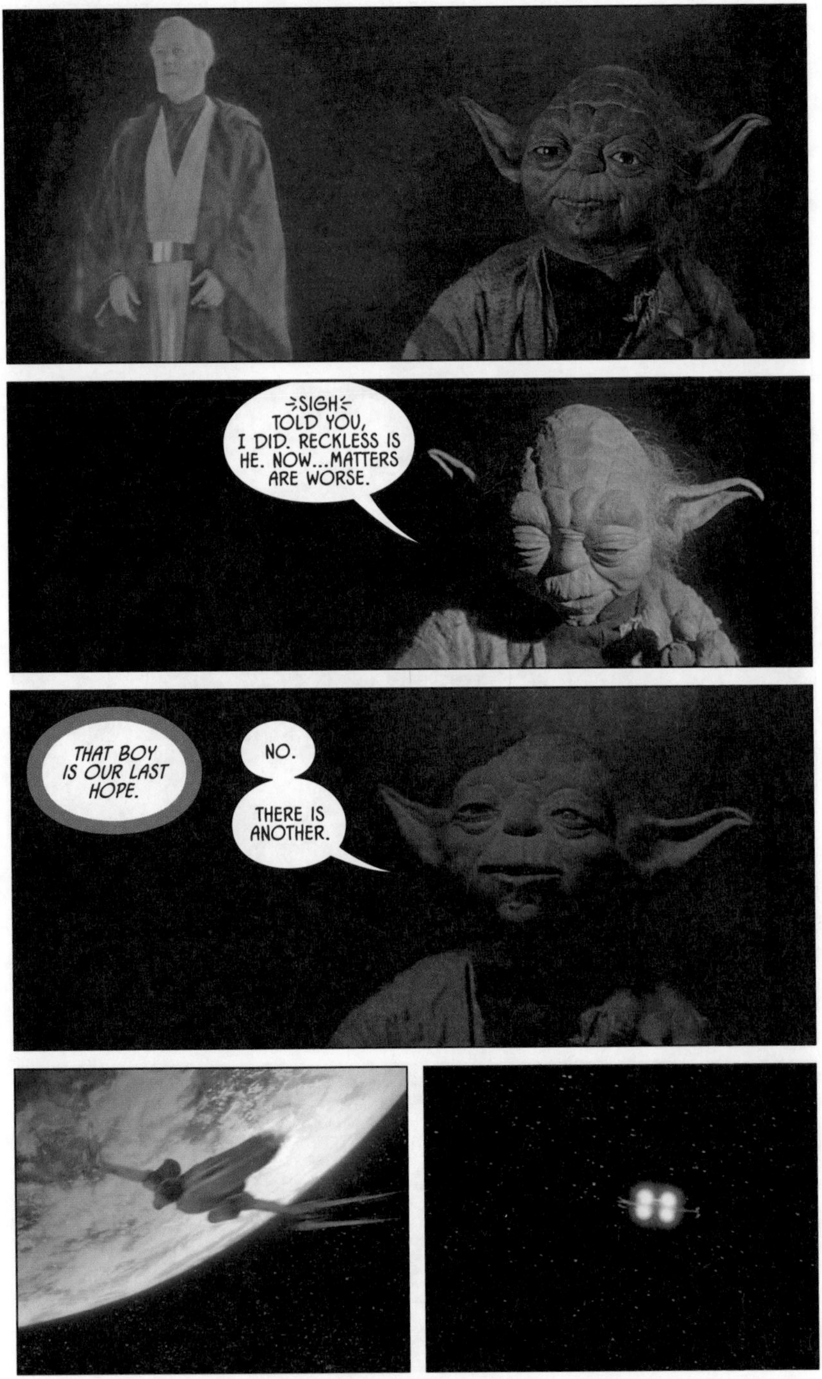

⇉SIGH⇇ TOLD YOU, I DID. RECKLESS IS HE. NOW...MATTERS ARE WORSE.
THAT BOY IS OUR LAST HOPE.
NO.
THERE IS ANOTHER.

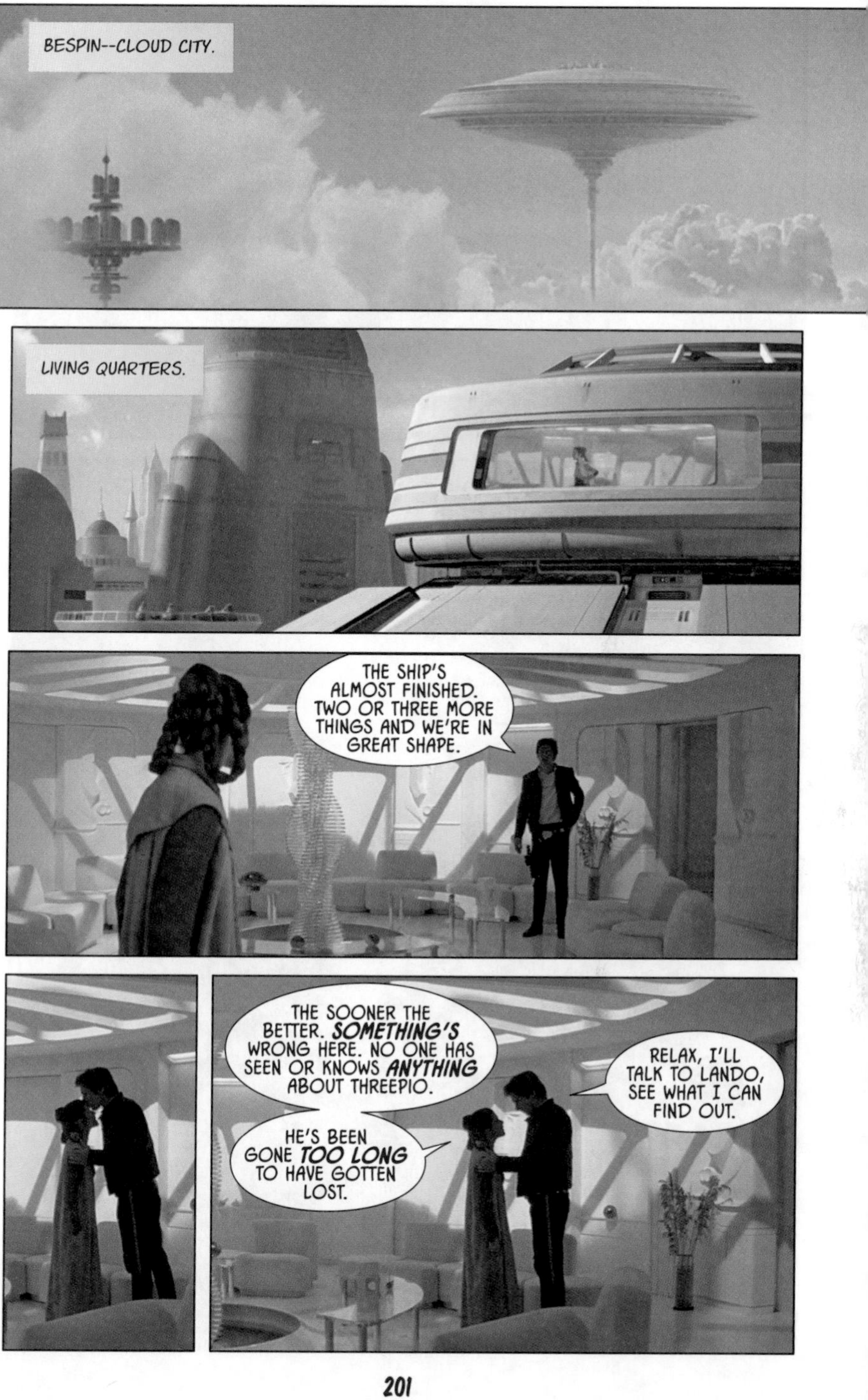

BESPIN--CLOUD CITY.
LIVING QUARTERS.
THE SHIP'S ALMOST FINISHED. TWO OR THREE MORE THINGS AND WE'RE IN GREAT SHAPE.
THE SOONER THE BETTER. SOMETHING'S WRONG HERE. NO ONE HAS SEEN OR KNOWS ANYTHING ABOUT THREEPIO.
HE'S BEEN GONE TOO LONG TO HAVE GOTTEN LOST.
RELAX, I'LL TALK TO LANDO, SEE WHAT I CAN FIND OUT.

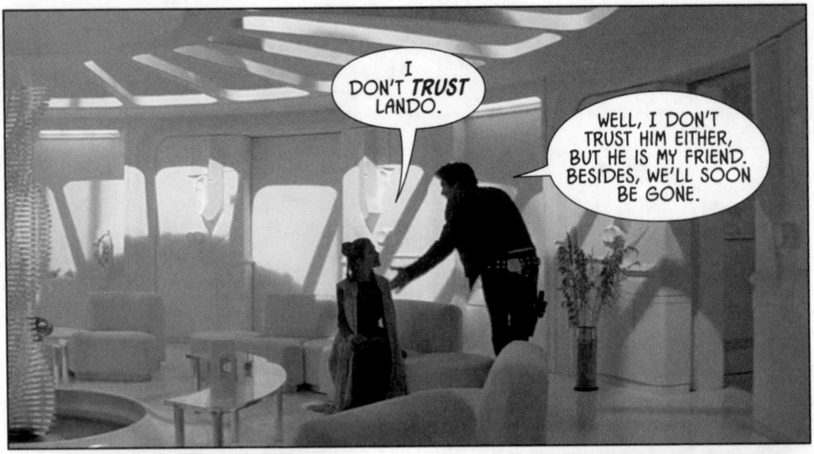
I DON'T TRUST LANDO.
WELL, I DON'T TRUST HIM EITHER, BUT HE IS MY FRIEND. BESIDES, WE'LL SOON BE GONE.

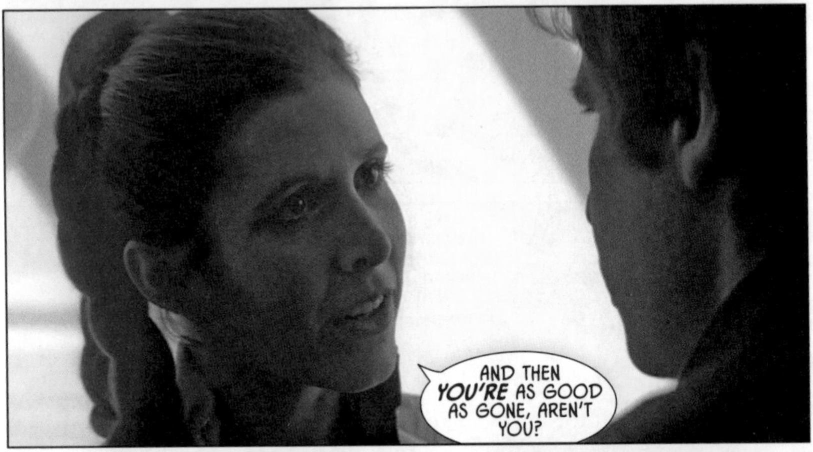
AND THEN YOU'RE AS GOOD AS GONE, AREN'T YOU?

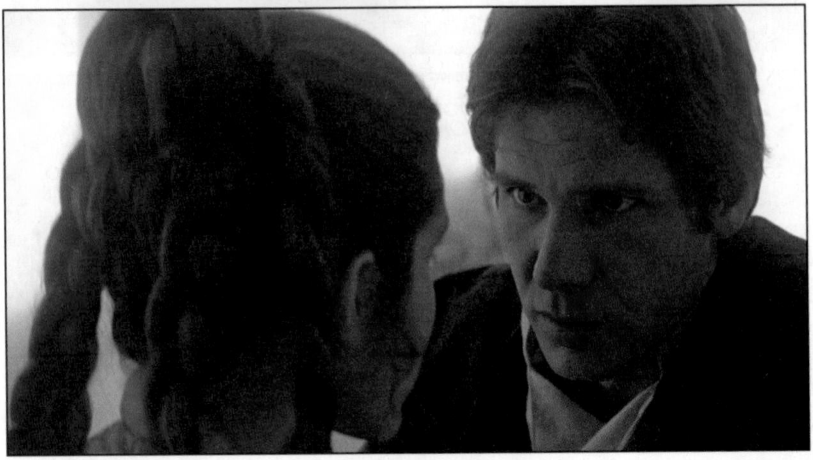

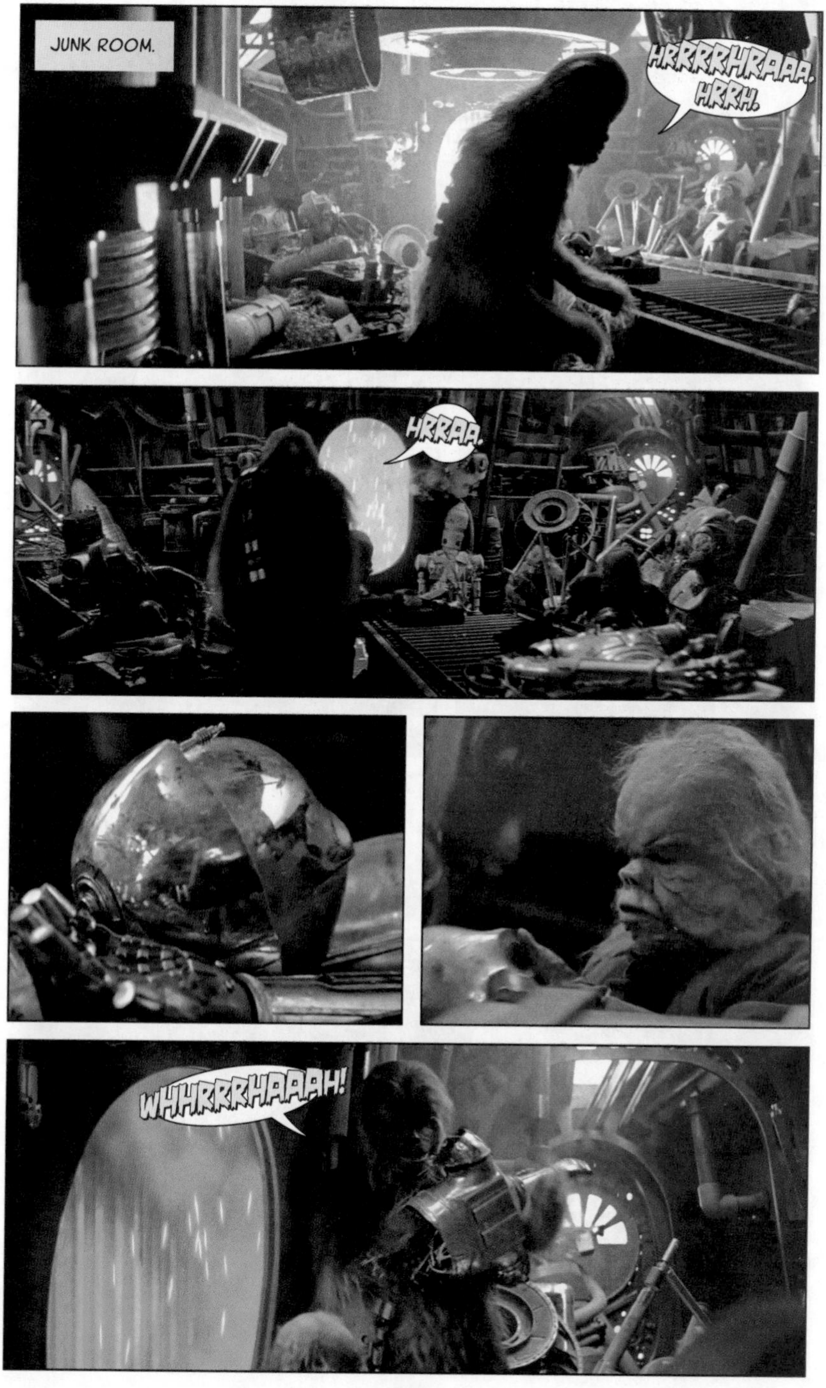
JUNK ROOM.
HRRRRHRAAA. HRRH.
HRRAA.
WHHRRRHAAAH!

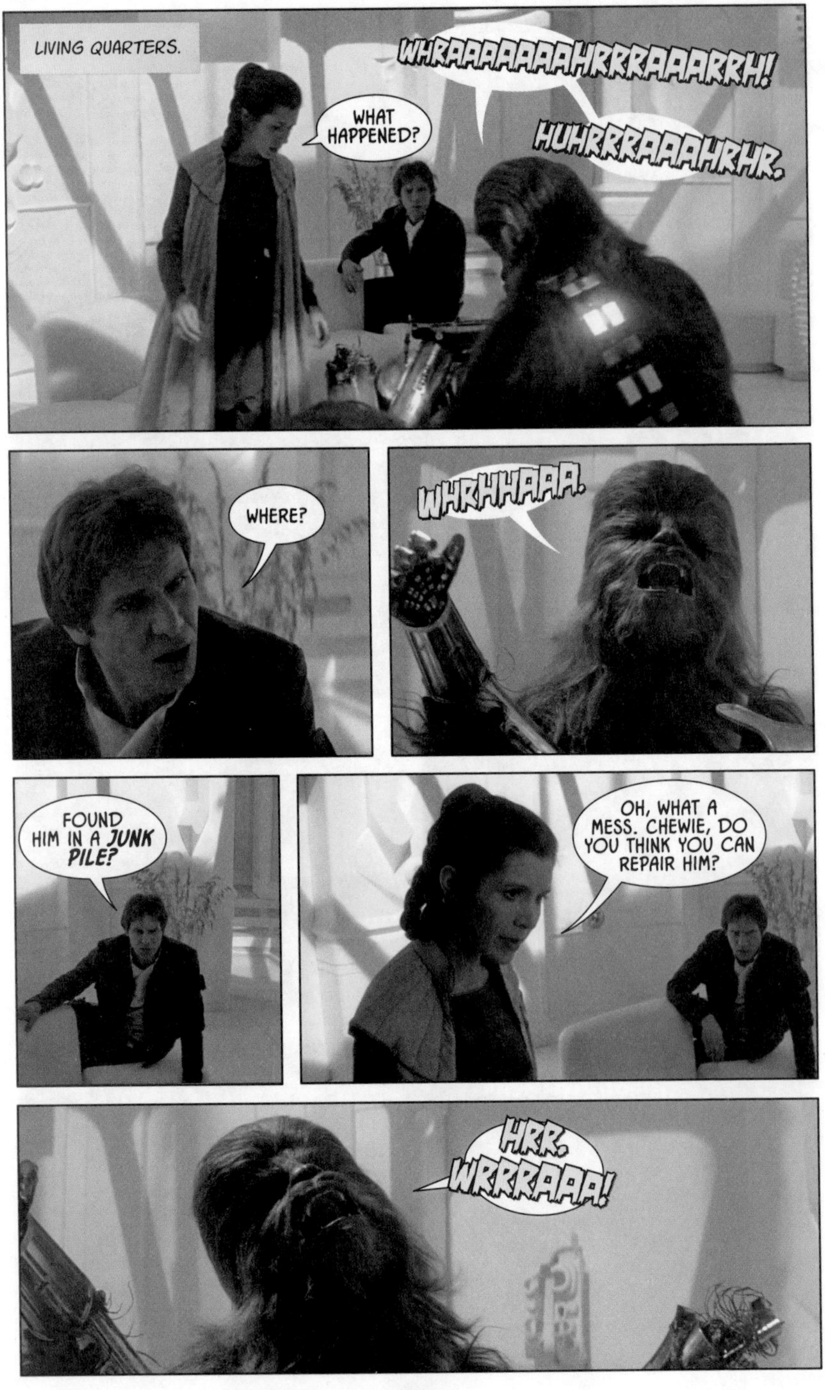
LIVING QUARTERS.
WHAT HAPPENED?
WHRAAAAAAAAHRRRAAARRH!
HUHRRRAAAHRHR.
WHERE?
WHRHHAAA.
FOUND HIM IN A *JUNK PILE?*
OH, WHAT A MESS. CHEWIE, DO YOU THINK YOU CAN REPAIR HIM?
HRR. WRRRAAA!

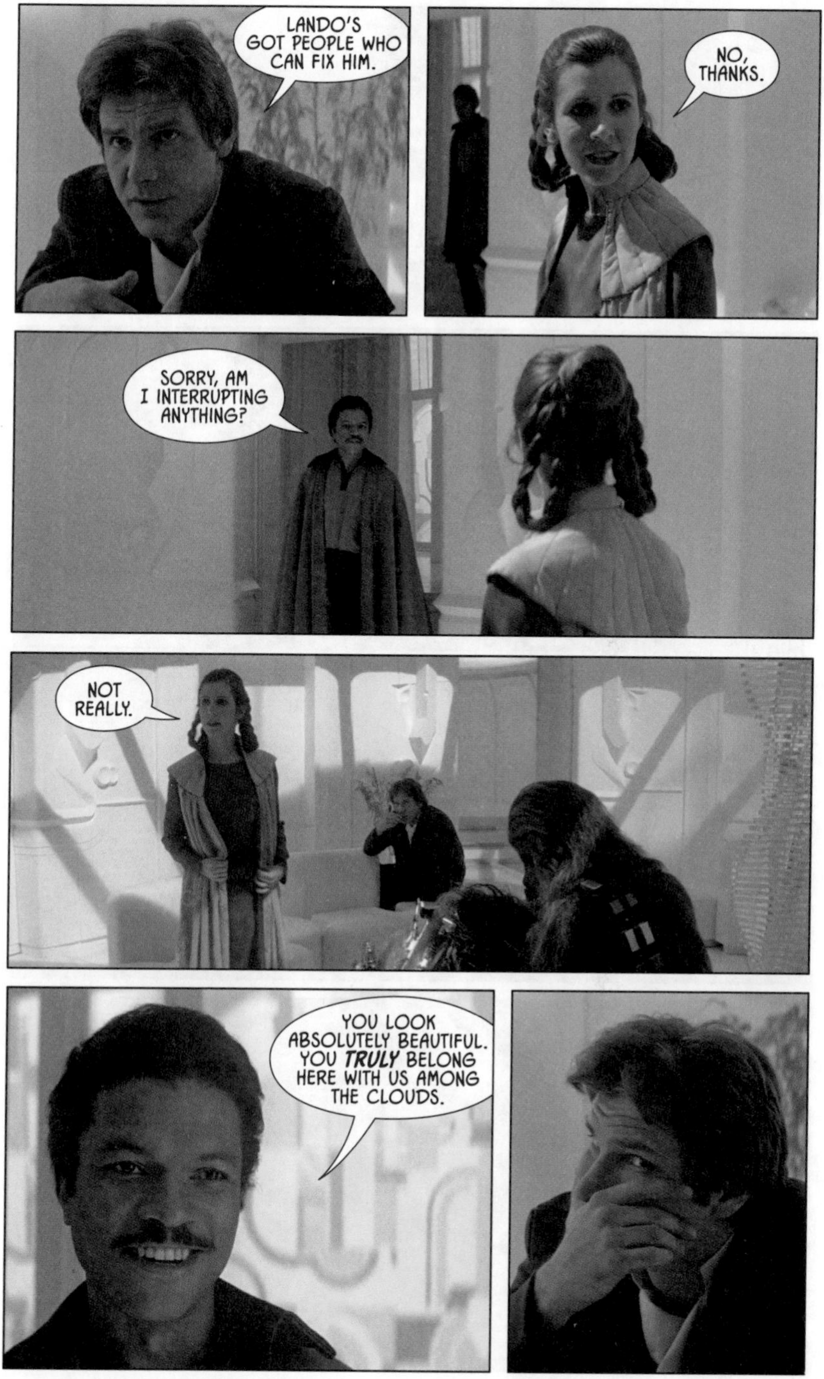
LANDO'S GOT PEOPLE WHO CAN FIX HIM.
NO, THANKS.
SORRY, AM I INTERRUPTING ANYTHING?
NOT REALLY.
YOU LOOK ABSOLUTELY BEAUTIFUL. YOU *TRULY* BELONG HERE WITH US AMONG THE CLOUDS.

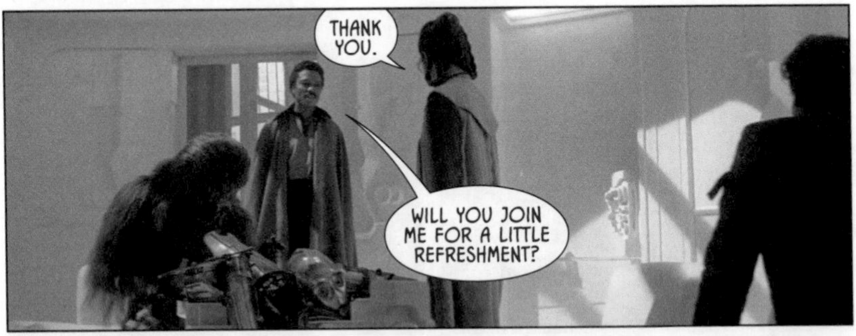
THANK YOU.
WILL YOU JOIN ME FOR A LITTLE REFRESHMENT?

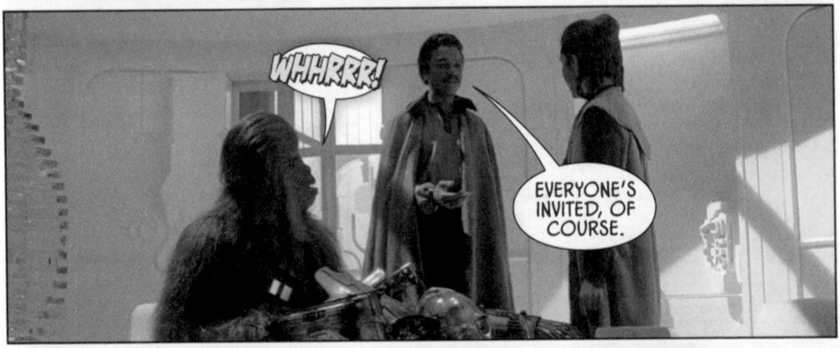
WHHRRR!
EVERYONE'S INVITED, OF COURSE.

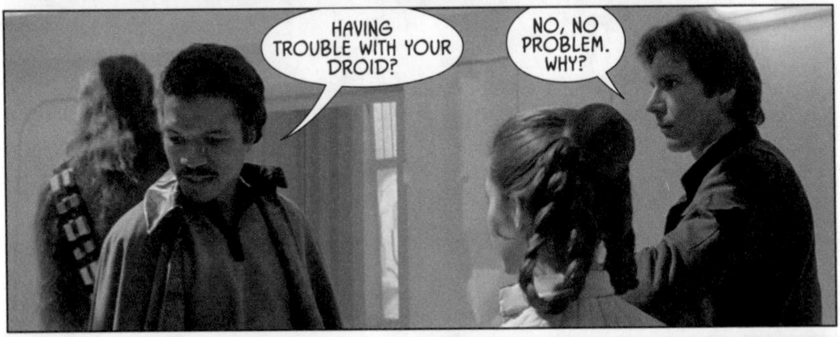
HAVING TROUBLE WITH YOUR DROID?
NO, NO PROBLEM. WHY?

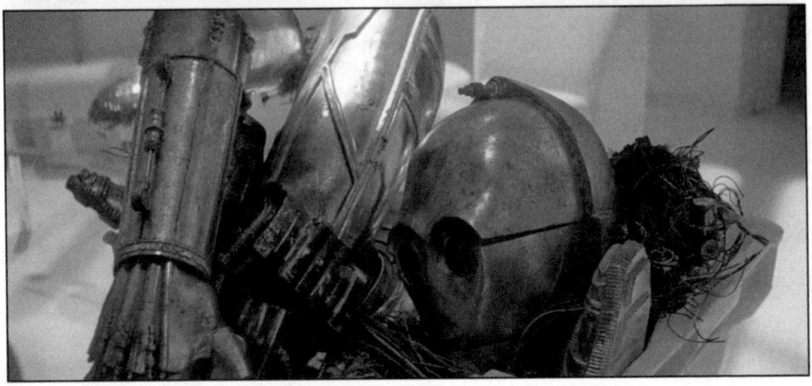

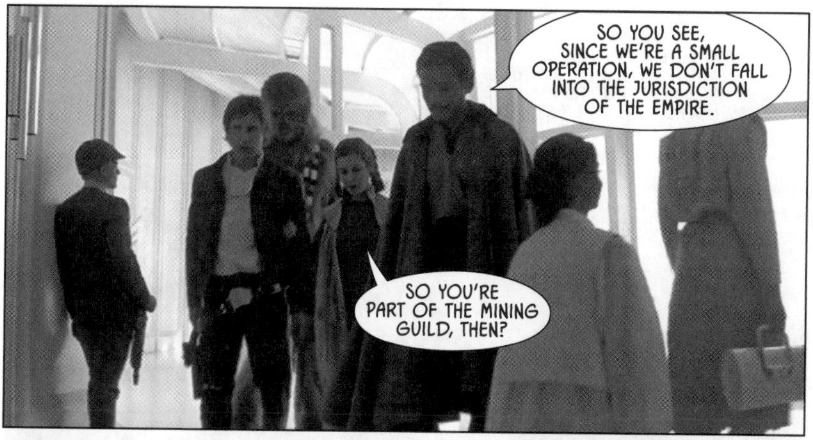
SO YOU SEE, SINCE WE'RE A SMALL OPERATION, WE DON'T FALL INTO THE JURISDICTION OF THE EMPIRE.
SO YOU'RE PART OF THE MINING GUILD, THEN?

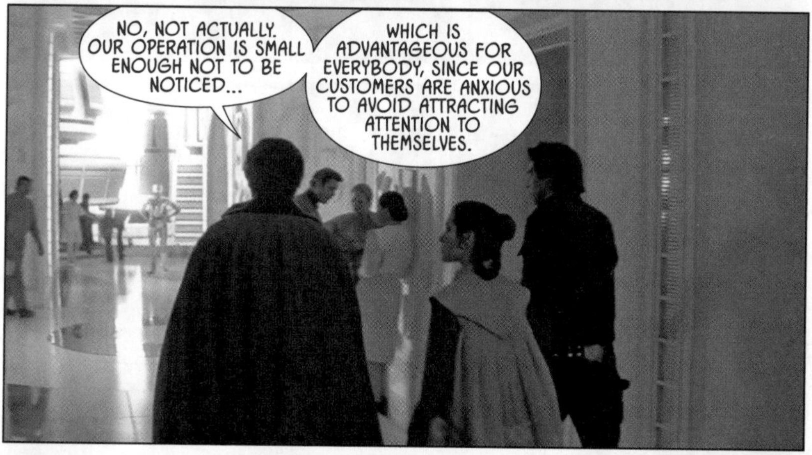
NO, NOT ACTUALLY. OUR OPERATION IS SMALL ENOUGH NOT TO BE NOTICED...
WHICH IS ADVANTAGEOUS FOR EVERYBODY, SINCE OUR CUSTOMERS ARE ANXIOUS TO AVOID ATTRACTING ATTENTION TO THEMSELVES.

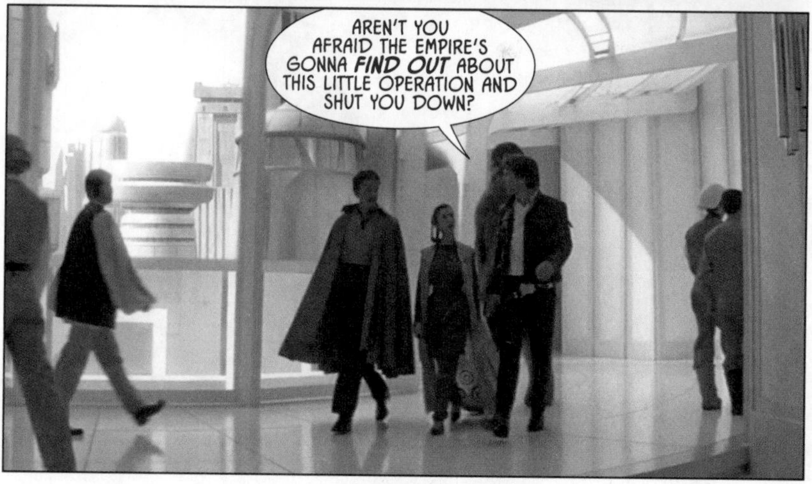
AREN'T YOU AFRAID THE EMPIRE'S GONNA FIND OUT ABOUT THIS LITTLE OPERATION AND SHUT YOU DOWN?

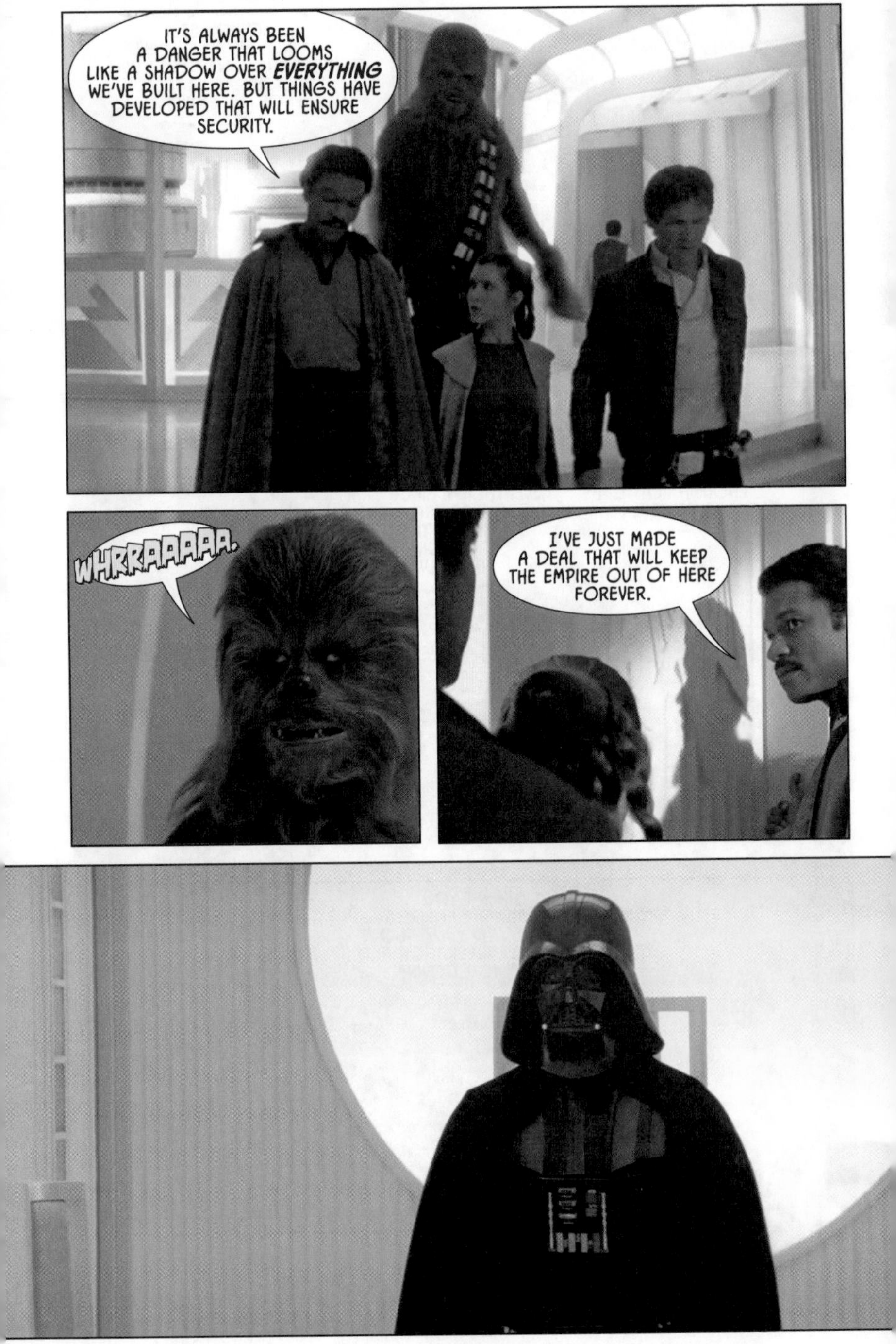
IT'S ALWAYS BEEN A DANGER THAT LOOMS LIKE A SHADOW OVER *EVERYTHING* WE'VE BUILT HERE. BUT THINGS HAVE DEVELOPED THAT WILL ENSURE SECURITY.
WHRRAAAAA.
I'VE JUST MADE A DEAL THAT WILL KEEP THE EMPIRE OUT OF HERE FOREVER.

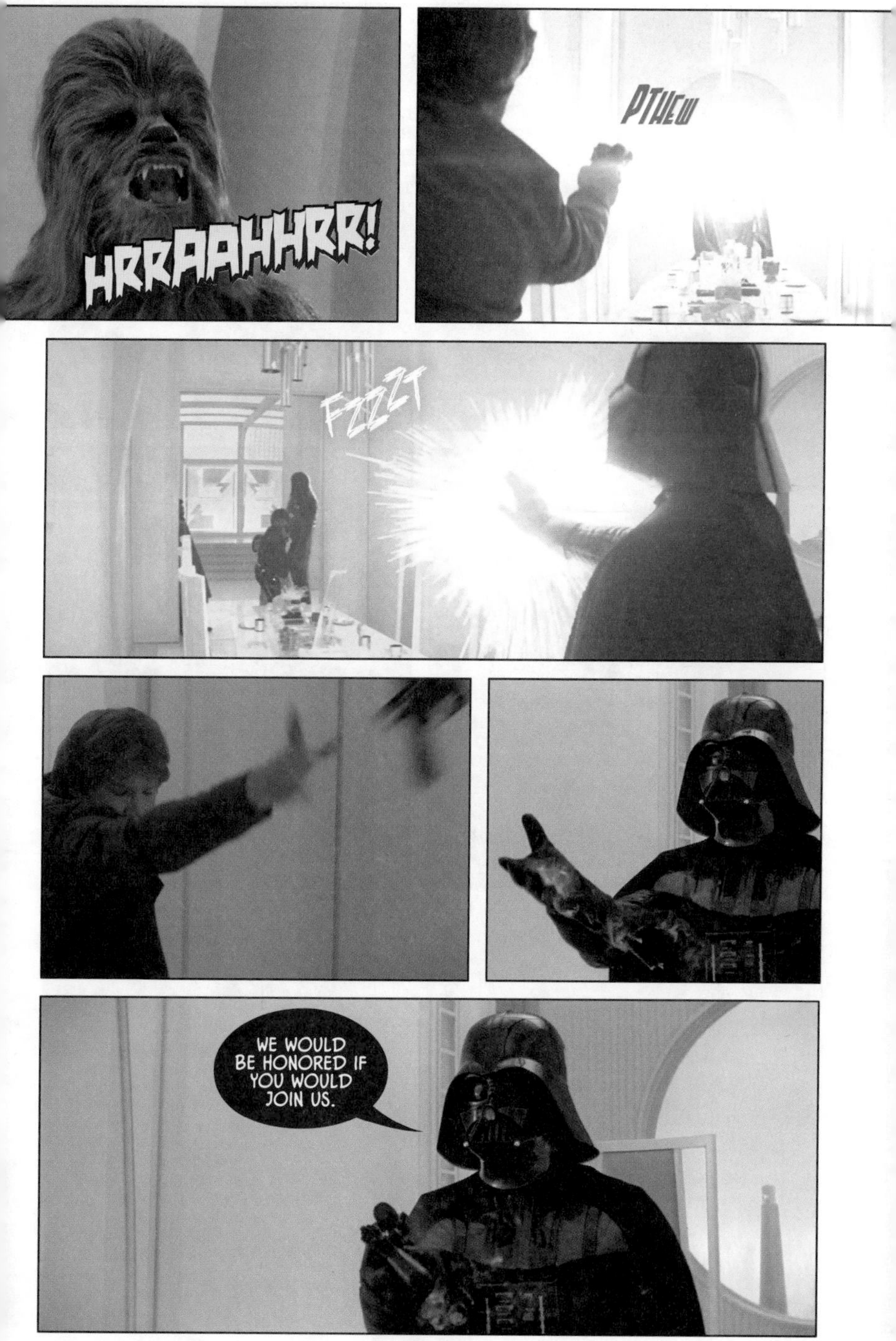
HRRAAHHRR!
PTHEW
FZZZT
WE WOULD BE HONORED IF YOU WOULD JOIN US.

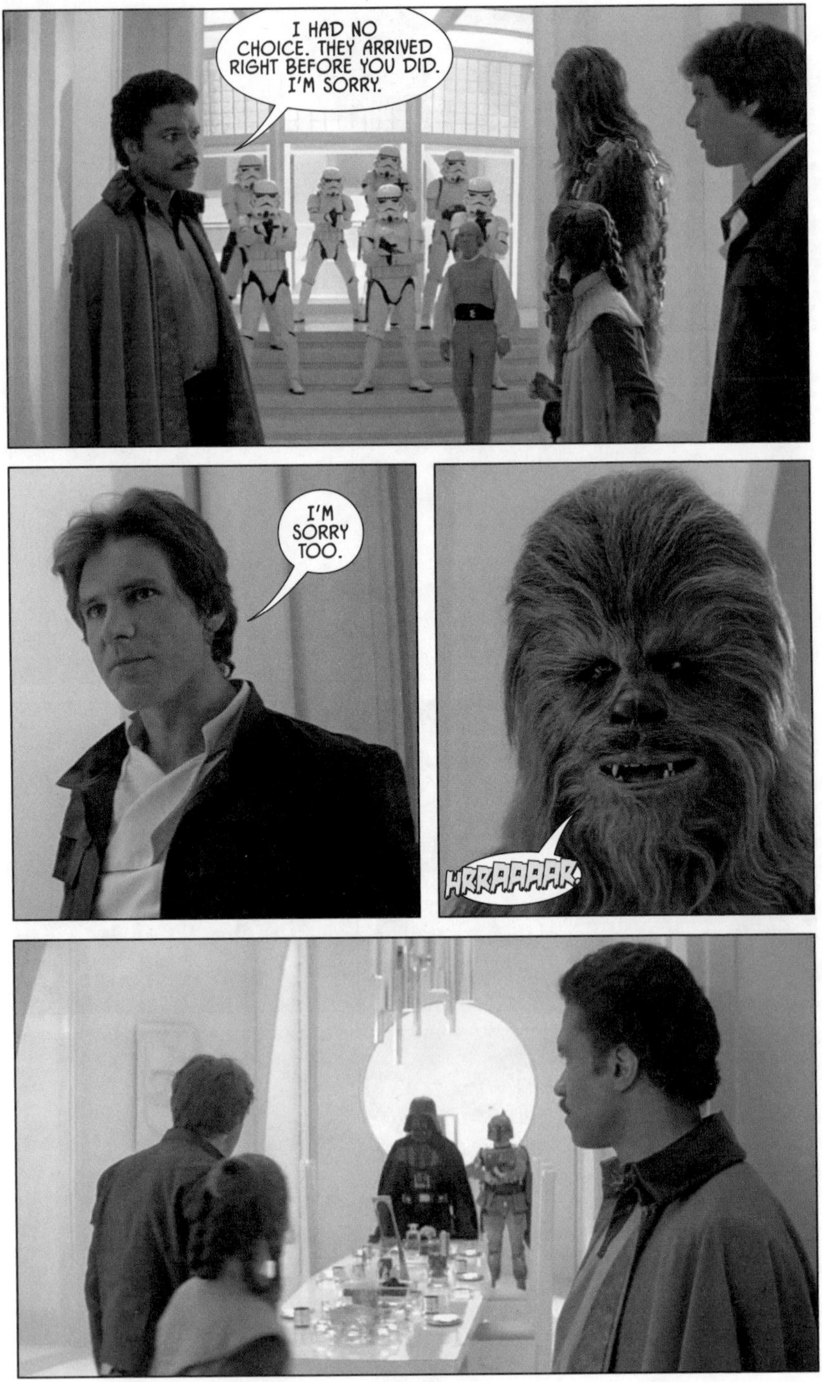
I HAD NO CHOICE. THEY ARRIVED RIGHT BEFORE YOU DID. I'M SORRY.
I'M SORRY TOO.
HRRAAAAR!

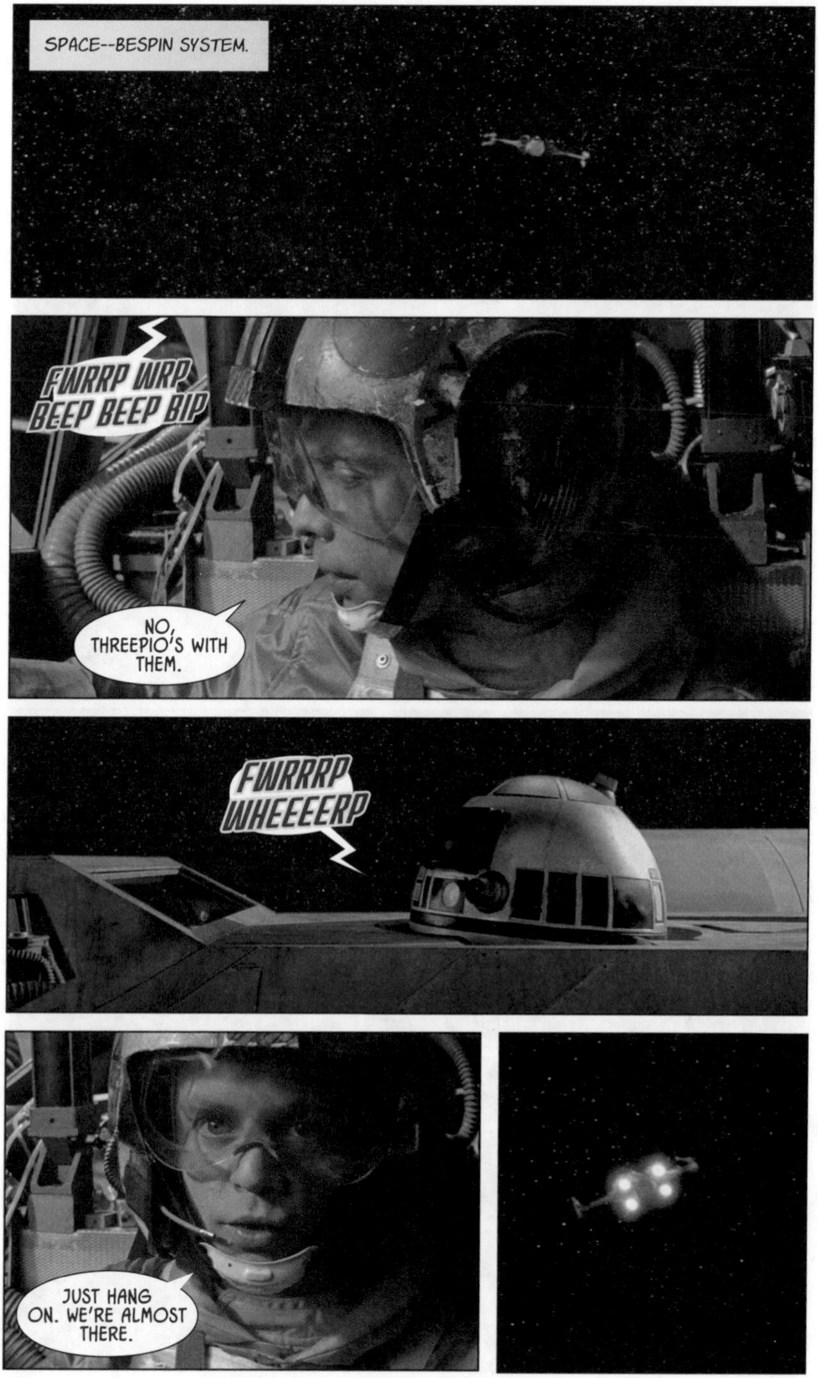
SPACE--BESPIN SYSTEM.
FWRRP WRP BEEP BEEP BIP
NO, THREEPIO'S WITH THEM.
FWRRRP WHEEEERP
JUST HANG ON. WE'RE ALMOST THERE.

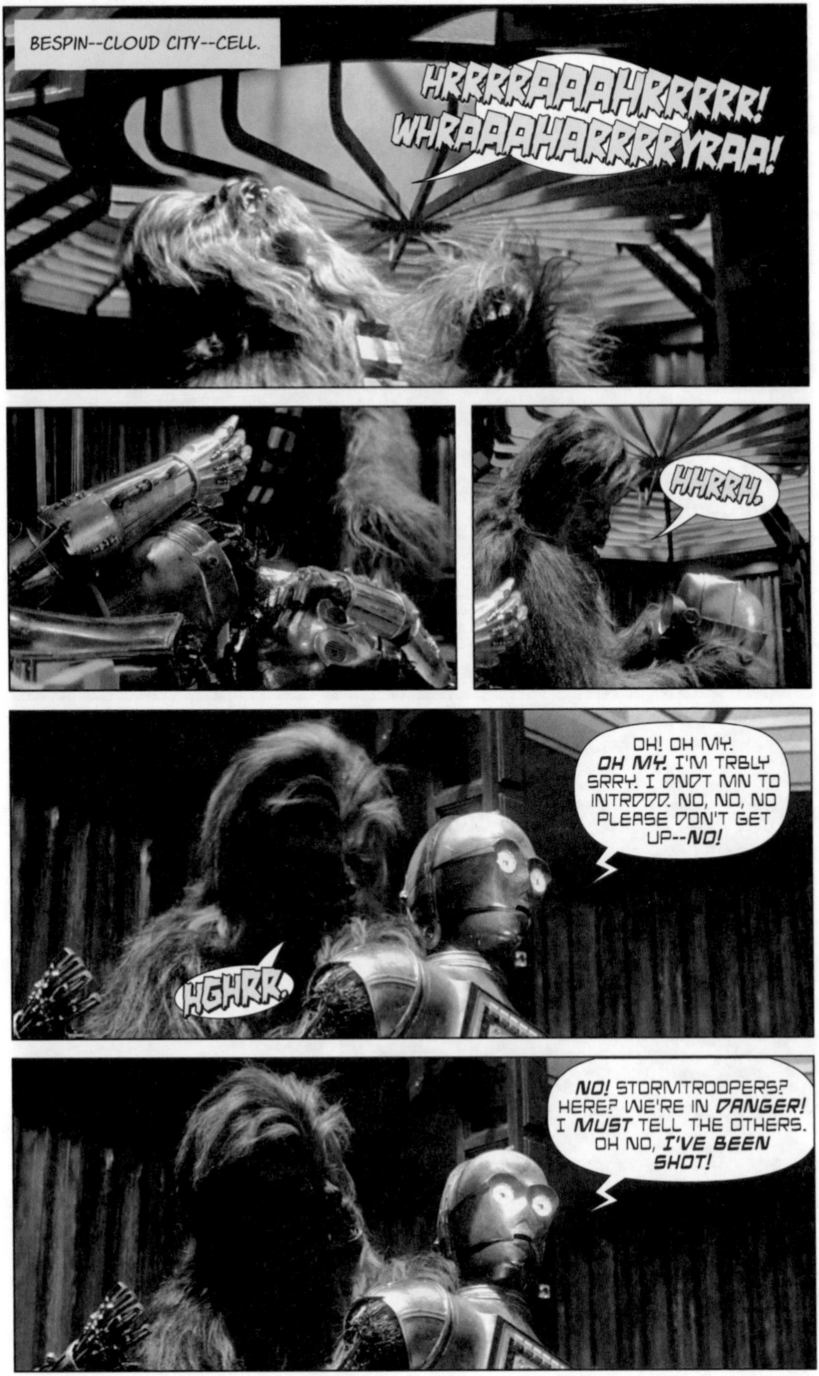

BESPIN--CLOUD CITY--CELL.
HRRRRAAAHRRRRR! WHRAAAHARRRRYRAA!
HHRRH.
OH! OH MY. OH MY. I'M TRBLY SRRY. I DNDT MN TO INTRDDD. NO, NO, NO PLEASE DON'T GET UP--NO!
HGHRR.
NO! STORMTROOPERS? HERE? WE'RE IN DANGER! I MUST TELL THE OTHERS. OH NO, I'VE BEEN SHOT!

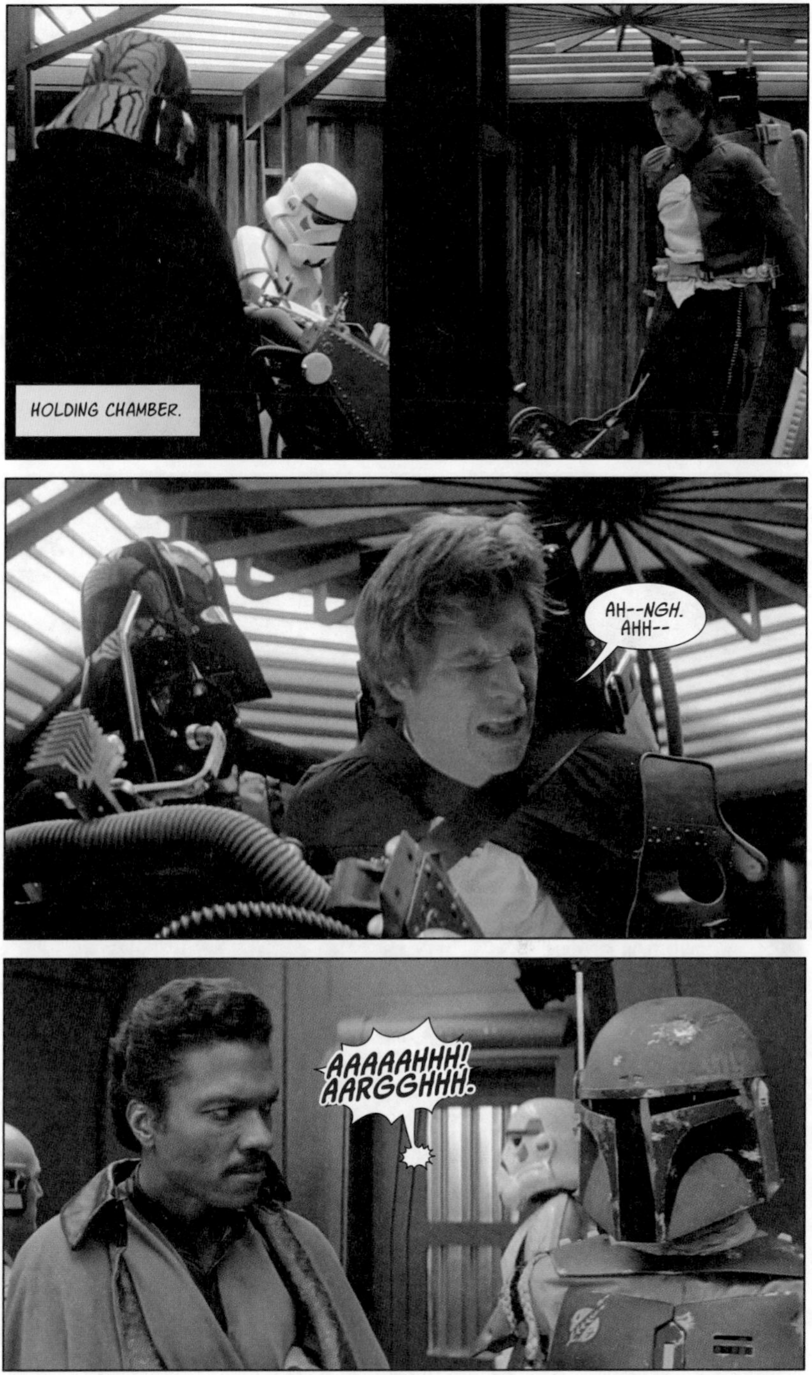
HOLDING CHAMBER.
AH--NGH. AHH--
AAAAAHHH! AARGGHHH.

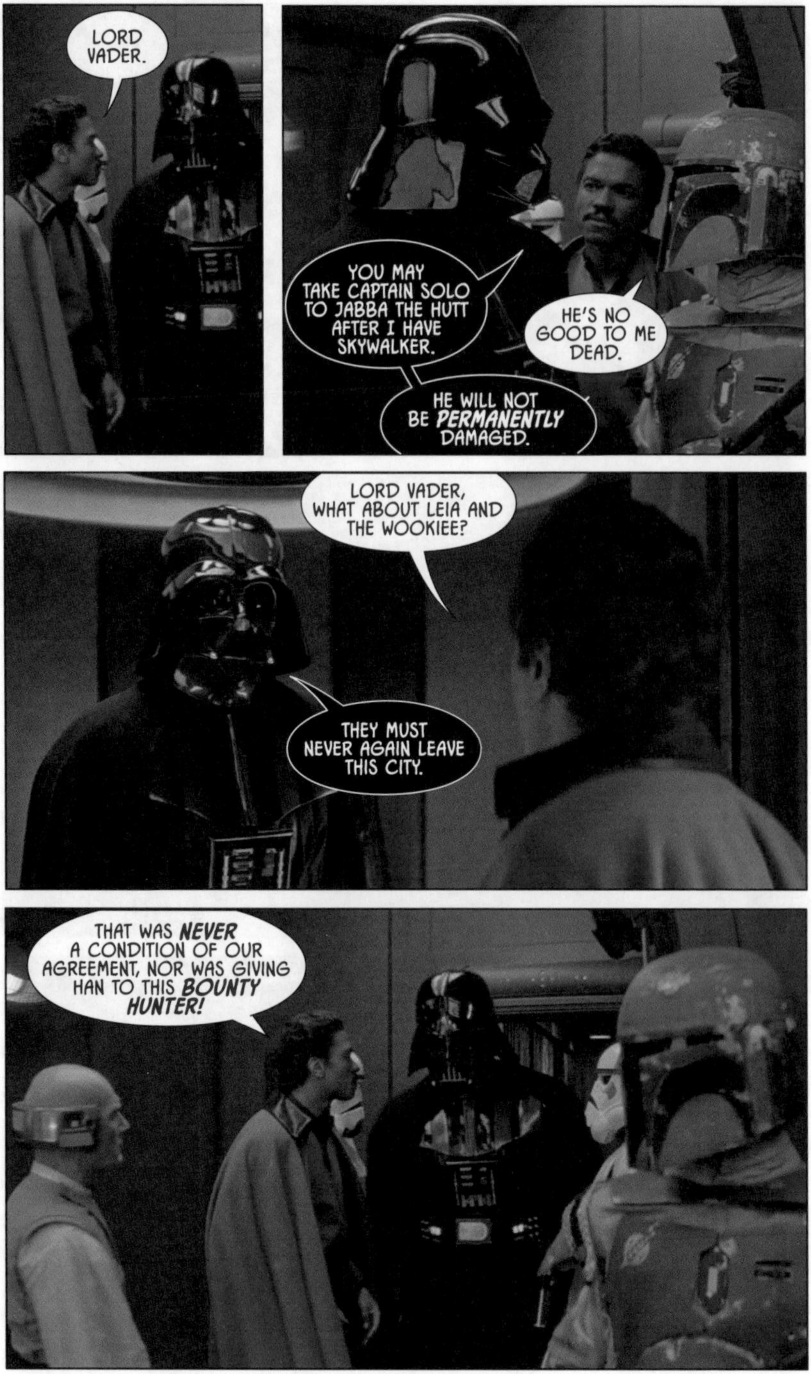
LORD VADER.
YOU MAY TAKE CAPTAIN SOLO TO JABBA THE HUTT AFTER I HAVE SKYWALKER.
HE'S NO GOOD TO ME DEAD.
HE WILL NOT BE **PERMANENTLY** DAMAGED.
LORD VADER, WHAT ABOUT LEIA AND THE WOOKIEE?
THEY MUST NEVER AGAIN LEAVE THIS CITY.
THAT WAS **NEVER** A CONDITION OF OUR AGREEMENT, NOR WAS GIVING HAN TO THIS **BOUNTY HUNTER!**

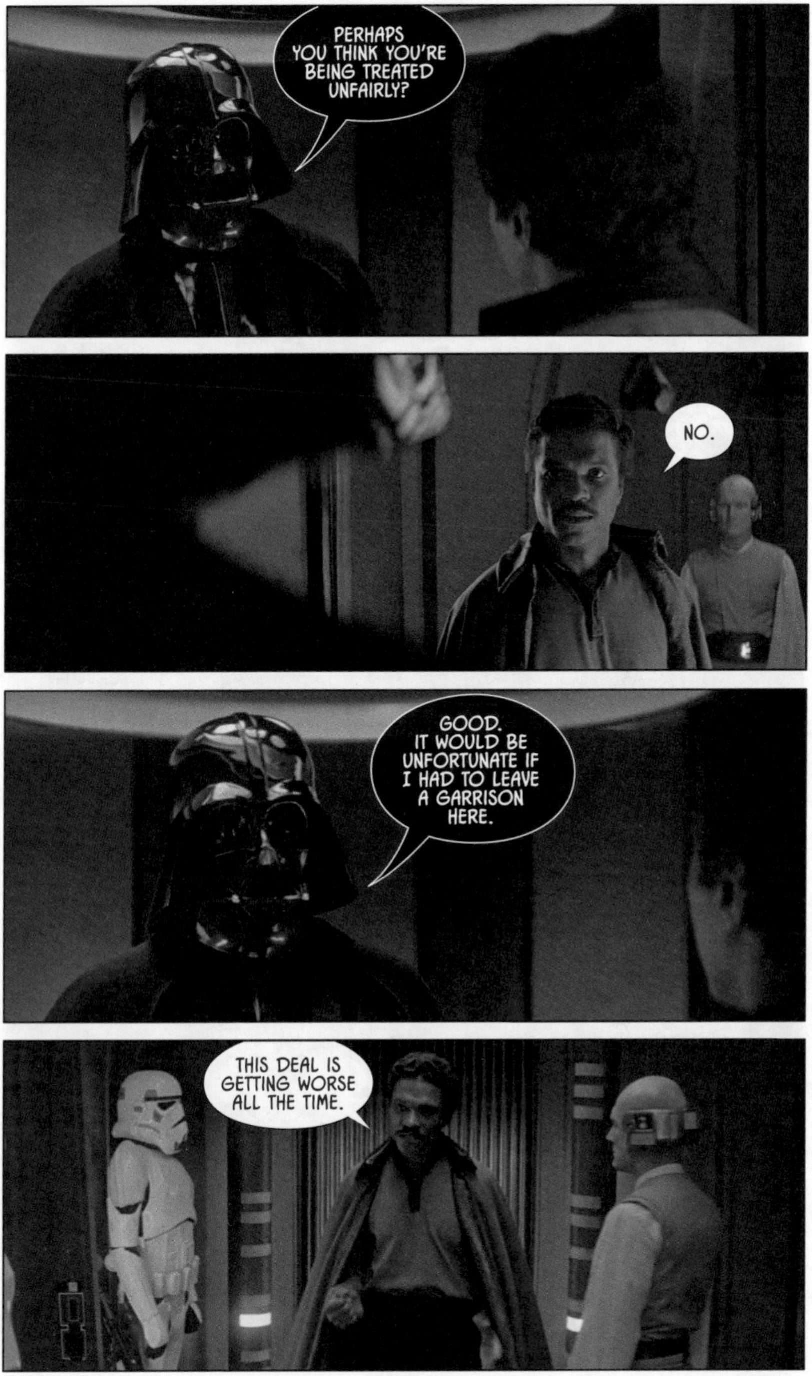
PERHAPS YOU THINK YOU'RE BEING TREATED UNFAIRLY?
NO.
GOOD. IT WOULD BE UNFORTUNATE IF I HAD TO LEAVE A GARRISON HERE.
THIS DEAL IS GETTING WORSE ALL THE TIME.

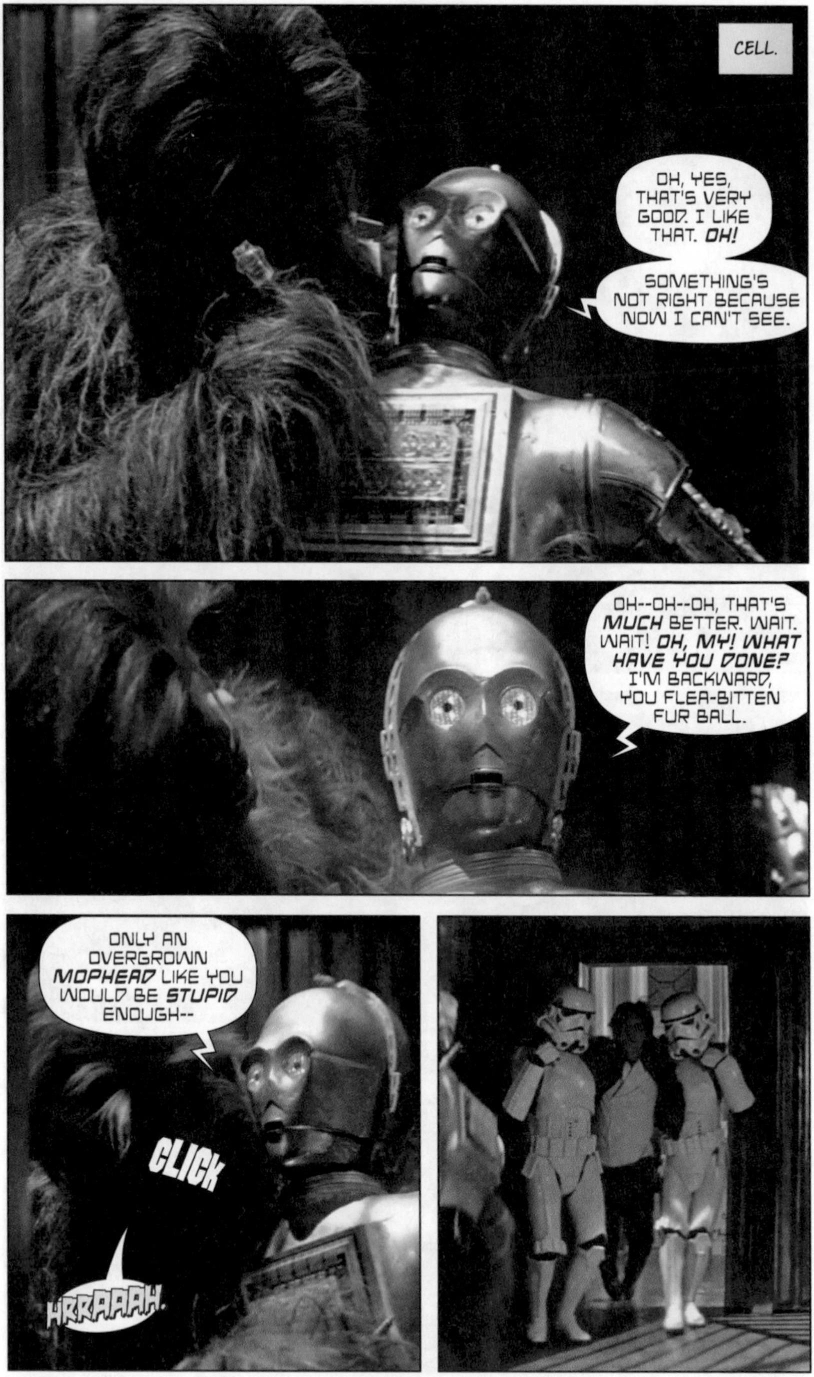
CELL.
OH, YES, THAT'S VERY GOOD. I LIKE THAT. OH!
SOMETHING'S NOT RIGHT BECAUSE NOW I CAN'T SEE.
OH--OH--OH, THAT'S MUCH BETTER. WAIT. WAIT! OH, MY! WHAT HAVE YOU DONE? I'M BACKWARD, YOU FLEA-BITTEN FUR BALL.
ONLY AN OVERGROWN MOPHEAD LIKE YOU WOULD BE STUPID ENOUGH--
CLICK
HRRAAAH.

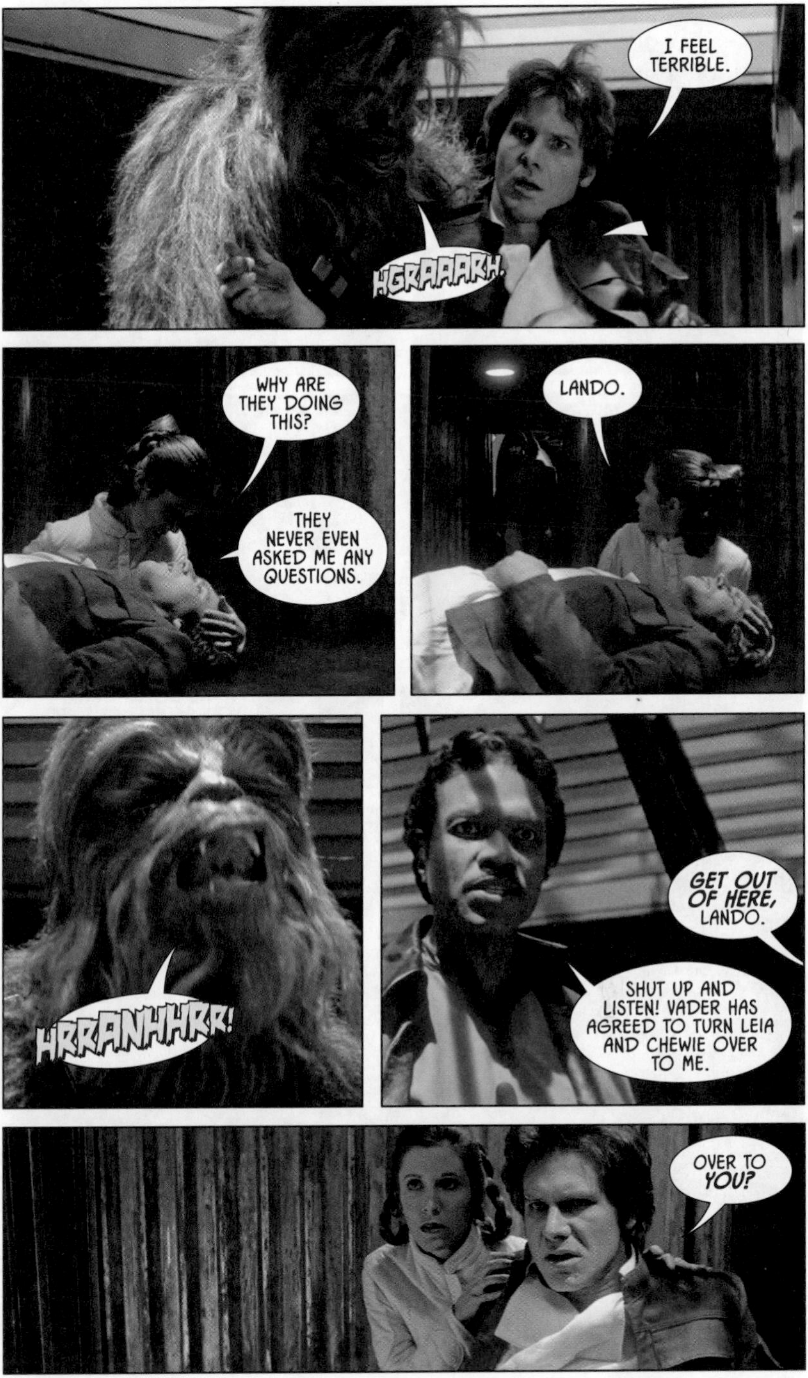

I FEEL TERRIBLE.
HGRAAARH.
WHY ARE THEY DOING THIS?
THEY NEVER EVEN ASKED ME ANY QUESTIONS.
LANDO.
HRRANHHRR!
GET OUT OF HERE, LANDO.
SHUT UP AND LISTEN! VADER HAS AGREED TO TURN LEIA AND CHEWIE OVER TO ME.
OVER TO YOU?

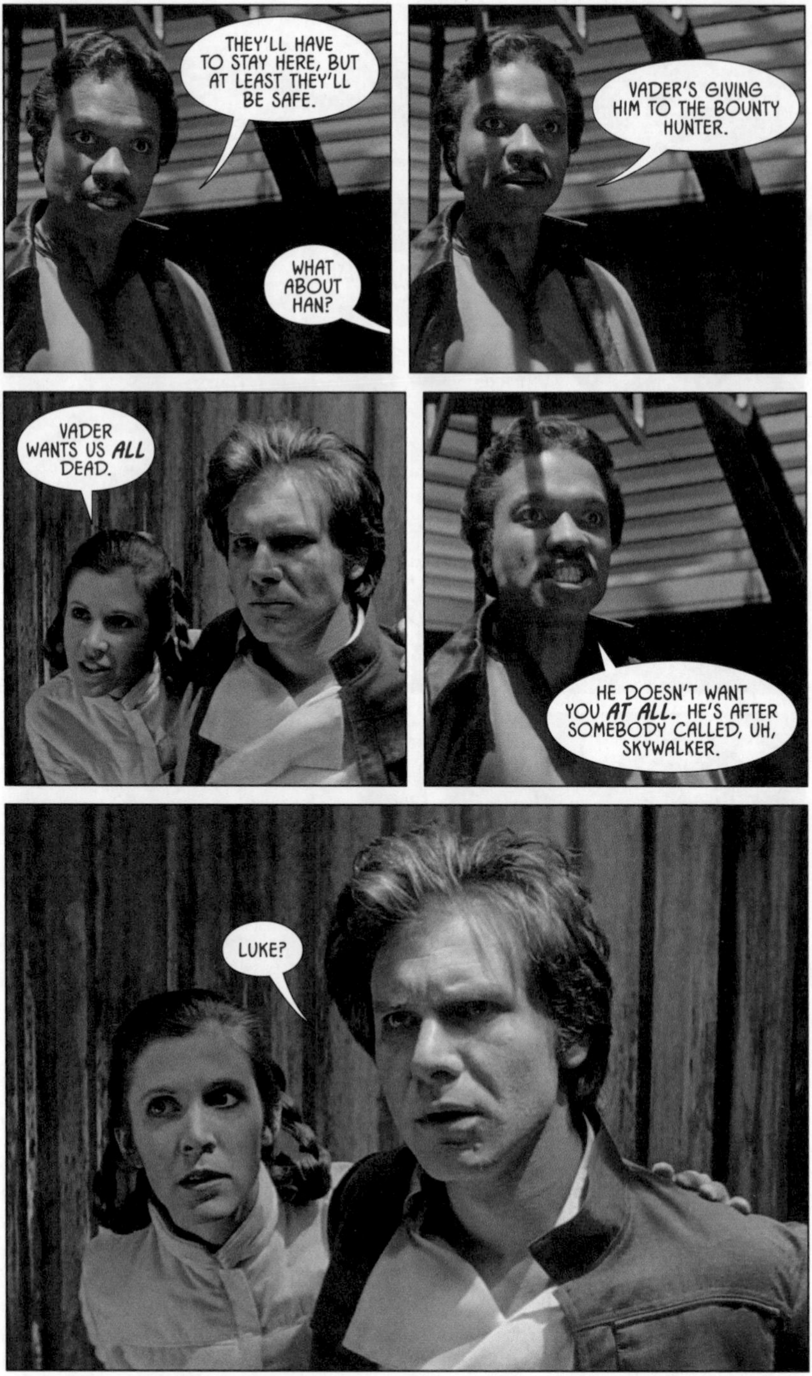
THEY'LL HAVE TO STAY HERE, BUT AT LEAST THEY'LL BE SAFE.
WHAT ABOUT HAN?
VADER'S GIVING HIM TO THE BOUNTY HUNTER.
VADER WANTS US *ALL* DEAD.
HE DOESN'T WANT YOU *AT ALL.* HE'S AFTER SOMEBODY CALLED, UH, SKYWALKER.
LUKE?

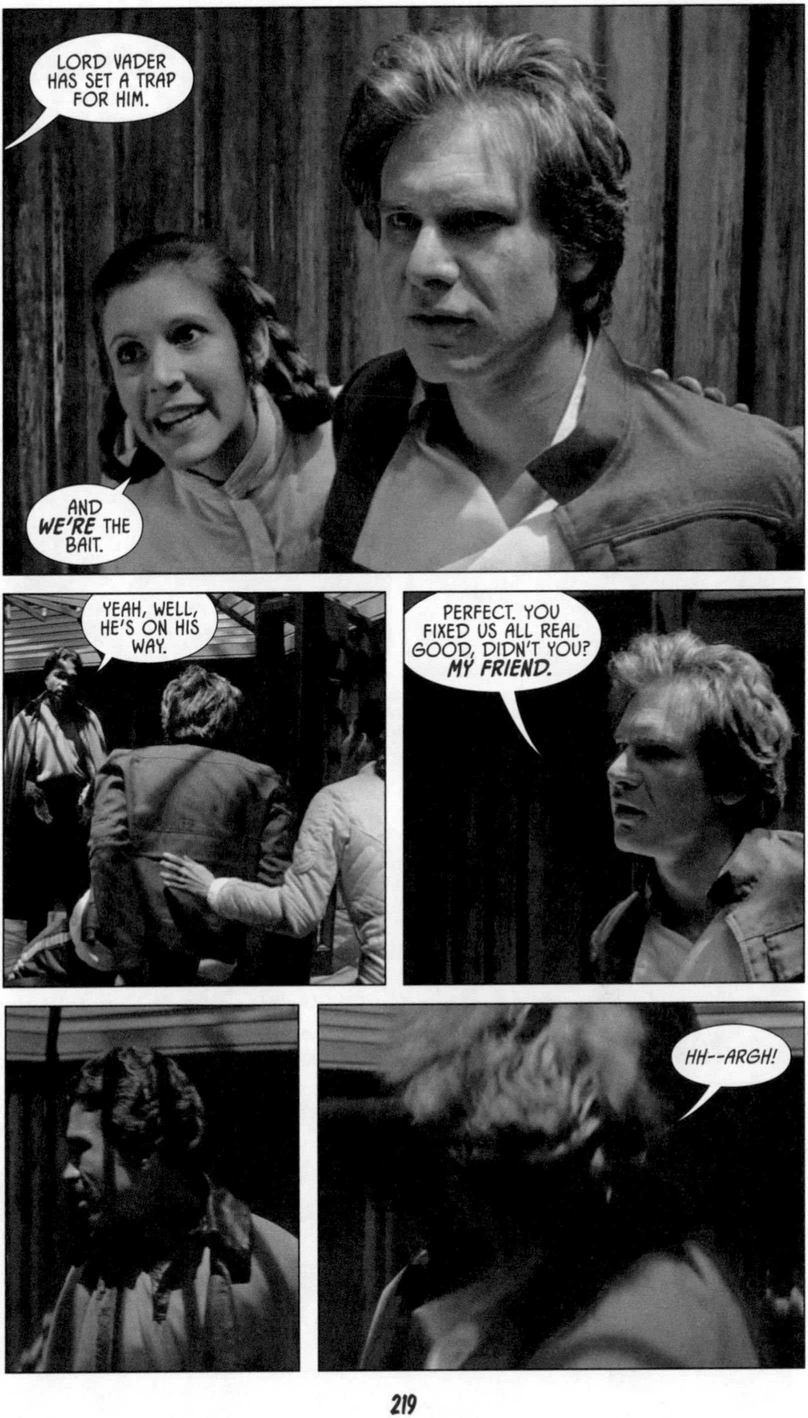

LORD VADER HAS SET A TRAP FOR HIM.
AND **WE'RE** THE BAIT.
YEAH, WELL, HE'S ON HIS WAY.
PERFECT. YOU FIXED US ALL REAL GOOD, DIDN'T YOU? **MY FRIEND.**
HH--ARGH!

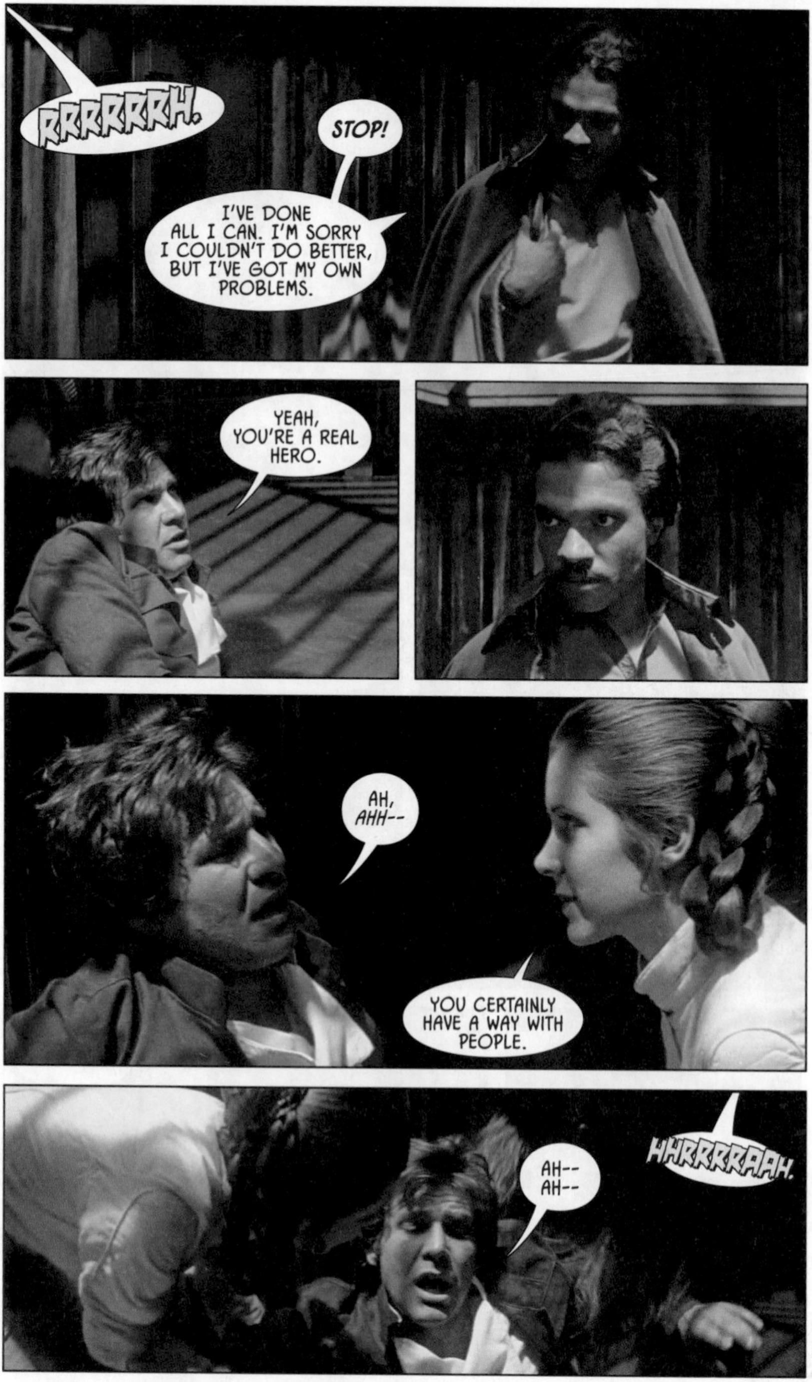
RRRRRRH.
STOP!
I'VE DONE ALL I CAN. I'M SORRY I COULDN'T DO BETTER, BUT I'VE GOT MY OWN PROBLEMS.
YEAH, YOU'RE A REAL HERO.
AH, AHH--
YOU CERTAINLY HAVE A WAY WITH PEOPLE.
AH-- AH--
HHRRRRAAH.

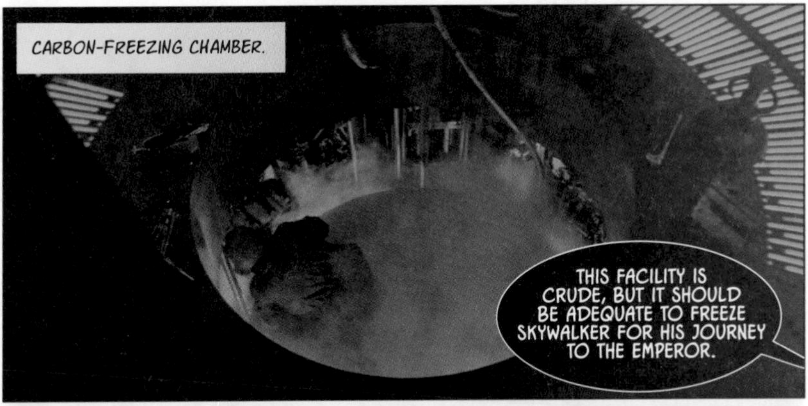
CARBON-FREEZING CHAMBER.
THIS FACILITY IS CRUDE, BUT IT SHOULD BE ADEQUATE TO FREEZE SKYWALKER FOR HIS JOURNEY TO THE EMPEROR.

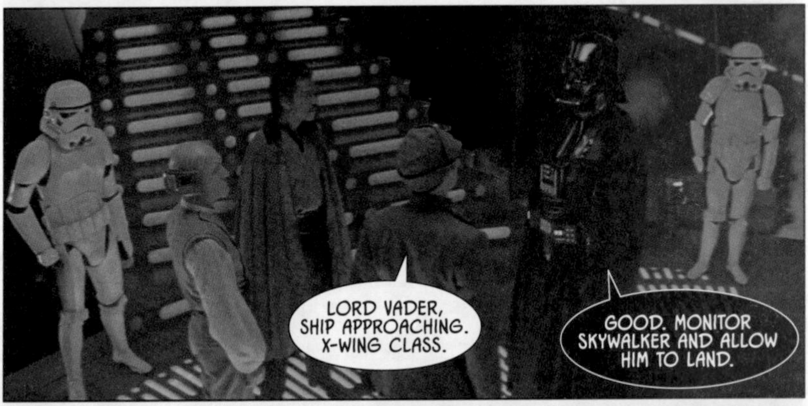
LORD VADER, SHIP APPROACHING. X-WING CLASS.
GOOD. MONITOR SKYWALKER AND ALLOW HIM TO LAND.

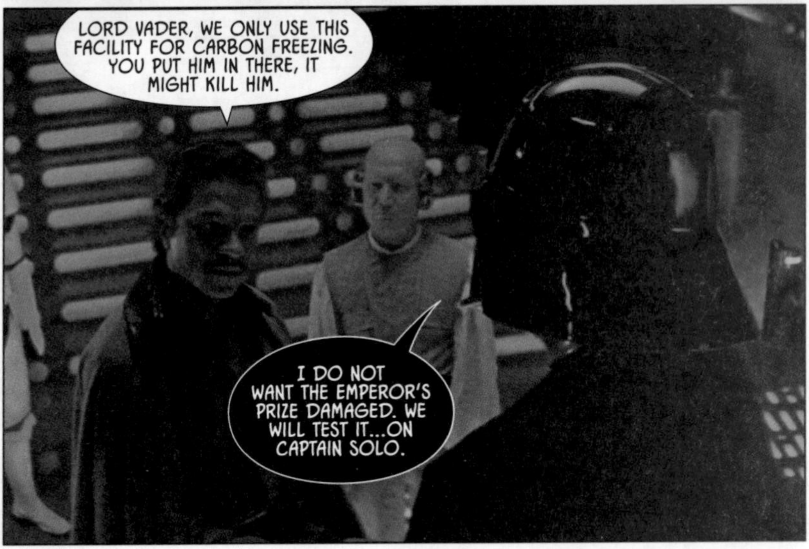
LORD VADER, WE ONLY USE THIS FACILITY FOR CARBON FREEZING. YOU PUT HIM IN THERE, IT MIGHT KILL HIM.
I DO NOT WANT THE EMPEROR'S PRIZE DAMAGED. WE WILL TEST IT...ON CAPTAIN SOLO.

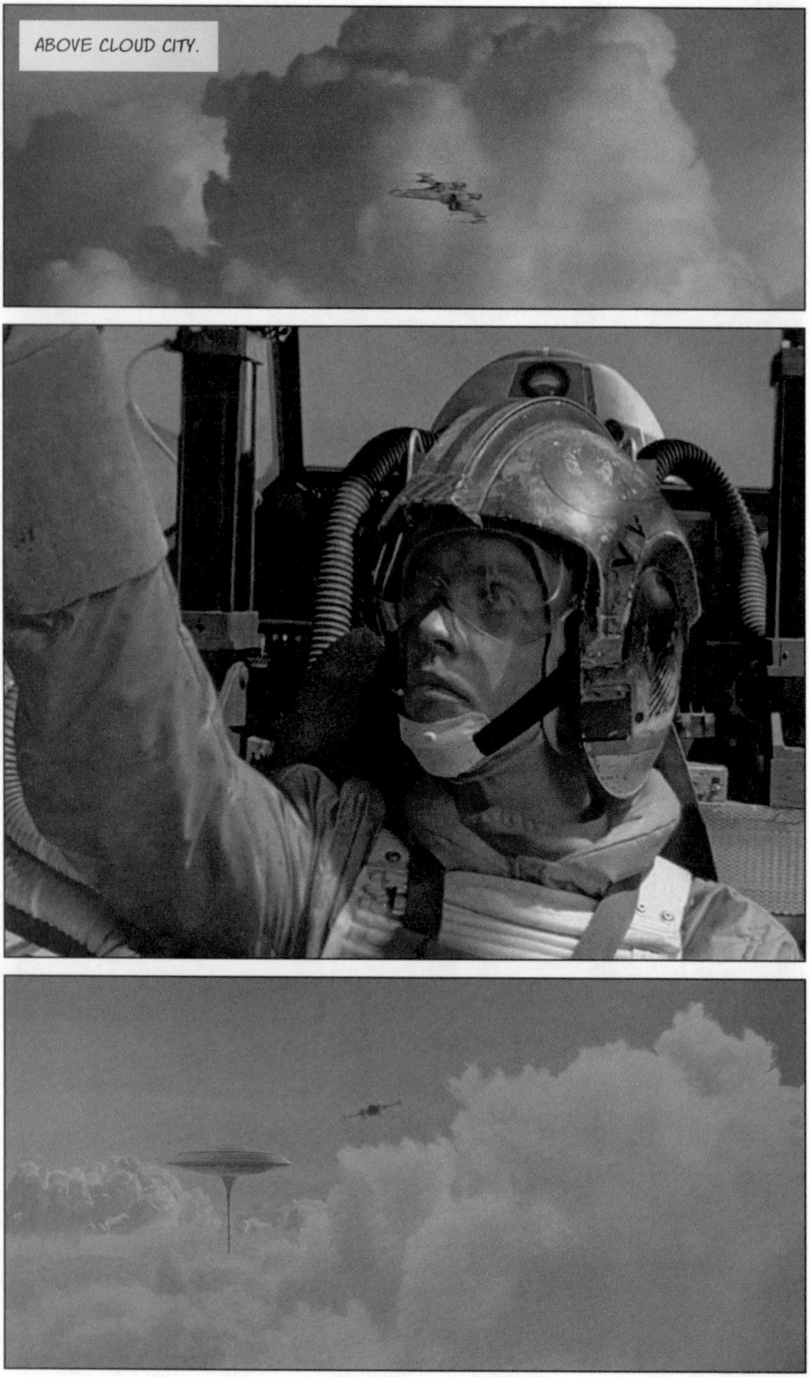
ABOVE CLOUD CITY.

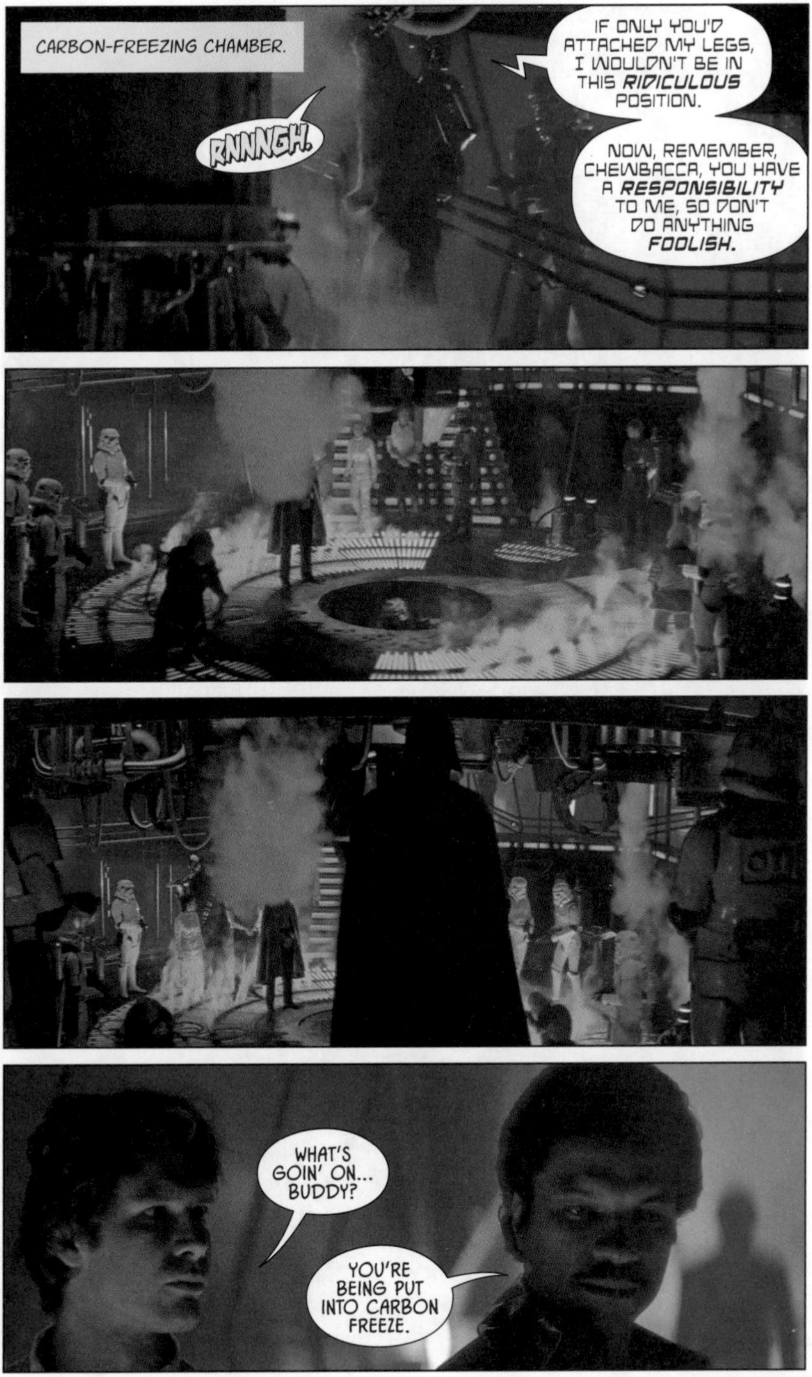
CARBON-FREEZING CHAMBER.
IF ONLY YOU'D ATTACHED MY LEGS, I WOULDN'T BE IN THIS RIDICULOUS POSITION.
RNNNGH.
NOW, REMEMBER, CHEWBACCA, YOU HAVE A RESPONSIBILITY TO ME, SO DON'T DO ANYTHING FOOLISH.
WHAT'S GOIN' ON... BUDDY?
YOU'RE BEING PUT INTO CARBON FREEZE.

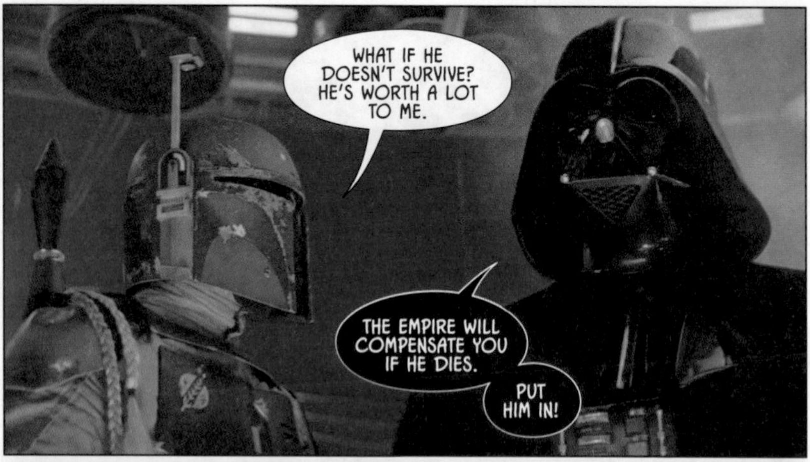
WHAT IF HE DOESN'T SURVIVE? HE'S WORTH A LOT TO ME.
THE EMPIRE WILL COMPENSATE YOU IF HE DIES.
PUT HIM IN!

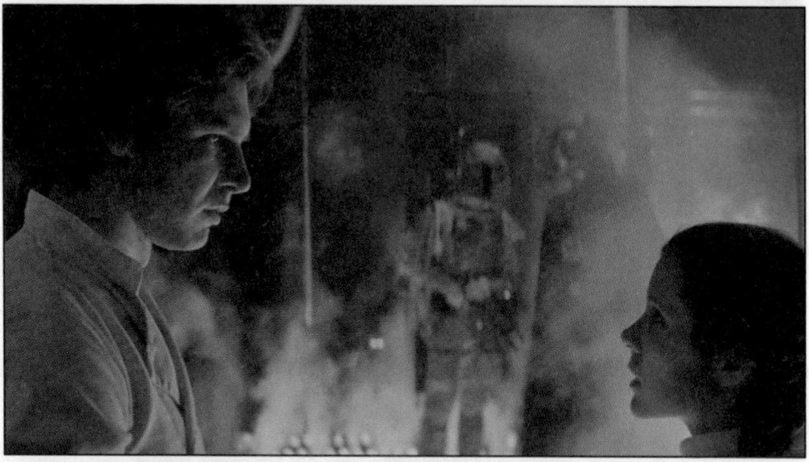

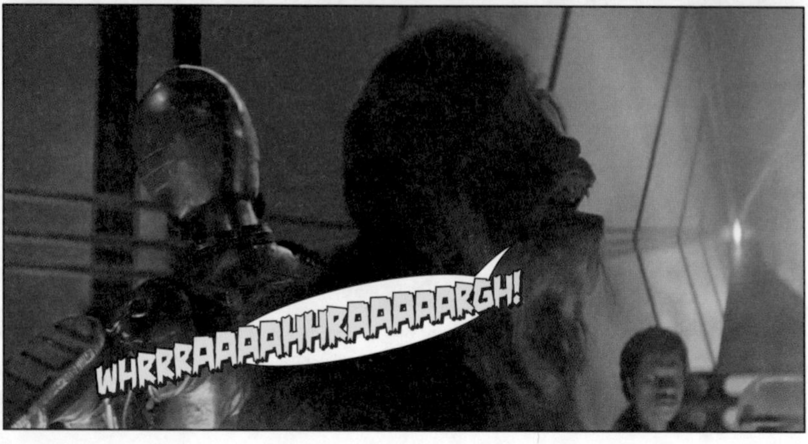
WHRRRAAAAAHHRAAAAAARGH!

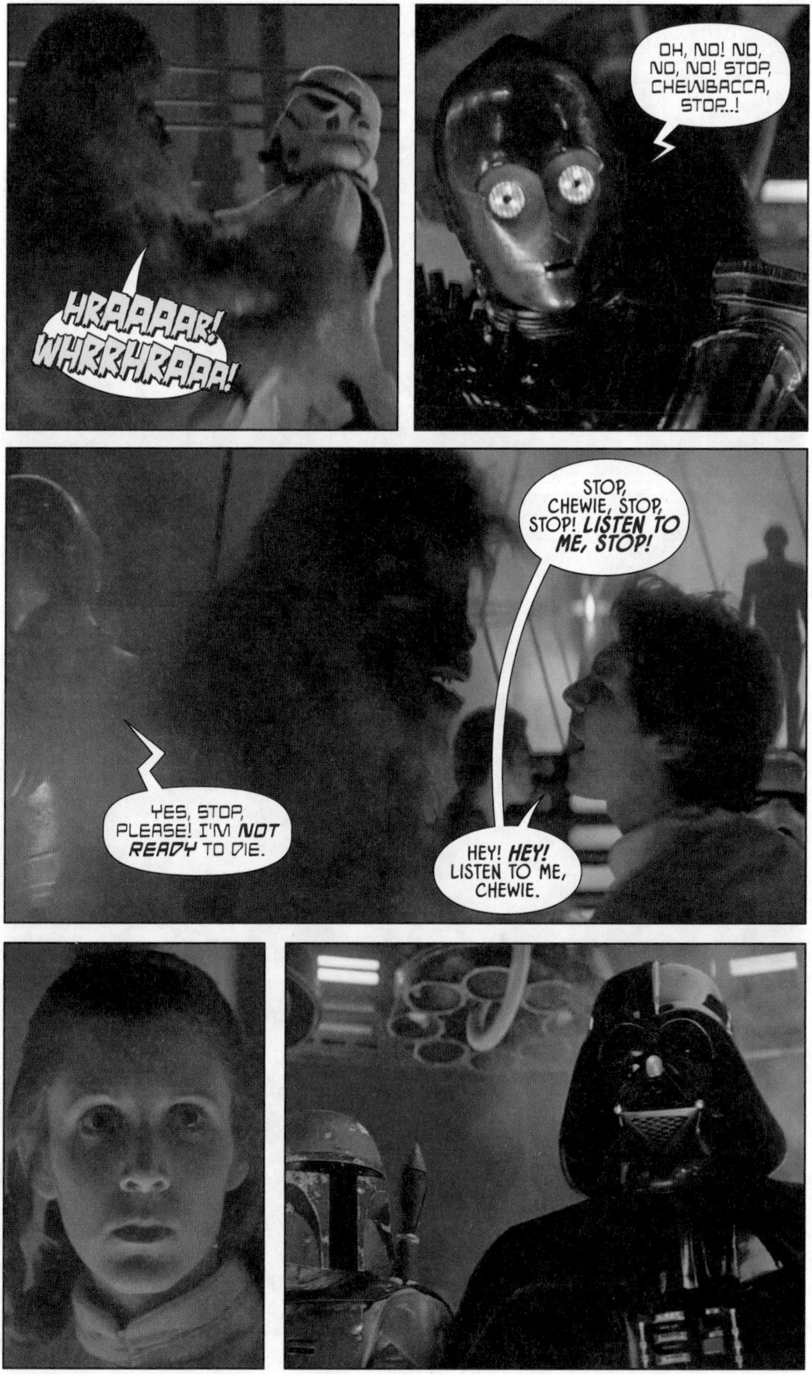
HRAAAAR! WHRRHRAAA!
OH, NO! NO, NO, NO! STOP, CHEWBACCA, STOP...!
STOP, CHEWIE, STOP, STOP! LISTEN TO ME, STOP!
YES, STOP, PLEASE! I'M NOT READY TO DIE.
HEY! HEY! LISTEN TO ME, CHEWIE.

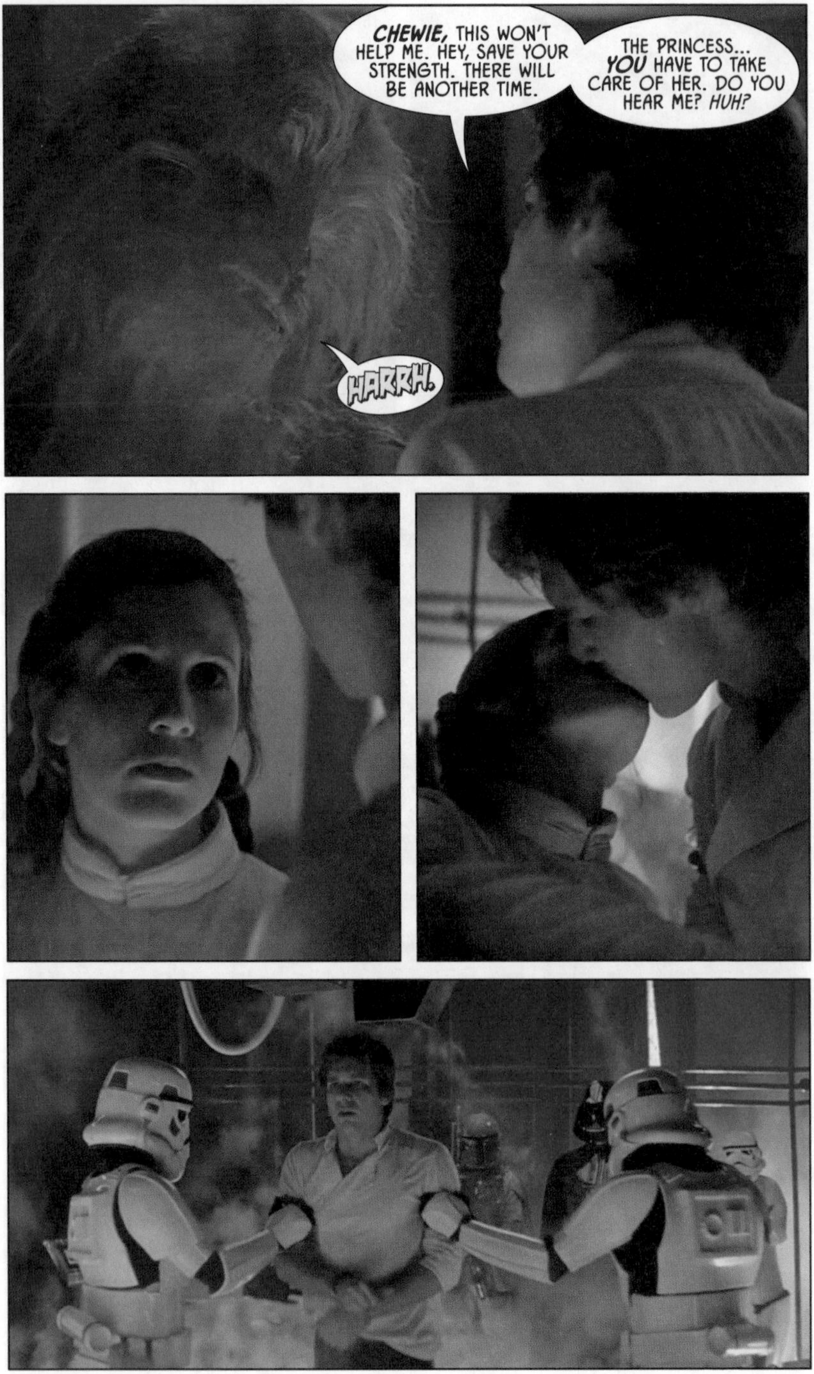
CHEWIE, THIS WON'T HELP ME. HEY, SAVE YOUR STRENGTH. THERE WILL BE ANOTHER TIME.
THE PRINCESS... YOU HAVE TO TAKE CARE OF HER. DO YOU HEAR ME? HUH?
HARRH.

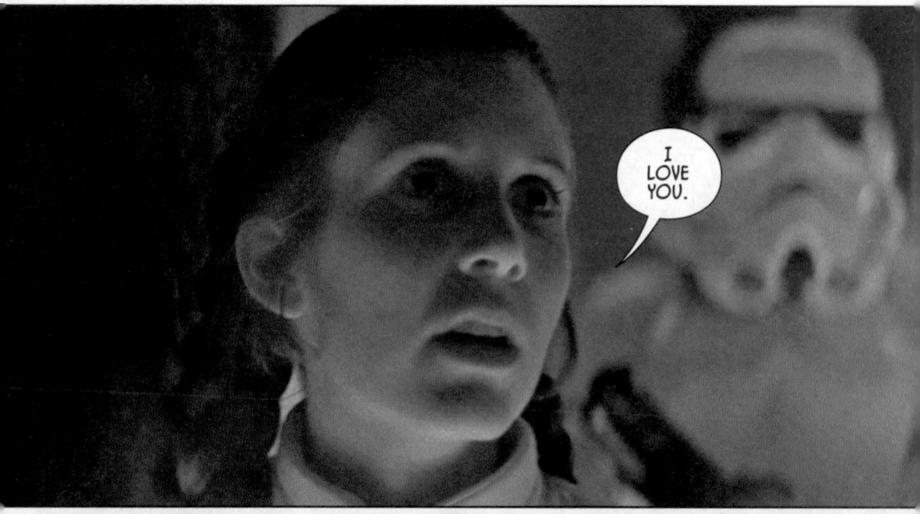
I LOVE YOU.

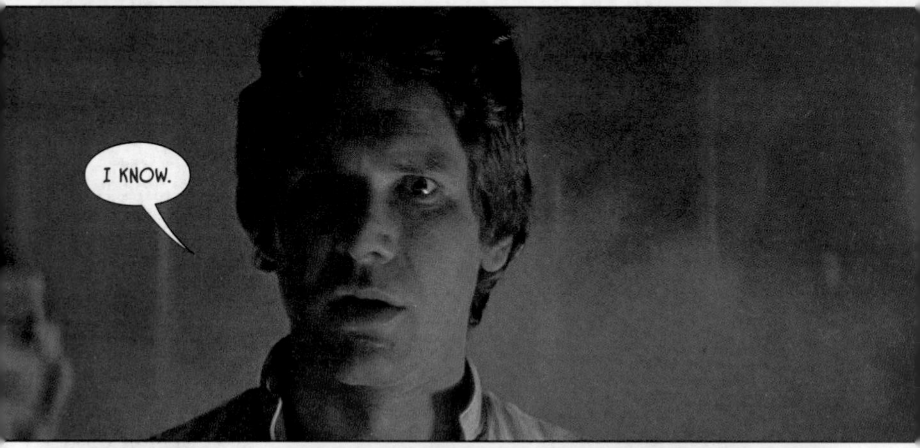
I KNOW.

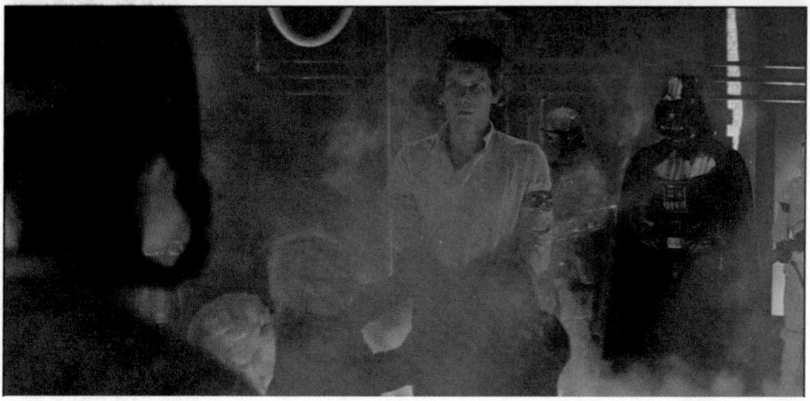

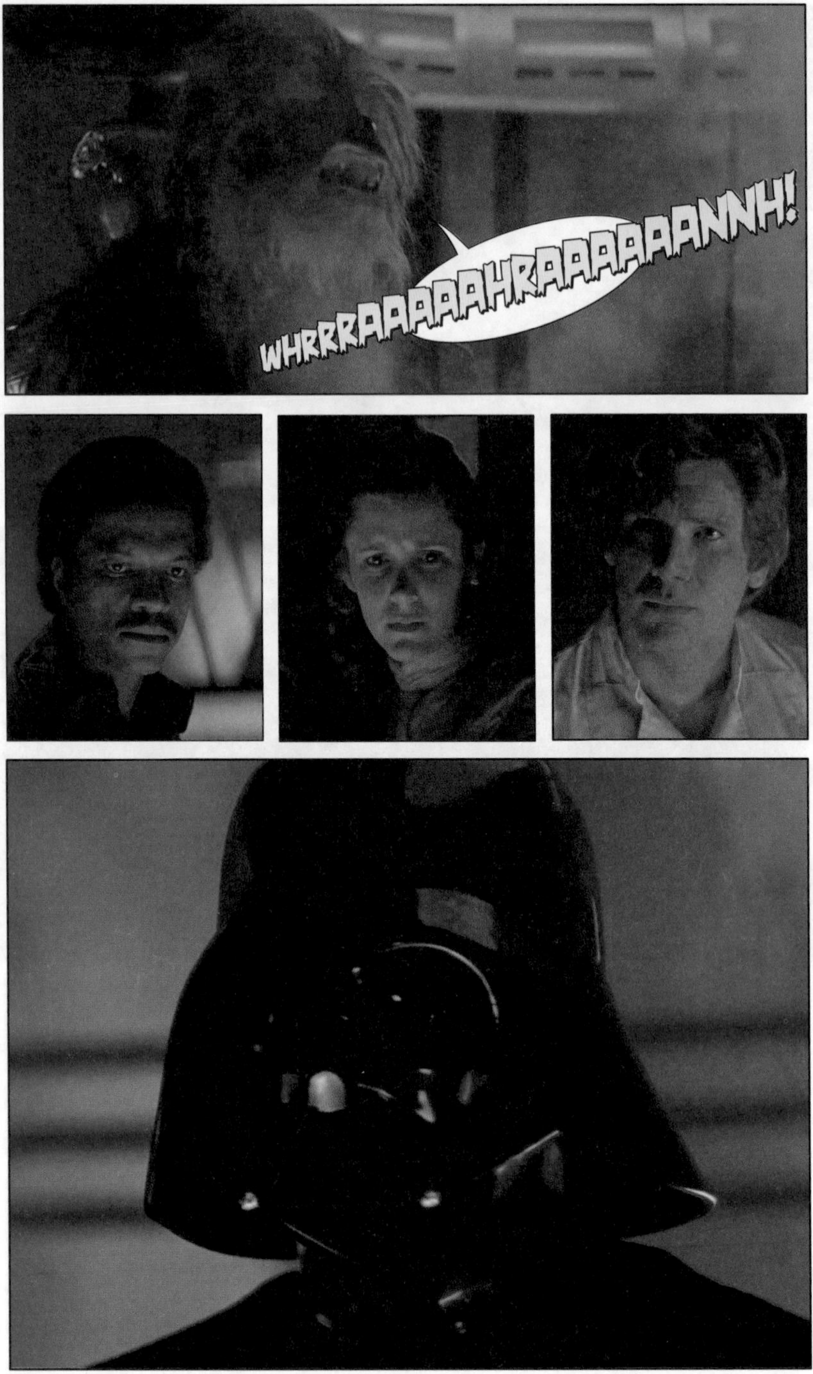
WHRRRAAAAAHRAAAAAANNH!

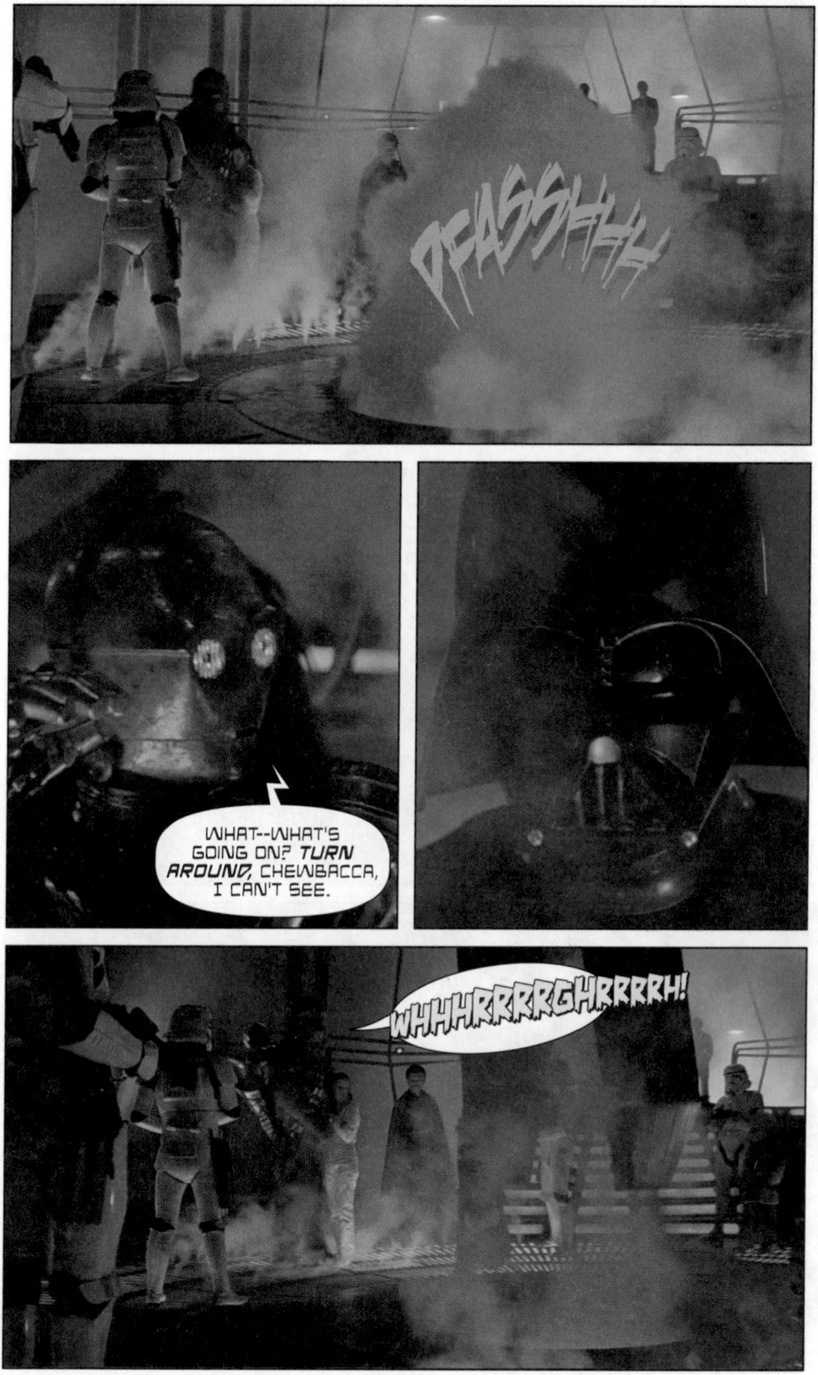
PFASSHHH
WHAT--WHAT'S GOING ON? *TURN AROUND,* CHEWBACCA, I CAN'T SEE.
WHHHRRRRGHRRRRH!

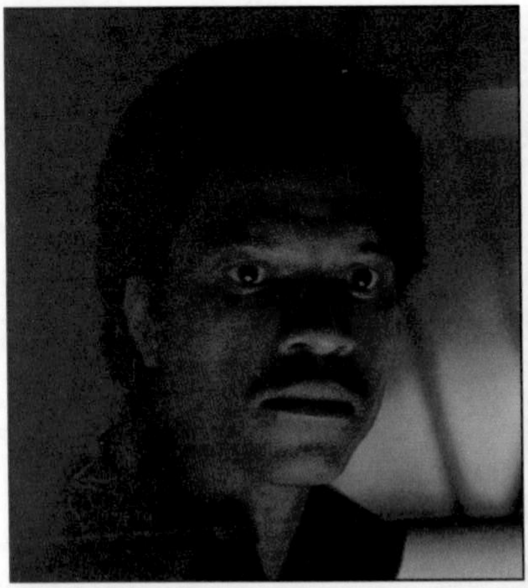
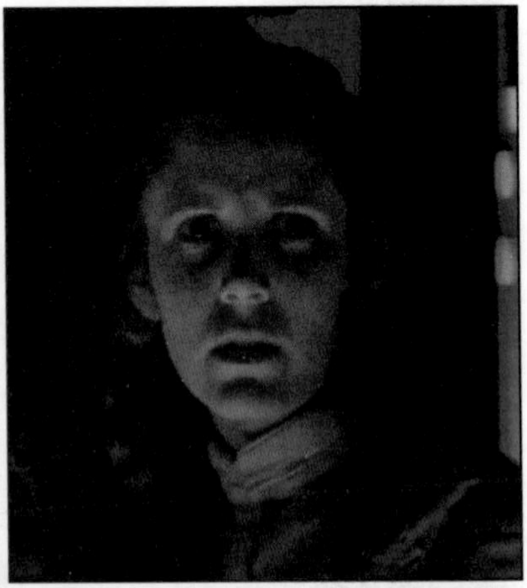
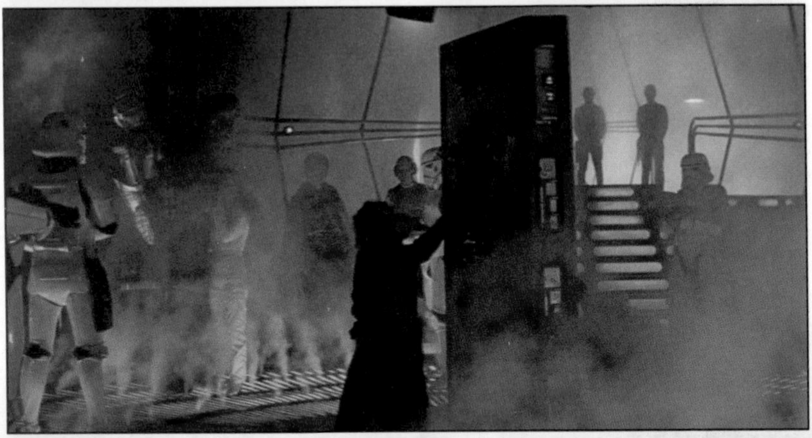
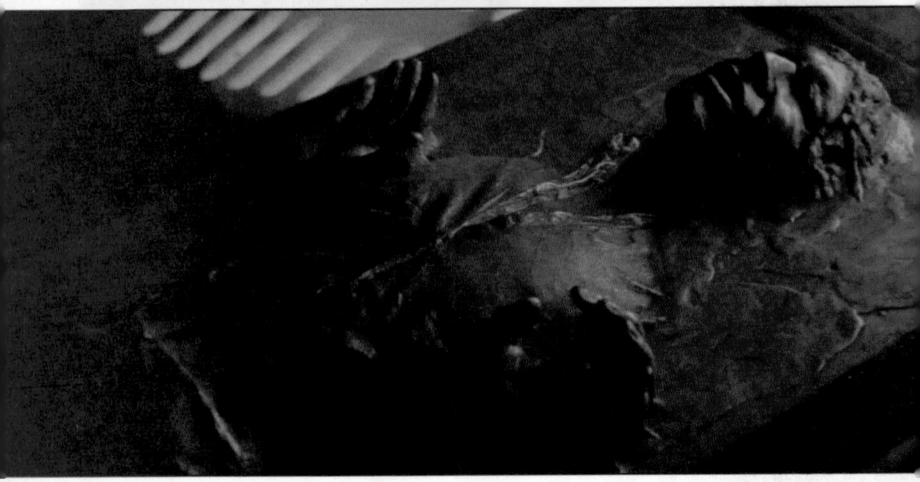

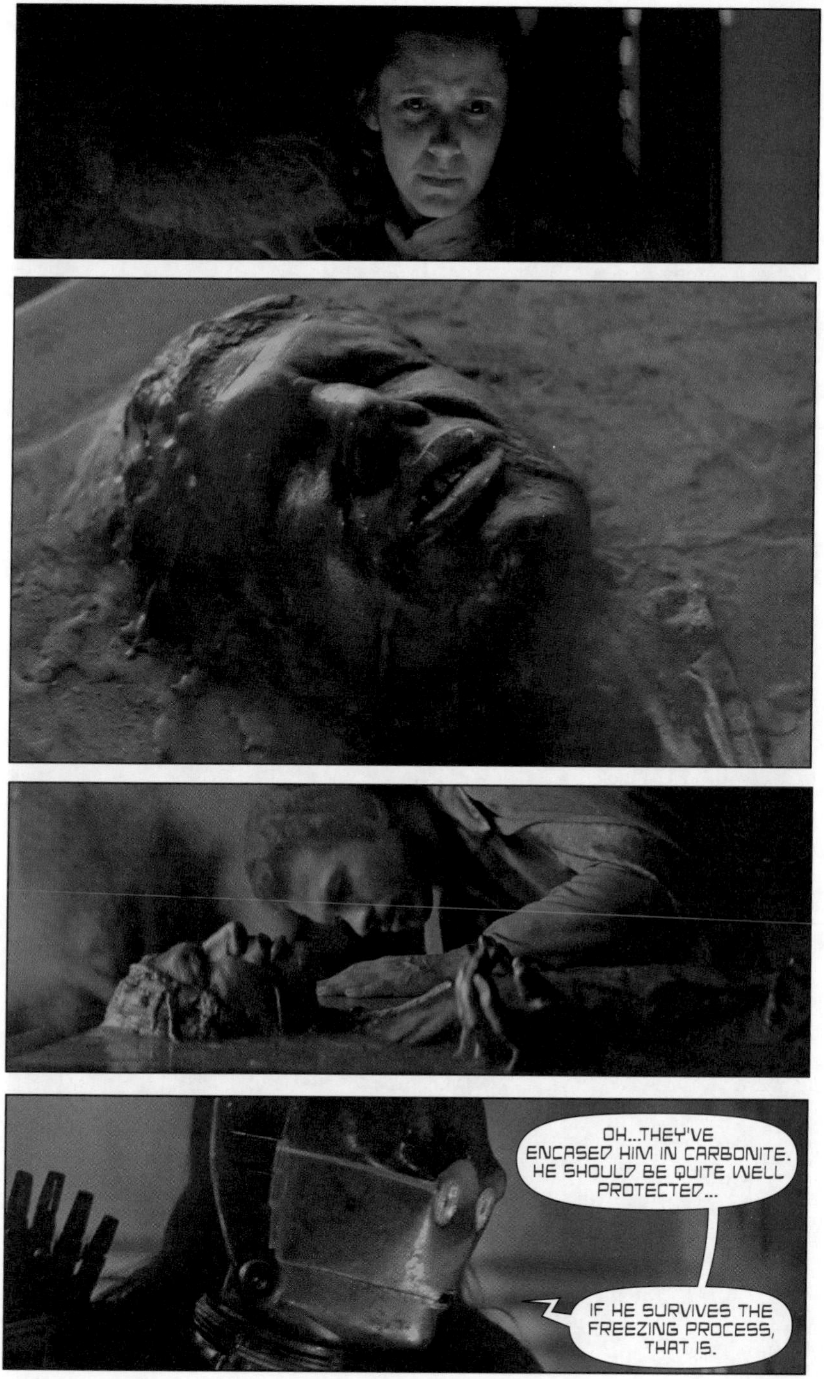
OH...THEY'VE ENCASED HIM IN CARBONITE. HE SHOULD BE QUITE WELL PROTECTED...
IF HE SURVIVES THE FREEZING PROCESS, THAT IS.

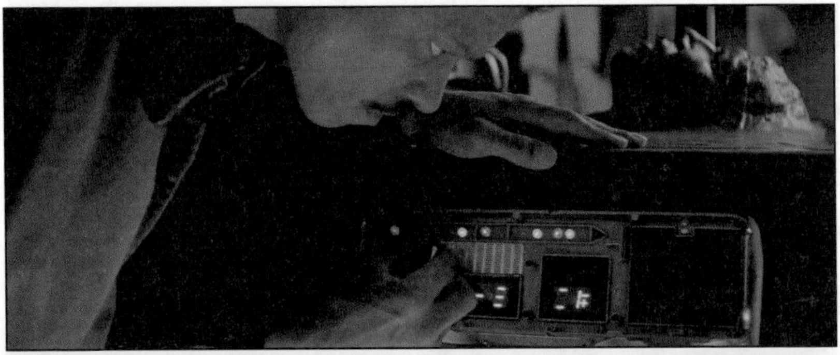

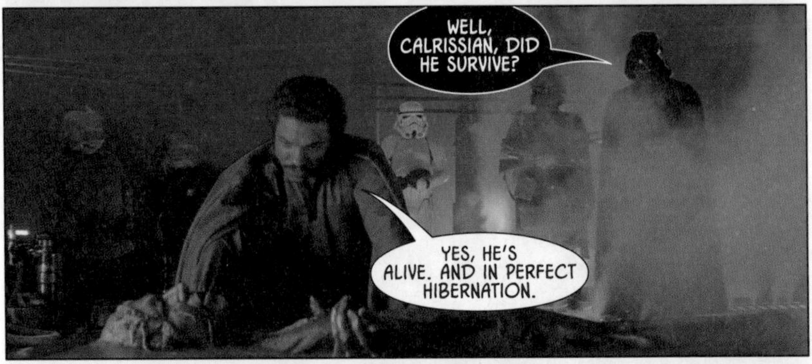
WELL, CALRISSIAN, DID HE SURVIVE?
YES, HE'S ALIVE. AND IN PERFECT HIBERNATION.

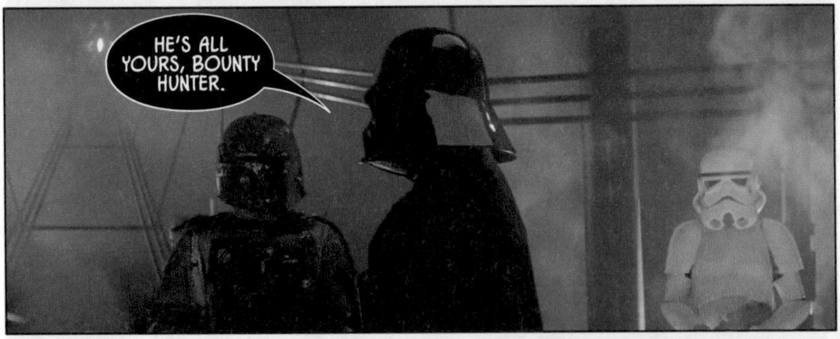
HE'S ALL YOURS, BOUNTY HUNTER.

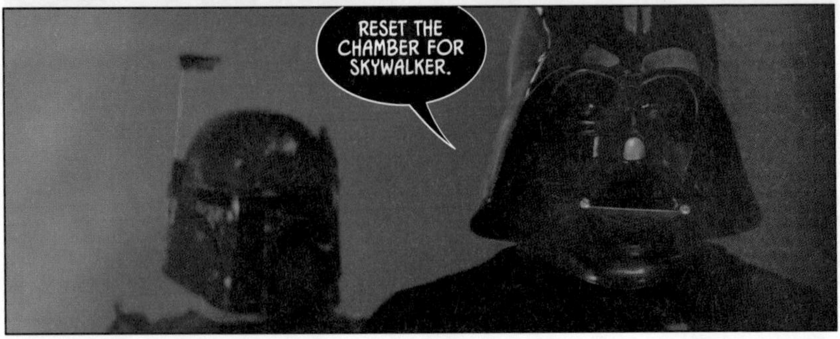
RESET THE CHAMBER FOR SKYWALKER.

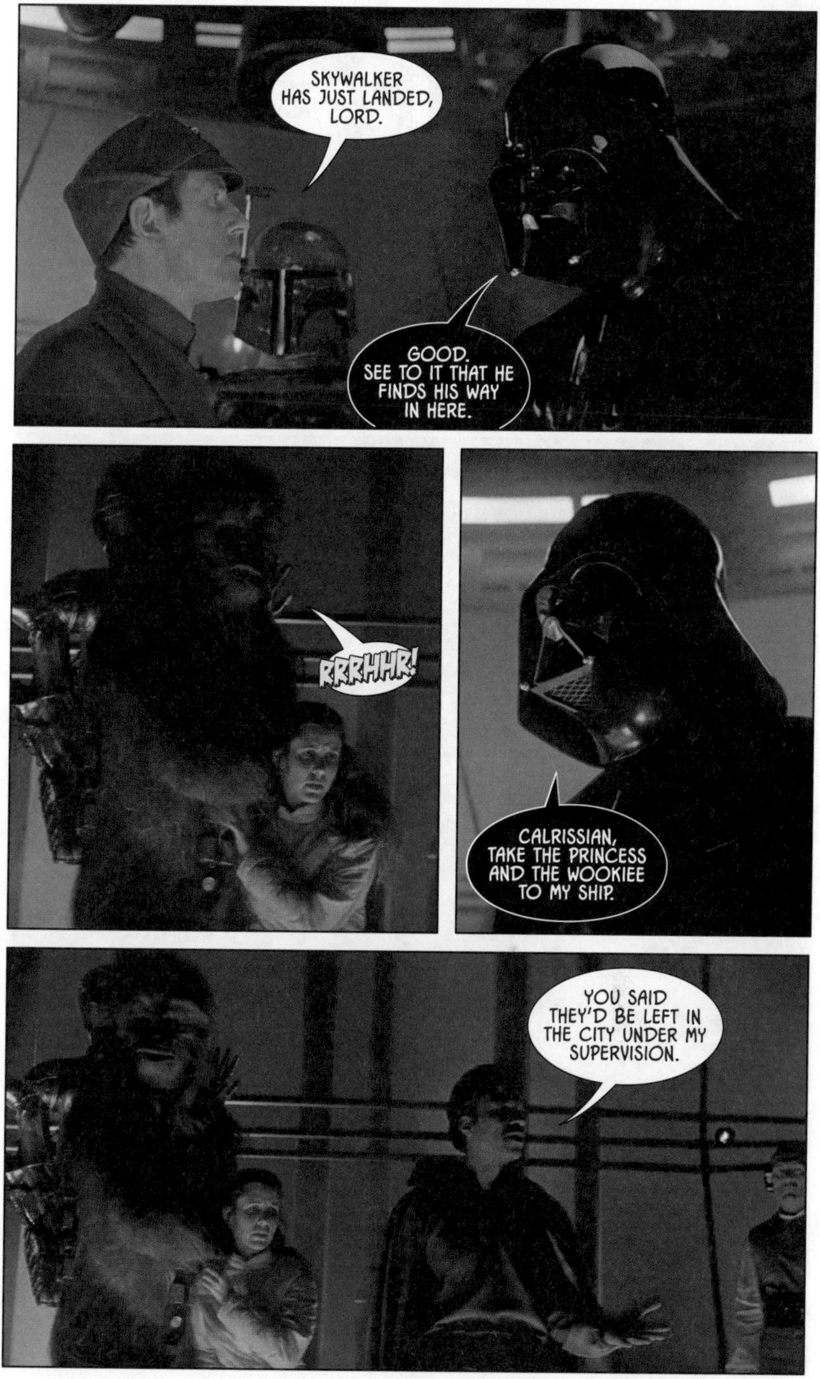
SKYWALKER HAS JUST LANDED, LORD.
GOOD. SEE TO IT THAT HE FINDS HIS WAY IN HERE.
RRRHHR!
CALRISSIAN, TAKE THE PRINCESS AND THE WOOKIEE TO MY SHIP.
YOU SAID THEY'D BE LEFT IN THE CITY UNDER MY SUPERVISION.

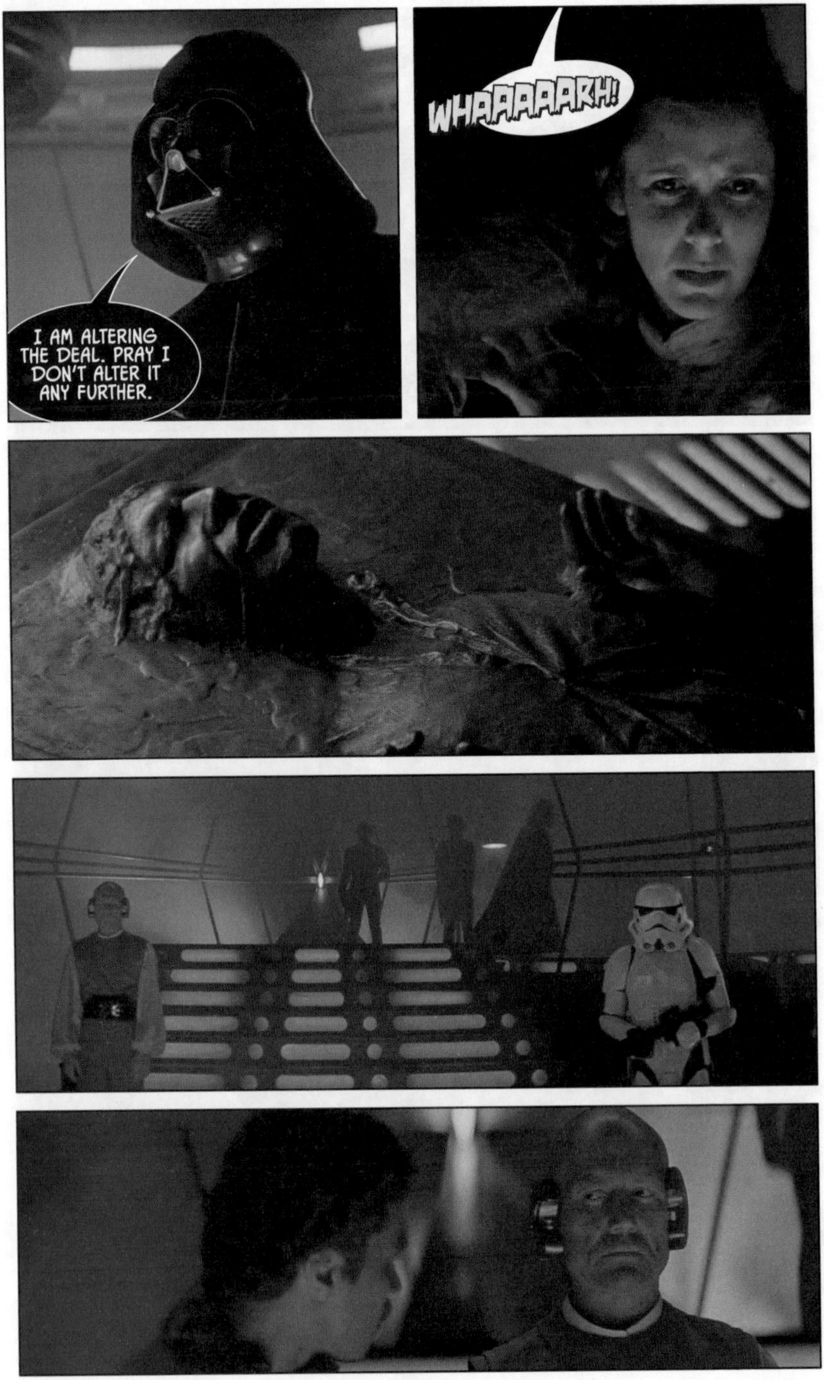
I AM ALTERING THE DEAL. PRAY I DON'T ALTER IT ANY FURTHER.
WHAAAAARH!

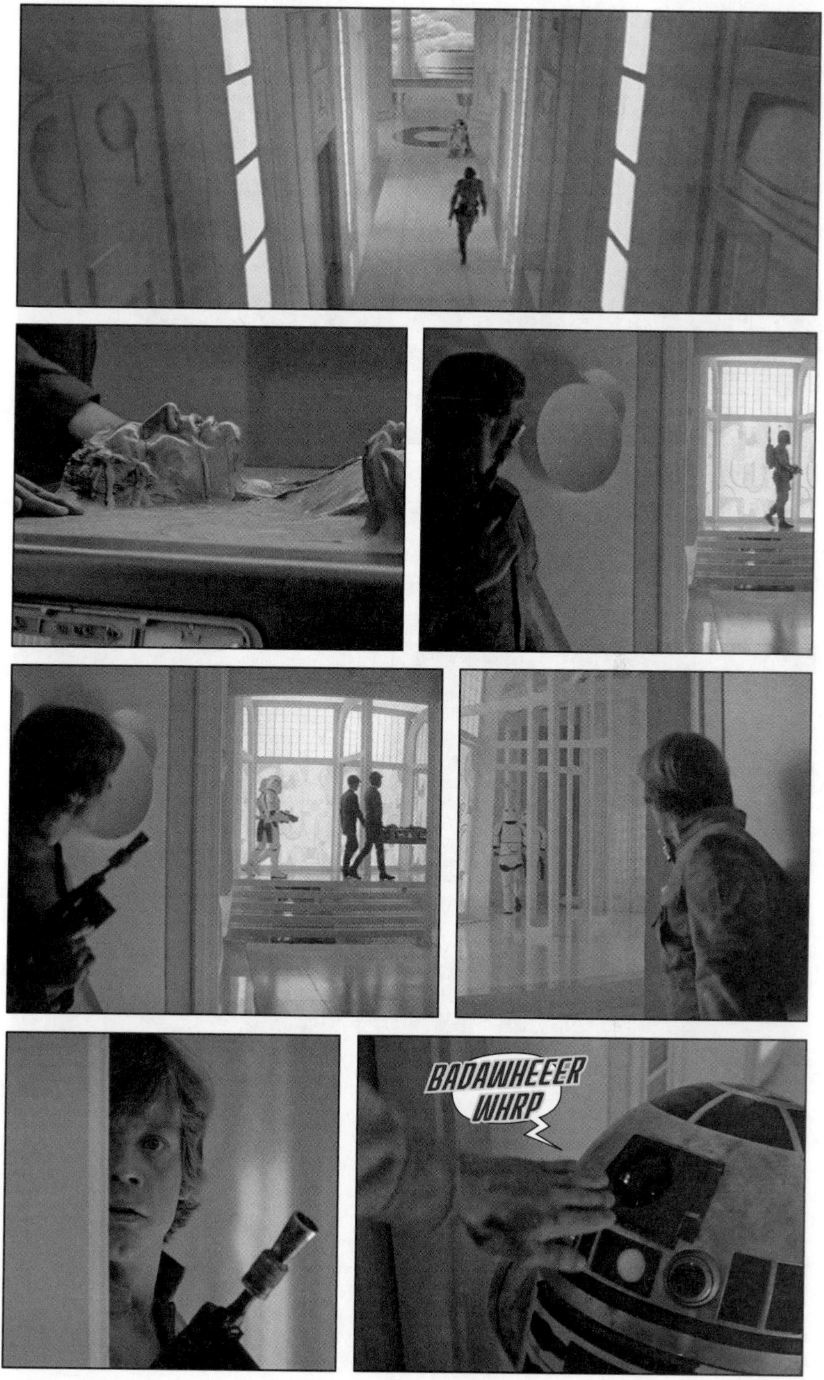
BADAWHEEER WHRP

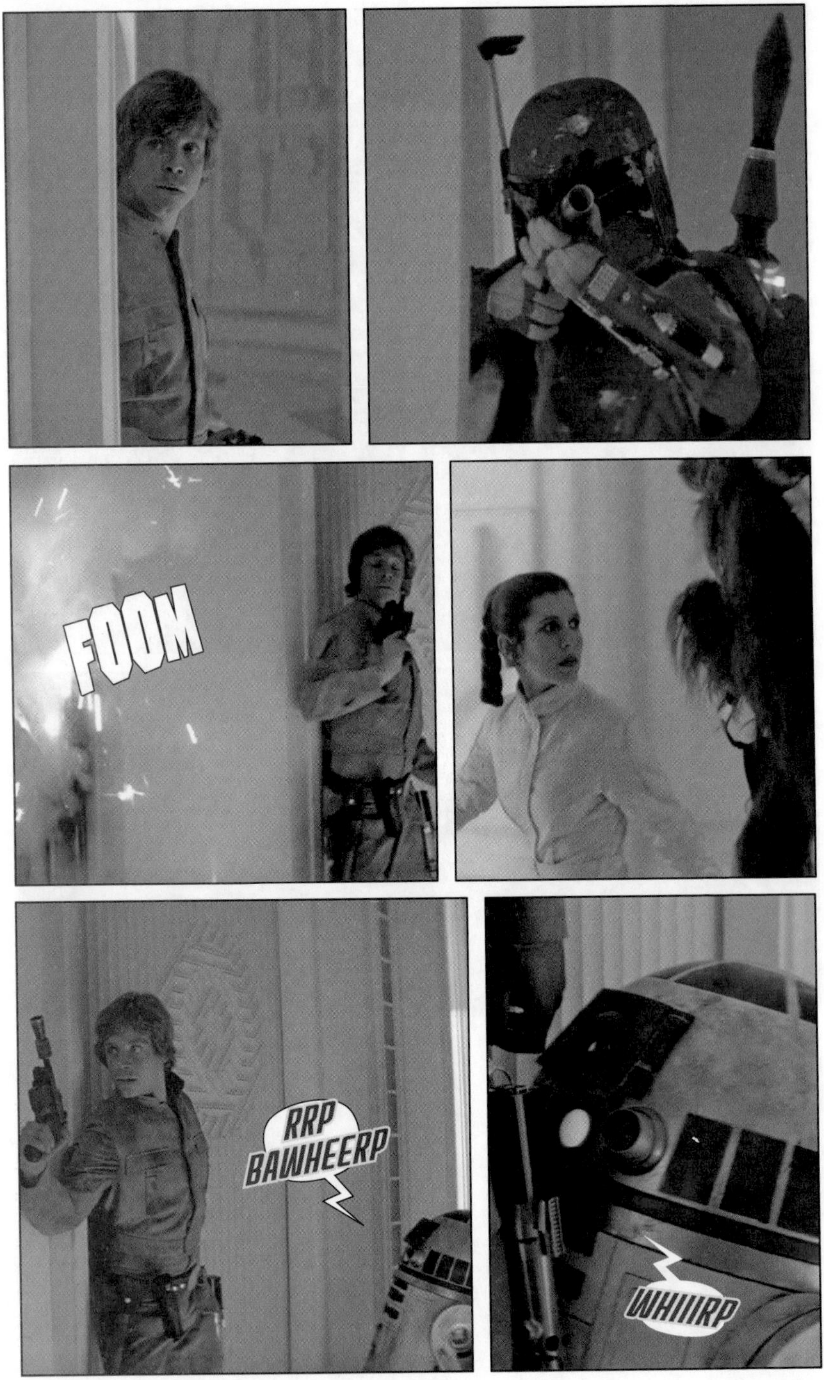
FOOM
RRP BAWHEERP
WHIIIRP

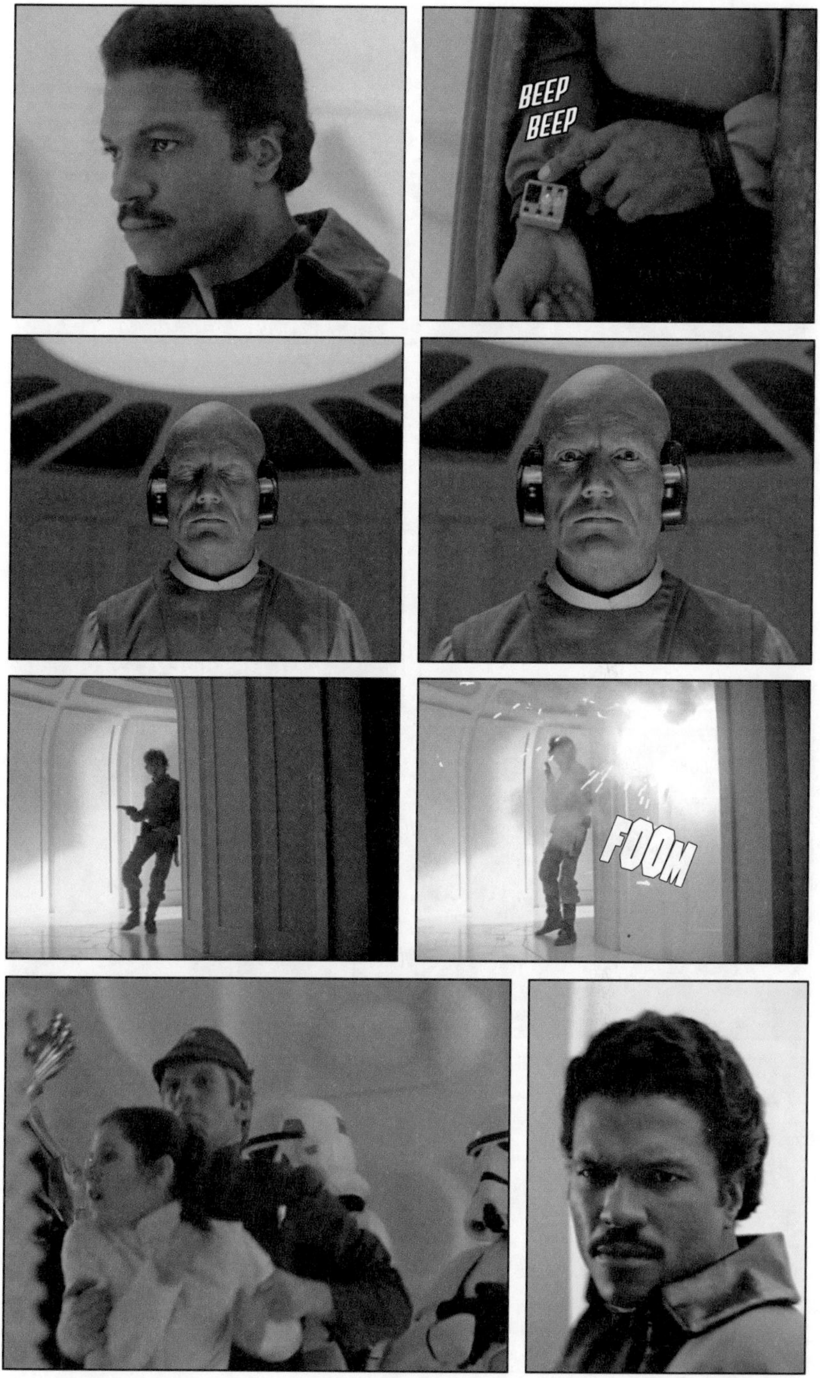
BEEP
BEEP
FOOM

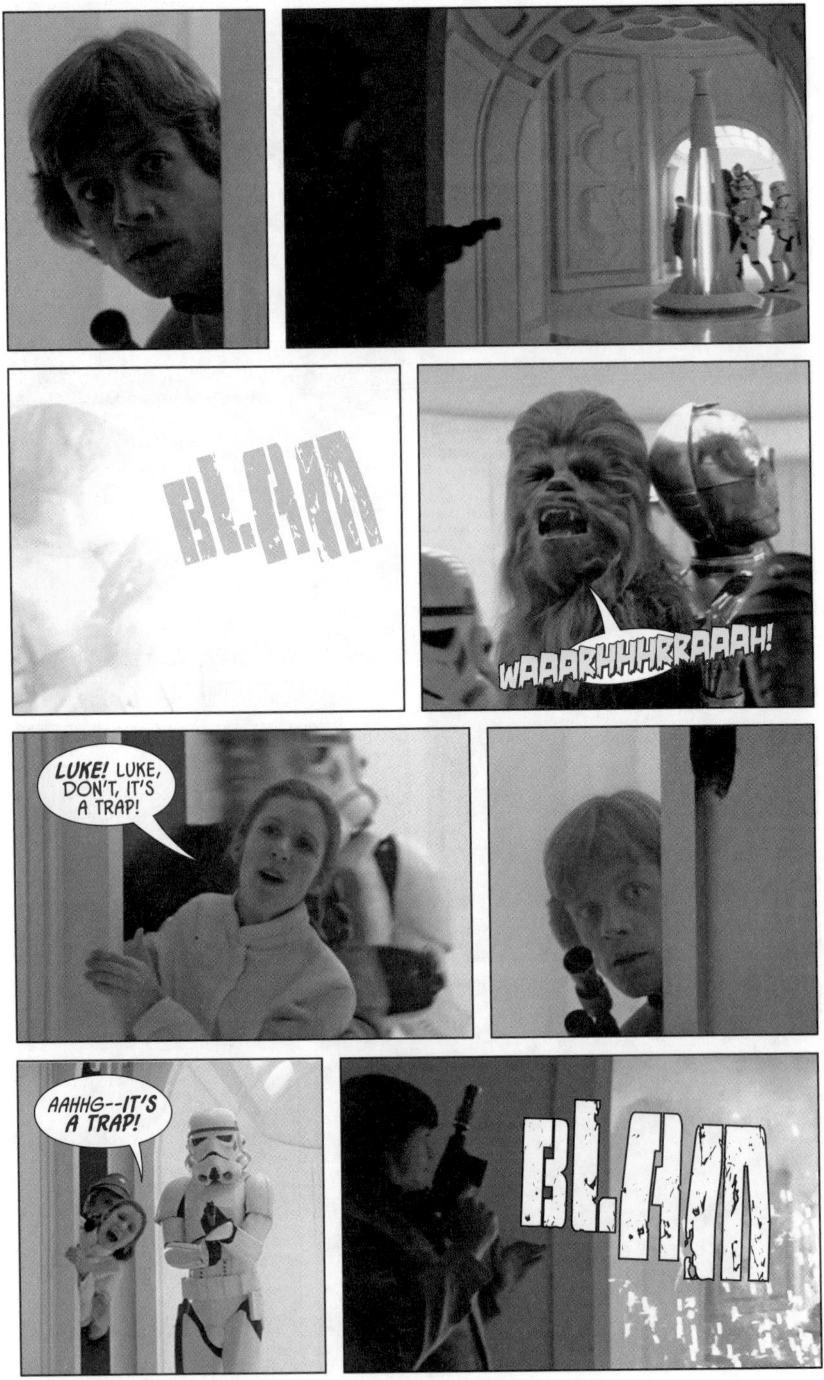
BLAM
WAAARHHHRRAAAH!
LUKE! LUKE, DON'T, IT'S A TRAP!
AAHHG--IT'S A TRAP!
BLAM

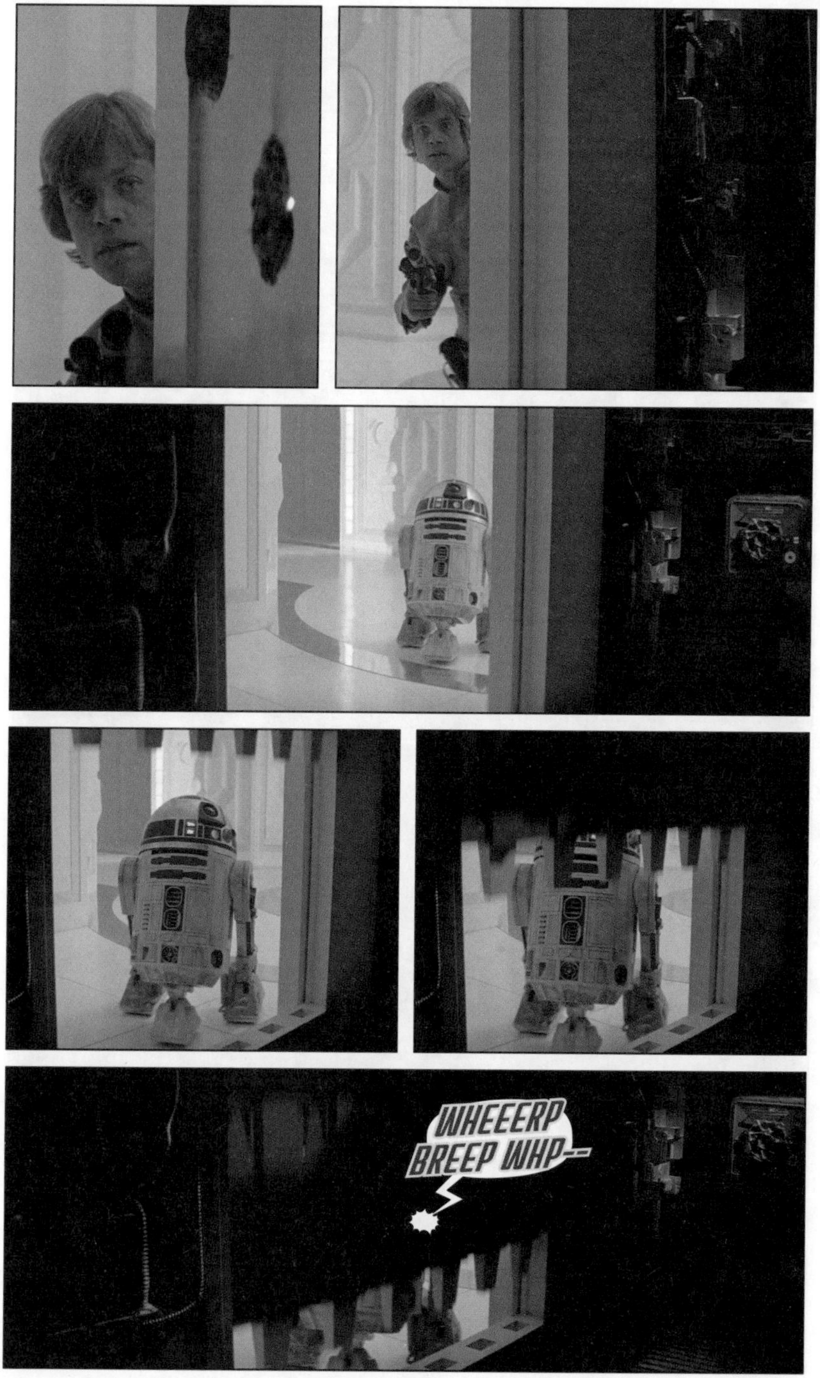
WHEEERP
BREEP WHP--

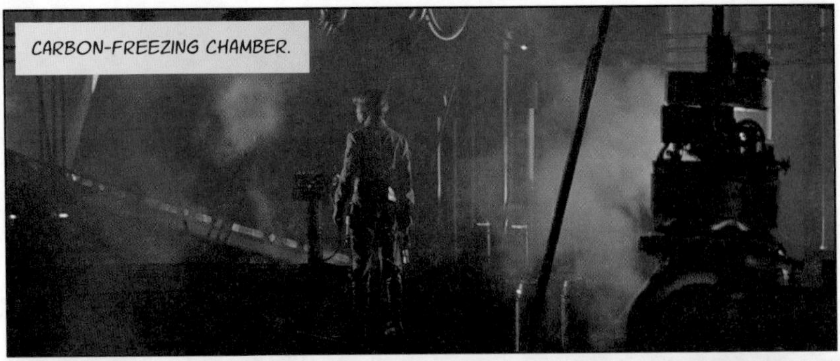
CARBON-FREEZING CHAMBER.

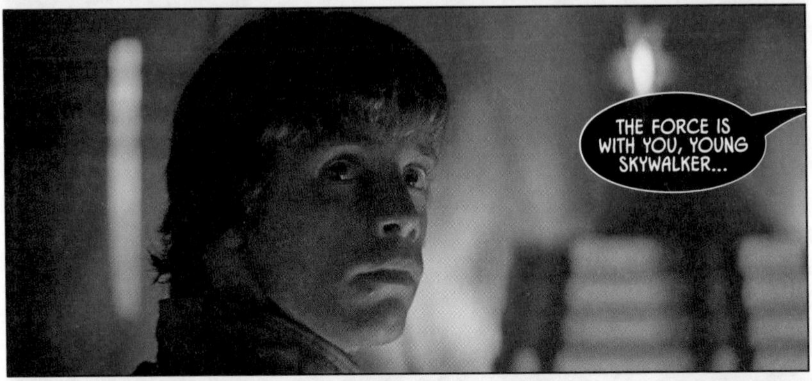
THE FORCE IS WITH YOU, YOUNG SKYWALKER...

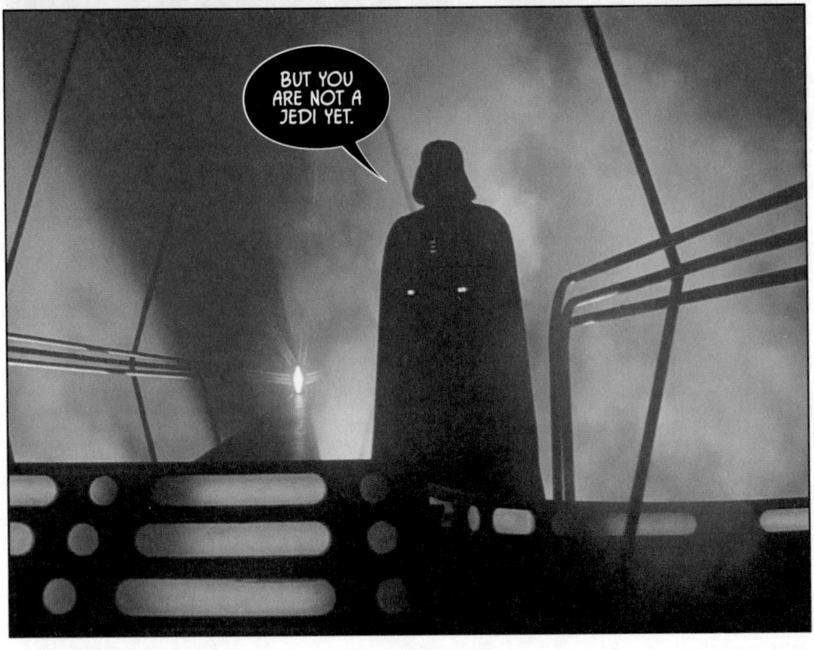
BUT YOU ARE NOT A JEDI YET.

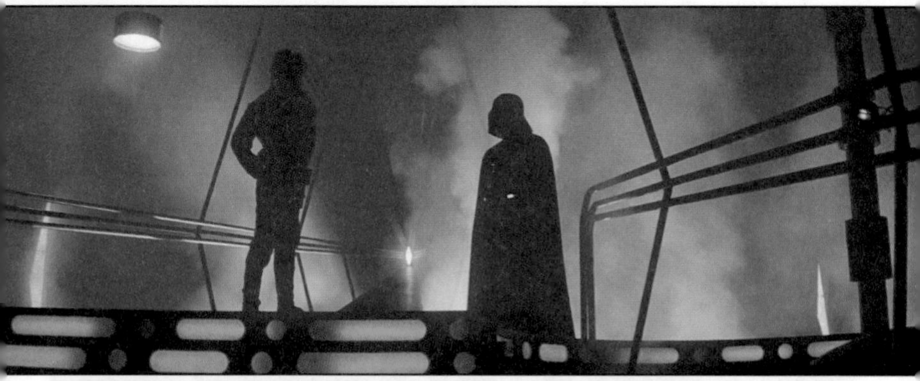

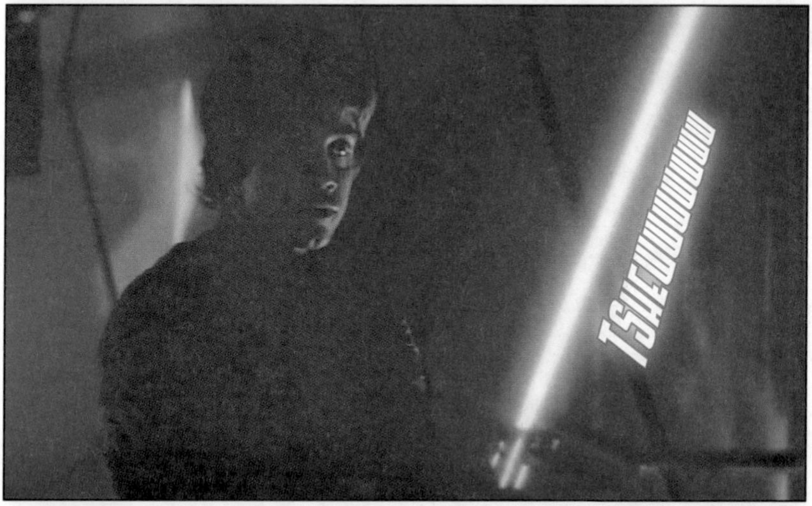
TSHEWWWWWWW

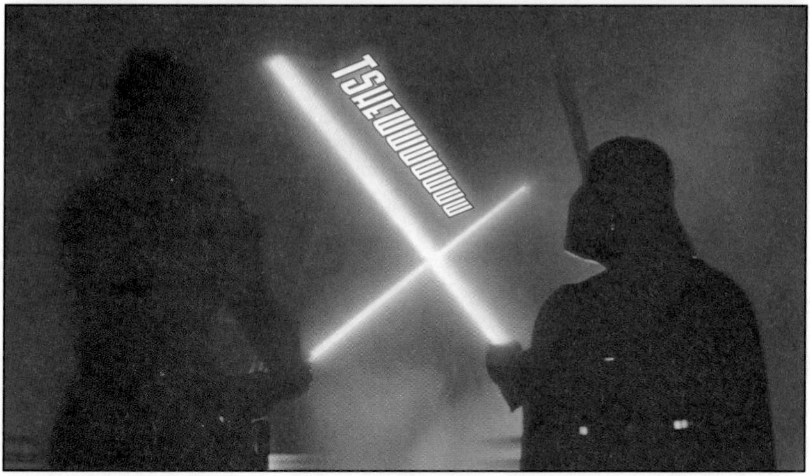
TSHEWWWWWWW

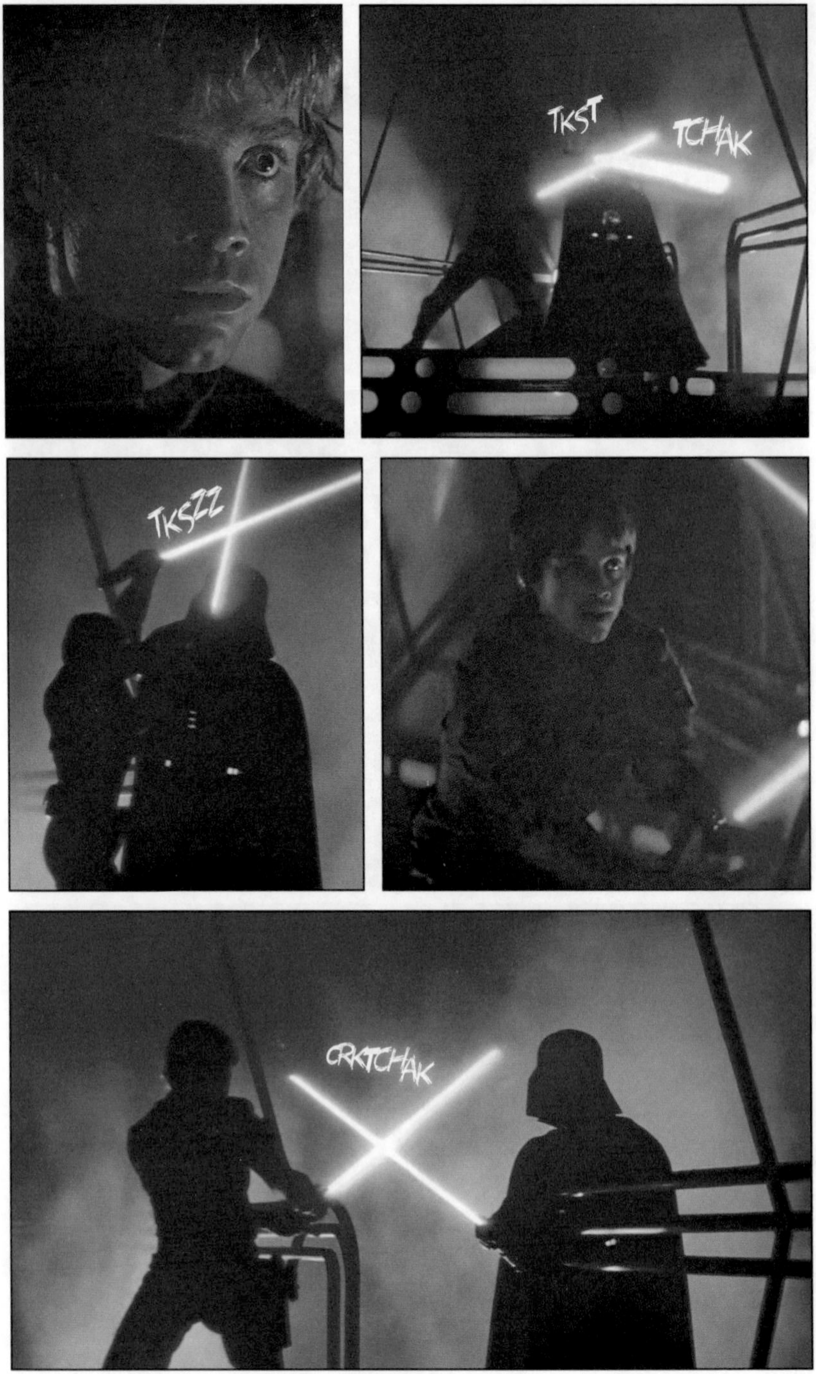
TKST
TCHAK
TKSZZ
CRKTCHAK

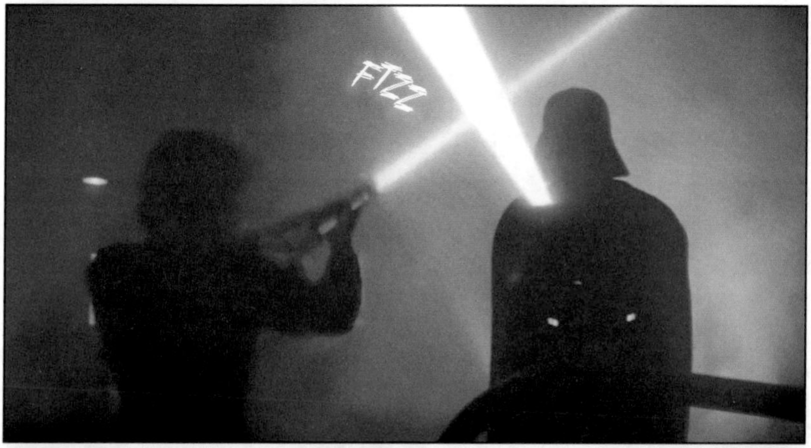
FTZZ
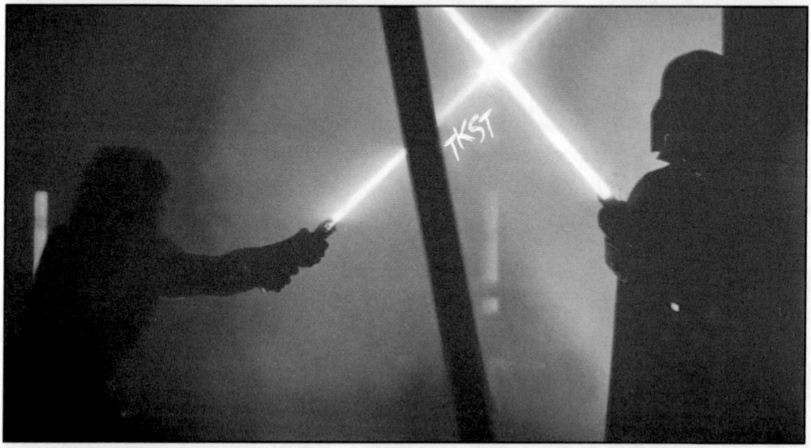
TKST
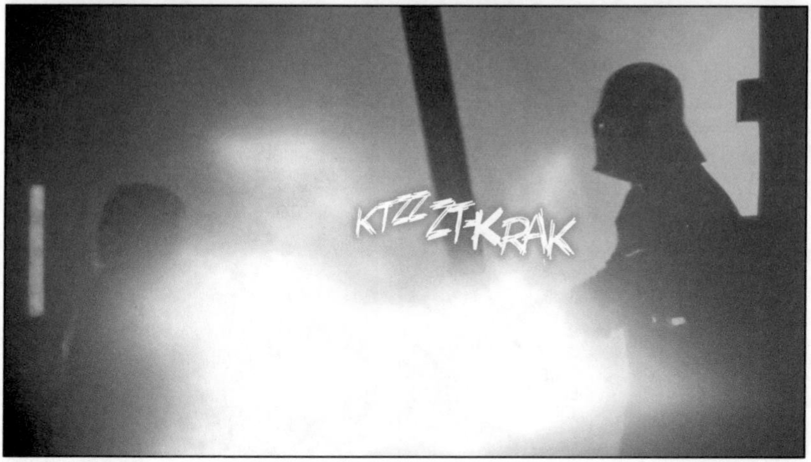
KTZZ ZT-KRAK

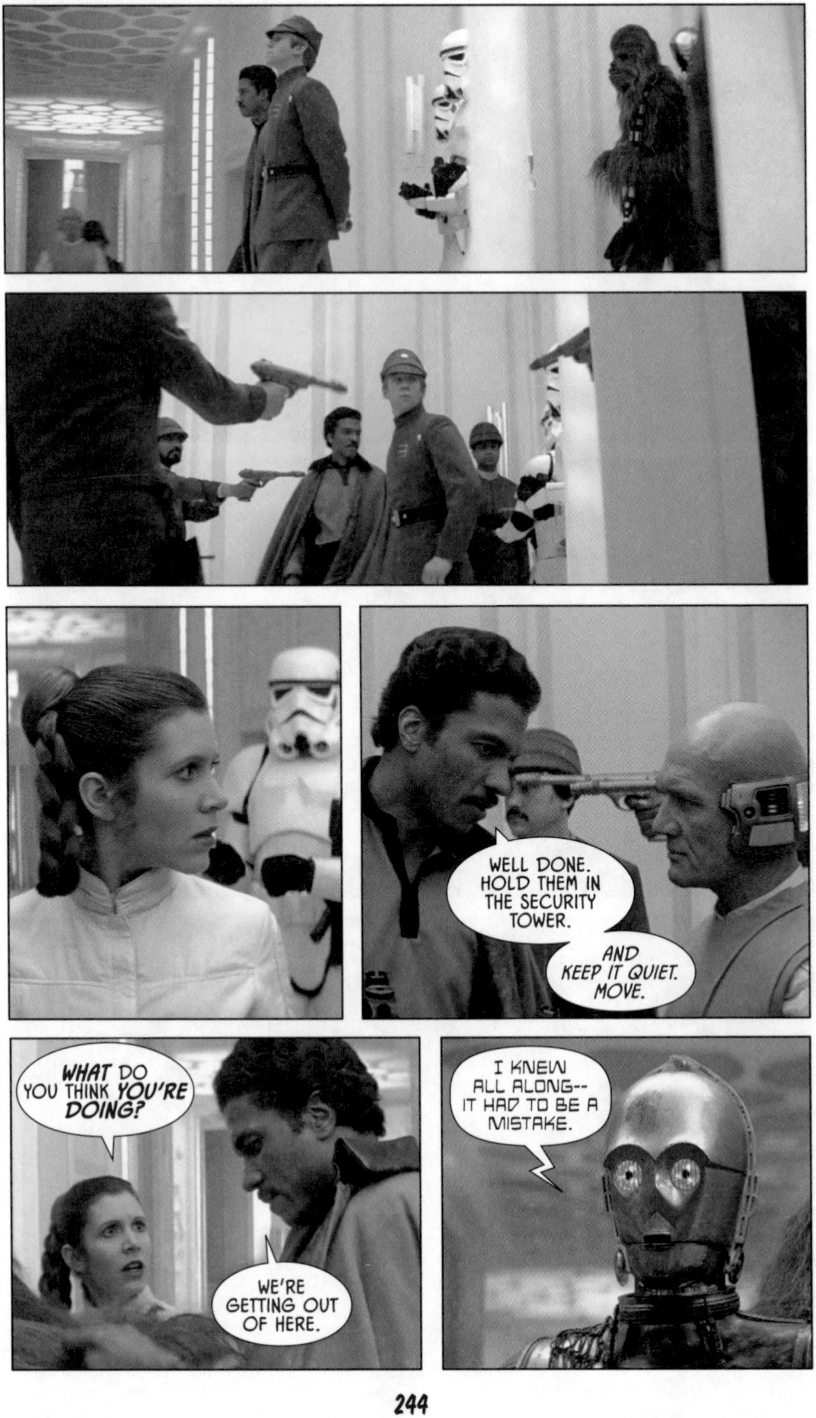
WELL DONE. HOLD THEM IN THE SECURITY TOWER.
AND KEEP IT QUIET. MOVE.
WHAT DO YOU THINK YOU'RE DOING?
WE'RE GETTING OUT OF HERE.
I KNEW ALL ALONG-- IT HAD TO BE A MISTAKE.

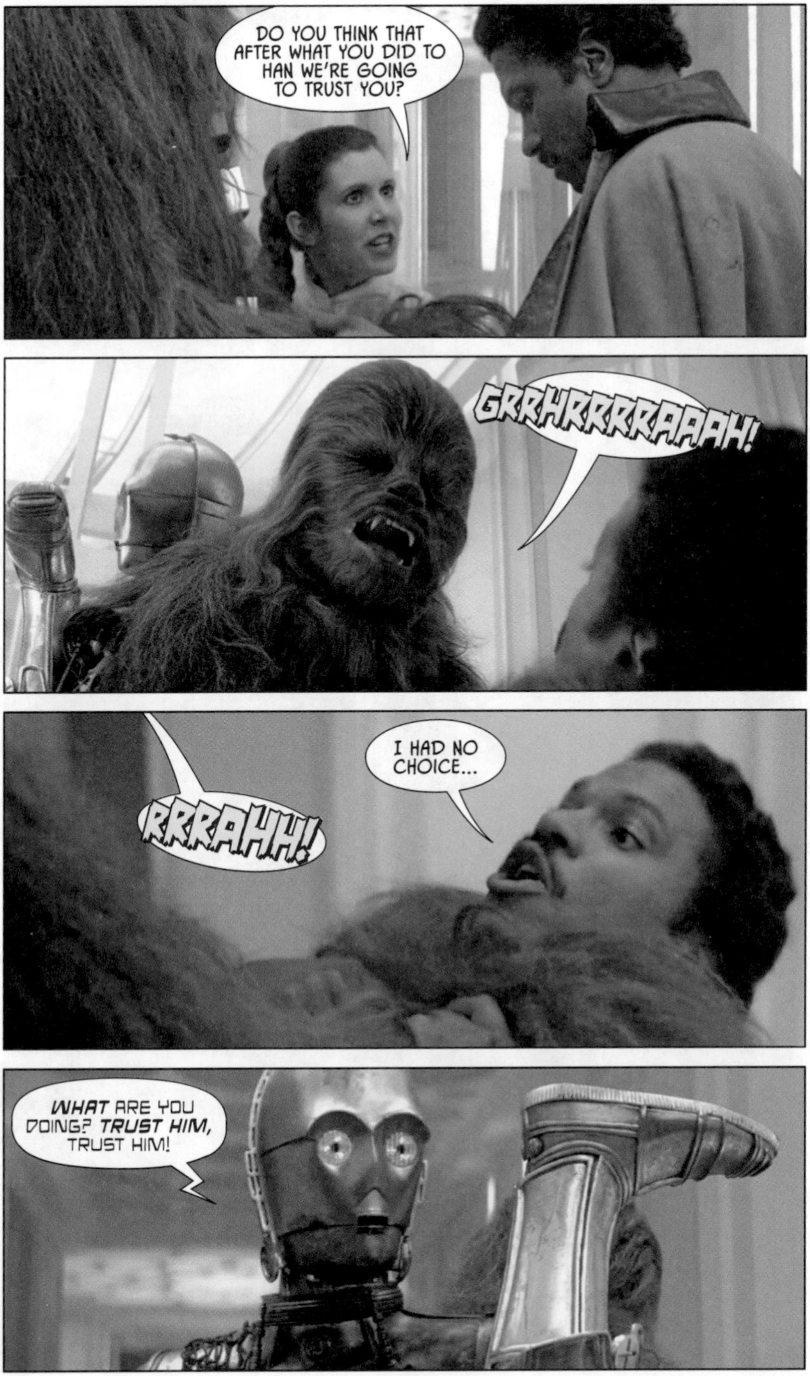
DO YOU THINK THAT AFTER WHAT YOU DID TO HAN WE'RE GOING TO TRUST YOU?
GRRHRRRRAAAH!
RRRAHH!
I HAD NO CHOICE...
WHAT ARE YOU DOING? *TRUST HIM*, TRUST HIM!

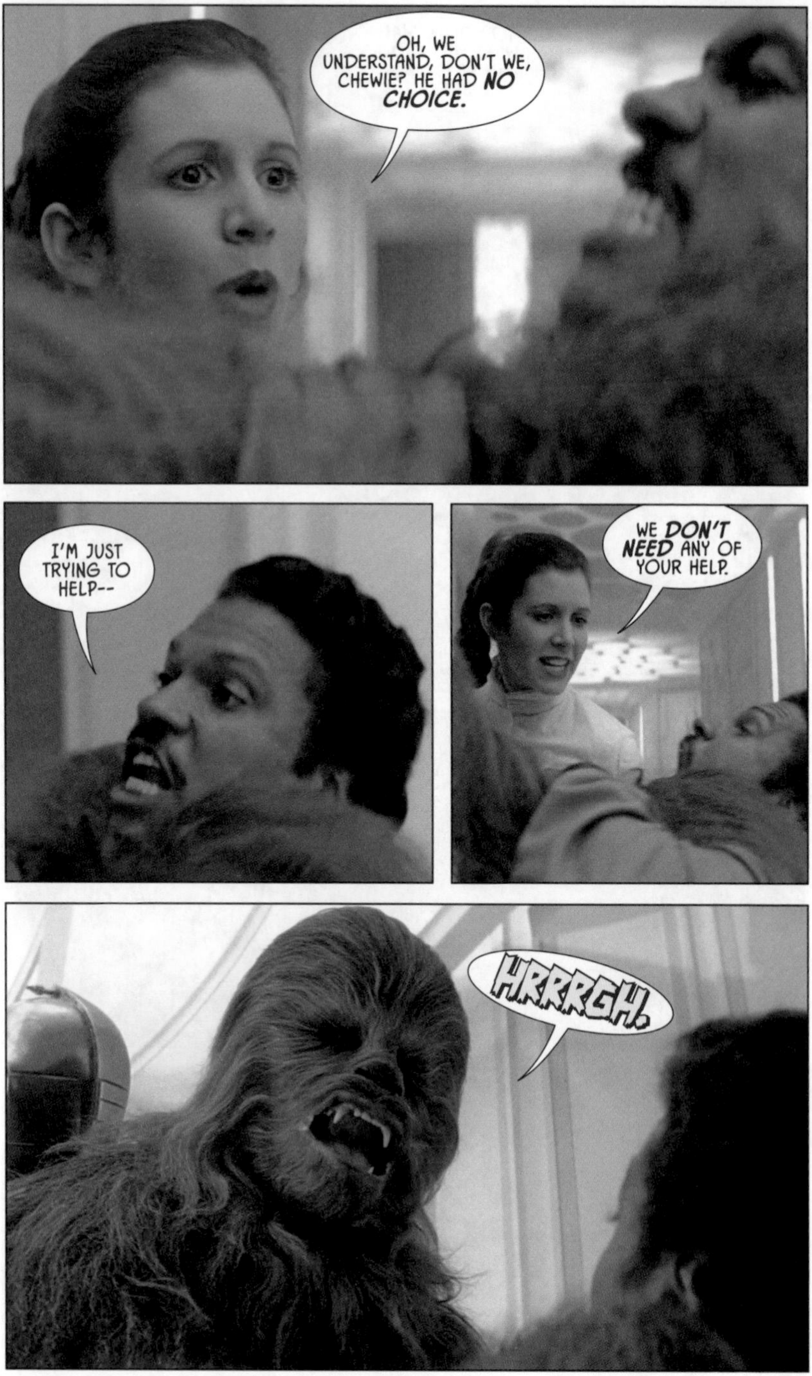
OH, WE UNDERSTAND, DON'T WE, CHEWIE? HE HAD NO CHOICE.
I'M JUST TRYING TO HELP--
WE DON'T NEED ANY OF YOUR HELP.
HRRRGH.

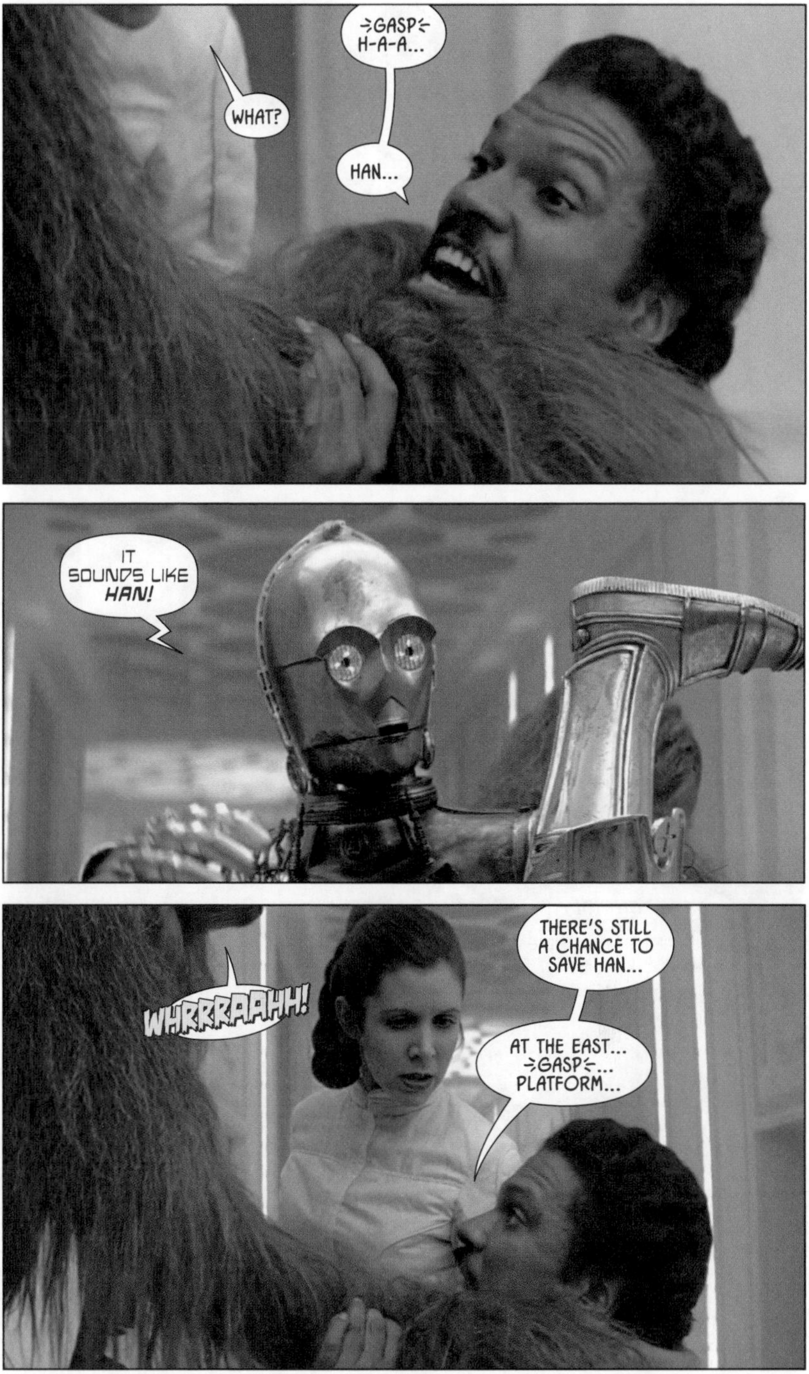

≑GASP≑
H-A-A...
WHAT?
HAN...
IT
SOUNDS LIKE
HAN!
WHRRRAAHH!
THERE'S STILL
A CHANCE TO
SAVE HAN...
AT THE EAST...
≑GASP≑...
PLATFORM...

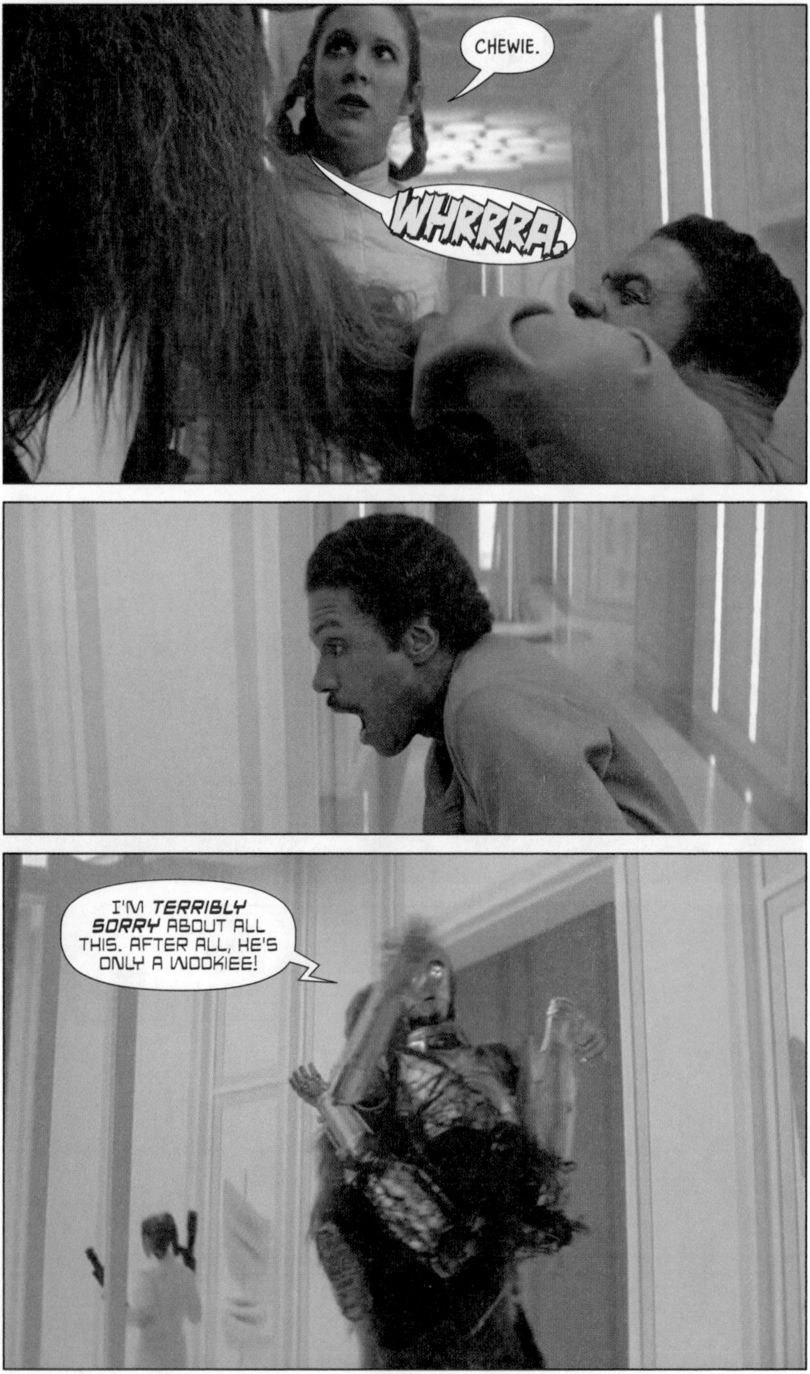
CHEWIE.
WHRRRA.
I'M TERRIBLY SORRY ABOUT ALL THIS. AFTER ALL, HE'S ONLY A WOOKIEE!

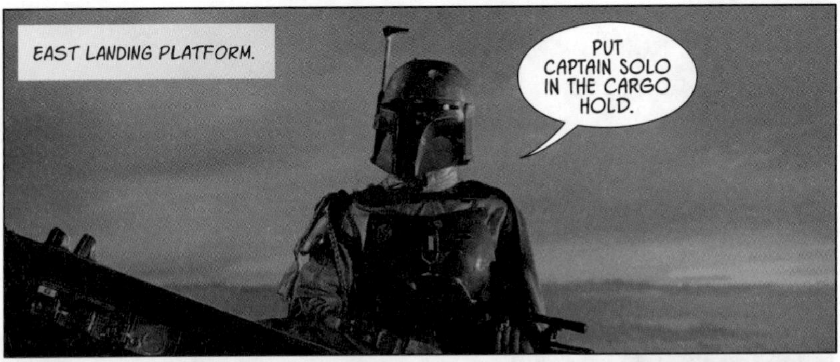
EAST LANDING PLATFORM.
PUT CAPTAIN SOLO IN THE CARGO HOLD.

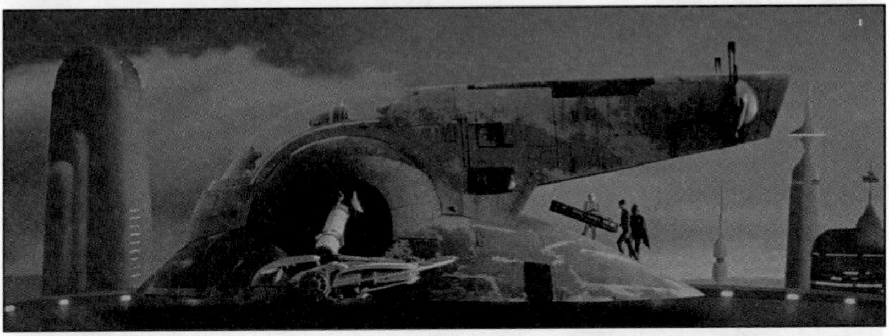

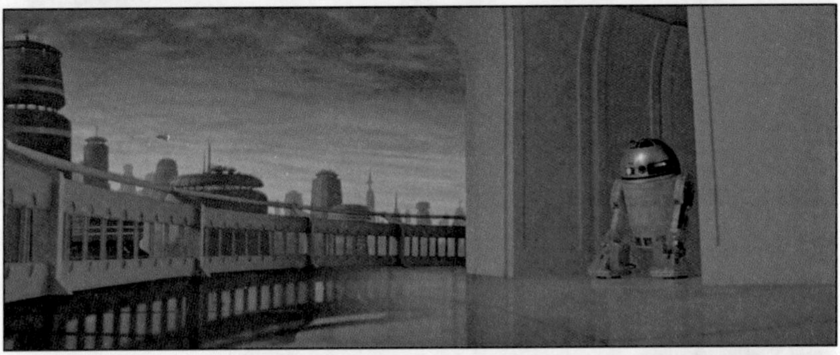

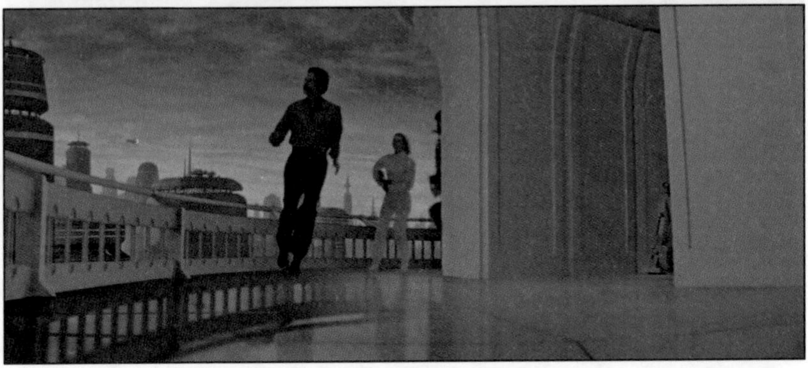

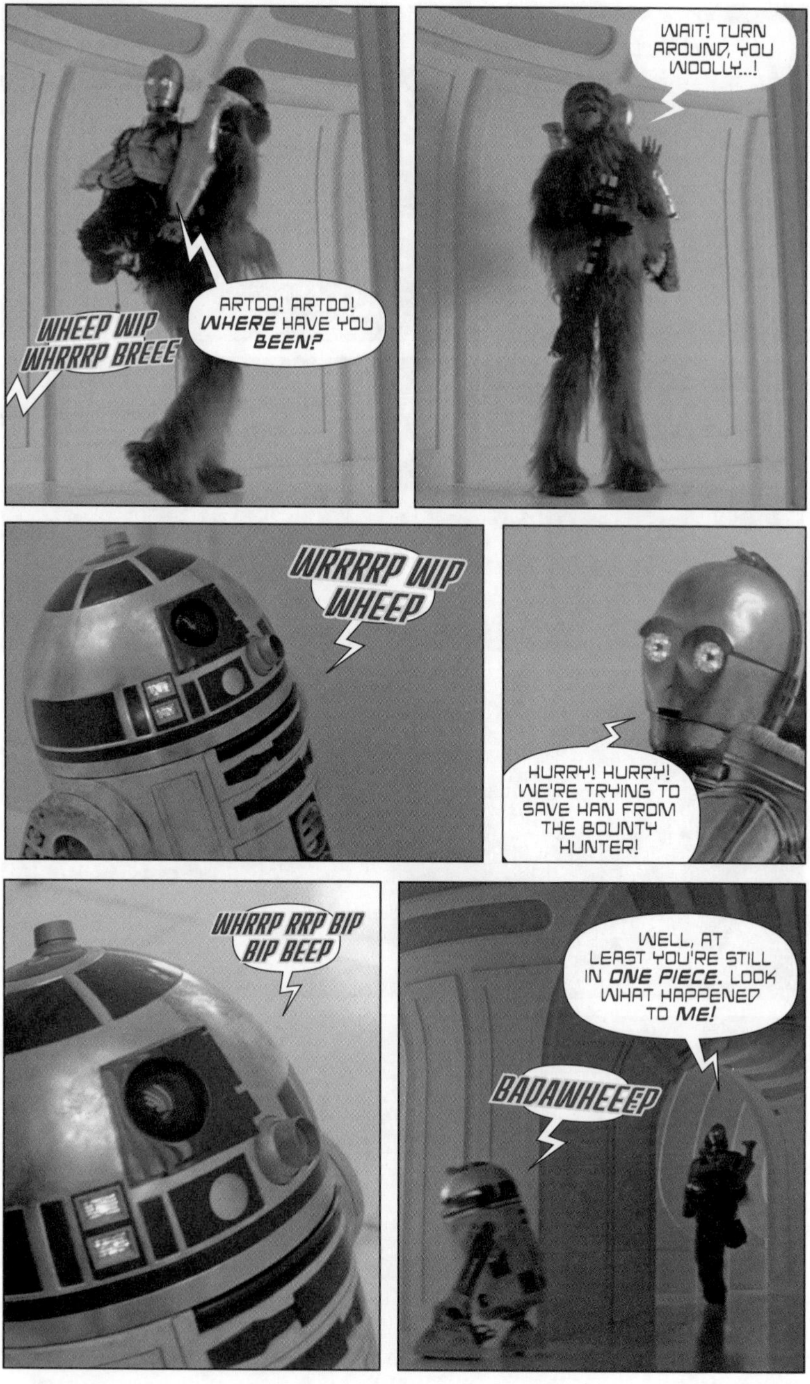
ARTOO! ARTOO! WHERE HAVE YOU BEEN?
WHEEP WIP WHRRRP BREEE
WAIT! TURN AROUND, YOU WOOLLY...!
WRRRRP WIP WHEEP
HURRY! HURRY! WE'RE TRYING TO SAVE HAN FROM THE BOUNTY HUNTER!
WHRRP RRP BIP BIP BEEP
WELL, AT LEAST YOU'RE STILL IN ONE PIECE. LOOK WHAT HAPPENED TO ME!
BADAWHEEEEP

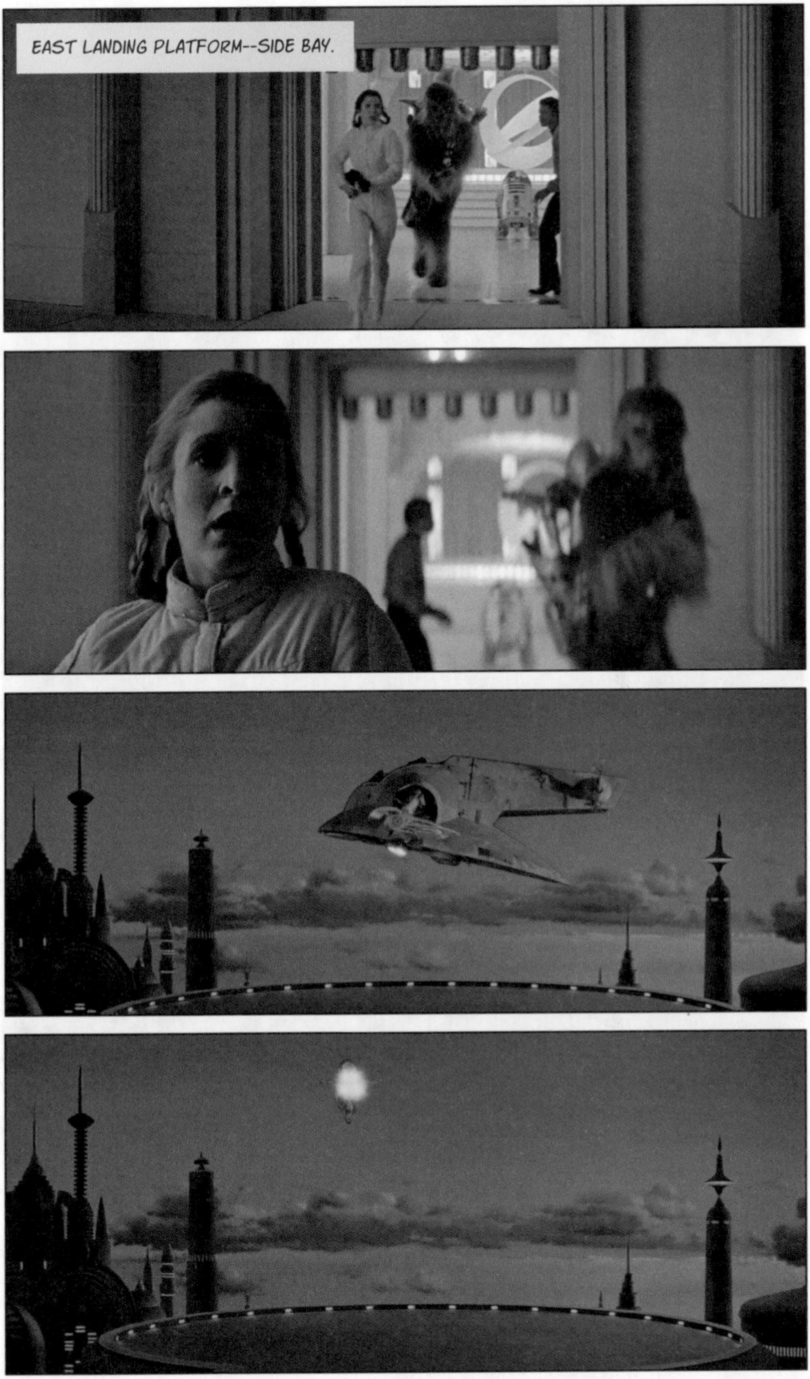
EAST LANDING PLATFORM--SIDE BAY.

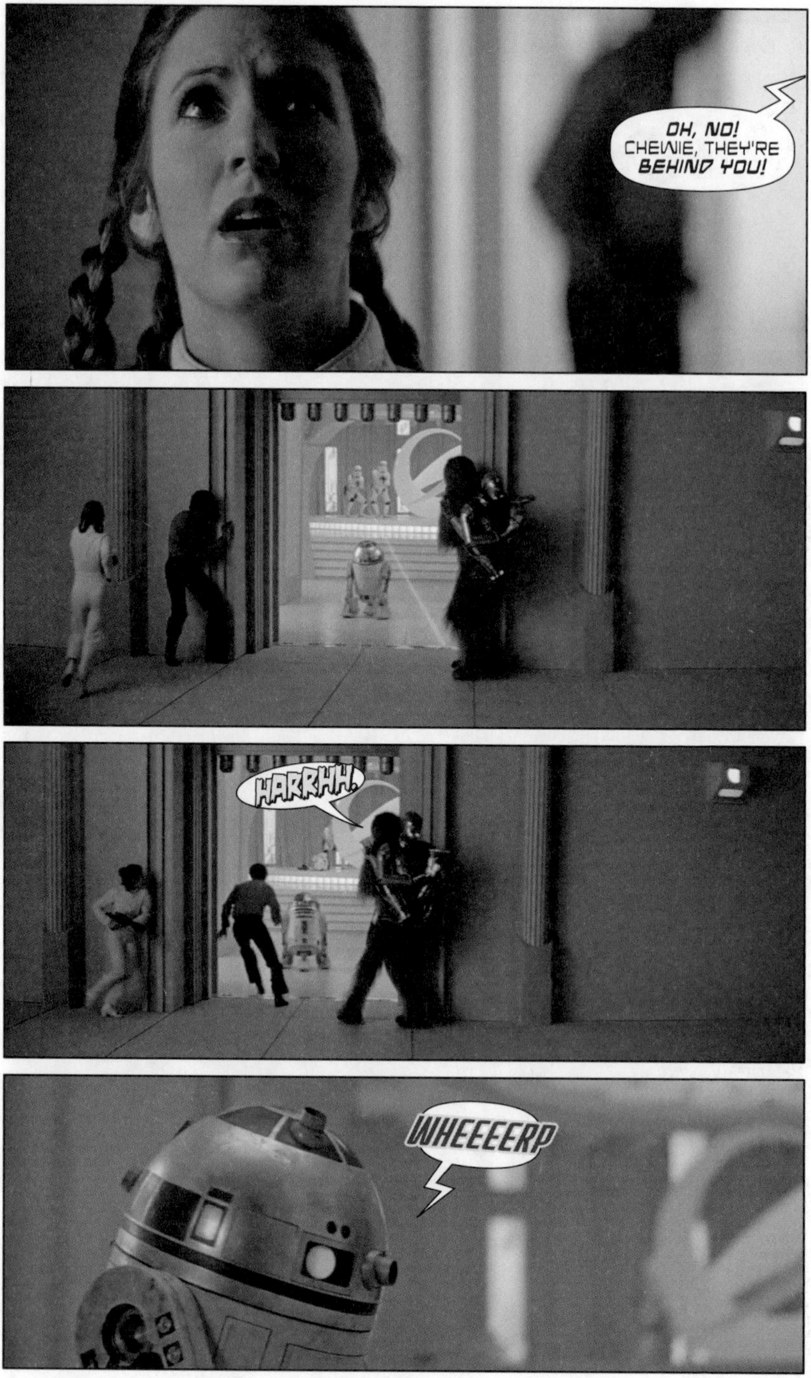
OH, NO! CHEWIE, THEY'RE BEHIND YOU!
HARRHH!
WHEEEERP

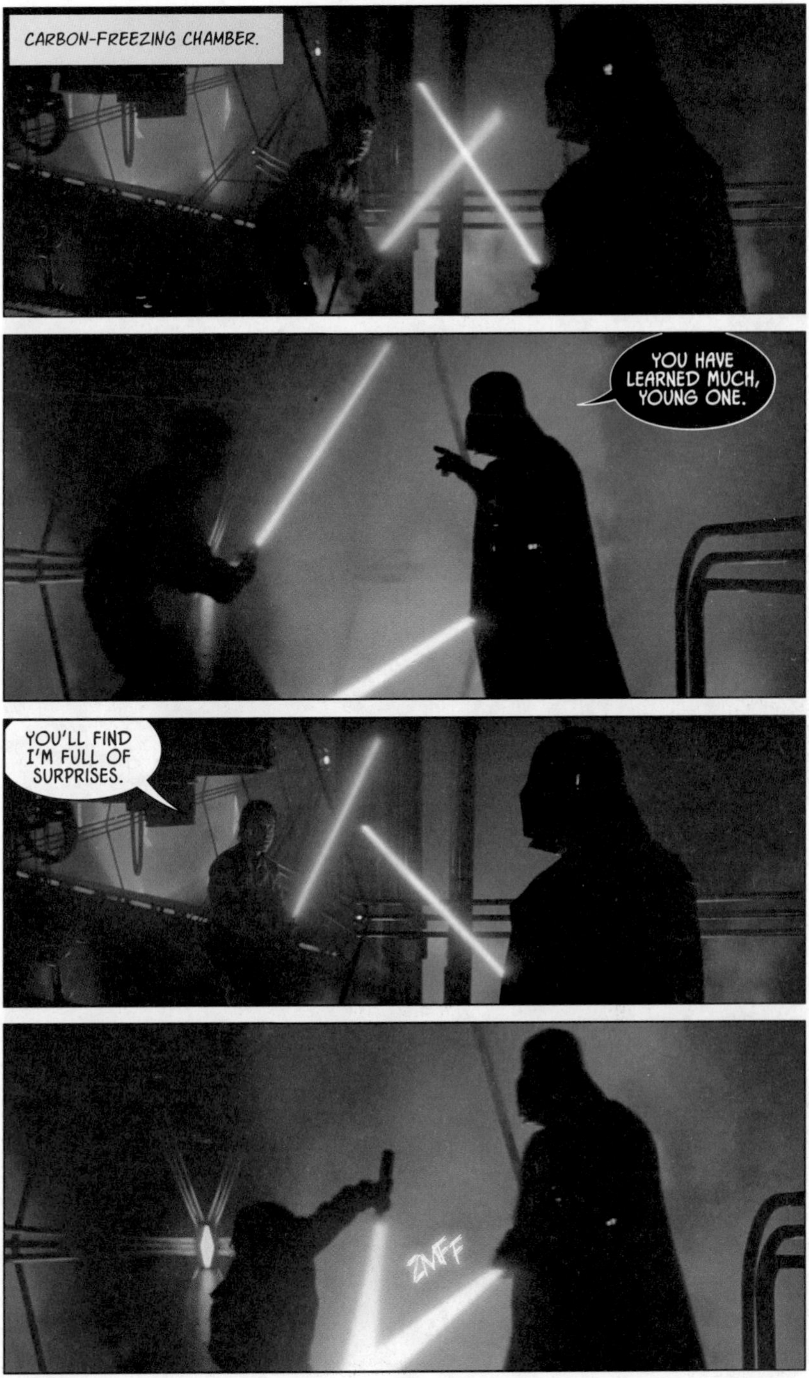
CARBON-FREEZING CHAMBER.
YOU HAVE LEARNED MUCH, YOUNG ONE.
YOU'LL FIND I'M FULL OF SURPRISES.
ZMFF

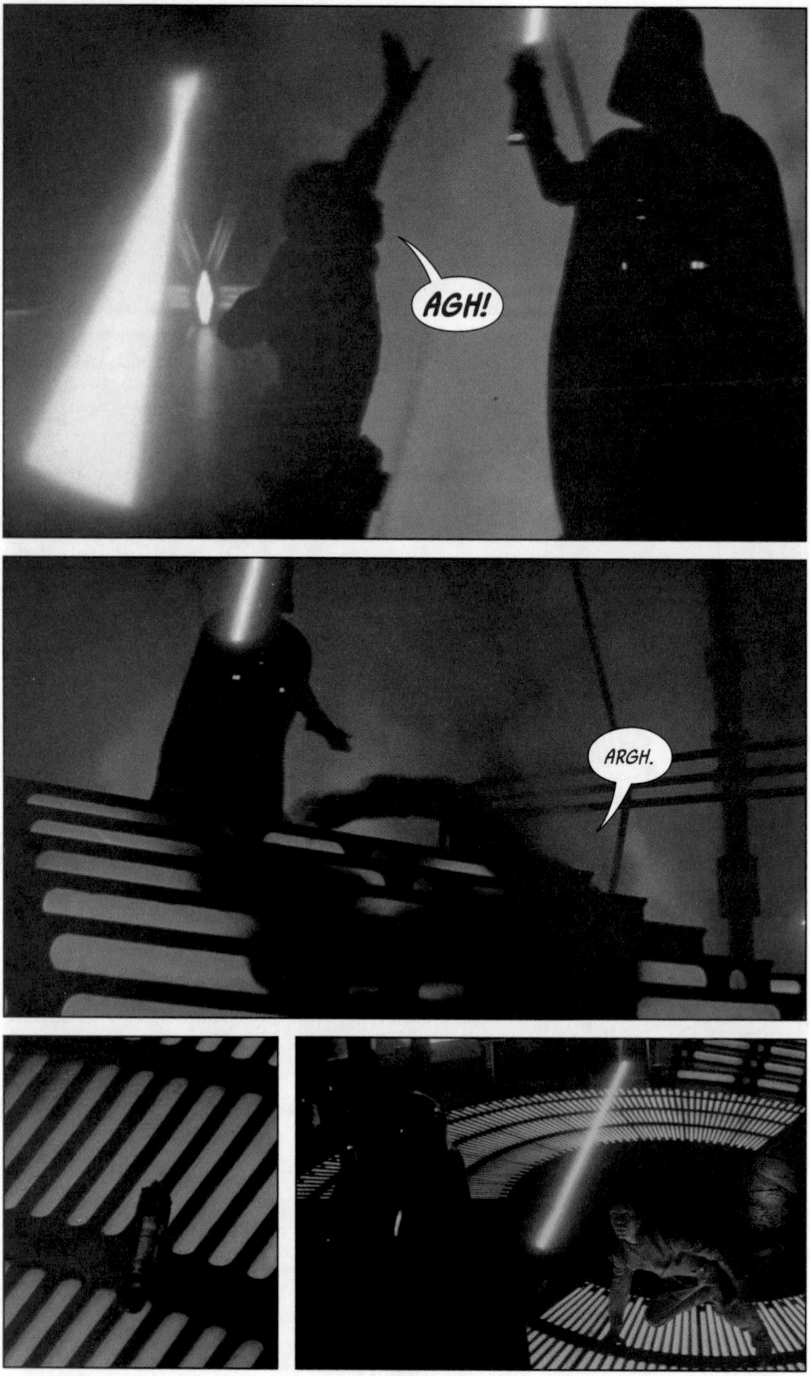
AGH!
ARGH.

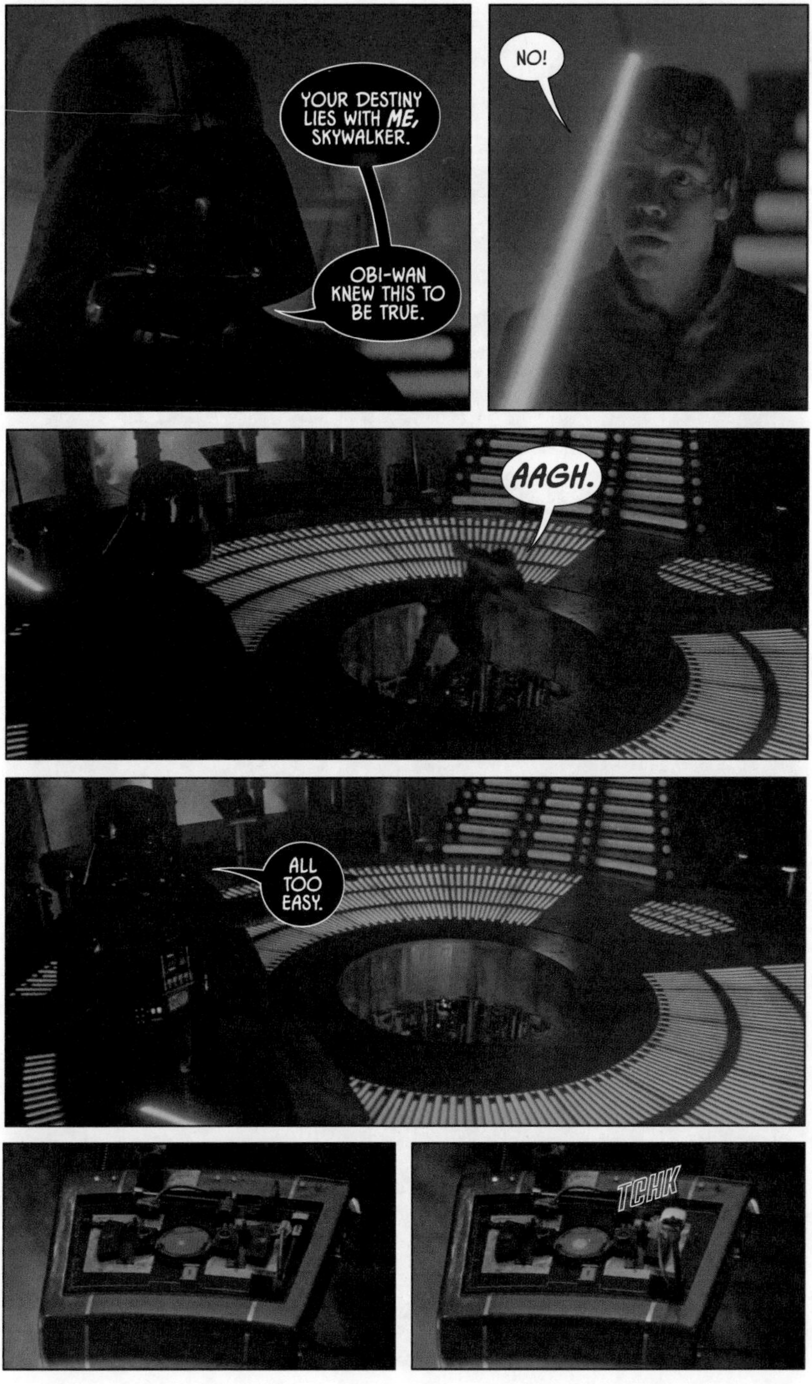
YOUR DESTINY LIES WITH *ME,* SKYWALKER.
OBI-WAN KNEW THIS TO BE TRUE.
NO!
AAGH.
ALL TOO EASY.
TCHK

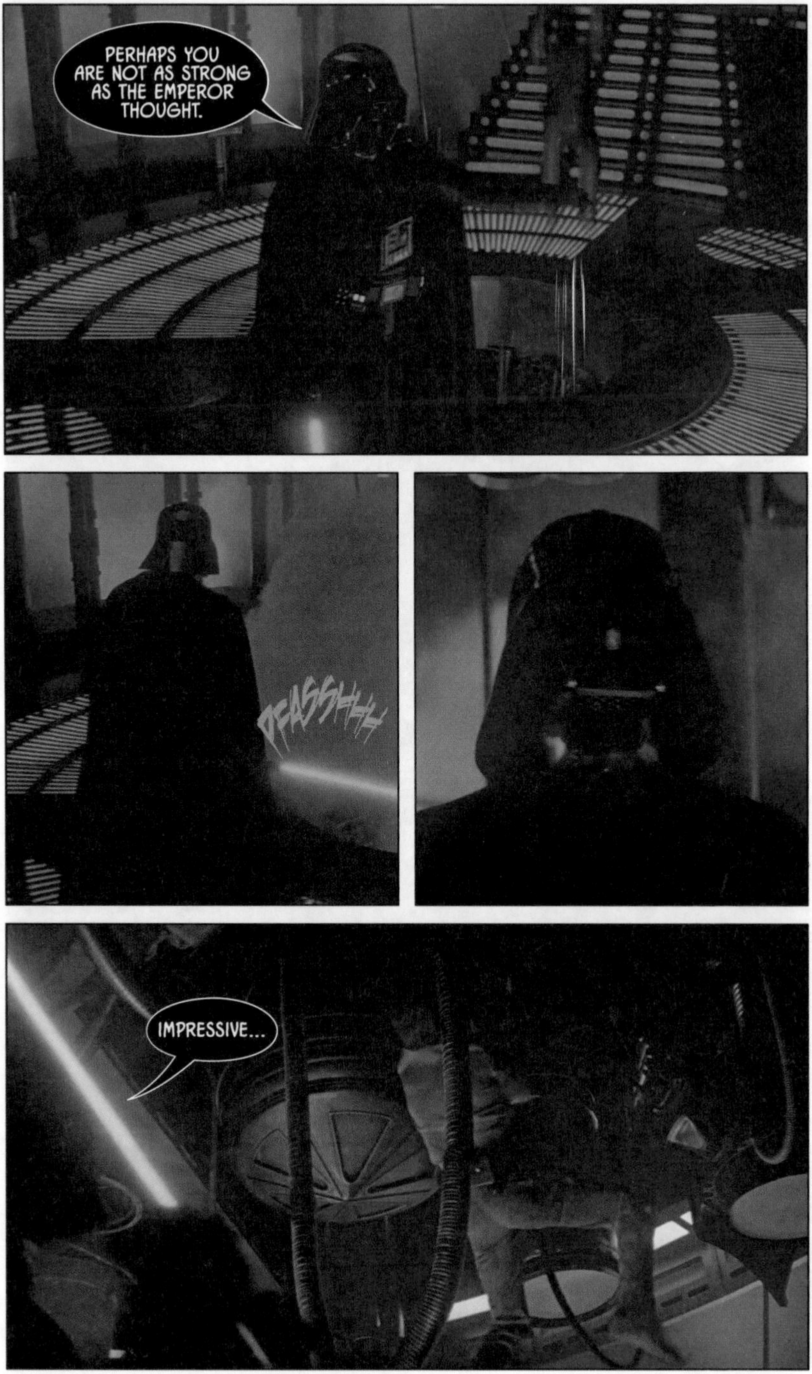
PERHAPS YOU ARE NOT AS STRONG AS THE EMPEROR THOUGHT.
PFASSHHH
IMPRESSIVE...

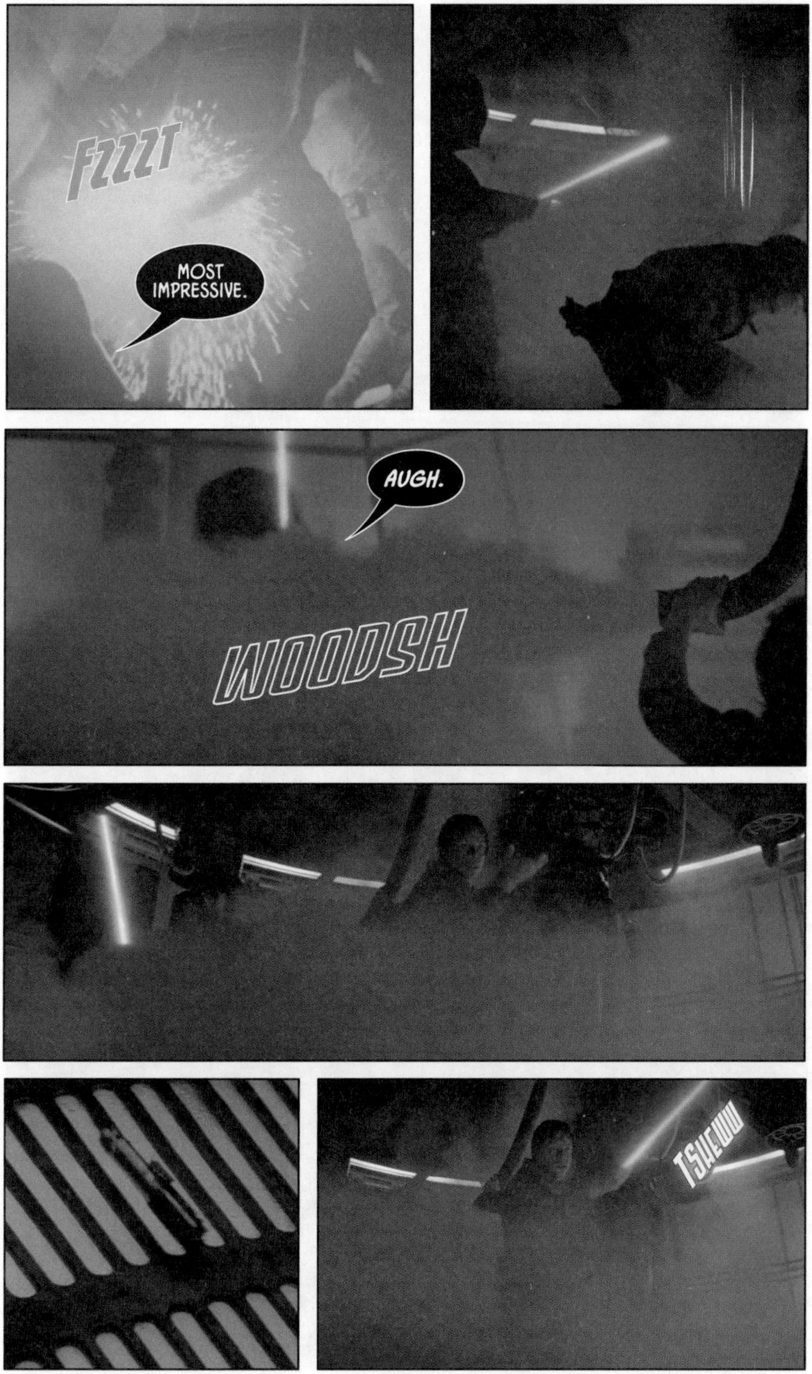
FZZZT
MOST IMPRESSIVE.
AUGH.
WOODSH
TSHEWW

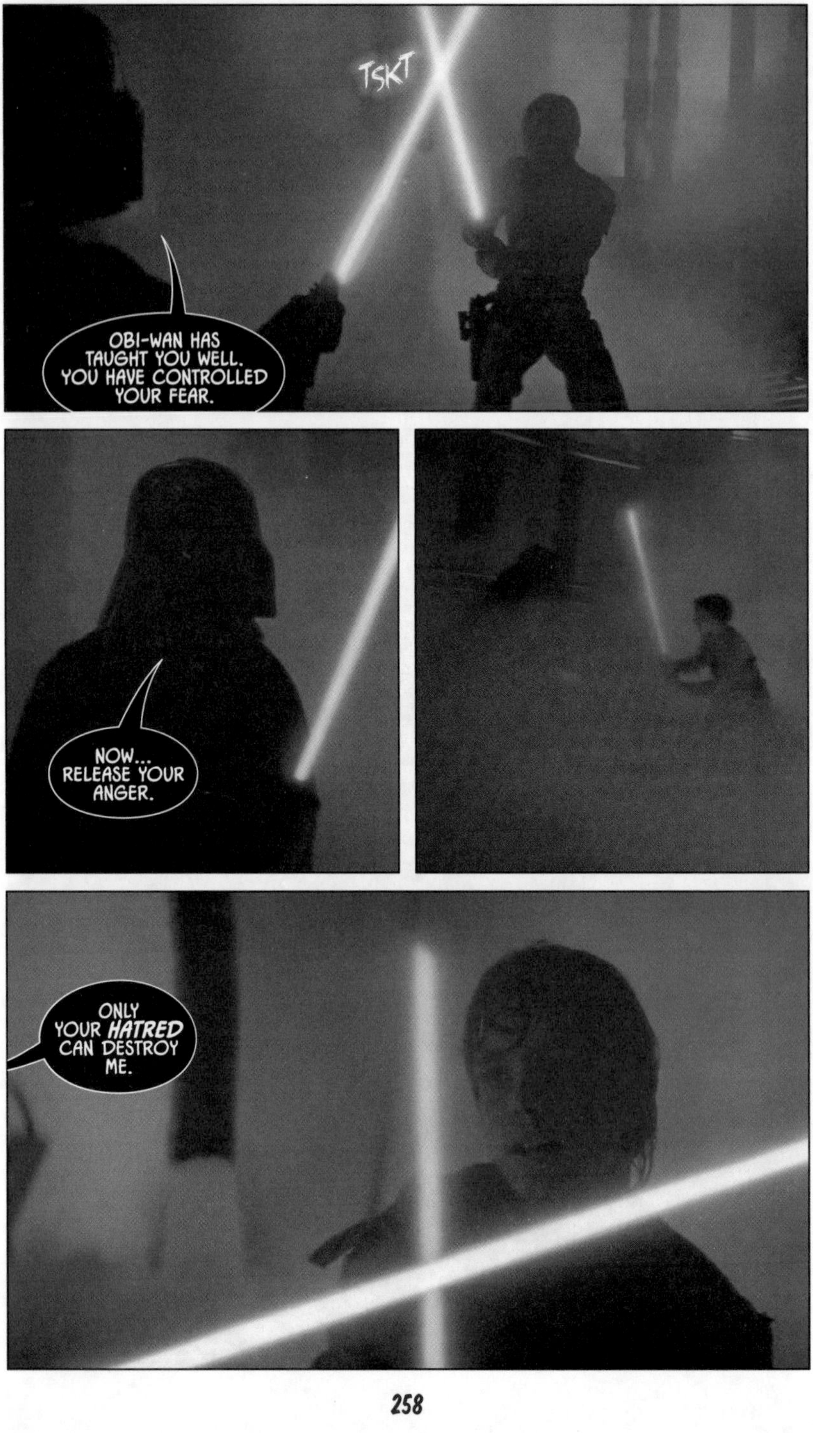
TSKT
OBI-WAN HAS TAUGHT YOU WELL. YOU HAVE CONTROLLED YOUR FEAR.
NOW... RELEASE YOUR ANGER.
ONLY YOUR HATRED CAN DESTROY ME.

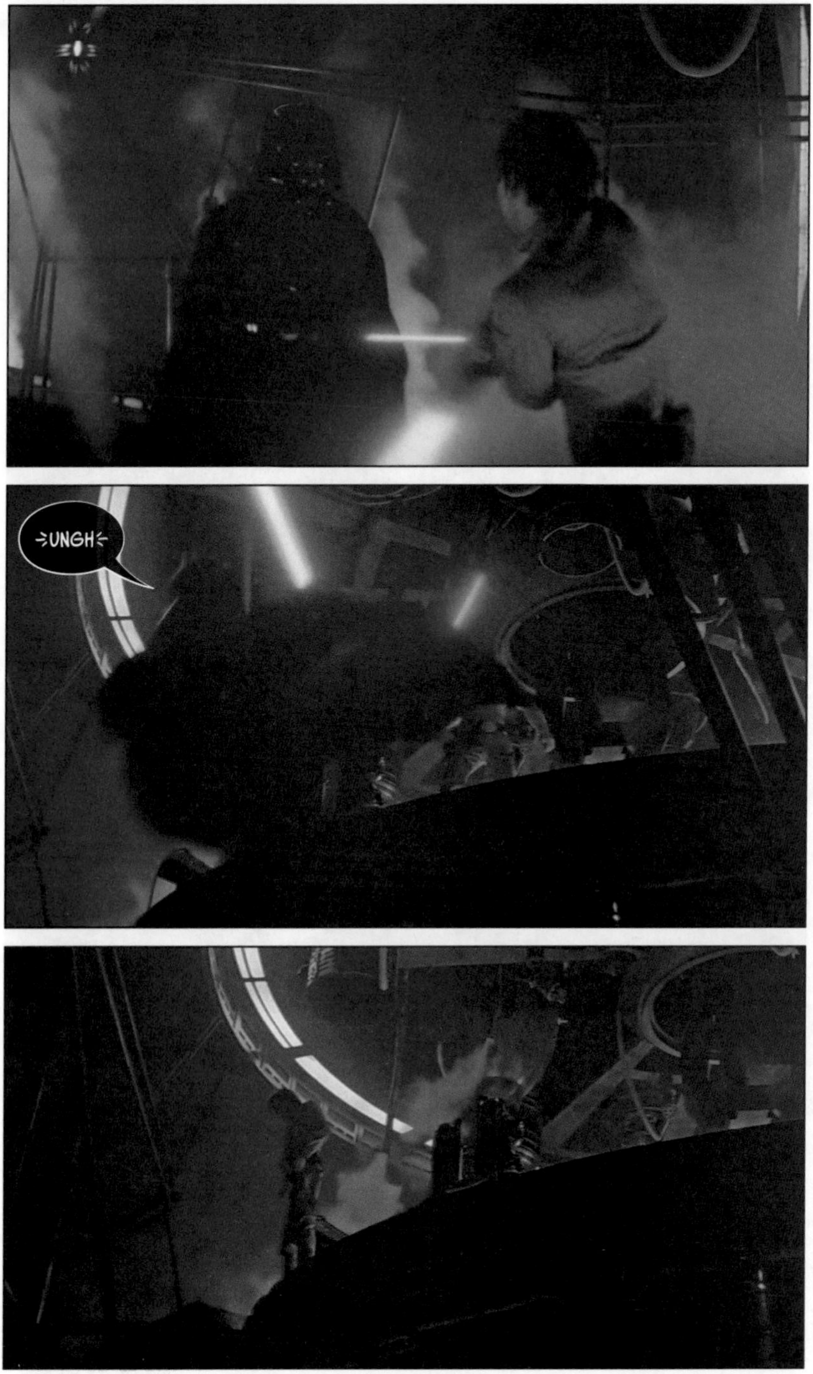
UNGH

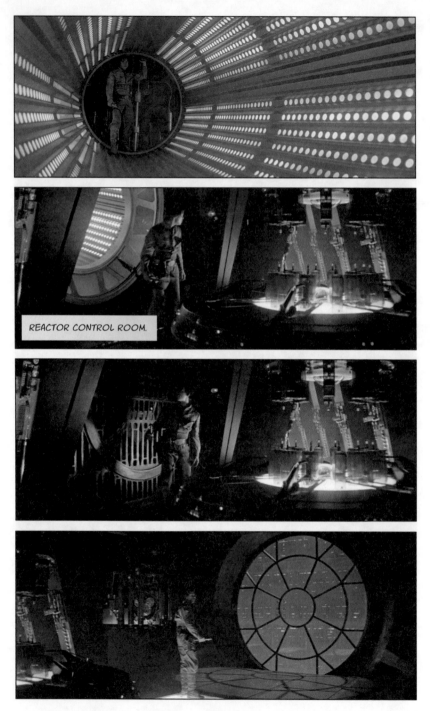

REACTOR CONTROL ROOM.

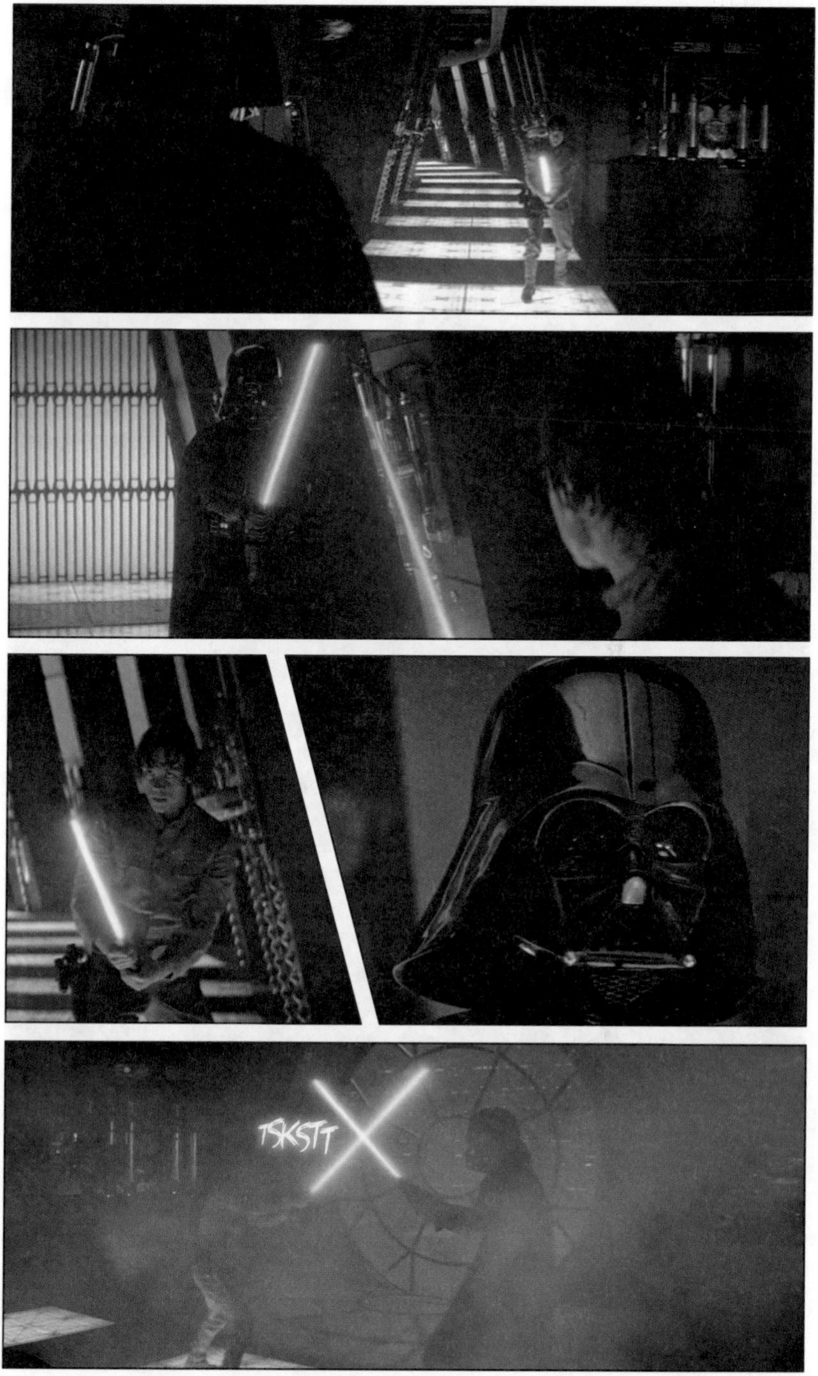
TSKSTT

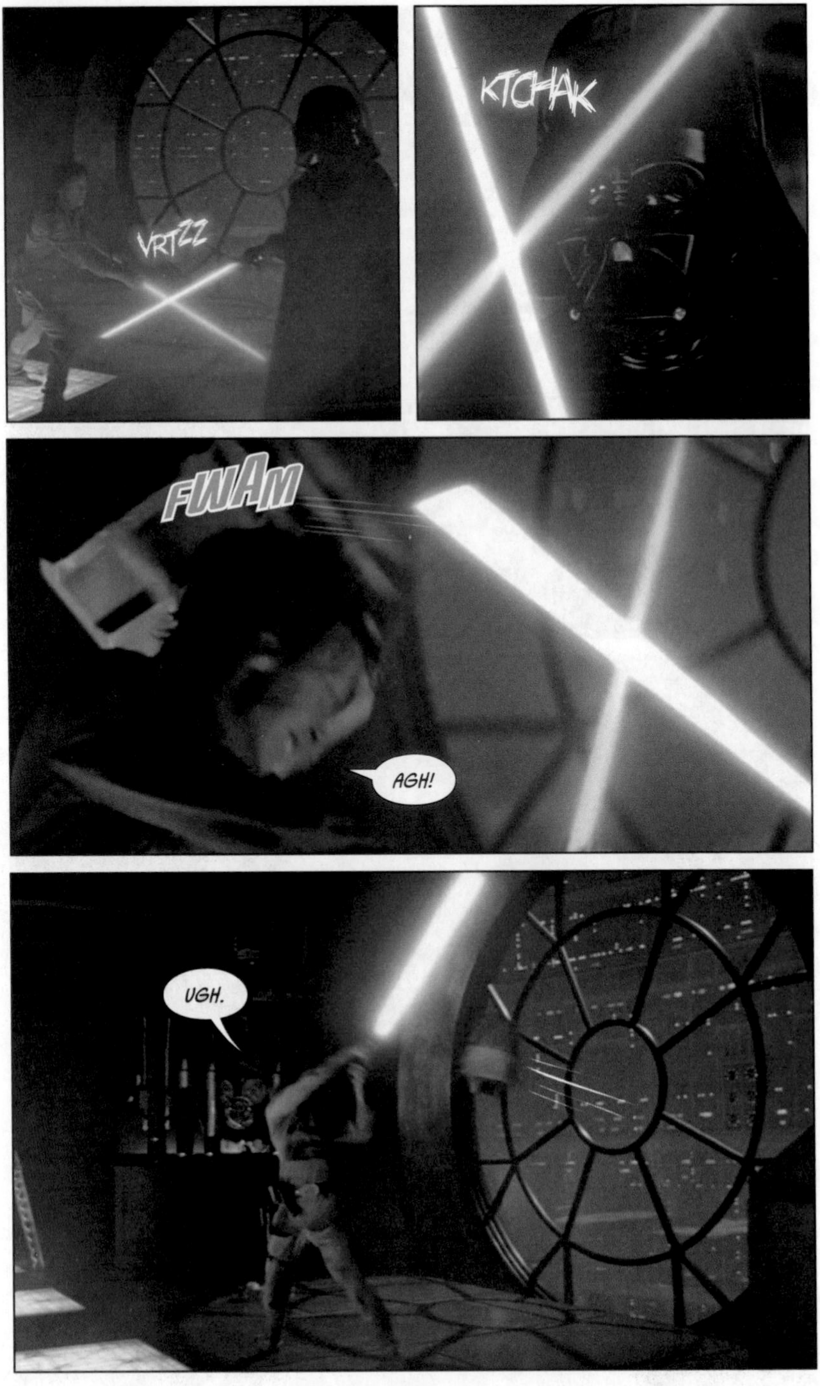
VRTZZ
KTCHAK
FWAM
AGH!
UGH.

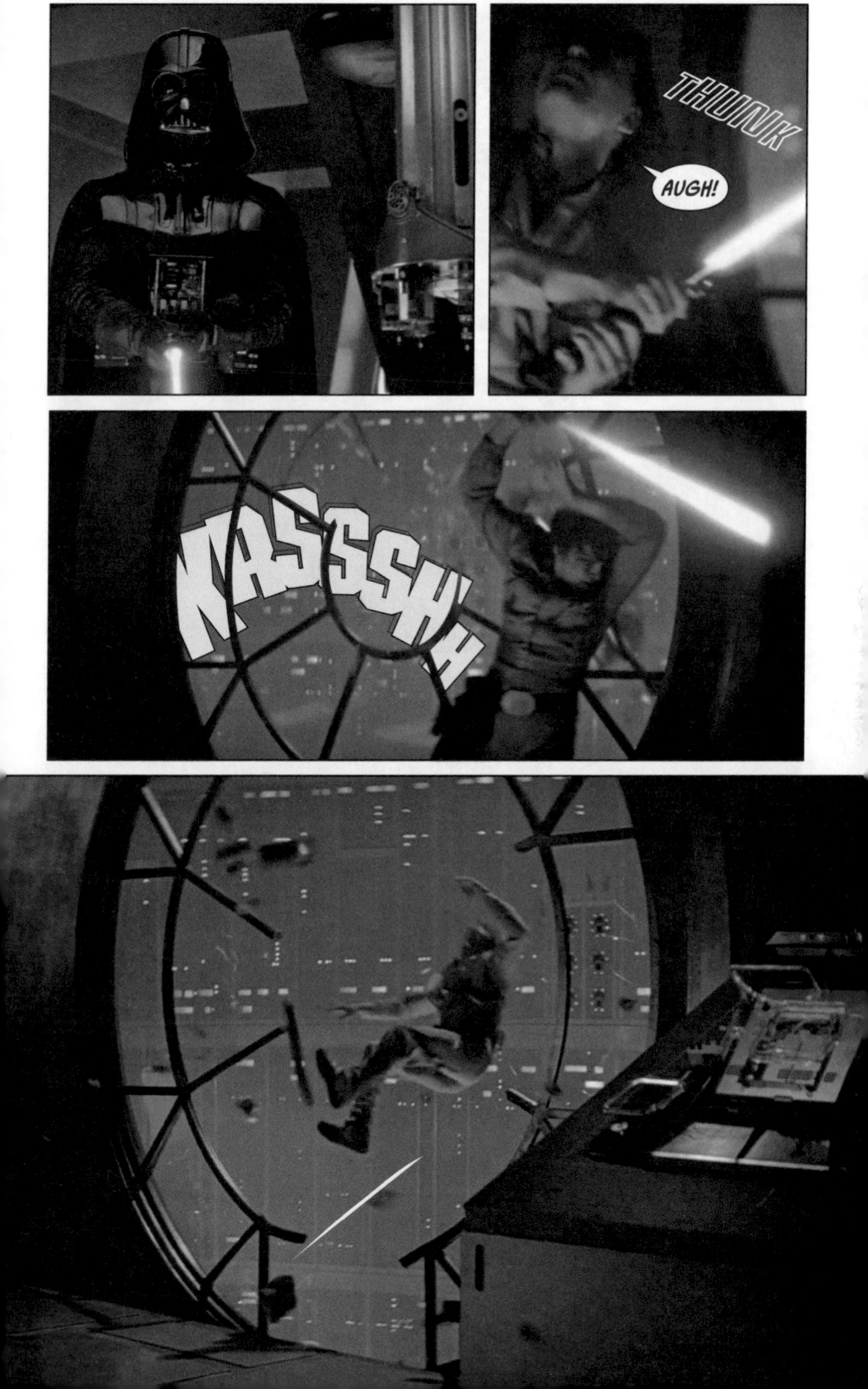
THUNK
AUGH!
KASSSHH

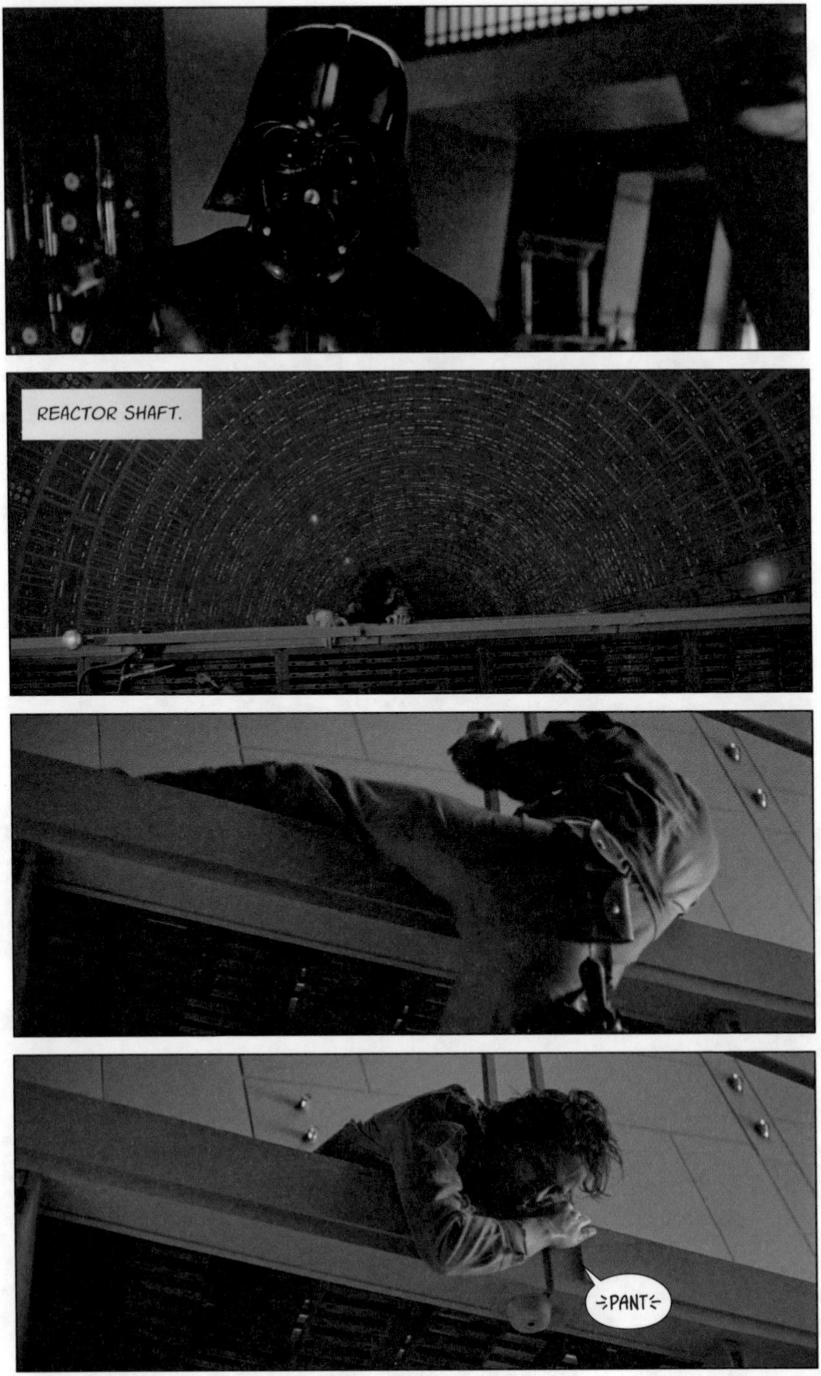
REACTOR SHAFT.
PANT

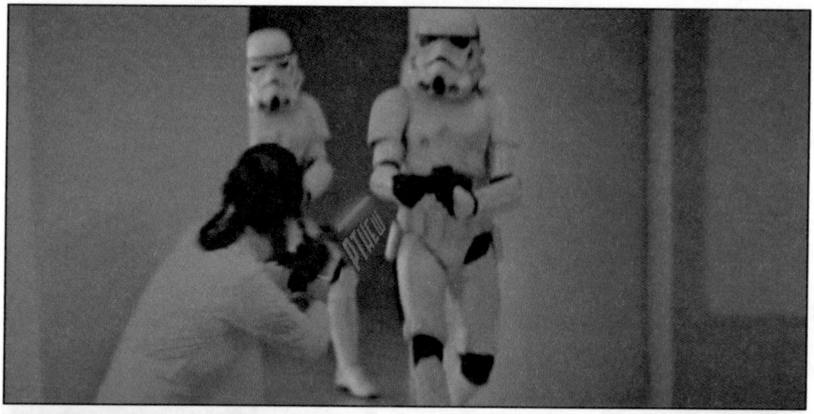
PTWEW
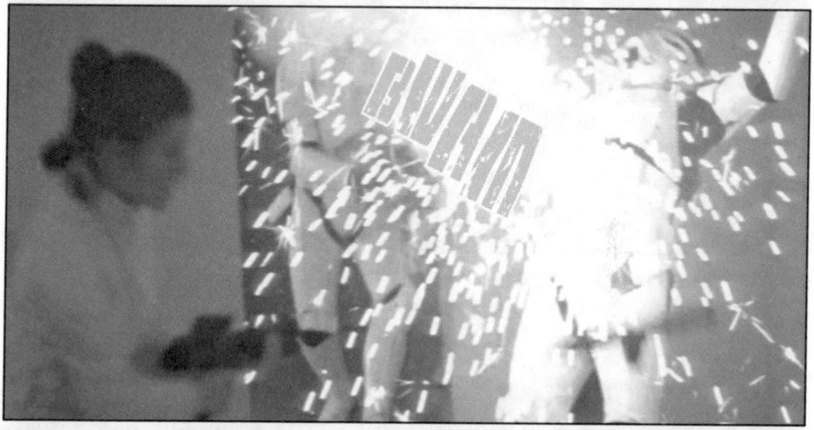
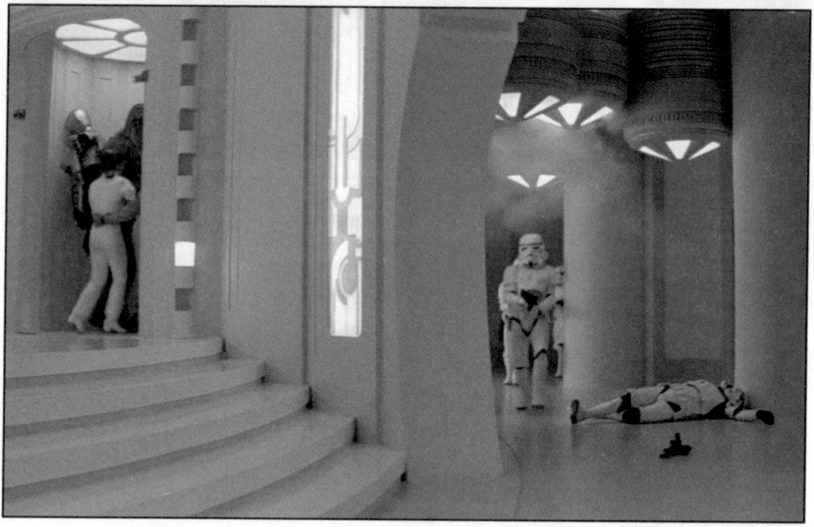

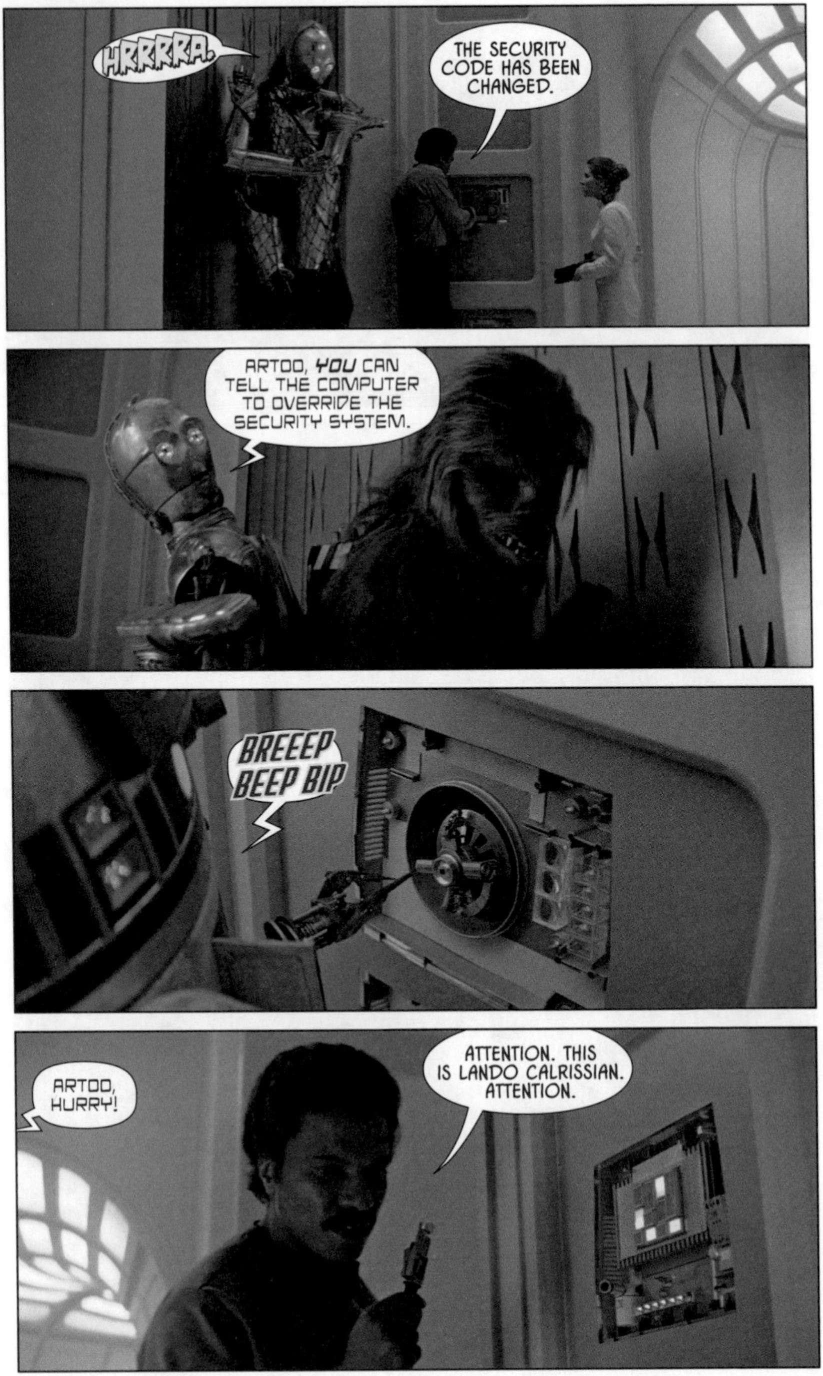
HRRRRA.
THE SECURITY CODE HAS BEEN CHANGED.
ARTOO, YOU CAN TELL THE COMPUTER TO OVERRIDE THE SECURITY SYSTEM.
BREEEP BEEP BIP
ARTOO, HURRY!
ATTENTION. THIS IS LANDO CALRISSIAN. ATTENTION.

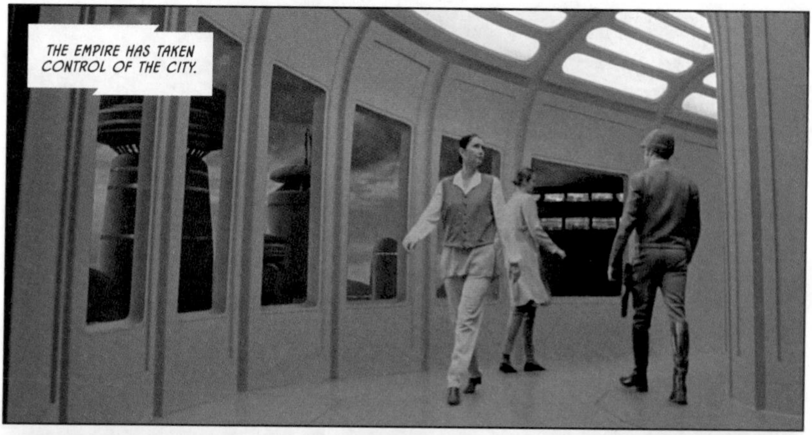
THE EMPIRE HAS TAKEN CONTROL OF THE CITY.

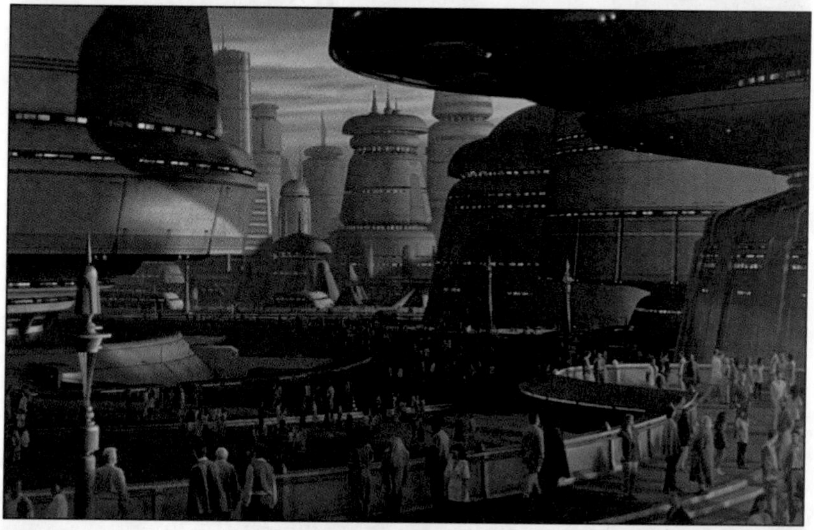

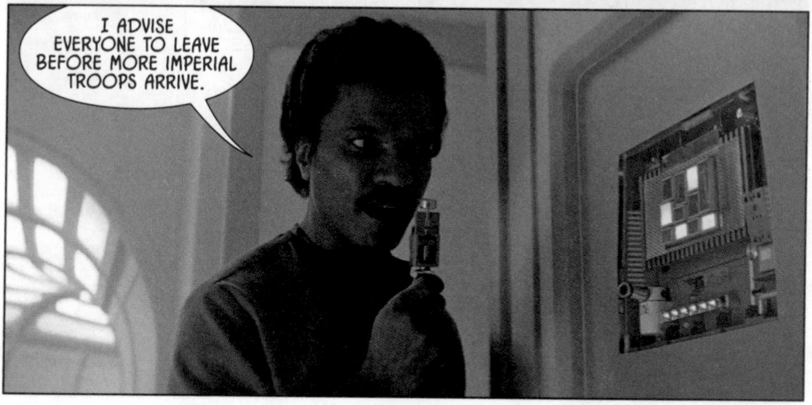
I ADVISE EVERYONE TO LEAVE BEFORE MORE IMPERIAL TROOPS ARRIVE.

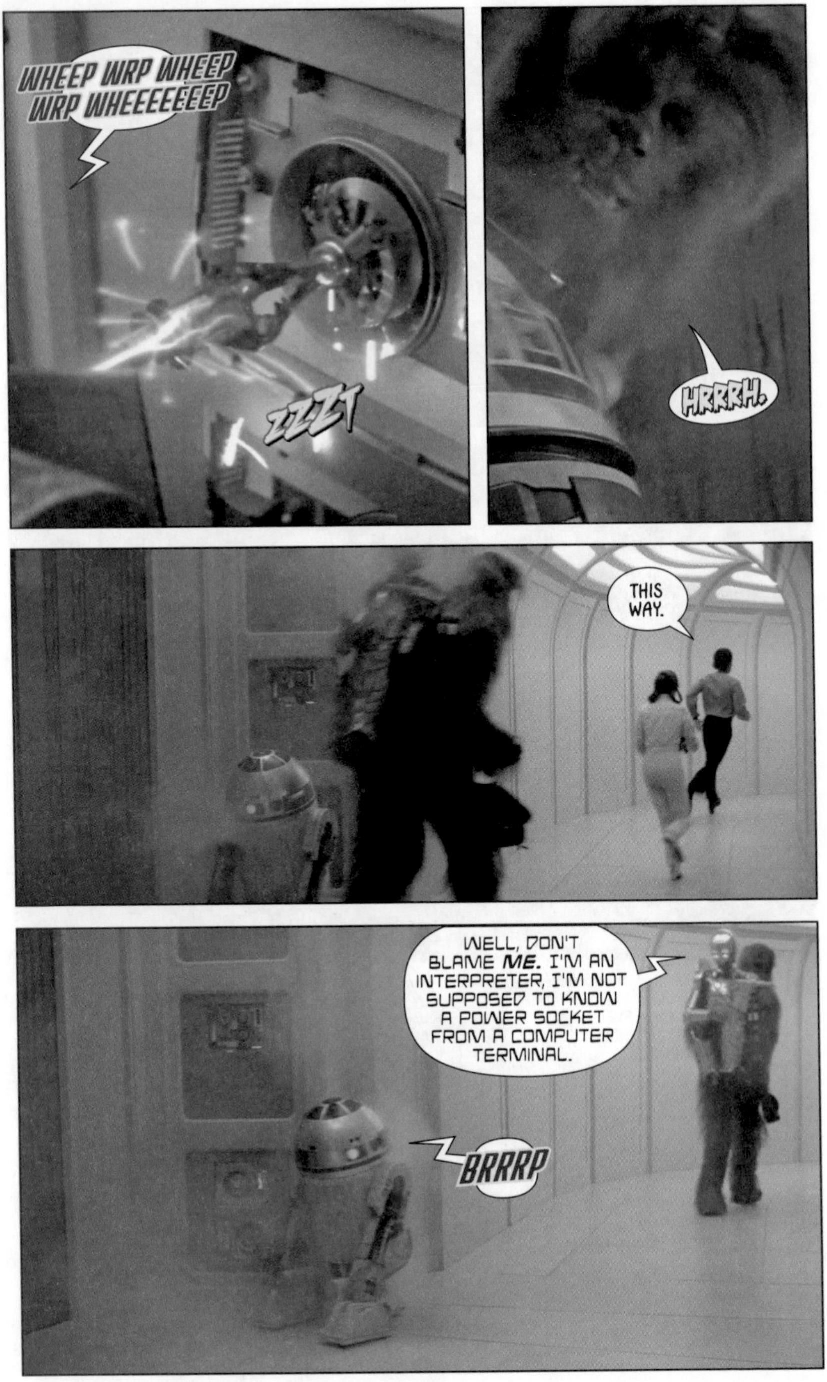
WHEEP WRP WHEEP WRP WHEEEEEEEP
ZZZT
HRRRH.
THIS WAY.
WELL, DON'T BLAME ME. I'M AN INTERPRETER, I'M NOT SUPPOSED TO KNOW A POWER SOCKET FROM A COMPUTER TERMINAL.
BRRRP

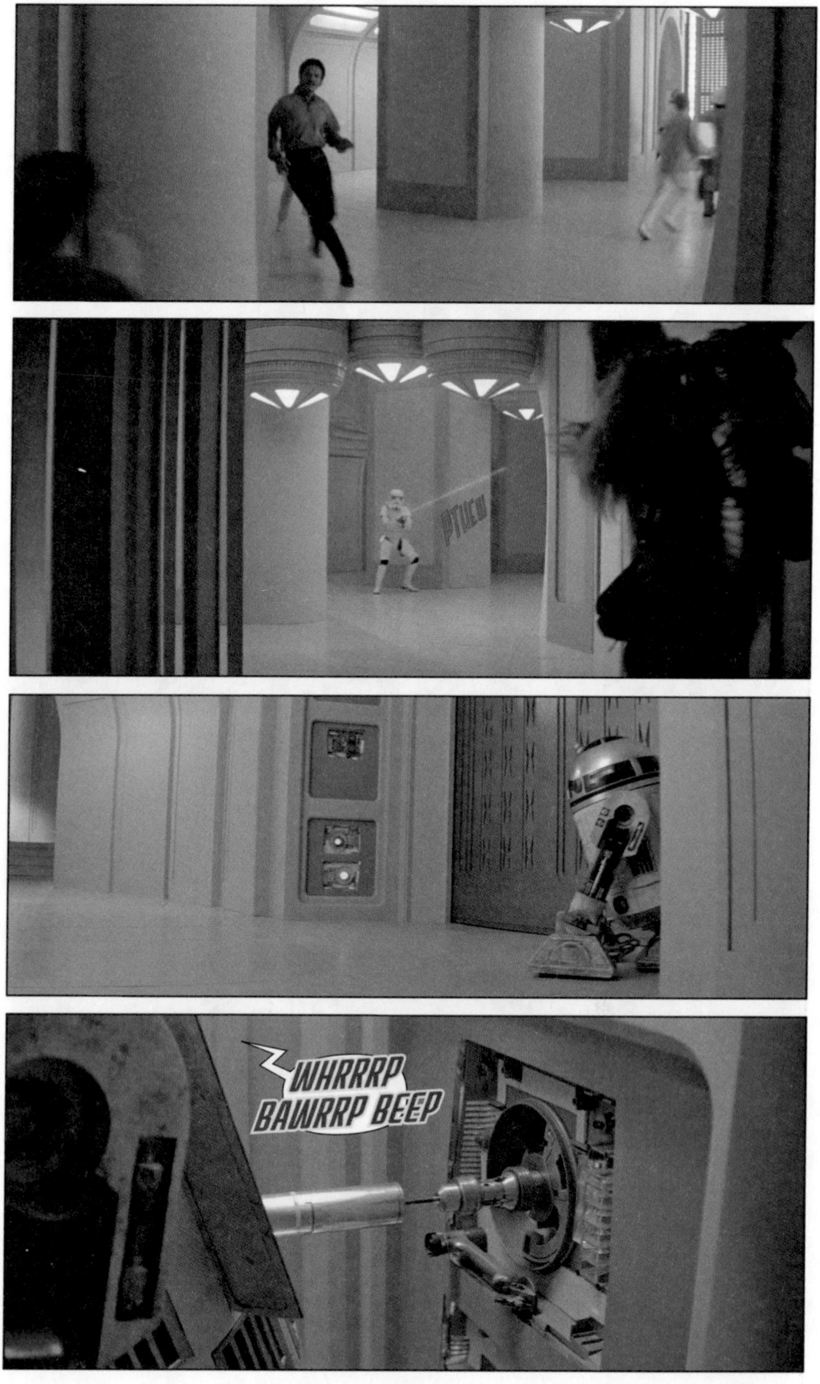
PTCHU
WHRRRP BAWRRP BEEP

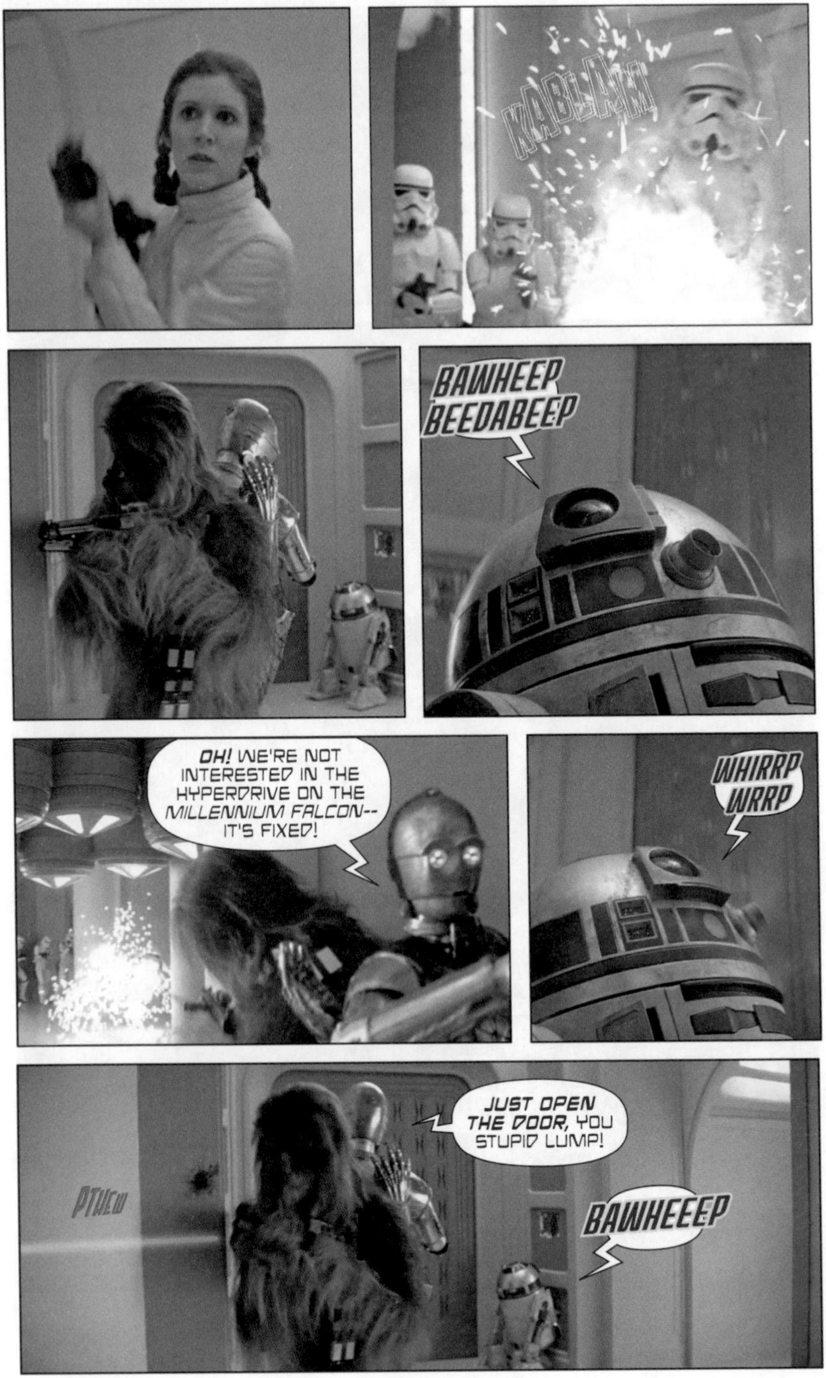
KABLAM
BAWHEEP BEEDABEEP
OH! WE'RE NOT INTERESTED IN THE HYPERDRIVE ON THE MILLENNIUM FALCON-- IT'S FIXED!
WHIRRP WRRP
PTHEW
JUST OPEN THE DOOR, YOU STUPID LUMP!
BAWHEEEP

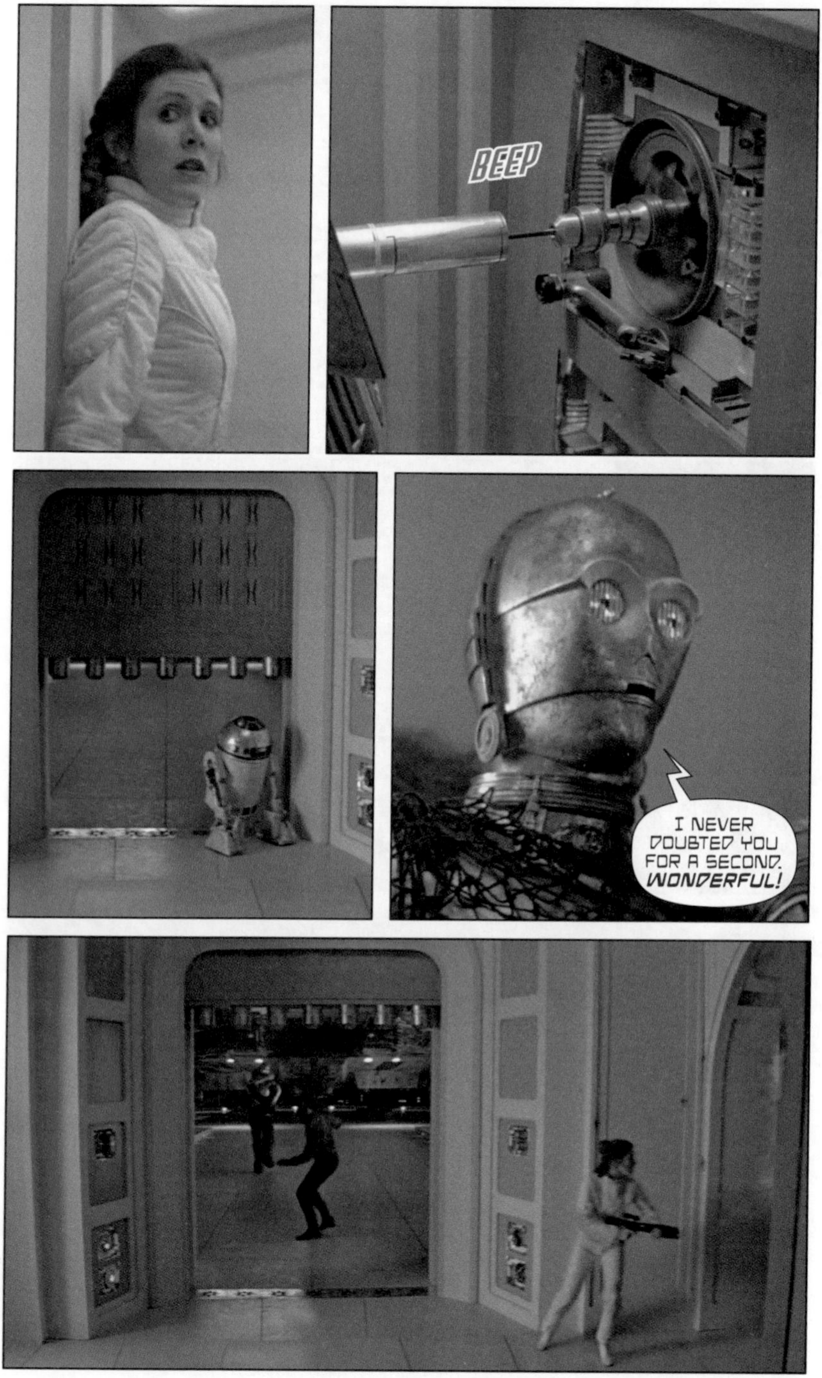
BEEP
I NEVER DOUBTED YOU FOR A SECOND. WONDERFUL!

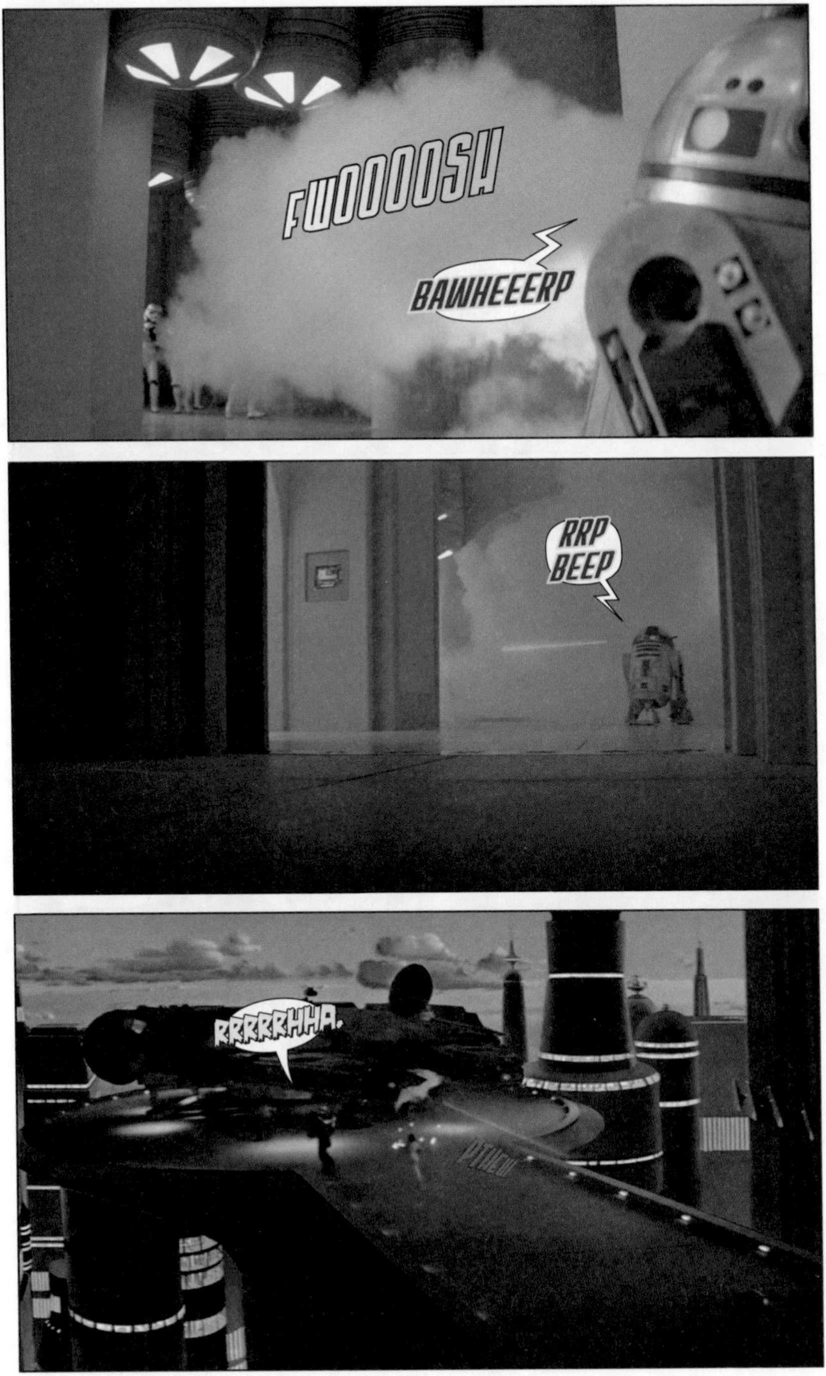
FWOOOOSH
BAWHEEERP
RRP BEEP
RRRRRHHA.
PTHEW

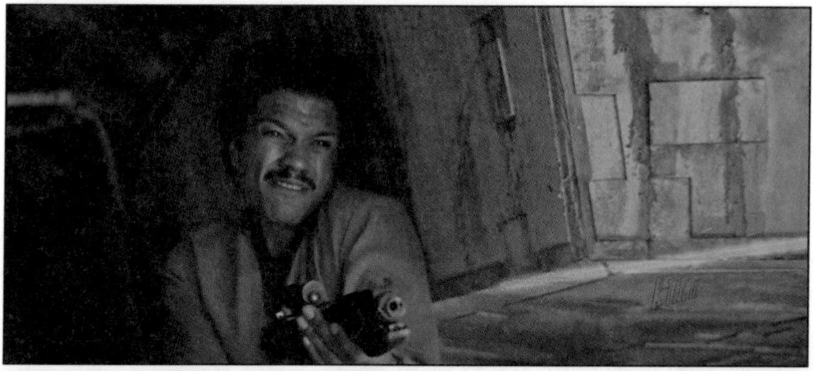

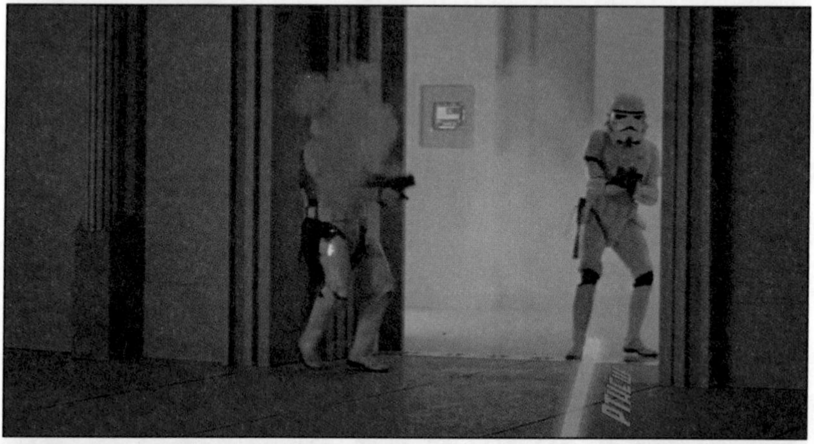

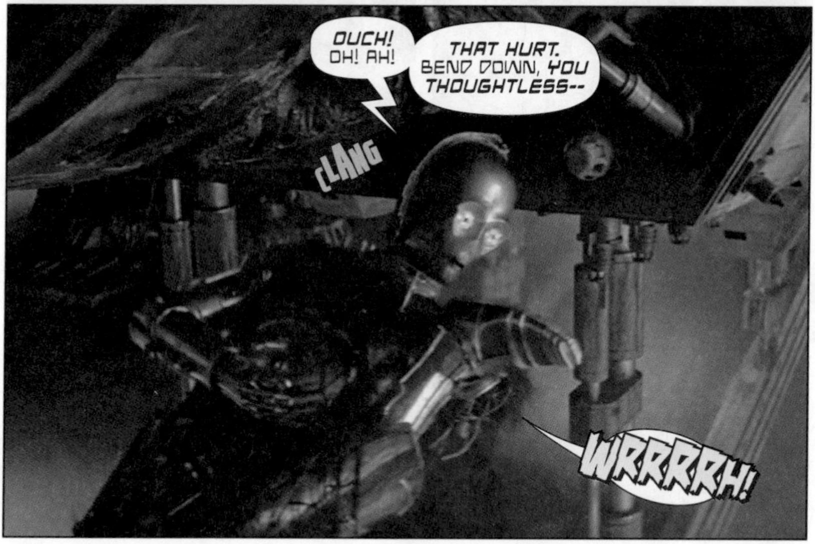
OUCH! OH! AH!
THAT HURT. BEND DOWN, YOU THOUGHTLESS--
CLANG
WRRRRH!

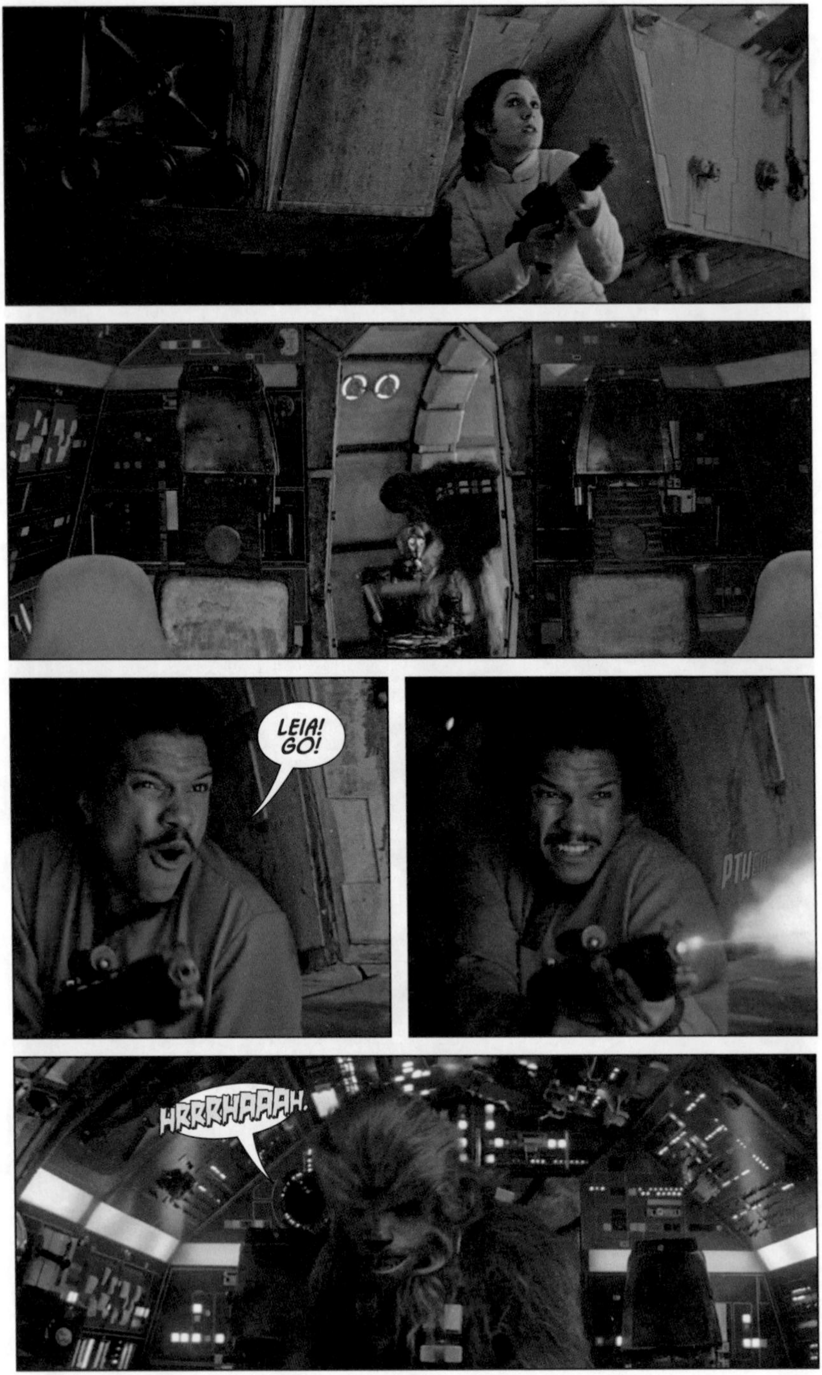
LEIA! GO!
HRRRHAAAAH.

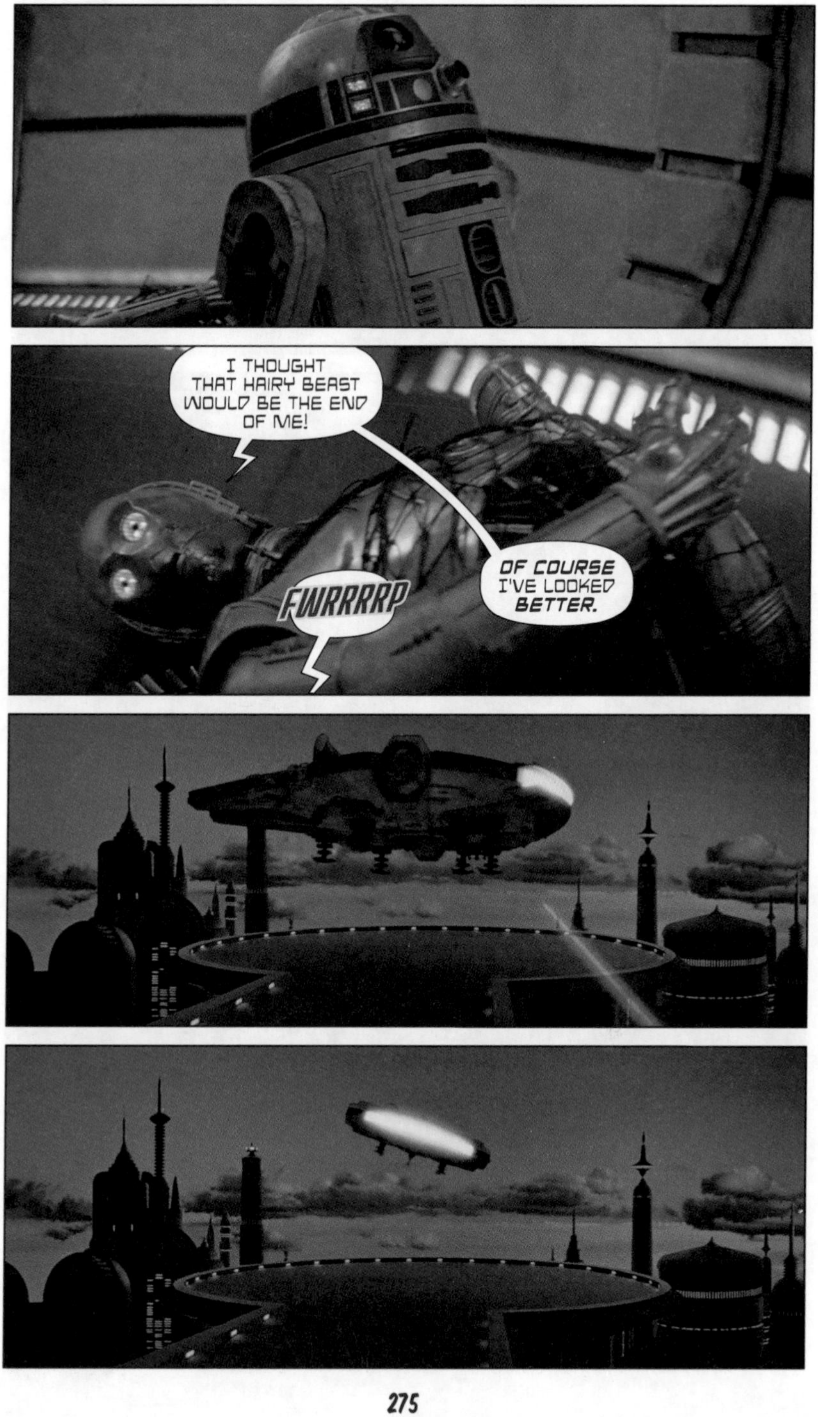
I THOUGHT THAT HAIRY BEAST WOULD BE THE END OF ME!
OF COURSE I'VE LOOKED BETTER.
FWRRRRP

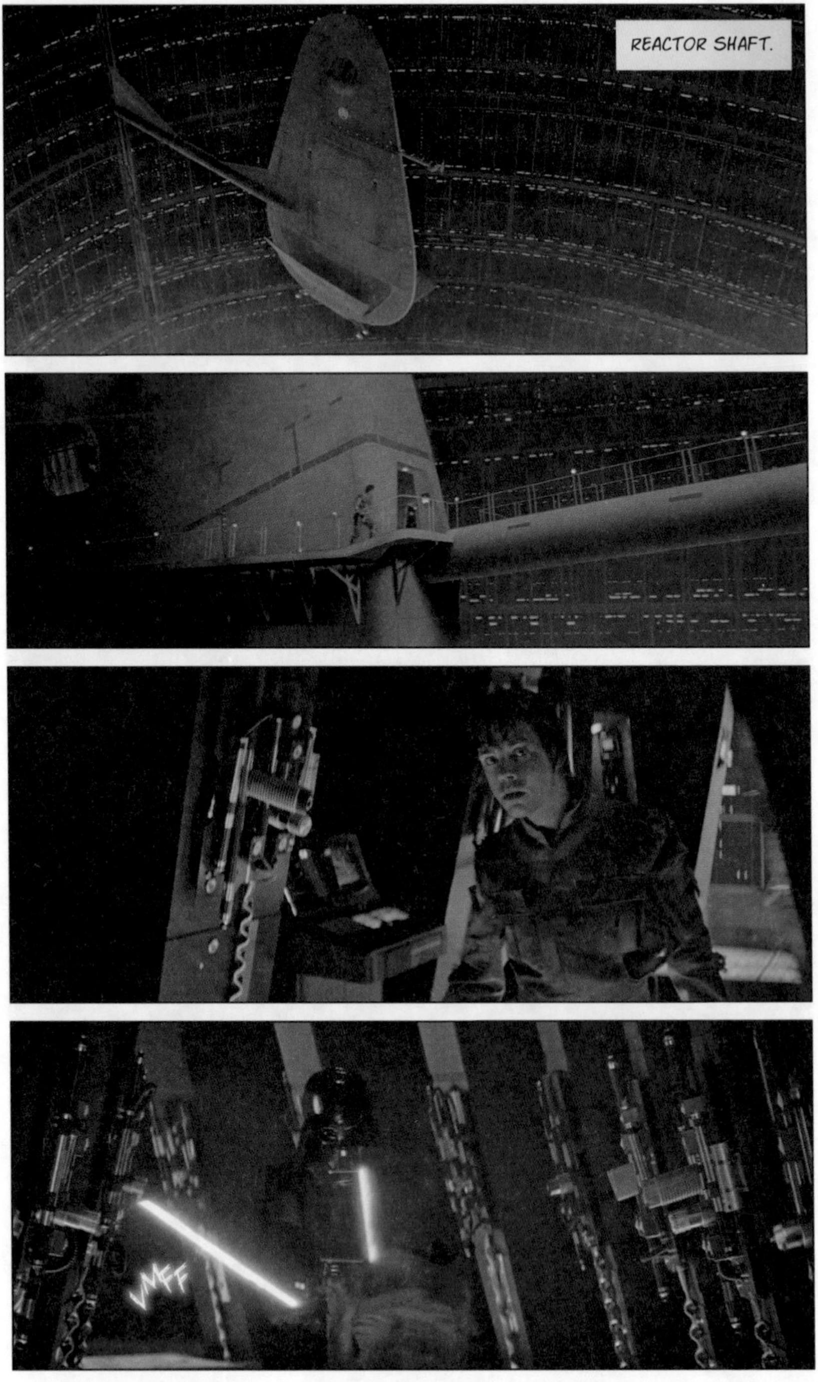
REACTOR SHAFT.
VMFF

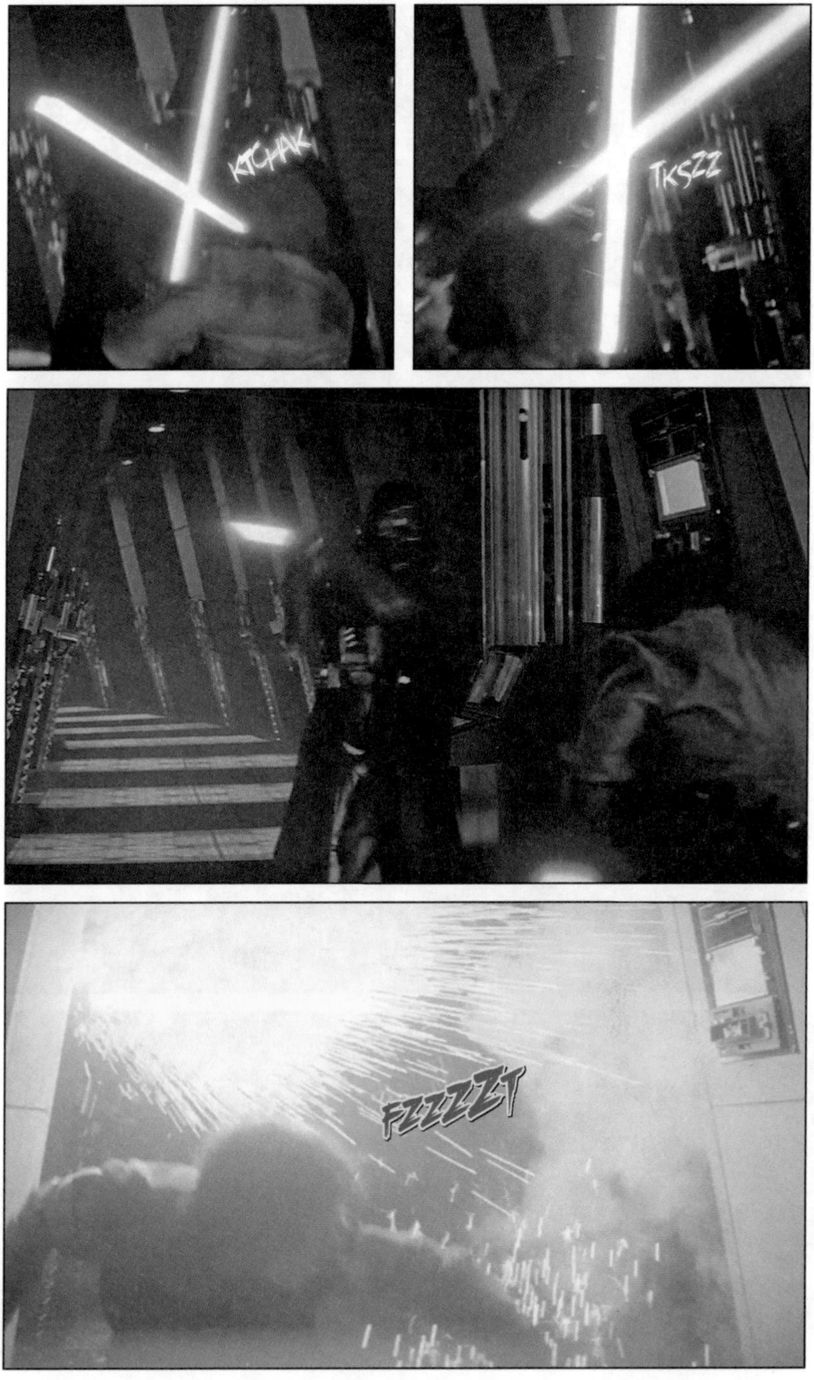
KTCHAK
TKSZZ
FZZZZT

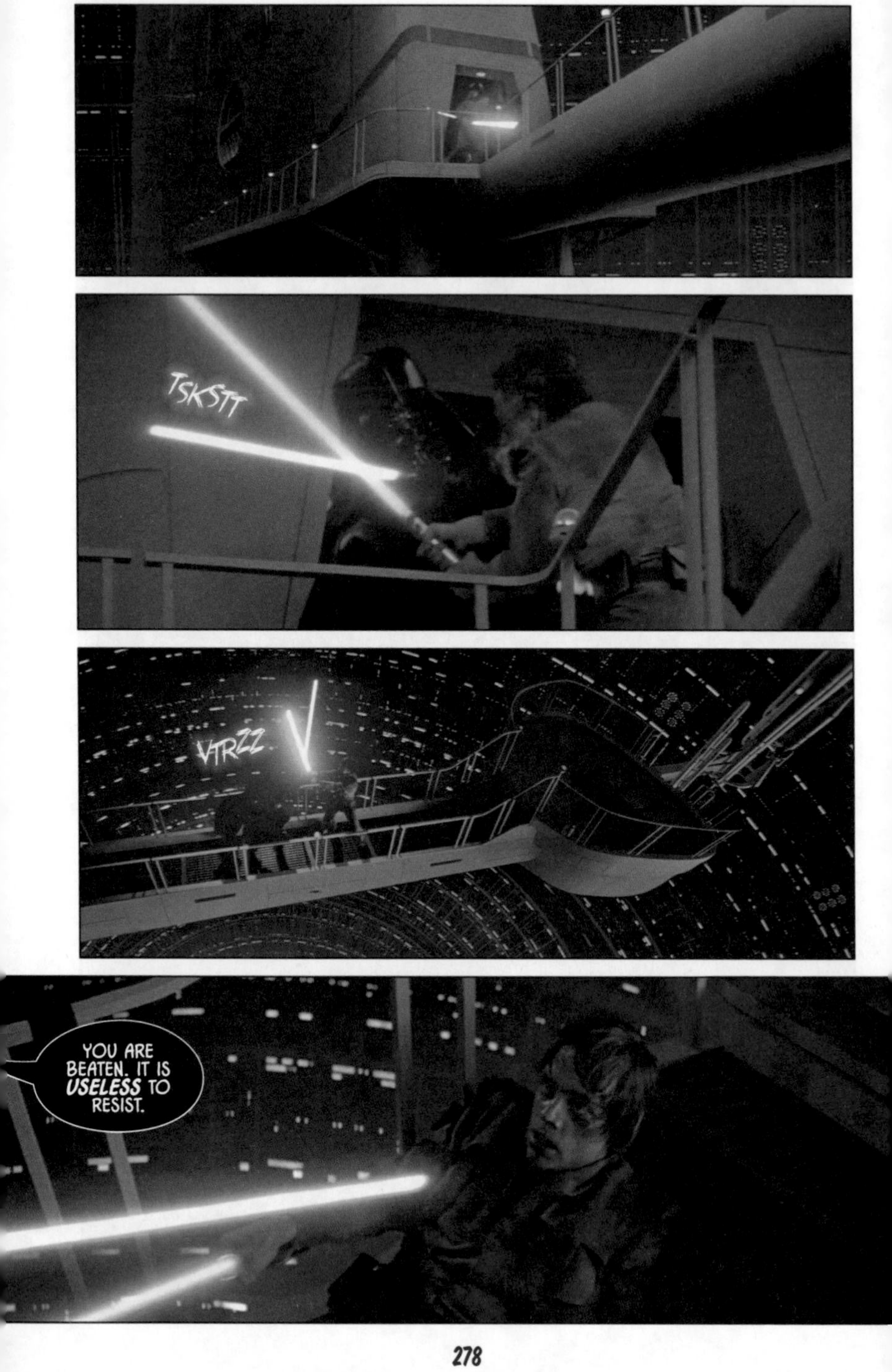
TSKSTT
VTRZZ
YOU ARE BEATEN. IT IS USELESS TO RESIST.

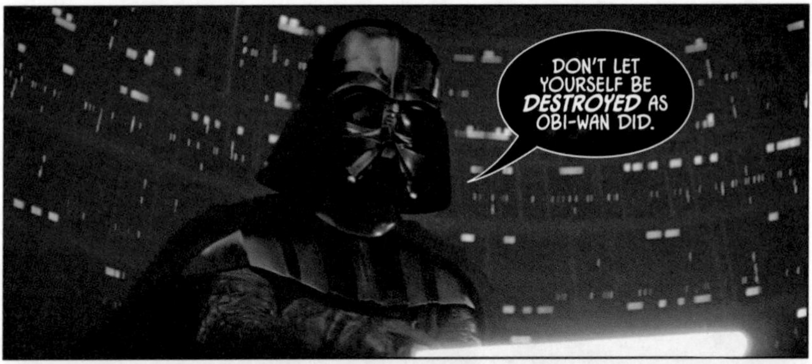
DON'T LET YOURSELF BE DESTROYED AS OBI-WAN DID.

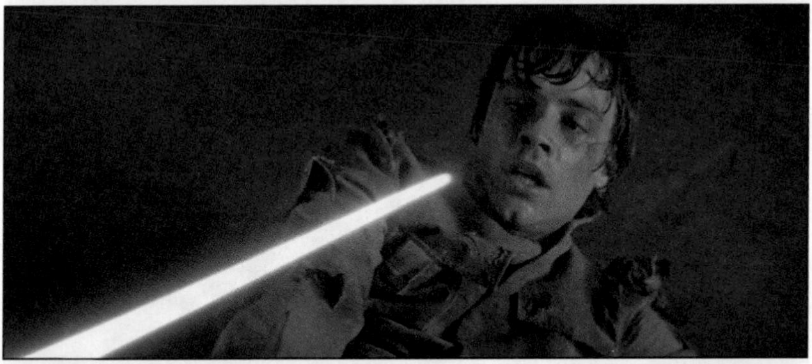

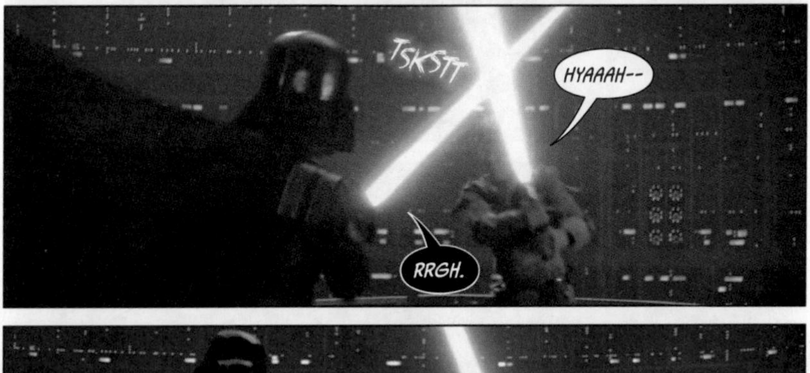
TSKSTT
HYAAAH--
RRGH.

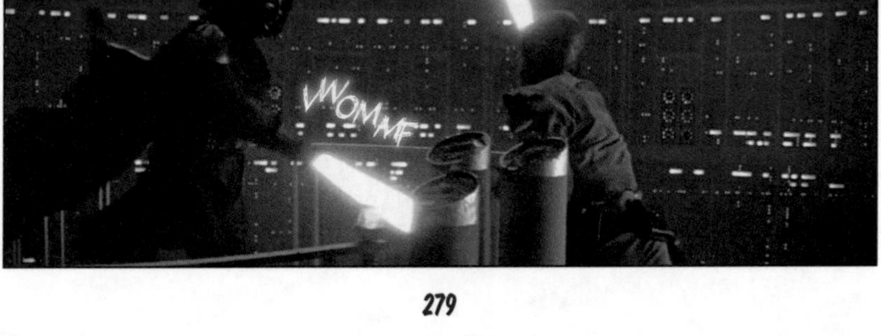
VWOMMF

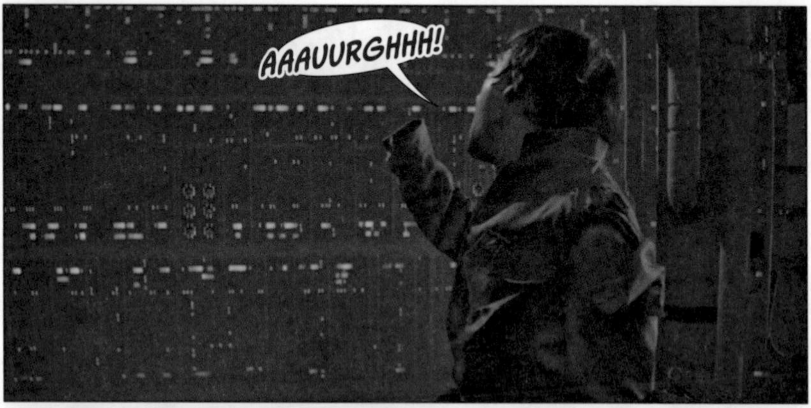
AAAUURGHHH!

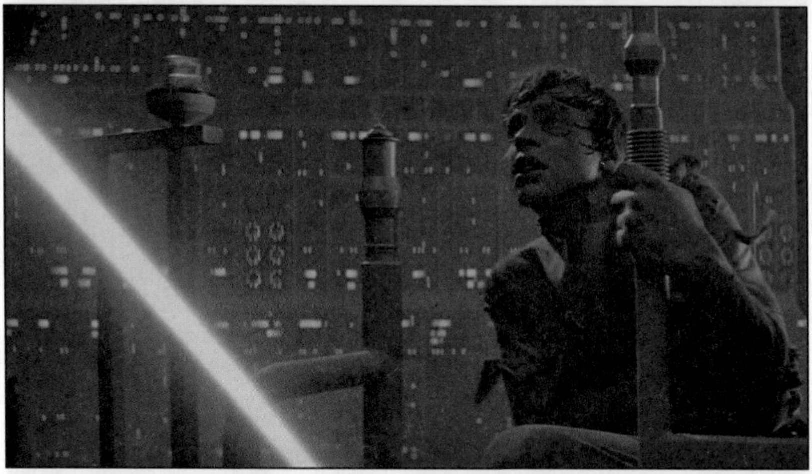

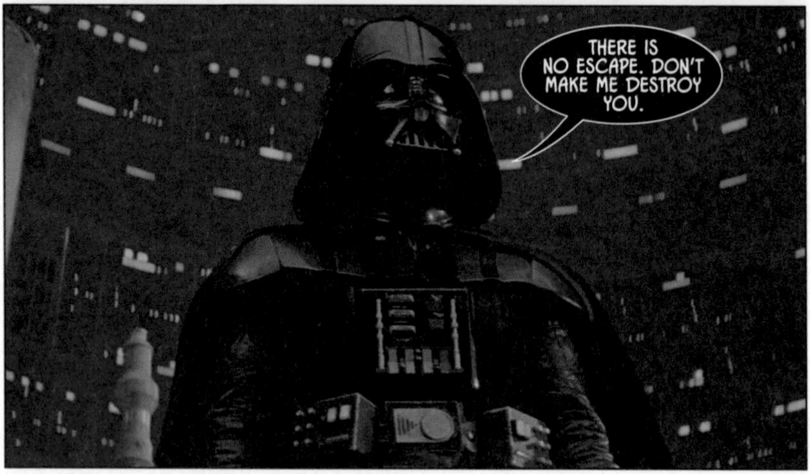
THERE IS NO ESCAPE. DON'T MAKE ME DESTROY YOU.

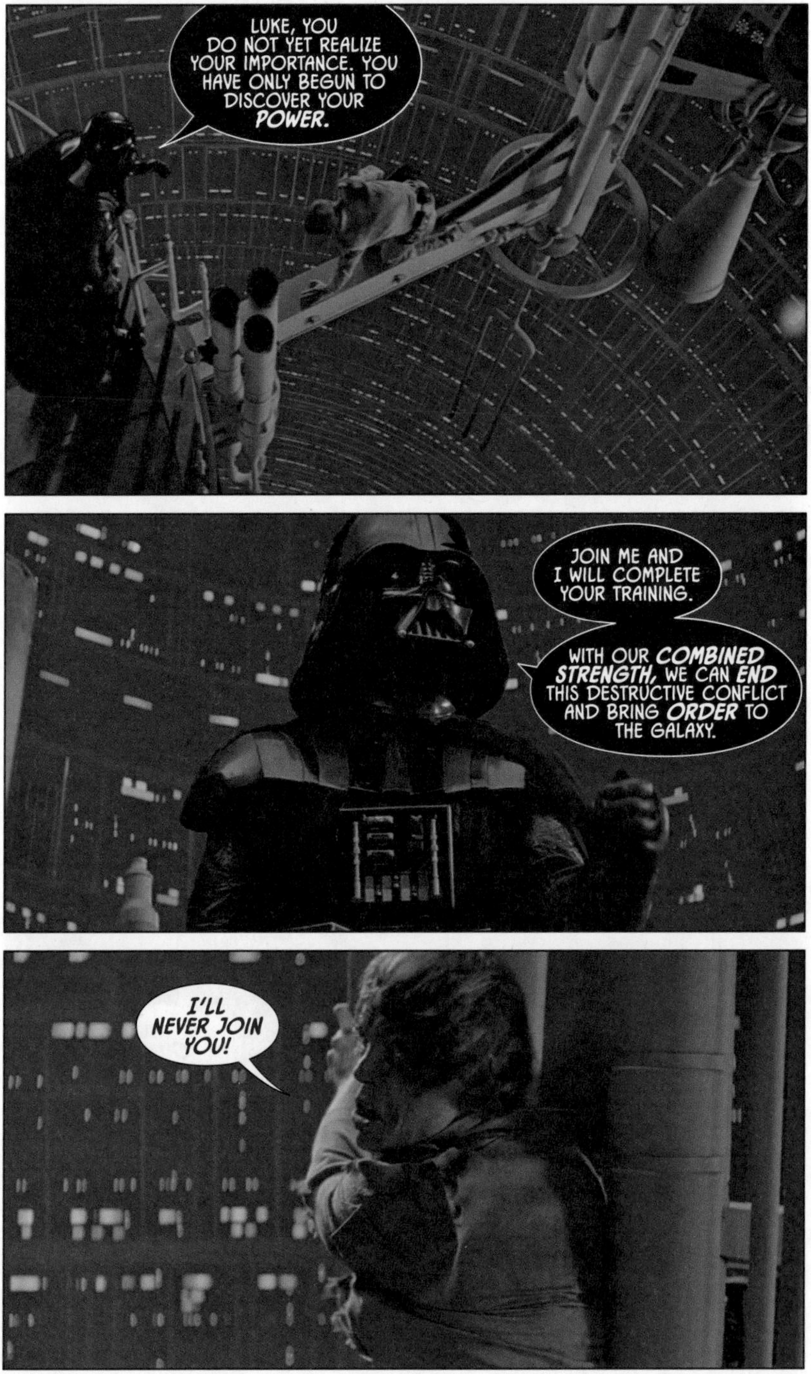
LUKE, YOU DO NOT YET REALIZE YOUR IMPORTANCE. YOU HAVE ONLY BEGUN TO DISCOVER YOUR POWER.
JOIN ME AND I WILL COMPLETE YOUR TRAINING.
WITH OUR COMBINED STRENGTH, WE CAN END THIS DESTRUCTIVE CONFLICT AND BRING ORDER TO THE GALAXY.
I'LL NEVER JOIN YOU!

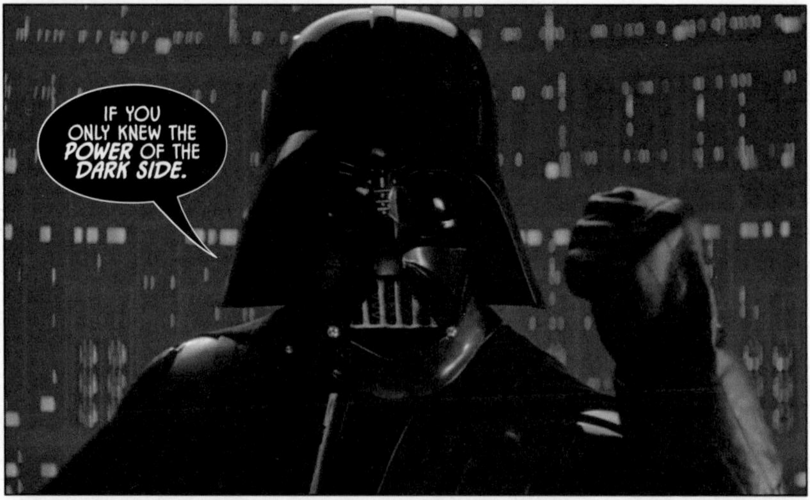
IF YOU ONLY KNEW THE POWER OF THE DARK SIDE.

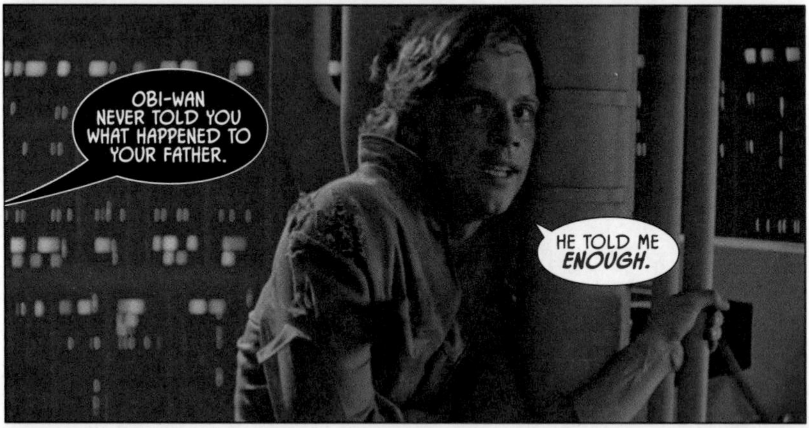
OBI-WAN NEVER TOLD YOU WHAT HAPPENED TO YOUR FATHER.
HE TOLD ME ENOUGH.

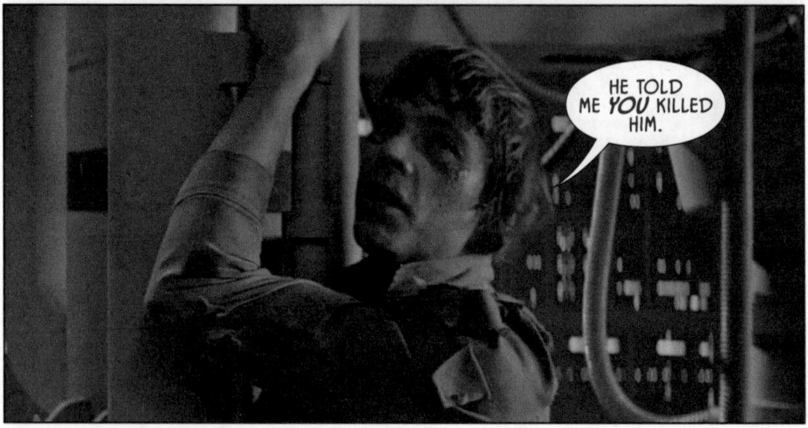
HE TOLD ME YOU KILLED HIM.

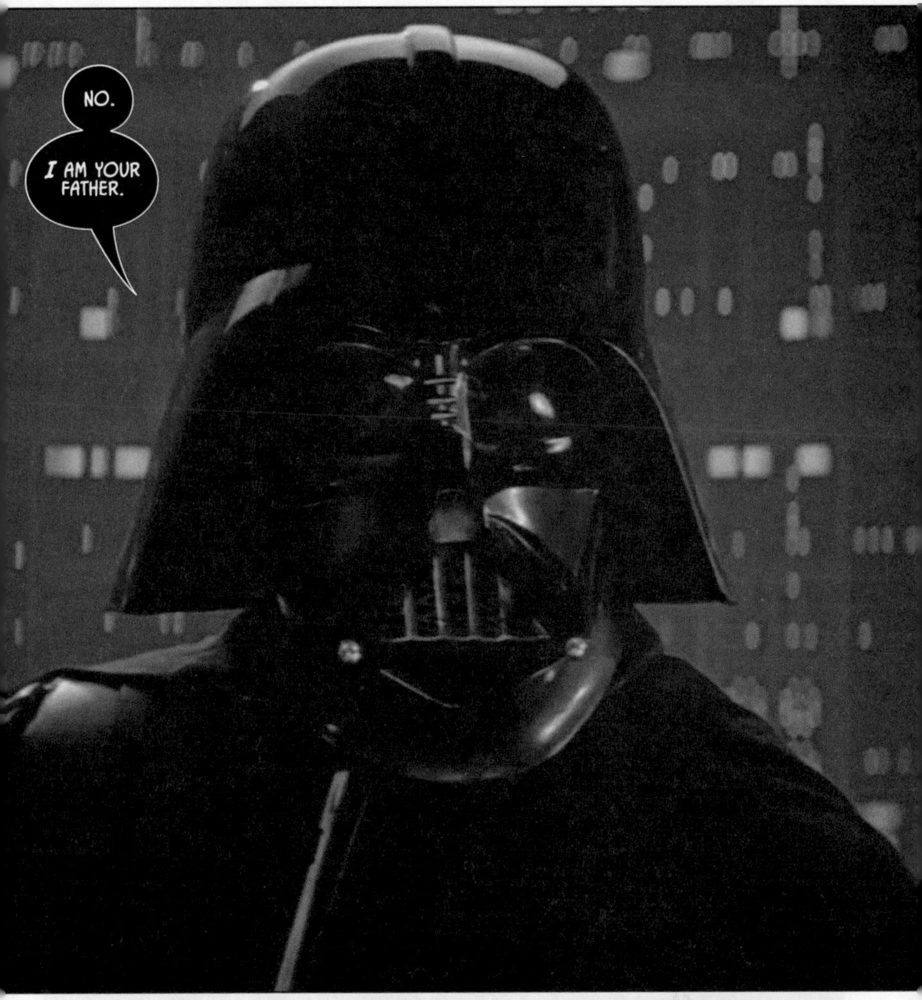
NO.
I AM YOUR FATHER.

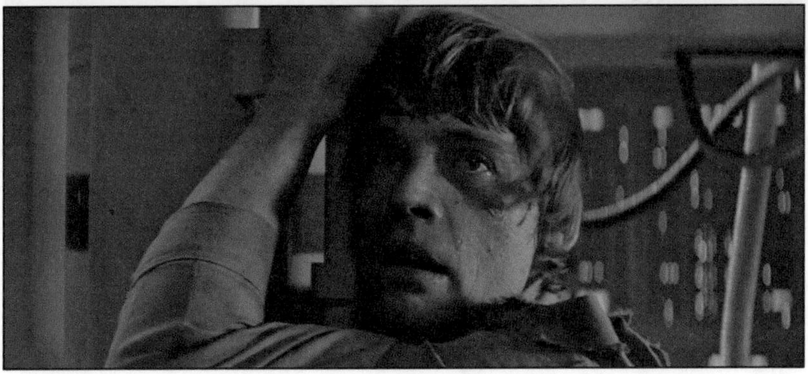

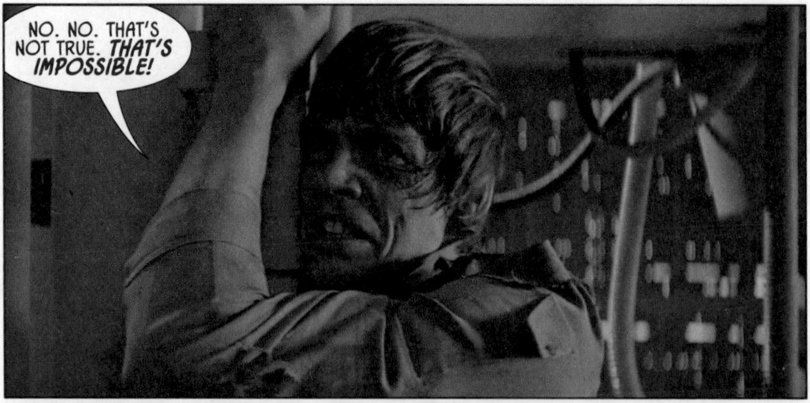
NO. NO. THAT'S NOT TRUE. THAT'S IMPOSSIBLE!

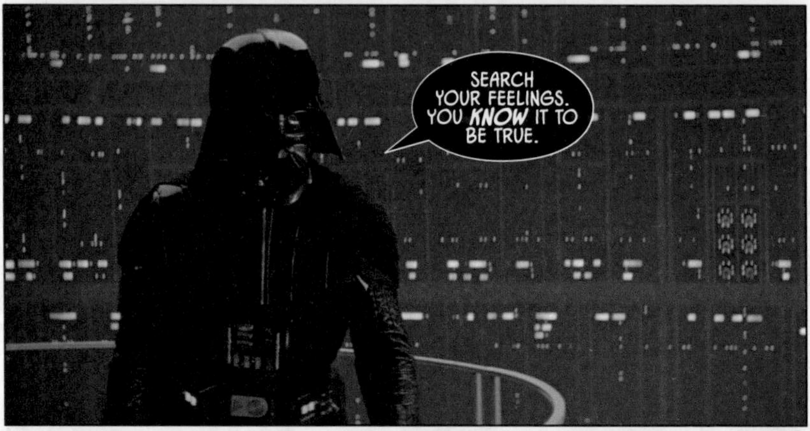
SEARCH YOUR FEELINGS. YOU KNOW IT TO BE TRUE.

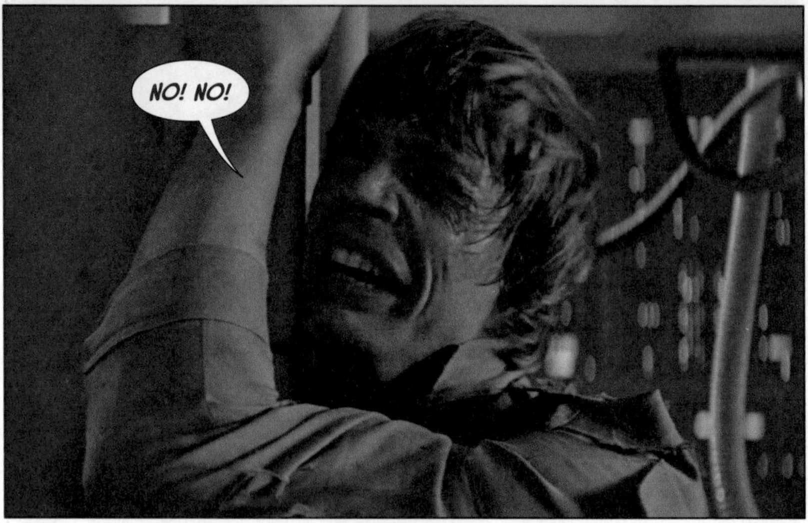
NO! NO!

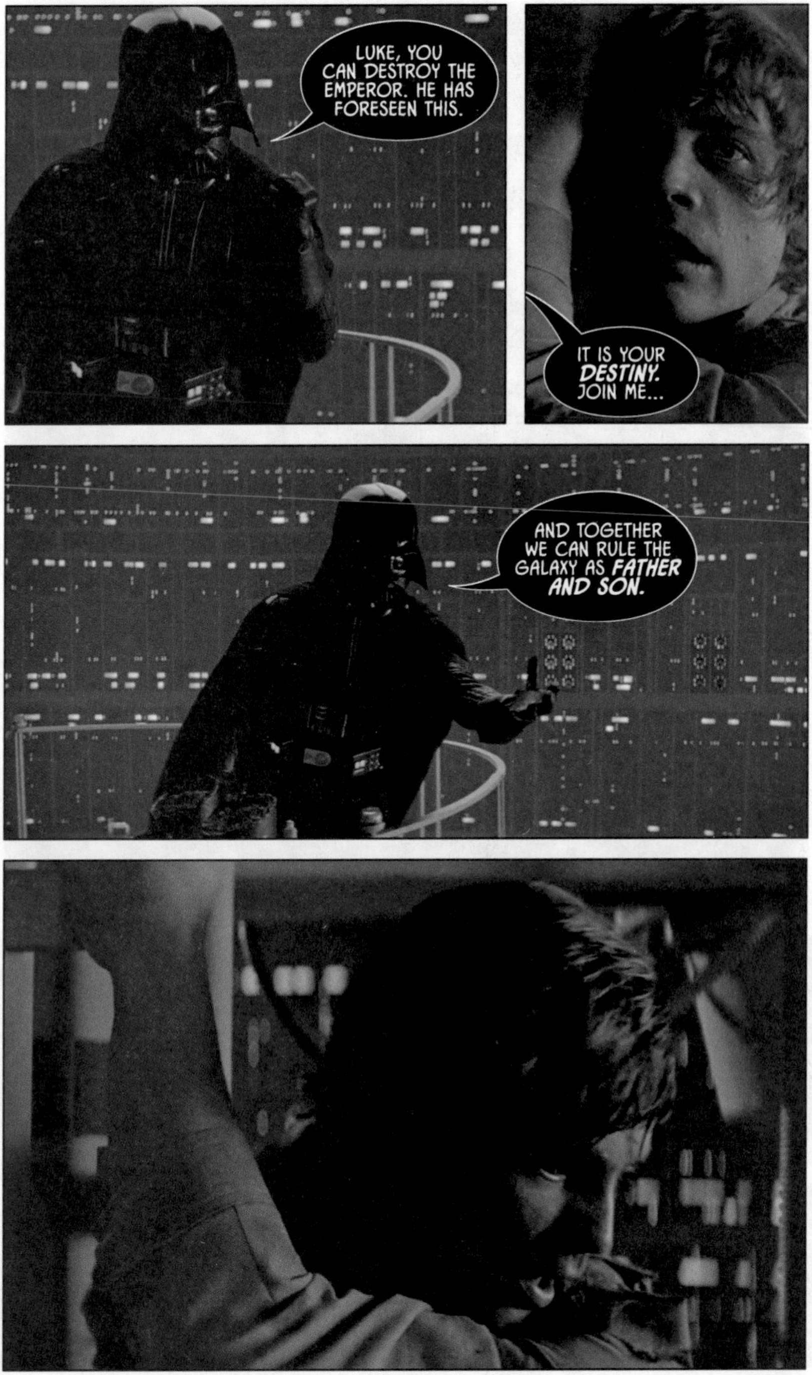

LUKE, YOU CAN DESTROY THE EMPEROR. HE HAS FORESEEN THIS.
IT IS YOUR ***DESTINY.*** JOIN ME...
AND TOGETHER WE CAN RULE THE GALAXY AS ***FATHER AND SON.***

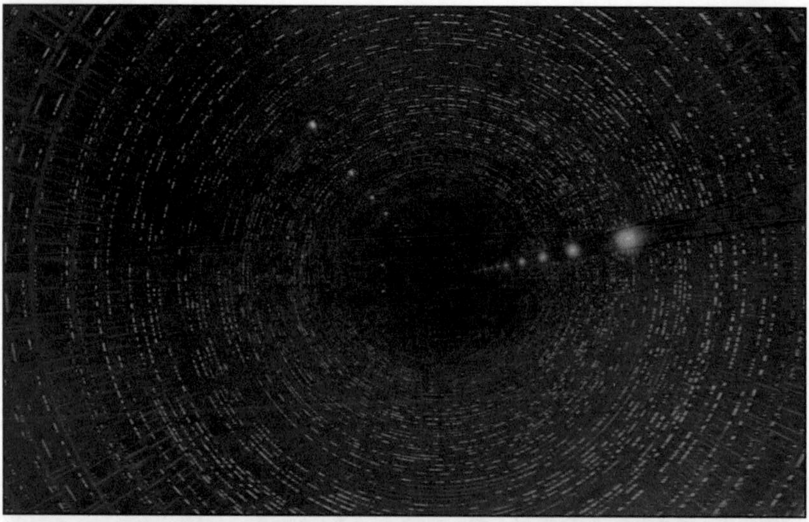

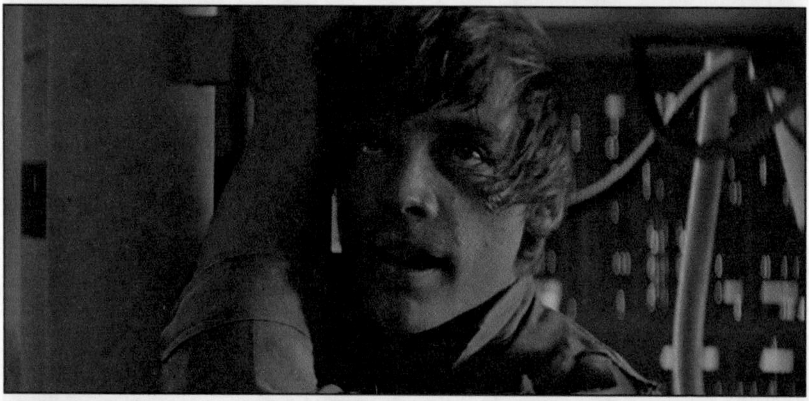

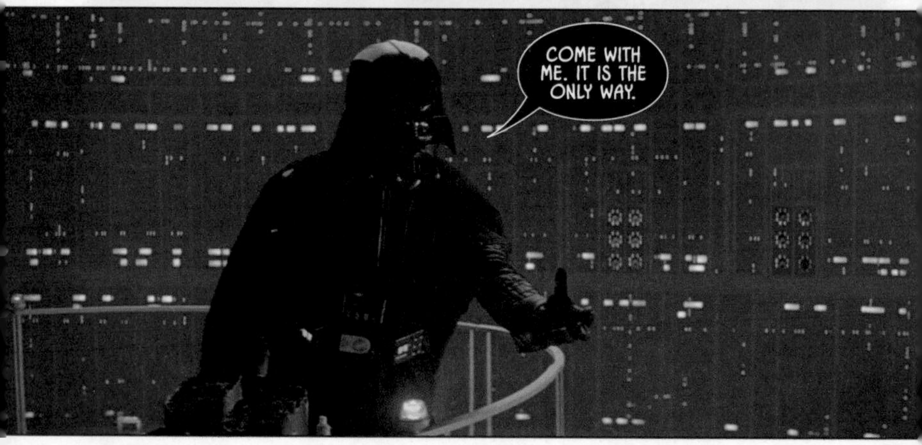
COME WITH ME. IT IS THE ONLY WAY.

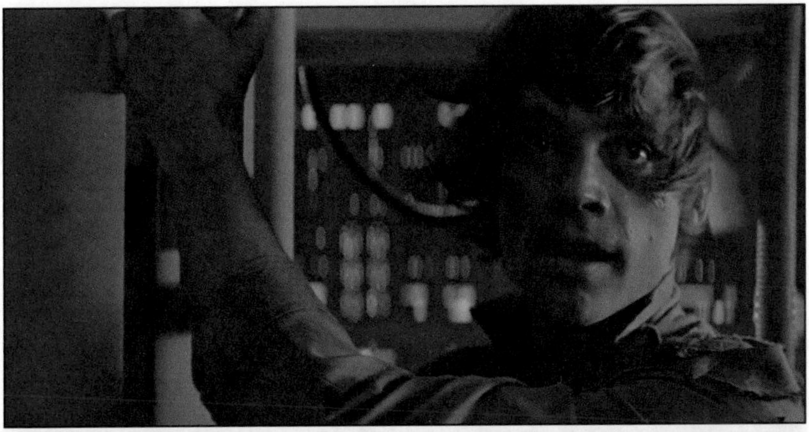

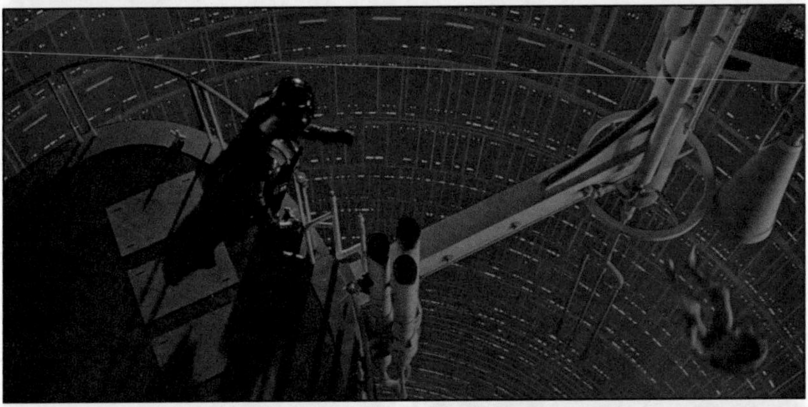

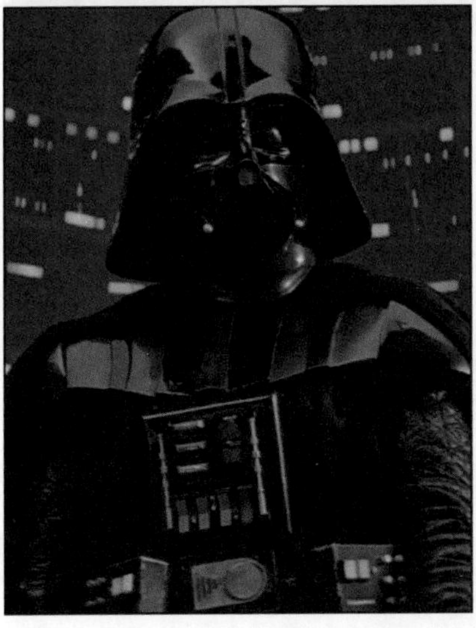

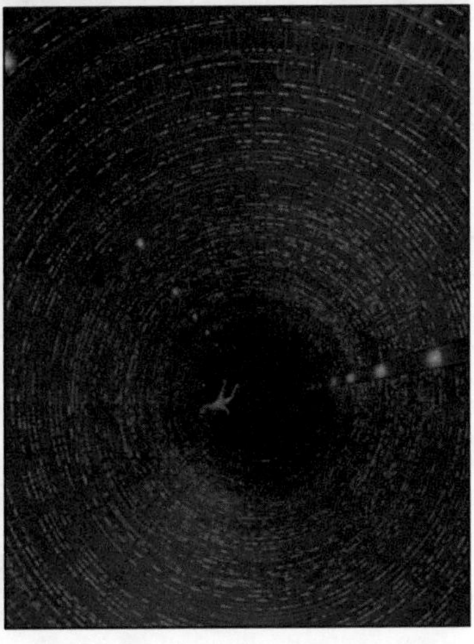

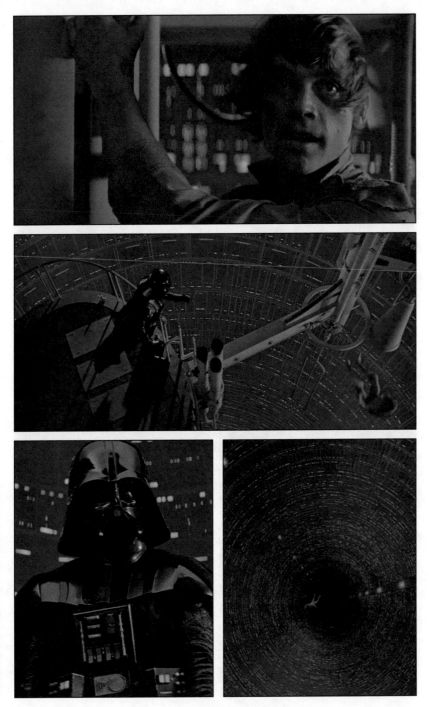

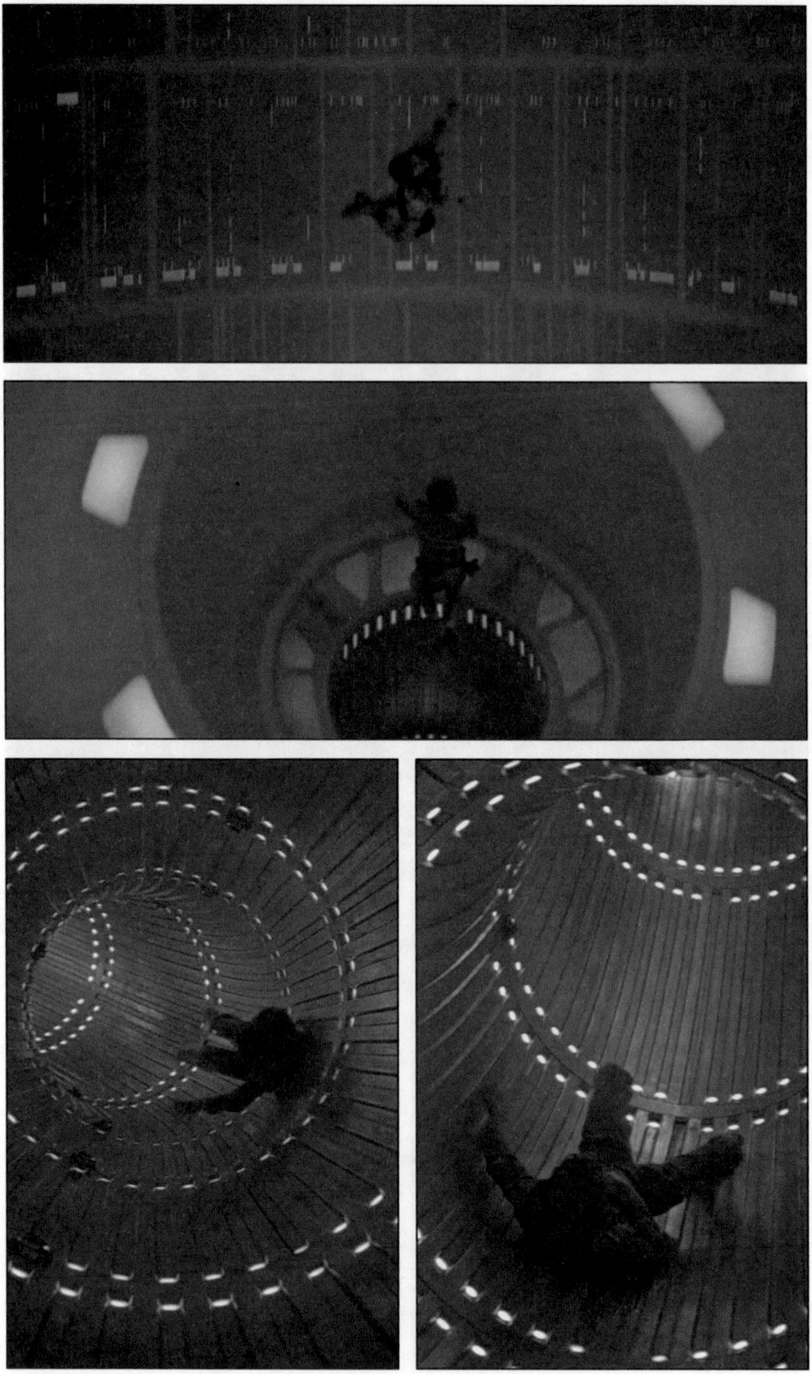

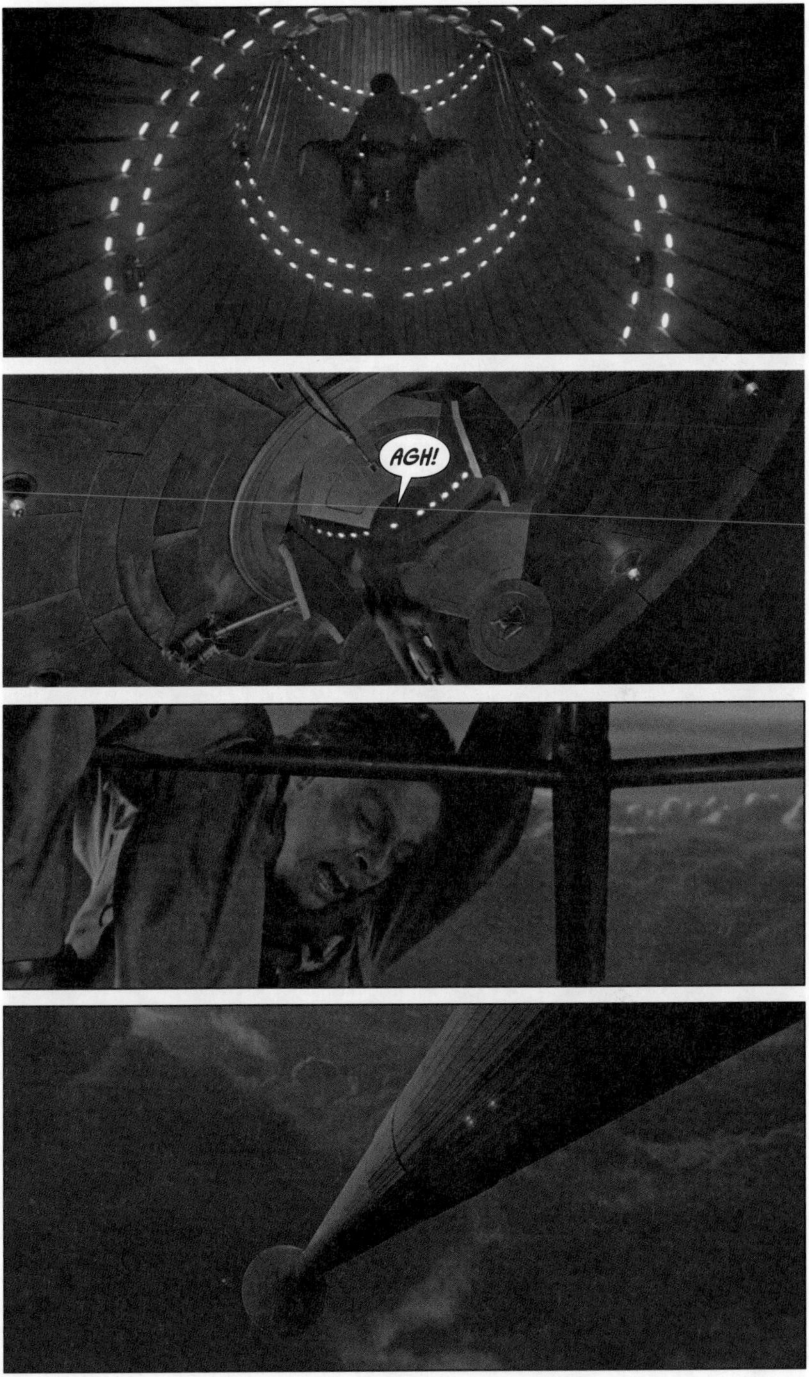
AGH!

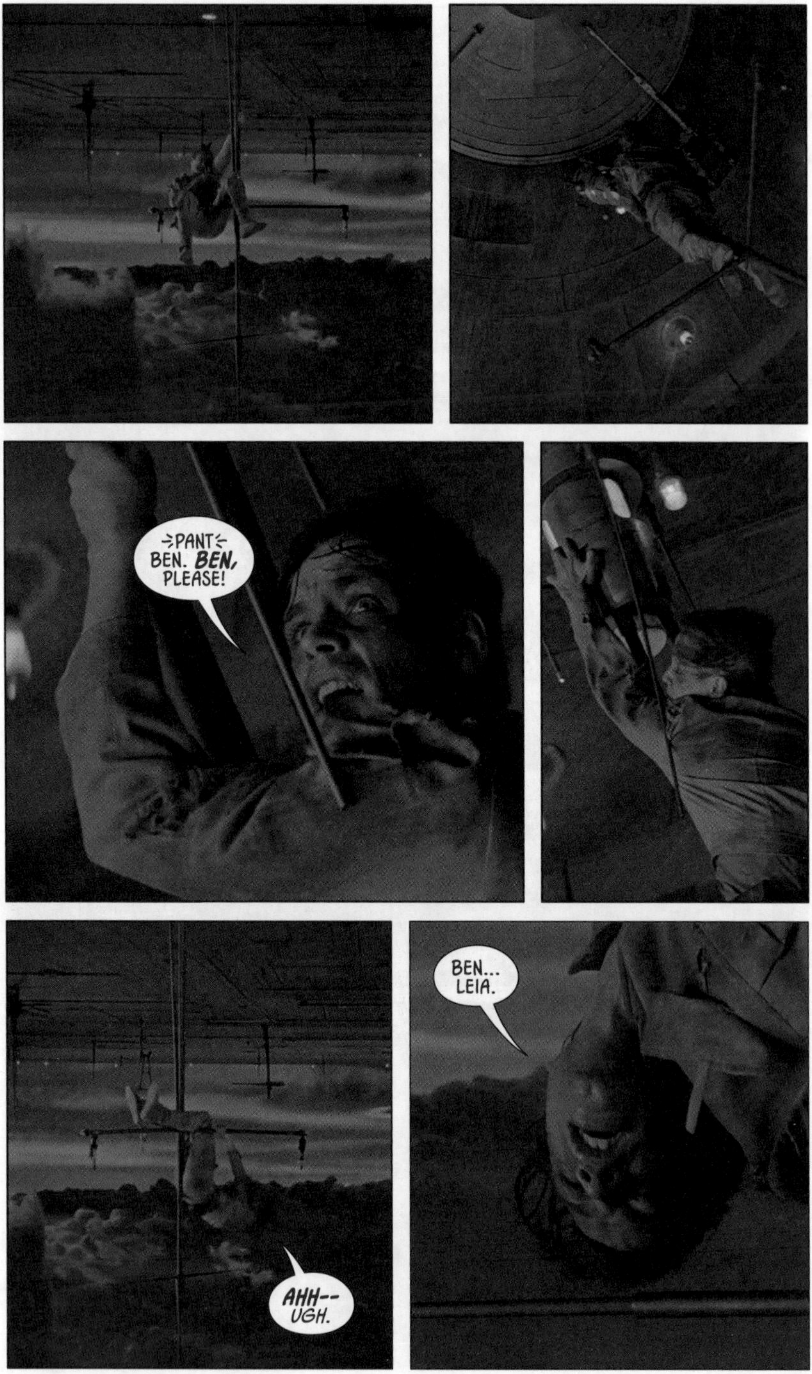

=PANT=
BEN. BEN, PLEASE!
BEN... LEIA.
AHH-- UGH.

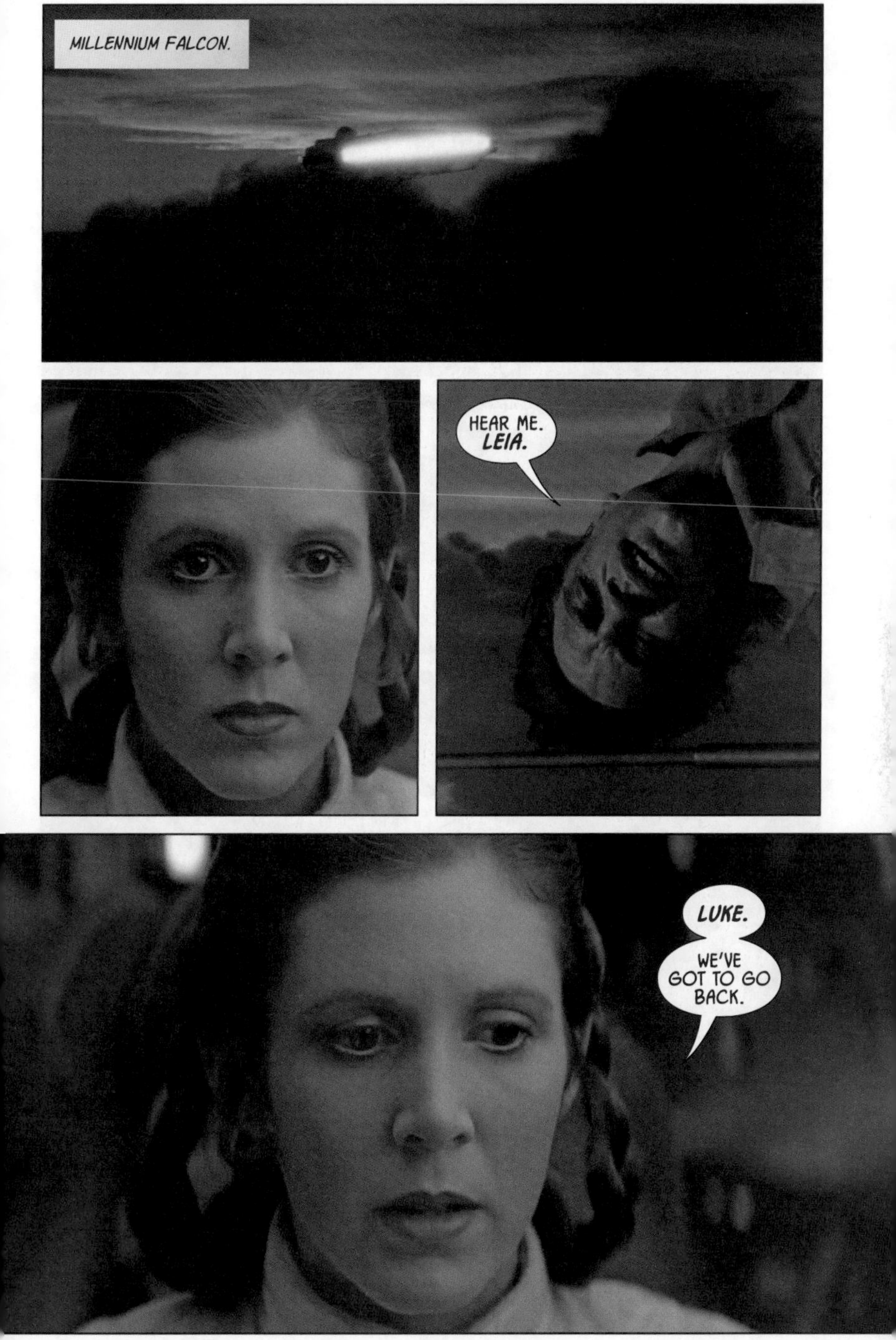
MILLENNIUM FALCON.
HEAR ME. LEIA.
LUKE.
WE'VE GOT TO GO BACK.

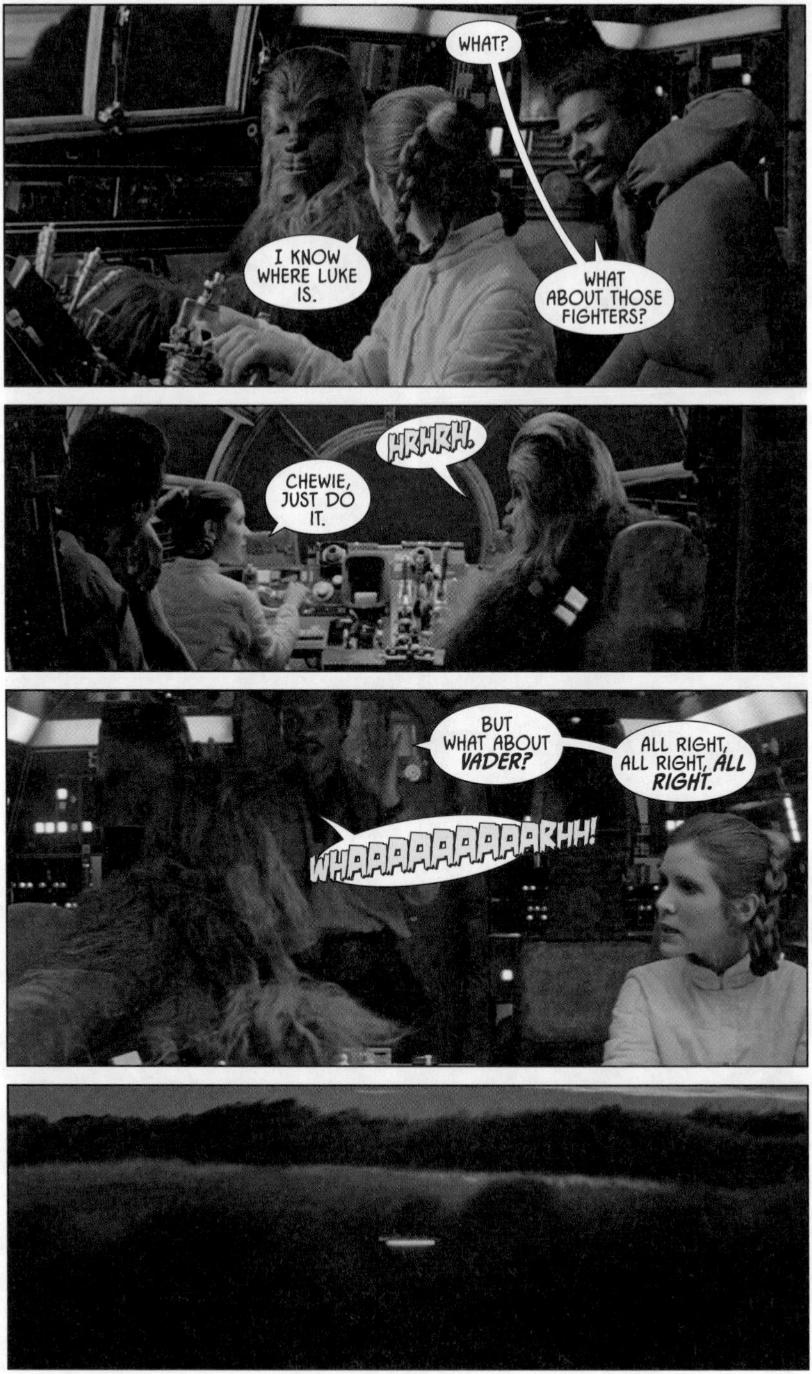
I KNOW WHERE LUKE IS.
WHAT?
WHAT ABOUT THOSE FIGHTERS?
CHEWIE, JUST DO IT.
HRHRH.
BUT WHAT ABOUT *VADER?*
ALL RIGHT, ALL RIGHT, ***ALL RIGHT.***
WHAAAAAAAAARHH!

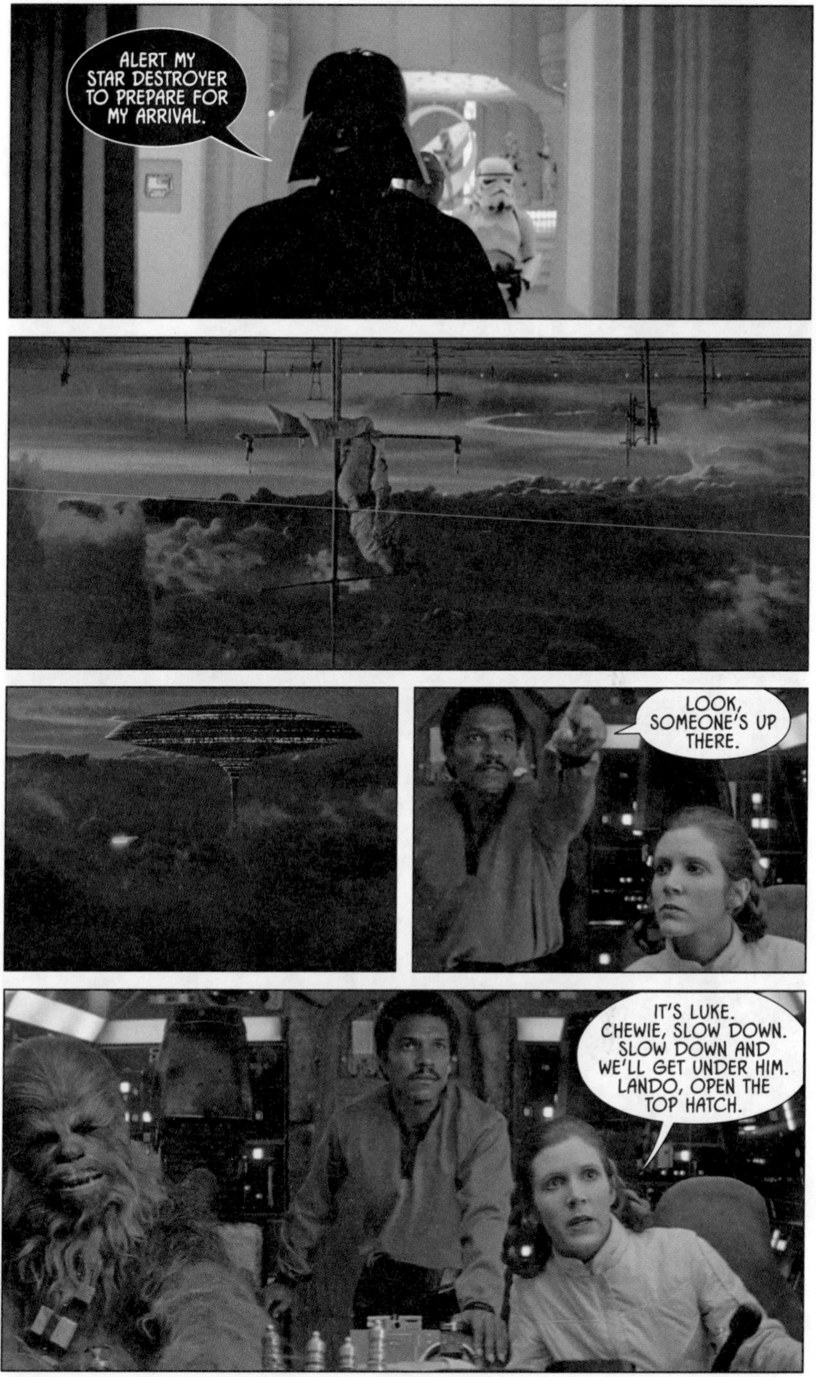
ALERT MY STAR DESTROYER TO PREPARE FOR MY ARRIVAL.
LOOK, SOMEONE'S UP THERE.
IT'S LUKE. CHEWIE, SLOW DOWN. SLOW DOWN AND WE'LL GET UNDER HIM. LANDO, OPEN THE TOP HATCH.

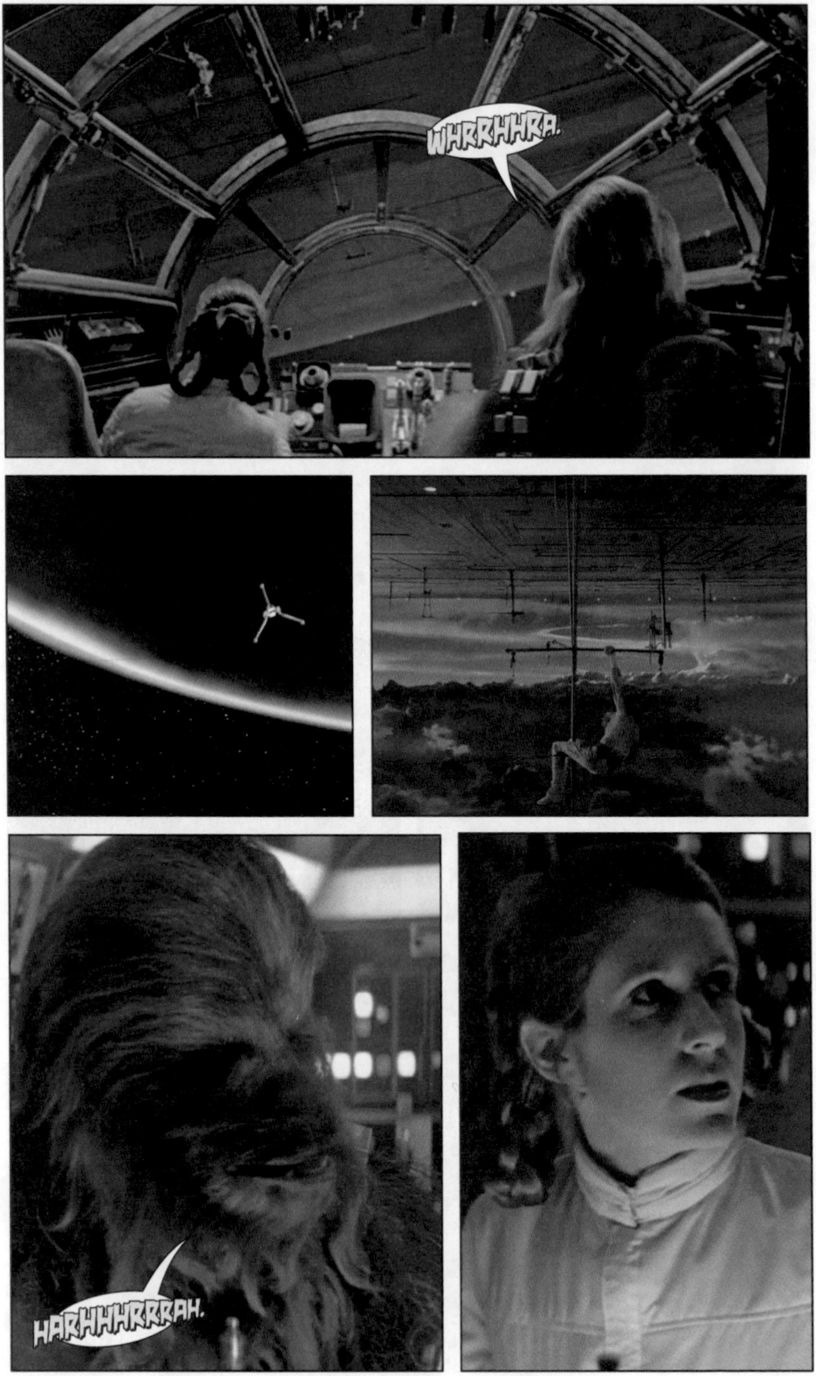
WHRRHHRA.
HARHHHRRRAH.

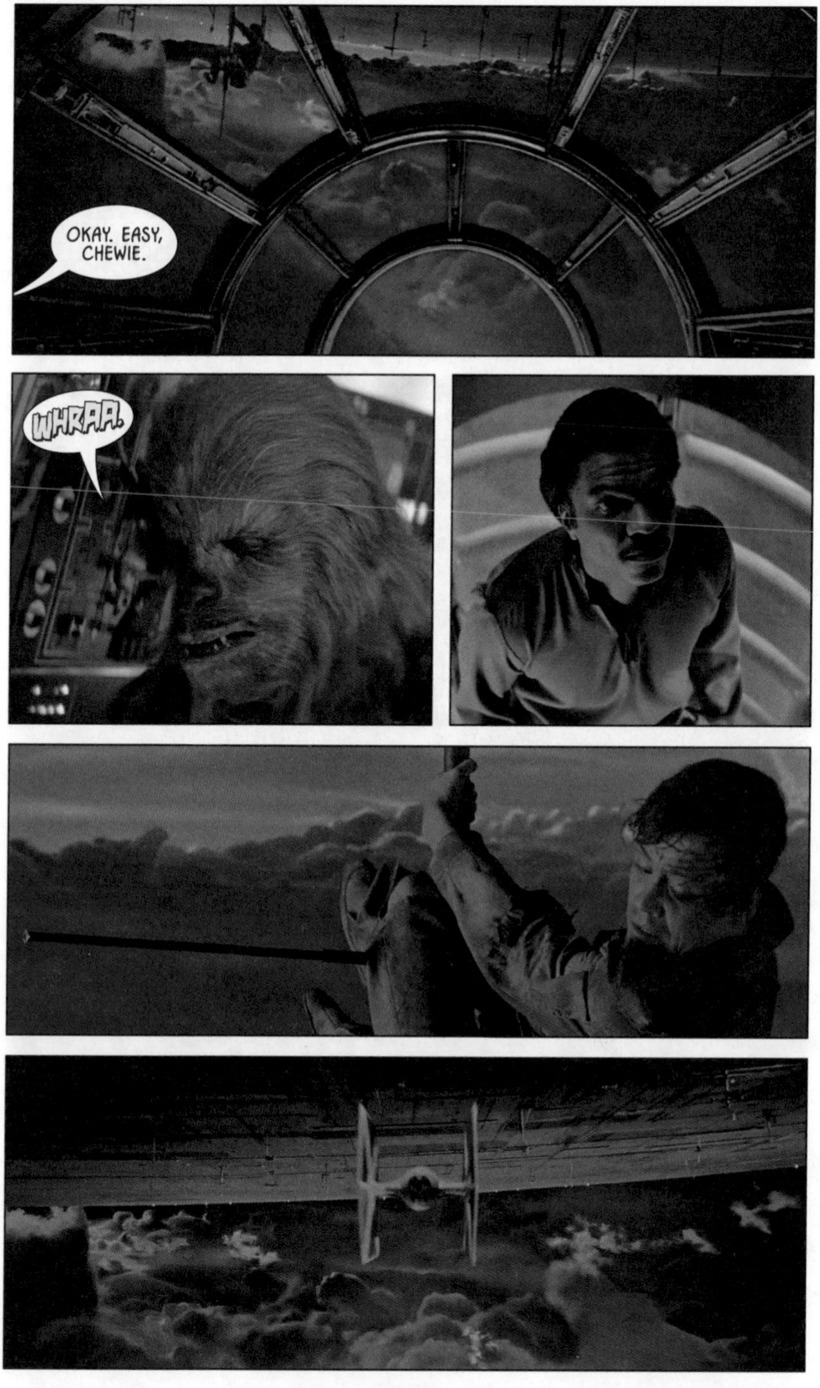
OKAY. EASY, CHEWIE.
WHRAA.

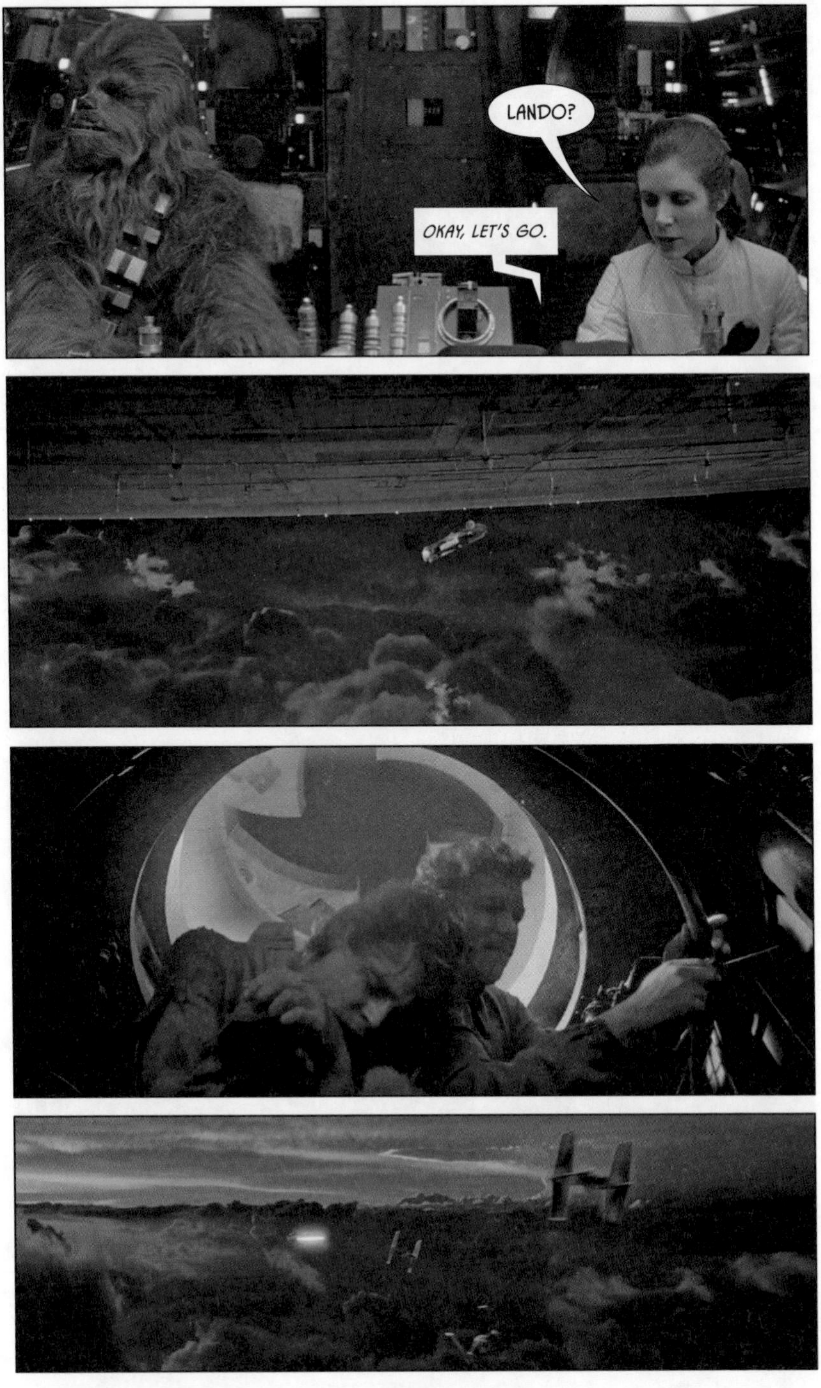
LANDO?
OKAY, LET'S GO.

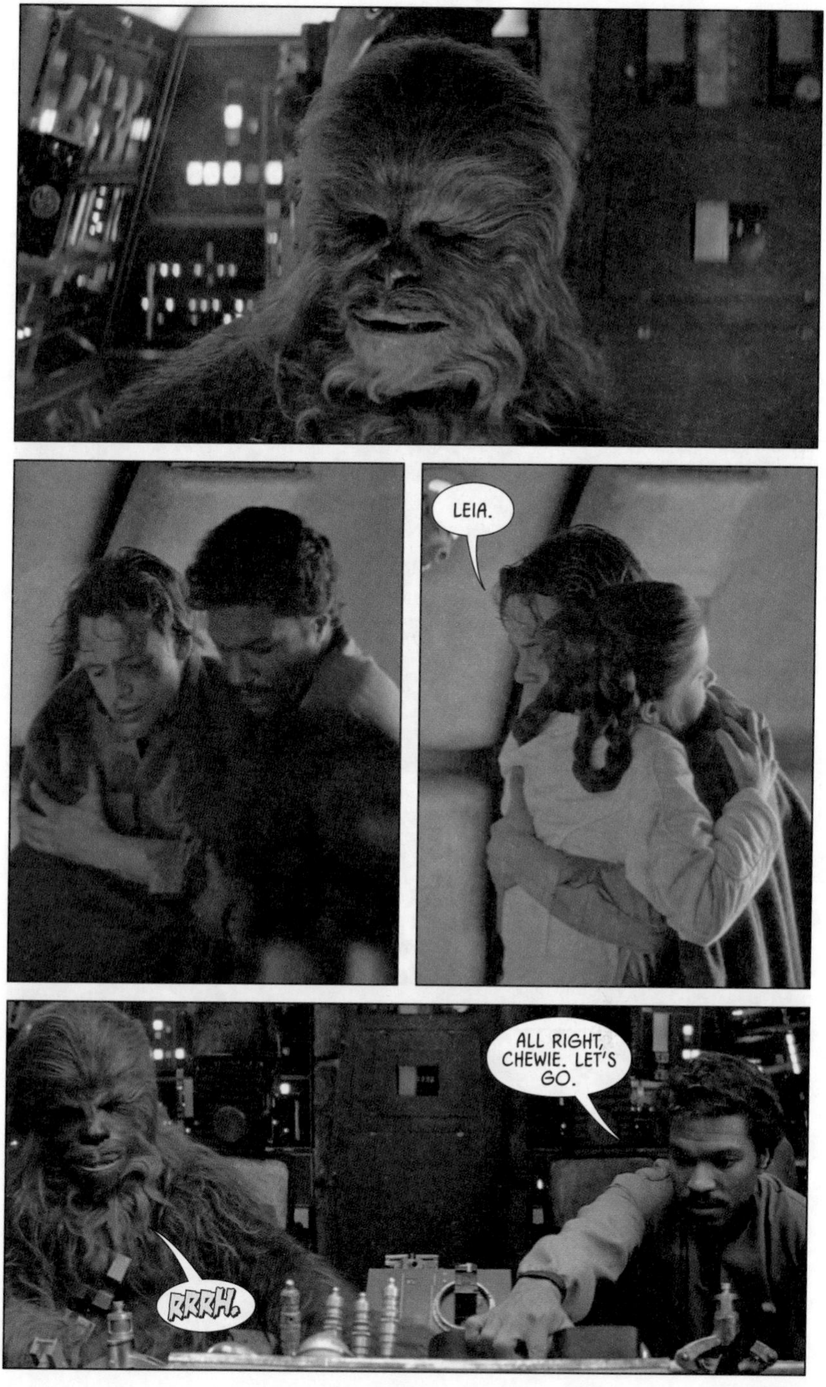
LEIA.
ALL RIGHT, CHEWIE. LET'S GO.
RRRH.

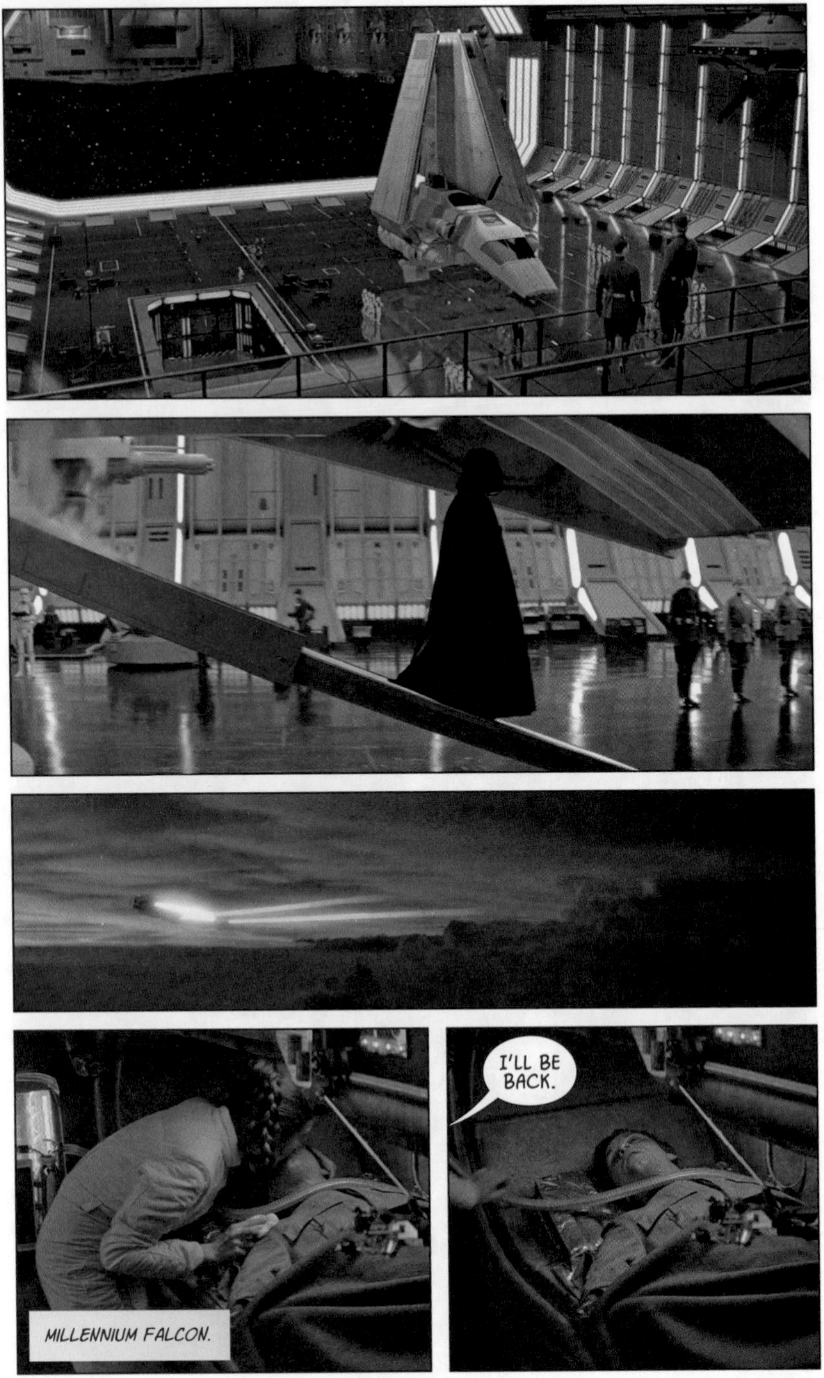
I'LL BE BACK.
MILLENNIUM FALCON.

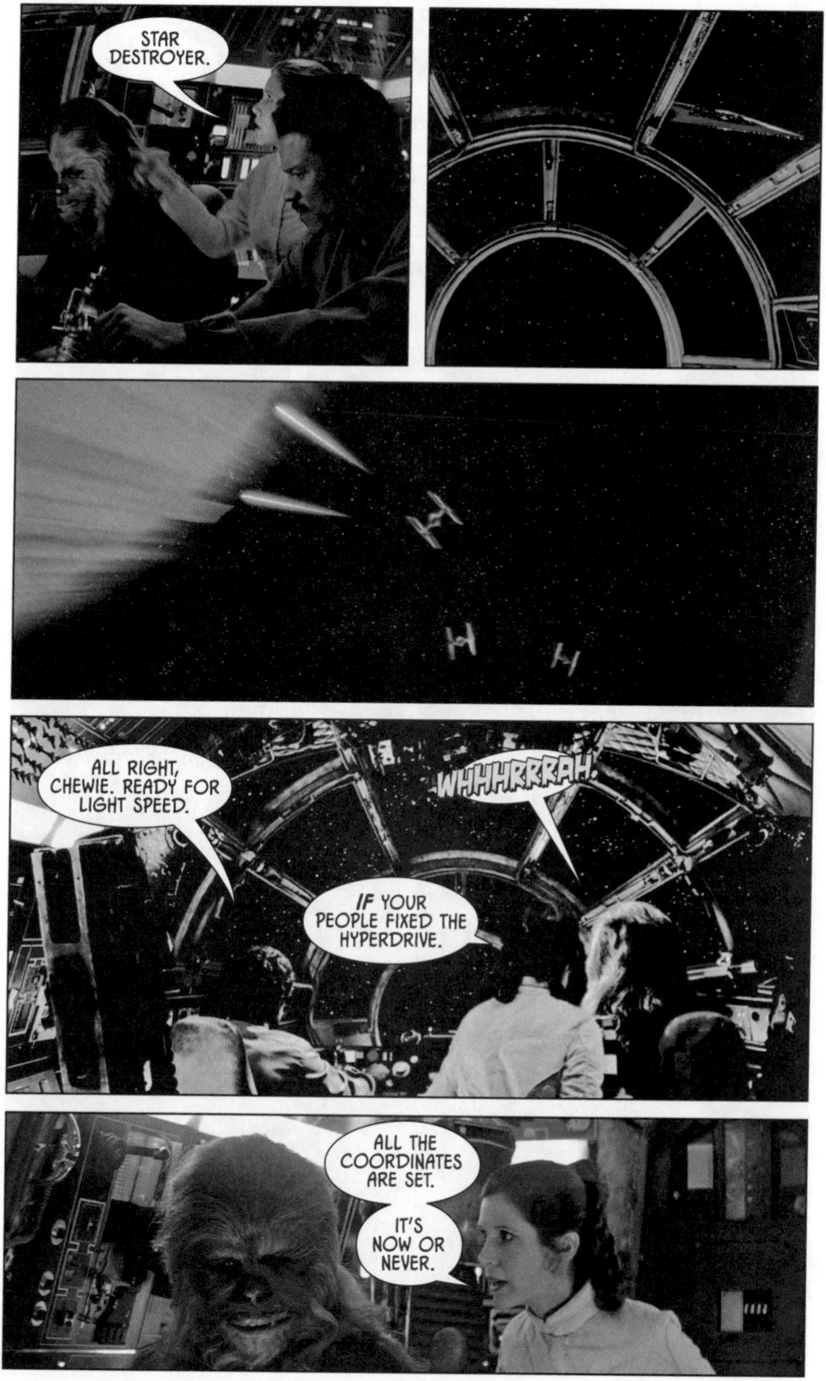
STAR DESTROYER.
ALL RIGHT, CHEWIE. READY FOR LIGHT SPEED.
WHHHRRRAH!
IF YOUR PEOPLE FIXED THE HYPERDRIVE.
ALL THE COORDINATES ARE SET.
IT'S NOW OR NEVER.

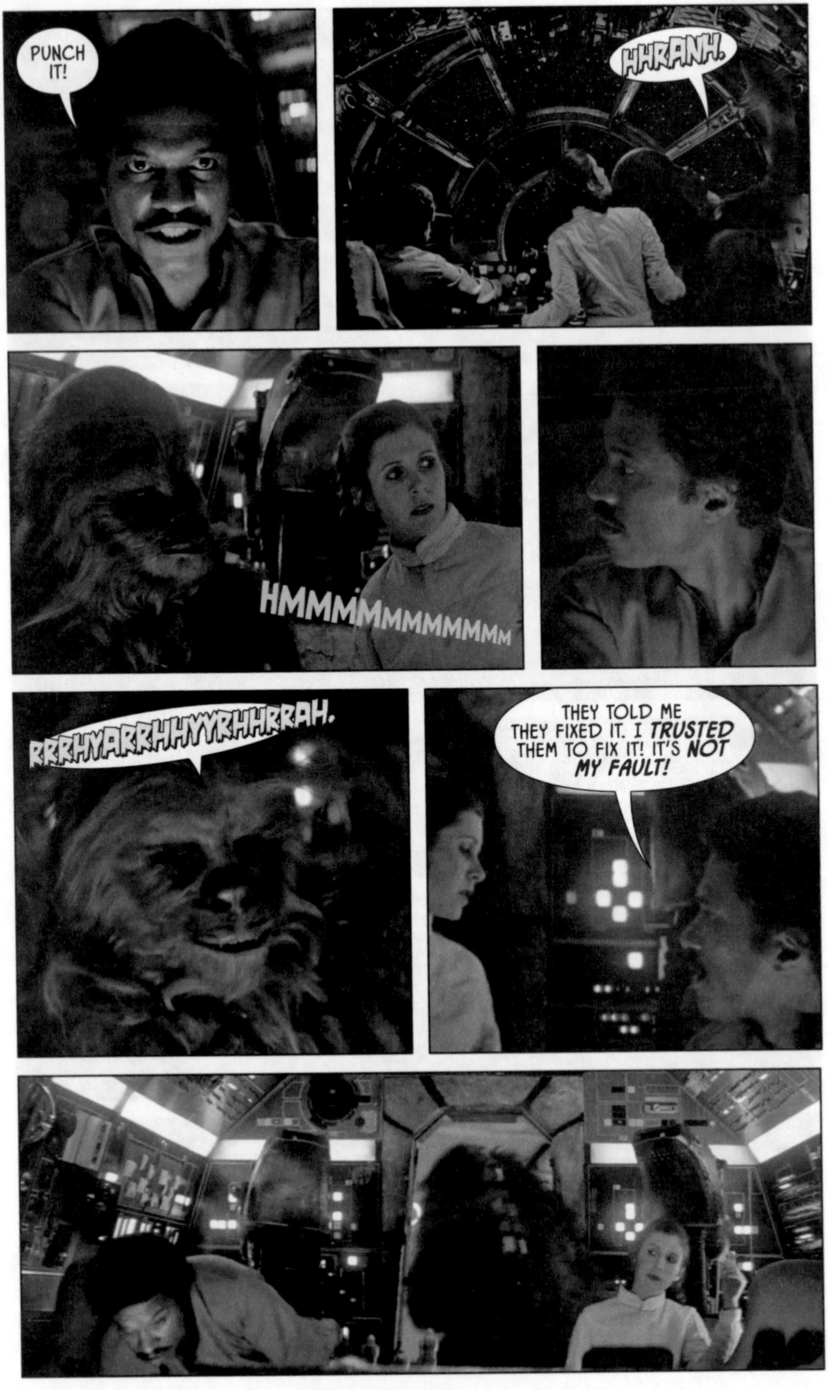
PUNCH IT!
HHRANH.
HMMMMMMMMMMM
RRRHYARRHHYYRHHRRAH.
THEY TOLD ME THEY FIXED IT. I *TRUSTED* THEM TO FIX IT! IT'S *NOT MY FAULT!*

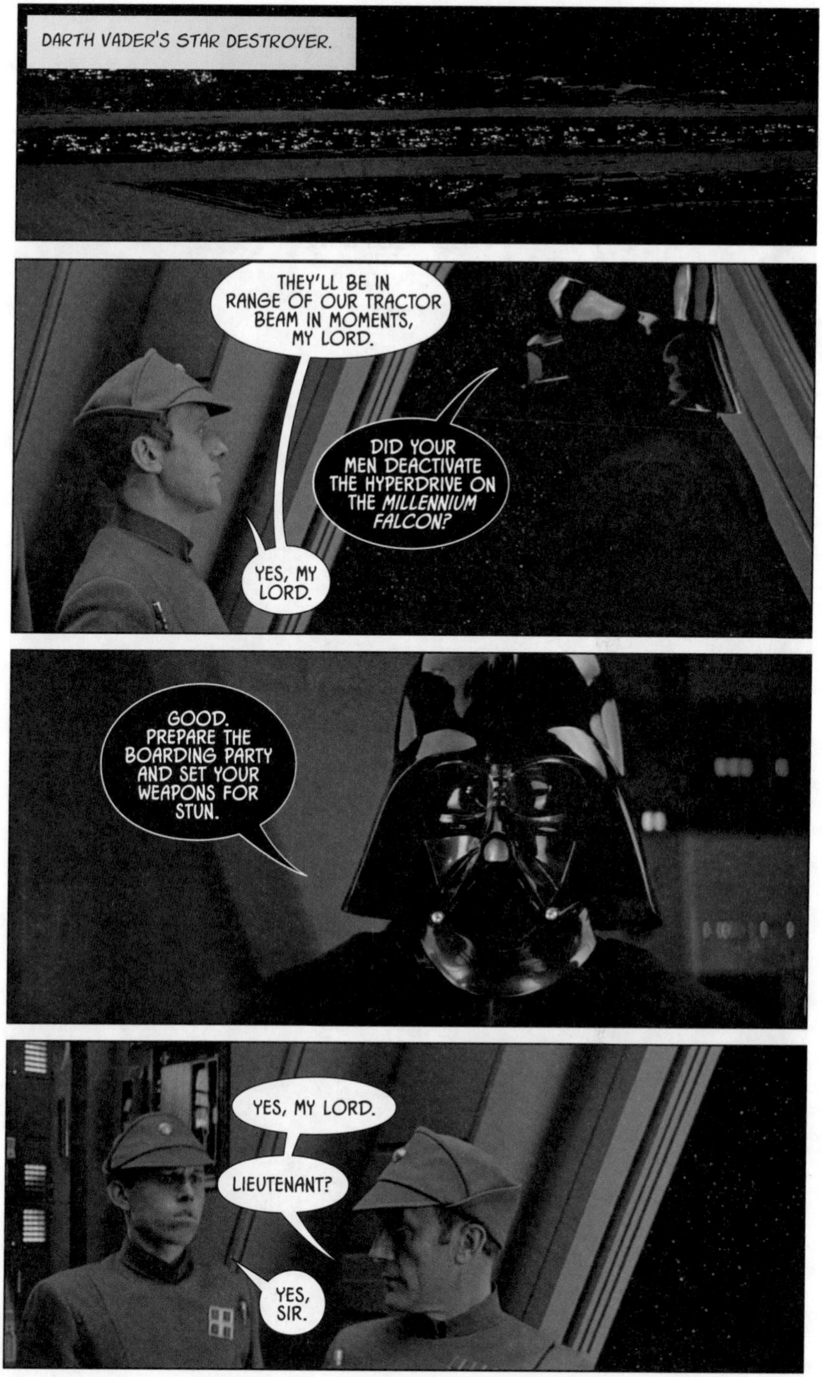
DARTH VADER'S STAR DESTROYER.
THEY'LL BE IN RANGE OF OUR TRACTOR BEAM IN MOMENTS, MY LORD.
DID YOUR MEN DEACTIVATE THE HYPERDRIVE ON THE *MILLENNIUM FALCON?*
YES, MY LORD.
GOOD. PREPARE THE BOARDING PARTY AND SET YOUR WEAPONS FOR STUN.
YES, MY LORD.
LIEUTENANT?
YES, SIR.

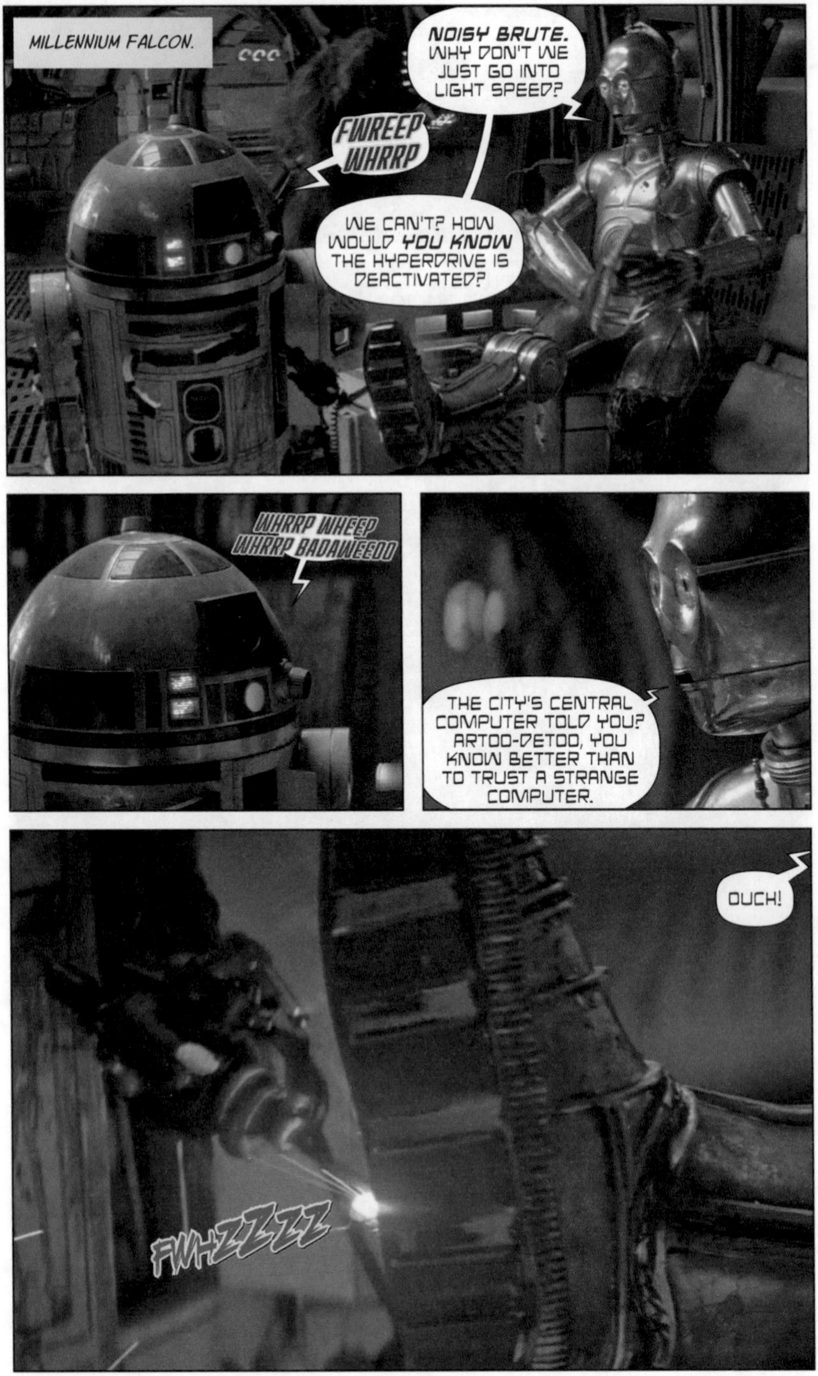
MILLENNIUM FALCON.
NOISY BRUTE. WHY DON'T WE JUST GO INTO LIGHT SPEED?
FWREEP WHRRP
WE CAN'T? HOW WOULD YOU KNOW THE HYPERDRIVE IS DEACTIVATED?
WHRRP WHEEP WHRRP BADAWEEOO
THE CITY'S CENTRAL COMPUTER TOLD YOU? ARTOO-DETOO, YOU KNOW BETTER THAN TO TRUST A STRANGE COMPUTER.
OUCH!
FWHZZZZZ

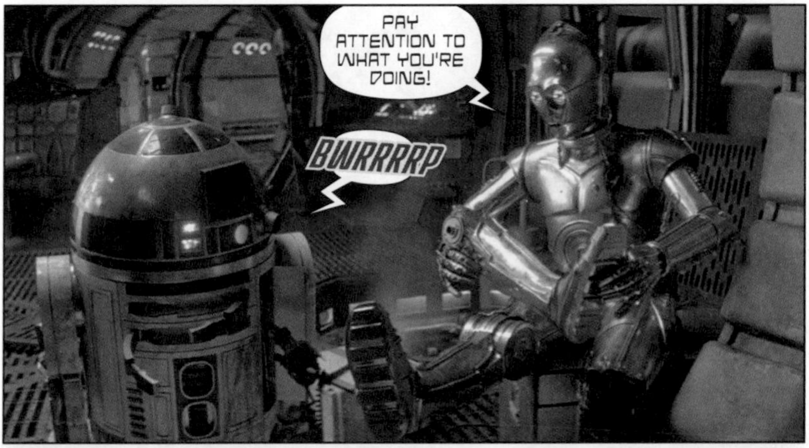
PAY ATTENTION TO WHAT YOU'RE DOING!
BWRRRRP

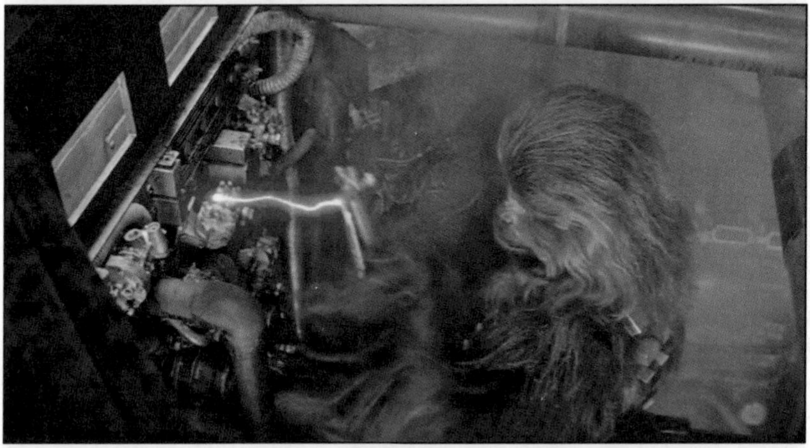

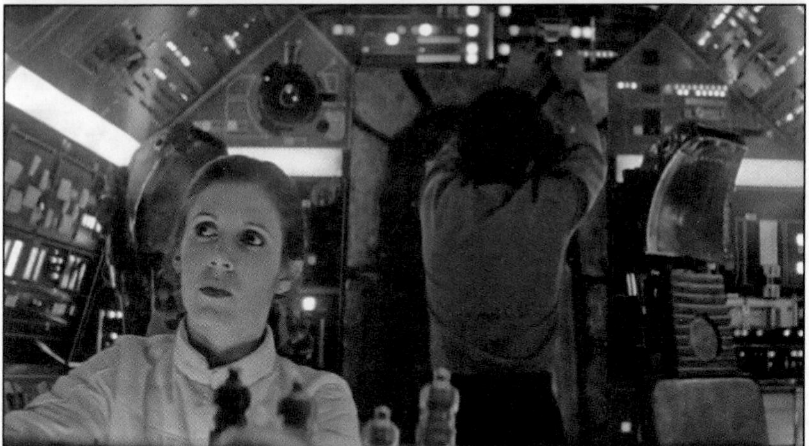

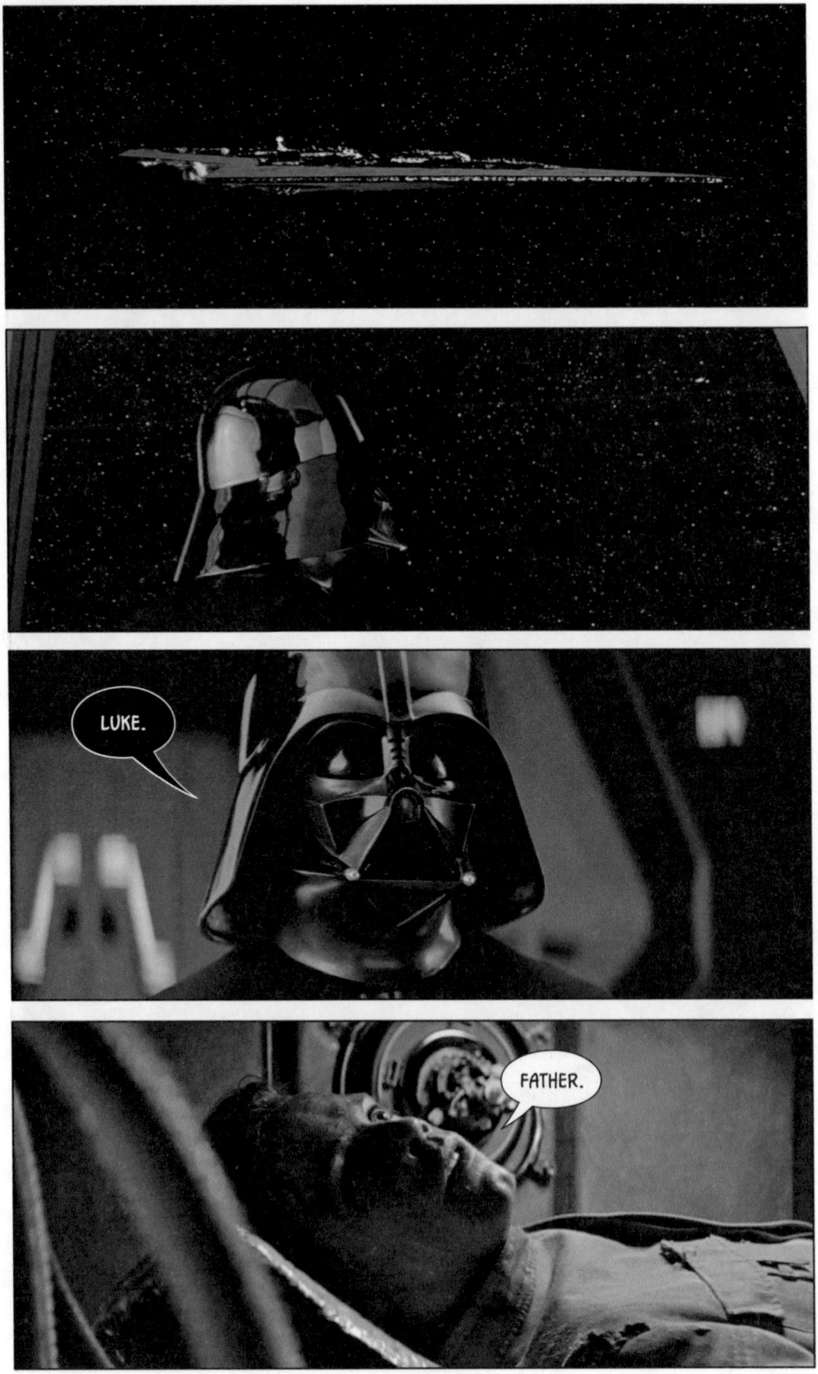
LUKE.
FATHER.

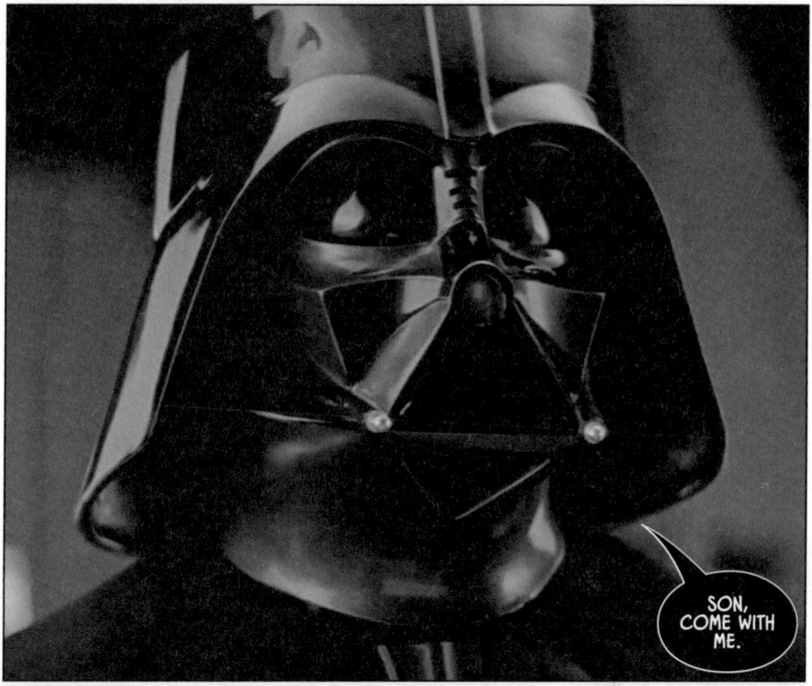
SON, COME WITH ME.

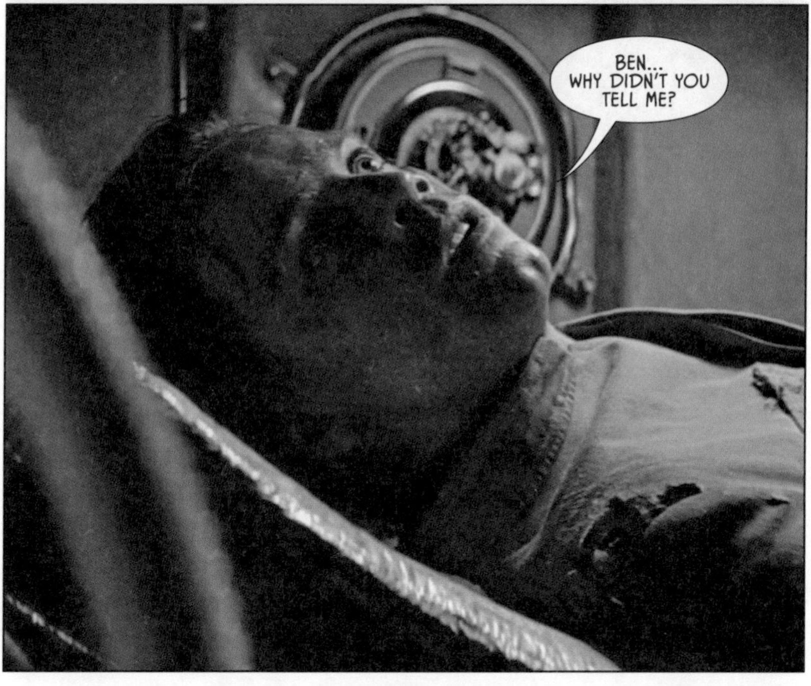
BEN... WHY DIDN'T YOU TELL ME?

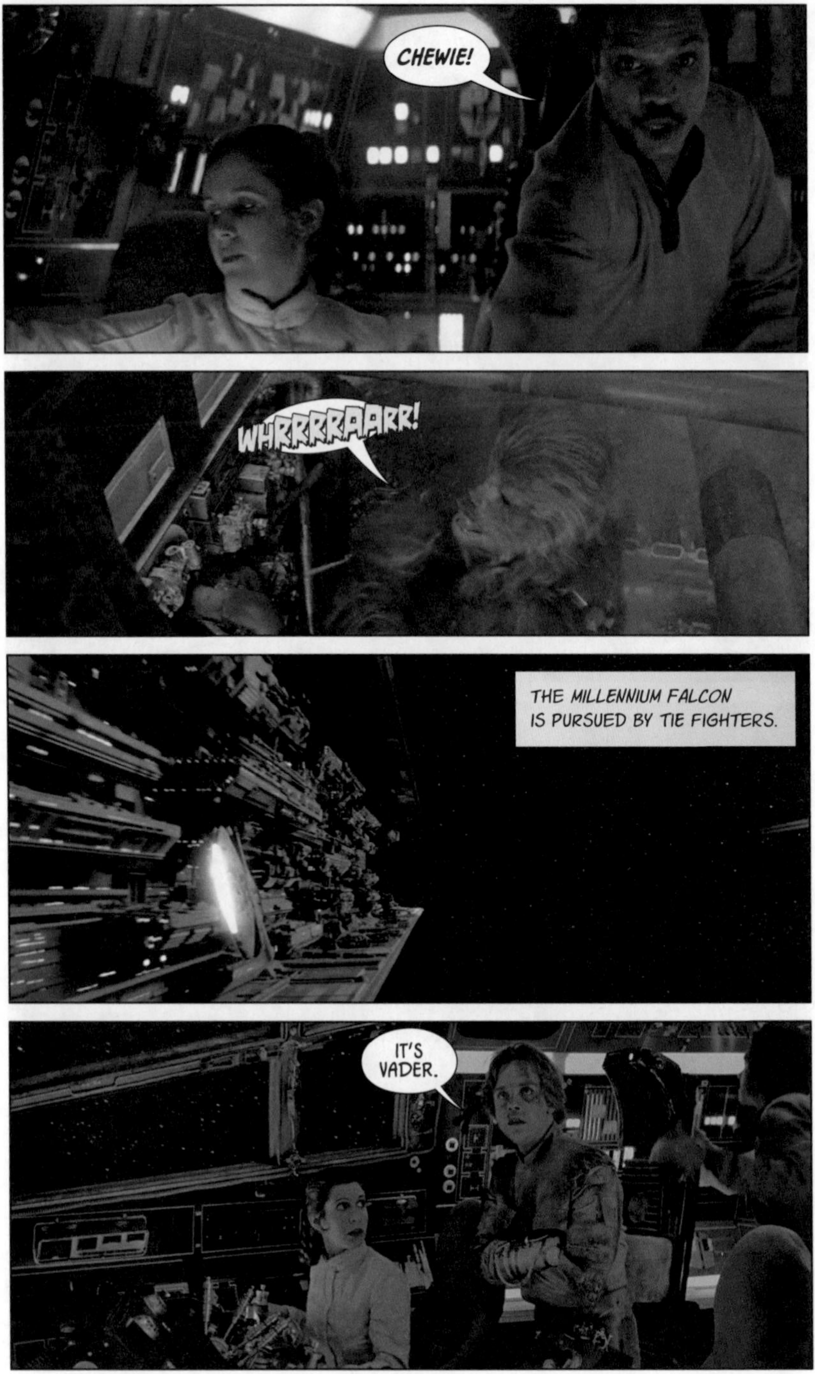
CHEWIE!
WHRRRAARR!
THE MILLENNIUM FALCON IS PURSUED BY TIE FIGHTERS.
IT'S VADER.

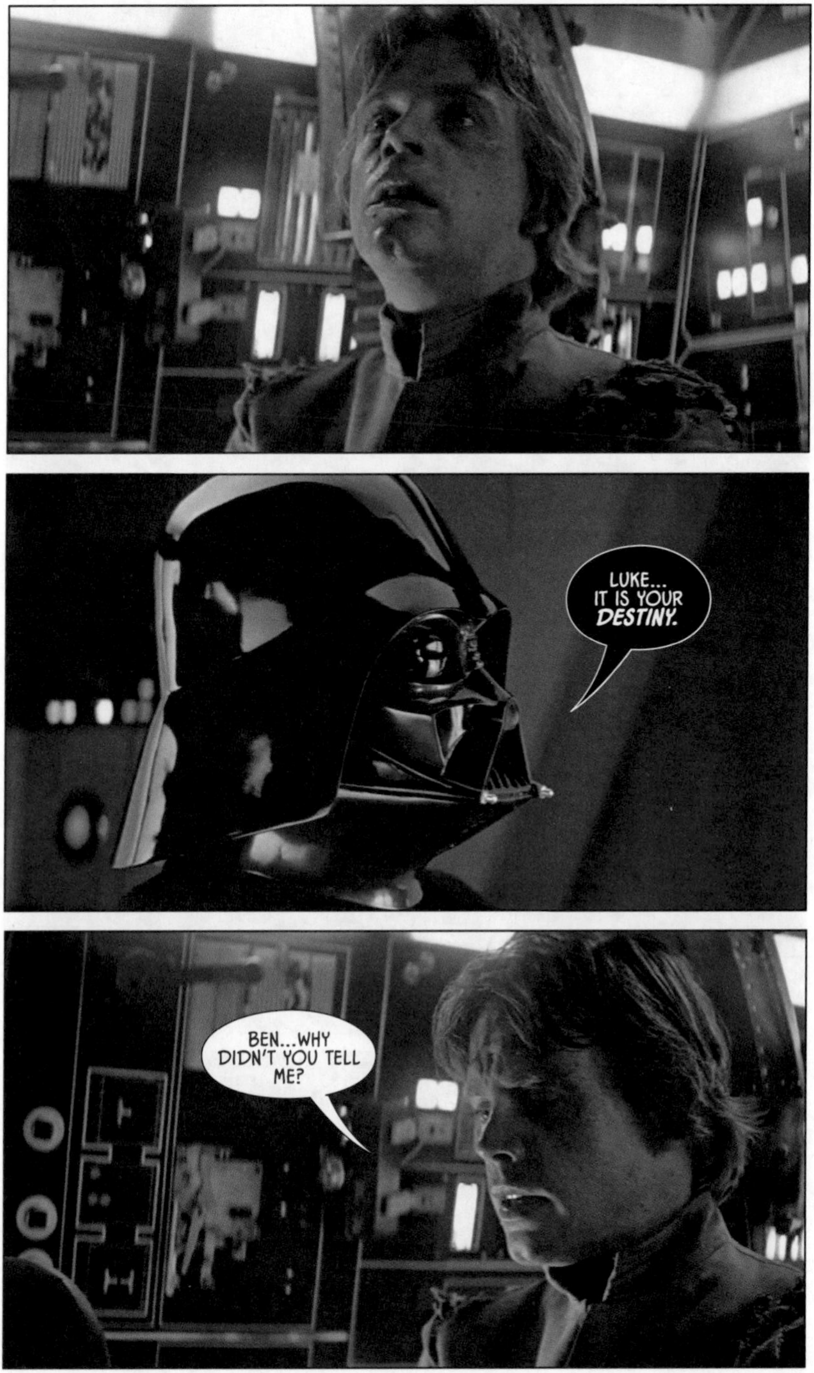
LUKE...
IT IS YOUR
DESTINY.
BEN...WHY
DIDN'T YOU TELL
ME?

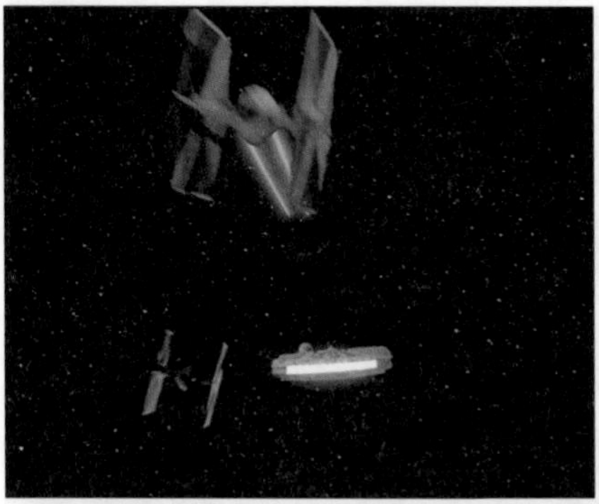

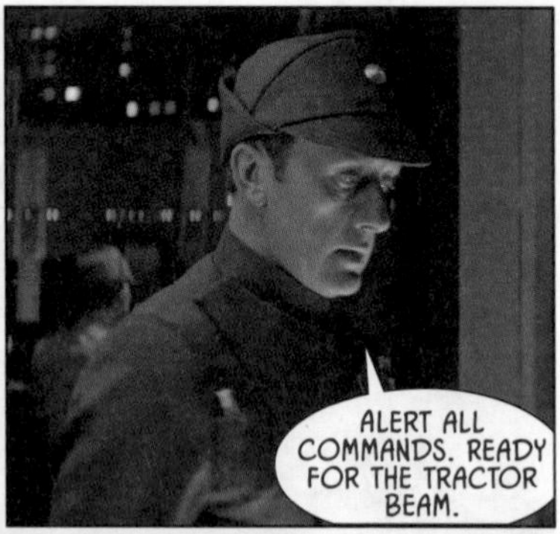
ALERT ALL COMMANDS. READY FOR THE TRACTOR BEAM.

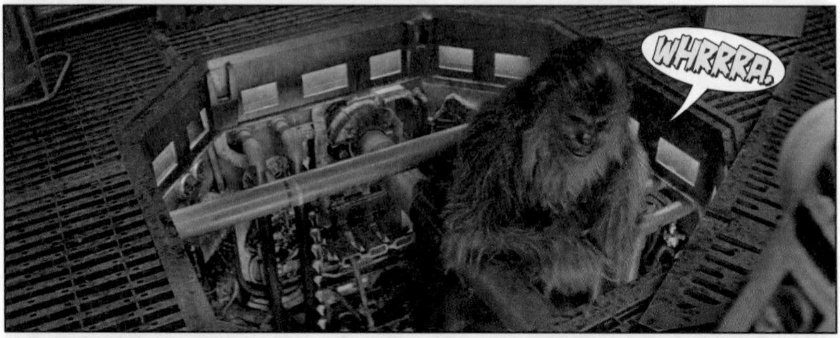
WHRRRA.

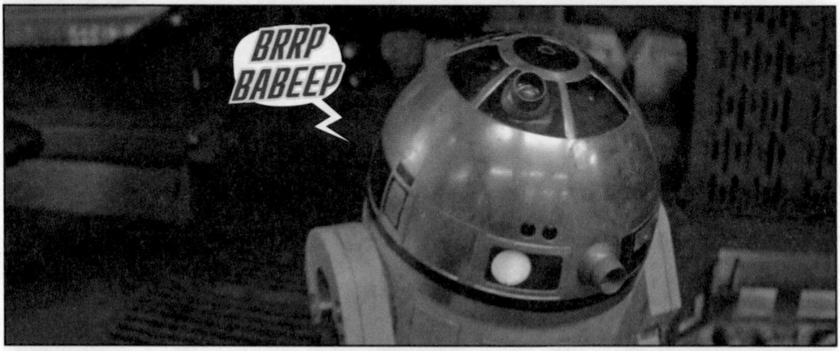
BRRP BABEEP

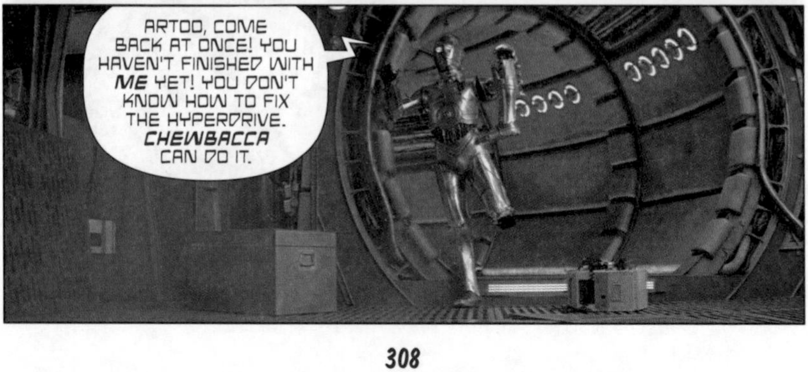
ARTOO, COME BACK AT ONCE! YOU HAVEN'T FINISHED WITH *ME* YET! YOU DON'T KNOW HOW TO FIX THE HYPERDRIVE. *CHEWBACCA* CAN DO IT.

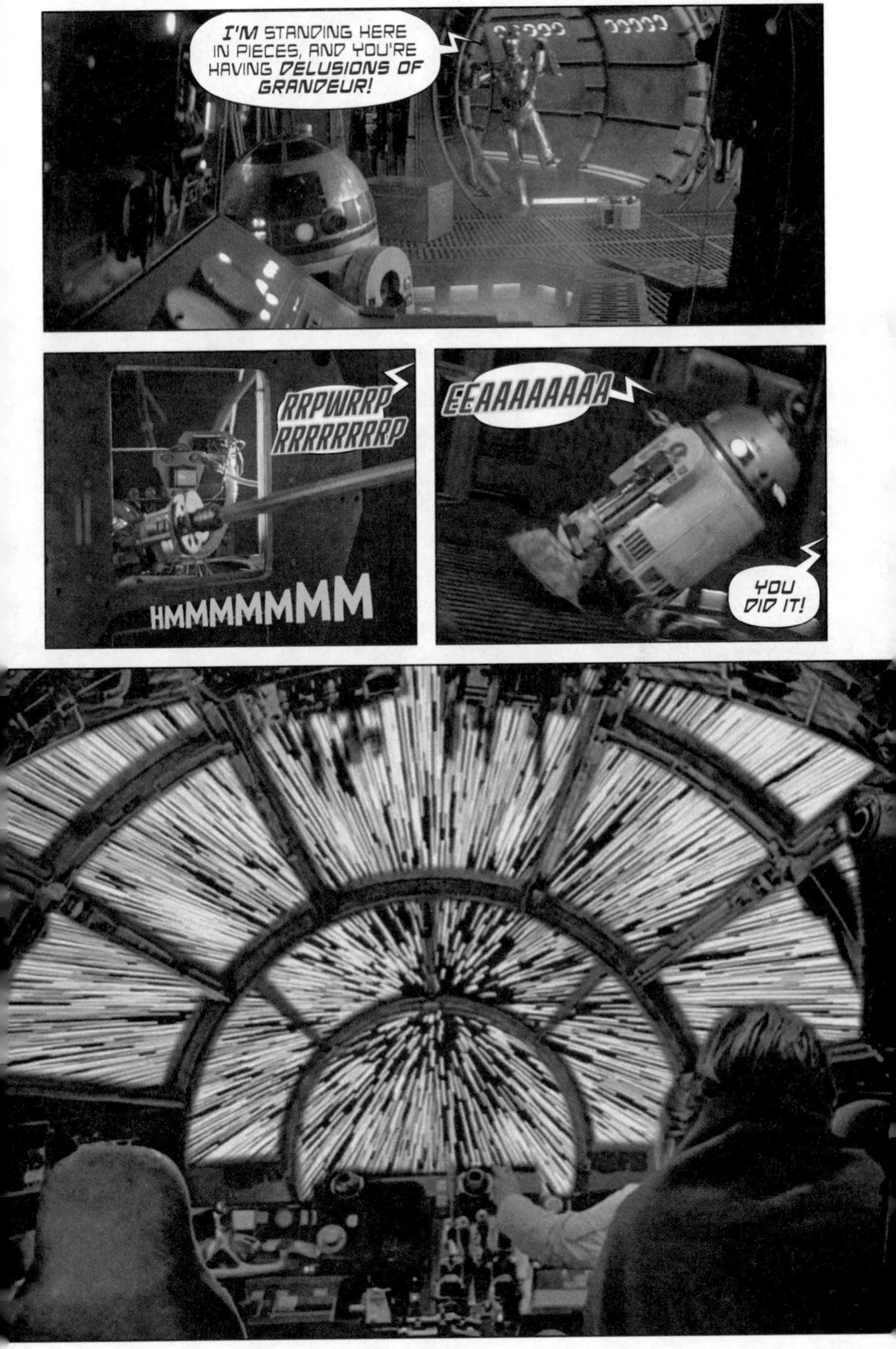
I'M STANDING HERE IN PIECES, AND YOU'RE HAVING DELUSIONS OF GRANDEUR!
RRPWRRP RRRRRRRRP
HMMMMMMM
EEAAAAAAAAA
YOU DID IT!

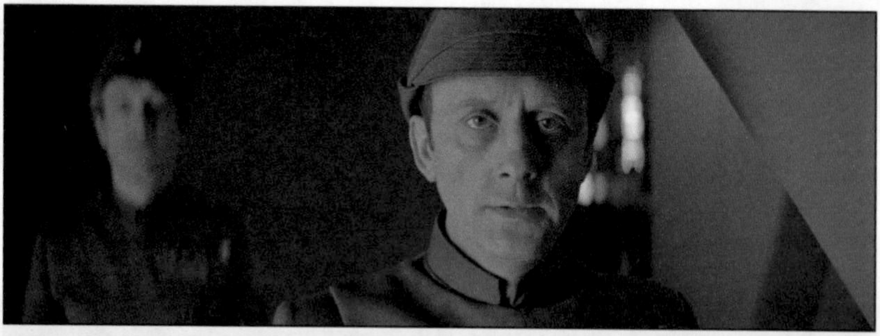

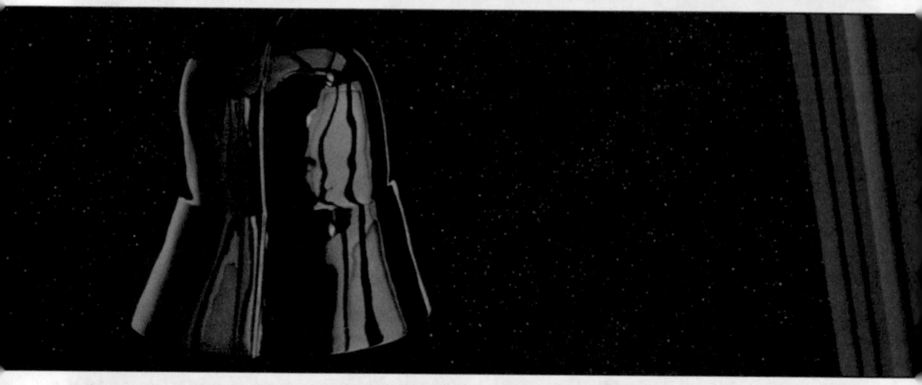

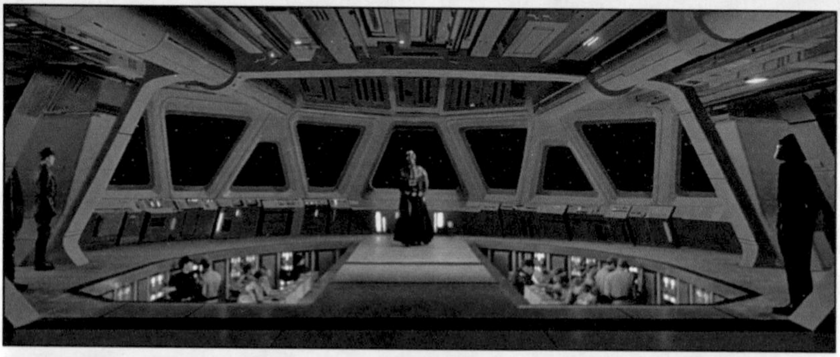

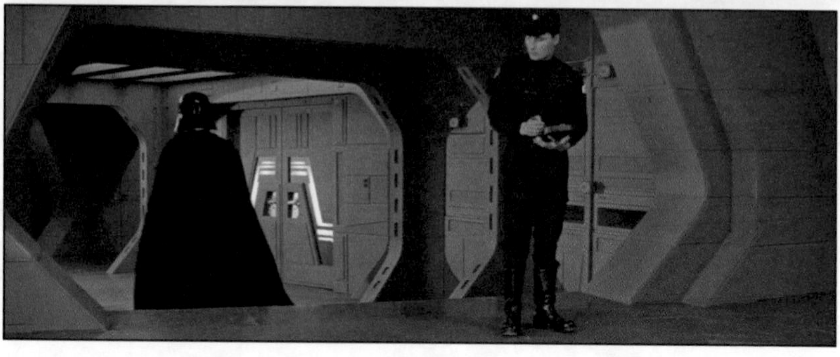

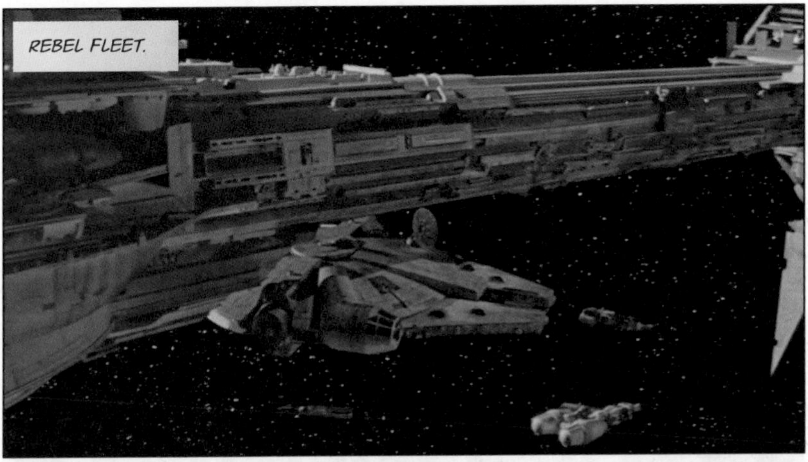
REBEL FLEET.

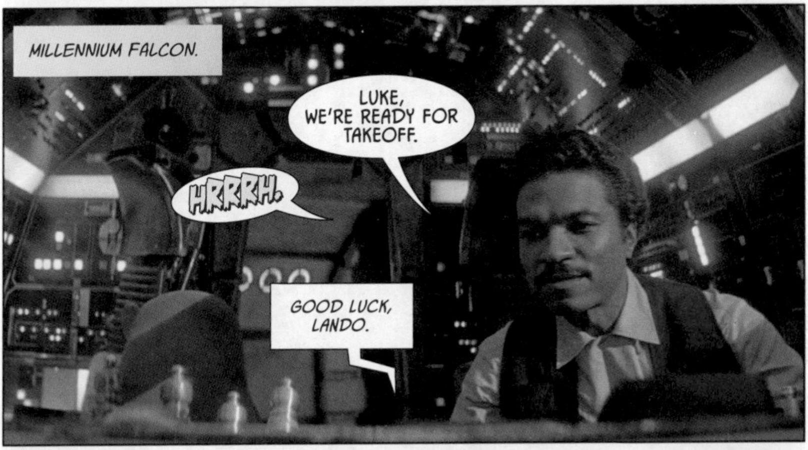
MILLENNIUM FALCON.
LUKE, WE'RE READY FOR TAKEOFF.
HRRRH.
GOOD LUCK, LANDO.

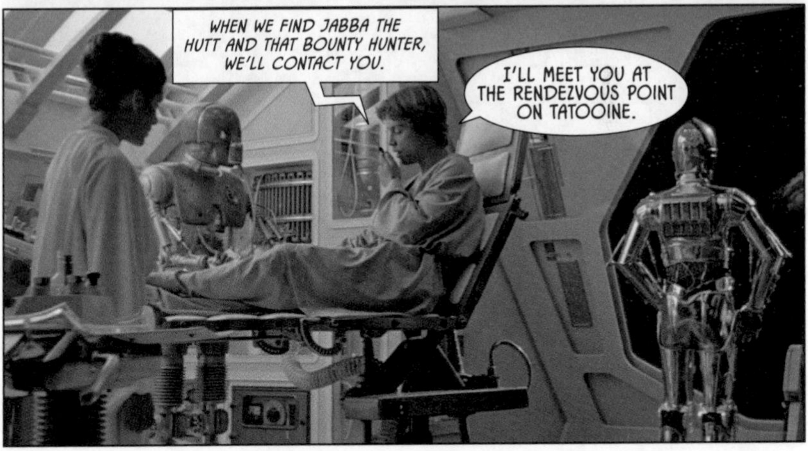
WHEN WE FIND JABBA THE HUTT AND THAT BOUNTY HUNTER, WE'LL CONTACT YOU.
I'LL MEET YOU AT THE RENDEZVOUS POINT ON TATOOINE.

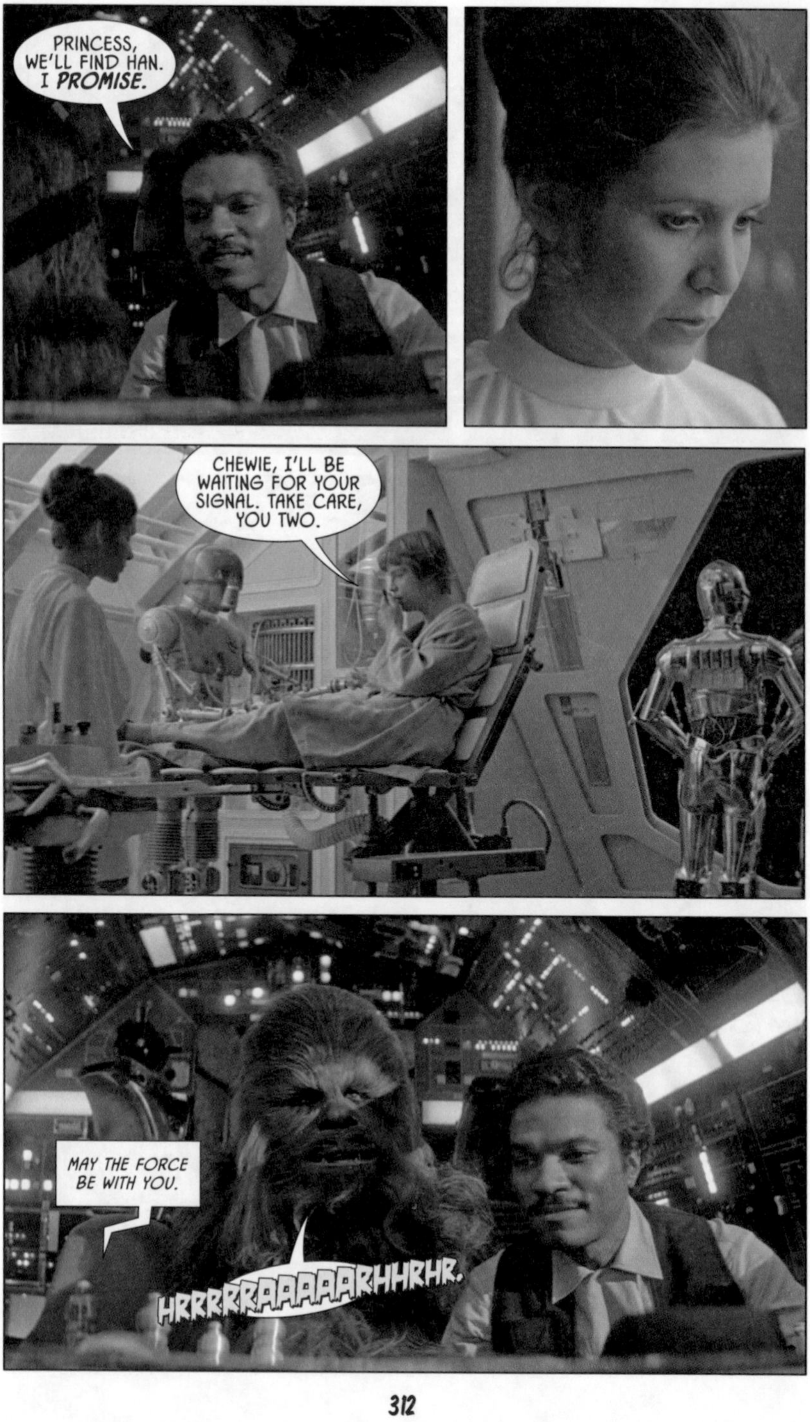
PRINCESS, WE'LL FIND HAN. I PROMISE.
CHEWIE, I'LL BE WAITING FOR YOUR SIGNAL. TAKE CARE, YOU TWO.
MAY THE FORCE BE WITH YOU.
HRRRRRAAAAAARHHRHR.

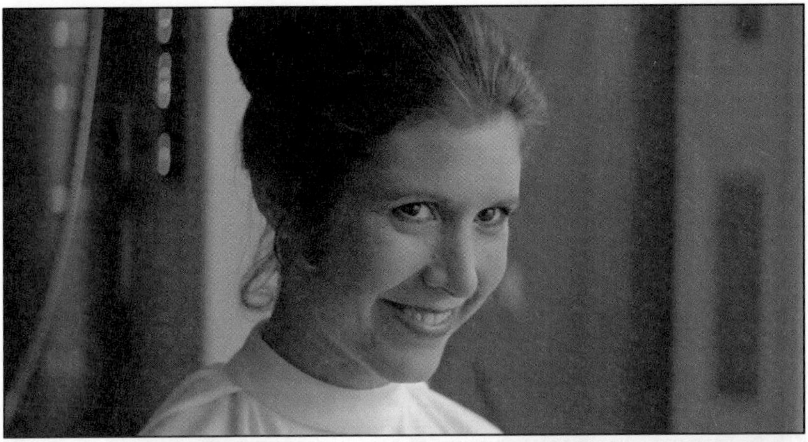

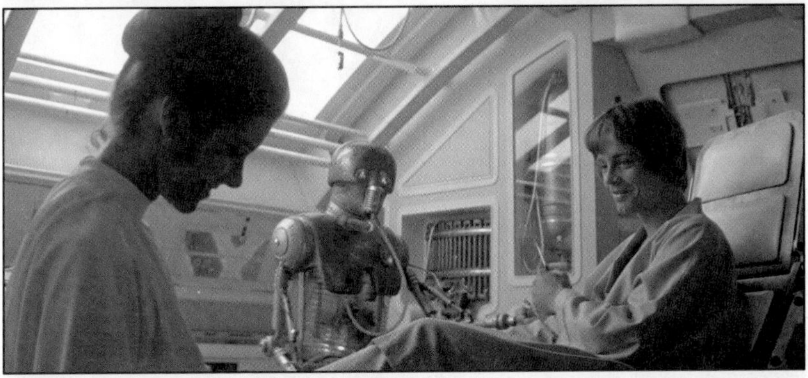

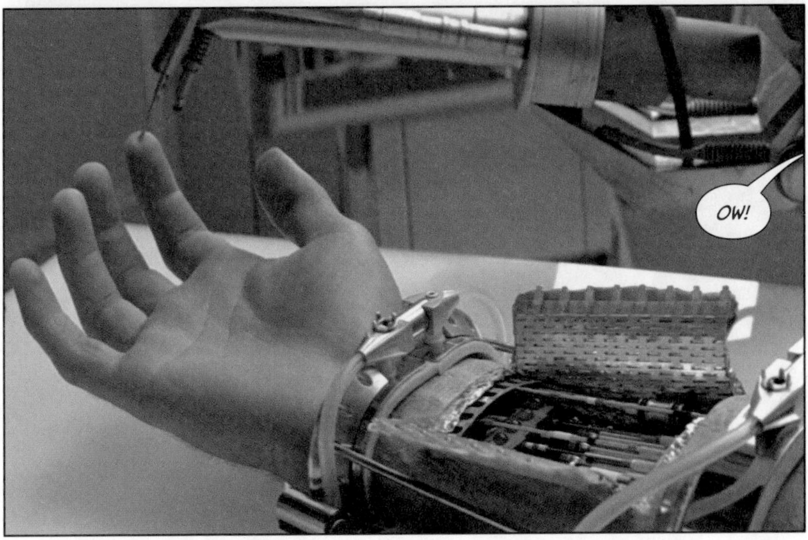
OW!

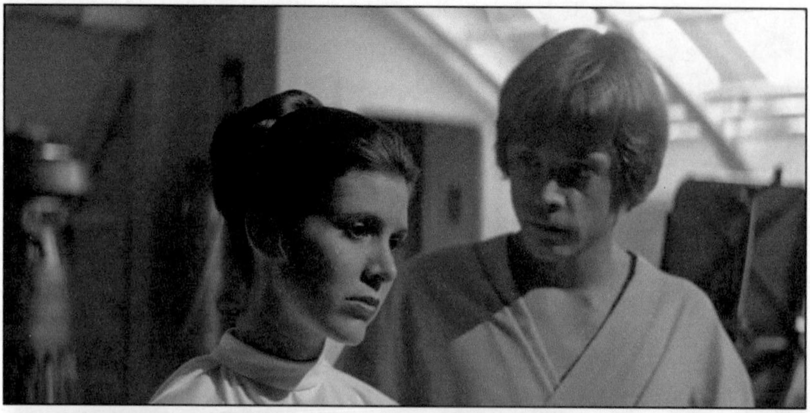

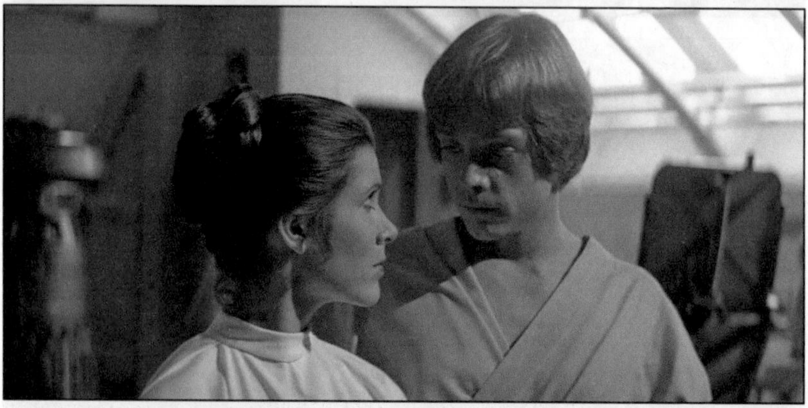

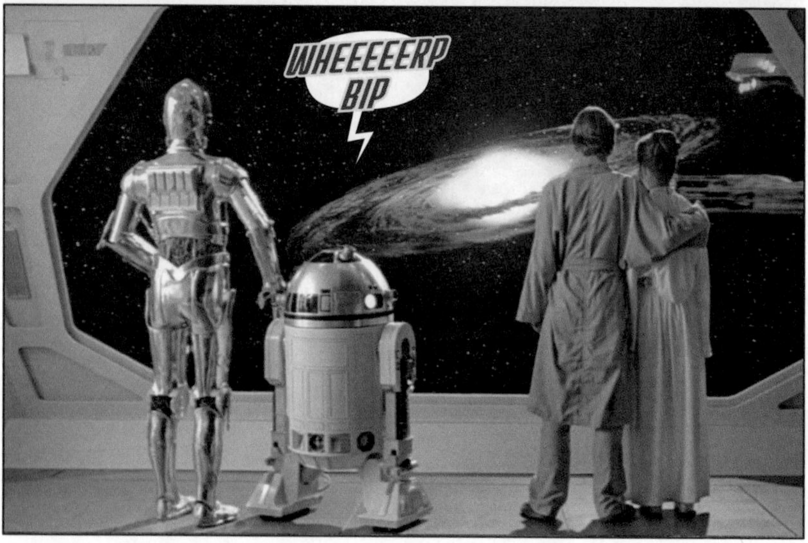

WHEEEEERP BIP

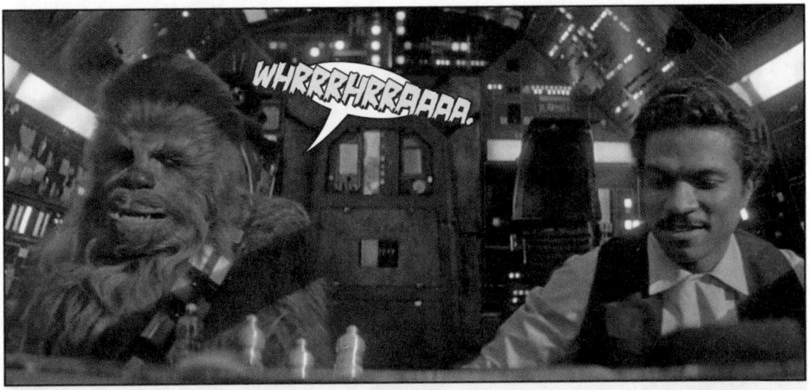
WHRRRHRRAAAA.

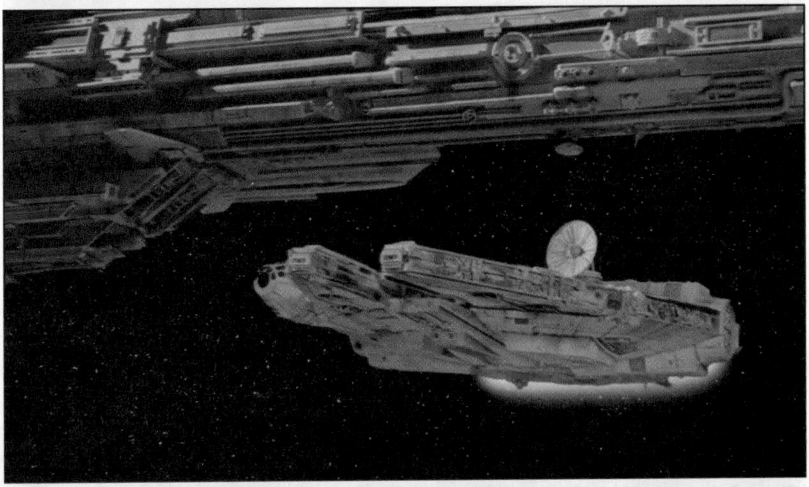

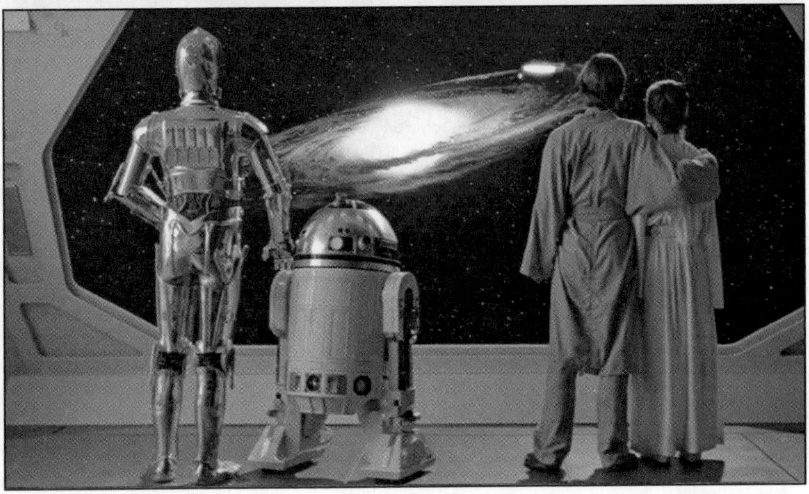

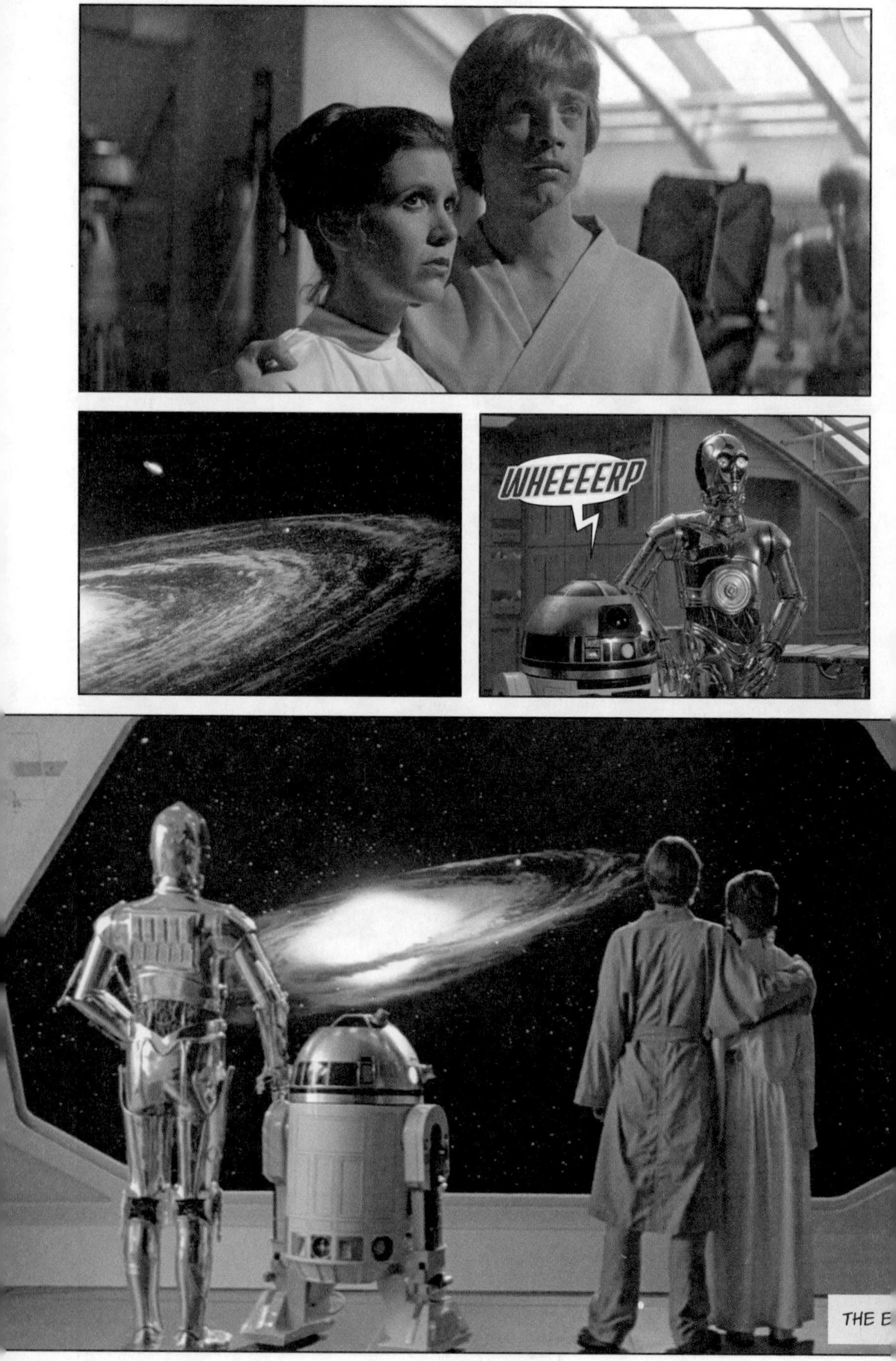
WHEEEERP
THE E